Minnesota Brothers

Minnesota Brothers

Four Stories of Swedes Who Find
Romance in Their New Homeland

Lena Nelson Dooley

BARBOUR
PUBLISHING

The Other Brother © 2002 by Lena Nelson Dooley
His Brother's Castoff © 2004 by Lena Nelson Dooley
Double Deception © 2004 by Lena Nelson Dooley
Gerda's Lawman © 2004 by Lena Nelson Dooley

ISBN 1-59789-108-8

Cover art by Corbis

All scripture quotations are taken from the King James Version of the Bible.

Published by Barbour Publishing, Inc., P.O. Box 719, Uhrichsville, Ohio 44683, www.barbourbooks.com

Our mission is to publish and distribute inspirational products offering exceptional value and biblical encouragement to the masses.

 Member of the
Evangelical Christian
Publishers Association

Printed in the United States of America.
5 4 3 2

Dear Reader,

Thank you for buying this book. I pray that you enjoy reading about the way the characters deal with the problems in their lives.

I live in Hurst, Texas, and I am married to the man God created for me. James and I will soon celebrate our 42nd anniversary. We have shared a lot of ups and downs in our life together, but God has always been the strong foundation through it all. One of the reasons I write is to show people that they can face hard times, and God will bring them through.

James and I have two grown daughters. I didn't get sons until the girls married. My sons-in-law are dear to me. I was thankful when my first two grandchildren were boys. We have a special relationship. An equally strong, but different, relationship is shared by my two granddaughters and me.

My husband and I are active in Gateway Church in Southlake, Texas. James is a greeter, and I volunteer in the bookstore. Where else? We enjoy a Family Life Group, where all ages share a loving bond. In addition, I'm involved in a Ladies' Life Group.

James and I have been interested in getting the message of Jesus Christ all around the globe. We have been on mission trips in Mexico, and I've been on one to Guatemala. We look forward to many more such opportunities.

Besides spending quality time with our family, James and I enjoy walking, going to movies, and getting together with friends. When I have time, I sew. I also knit, crochet, and read.

For many years I have spoken at women's groups and retreats as well as writing seminars and conferences. I have even spoken in other states and internationally.

Please visit my web site at www.LenaNelsonDooley.com.

Lena Nelson Dooley

This collection is dedicated to two wonderful editors—
Rebecca Germany and Tracie Peterson.
I've worked with Rebecca longer, both as the editor
at **Heartsong Presents** and then with Barbour fiction.
After Rebecca moved to her newer post,
I have worked with Tracie several years at **Heartsong Presents**..
Thank you both for helping me become a better author,
helping me tell the stories in such a way that they touched lives.
I wouldn't be who I am without you.
I respect you both and count it a joy to work with you.
I am blessed to know you.

The Other Brother

This book is dedicated to my two daughters,
Marilyn Van Zant and Jennifer Waldron,
who provided the catalyst that started me
writing inspirational romance novels.
Now they have given me the four
most wonderful grandchildren in the world.
And no book is ever written in our home
without the support of my wonderful husband, James,
whom I love more today than I ever imagined
when I married him in 1964.
He is the second most wonderful gift God ever gave me.

Chapter 1

April 1891

Olina Sandstrom stood by the railing of the *North Star*, her face turned away from the biting wind. A wayward curl persistently crept from her upswept hairdo and fluttered against her chilled cheeks. The wind flapped the hem of her heavy traveling suit as well, threatening to sweep her into the choppy sea. Thank goodness for the ship's railing. Even though the hard metal chilled her fingers until they were almost numb, she didn't want to let go.

The dark gray waters of the Atlantic Ocean spread from horizon to horizon. The ocean seemed to be a living thing, constantly moving and changing, never still. As waves lapped against the dark hull of the ocean liner, the deck where she stood dipped and rose in rhythm. It had taken Olina over a day to get used to the feeling. The movement unsettled more than her stomach. Never before had her foundation constantly shifted.

Oh, to be on land again, to feel safe. But would she ever feel safe again? Although Olina was excited to be on the grand adventure that would culminate in her reunion with her beloved, her heart was heavy with knowing what she had given up. Knowing what she had left behind, maybe forever.

The ocean fascinated Olina. Lars Nilsson's eyes were that shade of gray, and they were always alive with plans and new ideas. Even during storms, which had occurred more than once in the week since they had left Sweden, the ocean reminded Olina of Lars. When he was unhappy, his eyes took on that same brooding darkness. But when he was happy, they danced and flashed as the waves did when the sun sparkled across them. So day after day, Olina stood by the rail of the ship and longed for the time when she would look into those eyes again. It had been so long since she had seen them. This crossing seemed to be never ending.

"What are you looking at?" The soft voice of Johanna Nordstrom, Olina's traveling companion, penetrated Olina's concentration.

Olina gave a soft reply without looking away from the water that surrounded the ship. "The ocean."

"What do you find so interesting out there?" Johanna turned toward the churning water. Johanna had spent most of her time on the ship inside one of the salons. She told Olina that she preferred the warmth to the cold deck. Even in second class, the ship seemed luxurious to both of the young women.

Olina turned to face Johanna, one hand finally leaving the rail to swipe at a tendril that tickled her nose. "It reminds me of Lars. This voyage can't end soon enough for me. It has been so long since I saw him."

Looking out across the waves, Olina pictured Lars the last time they had been together. They had been alone in their favorite meadow. Soft green grass, dotted with tiny white flowers, spread around them. Jagged rocks broke through the ground cover farther up the slope, and the sound of the water in the fjord was a constant background melody punctuated by the calls of the birds that circled in the cerulean sky.

Lars came to tell her good-bye. When Olina started to cry, Lars pulled her into his arms. His gentle kiss brushed the hair from her temple. She didn't want to think of life without Lars. Ever since they were very young, they had known they would someday marry. Lars was an essential part of her. How could she go on without seeing him almost every day?

America was so far away. So far that she couldn't even imagine the distance. She just knew they would never see each other again. And it had taken years. Five long years.

"I'll work," Lars whispered against her coronet of braids, "and I'll save up until I can send you the money to come to America. Then we will be married. Even if it takes years, it'll be worth it." Lars placed a gentle kiss upon her willing lips before he left to meet his family at the docks.

Olina stayed in the meadow the rest of the afternoon. She relived every precious moment they had spent together. Every few minutes, she had touched the lips his tender kiss had covered for the first time, lost in the wonder of it.

"You know, Olina." Johanna's voice interrupted Olina's memories. "I haven't questioned you about your quick decision to accompany me to America. All you told me was that Lars had sent you the money for passage." Johanna patted one of Olina's icy hands. "I don't understand why none of your family came to see you off."

Olina wondered what she could tell her friend without making *Fader* sound bad. But Johanna deserved the truth. Without her help, Olina wouldn't be making this journey.

After turning away from the frothy water, Olina leaned on the railing, her hands still clutching it for support. "I wasn't trying to be mysterious. I just had a hard time talking about it." Thinking about it caused tears to pool in her eyes. She reached one hand into the pocket of her skirt and took out her pristine linen handkerchief to dab away the tears. "*Fader* didn't want me to go to America. He didn't understand. I love Lars so much, and there is no one else who can stir my heart as he does. I had to go to Lars."

The Other Brother

Olina swallowed a sob. "*Fader* told me that I was old enough to make my own decision. . .but if I went, he would disown me. No one in my family would ever be allowed to contact me. *Tant* Olga said he didn't mean it, so I waited awhile before I made my decision, hoping he would change his mind. He didn't." Olina wept so hard that she could not continue her explanation.

"He probably didn't mean it. He thought you would do what he wanted." Johanna pulled Olina into her arms and let her cry. "He'll change his mind when you get to America, and you can tell him how happy you are. If not then, at least when you and Lars have children, he'll want to know his grandchildren."

Olina was warmed by the embrace. Her mother often hugged her when she was still living at home. She hadn't realized how much she had missed it.

When Olina stopped crying, she moved from Johanna's embrace and dried her face with her handkerchief. "*Tack så*. A good friend you are, for sure."

The ship dipped, and Johanna grabbed the railing. "I'm sorry I didn't realize something was wrong. I was excited about going to America to be with Olaf. Even though I'm married, my mother didn't want me to travel alone."

Olina tried to smile at her friend. "You and Olaf hadn't been married long when he went to America, *ja*?"

"Only a few months."

"It must have been hard for you."

Johanna nodded. "It was. But your decision was a difficult one, too. I'm not sure I could have made it."

Olina studied the waves with their whitecaps. "It was the hardest thing I've ever done, choosing Lars over my family."

Gustaf Nilsson was angrier than he had been in a long time. "*Gud*, why did You let this happen?" When he was alone, Gustaf often talked to God. Was he ever alone today. Driving his wagon across the rolling plains in Minnesota toward Litchfield, all he could think about was taking the train to New York City.

Five years ago when his family had left New York, headed toward Minnesota, Gustaf had vowed never to set foot in that town again. It was too big for him. It was too dirty. . .and too noisy. . .and too crowded with people. Not at all the sort of place he wanted to be. He didn't like to be hemmed in. He needed fresh, clean air. He was a farmer. He tilled the land. And there was a Swedish settlement in Minnesota. That was why they had emigrated.

The winter before the move had been harder than usual in Sweden. With the crop failure that summer, the family finally heeded the pleas of their friends, who were already landowners in America, and sold everything they owned. God had been good to them in Minnesota. They bought a large farm, which Gustaf and Papa couldn't run alone. They had to hire several men to help them.

August, Gustaf's younger brother, had wanted to be a blacksmith. Papa thought it was a good idea, so August had moved to town. Then there was Lars, his youngest brother. Gustaf didn't want to think about Lars and what he had done. He didn't like to be this angry, but every time he thought of Lars, anger bubbled up inside him like the spring that had fed icy water to the family on their farm back in Sweden. But the anger did not cool him. It made him grow hotter and hotter. Even though the spring winds still blew, they couldn't touch the heat that was building in Gustaf.

"*Fader*, what am I going to do when I get there?" Gustaf looked into the wide blue sky, but the puffy white clouds didn't tell him anything. And he didn't hear the voice of God thundering the answer. Not that he expected it to. Gustaf had never heard the audible voice of God. He knew some people claimed to, but Gustaf always heard God's voice speak deep within his soul. That was where he hoped to hear something, but God was quiet today.

Why did Gustaf always have to clean up the messes Lars made? He knew he was the oldest, but that didn't mean he should have to leave the farm, where he had so many things that needed to be done, and travel to that awful place to meet that girl. Why hadn't she stayed in Sweden where she belonged? What would he do with the sturdy farm girl?

When the Nilssons had first arrived in Minnesota, the spring had been so wet that the roads were impassable. Lars had tried to go to town anyway. By the time Gustaf pulled the bogged-down wagon out of the mud, one of the axles had broken. He had taken it to town for August to fix before Papa found out. He hadn't minded that too much. Gustaf was glad August hadn't caused trouble like Lars had. One brother giving him grief was enough.

After a year, Lars decided he needed to work in town to make money to send for Olina. At first, Gustaf had been unhappy about that. So much of the time, Lars didn't complete what he was supposed to on the farm, and Gustaf was the one who finished the job. It was easier to do the whole thing himself. Besides, his sister, Gerda, helped more than Lars ever had.

Since he hardly ever finished anything he started, Gustaf had been sure that Lars would give up on the idea before he had earned enough money. That hadn't been the case. Lars took to merchandising. Before long, Mr. Braxton gave him more responsibility. Although it had taken another four years for Lars to save enough money to pay for Olina's passage, he never deviated from that plan. Then six months ago, Lars had sent Olina the money.

Soon after the letter was mailed, Mr. Braxton's brother from Denver came to Litchfield. He had been impressed with Lars's abilities, so he offered him a position in his mercantile. Lars moved to Denver. He said he would be better able to provide for a family with the increased income. The whole Nilsson family assumed that Lars had written Olina about the change in plans.

It took a long time for mail to cross half of the United States, the ocean, and part of Europe. However, Gustaf had expected to hear before now that Olina had arrived in Denver. He didn't know why it took her so long to start the journey. Yesterday, they had received two messages. A letter from Lars and a telegram from Olina to Lars. Papa had opened the telegram because he thought it might be something important.

Olina's note told them when she would be arriving on the *North Star* in New York City. The letter from Lars was disturbing. He had fallen in love with Mr. Braxton's daughter, and they would be married by the time the letter reached Minnesota. He said he had only thought he loved Olina. Until he met Janice, he had not known what real love was. He would write to Olina and explain things, but Gustaf knew it was too late for that. Olina was already on her way when Lars wrote the letter, if he did indeed write it.

Papa should have been the one to go to New York to meet Olina, but Mama didn't feel well. She had been extremely upset by the letter from Lars. Gustaf was sure that was the reason she felt so bad. She begged Papa to send Gustaf, so here he was.

Gustaf had half a mind to send Olina back where she came from. He would if she had enough money for the passage. He certainly didn't.

This would never have happened if Lars hadn't started working in that store. Why couldn't he love the farm as much as Gustaf did? Or if he had to work in a store, why had Lars not stayed in Litchfield with Mr. Braxton and his mercantile? Why did Lars wait to leave town until after he had sent Olina the money to come to Minnesota?

It was a good thing Gustaf's horses knew the way to town without much help from him. If they hadn't, he never would have made it to the train on time.

⟍

The seemingly never-ending journey was finally over. The ship docked at something called the Battery in New York. Such a huge place it was. So many docks. So many ships. So many people. Olina was overwhelmed. She had never heard such a din in all her life. It was so loud it was hard to distinguish one sound from another—voices speaking in many languages, which Olina couldn't understand, clanging, banging, the hooting of ships' horns, the clatter of horses' hooves on the brick streets.

"It's a good thing we came when we did." Johanna looked out over the crowd that had gathered as the ship docked. It was a constantly moving sea of humanity.

"What do you mean?" Olina took time out from trying to find Lars in the crowd to look at her friend. "What difference would another time make?"

Johanna turned toward Olina. "I was talking to one of the other passengers.

13

She told me that there are so many people coming to America that they are building a place on an island where they will process many of the emigrants. It's called Ellis Island, and it will be open for business in a few months. It'll take longer to be processed there before you get to come ashore. I want to be with Olaf as soon as possible." Just then she spied her husband's tall frame pushing through the crowd. She raised her hand as high as she could and waved her handkerchief.

It had taken long enough to get off the ship and through Immigration—much longer than either woman wanted it to take. But now Johanna was hanging on to Olaf's arm as Olina scanned the thinning crowd for Lars. Where could he be? She had sent a telegraph message before she boarded the ship. Surely he received it. It wasn't pleasant waiting here. Of course with fewer people around, Olina wasn't overcome with the strong smell of unwashed bodies as she had been when they first stepped on shore, but there were other unpleasant odors. Garbage and human waste were too strong for the ocean breezes to cleanse. Many of the men must have been drinking in nearby taverns before they came to the wharf. Stale alcohol mingled with all the other smells. Besides, the large ships blocked many of the breezes. There was also the odor of fish and fumes from the many boats. Olina thought about covering her nose with her handkerchief as some of the other women on the dock were doing, but she didn't.

Gustaf had lost his good humor before he left home. Now it was so far away he didn't know if he would ever find it again. He was angry and frustrated. The train ride had been long and noisy. No one could sleep with all the babble from the passengers. Add to that the chugging engine and the *clackity-clack* of the rails. Gustaf had nursed a headache since he left Minnesota. The stuffy cars didn't help him feel any better. When he went out on the platform between cars to get a whiff of air, it wasn't fresh. Smoke from the engine, which enveloped the train itself, was no more pleasant than the unwashed bodies and bad breath inside the car. When he turned to go back inside, a cinder caught in the corner of his eye. After he removed it, tears formed in the injured eye for over an hour. For sure, he didn't want people to think he was crying.

When he had finally reached New York, it was a race against the other passengers to find a cabby who could take him to the docks. He had gotten the slowest cabby in New York City.

"Hey." Gustaf reached up and tapped the driver on the shoulder.

The driver didn't take his attention off the road. "Sir?"

"You aren't driving around and around trying to make my fare larger, are you?" Gustaf didn't try to disguise his anger.

"No, this is the most direct route to the Battery. That's where you said you was going, ain't it?" The man leaned away from a right turn, easily controlling the horses and buggy. "It's not far now."

"I'm glad." Gustaf scooted back in the seat, holding on tight. If not, he might be thrown from the buggy as it lurched and groaned its way through the traffic. "I'm meeting a young lady, and her ship should have docked over an hour ago."

"Why didn't you say so? We wouldn't want to leave a lady waiting in that mob." The man flicked the reins across the rumps of the horses, and they trotted at a much faster pace.

Gustaf glared blankly. He was trying to remember what Olina Sandstrom looked like. He didn't want to spend a lot of time looking for her. Blond braids loosely encircled her head the last time he saw her. She had a round face with rosy cheeks and big blue eyes. He thought Olina's eyes were the prettiest of any of the girls in their village. She helped her family with farm chores, so she was strong. Butter and cheese, from the family dairy, and rich pastries had kept her figure rounded. She should be easy to spot in New York. He hadn't seen that kind of girl anywhere he had been in the city.

"Here we are. Would you like me to wait to take you and your lady to a hotel?" The cabby looked around the area. "I don't see any other conveyance that ain't being used by someone else."

"How much is that going to cost?" Gustaf could feel his purse shrinking as they talked.

"Tell you what." The cabby winked down at him. "I wait for half an hour, and I won't charge nothing but the fare here and to where you're going. If you ain't back by then, I'll have to take any fare I can get."

"It's a deal."

Gustaf loped off, seething inside. The cheeky cabby thought he was coming for his own lady, not for his brother's castoff. If that didn't cap the day. Gustaf hurried toward the wharves, where he saw several ships docked. There was the vessel she had sailed on. Quickly, Gustaf scanned the scattered clusters of people near the *North Star*. Not one of the women looked like Olina. What if she hadn't boarded the ship? What if he had made the journey in vain? Gustaf's anger built even higher than it had been—if that were possible. Had he wasted all this time and money for nothing?

Once again, Olina looked around the large wharf area. Where was Lars? She didn't know what she would do if he didn't come. She had so little money left. Johanna had insisted that they book passage in second class. She didn't want to travel in steerage, where everyone was treated like cattle, sharing rooms and bathrooms and who knew what else. Olina had enjoyed the relative luxury. She knew it was not like first class, but she had never known that kind of life, so she didn't miss it. But she would have missed the money it would have cost. Olina didn't have that kind of money to start with. Now she almost wished she had talked Johanna into steerage. At least she would have enough money to make her way to Minnesota on her own if Lars was unable to meet her in New York.

"I wonder what's keeping Lars." Olaf turned from his conversation with Johanna to talk to Olina. "You could go with us to the hotel. I'm sure there's another room available. Of course, tomorrow we'll be leaving for Cincinnati, but we'd be glad to have you with us tonight."

Olina looked at Johanna clutching her husband's arm as if she would never let go. She knew that the young couple didn't need her tagging along on their first night together in over a year.

"Lars wouldn't know where to find me if I went with you." Once again Olina looked around the wharf. "I think I'll wait a little longer."

"We can't leave you here alone." Johanna took Olina's arm. "It wouldn't be proper, and you might not be safe. I would worry instead of enjoying my husband." She smiled a secret smile at Olaf.

That smile made Olina uncomfortable, so she quickly looked away. That's when Olina noticed a man who seemed to be looking for someone. He was built like Lars, strong and muscular, and blond hair stuck out from under his navy blue cap. He looked a lot like Lars, but he was taller than she remembered Lars being. Maybe it was Lars. He could have grown taller since he had come to America. All that work and good food in the land of plenty. Maybe he had grown. Lars, or whoever he was, started toward them. Now he was close enough for her to see all of his face.

Just as Olina realized that, she looked into icy blue eyes. Sky blue and cold as the ice in the fjords in winter. They jolted her. But it wasn't Lars. His were gray, not blue.

◇

Gustaf recognized Olina's eyes the moment he saw them. It was a good thing. He never would have known who she was otherwise. She stood as if she were holding herself upright by the strength of her will. She was slender, with curves in all the right places. Instead of the braids he remembered encircling her head, her upswept hairdo was topped with a fashionable small hat that had ribbons and feathers and a small veil that was turned up. Wispy curls brushed her cheeks and neck.

Gustaf didn't know a lot about fashion, but he knew that the traveling suit she was wearing was fashionable. Olina had changed, all for the better. But she was fragile-looking, as if the journey had worn her out. As if she would wilt if given the chance. He couldn't tell her what he had come to tell her until she had rested. He would have to wait for the right time. But what *was* the right time to tell a woman who had come halfway around the world that she had been jilted?

Chapter 2

G ustaf?" Olina was surprised she hadn't realized who he was right away.
He nodded as he glanced at the luggage. "How many of these are yours?"

"Those two trunks and this carpetbag." After Olina pointed out the pieces, she looked past Gustaf, scanning the thinning crowd. "Where—?"

"I have a cab waiting. We need to hurry." Gustaf hefted one trunk up on his back.

"Wait." Olina's hand on his arm stopped him. "I want you to meet my traveling companion and her husband." She turned toward the Nordstroms.

Olaf held out his hand. "I'm Olaf, and this is Johanna."

"I'm pleased to meet you." Gustaf let the trunk slip back to the dock before he shook Olaf's hand.

"Do we have to hurry to catch the train?" Olina had a lot of questions she wanted answered. "And is—?"

"No," Gustaf interrupted. "Our train doesn't leave until in the morning."

"But where will you spend the night?" Johanna sounded worried.

Olina smiled at her. How like Johanna to be more concerned for her friend than herself.

"I hadn't thought of that," Gustaf answered. "I guess I was planning on waiting at Grand Central Station tonight."

"Why don't you come to the hotel with us?" Olaf said. "I'm sure they have another room."

Gustaf looked angry, but he agreed. "We can share my cab if we hurry. The driver said he wouldn't wait long for us."

Each man picked up a trunk and started toward the cabstand, leaving the women to guard the other luggage. When they returned for the other two trunks, Olina and Johanna went with them, each carrying a carpetbag, as well as their reticules.

The cab was crowded. Olina had to sit very close to Gustaf. After they had gone a couple of blocks, she leaned close to his ear. "Where is—?"

"That's our hotel." Olaf pointed toward a three-story building with a red brick facade.

When the three men had unloaded the baggage, Olaf and Gustaf went to the front desk.

17

"I booked you a room on the same floor as your friends, but on the other side of the hotel," Gustaf told Olina when they returned. "My room is on the next floor."

As they walked across the lobby to the staircase, the carpet softened Olina's tired steps. It was a good thing Gustaf had brought her here. Olina wouldn't have been able to afford a hotel room at all in this big city. New York City. It was so confusing and noisy.

After the baggage was stored in the three hotel rooms, the four went to the restaurant on the ground floor. Another time, Olina would have enjoyed the beauty of the place, aglow with gaslights on the walls, as well as candles on each table. Delicious smells wafted through the room, making Olina aware that she had not eaten much that day. She had been too excited, knowing they were landing in New York. She was supposed to see Lars waiting for her. That had added to her excitement, but that had not happened. Now here she was in a hotel restaurant with Gustaf. Maybe he would soon tell her where Lars was and why he didn't come to meet her.

As soon as they were seated, a young woman in a long black dress with a white apron and cap served them. Gustaf and Olaf were able to converse with her in English. Neither Olina nor Johanna understood anything they said. But the two men sounded as if they had spoken the language all their lives. Olina hoped she would be able to learn the strange way of speaking. It felt uncomfortable being an outsider. Surely Lars could speak English as well as Gustaf. Lars would help her learn. He wouldn't want her feeling uncomfortable around others.

The meal was congenial, but Olina waited for Gustaf to bring up Lars's whereabouts. Lars hadn't even been mentioned during the meal. Gustaf seemed rather aloof. Maybe he didn't want to talk about Lars in front of the Nordstroms. Olina was beginning to worry. She hoped Lars was not sick or injured. Just wait until Gustaf walked her to her room. She would get to the bottom of this.

All through the meal, Gustaf was distracted. He tried to carry on a sensible conversation with his companions, but his thoughts were otherwise engaged.

Here they were in a hotel, using up more of the hard-earned money he had brought with him. He felt each dollar as it slipped through his fingers, his precious store dwindling at an alarming rate. He had better get Olina back to the farm quickly, before he ran out of money. Why had he not brought more with him? He had enough put away that it wouldn't have hurt to bring extra so he wouldn't feel the pinch, but he had been angry. He only wanted to get the trip over with. He hadn't wanted to spend one penny more than was necessary, and he had planned to send Olina back to her parents. Besides, he would need his money when he and Anna married.

Gustaf hadn't thought about spending time at a hotel. He was going to go back to the train station and wait for the train to Minnesota, even if it took all night. When he first saw Olina standing there, he knew he couldn't treat her that way. Now look at the mess he was in. It was a good thing *Fader* had told him to buy both tickets before he left home. He had planned to turn Olina's ticket in and get his money back after he put her on a ship to Sweden. Now he barely had enough money for food until they got to Litchfield.

Gustaf hadn't even mentioned Lars to Olina. How could he bring up his name without exploding with anger? She didn't need to see that, not in her condition. She was so tired; she looked as if she was having a hard time staying awake. There was not one detail of her actions or appearance that escaped him.

If he could get his hands on Lars right now, he would likely hurt him. How could Lars do this to Olina? Why couldn't he be man enough to face this on his own?

Olina said she was hungry, but she didn't eat like the farm girl of his memory. She ate more like his mother did, with grace and poise. She had stopped eating before her plate was empty. She insisted the food tasted good, but she left some, as his mother often did.

What was he doing comparing her to his mother? Was he mad? How was he going to tell her about Lars? He would have to wait until the right time.

When Gustaf finished the last bite on his plate, Olina stood up. "I'm tired." She looked right at him. "Will you walk me to my room?"

Olaf stood when Olina and Gustaf did. Then he sat back down with his wife.

At the top of the stairs, Olina could wait no longer. "Where is Lars?" she asked as they walked down the hall.

"I'm not sure."

Olina stopped and placed her hands on her hips. "What do you mean, you're not sure? Is something the matter with him?"

Anger blazed from Gustaf. "Yes, something's the matter with him. He's married."

Olina couldn't believe her ears. Surely he hadn't said what she thought she heard. "Married?"

She didn't realize she had voiced the question until she saw the expression on Gustaf's face. He reached toward her, but she stepped back from him.

"Olina, I'm sorry. I didn't mean to tell you this way." He took her arm, but she pulled away.

"How could he be married?" The question ended on a squeak. Here she was worried that Lars was sick or hurt, and he had done this to her. Olina clutched her arms around her waist as if something inside hurt. And it did. Everything hurt.

She felt as if she couldn't stand up another minute.

Gustaf must have realized this, because he put his arms around her and pulled her against his chest. Olina began to sob. What was she going to do now?

Gustaf helped her walk to her room. "We need to talk. If we leave the door open, I can come in for a few minutes."

He eased her into a chair and hunkered on the floor beside her. Olina didn't look at his face. How could she? She didn't want to see pity there. First *Fader* rejected her, and now Lars had jilted her. How could God have let this happen?

"What am I going to do?" It was hard to get the words past the lump in her throat.

"What do you want to do, Olina?"

"I don't have the money to go back to Sweden."

Gustaf stood and walked over to the window. "I came to take you to Litchfield with me."

"Do your *moder* and *fader* want me to come?"

Gustaf turned from the window. He looked at her, but she didn't read pity in his expression. "Yes. They're not happy about what Lars did."

Olina sat up straighter. "What exactly did Lars do?"

"Didn't he write you at all after he went to Denver?"

"Denver?" Olina quickly stood and paced across the floor. "The last letter I received from him contained the money for my passage." She stopped walking and turned toward Gustaf. "What is he doing in Denver?"

"I don't want to talk about Lars right now." Gustaf stomped to the window again. "He's always making messes and leaving them for me to clean up. You are one of those messes, and I will take care of you, as I have all the others."

Olina could hardly believe her ears. "Did you just call me a mess?" She stood a little taller, the starch returning to her backbone. "I'm not sure I want to spend any time with you."

"Well, you're going to have to. . .until we get to Minnesota, at least!"

Why was he shouting at her? Did he want everyone in the hotel to know what had happened to her?

Olina walked over to the door. "I'll thank you to leave my room."

"All right. I'll go, but I'll be here to pick you up early in the morning so we can catch our train." At least he had moderated his tone. "When we get to Litchfield, you and my parents can decide what to do."

After Olina closed the door behind him, she resumed pacing the floor, sure she would never be able to sleep. Everything in her life had turned to darkness. *Fader* had rejected her because she wanted to come to America to marry the man she loved. She stopped by the window and stared out, unseeing.

How could Olina love a man who could do that to her? How could she turn off a love that had consumed most of her life? Here she was in a strange place where she couldn't even speak the language. Tomorrow she would board a train with the most insufferable man she had ever known.

Olina didn't remember Gustaf much from when they had been in Sweden. He was older than Lars and she, so he hadn't paid much attention to her, nor she to him. She never noticed him acting the way he was now.

Olina walked over and sat on the side of the bed. It had been so long since she had slept in such a soft one. She had been looking forward to it, but with what had happened today, she didn't know if she would sleep a wink.

Olina didn't like to feel helpless, but that was what she felt right now. Helpless and alone. Alone and unloved. How much worse could it get? She didn't want to know. She wished she couldn't feel anything. That's what she could do. Stop feeling anything. Then maybe the hurt would go away.

Olina knew she could trust no one except herself. She would have to face this alone.

☙

Gustaf had been quiet at breakfast, and then he had rushed Olina to Grand Central Station. What a large place it was! So fancy with arches and columns and all kinds of mosaic tiles. Olina had never seen anything like it. The ceiling seemed to be a million miles above them. People were everywhere, all talking in their own languages or the language of this new country. Occasionally, Olina heard a Swedish word as they made their way through the throng. It was like music to her ears, even though it was buried in the multilingual cacophony. The place was so large, they had barely made it to their train on time.

Olina was fighting a headache. The *clackity-clack* of the train was much louder than she had expected. Some people carried on conversations, which only added to the confusing din. She pressed her fingers to her temples as she tried to ignore all the noise.

This America was big. They had traveled for two days, and they hadn't reached Minnesota yet. At first Olina looked out the windows to see everything. . .and to keep from looking at Gustaf. Although she tried not to feel anything, every time she saw him, it brought all those feelings back; so she ignored him as much as she could.

There was a lot to see. Before they left the state of New York, Olina saw lots of trees—tall trees, many kinds that were new to her. As they traveled across other states, hills gave way to prairies with tall grasses blowing in the wind. Soon vast fields of wheat and other crops were interspersed with farmhouses and barns.

The train passed through small settlements as well as a few cities. It often stopped to let off and take on passengers. Soon the cities all looked a lot alike. They had crossed several states—Pennsylvania, Ohio, and Indiana—before they reached

Chicago, Illinois, which was the largest city since they left New York City.

Every so often, she sat back and glanced at Gustaf in the seat facing hers. Every time she looked at him, Gustaf was reading the newspaper he bought in Grand Central Station. . . or he was asleep. . .or he was reading from his Bible, which he had in the carpetbag he carried. The only time he talked to her was when he needed to tell her something about the trip or when they were getting something to eat. That was fine with her.

Although Olina tried not to, she missed Lars. She also missed *Mor*. . .and her brothers. She could not even keep from missing *Fader*, even though he had hurt her so much. Maybe if she closed her eyes and rested her head against the back of the seat, her headache would go away.

Gustaf glanced up when he heard the soft breathy sound. Olina's head rested on the window beside her. Her eyes were closed, and her lips were slightly parted. She must be asleep, because the soft sounds that came from her small mouth were almost snores, but not quite. Gustaf wished he sat beside her. If he did, he would ease her head from the hard glass onto his softer broad shoulder. He would love to cushion her sleep there.

What was he thinking? He loved Anna, didn't he? The sweet honey smell of Olina had teased him when they were in the cab, but he had tried to ignore it.

Gustaf pulled his Bible out of his carpetbag again. His thoughts were not the thoughts of a man who planned to ask Anna to marry him the next time they were alone together. The sooner he got this mess with Olina fixed, the better for him. Gustaf leafed through the book, trying to find something that would ease his mind. But he went from one verse here to another verse there without gaining the peace he was seeking.

How had Olina gotten under his skin so much? Was it because he wanted to make up for what Lars did to hurt her? When she broke down and cried at the hotel, it touched Gustaf's heart. What he felt was pity, wasn't it? Then the next morning, Olina was somehow stronger. He had watched her, and he could see an iron will that kept her from showing the outside world how much she had been hurt. He admired that.

Chapter 3

Would this train ride never end? The benches that had felt comfortable when they left New York were now almost too hard to bear. Olina squirmed, trying to find a softer spot, but to no avail. Most of her body was sore. She thought about Lars, and tears pooled in her eyes. When she thought about her family back in Sweden, the same thing happened. She would not cry. Crying didn't help anything. Olina wished she had something to read, but the newspaper Gustaf bought in New York City was in English. She couldn't read a word of it.

Olina's thoughts drifted to *Tant* Olga. What would she have done without her great-aunt?

About a year after Lars moved to America, *Tant* Olga asked if Olina would move into town to take care of her. At first Olina hadn't wanted to leave her beloved farm near the fjords. But she was glad when she did.

Tant Olga had fallen in love with a sailor when she was young. She married him against her family's wishes. *Farbror* Art had worked hard until he bought his own ship. As the wife of a merchant seaman, *Tant* Olga had enjoyed a life of plenty. Then her husband had been swept from the deck of his ship in a storm, leaving *Tant* Olga a wealthy woman. Art and Olga never had children of their own.

Tant Olga was an old woman when she asked Olina to live with her. She said she would pay Olina to take care of her. Olina had been worried that all she would do would be a drudge for *Tant* Olga. That had not been the case.

The two women, so far apart in age, were kindred spirits. *Tant* Olga helped Olina become the woman she was today. Climbing the stairs in the three-story house and eating smaller portions of foods that weren't so rich helped Olina slim down. *Tant* Olga taught Olina to be a lady instead of a farm girl.

They enjoyed taking outings. The two of them even read the newspapers together, because they wanted to know what was going on in the world. Olina had written about these things in her letters to Lars. They discussed current events through their letters.

When Lars sent the money to come to America, Olina hadn't known what to do. Her father had forbidden her to go. But *Tant* Olga hadn't. When *Tant* Olga learned that her nephew opposed the trip, she assured Olina that he didn't mean it. She was convinced that when Olina asserted her independence and started on the journey, he would come to his senses and change his mind. Her father had changed his mind after she married Art. Olina hoped that would be the case with her own *fader*.

She didn't want to think about her father. She didn't want to cry again, so she pushed thoughts of him out of her head. Instead, she returned to those days before her journey started.

Tant Olga helped her buy new clothes with the money she had saved. *Tant* Olga hadn't let Olina pay for anything she needed while she was staying with her, and she still paid her a wage for taking care of her. Over and over again, Olina told *Tant* Olga that she felt as though she were taking advantage of her, but *Tant* Olga didn't agree.

They studied the fashion books and bought the most popular fabrics. *Tant* Olga taught Olina how to sew and embroider and make lace. So when Olina made many of her clothes, they were the latest fashions, with extra touches. *Tant* Olga also helped her find a dressmaker who made other things for Olina when she was preparing for the journey to America.

Tant Olga even asked around until she found that Johanna needed someone to go with her so she could join her husband in America. Without *Tant* Olga's help, Olina wouldn't be on this train somewhere in the interior of the vast country of America.

The train whistle cut through Olina's thoughts.

"This is our stop, Olina." Gustaf's words followed the sound. "Welcome to Litchfield, Minnesota."

Olina peeked out the window as the train slowed. The town of Litchfield spread on both sides of the tracks. It looked like many of the small towns they had come through on the long trip from New York City. Olina saw a mercantile and a livery stable near the tracks on one side. Other buildings surrounded them. One looked like a hotel. Even a building that appeared to be a saloon was nearby. On the other side of the tracks, the buildings looked more like homes. She saw a church steeple sticking up from a grove of trees that obscured much of that side of the town.

When the train came to a stop, Gustaf took Olina's hand to help her stand. Olina couldn't explain the funny feeling she had every time Gustaf touched her. Maybe it was because she had been traveling so long.

Olina stood poised on the platform and looked around. Beyond the depot, dirt streets were trimmed with wooden sidewalks. Hitching posts stood sentinel in front of various buildings, but they were different from the hitching posts in most of Europe. These connected by a board. Many people were making use of both the sidewalks and the hitching posts. Single horses, horses with buggies, and horses with wagons were tied to several of the posts. Litchfield was a town full of life. Olina liked that.

The Other Brother

As Olina continued her perusal of the town, she noticed that there were several stores down one street away from the depot. Maybe Litchfield was a larger town than she had first thought. She turned, looking for Gustaf. She spied him claiming her trunks from the baggage wagon. He pulled one up on his shoulders as if it didn't weigh much, but Olina knew better. She couldn't get the trunks down the stairs at *Tant* Olga's. The wagon driver helped bring them down when she was going to the ship.

Gustaf deposited the trunk beside the two carpetbags, which he had placed on a bench that ran the full length of the depot. Then he went back for the other. Olina walked over to stand beside the luggage.

"I'm going to leave you here to guard our bags." He didn't look at her while he was talking. Instead, he looked around as if trying to see who was at the station. "I left my wagon at the livery. I'll go get it. You'll be safe waiting with our bags. I'll be back soon."

With long strides, he stepped off the station platform and marched to the livery. Olina sat beside the trunk. She was glad the bench was in the shade. The late morning sun was hotter than she thought it would be in April. Olina would be glad when they got to the Nilssons' farm. She could hardly wait to freshen up. And she wanted clean clothes. On the trip from New York City, she had changed her waist a couple of times with fresh waists she had packed in her carpetbag. But she had worn these clothes too long.

What she actually needed was a bath. She would love to soak in a bathtub, such as *Tant* Olga had in her upstairs bathroom, filled with tepid water. One like she used in the hotel in New York City. She needed to wash her hair. It felt as if it were sticking to her scalp. They couldn't get to the farm any too soon for her.

When Olina heard a wagon pull up beside the platform, she turned to see if it was Gustaf. It was, but he didn't look happy.

"I'm afraid we're not going straight to the farm. Mother sent a list to August at the livery, asking that I pick some things up at the mercantile. I hope that doesn't inconvenience you."

Why did he sound so formal? It made Olina uncomfortable. "No, that'll be just fine, for sure."

Gustaf helped her up from the bench, then took her arm and lifted her into the wagon. While she was busy arranging her skirt on the seat, Gustaf crossed in front of the team of matched black horses. He took time to whisper to the horses and caress their faces before he climbed into the wagon. The seat was wide, but Gustaf was a big man. His presence beside her seemed to crowd Olina.

"Just wait here," Gustaf said as he stopped the wagon in front of a store that was about a block from the train station. "I'll be right back." Gustaf stepped down and tied the horses to the hitching post.

At least he had parked in the shade. Olina was still hotter than she wanted to be. She glanced into the open door of the store. It looked cool inside. What could it hurt if she moved out of the heat?

With that thought, Olina clambered down from the wagon and stepped into the cool interior of the store. What a lot of merchandise they carried. Why, she could probably get anything she would ever need right here. Olina noticed a display of fabrics on a far wall. She made her way through the crowded store and started feeling the texture of various pieces.

A soft feminine voice sounded behind Olina. Olina turned and glanced at the blond girl who stood there. Then she moved as close to the fabric as she could. She had not understood what the young woman said. She guessed that she might want to get by.

"Olina Sandstrom?" Now the voice was excited.

Olina looked once again. "Were you talking to me?" she asked in Swedish.

"*Ja*," the girl answered and continued in Swedish. "Don't you know me? It's Merta Petersson. We used to live near you."

"Of course." Olina reached to hug the girl. Finally someone she knew and who spoke the same language she did. "But I would have never known you. How old were we when you moved? Seven or eight? You've really changed, for sure."

"You have, too." Merta nodded. "But I would recognize you anywhere. You always had the most beautiful eyes."

Olina blushed at the compliment. "Do you live here in Litchfield?"

"I do now. Until last week I lived on a farm with my family, but I got married." Now Merta was blushing. "How did you get here?" Merta looked around the store to see who was there. "Who are you with?"

"I'm with Gustaf Nilsson." Olina couldn't help wondering if Merta knew that Lars sent her the money to come to America, but she didn't want to ask her, in case she didn't. She also wondered if Merta knew about Lars's marriage. Gustaf had indicated that the family had just found out about it. Maybe no one else in town knew yet.

"Yes. I saw his wagon outside," Merta said. "I'm so glad you are visiting here. I hope we can spend some time together before you go home."

"I'm sure we can." Olina noticed Gustaf heading toward the door. "I would like that," she added before turning and following him out the door.

Chapter 4

Gustaf started the horses moving toward the edge of town. Olina had a lot to think about. Merta was married now.

She didn't even tell me what her married name was. Maybe Gustaf knows. "Did you see Merta in the store?" she asked as she turned her gaze toward him. "Yes."

"She told me she was married, but she didn't tell me her married name." "It's Swenson." The curt answer spurted from Gustaf's stiff lips.

What's wrong with him now? Is he always in a bad mood?

Olina hoped the farm wasn't too far from town. She was ready to talk to someone besides this sullen man. She took a deep breath to keep from sighing. How easy it would be to give in to the desolation that threatened to engulf her. At this moment, she had no one to depend on. No matter what awaited her at the farm, she would take care of herself.

She didn't know what the rest of the Nilsson family thought about what had happened. She wasn't even sure what Gustaf thought about it. Except he called her a mess that had to be cleaned up. He said he would take care of her, but she didn't want him taking care of her.

Olina liked this Minnesota. Although the land was flat with a few small rolling hills, it was beautiful. Tall green prairie grass blew in the gentle breeze. Dotted over the green were patches of prairie flowers. Some were white, some pink or yellow. Olina wondered what they were called. They were unlike any flowers she had seen in Sweden. No wonder everything looked so green. She often caught glimpses of water shining through the grass. The farms they passed had many of their fields in cultivation, covered with bright green shoots of some kind.

When they first left town, Olina asked a few questions, but Gustaf answered in monosyllables. Soon she gave up.

After the few attempts at conversation, Gustaf also rode quietly, thinking his own thoughts. He didn't point out the beautiful wildflowers, or the small lakes, or even the road to their neighbor's farm. He sat berating himself. Maybe if he had made Lars face his own mistakes, he would have learned to be more responsible.

He couldn't even imagine what Olina must be going through, but he was beginning to admire her. He wished he could be more help to her; but whenever he thought about the last few days, anger still boiled up inside him. He didn't know who he was angriest at, Lars or himself.

When they reached the farm, decisions had to be made about Olina. Would he have any say in what happened? He hoped that he would. He wanted to help this young woman who shared the wagon seat with him, so close that he could feel her even though they were not touching. Occasionally on the train, he caught a glimpse of the hurt that lingered deep within her. What could he have done to prevent it?

*

"Our farm starts right here." Gustaf pointed toward the fence line that divided the land on their right.

The sound of his voice, after riding so far without talking, startled Olina. She jerked, then turned to look where he was pointing.

"It's still a ways before we come to the drive up to the house."

How could Gustaf sound as if everything were normal? Maybe he was right. Soon she would face the whole Nilsson family. She didn't want to fall apart the first time someone spoke to her.

"The crops look good." Olina was surprised that her voice didn't tremble. "What is growing in that field?"

"This one has winter wheat," Gustaf answered. "We'll plant corn in the next field, though."

Olina didn't think she had ever seen corn growing. She wondered if she would be here to see it.

"Just past that field, we'll turn in and head toward the house."

Olina gazed over the fields toward a grove of trees growing back from the road. "Is the house up there among the trees?"

"Yes. We bought the farm from Ben Johnson's widow. They had been on the farm for a long time. He was the one who built the house. The trees keep it cool in the summertime and protect it from some of the harsh winds in the winter."

Olina tried to see the house from where they were, but it was too far away. "Why did Mrs. Johnson sell such a wonderful farm?" Olina turned to look at Gustaf.

"They didn't have children, and she was getting older. She couldn't run the farm by herself."

"Couldn't she hire someone to help her?"

"Yes, but she felt alone when Mr. Johnson died. She wanted to move back East with her sister. It was our good luck that she was ready to sell about the time we got here. No one else tried to buy it. It's a big farm, so it cost quite a lot. After we sold everything we had in Sweden to come to Minnesota, we had enough money to buy it from her."

The Other Brother

Gustaf turned the horses down a long drive bordered on one side by a plowed field and on the other side by another field of wheat. "She didn't want to move all of her furniture across the country. I think her sister had married a wealthy merchant in some city back East. She already had a nice house full of furniture. We were able to move in and live right away. Of course, over time, Mother has made the house into her own home."

When Gustaf chuckled at that, Olina was able to laugh along with him, at least a little. She remembered how homey Ingrid Nilsson's house always was. How happy it made Ingrid and her family.

It was a little laugh, but Gustaf felt part of the heavy weight he had been carrying slip with the sound of it.

Maybe, just maybe, Olina will be able to get over what Lars has done to her. And maybe someday she will forgive me.

Chapter 5

Gerda Nilsson must have heard the wagon coming up the long drive to the house, because she rushed out onto the porch. Olina was glad to see the friend she had grown up with. But the young woman standing on the porch was no longer the girl who had romped through the meadows with her. Gerda's hair was up in the new pompadour style that was coming into fashion. The pouf formed a soft blond halo that framed her delicate features, features that were so like the ones Olina remembered, and yet so different. But then, they both were.

As Olina climbed down from the wagon seat, her gaze was drawn to the two-story farmhouse so different from the houses she was used to seeing in Sweden. Farmhouses back home were usually only one story. Instead of rock that was used over there, this American home was built of wood and painted white. Dark green shutters framed the windows on both the lower story and the upper story. Porches at home were small, but this house had a covered porch that spread along the lower story, covering at least three-fourths of it. White columns supported the roof of the porch, and a railing connected the columns except where steps led up to the porch.

Olina thought it must be wonderful to sit in the inviting rocking chairs that were scattered the length of it. Three sat on either side of the front door. The house looked enormous to Olina, much larger than farmhouses in Sweden.

"Olina!" Gerda rushed down the steps.

"Gerda!" Olina scrambled over the side of the wagon, catching her foot in the hem of her skirt. She would have fallen if strong hands hadn't caught her. She didn't want to look at Gustaf. He might be able to see how much his touch affected her, even though she didn't want it to. Her emotions were too close to the surface.

Gerda threw her arms around Olina and held her as if she would never let go. "I'm so glad you're here. I've missed you so much." She sounded as if she were about to cry.

Maybe she would think that Olina was only emotional about seeing her. "I've missed you, too. It seems like forever since you left."

When the two girls finally pulled apart, tears were streaming down their faces. Gerda pulled a handkerchief from the pocket of her apron and gently wiped Olina's face. Then she dried her own tears.

The Other Brother

Gerda took Olina by the arm and drew her toward the porch. Flower beds spread in front, and young plants were beginning to bud. There were even a few rosebushes. Olina had always loved the smell of roses. She doubted that she would be here when the buds opened enough to share their delightful fragrance.

"*Mor* has just left to take dinner to *Far* and the hired men, but she left food in case you got here before she returned. She wanted to be here when you arrived, but the men have to be fed. I was glad she let me stay at the house and wait for you." Gerda opened the door that led into the formal parlor.

Gustaf followed them in, carrying Olina's smaller bag.

Olina liked the furniture, upholstered in wine-colored velvet. It was different from what she was used to in Sweden, but it was attractive. A thick carpet spread to within a foot of each wall. Even *Tant* Olga's house didn't have carpet. Everything matched so well, not like the hodgepodge of furniture her family had collected over the years. Lace curtains and doilies knitted the decor together. *Mor* would love to see this beautiful place.

"What room do you want Olina to have?" Gustaf was heading toward the hall that was behind the parlor.

"I wanted her to share mine so we could really catch up." Gerda glanced at Olina before she continued. "But *Mor* said we should give her the bedroom on the front corner. That way she can have her privacy, but we'll still spend time together when we want to."

Gustaf nodded and ducked through the doorway. In the hallway outside the parlor was the stairway. He climbed up the steep stairs as if they were level ground. Olina followed him at a slower pace.

"When you've freshened up, come down to eat." Gerda stood looking up after her friend. "I put fresh water in your room."

Olina met Gustaf as he came from the bedroom that would be hers. His presence made the narrow hall feel even narrower. Olina needed to have more room between them. Why did his presence unsettle her? He was like all the other men in her life. He didn't want her, but she felt drawn to him even though she wanted to push him away. She felt as if the dark hall did not have enough air. She was having a hard time taking a breath.

"I can wait to bring up your trunks." Gustaf looked down at her. "That way you'll have plenty of time to freshen up."

"What I really need"—Olina moved toward the beckoning doorway—"is a long, soaking bath. It feels as though it's been a lifetime since we were in New York."

"Wouldn't you like to eat first?"

Olina slowly nodded.

Gustaf pointed to another door halfway down the hallway. "That's the bathroom. We have a large tub in there. A man from Norway invented an automatic storage water heater a few years ago, and we've just installed one, so we don't have to carry hot water upstairs for the bathtub."

Again Olina nodded. Then she stepped into the bedroom that would be hers for a while. How long, she could only guess. She was going to have to make some decisions, but she didn't want to think about them right now. She pulled out her hat pin and removed her hat. Dropping her hat on the table by the bed, she walked over and looked out the window that faced the front of the house. There was another window on the side of the house, and a gentle breeze blew through the room. More lace curtains covered these windows, and matching lace draped across the bed. How inviting that bed looked. Maybe she should lie down and forget everything. But she couldn't. It was there in her heart. . .in her mind. . .in every part of her.

After picking up the pitcher of water, she poured some into the matching bowl. Both of them were decorated with hand-painted roses. As she splashed the water on her face, its coolness soothed her. Gerda must have filled the pitcher right before they arrived.

Taking off the jacket of her traveling suit, she looked down at her wilted, dusty white waist. It didn't matter. Gerda and Gustaf had already seen it. She decided not to change until after her bath. Olina picked up the rose-scented soap and washed her hands. She dried her face and hands with the embroidered linen towel that lay on the washstand beside the pitcher and bowl. How was she ever going to get through the evening? She crossed the hardwood floor and descended the stairs, trying to rein in her emotions.

Gerda and Gustaf kept the conversation light and informative as they all ate homemade bread and ham, accompanied by applesauce that Gerda and her mother canned last autumn. Olina learned a lot about the farm, the neighbors, and the many activities that occurred in the close-knit community. Although they were a ways from town, many of the neighbors were from Norway or Sweden, and they often got together. Women visited over tea or held quilting bees as well as other bees. They had helped Merta Swenson make her linens before her marriage. It sounded like a lot of fun, but Olina wondered if she would ever have fun again. Men helped each other harvest crops, build barns, or mend broken farming equipment. But no one could help fix her broken heart.

They had even established a school close by. The school building was also used to hold church services when the weather was too bad to get into town. Olina would have loved getting married here and establishing her family in this community. Now there would not be any family. At least not for Olina and Lars.

And who else was there? Unbidden, a face swam into Olina's mind. A face so like Lars, only more mature. A face with icy blue eyes, but she had seen those eyes warm when he had looked at his sister. Why was she thinking about Gustaf? He was nothing to her. Nothing but her best friend's brother.

Olina needed to make a decision. What was she going to do? What could she do? She had very little money. Not enough to go back to Sweden. The only thing she could do was write her father and beg his forgiveness for going against his wishes. If he forgave her, maybe he would send her the money to come home. That is, if he had enough money to send.

Olina was soaking in a tub of warm water when she heard Mrs. Nilsson return. The sound of voices rumbled below her, but she couldn't make out what they were saying. She did recognize their voices as both Gerda and Gustaf talked to their mother. Was their conversation about her? Soon the talking ceased, and Olina heard Gerda and Gustaf leave the house.

Tears streamed down Olina's face and plopped in the cooling bathwater. She felt chilled, inside and out. She got out of the bathtub and pulled the plug. As the water gurgled down the drain, Olina dried off and put on fresh clothes. At least she felt better being clean again. Tonight, when she was once more alone in her room, she would write her father a letter.

Mrs. Nilsson was waiting in the kitchen for Olina when she came down the stairs. She opened her arms and gathered Olina close.

"My precious child." There was a catch in her voice. "I'm sorry that my son treated you so wrong." By the end of the second sentence, both Olina and Mrs. Nilsson were crying.

Olina quickly regained her composure and pulled out of the embrace. She reached for the handkerchief she had earlier stuffed into her sleeve. After wiping her face, she turned toward the woman she once thought would be her mother-in-law.

Mrs. Nilsson was also wiping tears from her cheeks. "Since we received the letter, I have asked myself if I did something wrong when I was rearing Lars. How could my son have done something so irresponsible and hurtful?"

"For sure, it's not your fault that this has happened," Olina said. "But I don't know what I'm going to do now."

Mrs. Nilsson pulled a chair out from the table for Olina. "After supper tonight, we'll have a talk with Bennel. He'll know what we should do."

Evidently Gustaf had gone out to help Mr. Nilsson in the fields, because they both came in for the evening meal at the same time. Mr. Nilsson didn't say anything about Lars to Olina before they ate, but when the meal was over, he asked Olina and Mrs. Nilsson to accompany him into the parlor. Gustaf followed them. Evidently his *fader* didn't mind, because he didn't tell him to go away.

Mr. Nilsson indicated that Olina should sit on the sofa beside his wife. Mrs. Nilsson took Olina's hand and squeezed it. Olina knew she was trying to make Olina relax, but she couldn't. Maybe it was because of what her *fader* had done to her. Mr. Nilsson felt too much like her *fader*. The stern expression on his face caused her to be nervous.

"First, Olina, I want to apologize to you for what my son did. I can imagine that you are extremely hurt."

Olina could tell that he meant what he said. She nodded.

The expression on Mr. Nilsson's face softened. "I can never make up for what Lars did, but I want you to know that we love you as if you were our own daughter. You have a home here as long as you want one."

"Thank you." It was hard for Olina to get the words out because her throat was dry.

"We'll do anything we can to help you." Mr. Nilsson got up from the chair where he was sitting and stood beside his wife, placing his hand on her shoulder. "While you are in our home, we hope you'll think of us as your parents."

Olina bowed her head a moment before she raised it and answered. "Thank you. I'd like that."

Mrs. Nilsson patted Olina's hand, which rested on the sofa between them. "Do you have any plans for now?"

"Well, I don't have the money to go back to Sweden." Olina tried to swallow the lump that had come in her throat. "I plan to write *Fader* a letter tonight, asking him to help me come home." Olina couldn't tell them what her father had said before she left Sweden. She hoped she never would have to tell anyone.

Gustaf didn't say anything while this conversation was going on, but Olina could feel his gaze on her. She glanced and caught an expression on his face that she had never seen before. It made her feel as if he cared what happened to her, not at all like the man in New York City who called her a mess.

Chapter 6

Olina wondered how long she would have to wait for an answer to her letter. Knowing it would take a long time, she tried to hide her hurt from the members of the Nilsson family. She thought she was doing it quite well. However, after only a few days, Gerda came to her room a little while before supper.

"Olina." Gerda sat on the side of Olina's bed and watched her friend as she fussed with her hair. "I haven't wanted to pry. I wanted to wait until you shared with me, but you haven't." Gerda got up and went to stand behind Olina, looking directly into the reflection of her face in the mirror. "It's hard for me to watch you hurting so badly. We've been friends a long time. Can't you let me help you?"

Olina turned from the mirror and walked over to the window. She pulled back the curtain that gently blew in the breeze, trying to find something to fix her gaze on. Although her focus wandered from the birds in the trees, to the open barn door, to the sparkle of water barely visible beyond the roof of the barn, none of these things interested her. She paused a minute before answering, trying to decide how much to tell Gerda. Then she turned to face her dear friend.

"Oh, Gerda." A shuddering breath shook her frame. "I haven't known what to say. . .or if I could say anything without crying." The sentence ended with a soft sob.

Gerda pulled Olina into her arms and hugged her, gently rubbing her back as she broke into sobs muffled against Gerda's soft calico dress. The soothing touch brought comfort to Olina. It had been too long since someone who loved her had held her. She missed her mother's touch. *Tant* Olga had hugged her occasionally, too.

When Olina stopped crying, she pulled away and swiped, with both hands, at the tears on her face. Gerda picked up a soft white handkerchief and helped Olina mop away the moisture that had completely covered her face and soaked the shoulder of Gerda's dress.

"Oh my, I must look a fright." Olina turned toward the oval mirror on the wall. "My face is all puffy and red." She patted some hairs into place before turning back toward Gerda. "I don't think I'll have any supper tonight. I'm not really hungry." She didn't want anyone else in the family to see her like this.

Gerda gazed deep into her eyes before turning toward the door. "I know you helped feed the chickens and gather the eggs. And you insisted on hanging the clothes on the line for Mother. That's enough to work up an appetite. I'll make both of us sandwiches out of cold roast beef and cheese. We'll grab an apple apiece and go down to the creek for a picnic supper."

Olina had no answer for her except to nod. After Gerda left, Olina glanced down at her white blouse that had become soiled when she was gathering the eggs. While Gerda went down to fix their supper, she changed into a soft green calico. Looking at the white collar and cuffs trimmed with lace that she usually wore with the dress, she decided to leave them off. She was glad that she had plaited her hair and wound it around her head that morning. It was suitable for a picnic on the banks of a stream.

After tramping down the fencerow of a large field, the two girls ambled out across a pasture toward the grove of trees that lined the banks of the stream. Each girl carried her supper in a small tin lard bucket. Gerda told her that they were the ones the Nilsson children had used when they were younger to carry their lunches to school. It made Olina feel young and almost carefree. But not completely. She could not bury her hurt that deep.

The day had been warm for late spring, and it was a long walk. Both girls began to perspire before they entered the cool shadows of the trees. Taking a well-worn path through the underbrush, they soon arrived at the bank of the flowing water. A small sandbar led from the verdant growth to the stream, and a few large stones jutted out into the water. One even formed a flat shelf above the flow.

Gerda walked out on the stone shelf that was still warm from the sun, although it was now shaded from the branches of the trees that hung over it. Olina followed her, watching bubbles and gurgles burst from the water as it swirled around the rocks. Gerda sat cross-legged on the rock and arranged her skirt to cover her legs. Then she put her lard bucket in her lap. After prying off the lid with a stick she had picked up as they walked through the woods, Gerda pulled out a sandwich wrapped in paper.

Olina did the same. Before she laid her sandwich on the full skirt that spread around her on the rock, she took a bite. It tasted heavenly. Olina hadn't realized how hungry she really was. After taking another bite, she looked back into the bucket. It contained more than just an apple. She pulled out another lump of paper and unrolled a sweet pickle. When Olina sank her teeth into it, pickle juice dripped down her chin. She reached up with her free hand, trying to catch it before it stained her dress.

"This tastes good." Olina wiped her mouth on a napkin that was also in her bucket.

"Mother and I made those last summer." Gerda unwrapped her own pickle. "It's a recipe Anna Jenson gave us. We all like it, especially Gustaf." Gerda took a bite of her sandwich. After she finished chewing it, she said, "Of course, Gustaf likes everything Anna makes."

Olina looked up. "Is she a wonderful cook?" She didn't know why she was so interested, but she was.

"Oh, she's a good cook," Gerda answered, "but I think Gustaf would like it even if it wasn't that good. He likes everything about Anna. The whole family expects them to marry sometime soon."

Olina didn't know why that should bother her, but it did. She looked up at Gerda, who was now digging other packages out of her bucket. "Why did you say that?"

Gerda looked up. "Say what?"

"That the family expects them to marry. Has he asked her to marry him?"

Gerda went back to unwrapping her supper. "I don't think so. She would have told us. . .or he would have. They're together a lot. I think he's calling on her."

Olina nodded even though Gerda wasn't looking. She took a bite of the sandwich again, and what had tasted heavenly a few minutes ago now turned to sand in her mouth, making her throat dry. She looked around for something to dip the water with.

Gerda dipped her empty bucket into the cool, moving water and handed it to Olina. "Drink this. You look as though you need it right now."

Olina turned the bucket up and gulped the soothing water, dripping some down the front of her dress. Then she emptied her own bucket of food and handed it to Gerda. "Here you can use mine."

The rest of the meal was eaten in silence by the two girls. Olina tried to force the food past the large lump in her throat. At any other time, the sandwich, pickle, chocolate cake, and apple would have tasted good. But not tonight. They were only so much sawdust to chew and wash down with lots of water. She was glad when all the packages were empty. She hadn't wanted to hurt Gerda by not finishing what she had fixed for them.

When Gerda was through with her food, she pulled off her shoes and stockings and dangled her feet into the water. "Are you ever going to talk to me? I know Lars hurt you, and I know that Gustaf didn't tell you about it as soon as he should have. But I thought we were best friends. I want to help you if I can."

Olina followed Gerda's lead and soon splashed her feet in the refreshing stream. As they sat there, Olina did reveal part of her heart to her friend. They discussed Lars and how he had hurt her and how Gustaf had treated her in New York City and on the trip to Minnesota. But Olina couldn't tell her friend about her own father rejecting her. Or that she no longer felt she could trust God.

Since it was such a warm spring day, Gustaf soon worked up a sweat. He loaded the wagon full of hay and took it to the pasture where the dairy cattle were kept. There he scattered the hay into four piles in different parts of the pasture, helping supplement the meager grass. Then he plowed the only field that hadn't been done before he went to New York. All the time he was following the horses pulling the large implement, he thought about that fateful journey, his anger on the trip there, and his confusion on the journey back.

It wasn't long before his thoughts settled on Olina. He would never be able to remove some images from his memory. Olina as she stood on the dock waiting for Lars. Olina at dinner at the hotel. Olina in the hall of the hotel when he had blurted out the truth about Lars. How different Olina was the next morning. She had strength and poise.

He couldn't understand what it was about her that drew him. But something did. Olina filled his thoughts as Anna never had. He couldn't remember thinking about Anna so much while he was working. He had a hard time concentrating on making the rows straight while his thoughts were in captivity to Olina.

What was he going to do? He knew that everyone, including Anna and his family, expected him to ask Anna to marry him. He wasn't sure he could do that now. How could he hurt her that way? Anna had meant a lot to him for a long time. But did he love her enough to marry her? That was a question he would have to answer soon. When he tried to bring her image to mind, Olina's face sometimes took its place. A lot of good his thoughts of Olina were. She didn't trust him, and he didn't know if she ever would. How could he have said those things to her in New York? What had he been thinking?

Gustaf didn't know what he was going to do. He knew that what he already felt for Olina was a major impediment to his stagnant relationship with Anna.

Gustaf worked even harder trying to clear the thoughts from his mind, but they wouldn't leave. He was glad when he finished the last row of the field. After unhitching the plow, he drove the horses into the barn before removing their harness. While he rubbed them down, he decided to go to the creek to take a swim before supper.

Because his mind was on other things, he didn't notice that the prairie grass, on the way to the grove of trees, was trampled down. It never entered his mind that someone had beaten him to the quiet haven.

As Gustaf walked the path through the underbrush, he pulled down his suspenders. Then he stripped off the sweat-soaked shirt and threw it onto a bush near the end of the path. He had started unbuttoning his trousers when he emerged from the woods and first heard the soft murmur of feminine voices. Startled, he froze just as Olina turned her eyes toward the rustle he made coming through the brush.

Shock registered on her face as her gaze swept from his unbuttoned waistband across his naked chest to his face. Blood rushed to color her cheeks, and she swiftly looked away.

Gustaf's first inclination was to cover up, but his shirt was nowhere near him. So he dove into the deep swimming hole formed by a small cove on the creek. He didn't even take time to remove his work boots. He was thankful that the creek wasn't over his head there because his heavy boots pulled his feet to the bottom, and he stood chest high in the water.

"Gustaf, what are you doing here?" Gerda started gathering up the scattered papers and putting them in her bucket. "We didn't know you were coming for a swim."

"I didn't know you were here, either." Gustaf pushed his wet hair back over his head.

"Is that why you went in swimming with your boots on?" Gerda covered her mouth to hide a giggle.

Gustaf looked down into the clear water. "Well, so I have. No wonder I'm having trouble swimming." He burst out laughing. The sound reverberated from the rocks and trees that surrounded them.

Gustaf noticed that Olina was laughing, too. A high musical sound. It was wonderful to hear. Before they had left Sweden, she had been a happy, fun-loving girl. He had often heard her laugh peal across the fields as she and Lars, or she and Gerda, were playing. He hadn't realized how much he had missed the sound of it until it wafted across the water to him. Maybe his being all wet was a good thing if it could start her laughing again.

Gerda and Olina both pulled their feet from the water and picked up their shoes and stockings. After looping their buckets over their arms, they started back toward the path.

"We'll let you swim in peace." Gerda smiled at her brother before following Olina through the opening in the bushes.

As they walked away, Gustaf could hear them giggling as if they were little girls. He was sure they were discussing him, but that was all right. Olina was laughing again.

The day after they washed the clothes, Mrs. Nilsson wanted to wash all the sheets and towels. Olina was glad to help her. While the water was heating, she went upstairs and started taking all the sheets off the beds. She made a pile in the hall at the top of the stairs. When she finished in the last bedroom, she spread out one of the sheets and placed the others on it. After pulling the corners together, she tied them in a soft knot and picked them up to carry downstairs. It was hard to see around the large bundle, and her mind was on her problem.

When Olina had gone down about half of the steep stairs, her foot slipped, and she was unable to regain her balance. Her elbow struck one of the stairs, and a pain shot up and down that arm. She shut her eyes and groaned as she hit another step.

Something stopped her descent, and a concerned voice sounded near her ear. "Olina, are you all right?"

Olina opened her eyes and stared up into Gustaf's face, which was very near hers. "I think so."

She lost her precarious hold on the bundle, and it fell to the bottom of the stairs. Gustaf eased himself down on the step beside Olina. He reached up and wiped a tear that had made its way down her cheek.

"You're crying. Are you sure you're not hurt?"

Olina rubbed the elbow and couldn't keep from wincing. It did hurt. "I hit my elbow on the stairs."

Gustaf carefully assisted her to stand. "Is that all that hurts?"

"I think so."

"Can you walk?"

Olina nodded.

Gustaf helped her the rest of the way down the stairs. He took her into the kitchen and pulled out a chair. "Sit here. Let me look at your elbow."

His touch was gentle as his fingers probed the area. "I think your arm is swelling."

He went to the sink and dipped a towel into cool water. When he came back, he made a pad with the wet cloth and tied another around it to keep it on her arm.

Olina watched all these ministrations with interest. This man was different from the man who met her in New York City. She never would have thought that Gustaf could be so caring, especially to her.

"Thank you." Olina started to get up.

His hand on her shoulder kept her in the chair. "You need to sit here and let the cool water ease your pain."

"But your moder is waiting for me to bring her the sheets to wash."

Gustaf glanced to the bundle that lay in a heap in the hall between the kitchen and the parlor. "I'll take them to her. She would want you to take care of yourself."

Olina watched in amazement as Gustaf hefted the bundle onto his shoulder as if it were as light as a feather and carried it out the back door. Maybe she should rethink her opinion of him.

☙

Gustaf wasn't sure why he went into the house at that moment, but when he saw Olina's foot slip, his heart jumped into his throat. He rushed to stop her from tumbling all the way to the bottom of the stairs. She would have hurt more than her elbow if that had happened. Something deep inside him reached out to her. It wasn't just her beauty that called to him.

Olina had faced her terrible dilemma with more strength than most men would have had in the same circumstances. He admired the way she fit right into the family, sharing the workload with *Mor* and Gerda. Of course, she was kind of quiet when the family was all together, but he was sure she had a lot to think about. It would be awhile before she had an answer from her father. Gustaf hoped that when it came, Olina's troubles would be over. But something within him didn't want her to leave Minnesota.

After supper, the family went into the parlor. Mrs. Nilsson picked up her knitting, and Mr. Nilsson read to the family from the newspaper he had picked up in town. Gerda and Olina sat on the sofa. Gustaf sat on the floor beside it.

"How is your arm, Olina?" he asked when his father stopped reading out loud.

She looked down at his upturned face. "It's much better."

"I'm glad."

Mr. Nilsson folded up the newspaper and laid it on the table beside his chair. "What happened to Olina?" He sounded compassionate.

"She was helping me," Mrs. Nilsson told him, "and she fell on the stairs."

"But Gustaf stopped me from going all the way down." She turned back to Gustaf. "I didn't thank you, did I?"

This was the first time Olina really took part in the conversation. She felt more comfortable and a part of the family.

The next day, Olina was helping Mrs. Nilsson once again. Several times during the day, Gustaf came by wherever she was and spent a few minutes talking to her. Soon this became a daily habit. The friendship continued to develop, but Olina wanted to be careful. Of course, it was just a friendship. Gustaf was spoken for, wasn't he?

Chapter 7

Olina had been in Minnesota for three weeks. The Nilsson family planned a party to introduce her to the neighbors. Olina dreaded that celebration. She didn't know how she could face all the people when they found out that she had come to America to marry Lars. Maybe if she had a headache or stomachache or something, she wouldn't have to go. Everyone else could enjoy the gathering whether she was there or not. Then she found out that the doctor was coming. If she pretended to be sick, Mrs. Nilsson would have him look at her. He would surely know that nothing was wrong with her.

Things had gotten better since the day she and Gerda had the picnic. Maybe she could make it through the party. If things got tough, she could remember how Gustaf looked when he jumped into the water, the way the cool stream had darkened his white blond hair to a honey color. But that memory also recalled his broad, muscular chest liberally sprinkled with blond hairs. With that picture came feelings that Olina didn't understand, a tightness deep within her that she had never felt before. It made her feel breathless. She had to remind herself that she didn't trust men. Besides, Gustaf was promised to Anna, wasn't he?

At least the party would bring one good thing. She would finally get to see this Anna. What would she look like? She wondered if Anna was prettier than she was. What did it matter? She didn't mean anything special to Gustaf, and he wasn't special to her. Was he?

❧

The schoolhouse looked festive when Olina and Gerda walked in. Whenever there was a party, the whole farming community helped. Chains made from colored paper draped around the rafters, and lanterns hung on hooks all around the walls. The young women were drawn toward long tables made from lumber laid across sawhorses and covered with tablecloths in various colors. Holding down the cloths were fancy dishes containing all kinds of goodies. Everyone must have brought her most cherished glass plates and bowls. Cakes and pastries took up half of one table.

Olina loved pastry, especially *munk*. The fried pieces of slightly sweet dough were especially good when they were rolled in sugar as soon as they came from the kettle. She could even see that one plate held *äppelmunk*, tasty doughnuts filled with apple bits and cinnamon before they were fried. She couldn't identify all of the kinds of cake, but she did see *gräddbakelse*. This cream cake was a favorite of hers. Olina knew she would have to be careful not to eat too much or she would look just as she had when she first went to live with *Tant* Olga.

Every one of the neighbor women had fixed several of their best recipes for the party. Olina decided that a large crowd must be coming to eat that much food.

"How many people will be here tonight?" she asked Gerda as they hung their shawls on two of the empty hooks on the wall near the door.

Turning around, Gerda looked across the group that already filled the room. "Everyone is here." Then she looked again. "But I don't see Anna. The Jensons are late as usual. I think Anna likes to make an entrance."

The two friends walked over to the table where Mrs. Nilsson was pouring apple cider into a variety of cups. "Here, Olina." Gerda handed her a cup before she took one for herself. "Mrs. Swenson, Merta's mother-in-law, makes the best cider."

Just as Olina reached for the proffered beverage, a large family came through the door accompanied by a lot of noise.

"There are the Jensons." Gerda took a slow sip of cider. "The one with the dark hair is Anna."

Olina was surprised. Anna Jenson was pretty enough, with bright eyes and a smiling face, but she stood tall and sturdy. Olina could tell by looking at her that she was a hard worker and strong. Her upswept hair braided and looped into a figure-eight bun low on the back of her head. Her laugh, though infectious, was a little too loud.

Olina looked around for Gustaf. She was surprised that he hadn't gone to greet his intended. If Olina were promised to someone, she would want him by her side at a party, especially one given to introduce a new girl to the community. Now why was she thinking about that? It didn't matter to her what kind of relationship Anna and Gustaf had, did it?

The night was a great success. Olina enjoyed meeting the neighbors, and they welcomed her with open arms. Some of the neighbors had emigrated from the same area where she had lived in Sweden. She renewed acquaintances with them. After inquiring about her family, they moved on to asking her how she liked Minnesota. No one wondered why she came, so she soon relaxed and enjoyed herself, pushing to the back of her mind and heart the fact that she was still hurting. She needed to get on with her life. Maybe soon her visit would be over, after her reply from her father arrived.

❦

When Anna and her family came in the door, Gustaf started to go to her, but his attention was drawn to Olina, where she stood by Gerda, drinking cider. He couldn't keep from comparing the two women.

Anna was familiar and comfortable. Olina caused something inside Gustaf to tug his heart. The last week or so, their friendship had grown, and he liked that. But would a man who intended to marry one woman develop such a strong friendship with another? Of course not. He knew he couldn't pursue the feelings Olina caused until he talked to Anna. He would wait until the end of the evening and ask if he could drive her home. Gustaf didn't want her hurt at the party, and what he needed to say to her would be upsetting. He knew that if he loved her as a husband should love his wife, he wouldn't be so interested in Olina. Anna deserved more than that from the man she would marry.

During the evening, Gerda or her mother made sure Olina met everyone in attendance. When the dancing started, accompanied by a fiddle and an accordion playing some American music and some Scandinavian music, Olina was never without a partner. All the young men, and even some of the older men, asked her to dance. All the men except Gustaf.

That Gustaf didn't dance with her shouldn't have mattered, but it did. Why did he stay so far away from her? Olina watched him covertly all through the evening. He didn't dance with Anna any more often than he did with the other young women. Maybe Gerda was wrong. Maybe there wasn't an understanding between them. And what difference did that make to her? Nothing. Not any difference at all.

However, several hours later while the women were gathering up their nearly empty dishes, Olina noticed Gustaf talking earnestly with Anna. Anna stood smiling up at him. Although Anna was a tall woman, he was several inches taller. After a moment, they walked together to the hooks along the back wall. Gustaf took a long blue cape off one hook and draped it around Anna's shoulders. Then they left together.

A dull ache started in Olina's heart. Trying to hide it, she helped Mrs. Nilsson gather up all the things they had brought.

"Where is a broom?" Olina asked as she put the last tablecloth in the basket. "I'll sweep the floor. Most everyone is gone."

"Oh no, you won't." Gerda took the basket from her hands and started out the door to take it to the wagon. "You were the guest of honor. You won't be cleaning up," she called back over her shoulder.

"It's all right." Mrs. Nilsson was standing beside Olina now. "Tomorrow Gerda and Merta will come and clean up the schoolhouse. No one wants to stay tonight, and they already planned to do it that way."

Olina allowed herself to be led out of the warm building into the cold of a spring midnight in Minnesota. Stars twinkled in the clear inky sky above. Shivering, she pulled her woolen shawl tighter around her and threw the loose end across her shoulder. She had done a good job of not thinking about Lars, but for a moment, she couldn't stop thinking how good it would feel to have his arms around her to help keep out the cold. She imagined glancing up into his gray eyes, but instead the eyes she saw in her mind were glittering, icy blue.

Anna smiled up at Gustaf. "I missed you while you were on your trip to New York. I've been surprised that you haven't come over since you returned. You've been back three weeks, haven't you?"

Gustaf's nod was accompanied by a grunt of assent.

"I suppose you've been busy catching up with the things that didn't get done while you were gone."

"That's right." Gustaf steered her toward the door. "I'm glad you wore this cape. It'll be warm on the ride home." Gustaf was trying to change the subject, but this was not a good subject to change to.

"Well, you could keep me warm," Anna purred in a voice unlike her usual clear one.

It was a good thing Gustaf was walking behind her. She couldn't see him gritting his teeth. How was he going to do this without hurting her too much? Even though the cold air caressed them as they walked to the buggy, Gustaf was beginning to sweat. This night was going to end in disaster. It wouldn't end well for him and not for Anna, either.

After helping Anna into the buggy, Gustaf walked around in front of the horses, giving them an encouraging pat as he passed. When he climbed up on the seat, he noticed that Anna was sitting closer to the middle than the side. Gustaf didn't want to sit so close to her.

He didn't want her upset the whole way home. It would take about half an hour to get to the Jenson farm. He would wait until they were within sight of the farmhouse to talk to her.

As they drove along, Anna kept up a steady stream of chatter. Gustaf wasn't sure what she was talking about because he was trying to think how to say what he needed to say with the least amount of hurt. He hoped his occasional comments of "yes," "right," and "interesting" were appropriate and at the right time.

When they were still about a mile from the Jenson farmhouse, Anna broke through his thoughts. "All right, Gustaf." Her voice was louder and harsher than it had been on the rest of the trip. "Are you going to tell me what's bothering you?"

Gustaf pulled the team off the road and parked under a tree. He tied the reins to the front of the buggy and sat there a minute. Then he turned to look at Anna in the dark shadows. Her luminous eyes sparkled through the darkness. "What makes you think something's the matter?" It was a stupid question. They had spent enough time together for her to read his moods.

"I've been carrying on a one-sided conversation all the way home. You haven't heard a single word I've said." Anna sat with her arms crossed defiantly across her chest.

Gustaf wanted to deny her allegation, but then thought better of it. "You're right. My thoughts have been engaged otherwise."

"And who has engaged your thoughts?"

Gustaf was amazed that her question had cut straight to the root of the problem, but he didn't want to tell her that right now.

Sensing his hesitation, Anna continued, "Are you going to tell me what's going on?"

"Anna." Gustaf tried to take her hand in his, but she pulled stiffly to the far end of the buggy seat. He was afraid if he reached for her again, she might tumble off into the dirt. He didn't want that.

"I've been thinking about our relationship." Gustaf stopped and cleared his throat, trying to dislodge the large lump that had taken up residence there.

"And?" Anna wasn't going to make this any easier.

"And. . ." Gustaf tried again. "And I think. . .maybe. . .we shouldn't spend so much time together."

"Is there someone else?" Anna's bitter question surprised Gustaf.

"What kind of man do you think I am?" he asked in anger.

"I don't know what kind of man you are." Anna shivered, but she pulled even farther away from him, if that were possible. "I thought—" Anna stopped to swallow a sob. "I thought we had something. You've been calling on me for some time now."

An owl hooted in a nearby tree, and the wind picked up, swishing the branches above their heads.

"Well. . .I have been." That lump had grown to be a boulder. "Calling on you, I mean." Why did this have to be so hard to say? "I'm not sure we're supposed to be together for life."

Even in the dark, he could see Anna glare at him. "What is that supposed to mean?" Her tone was harder and more brittle. "I thought you were going to ask me to marry you tonight." Anna ended on a sob, and Gustaf could see the tears glistening on her cheeks, making trails that she didn't wipe off.

It felt as if there were a dagger in his heart. He reached out to her but hesitated when he saw her expression. Gustaf pulled his big white handkerchief from his back pocket and handed it to her, knowing she wouldn't want him touching her right now. As she mopped her tears away, they were replaced by others.

"I know that's what you thought, and that makes this even harder." Gustaf tried to sound gentle, but he didn't. The words sounded harsh to his own ears. "You're important to me, but I know I don't love you the way you should be loved by your future husband. You deserve better than that. Can't we remain friends?"

"And are we friends right now?" Anna's question was forced from between stiff lips. "Is friendship what we have had all this time? Nothing more?"

Gustaf bowed his head and covered his face with both hands. Could the evening get any worse? "I'm so sorry. I didn't want to hurt you." He wasn't even sure Anna heard his muffled words, so he looked up, dropping his hands into his lap.

"Would you please take me home now?"

Gustaf untied the reins and clucked to the waiting horses. Ominous silence accompanied them the last mile to the farmhouse, covering them in an oppressive blanket. When the buggy stopped, Anna didn't wait for Gustaf to help her down. Instead, she scrambled over the wheel, almost falling in her haste.

"Wait, Anna. I'll help you." He tried to follow her.

"Don't bother," she yelled back over her shoulder and ran into the house.

Gustaf hoped some day she would speak to him again.

Chapter 8

After the party, Olina settled into life on the Minnesota farm. She gladly helped with her share of the chores. It was good for Gerda and Olina to be together again. It was as if they had never been separated. Gerda helped Olina become a part of the community, and Olina caught Gerda up on what had happened in the old country after the Nilssons left.

Before long, the two girls spent most of their evenings doing needlework as they talked. Gerda took an interest in all the fashionable clothes Olina had brought with her from Europe.

"Stand still, Olina." Gerda walked around her friend, looking at the darts and flounces on the dark green traveling suit Olina was modeling. "I want to see how she made this."

"I could take it off." Olina unbuttoned the suit. "That way we could look at the seams from the inside. The jacket is lined, but the waist and skirt aren't." When the coat was completely removed, it revealed a soft creamy cotton waist with a lace-edged, ruffled jabot gracefully draping around Olina's neck.

Just then, the back door burst open and Gustaf entered, followed by his brother August. Gerda and Olina watched them from the parlor.

"I tell you, Gustaf." August raised his voice. "You'll never get him to sell it."

"What need does he have for a plow horse?" Gustaf sounded disgusted. "That horse will stay in his barn and pasture and never do another day's work." He threw his cap on the table, stomped over to the sink, and started washing his hands. "I could use another plow horse."

August glanced through the door to the parlor and saw the two girls. "Gerda, how are you?" He rushed to his sister, picked her up, and twirled her around, then set her on her feet. "It's been a long time since I saw you."

Gustaf followed him, drying his hands as he went. "You saw her on Sunday. It's only Thursday. That's not a long time."

He stopped short when he saw Olina. She was standing between him and the window. The sun coming through the pane gave her a gilt edge, turning the soft hairs that had escaped her chignon into a golden halo. The cream-colored blouse and dark green skirt looked like something from one of the *Godey's Lady's Book*s Gerda often received. Olina took his breath away.

It had been like this ever since he talked to Anna. He had felt a freedom from his ties to her, releasing all the pent-up feelings for Olina he had been fighting before.

Sometimes the pain he glimpsed deep in her eyes, when she didn't know anyone was looking, cut him to the quick. He knew Lars had hurt her, but Gustaf felt that there was even more hurt he didn't know about. What could it be?

Besides, Olina didn't ever participate in worship when they were in church. The Sandstrom family and the Nilsson family had been part of the same church in Sweden. Both families fully participated in everything together. During the services now, Olina looked as if she had been turned to stone. If only he could reach across the barriers and ease the pain in her. But how could he do that? He prayed for her every day. He tried to reach out to her in subtle ways.

"Are you men coming in for the evening?" Gerda turned from August to Gustaf.

"We thought we'd sit and talk awhile before August returns to town." Gustaf lowered himself onto the horsehair sofa. "Do you girls want to visit with us?"

Olina looked at Gerda. "If we want to discover how the seamstress made this suit, maybe we should go up to my room." She swept out of the parlor and up the stairs without waiting for an answer.

When the two young women reached the bedroom, Olina stepped out of the skirt. She handed the garment to Gerda before also shedding her waist and putting on her dressing gown.

"Look at all the tucks and ruffles she made on this waist." She knew she was hiding from Gustaf, but she didn't like the way he unsettled her. The feelings aroused by being near him were at war with the decision she made not to trust a man again. Turning from her musings, she looked into the questioning face of Gerda. "I wonder how long it took her to finish the waist of the suit."

This question didn't deter Gerda. "Olina, what's the matter?"

Olina looked away and picked up the garment she had been talking about.

"Oh, don't worry." Gerda stood looking into Olina's troubled eyes. "I don't think anyone else has noticed. But I've known you too long not to see that something more is wrong."

Olina crumpled onto the side of the bed. Gerda sat beside Olina and pulled her into her arms. How could she comfort her? She didn't even know exactly what was wrong.

"You can tell me what it is. I'll keep your secret." The whispered words went to Olina's heart. "Sometimes it helps to have someone to talk to. Someone who knows everything. You know that nothing you could tell me would ever change the way I feel about you. We're too good of friends for that, *ja*?"

Olina nodded as she raised her head from her friend's shoulder. "I have been carrying this a long time, and it has become an unbearable burden. . . . But I don't know where to begin."

"Since I know about Lars"—Gerda reached up to brush back the hair that had fallen across Olina's forehead—"why not tell me what else is bothering you?"

Olina stood and walked across the room. She stood at the window and pulled back the filmy curtains. Dusk was falling on the farm, wrapping all the buildings and trees in shadows. She stared into the shifting darkness.

"It's hard to tell you that my own father doesn't love me."

Gerda's quickly indrawn breath preceded her question. "How can you say that? Your family has always been close."

"I thought so." Olina looked toward the sky to see the first twinklings of starlight. "But you know that Father was always stern. He's a very controlling man."

Gerda stood and crossed the room to stand beside her. "That doesn't mean he doesn't love you."

Olina turned and gazed into her friend's face. "He disowned me when I chose to come to America and marry Lars."

Gerda stood speechless. Olina could see that she was trying to digest what she had just heard. "Disowned you? What do you mean?"

"He told me that I was no longer a part of the family. . .that I was to have no contact with anyone in my family." She paced back and forth across the bedroom before returning to stand beside the window.

"What about your mother and your brothers?" Gerda demanded.

"They could say nothing. Father was in a high temper. I think he thought I would change my mind, but I couldn't. Lars and I were so in love." Olina finished on a sob, dropping to the floor. She crossed her arms on the windowsill and placed her chin on her hands. "At least *I* was in love with *him*," she wailed.

Gerda dropped beside Olina and once again held her in her arms. "Your father will change his mind."

Olina looked up. "That's what *Tant* Olga said. She said he'd change his mind when we had his grandchildren. But now that will never happen." Olina felt completely drained. "How could God have allowed all this?"

The question hung in the air between the two young women. A question without an answer.

Gerda got up and started picking up the clothing they had dropped at various places around the room. "Olina, didn't you write your father a letter right after you arrived?"

Olina nodded. "I told him what happened, and I asked him to send me the money to come home. I told him I would work and pay back every cent as soon as I could."

"Well, see. Everything will be all right. He'll send you the money." Gerda folded the skirt and laid it across the end of the bed.

Olina stood and picked up the crumpled waist from where the two girls had sat on it. Smoothing out the wrinkles the best she could, she put it beside the skirt. "But what if he doesn't? What will I do then?" She turned a forlorn face toward her friend.

Gerda took Olina by the shoulders. "He will. He has to." She let go and picked up the jacket. "But if he doesn't, you'll stay right here."

"I can't stay here. I would be a burden to your family."

"A burden? I don't think so." Gerda turned the jacket wrong side out. "You've been doing your part. Besides that, maybe we could move to town together and become seamstresses. We're both good at making quality clothing. The only ready-made clothing at the mercantile has to be ordered from other places, and they never fit right. We could probably make a good living as seamstresses. The only way Father will let me move to town is if I have someone to live with. It would work out well for both of us." Gerda smiled at Olina. "Besides, it won't come to that. You'll be going home before you know it. So let's do all we can to learn how she made your lovely clothes. *Jaha?*"

Chapter 9

When Olina came, the Nilsson family had started speaking Swedish most of the time around Olina so she would not feel left out. Olina asked Gerda to help her learn English, and Gerda was good about helping her. After the second week, she asked the whole family to speak mostly English so she could learn it. Even if she went back to Sweden, she would be glad she knew the language. Olina was surprised how quickly she picked it up. It wasn't easy, but when she heard it all the time, it was easier to learn. Now that she had been there nearly two months, only a few Swedish words crept into their conversations.

Gerda and Olina took each of the garments Olina had brought as part of her trousseau and studied it inside and out. They drew diagrams of how each piece was shaped and how the pieces fit together. Then they made new summer dresses from some fabric they had at the farm.

"*Moder*," Gerda called out as the two girls came down the stairs carrying one of the new dresses, "come see what we have for you." Both girls were excited.

Mrs. Nilsson wiped her hands on her big white apron as she came from the kitchen into the hallway. "Now what could you possibly have for me? No one has been to town today."

"We wanted to surprise you." Olina held the dress up by the shoulders. It fell to the floor in a graceful sweep. "Here, try it on."

Mrs. Nilsson was surprised but pleased. "All this time I thought you girls were making something pretty for yourselves."

"We did." Gerda twirled to show off her new dress. "This is mine." Balloon sleeves, gathered at the shoulder and tightly cuffed at her wrists, had five rows of tucks running the entire length. Intricate white lace set off the powder blue material with a dainty flower pattern. The dress was full at the bust but had the new wasp waist that was accented by the full skirt. Yards of material gathered at the waist and swept to dust the floor with a lace trimmed ruffle flounce.

"See, Mrs. Nilsson, we made you one like hers." Olina held it out to her. "Only in an old rose floral print."

"I'm too old to wear such frippery." Mrs. Nilsson couldn't keep a smile from flitting across her face as she reached for the dress and held it up in front of her.

"You are not." Gerda hugged her mother. "It'll look good on you."

The girls went into the parlor to wait for Mrs. Nilsson to return. Someone had brought in the mail, and it contained a new *Godey's*. The two girls pored over the pages while they waited.

"Mrs. Johnson gave me a stack of these magazines that she had collected over the years. I had a good time looking through them. I don't think the book is as good since Sarah Hale sold it." Gerda was looking at some of the pictures. "I'm not sure how long I will continue to take it."

"It does help you keep up with fashion, doesn't it?"

"Anna has been taking another magazine. It's called *Ladies' Home Journal*. I'm sure she would let us borrow one to compare them."

Just then Mrs. Nilsson came in wearing the new dress. "This is wonderful." She smoothed the fabric over her hips. "You put more lace on mine than you did yours." Lace lined the tucks on her sleeve and outlined the waspish waist. The delicate rose color of the dress brought out the natural color in her cheeks, making her look younger. "I'm sure you had a hand in this." She smiled at Olina.

"Gerda helped. And she picked out the fabric for you. It does look good." Olina had a feeling of accomplishment when she looked at the beautiful picture made by the woman standing before her.

Mrs. Nilsson continued to finger the delicate lace. "When the other women see these dresses and how well they fit, you'll probably have some asking you to make them a dress."

That sounded good to Olina. If her father refused to send her the money to come home, maybe she and Gerda could work together.

"What have we here?" Mr. Nilsson's voice boomed, preceding him from the hallway into the parlor. "Who is this vision of loveliness?" He picked his wife up from behind and twirled her around before setting her feet back on the floor.

"Bennel, behave yourself." Mrs. Nilsson blushed and patted a hair back in place.

"Where did my Ingrid get this pretty dress? I haven't seen it before, have I?" His expression told the girls how much he liked the garment.

"No. The girls made it for me as a surprise."

Mr. Nilsson looked astonished. "I thought you had to try it on several times to check the fit."

"I did, too. But they made it in secret, and it fits so well." She turned around so he could see the dress from every angle.

"You girls are good." Pride tinged his voice. "Very good."

"Mother," Gerda interrupted, "we used the last of the lightweight fabric we have here. Maybe Olina and I need to go to town and pick out some more."

"I could take you," Gustaf said from the hallway.

His voice startled Olina. When had he come in? She hadn't heard the door open. She had been too wrapped up in what was going on.

"I'm going to town tomorrow." Gustaf was drying his hands on a towel from the kitchen, so he had been in the house long enough to wash his hands. "You girls can ride along. How about it?"

"Sure," Gerda answered before Olina could decline.

Olina knew she should refuse. She had little money. She wanted to keep what little she had in case her father refused to send her the money to go home.

All eyes had turned to her, and she needed to give an answer. It might not hurt to ride along with them. She might have to tell Gerda why she was not spending her money, but she didn't want the rest of the family to know that *Fader* had rejected her when she left Sweden. That was one secret she was in no hurry to share.

After supper, the girls were upstairs in Olina's room looking at more of the drawings they had made. Gerda picked out four of them.

"I want to get fabric to make these four for me." She pointed out two more of them. "Mother would look good in these. What kind of fabric are you going to buy?"

Olina looked at the floor for a minute. She traced the pattern in the carpet with the toe of her black high-top shoe. "I won't be buying any."

"Why not?"

"I don't want to spend the money I have left. I might need it."

"Don't worry about that. We'll get you some fabric with our order."

"I couldn't take it." Olina looked up at her friend. "Besides, I have all these new clothes I brought with me."

Soon after breakfast, Gustaf pulled the wagon to the front of the house. The day was fresh and new as the girls stepped out into the brisk morning air. The sun had come up, and the rooster was still occasionally crowing as he pranced across the yard.

When they reached the wagon, Olina was trying to figure out how she could get up without Gustaf touching her. Then he placed his hands on her waist and swung her effortlessly across the wagon wheel. In the blink of an eye, she was sitting on the bench seat beside Gerda.

Gustaf walked around the front of the wagon. He stopped by each horse and gave it a bite of something he had in his pocket. Olina watched him, all the while still feeling where the heat of his hands had touched her. Her skin burned, and her stomach was in turmoil. This was going to be a long day.

"You haven't been to town except to go to church, have you, Olina?" Gustaf's voice broke through her thoughts.

"No, not since the day I arrived," she whispered.

"How long have you been here?" Gustaf picked up the reins and clicked his tongue to start the horses.

Was the man going to ask her questions all the way to town? "It's been about two months, hasn't it?" she said.

Gerda looked at Olina and must have noticed how uncomfortable she was, because she changed the subject. "Gustaf, we haven't seen Anna since the night of the party. And you have not gone over to the Jensons', have you?"

Gustaf's face seemed to close up. "No," he grunted.

"I'm not trying to make you mad." Gerda looked frustrated. "I was just wondering."

Gustaf heaved a gigantic sigh. "Well, wonder no longer, little sister. I have not said anything about it, but Anna and I are not seeing each other anymore."

Why did that relieve Olina? It shouldn't make any difference to her, but a small weight lifted from her heart.

When they reached Litchfield, Gustaf took the young women to the mercantile. He needed to get some work done at the blacksmith's, and he was going by the bank. He promised to return for them in time for the three of them to go to the restaurant at the hotel for lunch.

Gerda pulled Olina along with her as she rushed to see if there were any new bolts of fabric on the shelves. Looking past Gerda, Olina spied several bolts of colorful silk on the shelf beside the cotton bolts.

"Oh, look, Gerda." She pointed to a color that was neither pink nor lavender. "Isn't it lovely?"

Gerda reached for the bolt just as Mrs. Braxton came to help them. "Is this new?"

"We have never had silk this color before. They call it mauve. I think the name is French. Would you like me to cut you some?" Mrs. Braxton reached for the scissors under the counter. "We have refinished this counter so it won't damage the silk."

Olina smoothed her hand across the wooden counter. "It feels nice. It shouldn't snag anything."

Gerda put her finger on her cheek and thought a minute. "I want ten yards of the silk."

"What are you going to make with it?" Olina fingered the fabric, enjoying the smoothness.

"I want to copy one of the dresses you brought with you, and I think I'll make a matching bonnet."

Mrs. Braxton looked at the new dress Gerda was wearing. "Where did you get the pattern for that dress you have on? I like the sleeves. I might want a similar dress myself."

Gerda waved toward her friend. "Olina brought a lot of new clothes with her. We've been studying them. This is the first one we duplicated. Hers was made from a soft, lightweight wool. But it made up really well in this cotton."

"Do you think you could make one to fit me?" Mrs. Braxton turned around so the girls could study her figure. "You could take measurements today."

Gerda looked at Olina with a question in her expression. Olina nodded slightly. It would give her something to do until she heard from *Fader*.

"I think we could manage that." Gerda turned toward the shop owner's wife. "What fabric do you want us to use?"

Mrs. Braxton reached up and removed a bolt of emerald green silk. "I want it out of this. If you make it for me, I'll give each of you enough fabric to make yourself a dress. . . . Or I could pay you instead."

"I would love to have this sea green silk." Olina held it against herself. "Would I look good in it?"

Gerda nodded. "And I want this. . .what did you call it?"

"Mauve."

"Yes, I'll take the mauve. We each want ten yards."

Mrs. Braxton began cutting the fabric as Gerda and Olina chose thread, buttons, and lace to trim the dresses. Mrs. Braxton added an extra packet of needles to the order before she wrapped it. Then she took the young women upstairs to her living quarters. They spent an hour visiting with Mrs. Braxton while they measured her for her dress and shared a cup of tea with her. They returned downstairs to buy several pieces of calico and gingham to take home. They had finished getting all the notions they needed when Gustaf came for them.

"Are you ready for lunch?"

When Olina heard his voice, she looked up. For a moment she felt drawn to him. What was she thinking? She didn't even trust him. She couldn't risk getting hurt again. All of her pain was still too new. She had tried to deal with it the best she knew how, but she would never risk being hurt like that again.

The three went across the street and entered the dining room of the Excelsior Hotel. It wasn't as luxurious as the hotel where they had stayed in New York City, but it was nice. During the meal, several people Olina had met at the party came by the table to visit with them. Lunch passed rather pleasantly.

Just after they finished dessert, Gustaf reached into his pocket for his money. When he did, something crinkled. "I forgot. I picked this up at the post office when I went in to mail some letters." He handed a letter with a Swedish postmark to Olina. "It looks as though you have a letter from home. I know you'll be glad."

Olina didn't want to be impolite, but she couldn't help it. While Gustaf paid the waitress, she tore into the envelope. The thickness of the envelope felt as if the letter would be long and newsy. Instead, the letter she had written home dropped onto the table, unopened. Accompanying it was a short terse note.

The Other Brother

The person whose return address is on this envelope is considered dead. The Sandstrom family does not want to receive any more mail from that person.

Olina sat and stared at her father's signature on the bottom of the note.

Gustaf had turned to say something to Gerda when he heard Olina gasp. As he whipped back around, he saw that every bit of color had drained from her face. Her eyes were glazed with unshed tears. Gustaf wanted to shield her from other people, so he got up, gathered the dropped papers from the table, and helped her from the chair. Placing himself between her and the other people in the room, he ushered Olina out the door and through the lobby to the waiting wagon. Gerda followed right behind them.

This time, Gustaf picked Olina up first and put her on the middle of the wagon seat. Gerda could sit on the outside to shield her from curious onlookers. As soon as he was in the wagon, he started the horses toward home. He didn't stop until they pulled up in front of the house.

No one had said anything on the way home. Olina sat quiet and still. When he helped her down from the wagon, she rushed into the house.

"Go to her, little sister. She needs someone." Gustaf drove the wagon to the barn, praying for Olina all the way.

Chapter 10

He really means it. Olina paced her room, tears streaming down her face. *How can I go on like this?*

Olina wished she could still depend on God. Knowing God was with her had given her comfort when she was younger. She needed comfort now as never before. Gerda had tried to help her, but what could anyone do? Olina dropped in a heap beside her bed, leaning her head on the flower garden quilt that draped to the floor. Her shoulders slumped against the side of the bed.

Thinking hurt so much, so Olina tried to clear the horrid thoughts from her mind. However, memories flitted in and out of her head. As she rejected one, another attacked her from the other side. *Fader's* harsh words the last time she had seen him rang through her consciousness undergirded by the written words on the letter she clutched in a crumpled ball, unable to let go of it. Olina had no hope.

Child, please let me help you. Olina had heard that voice before, but today she turned a deaf ear to it. *I know the plans I have for you.* Olina put her hands on her ears as if to shut out an audible voice and moaned loud enough to drown it out.

Olina stayed in her room for two days, not letting anyone come in except Gerda when she brought food and fresh water. Gerda would return later in the day to pick up the dishes, often containing most of the food, uneaten. But Olina did eat enough to keep from starving. If Gerda hugged Olina, she let her, but when Gerda tried to talk, Olina wouldn't listen. She would busy herself rearranging her silver-handled hairbrush and mirror on the dresser or opening a drawer and moving things around, but she never touched the wad of paper she had finally dropped beside her bed.

The third day, Olina came downstairs after the family had eaten breakfast. When she arrived in the kitchen, Mrs. Nilsson looked up expectantly.

"I don't want to talk about it right now." Olina tried to keep her hostess from asking any questions. "If it's all right, I'll tell the whole family after dinner. That way, I only have to say it once."

Mrs. Nilsson nodded and turned back toward the cabinet. "We have some bacon and biscuits left from breakfast. Are you hungry? I could fix you some eggs." She picked up the cast-iron skillet and placed it on the stove.

"No, thank you." Olina went to the cupboard and got out a plate and glass. "I don't want any eggs, but the biscuits and bacon sound good." She helped herself.

"Would you like some butter and jelly on your biscuits?" Mrs. Nilsson placed a jar of jelly on the table beside the dish of butter.

"That sounds good." Olina pulled out a drawer and picked up a knife and spoon.

"Well, sit down and enjoy your breakfast." Mrs. Nilsson reached for the glass Olina had left on the cabinet. "I'll go to the springhouse and get you some milk."

Olina turned. "Oh, I can get the milk."

"Let me wait on you this one time." Mrs. Nilsson patted Olina on the shoulder. "You haven't let me do much for you since you came here." She turned and started out the back door, but she turned back. "Olina, I want you to know that we've all been praying for you. We were worried, but Gustaf convinced us to let you take your time. He told us that you would talk to us soon." Then she walked into the bright summer sunshine.

Olina sank into a chair by the table. Maybe this wouldn't be so bad. She had been able to function and even carry on a conversation without bursting into tears. If she could get through the day and then the evening, she might make it. Olina hadn't realized how hungry she was. She had eaten two biscuits and two slices of bacon by the time Mrs. Nilsson returned.

"Would you like to finish these other two biscuits and the rest of the bacon?" Mrs. Nilsson picked up the uncovered plate and placed it on the table in front of Olina. "Then I could go ahead and wash up all the dishes."

After breakfast, Olina helped Mrs. Nilsson clean the kitchen before she went out to gather the eggs. Performing regular chores brought the illusion of normalcy to Olina. Egg production had picked up. Although the chickens had a nice house with wooden nests filled with straw, a few of the hens laid their eggs in strange places. When Olina had filled the egg basket from the nests in the henhouse, she searched the weeds that grew along the fence between that building and the barn. There she found three more eggs. Olina went into the barn and looked in the scattered hay at the base of the mound that filled one end of the barn. Four more eggs were added to her basket before she returned to the kitchen.

"Those hens." Olina set the basket on the cabinet. "Why don't they use the nests you've provided for them?"

"I've wondered that myself." Gerda came into the kitchen and put the empty laundry basket on the table.

Olina turned to look at her friend. "At least the ones that lay their eggs somewhere else always lay them in the same places."

Gerda's gaze held Olina's for a minute or two before she turned away. "*Ja*, that's a good thing. It would take a long time to gather the eggs if we had to search everywhere for them."

Olina was glad that she had seen understanding in Gerda's expression before she turned away. Having a friend who loved her no matter what could get her through the rest of the day.

☙

Dinner was delicious that night. Mrs. Nilsson had baked two large hens. She served them on a platter surrounded by potatoes and carrots. That afternoon, she had also baked fresh bread and an apple pie. It was a feast worthy of a special occasion. Olina tried to eat the wonderful food, but after a few bites, she pushed it around her plate instead of putting it in her mouth. When she thought about the evening ahead, her stomach started jumping and her throat tightened, making it hard to swallow her food.

Mrs. Nilsson looked around the table. "Olina would like to talk to us in the parlor when you're all finished eating."

Gustaf looked up and stared at Olina. Surely he would look away soon. However, he didn't. And Olina couldn't look away, either. Everything in the room faded from her consciousness. It was as if there were only two people in the room, Gustaf and herself. The moment stretched into what seemed like an eternity, and Olina felt more confused than ever. If anyone else noticed, they didn't comment on it.

"We'll help you clean up, *Moder*." Gustaf got up from his chair and picked up some empty dishes from the table.

"You don't have to do that." Mrs. Nilsson reached for them.

"Yes, we do." Gustaf continued toward the sink with his hands full. "That way we'll all get to the parlor at the same time."

Even Mr. Nilsson helped. Gustaf and Gerda started talking about what they had done during the day. Soon the dishes were washed and put away. Mrs. Nilsson removed her big white apron and hung it on a hook beside the back door.

By the time Olina reached the parlor, the only place to sit was beside Gerda on the sofa. When she was seated, everyone turned toward Olina. The time had come for her to share. She closed her eyes and took a deep breath. Before she opened them again, Gerda reached over, took her hand, and squeezed it.

☙

Gustaf's heart ached as he watched Olina prepare to talk to them. When he had looked at her during dinner, he could see the wall she had erected around her heart. It was painted with painful strokes trying to hide what was inside, but he could see more hurt than he ever wanted to feel himself. He wondered how she could take it. She didn't look that strong, but she must be.

When Gustaf had gone into the kitchen for dinner, she had been standing beside her chair. He thought she looked fragile when he had met her on the dock, but that woman would look strong beside the woman standing by the table. She had to have inner strength to stand there, as if nothing were wrong. But something was wrong, terribly wrong. *Gud, what can I do to help her? Please tell me.*

He wished he could sit beside her, where Gerda was. He wanted to be the one to comfort her and take away her pain. This feeling was new and stronger than anything he had ever felt for a woman. Was this love? If it was, what could he do about it if she wouldn't let him come near her?

Just love her, My son. She needs so much love.

When Olina opened her eyes, Gustaf tried to communicate that love to her through his expression. He knew he would have to go slowly and let God heal Olina's hurts before he could ever say anything to her about his feelings. That thought caused his heart to beat a little faster. Gustaf felt hope for a day when Olina might be his wife.

Olina glanced at Gustaf. He was looking right at her. His expression was trying to tell her something, but she felt uncomfortable, so she quickly looked away. What was he trying to communicate to her?

Olina took a deep breath again. Still holding Gerda's hand, she looked at Mr. Nilsson and then Mrs. Nilsson before fixing her gaze on the pattern in the carpet. As she began to talk, she studied the design.

"I'm sorry I have not been sociable these last two days."

Gerda didn't let her continue. "Olina, it's all right."

"Yes," Mrs. Nilsson added. "You have no need to apologize."

Olina nodded. "Thank you." She looked into Mrs. Nilsson's sweet face. "I seem to have a serious problem." For a moment she couldn't go on. A large lump formed in her throat, and she couldn't get any words around it.

Gustaf jumped up from the chair where he was sitting and went to the kitchen. He could be heard rummaging around before he returned with a glass of water. When he reached toward Olina, she gladly took the proffered liquid refreshment.

After a few sips of the cool well water, she was able to continue. "My father didn't want me to come to America. He told me that if I did, he would disown me. I didn't think he really meant it. . .until I received the reply to my letter."

Olina's hands started shaking, so she set the glass on the table beside the sofa. "He didn't even open my letter. Instead, he wrote that the person who mailed it was considered dead by the family. He doesn't want me to write again."

A sob was working its way up Olina's throat, but by sheer will, she swallowed it. She wouldn't cry in front of everyone.

"I have no home."

"You certainly do," Mr. Nilsson thundered. "Your home is right here." He jumped out of his chair as if catapulted and stomped toward the hall. He leaned one hand on the door frame, looking as if he needed the support. With his head down, he paused before he turned around and continued. "We are your family now." He looked as if he wanted to say something more, but instead, he turned and walked through the kitchen. Before he went out the back door, Olina saw him grab his hat from the hook and slam it on his head.

Mrs. Nilsson spoke softly. "You'll have to forgive him, Olina. When he's disturbed, he tends to get too loud."

Olina nodded. "That's all right."

"He really does love you." Mrs. Nilsson got up from the rocking chair and walked over to Olina. "I know you are concerned about not having any money. You're doing your share around here, so you will be treated like the others."

Olina started to say something, but Gerda interrupted. "Besides, we've started making dresses. Perhaps we'll soon make enough money to live on."

Gustaf had been sitting listening to everyone else. When he heard what Gerda said, he stood up and made a noise that sounded like a snort. Olina looked up at him, and he said, "Neither one of you needs to make enough money to live on. We'll take care of you." Then he followed his father out the back door.

What was it about men that they felt they had to take care of women? The two men who should have taken care of Olina hadn't. She never wanted to have to depend on a man again.

Chapter 11

Gerda and Olina were hanging clothes on the line when they noticed a horse-drawn surrey turn from the country road and start up the long drive to the house. With her right hand, Gerda shaded her eyes from the bright sunlight and gazed at the approaching vehicle.

Olina removed a wooden peg-shaped clothespin from her mouth and secured a sheet to the rope line. "Is that someone you know?"

"The surrey belongs to the Braxtons." Gerda picked up another pillowcase from the laundry basket. "It looks as if Mrs. Braxton is driving, and she has another woman with her. Did *Moder* say anything this morning at breakfast about expecting company?"

"I didn't hear her." Olina stopped and, while Gerda hung the final piece of laundry on the line, watched the two women as they moved closer and closer to the house.

Gerda picked up the empty laundry basket. "I thought maybe I wasn't paying attention. Come on. We don't often get unexpected company."

The young women went in through the back door before the knock sounded on the front. Mrs. Nilsson looked up from the stove, where she was stirring a pot of stew.

"Now who can that be?" She patted a stray lock of hair into place and started untying her apron strings. "Did you see anyone drive up?"

"Mrs. Braxton and another woman," Olina answered while Gerda hung the laundry basket on a hook beside the back door.

Gerda turned to her mother. "I think it might be her sister-in-law. The one who is married to Mr. Braxton's brother."

Mrs. Nilsson brushed her hands down her skirt to smooth it. "The one from Denver?" When Gerda frowned and glanced at Olina, she stopped talking.

"I forgot they were coming to town for a visit." Mrs. Nilsson started toward the front door.

"Denver?" Olina looked at Gerda. "Is he the man who owns the store where Lars went to work when he moved to Denver?"

Gerda slowly nodded, not taking her gaze from her friend's face.

Olina took a deep breath. "I think I'll go to my room." She hurried through the hall and up the stairs before Mrs. Nilsson had invited her guests into the house.

"Do come in." Mrs. Nilsson opened the door wide and gestured toward the parlor.

The two women preceded her into the room. After sitting on the sofa, they started removing their gloves.

Mrs. Nilsson sat in her favorite rocker. "It's always a nice surprise to have guests come to your door. Besides, I want to know how Lars is doing."

Mrs. Braxton glanced at her sister-in-law, who said, "He was fine when we left Denver."

"Actually. . ." Mrs. Braxton looked around. "We were hoping to talk to Gerda and Olina."

Gerda was starting up the stairs to check on Olina when she heard her own name spoken. She came back down the steps and entered the parlor.

"Gerda is right here." Mrs. Nilsson looked at her. "Do you know where Olina is?"

"She went upstairs." Gerda sat in the straight chair where she could see both the staircase and the other women in the parlor.

"Let me go put some tea to steep while you talk to Gerda." Mrs. Nilsson started toward the kitchen. "Then I'll go see about Olina."

Olina was standing at her favorite place beside the window, watching two birds with their babies in a nest in the tree by the barn, when she heard a soft knock on her door. She had been expecting someone, but she had figured it would be Gerda, not her mother. Gerda always knocked harder. Olina glanced one more time at the industrious birds before she started toward the door. *I wish I could be like you. You don't seem to have a worry in the world.*

Olina took a deep breath before she opened the door and peeked around the edge. "Yes?"

"The ladies would like to see you and Gerda." Mrs. Nilsson's compassionate look went to Olina's heart. "But you don't have to come down. . .if you don't want to."

Olina sighed. "It's okay. I have to face people sooner or later." She fluffed her hair where the kerchief had mashed it while she was hanging up the clothes. "I'm feeling better since I told your family everything last week." She stepped through the door and closed it behind her.

Mrs. Nilsson put her arm around Olina's waist. "I'm proud of you, Olina."

They went down the stairs together. When they entered the parlor, Mrs. Braxton looked up eagerly.

"Olina, there you are." She stood and took Olina's hand in both of hers. "My sister-in-law wanted to meet you two."

Olina looked at the other woman still sitting on the sofa. The woman was smiling at her. Olina wondered how much she might know about what had

The Other Brother

happened—if she knew that Olina had come to America to marry Lars.

"Olina, this is Sophia." Mrs. Braxton took Olina by the arm and led her farther into the room. "She was wondering how long it would take you and Gerda to make her some dresses."

Olina looked at Gerda. This was what they had been hoping for. "How many dresses are we talking about?"

Sophia Braxton rose from where she was sitting. "We're going to be here in Litchfield for a week before we return to Denver. We were in Chicago, but I didn't see any clothes there that could compare with the dress you made Marja." She looked at her sister-in-law. "Without a dressmaker, I can't get clothes that fit as well as her dress does. I would like to have as many dresses as you can make during the week we are here. I understand that you brought several European fashions with you when you came."

Olina wondered if she looked as surprised as Gerda did. How many dresses could they make in a week? They didn't know.

Marja looked from one girl to the other. "I have an idea."

"What?" Olina and Gerda both said at once.

Marja clapped her hands before clasping them under her chin. "You girls could stay in town this week. That way you would be close if you need to do any fitting."

Olina was amazed. She never would have thought of that.

"But where would they stay?" Mrs. Nilsson looked worried.

"They could stay at the hotel." Sophia stood up. "What a wonderful idea. Adolph could rent the room next to ours. I think it's empty."

The idea presented interesting possibilities to Olina. If all they did that week was sew, they might make quite a bit of money.

Marja chuckled. "I'm full of ideas. The price on treadle sewing machines has dropped, so we ordered one for the store. It came last week. Maybe you girls could use it. I've heard that you can sew much faster that way."

Olina looked at Gerda. Sew with a machine? She had never used one. All the dresses she had made were by hand. "I wouldn't know how to use it."

"It has a manual." Marja patted Olina's arm. "We could learn how to use it together. That would help Mr. Braxton and me sell more of the machines—if we know how they work."

It would be a change from staying on the farm. Maybe it was not a bad idea. Olina turned toward Mrs. Nilsson.

"Do you think Mr. Nilsson would mind?"

"We could ask him."

When the men came in for dinner, Gerda and Olina had a hard time keeping their questions to themselves. They wanted to blurt out what Mrs. Braxton had said, but they knew they needed to wait. It seemed as if the men took an eternity washing up, but finally, they were all seated around the table. After the blessing, Mrs. Nilsson started passing food around the table.

"We had some visitors today." She smiled at the girls as she made the casual comment. "Marja Braxton and her sister-in-law Sophia came by."

Mr. Nilsson put a large scoop of gravy on his mashed potatoes, then passed the gravy boat along to Gustaf. "What did Mrs. Braxton have to say? Did she have any news of Lars?" After realizing what he had said, Mr. Nilsson blushed and looked at Olina.

Mrs. Nilsson took a bite of her baked chicken. She chewed and swallowed it before answering. "She said he was fine when she left Denver. She didn't come to see me. She wanted to talk to the girls."

Mr. Nilsson looked first at Gerda, then Olina. "Why would she want to talk to our lovely girls?"

Gerda giggled. "She wants us to sew for her sister-in-law."

"You remember when the girls made the dress for Marja?" Mrs. Nilsson put her hand on her husband's arm. "They did such a good job that she recommended them to Sophia."

Mr. Nilsson nodded. "Good work speaks for itself."

"They want the girls to spend the week in town so they can sew all week for Sophia."

The girls held their breath while they waited for Mr. Nilsson to answer. However, they knew he couldn't be rushed.

Mr. Nilsson thought for a moment. "That might not be a bad idea. Where would they stay? Do the Braxtons have enough room for all the extra people?"

"Well." Mrs. Nilsson took a drink of water. "The Braxtons' living quarters are small, so Adolph and Sophia are staying at the hotel. They want to rent the room next to them for the girls."

Mr. Nilsson put his fork down and rested his forearms on the table. He looked from his wife to his daughter to Olina. "Is that right?"

"Oh, *Fader*, Mrs. Braxton has a treadle sewing machine in the store." Gerda pleaded with her father. "She wants us to use it so we can get several dresses done this week. Would it be all right if we go? Please?"

Mr. Nilsson looked at his wife. "Do you think it's a good idea? I wouldn't want anything to happen to the girls."

Mrs. Nilsson nodded. "I'm sure Johan and Marja and Adolph and Sophia would protect them."

"Let me think about it a bit." Mr. Nilsson picked up his fork.

"If you decide it's all right, I would be glad to take Gerda and Olina into town in the morning." Gustaf looked at his father. "I need to pick up a plow August is fixing for me. He said it would be ready by tomorrow."

Mr. Nilsson took another bite and laid his fork down while he chewed his food. He looked at Gerda then Olina. "I think that is a good idea."

Gerda jumped up from her chair. "That's wonderful." She went to her father and hugged him.

Olina had finished packing her carpetbag when Gerda knocked on her door. "I can hardly believe Father agreed to let us go. It'll be so much fun."

"It will be a lot of work, too." Olina smiled at her friend's enthusiasm. She walked over to the window for a last look at the birds. "I wonder if the babies will learn to fly by the time we get back from town."

"What?" Gerda came up beside her.

Olina pointed toward a fork in a high branch. "See that nest? I have been watching the birds with their babies."

"Maybe they will." Gerda picked up Olina's bag. It felt light. "You aren't taking much for a week's stay."

"I don't need much to work all day." Olina laughed.

Gerda stopped at the door and turned around. "We'll do more than just sew all the time. There's always something going on in town."

Olina wasn't interested in what was going on in town. She wanted to see how much money she could make as a dressmaker. Maybe she could soon support herself. But would Mr. Nilsson let her live on her own?

The ride into town was a happy affair. Gustaf and Gerda teased each other and told funny stories. Olina relaxed and enjoyed the camaraderie. She missed being around her brothers, and this brought back pleasant memories. If only she could keep from thinking about *Fader* and the pain he had caused her. Because of him, she would never see her brothers again. She couldn't think about that or she would cry. So she shut out those thoughts and chuckled at Gerda and Gustaf.

When Olina first laughed, Gustaf almost fell off the wagon seat. He thought he would never hear that laugh again. Ever since Olina had told them about her family, she had hardly smiled when he was around. He didn't know if she smiled at other times. He turned to look at her.

She was wearing a light green dress and bonnet. Probably one she and Gerda had been working on. He remembered their buying green fabric when they went to town. The color brought out the peachy texture of her skin. A light wind tugged some of her hair free from the confines of the hat, and the sun shining through it made it look like liquid gold floating in the air around her head. She was so beautiful. It almost hurt to look at her. He wanted to take her in his arms and hold her close, but he knew he couldn't do that yet.

"Gustaf." Gerda was looking at him. "You haven't answered my question."

He dragged his gaze from the beautiful image he was enjoying and glanced at his sister. "What did you ask?"

"See," she said to Olina. "He wasn't even listening to me."

Olina laughed. "I guess not."

"Well, what did you want to know?" Gustaf tried to sound gruff.

"How long will you stay in town today?"

Gustaf looked at Olina again. A sinking feeling settled in his stomach. He didn't want to leave her in town. Every day he looked forward to sitting across from her at the dinner table. Often he saw her during the day as she worked around the farm, gathering eggs or hanging up clothes or walking around and enjoying the outdoors. He was always finding excuses to work near her so they could talk to each other. The longer he was around her, the more he found to admire about her.

"I may be there most of the day." He turned toward the outskirts of town that were up ahead. "If that's all right with you."

"Of course it is." Gerda hugged his arm. "You can help us get settled. That way you can assure Father that we are all right."

"Sounds like a good idea." Gustaf smiled. *A very good idea. Maybe I'll have to find several reasons to come to town this week so I can assure Father that they're all right.* But he didn't fool himself. He wanted to come to town to see Olina as much as possible. *Yes, this week could get interesting.*

Chapter 12

When Gustaf stopped the wagon in front of the mercantile, Marja and Sophia Braxton hurried out the front door. They must have been as eager as Gerda and Olina, since they had been watching for them.

"Mrs. Braxton." Gustaf doffed his cap. "Should I take the girls to the hotel? Their bags are in the wagon."

"What a wonderful idea." Marja clapped her hands. "Sophia and I'll walk over right now."

"I'm sorry I can't offer you a ride." Gustaf gave a rueful smile. "The wagon seat is full. If you want to wait, I can come back for you."

"It's not far, and the walk will do us good." Sophia waved them off.

Gerda's eyes sparkled as she looked around. "I'm so excited. I didn't think Father would let us do this."

Gustaf chuckled. "You're a grown woman, Gerda. Father wants the best for you. He's just careful because sometimes there are rough men in town."

"I know." Gerda put her hands around his powerful arm and looked up into his face. "We'll be careful." She turned to look at her friend. "Right, Olina?"

"Of course." Olina made the mistake of looking at Gustaf. His gaze was fastened on her, and when she looked at him, she was drawn to those blue eyes. Sometimes they could look so icy, but now they held the warmth of a sunshiny day. That warmth reached all the way to her toes. She couldn't look away, even if she had wanted to. But she didn't want to. That warmth was melting something deep inside her as the sunshine melted ice in the fjords back home.

Home? Where was home? Was it in Sweden? Or was it right here in Minnesota with people who accepted her for who she was? People who didn't try to change her. Yes, it was starting to feel like home. With a tremulous smile, Olina finally looked away from Gustaf's mesmerizing eyes. Today was a new day. Minnesota was her new home. Olina was going to make the best of it.

Child, let Me help you.

Olina almost heeded the quiet voice. Almost, but not quite.

When Olina smiled, Gustaf could feel it touch his heart. It felt like the wings of a butterfly as it flitted across the flowers Gerda planted around the front porch. Soft, gentle, but a smile nonetheless. Olina needed to smile more. Maybe this was

69

the start of something in her life. She looked as if she had made a discovery. . .or a resolution. Gustaf didn't know which. But whichever it was, it would have far-reaching consequences in her life. He hoped those consequences would include him. *Please*, Gud.

Adolph Braxton was waiting in the hotel lobby for them. He took them up to the third floor, the top floor. "We wanted to be away from the noise in the street."

He opened the door to a large room that was at the back corner of the hotel. Windows on adjoining walls bathed the interior with sunlight.

Olina walked over to check the view. Since the hotel was taller than the building next door, she could look across the rooftops. The hotel was at the end of Main Street, so the windows at the back overlooked an open field.

Olina turned around. "This is a wonderful room. We'll have lots of light to work by."

Just then, Marja and Sophia walked in. Marja smiled and clapped her hands. "We thought this would be just right. Sophia and Adolph moved next door so you girls could have this room."

"You didn't have to do that," Gerda exclaimed.

"Nonsense." Sophia put her arm through her husband's. "This room is the largest in the hotel. It'll give you plenty of space to work. Our room is nice, too." She smiled up at her husband. "Right, dear?"

Adolph nodded. It looked to Olina as if his fair skin blushed a little under his bushy sideburns.

"We'll bring the sewing machine up later today," Marja said.

"Mrs. Braxton." Gustaf walked to the door. "Would you like me to bring it in my wagon? I would be glad to."

With a harrumph, Adolph said he would help Gustaf, and the two men left. Olina looked around. Heavy drapes hung at the windows. Olina walked over and discovered ties hanging high beside the window. She used them to hold the drapes open and allow the maximum of light to enter the room. Gerda went to the large canopy bed that was in one corner of the room. She sat on the side. Olina turned and surveyed the room. Even with the substantial wardrobe on the wall near the door and the table that sat against the other wall without a window, there was lots of space. There were even two straight chairs by the table. This would be a wonderful place to work.

"This room is as large as some people's houses," Gerda said as she walked to one of the two rocking chairs that flanked a small round table.

Sophia sat in one of the rockers. "That's why we wanted you to have this room. You can spread out all over while you are working."

While they were waiting for the men to return, Olina and Gerda showed their drawings of the clothing to the two Mrs. Braxtons. Sophia exclaimed over most of them.

"How am I ever going to choose which dresses for you to make for me?"

Marja Braxton sat on one of the straight chairs. She folded her hands in her lap. "That is a real problem. When Gerda and Olina made my new dress, I had only seen the one style."

Olina stood looking out one of the windows at the back of the hotel. She could see a cluster of trees in the field. As the wind gently blew the branches, birds flitted in and out among the treetops, much as the birds at the farm had. It would be pleasant to watch them when she needed a break from the tedium of sewing. But maybe it wouldn't be quite so tedious when they used the treadle machine. She hoped not.

Olina turned back toward the other three women. "I have an idea, Mrs. Braxton."

"What?" Both women spoke in unison.

Marja laughed, then added, "You should call us Marja and Sophia. It would be a lot easier."

Sophia nodded. "I agree. Now, Olina, dear, what was your idea?"

Olina spread the drawings out on the table. "You should pick your favorite drawing. Bring us the fabric you want to use. We'll start on that dress. Then you can choose the next favorite. That'll give you a little time to decide what fabric to make it from while we are working on the first. We'll make as many as we have time to this week, doing them one at a time like that."

Marja clapped her hands. "What a wonderful idea. Olina, you are a smart girl. I'm so glad you came to Minnesota." She pulled Olina into her arms and hugged her hard.

That hug reminded Olina of her mother. Maybe the people here did accept her for who she was. She could make a home for herself. Perhaps in time, she would find peace in her heart again.

When the men returned with the sewing machine, Olina was amazed. She had never seen anything like it. The black iron machine was attached to a small wooden table with iron legs. Under the table, a mesh contraption near the floor was attached to the machine above it. She had no idea how it could work, but she was eager to find out.

"Where is the manual?" Marja looked at the two men.

"Right here." Gustaf pulled a booklet from his back pocket and handed it to her. "Sorry I had to fold it, but I couldn't carry it and the machine at the same time."

Marja gave it to Olina. "Tonight you girls can read this and try to see how it works. Sophia and I will come in the morning for you to take her measurements.

We'll bring the first fabric and notions." She clapped her hands. "Oh, I'm getting so excited."

"So am I," Sophia agreed as she took Marja's arm. "We need to go look at the fabric in the store. I have my eye on a couple of those drawings." Adolph quietly joined the two women as they walked down the hall chattering about the different dresses.

Gustaf turned to Gerda, but he watched Olina out of the corner of his eye. "Could I take you and Olina to lunch downstairs?"

Gerda stood up. "Is it noon already? Where has the morning gone?"

"One, it took awhile to get to town." Gustaf counted on his fingers. "Two, we had to move your bags into your room. Three, we brought that heavy machine up two flights of stairs. That took time."

"Oh, you." Gerda playfully hit his arm. "That's not what I meant."

"I know." Gustaf laughed with her. Then he turned to Olina. "May I escort you to lunch?" When Olina nodded, he continued, "We'll let my sister come with us if she'll behave herself."

Olina couldn't help herself. She burst out laughing with them. It felt so good to share a fun time. Maybe her heart could heal.

In the dining room, they were served a rich beef stew with hot corn bread slathered with fresh butter. While they were eating, several people from church stopped to visit. When they found out that the girls were staying in town for a week, they issued many invitations. Gerda and Olina wouldn't have to eat at the hotel very often, and they would have time to renew acquaintances and establish new friendships.

"I guess we'll not be sewing all the time." Gerda smiled at Olina.

"We need to sew a lot." Olina kept thinking about the money they would earn.

"I know that Marja and Sophia won't expect us to sew all our waking hours as if we were slaves."

When the waitress brought apple cobbler for dessert, she asked if they had heard about the brush arbor meeting that was going on that week. Olina didn't know what she was talking about, so Gustaf explained.

"We don't have many of these since we have our own church building. Traveling evangelists hold meetings in an open-air structure with a roof made out of tree limbs. I've heard that wonderful things happen at them." He got a faraway look on his face. "I've always wanted to attend one, and I hear this preacher has a powerful message." He looked back at the young women. "I think I'll come to town for the meeting tomorrow night." Turning toward Olina, he asked, "May I escort the two of you?"

Before Olina could decline, she heard Gerda accept with eagerness. How could she not agree to accompany them? Maybe later she could think of a way out of it.

Thank You, Father. On the way home late that afternoon, Gustaf was glad he had a reason to come to town tomorrow. He would have thought up some excuse, but this meeting was a good opportunity. He couldn't imagine worshiping out in the open like that. The services in their church were formal. This sounded as though it would be a chance to relax and worship with abandon. Of course, he sometimes did that when he was out working in the fields. He would take a break and sit under the shade and sing praises to the Lord. He had even been known to walk around praising the Lord with a loud voice, but only when he knew no one was near.

Gustaf had heard people talk about the old-time brush arbor meetings and how they would consist of a lot of praise and worship; the ministers presented the gospel in a forceful but understandable manner. Gustaf wanted to hear that kind of sermon. And he wanted to see Olina touched in a service. Maybe this meeting would be the time God could reach her in a new way, bringing healing to her wounded heart.

Chapter 13

When Marja and Sophia arrived the next morning, the four women spent an hour learning to use the sewing machine. It wasn't as hard as Olina had feared it would be. Then Olina and Gerda measured Sophia. After Sophia showed them which dress she wanted them to make out of the fabric they brought, she and Marja left the young women to their work.

Olina and Gerda cut out the bodice first. While Gerda cut out the rest of the dress, Olina started sewing the bodice, using the machine. By lunchtime, the dress was far enough along that the girls were sure they could finish it that day.

With a spring in their steps, Gerda and Olina started down the stairs to see what the restaurant was serving for lunch. Before they reached the bottom step, Merta Swenson came through the front door.

After greeting them, she asked, "Have you eaten yet?" When they shook their heads, she continued, "I want you to come to my house for lunch."

Merta served them chicken and dumplings, followed by gingerbread. This visit was the break from sewing that Gerda and Olina needed. After they were finished eating, Merta accompanied them on the walk back to the hotel.

"Remember how you said that you would like to move to town and be dress-makers here?" Merta asked as they reached the hotel.

"Yes," Gerda answered, and Olina nodded.

Merta pointed to a house down the road a ways, but still clearly visible from town. "The Winslow house is for sale. An older widow lived there, but her son wanted her to move to California with him, so she did."

Gerda studied the cottage for a minute. "From here, it looks as though it's in good shape."

"It is," Merta agreed. "Everyone in church made sure she was taken care of. Some of the men are still taking care of things at the house until it sells."

Olina could tell that it was a nice place and not at all small. She turned to Merta. "Do you have time to walk down there with us?"

"Please do." Gerda stepped off the wooden sidewalk. "We could look around, couldn't we?"

Merta took Olina's arm and pulled her with them. "It's not far. It won't take long."

The three young women walked along talking as they approached the cottage, set back from the road and surrounded by trees. When they reached the gate, Olina opened it and walked up on the front porch. It covered over half of the front of the house, with the front door at the end by whatever room projected beyond the porch. Olina stood in one of the two arches of the porch, which were held up by columns. She liked the shrubbery growing at the end and flowers beginning to bloom in the flower bed in front.

"I like this porch." Olina turned and looked back toward town. "It would be pleasant to sit out here in the cool of the evening." She slid down to sit on the top step. "I wish I had the money to buy this house, but I don't."

"Neither do I." Gerda sat beside her. "Maybe Father and Gustaf could work out a deal with the owner. I would like to move closer to town. This is far enough out from town to be away from all the noise but close enough to be safe and convenient." She stood up and stepped away from the house. After turning, she looked up at the second story. "Merta, have you ever been inside?"

"Oh, yes." Merta joined her and looked up, too. "The second floor has two bedrooms in the front. There are two smaller rooms behind them. She used them for storage." Merta pointed to the room that was beside the porch. "That is the parlor. On the other side, she had a library. I think she used to be a schoolteacher, so she had lots of books. Behind those two rooms are a kitchen, with a large area for a table and chairs, and a big pantry."

Olina stood up and looked back toward town. "It sounds perfect. If only. . ."

"We need to pray about this. Maybe the Lord wants us here." Gerda took hold of both Olina's hand and Merta's. Then she asked God to provide a way if He wanted them to live in this house.

Just as Gerda and Olina sewed the last button on the dress, a knock sounded at the door.

"That must be Sophia." Olina was glad for the opportunity to get up and move around. She stretched her arms over her head for a minute before she opened the door. "You're just in ti—" She stopped with a startled gasp.

"Well, what a welcome." Gustaf's laughing gaze met hers. "I didn't know you were expecting me."

Olina could feel her cheeks redden. She wanted to hide them, but she couldn't look away from him. She liked to see the merriment in his eyes. Was that something more? Whatever could it be? She shook her head. Why did Gustaf have this effect on her? Maybe it was because she had not expected to see him filling her doorway.

"We thought you were Sophia." Gerda jumped up and came over to hug her brother. "But I'm glad you're here, even though I don't know why." She stepped back. "Come in."

Gustaf seemed to fill the room, too. Olina turned back to the dress they had dropped in a heap on the bed. She picked it up and started folding it as she listened to Gustaf and Gerda.

"Do I have to have a reason to come see my little sister?" With his finger, he flicked a curl that was drooping on her forehead.

Gerda playfully hit him on the arm. "You are a big tease. Isn't that right Olina?"

Olina looked at Gerda. "Yes, he does tease a lot."

"So what brings you to town?" Gerda came over to help Olina finish folding the dress.

"Remember yesterday at lunch, I said I would be coming into town for the brush arbor meeting." Gustaf looked from Gerda to Olina. "I came a little early. I wanted to check on the two of you so I can assure Father that you're all right."

Gerda rolled her eyes.

"I thought maybe you two lovely ladies would join me for dinner before the meeting." Gustaf looked at Olina, waiting for her to answer.

They did have to eat. Olina picked up the dress and moved it to the table. With her back turned to Gustaf, she answered, "We could do that."

All afternoon Olina and Gerda had been smelling roast beef cooking. "I think we are having roast." Olina sniffed the air. "It smells like they are cooking yeast rolls. It should be good."

Their meal was a congenial affair. Gustaf and Gerda kept up a lively conversation. Although Olina was quieter, she enjoyed listening to them.

"Gustaf." Gerda sounded excited. "Merta, Olina, and I went to the Winslow house today."

Gustaf swallowed a mouthful. "Why did you do that?"

"It's for sale." Gerda buttered a hot roll.

Gustaf looked at Gerda then at Olina. "Why would you be interested in a house that's for sale?"

"I know that we don't have the money to buy it." Gerda put down the roll and clasped her hands in her lap. "But Olina and I would like to move closer to town."

Gustaf raised his eyebrows. Olina looked down at her plate, but she peeked at Gustaf through her eyelashes. He turned toward Gerda.

"Why is that?"

"Oh, Gustaf." Gerda placed her forearms on the table and eagerly leaned toward him. "There's no dressmaker in Litchfield. Olina and I think we could make a living here."

Gustaf looked thoughtful. "You might be able to."

"It's no use to think about it though." Gerda sighed and picked up her forgotten roll. "Father would never let us do it. But the house would be perfect for us. The woman who lived there was a teacher, and she had a library with lots of windows. That room would make a wonderful workroom for us."

Just then the waitress brought their dessert to them. In a moment, she returned with a large pitcher of water to refill their glasses and a cup of coffee for Gustaf.

When they had finished eating rice pudding with raisins and cinnamon, Gerda wiped her mouth with the napkin. "I would like to go to the meeting with you, Gustaf."

"I had hoped you would say that." He turned toward Olina. "What about you?"

"Of course she'll go. She won't want to sit alone in the hotel room." Gerda got up from her chair. "We need to go freshen up before we leave. What time does it start?"

"You have plenty of time." Gustaf helped Olina push her chair away from the table. He walked them into the lobby. As he watched the two go up the stairs, he called after them, "I'll be waiting right here for you."

When the young women came back down the stairs, August had joined Gustaf. The two men looked as if they were praying together. Surely they weren't doing that right there in the lobby of the hotel. They must be having a private conversation.

"Wonderful." Gerda pulled Olina across the lobby. "August is here, too."

The two men glanced up when they heard Gerda's exclamation. August grabbed her in a bear hug and swung her feet off the floor. When he put her down, he turned toward Olina. "You look nice tonight. I'm glad Gustaf talked me into going with the three of you."

Olina looked at Gustaf. Once again, she felt a blush rise to color her cheeks. She had known other women who didn't turn red every time a man looked at them. Why couldn't she be like them?

The evening was cool but pleasant when they arrived at the structure covered with fresh branches. Olina hoped that the four of them would sit on the back bench, but Gustaf led them down the center aisle. He stopped about halfway between the back and the front. He motioned for August, Gerda, and Olina to precede him on the bench, leaving him sitting on the aisle. He probably needed to sit there so he would have somewhere to put his long legs. The benches weren't far apart.

Olina wondered if many people would come to the meeting. Soon most of the benches were full, and men stood outside the arbor looking in. Olina was glad. At least they wouldn't be conspicuous. When everyone was crowded into the structure, it warmed up a bit.

A large man with snow-white hair stood from the front bench and stepped onto the short platform. When he turned around, he unbuttoned his black frock coat and raised his hands. All talking ceased. His booming voice led in an opening prayer. Olina had never heard a prayer like the one he prayed. He sounded as if God was his friend, not just someone who lived in heaven and kept His distance. In the Swedish church they attended here, as well as the church back in Sweden, God had seemed far from Olina.

She used to love Him. She had liked learning about Him, but she hadn't thought of Him as a friend. When this man said, "Father," his voice held love and warmth, not just awe. Olina didn't know what to think about that.

After the man finished praying, he started singing a song Olina had never heard before. However, the words and the music touched something in her that she had been hiding. The first line, "Love divine, all loves excelling, Joy of heaven to earth come down," awakened a longing. Olina felt uncomfortable. If she had been sitting on the back bench, she would have slipped out and returned to the hotel room. The longer the singing continued, the more uncomfortable she became. Her mother had always told her not to squirm in church, but the wooden bench was hard even through the layers of her clothing.

When the first song ended, the leader started another without announcing what it would be. That didn't bother the other people. By the second word, most of them were singing with him.

Olina didn't sing along. She had never heard this song, either. She didn't want to "survey the wondrous cross." Olina didn't want to think about Jesus dying for her. She didn't want to think that He loved her. By now she was fidgeting a lot. Maybe she could tell Gerda that she needed to use the necessary.

When the singer started the third song and everyone joined in, Olina couldn't shut the words out of her mind. "Amazing grace, how sweet the sound." How she would like to believe in that amazing grace, but she knew that God had not protected her from grievous hurt.

❧

Gustaf was attuned to Olina's every move. He could tell that she was uncomfortable. Maybe it would have been better not to bring her. He and August had prayed for Olina while they waited for the two young women to come down to the lobby. Perhaps it wasn't the time for God to speak to her yet.

Gustaf had been humming along after he caught on to the melody of the songs. The words had gone right to his heart, making it joyful, but that didn't seem to be the case with Olina. Maybe he should offer to walk her back to the hotel. But something stopped him from asking her.

❧

The last song started. "Holy Spirit, Truth divine, dawn upon this soul of mine; Word of God and inward light, wake my spirit, clear my sight."

Those words calmed Olina. Could the Spirit of God clear her sight? By the time the song ended, she had stopped fidgeting. She let the music pour over her, hoping it would indeed bring her lasting peace. But how could she trust God?

When the singer finished, he returned to his seat on the front bench and another man stepped onto the platform. He was a small, wiry man carrying a big black Bible under his arm. He turned and looked out across the group that was gathered. It seemed to Olina that his gaze stopped when he reached her. For a moment suspended in time, he continued to look at her before he continued on across the crowd. She felt as if he could see everything in her heart. Why was he interested in her?

He stood there for several moments. The crowd was quiet except for a mother in the back shushing her fussy baby. After the long pause, the preacher cleared his throat, pulled a large white handkerchief from his pocket, and mopped beads of perspiration from his forehead. Then he opened the Bible near the middle.

"I'm going to read to you from the book of Jeremiah, the twenty-ninth chapter, verses eleven through thirteen." Once more, he cleared his throat before continuing. " 'For I know the thoughts that I think toward you, saith the Lord, thoughts of peace, and not of evil, to give you an expected end. Then shall ye call upon me, and ye shall go and pray unto me, and I will hearken unto you. And ye shall seek me, and find me, when ye shall search for me with all your heart.' "

When he once again cleared his throat, the singer moved to the platform and handed the preacher a tin cup of water. After taking a swig, he gave it back to the man with a whisper of thanks. "I'm also going to read the first part of the fourteenth verse: 'And I will be found of you, saith the Lord.' "

Olina didn't remember those words from the Bible. Maybe it was because she didn't really like the Old Testament. It was harder for her to understand than the New Testament. She hadn't paid much attention when *Fader* read to the family from the Old Testament. But she thought she would have remembered those words. They had lodged in her heart after the preacher read them.

"I believe God is talking about His plans for us." The preacher closed the Bible and walked back and forth across the small platform. "God has plans for us, and they are plans that are good, not bad. He knows what He wants to happen in our lives. Sometimes it doesn't seem that way, but in the end, the good He intends will come to pass."

Could this be true? Olina didn't know. She only knew that God had allowed so much to happen to her. If He wanted good to come from it, when was it going to happen? Olina didn't hear any more of the preacher's sermon, but his opening words kept ringing through her heart and mind. God had plans for her good. Did He? Could she trust Him to bring them about?

Chapter 14

When Sophia and Marja came to the hotel late Monday afternoon, Olina and Gerda had finished two dresses that day. These would be the last, since Sophia and Adolph were leaving on the train Tuesday morning. Because they had been so busy, the week had flown by.

On Wednesday and Thursday, Olina and Gerda had made one dress per day. Once they became used to the sewing machine, everything went more quickly. Starting on Friday, they were able to finish two dresses per day. They had taken turns with each new dress. On one, Gerda cut out the dress while Olina sewed the pieces together. On the next one, they switched places. That way they both learned to use the machine. They shared the handwork, sewing on buttons and hemming.

"I can hardly believe I have eight new dresses at one time. These will last me for years." Sophia held up the light blue dimity, and its full skirt spread around her. "I've never had such a fine wardrobe as this." Her smile warmed Olina's heart. "What are you girls doing tonight?"

Olina looked at Gerda, who was making a bundle of the fabric scraps. She would take them home so her mother could use them in a quilt. "We'll be packing, getting ready for Gustaf to come for us tomorrow morning."

Sophia glanced down at the dress again. "I want to wear this before I leave town. Adolph and I would like to have you girls as our guests for dinner tonight."

Marja clapped her hands. "What a wonderful idea. We could all eat together."

"Of course," Sophia agreed. "It can be a dinner party. I'll check with the hotel to see if we can get festive food for tonight."

Sophia and Marja gathered up their things. They had started toward the door when Sophia turned back.

"I almost forgot to give you this." She opened her reticule and pulled a sealed envelope from it, thrusting it into Olina's hands. "I've put a little bonus in this along with what I agreed to pay you. You've done such a good job."

Before the young women could demur, Marja and Sophia had bustled out the door, chattering about the plans for the evening.

Gerda looked at Olina, who was using both hands to test the weight of the envelope. Olina could tell that it held quite a bit of money.

The Other Brother

"Well, look at it, Olina." Gerda was anxious.

Olina was careful not to tear the paper as she looked inside. Several green-backs spilled from the envelope onto the bed. Olina dumped the rest and sat beside the pile to divide it into two stacks. She had never seen that much money at one time in her whole life. At first, she just sat and looked at it. *What a blessing!* Now why did she think that? Did she still believe in blessings?

Since the first night of the brush arbor meetings, Olina had pondered the words of the evangelist. She wanted to read the words he shared from the Bible in her mother tongue, but she had not brought her Bible with her. Because of what her father had told her, she had left it at her aunt's house. After that Wednesday night meeting, Olina had written her aunt a letter, asking her to send the Bible to America. She wanted to wait to face the words until it came, but they kept popping into her head at the oddest times.

The preacher had said things on Thursday and Friday night that piqued her interest, but none as strongly as that first night. Did God have plans for her? If so, what were they?

"This is a lot of money." Gerda's comment interrupted Olina's musings.

"Yes, it is." Olina still stared at the two piles.

Gerda sat on the bed across from Olina, the money between them. "I have an idea."

Olina looked up at Gerda. "What?"

"Do you remember how much Marja said the sewing machine cost?"

Olina nodded.

"Look at all this." Gerda picked up her share of the bounty and let it drift back to the bed. "If we put our shares together, we could buy that machine and still have plenty of money left."

Olina's eyes widened as she looked at her friend. She hadn't even thought about anything like that. Maybe Gerda's idea was a good one.

"Remember at church?" Gerda started stacking her money in a neat pile. "When the other women saw Marja's and Sophia's new dresses, we got orders from four other women."

Olina was getting interested. "We could make those dresses much faster with the machine." She walked over to the piece of equipment and rubbed her hand over the wooden table that held the machine head. "If we are going to be dressmakers, we need this."

Gerda joined her. "It would be wonderful if somehow we could move to the house we saw and sew from there." She got a dreamy look in her eyes. "We did pray and ask God to provide for us. Look what He has already provided."

Olina could only agree. Maybe, just maybe, she had been wrong, and God had not deserted her as she had thought.

The party that evening was festive. The glow of candlelight glistened from polished silver and crystal goblets, and a floral centerpiece graced the table. Instead of the roast beef most people were having for dinner, they each had a tender steak, surrounded by fresh vegetables. The dainty rolls were fluffy and browned to perfection. Dessert was a light chocolate pastry with a custard filling. Olina had never tasted anything like it.

While the guests enjoyed their meals, several people came over to talk to Olina and Gerda. Some of them were visiting with Sophia and Adolph before they went back to Denver. Other couples came for the wives to look at the dresses all four women wore. Olina and Gerda had worn the pastel silk frocks they had made before they had come to town to sew for Sophia. Three more women wanted to talk to them about making them dresses.

"Marja," Gerda said as they were getting ready to go up to their rooms. "You said that Johan would pick up the sewing machine in the morning when we are getting ready to leave."

"Yes, dear, I hope that's all right." Marja patted Gerda on the arm.

"Well, Olina and I have decided that we want to buy the machine with the money we made this week."

Marja clapped her hands. "What a wonderful idea." Then she put her arms around both young women. "You have so many more dresses to make already."

The three women started up the staircase. "We thought it would be a good investment," Olina added.

"I'm glad Johan came to help me carry that heavy machine down to the wagon." Gustaf made a clucking sound to the horses, and they started out of town. "Here I thought I had carried it on those stairs for the last time." He chuckled. "It's a good thing we needed to pick up some feed for the horses. If not, I would have brought the buggy, not the wagon."

Gerda was seated between Gustaf and Olina on the wagon seat. She poked Olina with her elbow. "He always has something to complain about, doesn't he?" The young women giggled. "I think he likes helping us."

Olina peeked around Gerda to see that Gustaf was looking right at her. "Do you agree?" he asked.

Goose bumps ran up her arms. "I think. . ." Olina swallowed and looked away.

"What do you think, Olina?" Gerda seemed oblivious to the charge in the air.

"I think that Gustaf does like to help. . .us." Olina ducked her head. "But I don't think he complains much. At least I don't hear him."

When a robust laugh burst from Gustaf, another feeling ran up Olina's spine. She was not sure what it was, but she knew that she liked to hear Gustaf's hearty laugh. It sounded musical to her, like the symphony she and *Tant* Olga attended before she came to America—rich, full, and heartwarming. At least it warmed her heart today. But it wasn't just the laugh. That was only part of what warmed her heart. After all, she and Gerda really became professional dressmakers when they bought that treadle sewing machine. Her life was taking shape. It had a purpose now.

Ingrid Nilsson prepared a special feast to celebrate the return of the young women. Even August came home to have dinner with them. He said that Gustaf invited him when he came to town to pick them up. The meal was a lively, happy time, with much talking and teasing among the Nilsson family. However, Olina remained silent, listening to the others and remembering such evenings with her family back in Sweden. The times she thought of them were not as often, but since writing the letter to *Tant* Olga, Olina couldn't get them off her mind. A veritable smorgasbord of thoughts tumbled through her head. Dressmaking. The house on the edge of town. Her family. In the midst of all those thoughts, Gustaf's face often appeared.

"Isn't that right, Olina?" Gerda's voice penetrated her reverie.

Olina looked at her friend.

"I was telling Father about all the women who want us to make dresses for them." Gerda smiled at Olina.

"Oh yes. It's amazing. Even with the sewing machine, we will be busy for a couple of weeks." Olina could feel a blush creeping up her neck. She should pay attention to what the others were saying.

"By the time we're finished," Gerda added, "perhaps more women will want our dresses."

"What sewing machine?" Mr. Nilsson had a puzzled expression.

Olina looked at Gerda, wondering if she shouldn't have said anything about the machine. She assumed that Mr. Nilsson knew about it by now.

"Olina and I used some of the money we made this week to buy the treadle sewing machine Mrs. Braxton let us use to make her sister-in-law's dresses." Gerda smiled at her father.

Olina noticed that the puzzlement in his face softened. "Since we have so many other dresses to make, it was a good investment."

Mr. Nilsson's face softened even more. "That is so, for sure. You girls used your heads." He took another bite of creamy mashed potatoes. "*Ja*, it was a good investment."

"I made a good investment this week, too." Everyone stopped eating and looked at Gustaf as he continued. "Father, remember the Winslow house right outside town?" He waited for his father to nod. "Brian Winslow moved to California."

"I remember hearing that," Mr. Nilsson said.

Mrs. Nilsson passed the fried chicken to August, who didn't have any more on his plate. "I heard that he took his mother with him."

"He did." Gerda picked up another hot roll and buttered it.

Olina wondered where this discussion was headed. She didn't have to wait long to find out.

Gustaf put his fork on his plate and tented his fingers over it. "The Winslow house was for sale. I talked to their lawyer last week. This morning I signed the papers making the house mine."

Olina and Gerda looked at each other with stunned expressions. Gustaf had bought their house. The house they had prayed for God to find a way for them to rent. A plan was forming in Olina's mind, and she could tell that Gerda's thoughts were running along the same lines. Maybe. But it could never be. Mr. Nilsson wouldn't agree to let two young women live alone, even though it was near town.

"Gustaf." Mr. Nilsson laid his fork down and looked at his son. "Why did you buy the house?"

Gustaf looked at his father, man to man. "The price was reasonable, and I had more than enough money saved. Some day, I may want to live there with my wife."

"Son, you know that you'll always have a home here on the farm."

Gustaf smiled. "I know that. But when I marry, we might want to live closer to town. It wouldn't mean that I couldn't work the farm. It's not that far from here."

August couldn't let that comment pass. "Just when are you planning on getting married?" He jabbed Gustaf in the ribs, laughing.

Gustaf ignored the teasing. "I don't know when God will have me marry, but I know He doesn't want me to be a solitary man all my life."

He looked at Olina when he made that solemn declaration. Her heart began to beat double time at the sound of his voice and the words he said.

"What will you do with the house right now?" Mr. Nilsson took the conversation back to the heart of the matter. "It isn't good for a house to sit empty for long."

"I know that." With a smile, Gustaf glanced at Gerda and then Olina. "Since the girls have several clients in town, they could live in the house."

Olina expected a negative exclamation from Mr. Nilsson about that statement. Her father would have vehemently denied the request. But the room was silent except for August's fork scraping on his plate. Everyone else in the room had stopped eating. The silence lengthened while Olina held her breath.

Finally Mr. Nilsson answered Gustaf. "I'm not sure I like that idea. The girls are under my protection, and I don't want anything happening to them."

"Father, I know that." Gustaf once more leaned his forearms on the table with his fingers tented over his plate. "Look at Gerda and Olina. They aren't girls. They are women."

Mr. Nilsson looked at Olina first then turned his attention toward his daughter. Olina could tell that he was seeing them differently than he ever had before.

"You're right, my son, but they still need protection."

Gustaf nodded. "That can be arranged. Several men in the church have been looking after the property since the Winslows left. I'm sure they would help look after the young women."

It sounded to Olina as if Gustaf emphasized the words *young women*.

August put down his fork. "I could check on them every day, too, Father. It would be nice to have part of the family living closer to me."

"I know we don't have locks on this house," Gustaf continued, "but I had locks installed on that one. It would make Gerda and Olina feel safer at night."

August looked at Gerda with a smile. "I could make a big dinner bell for the girls to hang outside. Then if they need help, they can ring it. I could hear it from where I work and where I live."

Mr. Nilsson looked around the table at each of his children. "You have all given convincing arguments." Then he looked at Olina. "Is this what you would like to do, Olina?"

A large lump had grown in her throat, and she couldn't get any words around it, so she nodded. Mr. Nilsson studied her face as if he was trying to read her thoughts. Then he picked up his fork. "Let's finish this wonderful meal so we can have a piece of that apple pie I smelled as I came into the house. I'll think on this discussion and give you my decision in the morning."

Chapter 15

Gustaf knew that his father was a fair man with a strong sense of responsibility for his family. He would pray about the decision he had to make before morning.

Gustaf had prayed before he bought the house. God hadn't given him that check in his spirit that helped keep him from making wrong decisions. He felt complete peace about buying the property and couldn't help thinking about the possibility that he would one day live there with Olina as his wife. The house was perfect for a newlywed couple. Olina could continue to be a dressmaker if she wanted to. When God blessed their marriage with children, he would build onto the house to accommodate however many children God blessed them with. There was plenty of room for expansion.

He imagined little girls with blond curls playing in the yard and even swinging from limbs of trees. When they were younger, Gerda and Olina had climbed trees right along with their brothers. His sons would accompany him to the farm to help their grandfather.

What was he thinking? In his mind, he had children when he didn't even know whether Olina would ever forgive him. If she did, she might never come to love him as he already loved her. He needed to turn his thoughts to more profitable pursuits.

Gustaf got on his knees with his Bible open on the bed beside him. He prayed for a few minutes. Then he read a passage of Scripture about God hearing and answering prayers before he returned to his supplications. After over an hour spent in the presence of his heavenly Father, peace descended over Gustaf's soul. He knew that no matter what his earthly father decided, it would be the will of the heavenly Father. Clothed in that peace, Gustaf climbed into his bed and fell into a deep, restful sleep.

Olina paced the floor of her room thinking about the discussion at dinner. Could it be possible that Mr. Nilsson would let them move to the house?

Trust Me, Olina. The voice sounded in her mind. A voice that was getting harder to ignore since the first night at the brush arbor meeting. Did God have a plan for her? Did it include living in the house? Olina never imagined that it would be so simple to establish herself as a dressmaker. Had God been a part of that?

The Other Brother

She wanted to pray for Mr. Nilsson as he made the decision, but it had been a long time since she trusted God enough to ask Him for anything. She knew that Gerda was probably praying right now if she hadn't already gone to sleep. Maybe even Gustaf was talking to God about his father's decision. Olina hoped so. Gerda and Gustaf still trusted God. He would listen to them.

I will listen to you, too, Olina.

Olina wished that were true, but she had ignored God for so long, how could He want to hear what she said?

When Olina awoke, she could tell that she had overslept. The sun, streaming through her window, was too high in the sky for it to be early morning. She quickly dressed and went downstairs to the kitchen, where she was met by the smells of bacon and biscuits.

"I'm so sorry I overslept."

Mrs. Nilsson turned at the sound of Olina's voice. "That's all right, Olina. We decided to let you sleep until you awoke. Gerda heard you moving around in your room late into the night."

Olina frowned. "I didn't want to disturb anyone."

Mrs. Nilsson put her arms around Olina and pulled her into a maternal hug. "Olina, dear, you didn't disturb anyone. I think Gerda was awake a long time, too. She was probably praying about her father's decision." She patted Olina's arm before turning back to the skillet on the woodstove. "I've kept the bacon and biscuits warm. Would you like one egg or two?"

"Only one, but let me cook it." Olina started toward the extra apron hanging on the hook beside the back door.

"No, please let me do this for you." Mrs. Nilsson broke an egg into the skillet. She started basting the egg with the warm bacon grease as she continued. "After all, I won't be cooking for you much longer."

Olina sat down hard in the chair she had pulled out from the table. "Do you mean what I think you mean?" She was afraid to believe what she had heard.

"Yes, dear. Bennel said that you and Gerda could move into Gustaf's house."

Olina was speechless. It was too wonderful to imagine. Was this part of God's plans for her? Whether it was or not, Olina was ecstatic. She couldn't hold back a giggle that bubbled from deep within.

"I'm glad that makes you happy." Mrs. Nilsson set the plate of food in front of Olina. "Now eat up. Gustaf and Gerda are finishing the chores, so the three of you can look at the house. They want to see what needs to be done to get it ready for you to move in."

Olina was so excited that she thought she couldn't eat, but when she took the first bite of the light fluffy bread, it whetted her appetite. By the time Gerda and

Gustaf came in from outdoors, she had cleaned up everything on her plate.

Gerda burst through the back door like a whirlwind. "Olina, has Mother told you?" When Olina nodded, she continued. "Isn't it wonderful?" She ran around the table and pulled Olina up into a hug. Olina felt as if Gerda were cutting her in two with her strong arms, but she hugged Gerda back just as hard.

Gustaf soon followed Gerda into the kitchen. "If you girls. . . young women. . . would get ready, we'll be off to town."

Gerda and Olina turned to look at him. His smile was as big as theirs.

"We'll be ready in ten minutes. Right, Olina?" Gerda hurried out into the hall.

Olina couldn't tear her gaze from Gustaf. He looked so strong and masculine. The freshness of the warm summer morning surrounded him, and his eyes communicated something to her soul. She didn't know, or recognize, what it was, but she liked it. It made her feel fresh and warm as the morning.

While Gustaf unlocked the front door of his house, Olina stood on the porch looking out toward the road. Everything around them was in the full bloom of summer. Trees were clothed in various shades of green above their brown or gray trunks. Birds sang in some of the trees. Prairie grasses, blowing in the wind, were dotted with white, pink, and yellow wildflowers. When she looked down the road to her right, Litchfield looked rooted in the prairie as much as the trees were. It felt as if it were part of the landscape, a close neighbor to keep the house from being lonely. Taking a deep breath of the fresh air, Olina let out a sigh of contentment. This would soon be her home. But she had to ask Gustaf one question.

Olina turned to look toward him, only to find him smiling at her. Gerda had already entered the house.

"So, how much rent are you going to charge us?"

The look that passed over his face was one of hurt then understanding. "I won't charge rent to anyone in the family."

"Oh, but I'm not—"

Before Olina could finish, Gustaf interrupted with a teasing comment as he walked over to stand in front of her. "But you can cook me a hot meal every once in a while. That would be a fair rent."

Olina had to look up to meet the challenge in his face. "Why would you need a hot meal when your mother cooks so well?"

Her question, which had started on a strong note, ended with a soft breathy word. Gustaf leaned closer as if he were having a hard time hearing her. Olina didn't know whether to step back or stay where she was. He was entirely too close for comfort. But she would not allow him to cause her to move.

"Does that mean I can't enjoy another woman's cooking?"

There he was emphasizing the word *woman* again. Olina liked the fact that he knew she was a woman, but that knowledge caused unfamiliar feelings within her. She couldn't decide whether they were comfortable feelings or not.

His gaze held hers, and time stood still. The fragrance of soap and something else that Olina couldn't define enveloped her in a world inhabited by the two of them. Olina couldn't ever remember any man she had known smelling quite like that. Sweat, she had smelled, and soap, but not this masculine aroma. It was heady and scary at the same time.

Gustaf reached toward her when the sound of Gerda's voice came from inside the house. "Olina, look. The house has furniture in almost every room."

Gustaf pulled back as Olina turned toward the door.

"Yes, there was too much furniture to take to California, so they left most of it. If the person who bought the house didn't want the furnishings, they would have been sold at an auction for the Winslows. I thought we could use most of it."

Olina was still dazed by what had happened on the porch, but she looked around her, trying to get her bearings back. The Chesterfield in the parlor looked to be in good condition. She decided to try it out. It might help to sit for a minute. While she walked to the sofa, she looked at the chairs and tables arranged around the room. A large rug covered the floor. The room had a homey feel.

Olina dropped onto the comfortable sofa. She ran her finger across the table that sat beside it.

"Merta swept and dusted the house for me yesterday while I was in town." Olina raised her head at the sound of Gustaf's voice from the doorway. Now that she was across the room from him, she had her equilibrium back.

"That was nice." Olina didn't look into Gustaf's eyes. She focused on the wall beside the door.

"I told her someone might be moving in pretty soon." Gustaf looked at the wall, too. "Do you think we should put up new wallpaper?"

Gerda walked up behind him. "This wallpaper is lovely. Isn't it, Olina?"

Olina nodded, for the first time noticing the ivy pattern. "Everything is wonderful."

Gustaf stepped into the room. "Do you think the curtains need washing?"

Gerda walked over and lifted the edge of one. "Of course they do. They'll be filled with dust. Come, Olina. Let me show you the rest of the house."

After the tour, the trio decided to have a workday the next day. They would bring all the things needed to wash the curtains in the house. Their search of the cupboards revealed that there were enough dishes, pots and pans, and utensils for the young women to set up housekeeping. They could add to them as needed. One of the closets even held bed linens. They would want to wash them when they washed the curtains.

The room that Mrs. Winslow used as a library had shelves on two walls and windows on the other two. It would be ideal for the sewing room. They could utilize the shelves to showcase fabrics and notions, and the windows gave it a light, airy feeling. Since the room contained no furniture, there was plenty of space for a cutting table, the sewing machine, and whatever chairs Gerda and Olina needed in their business. It might take them a little time to completely furnish it as they would like, but the possibilities made both girls excited.

"It won't take long to get the house ready to move in," Gerda gushed. "One or two workdays, and we'll be living here."

She hugged Olina hard again. Olina felt like dancing as she had when she was an excited little girl. But today she was no longer a girl. She must act as a woman would. She never wanted Gustaf to think of her as a little girl again.

The whole family decided to participate in the workday at Gustaf's house. Even August took the day off from the blacksmith's. Mrs. Nilsson decided to cook dinner at the house, and Mr. Nilsson wanted to check everything out before Gerda and Olina moved in.

After chores were finished, they piled into the wagon. Mrs. Nilsson sat on the seat between Mr. Nilsson and Gustaf. Gerda and Olina sat in the back of the wagon surrounded by cleaning supplies and various items they were taking to the house.

When they stopped the wagon, they sat for a minute while Mr. and Mrs. Nilsson looked at the cottage and its surroundings.

Mrs. Nilsson was the first to break the silence. "Oh, Gustaf, I like it. It's so pretty from the outside."

Mr. Nilsson nodded his agreement before he stepped to the ground. While he was helping his wife out of the wagon, August called to them from down the road toward town.

They all pitched in, and soon the windows were open wide, letting in the summer breeze to air out all the rooms. While the women put water on to boil, the men took down the curtains. August tested the clothesline to make sure it was stable. Then he used a wet rag to wipe the dust off the wire before the women hung clean items over it.

When the first load of water was hot, Mrs. Nilsson put another pot on the back of the stove to heat. She placed the pot of beef stew that she had brought from home on the front of the stove to heat for lunch.

About the time they were going to stop to eat, Merta pulled up in her buggy. Two other women from the church were with her. They brought hot corn bread and butter, lemonade, and a pound cake. The women insisted on taking over the work in the kitchen, making Ingrid sit down and rest while they served everyone.

Lunch was like a party to Olina. She enjoyed having Merta there, but she also got to know the other two women better.

The Other Brother

"Are you a good cook?" August asked Olina. "I've eaten some things that Gerda made that weren't so good."

Gerda, who was sitting beside him, hit him playfully on the arm. "That was a long time ago."

"Yes, both Mother and *Tant* Olga insisted that I learn to cook." Olina smiled at August. "Maybe you could eat with us sometime since we're so close now."

"That would be wonderful," Gerda exclaimed. "I would love to fix you breakfast and dinner every day. I'm not sure about lunch every day, though. We'll be busy in the daytime. We have a lot of orders to fill."

"I might take you up on that." August smiled as if he had been given a special present.

And I might take you up on it sometime, too. For the first time in his life, Gustaf envied his brother.

Chapter 16

It took only one day to finish getting the cottage ready, so Gerda and Olina planned to move on Friday. Mrs. Nilsson gathered some of her kitchen items to add to the things left in the house. She also packed a few towels, more sheets, and two good goose-down pillows.

With Gerda and Olina in her bedroom, she opened the large cedar chest. Inside were a number of handmade quilts. She let each of the young women pick two for their own beds. While adding some cutwork kitchen towels and crocheted doilies to the growing stack, she furtively wiped a tear from the corner of her eye, but Olina noticed the movement.

Perhaps her own mother had shed tears about her daughter leaving home. For a moment, Olina's heart yearned to see her mother's dear face. *Please,* Gud, *let me see* Mor *again, at least once.* After she had that thought, Olina realized that it was a prayer.

When they had unloaded the first wagonful of things at the house, Gustaf and his father returned to the farm to bring another load. Olina was surprised that there was more than would fill one wagon. In addition to her hand luggage, she had brought two trunks full of things with her when she moved from Sweden. Gerda had a lifetime of possessions to move. She didn't seem to be leaving anything at her parents' home.

Mrs. Nilsson insisted on giving a large table to Gerda and Olina for them to use in the sewing room. Besides that, she gave them two rocking chairs that were in the attic of the farmhouse, along with two straight chairs. Olina couldn't imagine that they would need anything else at their new home. Her small hoard of money wouldn't have to be used for furnishings. That was a blessing.

When the men returned and unloaded the wagon the second time, Merta arrived. She said that some of the women had prepared lunch for them. They had the table set at Merta's house waiting for them to come.

"We can't possibly go looking like this." Olina pushed a stray curl back under the scarf she had tied around her head.

"Yes, you can." Gustaf touched her cheek with one finger, rubbing at a spot. "You have some dust on your face, but it won't take you long to clean up."

Olina turned away to hide the blush she could feel staining her cheeks. More than her cheek was affected by the touch of his finger.

The Other Brother

"Of course not," Gerda agreed. After filling a white pitcher with a rose pattern on the side, she picked up the matching bowl and invited her mother to accompany her to her bedroom to freshen up.

Olina soon followed with a pure white bowl and pitcher of fresh water for her own bedroom. Setting it on the washstand, she peered into the looking glass on the wall above it. After removing the scarf, she fluffed her hair with her brush and pulled it back, tying it at the nape of her neck with the scarf. That would have to do. She didn't have time to put it up properly.

Olina was descending the stairs when Gustaf returned from washing at the pump in the kitchen. He caught his breath when he looked up at her. He hadn't seen her like that since she arrived in America. Even though her hair was tied back, curls cascaded past her waist. It reminded him of the bubbling waterfall on the farm in Sweden as it sparkled in the sun. He had seen her many times back in Sweden. When she hadn't had her hair in braids as a young girl, she wore it tied back, but he didn't remember it like this. Gustaf wished he had the right to run his fingers through the silky-looking strands. He just had to imagine what they would feel like curled around his fingers.

"Is everyone ready?" His father's voice sounded from behind him.

Gustaf was glad that his father hadn't been watching his face. He knew Gustaf too well, and he might realize what Gustaf was thinking. Gustaf wasn't ready to discuss his feelings for Olina with anyone, especially not his father.

While they were eating, the women from church asked if there was anything else they could do to help Gerda and Olina get settled in the Winslow house.

"I guess it's no longer the Winslow house." Gustaf couldn't keep the pride out of his voice. "From now on, it will be the Nilsson house."

Olina knew what he was saying, but she was not a Nilsson. It felt different to be living in a Nilsson house when Gustaf owned it instead of his father, but she wasn't yet ready to explore the reason.

Two of the women had talked to Gerda and Olina about sewing for them. They made arrangements to bring fabric to the cottage on Monday so that Gerda and Olina could get started making their dresses. Olina felt so professional. She thought Gerda felt the same, because they shared a secret smile across the table.

It didn't take long for Gerda and Olina to settle into a routine. In the mornings, after doing whatever cleaning the house needed, they started sewing on dresses for customers. Working together, they had no trouble finishing a dress, sometimes more, in a day. As women began wearing their new frocks, more were ordered, both by the same women and others. By the end of the first month they lived in the house, their business was thriving.

August quickly formed the habit of eating breakfast with the young women. Sometimes when they were busy, he would invite them to join him for lunch at his boardinghouse. The food there was good, and it kept Gerda and Olina from having to take time to cook. They took turns fixing dinner.

It soon became apparent that Gustaf meant what he said about the rent being a hot meal. It wasn't at all unusual for him to arrive in town to share lunch or dinner with them four or more times a week. Not that Olina minded. It was pleasant to have him around. When he was there, he checked to see if there were any repairs that needed to be done at the house.

Two months had passed when Gustaf arrived carrying a package. "Olina, I have something for you." He strode into the sewing room and stopped short. She was standing on a straight chair, trying to reach something on a high shelf. "What do you think you are doing?" His voice exploded.

The loudness and harshness must have startled Olina, because she lost her balance, teetering on the chair before her feet flew out from under her. Gustaf hurled the package to the floor and lunged toward her, barely catching her. He pulled her hard against his heaving chest. What a scare she had given him. He didn't realize how hard he was clutching her to himself until he heard her soft sob. That sound cut right to his heart.

Gustaf loosened his hold, cradling her gently against his still pounding heart. "I'm so sorry. I didn't mean to hurt you."

Olina hiccoughed. "You scared me," she whispered against his chest.

Gustaf set her on her feet, but he didn't let her go. She felt so right in his arms. He tried not to sound harsh. "What you were doing was dangerous. I was afraid you would fall."

She pushed against his chest until there was room between them. "Actually, you caused me to fall. Your shout startled me." At least she didn't sound as though she were accusing him of anything bad.

"Do you often climb like that?" Gustaf stepped away from Olina, giving himself room to breathe.

"Only when I need something from a top shelf." She looked defiantly up at him.

"I can get you anything you want."

"What about when you are not here?" The question came out in a whisper.

"I will bring you a step stool the next time I come." Gustaf looked at the package lying on the floor near the wall. "I brought you something. It's from Sweden."

Olina looked from his face to the box.

"My Bible. *Tant* Olga has sent my Bible." Olina grabbed the box and clutched it to her heart. "Thank you for bringing it to me."

Gustaf was confused for a moment, then he nodded. He was surprised but encouraged by Olina's actions. He had been praying for her so long, worrying about her relationship with the Lord. The fact that she had asked her aunt to send her Bible must be a good sign. He decided it would be best to let her open the package alone, so he said a quick good-bye and went to look for Gerda.

Olina knew that Gerda would come back into the house at any moment. She had been out checking the small garden they planted. Olina wanted privacy when she opened the box, so she took it up to her bedroom and closed the door.

Dropping into the rocking chair by the window, she continued to hold the package close as tears streamed down her cheeks. She wasn't sure she was ready to read the words for herself, but she knew she must.

Olina took the package and laid it on the bed. She wondered why *Tant* Olga had used such a large box to send the Bible. When she opened it, she found out. Letters and two smaller parcels accompanied the book. One letter was in *Tant* Olga's handwriting, but the writing on the other cried out to her heart. It had been so long since she had seen anything her mother had written.

Grabbing that letter, Olina returned to the rocking chair. Very slowly, she read her mother's words, savoring every one of them.

> *Olina,*
>
> *I miss you very much. Olga has let me read your letters. I am so sorry about Lars, but Olina, you are better off without him. If you had married, he might have hurt you later. I am praying for God to heal that pain in your heart.*

Olina paused and gazed at the fluffy clouds floating in the azure sky. She felt disappointment from what had happened with Lars, but the deep hurt was no longer there. When had that happened?

> *Peter has gotten married. I don't think you know the girl. Mary's family had moved here not long before you left for America. They are living with us on the farm. Of course, he is working the farm with your father and John.*
>
> *Speaking of your father, I pray daily that he will change his mind about you, but he hasn't yet. Olga said she will pass on my letters to you. And you may write me at Olga's. I visit her as often as I can.*

It was as if Olina could hear her mother's voice as she read. When she finished the rest of the letter, she placed it lovingly among her handkerchiefs. She knew that she would take it out and read it many times. Tonight she would write a long letter in return. Hope about her family crept back into Olina's heart.

She went over to the bed and picked up one of the small packages. Turning it over, she saw her mother's handwriting on it. *This belonged to your grandmother. I want you to have it.*

Olina quickly tore the paper from the box. It contained a cameo brooch set in gold. Olina held it in her hand, carefully studying the dainty carved features of a young woman. Her mother's thoughtfulness touched her heart. She would treasure this link with her past.

The other small package was from *Tant* Olga. The cameo earrings it contained had to be carved by the same craftsman. Olina quickly opened *Tant* Olga's letter. In it she told that the brooch and earrings had been a set when they were first purchased.

After reading *Tant* Olga's letter, Olina opened her Bible. The pages fell open to the words she was looking for. She read the verses again and again. The evangelist was right. God did care about what was going on in her life. Olina had never heard anyone explain those particular verses in quite that way, but there was no doubt in her mind what the words were saying.

Father God, forgive me for doubting You. I have been so hurt. Please help me get past that hurt to what You have for me.

It was a simple prayer, but a peace Olina hadn't felt for a long time invaded her heart, returning it to familiar territory. Olina still didn't know what would happen about her father, but her heavenly Father was once again in her life. However, she wondered if He had ever left. Maybe she had just shut herself off from His presence.

Chapter 17

Life in the little house bustled. Besides the thriving dressmaking business, Gerda and Olina often had women from town call on them. Sometimes women from the surrounding farms also stopped by on their way to or from town. When that happened, the two young women took time from their busy schedules to share conversations accompanied by refreshments. Olina liked using her grandmother's china teapot to brew the invigorating tea they all enjoyed. Gerda was the one who liked to bake, and she kept a pie, a cake, or dainty pastries on hand for those times of fellowship.

Soon after Olina's Bible had come from Sweden, Gustaf arrived at the house just as she was making herself a light lunch. That day Gerda had gone into town to help Merta make new curtains for her kitchen.

"Are you hungry?" Olina asked when she answered Gustaf's knock. After he nodded, she continued, "I can make us a picnic, and we can eat down by the stream."

Gustaf helped Olina gather together the cold chicken, applesauce, and bread. They put them in a basket, along with a tablecloth to spread on the ground.

After they had finished eating, Olina asked Gustaf, "Do you think that God has specific plans for each person?"

Gustaf took a moment to think about her question. Olina was glad. She wasn't looking for the easy, quick answer.

First, Gustaf asked her a question. "Why are you asking me this?"

Olina watched a cloud that resembled a calf drift across the sky above them. It was hard to put her thoughts into words. "A lot has happened in my life that didn't seem to be good at the time."

Gustaf nodded as if he agreed.

"When we went to the brush arbor meeting, the preacher said that God has plans for us. He read a scripture that I had never heard before, and he said that it was about the plans God has for us. Do you remember?"

"Vaguely." Gustaf looked as if he were trying to remember.

"That is one reason I asked *Tant* Olga to send me my Bible. I wanted to read those verses for myself." Olina wasn't sure she should have started this conversation. It was hard to put into words. "I have memorized the words now."

"Tell them to me." Gustaf sounded eager.

" 'For I know the thoughts that I think toward you, saith the Lord, thoughts of peace, and not of evil, to give you an expected end. Then shall ye call upon me, and ye shall go and pray unto me, and I will hearken unto you. And ye shall seek me, and find me, when ye shall search for me with all your heart.' Do you think God was talking about His plans for us like the preacher said?"

Gustaf didn't answer right away. "It could mean that. I know that when I try to make a decision without asking God about it, I often make the wrong decision."

"How do you know whether your decision is right or wrong?"

"Olina, when a decision is the one God would have me make, He gives me peace deep in my heart. It is hard to explain, but that's what it is. Real peace."

When Gustaf left, Olina didn't go back to work. Instead, she took out her Bible and read the verses again. Since her Bible had come from *Tant* Olga, Olina read it every day. Her relationship with God had grown.

It had been so long since she had read the words of God that her thirst was almost unquenchable. She looked forward to Sunday when the Nilsson family attended services at the Lutheran church in Litchfield. Every Sunday Olina listened eagerly to the words spoken by the pastor. Her whole outlook on life had changed dramatically.

"Olina." Gerda came down the stairs wearing her bonnet and carrying a basket on her arm. "I'm going to the mercantile. We have no more eggs, and we'll soon be out of flour. Do you need anything?"

Olina looked up from the hem she was stitching. "We only have one more needle. It's surprising how many we break."

Gerda laughed. "Maybe we work them too hard. They can't keep up with our speed."

Olina put the dress down on the table and walked over to the sewing machine. "I've been wondering what we would do if the machine needle breaks. Maybe we should have Marja order us a couple of replacement needles just in case something happens."

"That's a good idea." Gerda took a list from her pocket and wrote on it. "Do you want to come to the store with me?"

Olina picked up the dress again. She sat in the chair by the window and reached into the sewing basket at her feet, taking out the spool of thread. "We promised this dress today, but we don't know when she'll come for it. I think I should work on the hem. I want it finished whenever she comes to pick it up."

After Gerda left, Olina's fingers flew as they made the dainty stitches for which she and Gerda were so famous. Although her hands were busy, her mind kept wandering. It had been three days since Gustaf had come to eat with them. She wondered where he was and why he had stayed away so long. For a moment, she dropped the dress in her lap and looked out the open window. Gustaf's face filled her thoughts as if he were standing there. She could even feel the touch of his hand against her waist. He had been walking beside her on Sunday. When they walked up the steps at church, his hand had touched her back as he guided her. Olina wondered if he even noticed. Probably not. She picked up the dress and continued working on the hem. She should keep her mind on what she was doing and not daydream.

Gustaf drove the wagon into town to pick up supplies for his mother. It was the first day that week he could get away from the farm. One of the hired men was sick, and Gustaf had to do this man's work as well as his own.

He was glad that the horses knew the way to Litchfield. It allowed his thoughts to ramble wherever he wanted. They naturally turned toward Olina. When he was finished in town, he planned to stop by the Nilsson house to check on things, especially Olina. Maybe he would stay for dinner.

Sunday, when they had started up the steps at the church, Olina had stumbled on the second step, and he had touched her to steady her. While it had helped Olina, it did nothing to steady the beat of his heart. Just thinking about it, his hand tingled as it had on Sunday. Whenever there was any kind of physical contact between them, his heart beat double time. Gustaf would hurry gathering the supplies so he could see Olina sooner.

The eastbound train was leaving town when Gustaf pulled up in front of the mercantile. Trains fascinated him. He didn't think he would ever tire of riding them. At the sound of the whistle, Gustaf looked down the street toward the station. A couple standing on the platform beside a pile of luggage looked familiar. At least the man did. If he didn't know better, Gustaf would have been convinced that the man was Lars. But Lars was in Denver. They had received a letter from Lars two weeks earlier, and he had not said anything about coming to Minnesota.

The tall man raised a hand and gave a broad wave to Gustaf. Instead of getting out of the wagon, he clucked to the horses, urging them toward the station. Soon he was convinced that the man was Lars. That must be his wife with him. Gustaf had never seen her. She was almost as tall as Lars.

Gustaf had not stopped the wagon before Lars leapt from the platform into the street and shouted, "I thought that was you, big brother." Lars stood as if waiting for him to jump from the wagon, but Gustaf just sat where he was.

"Lars, what are you doing here?"

Lars laughed. "You sound as if you aren't glad to see me."

"Of course, I'm glad to see you. I'm a little. . .surprised."

"That's what we wanted to do. Surprise everyone."

Gustaf frowned. "Surprises aren't always a good thing. There are some people who might be uncomfortable by your surprise."

"Who would that be?"

Gustaf jumped down from the wagon seat and spoke quietly to Lars. "Do you know that Olina is still here?"

"Yes." Lars looked a little uncomfortable. "I need to talk to Olina face-to-face."

"That might not be a good idea." Gustaf tried not to sound too angry, but when he thought about what Lars had done to Olina, the anger came anyway.

Lars spoke to Gustaf, man to man. "It's something I have to do. I'm not proud of what I did to Olina. I need to make amends for it."

"Lars, is everything all right?" The feminine voice called from the station platform.

Lars gestured toward the woman standing on the platform, and Gustaf looked up at her.

The woman smiled.

"Come meet my wife." Lars took Gustaf by the arm and pulled him along up the steps. "Janice, this is my oldest brother."

She placed her gloved hand into Gustaf's. "I think I would have known you anywhere, Gustaf. Lars has told me so much about you." Her voice had a lyrical quality to it.

Gustaf hadn't known what to expect in his sister-in-law. She was tall and willowy. Her friendly face was surrounded by abundant black hair, styled in the current pompadour fashion. Her eyes were her most arresting feature. They were green, sparkling with life. For a moment Gustaf questioned his brother's sanity. Janice was beautiful, but she didn't come close to Olina in any area that he could see.

Gustaf gave Lars and Janice a ride to the hotel. They had decided to stay there for the first few nights of their visit. They thought it would make everything less awkward. It was a good thing that Gustaf hadn't yet bought the supplies. There wouldn't have been room in the wagon for all of their luggage and everything he came to pick up.

When they came back out of the hotel after taking the luggage up to their room, Gerda was walking down the sidewalk near the mercantile. She saw Lars before he saw her, and she came hurrying across the street, calling out to them.

Gustaf suggested that Gerda, Lars, and Janice go into the hotel. He told them he would pick up Olina and bring her back so they could have lunch together. When Gerda looked concerned, he told her that he would prepare Olina for the confrontation.

As Gustaf drove the wagon toward his house, he started praying for Olina. He wanted to warn her about Lars, and he wanted to be with her when she learned that he was in Litchfield. If need be, Gustaf was prepared to stay at the house with

Olina until she didn't need him anymore. He hoped that Lars and Janice's presence wouldn't set Olina back in her walk with the Lord. Most of all, Gustaf didn't want Olina hurt again.

Olina was finishing the last stitch in the hem of the ruffled skirt when she noticed Gustaf's wagon coming from Litchfield. She hadn't seen him go by on the way to town. It was hard to miss him now. He was driving fast. That was unusual for Gustaf. He was always careful with the horses. Olina stood up and stretched. Then she took the dress to the table to fold it. She was glad that she could see outside from every spot in the room. With one eye on what she was doing, she kept part of her attention on the wagon that was approaching the house.

When Gustaf stopped the wagon in front, Olina went to the door. Maybe he was coming to eat lunch with them. It was too bad that they hadn't cooked anything today. Olina was planning to make a sandwich with some of the tomatoes out of the garden and the piece of ham left from breakfast. That would barely feed her. It wouldn't be enough for a hardworking man like Gustaf.

Olina opened the door just as Gustaf stepped onto the porch. "Hello. Have you come for—?" The look on Gustaf's face stopped the question in midsentence. She rushed through the door. "Oh, Gustaf, what's the matter?" Without thinking, she reached up and cupped her hand on his cheek.

Gustaf placed his calloused fingers on top of hers as if to hold them in place. "Olina, I must talk to you."

"You're scaring me. Whatever has happened to cause you this distress?" Olina couldn't pull her gaze from his.

He looked as if he were worried about her. Why would he be worried about her? Had he heard something in town? She glanced down at his other hand. It didn't hold any mail, so it couldn't be anything bad about her family.

Gustaf pulled her hand from his face and held it in both his hands. "Let's sit here."

Olina and Gerda loved sitting on the porch in the cool of the evening, so Gustaf and August had built a wooden swing for them. Gustaf guided her toward the swing. When they were seated, he leaned his forearms on his knees and clasped his hands.

"I've come to tell you something."

Olina was exasperated. "So tell me. Don't keep me wondering any longer."

Gustaf leaned back and placed his arm along the back of the swing. "Someone came to Litchfield on the train that just went through."

"So?" Olina knew that people often came to Litchfield on the train. She looked up into his troubled eyes and waited.

"It was Lars and his wife." The statement hung in the air between them while Gustaf seemed to be studying every expression on Olina's face. What was he looking for?

"Lars. . .and his wife?" Olina was puzzled.

"Yes." Gustaf took one of her hands in his.

"I didn't know that he was coming home."

"No one did." He rubbed the back of her hand with his thumb while he continued to study her. "It's a surprise visit."

Olina waited for the hurt to settle in her chest, but all she felt was surprised. *Oh, Father, did You take that hurt away, too? Will I be able to forgive Lars as You have forgiven me?* "Where are they?"

Gustaf must have been holding his breath, because he had to let it out to answer her. "I left them at the hotel with Gerda. Do you feel like going into town to see them?"

Olina stood up and walked to the porch railing. She leaned against it, looking toward town as if she could see into the hotel. Then she turned back to Gustaf. "It was inevitable that this would happen. We might as well get it over with, but I need to freshen up a bit."

Gustaf's smile went right to Olina's heart. "I'll be here when you are ready."

"I'll hurry."

Gerda, Lars, and his wife were sitting in the lobby visiting when Gustaf and Olina arrived. Lars stood as if he had been watching the door for them. Standing across the room from her was the man she had planned to marry. For a moment, all the pain lanced through Olina's heart. How was she going to get through the next few minutes? She just had to. She closed her eyes and took a deep breath. Did she need to stop all feeling again as she had before? Would it help?

Lars introduced Olina to Janice. *What does he see in her that he didn't see in me?* Olina recognized the wariness in Janice's expression. It wasn't her fault, was it? Lars hadn't been a real man. He hadn't taken responsibility for his actions, and two women were paying a price for that irresponsibility. When Lars met Janice, did he even tell her about Olina?

After introducing Olina to Janice, Lars asked Olina if she would take a walk with him. She looked at Janice, who nodded.

They walked around the hotel and out across a field toward a small grove of trees. When they reached the shade, Lars stopped Olina with a gentle touch on her arm. She turned toward him.

"Olina, we came to visit with our family, but you're the main reason I've come."

She looked up at him and waited. It was a minute or two before he continued. During that time, he studied her as if he were looking for something specific.

"I know that I did you a grave injustice." Lars seemed ill at ease. He shifted his weight from one foot to the other. "I was blind to my faults. And I was impulsive."

Olina nodded. She agreed wholeheartedly.

"I should have met you in New York City. I apologize for that. Can you forgive me?"

Olina gazed up at a cloud that was drifting by. It looked like a little lamb, gamboling in the pasture around his mother. The lamb reminded her of Jesus, who died to bring her forgiveness.

Looking back at Lars, she whispered, "Yes, I will work on forgiving you." She paused, then continued. "Why did you go to Denver in the first place, Lars?" She had to know.

Once again, Lars shuffled his feet in the grass. "I thought we could start our new life together in Denver. I was offered a better-paying job, and I planned to get us a home, then come back here before you arrived. I planned for us to be married here and then go to our new home." He looked everywhere but at her, taking a long time before he blurted, "I thought I loved you, Olina, but I didn't know what love really was until I met Janice."

Olina waited for the pain to lance though her midsection. She felt disappointment but not the agony she expected. "And what is love. . .really?"

"It's not just that she's beautiful. You're beautiful, too. Janice and I were made for each other. She has strengths where I have weaknesses, and I have strengths in the areas where she is weak. I know God created someone for you, just as he created Janice and me to be together."

When Lars said that, Olina looked across the field toward town, and her thoughts drifted to Gustaf. Could he be the one?

"I have great fondness for you." Lars's voice sounded stronger, more sure. "You will always have a special place in my heart."

Olina glanced back at him. "Maybe that's not good."

"Janice knows all about you. . .us. . .what we were to each other. At least now she knows. I was not man enough to tell her about you until after we were engaged." Lars rubbed the back of his neck. "We were not meant for each other, you and I. We just thought we were. I know it'll be hard for you to forgive me for all of this, but that's what I came here for. To apologize to you face-to-face. I pray that someday we can be friends."

Olina glanced at the grass, then across the field to some cows that were grazing in the adjoining pasture. "I'll not deny that you hurt me very much. I don't know when I've ever been so hurt." She looked down at her skirt that the gentle wind was swirling around her ankles. "I'm trying to forgive you. In time, maybe we'll be comfortable around each other." She gazed up at Lars. "We should go back. I don't want the others to be worried about us."

Lars took her arm and guided her back to the front of the hotel.

On the way across the field, Olina thought about all she had gone through. Had God allowed those things to happen because He had created someone for her, someone besides Lars? Was he here in Litchfield, Minnesota, right now?

What about Janice? She had been caught in the middle of the dilemma Lars had caused by his irresponsible actions.

Just as she stepped up on the wooden sidewalk, Olina said, "I'm glad you've come. I do want to get to know your wife."

When Gustaf drove Olina home, Gerda stayed in town with Lars and Janice. He was glad, because he wanted to talk to Olina alone.

After stopping the horses by the front gate, Gustaf turned to Olina. "Are you all right?"

Olina looked up at Gustaf. "You mean about Lars and Janice?"

"That. . .and about Lars being here. . .and about Lars and you."

Olina blinked as if her eyes were watering. "There is no 'Lars and me.' "

Gustaf reached over and took both her hands in his. "I know that, but how are you handling everything?"

When Olina looked down at their clasped hands, so did Gustaf. Hers looked so small and smooth, engulfed in his large, calloused ones. He would gladly take all the pain out of her life, but he knew he couldn't.

Olina looked back up at him. "I want to forgive Lars, but it is so hard, for sure. How can I completely forgive him? The hurt goes deep."

Gustaf didn't know if he had an answer for her, so he got out of the wagon, then helped Olina down. They walked to the front door in silence.

"Let's look in the Bible, Olina." Gustaf opened the door and waited for her to enter.

Olina went into the parlor and picked her Bible up from the table where she had put it when she finished reading it last night. "What do you want to show me?"

Gustaf sat on the sofa, and Olina sat beside him. Gustaf searched for a verse. "In Matthew, chapter six, it says, 'And forgive us our debts, as we forgive our debtors.' "

Olina nodded. "I remember reading that. It's where Jesus teaches His disciples how to pray, isn't it?"

"Yes. But it was more than that." Gustaf cleared his throat. He didn't want to hurt Olina, but he wanted her to understand what he was talking about. "I believe it means that if we don't forgive others, then the Lord won't forgive us."

"That's a hard word, Gustaf."

"I know, but when you forgive others, it allows your forgiveness from God to flow freely. Does that make any sense?"

Olina nodded. "I see what you mean. And I think I agree, but it's not easy sometimes."

Gustaf stood and walked to the front window. "God didn't say that everything would be easy, but it would be worth it. I had a hard time forgiving Lars for what he did. God used this verse to teach me that I had to. It took me awhile, and I thought I had totally forgiven him."

Gustaf rubbed the back of his neck with one hand. "Then today when I saw him on that platform. . .and knew that his coming could cause you pain, my anger came back. While I was coming for you, God reminded me that I had forgiven Lars. If you are never able to forgive Lars, there'll be a root of bitterness growing inside your heart. Soon it will consume you." He turned back toward Olina. "You don't want that, do you?"

Olina shook her head. "No, I don't. Would you pray for me?"

"We can do that right now." Gustaf sat back down beside Olina. "Father God, please help Olina turn loose the bitterness and unforgiveness she has in her heart. Give her Your strength. Let Your love for Lars flow through her heart and take its place. We pray this in Jesus' name. Amen."

Chapter 18

Lars and Janice stayed at Litchfield for a month. Because Lars decided to help with the harvesting at the farm, after a few days, he and Janice moved into the house with his parents. Gerda and Olina became friends with Janice. Often when the men were working at the farm, Janice spent the day at Gerda and Olina's home, even helping them with handwork or cooking lunch for them while they finished a garment. In the evenings, Gerda, Olina, and August ate dinner at the farm. Everyone wanted to make the most of the time Lars and Janice were there.

One Friday night in September, all the family was gathered around the table enjoying another one of Mrs. Nilsson's wonderful meals. Gerda noticed that Gustaf seemed preoccupied. She wondered what was bothering him, but she didn't have long to worry.

"A few of the shingles on my house look as if they're damaged." Gustaf took another bite of the chicken and dumplings. Olina knew it was one of his favorite foods. He looked thoughtful while he chewed. "Since we don't have any other fields ready for harvest right now, I think I'll go over and fix the roof tomorrow." He looked around the table at his brothers. "Do you want to help me?"

Lars put down his fork and frowned. "I would like to, but Janice promised her aunt and uncle that we would spend the day with them."

Janice smiled at her husband. "It would be all right if you want to help your brother. I can go without you."

"No," Gustaf said. "You haven't spent much of your time here with the Braxtons. It's only right that you both go tomorrow."

"I can help you." August reached for another hot roll. "I haven't had a day off, except Sunday, for a long time. We aren't very busy right now."

Gustaf smiled. "Then it's settled. I'll feel better about the girls spending the winter in the house if I know the roof is safe."

The next morning, Gustaf and August arrived in time for breakfast. Gerda had told Olina that they would, so the young women had cooked extra bacon and biscuits. Gerda started the scrambled eggs while the men washed up for the meal.

Breakfast was fun, with light banter going around the room and keeping everyone laughing between bites. Olina looked at Gustaf. She liked having him sitting across the table from her. It was familiar and something she would like to continue for her whole life. Where had that thought come from? She sat stunned, wondering what it meant.

August pushed his chair back from the table. "We'd better get started if we want to finish today."

"Okay, brother." Gustaf clapped him on the back before he went out the door toward the wagon.

Olina sat for a minute more, still stunned by the direction of her thoughts. Gerda quickly cleaned off the table. Olina jumped up and started washing the dishes while Gerda dried them and put them away.

"I'm going to the mercantile this morning." Gerda hung the tea towel on a hook near the sink. "Do you want to go with me?"

"Not today," Olina said. "Last week I bought a piece of wool to make myself a suit. I haven't even had time to cut it out. I want to get it made before the weather gets any colder."

"Do you want me to get anything for you while I'm there?"

Olina followed Gerda out of the kitchen. "Would you check and see if they have any cotton sateen? I want to make a new waist to go with the suit."

Gerda stopped and put on her bonnet and shawl. "What color?"

"The wool is navy. Maybe a light blue, pink, or even white would go with it."

Olina went into the sewing room and pulled the fabric from the shelf. She planned to make a skirt that wasn't as full as she wore in the summer. She liked a little flare, but if it wasn't too full, the skirt would be warmer. The wind was bad about blowing full skirts around, and the wind already had a bite to it. Olina wanted to make a fitted jacket with fitted sleeves. That style was also warmer than looser styles. If she had enough fabric, Olina was going to add a peplum to the bottom of the jacket. Maybe she would scallop it to give it more interest. She could even add scallops to the opening of the jacket, with a buttonhole in each scallop. The more she envisioned the new creation, the more excited she became. Spreading the fabric on the table, Olina went to work cutting out the suit.

Gustaf and August quickly gathered the needed tools and wooden shingles from the wagon. While Gustaf carried them to the side of the house, August hefted the ladder on his broad shoulders.

It took several trips up and down the ladder before the men had moved all they needed to work with onto the roof. Soon they were pulling away rotted shingles and nailing new ones into place. While they worked, the brothers talked and laughed. They had always gotten along, and they worked well together.

It took them most of the morning to finish the back of the roof. Then they moved across to the front. Gustaf placed his tools and nails within easy reach, but they had used most of the shingles they brought up earlier.

"I need more shingles." Gustaf stood and stretched his muscles. He wasn't used to all this hammering and crawling on his knees. He rotated his right shoulder while holding it with his left hand. "How about you?"

"Sure." August laid his hammer down and pulled a bandanna from his back pocket to wipe the sweat from his forehead. "I've used most of mine."

"I'll go down and get some more." Gustaf started over the top of the roof, but one of the shingles he stepped on broke, and he lost his balance. Standing on a slope wasn't easy, and he couldn't regain his balance. He tried to clutch at anything that would stop him as he tumbled down the few feet to the edge of the roof, then he plunged through the air. A primitive cry forced its way from his throat before he hit the ground two stories below. Then everything went black.

At first, the sound of the pounding had bothered Olina, but soon the rhythm was soothing. One of the men hit a nail, followed immediately by the other man's pound. It didn't take Olina long before she knew which pound was which. Although Gustaf hit the nails with power, because of his work at the blacksmith's, August's pounds were harder. *Ba boom. Ba boom.* The rhythm continued. It was a comforting sound, much like her mother's heartbeat when she had held Olina close as a child. The sounds would stop as the men moved to another spot, only to resume again.

Olina tried to keep her thoughts from wandering to Gustaf. She didn't want to make any mistakes as she cut out the suit. If she was careful, she could make the outfit the way she wanted and still have enough fabric left to make a matching reticule. She could line the purse with the fabric from the blouse she would make to go with the suit.

There was never a minute when Olina wasn't aware that Gustaf was on the roof above her. She knew when the men moved to the area above the sewing room, even though a bedroom was between the roof and the room where she worked. Once again the pounding stopped. She imagined the men taking a break.

"Aaiiee!"

The primitive scream was followed by a dull thump right outside the sewing room. For a moment Olina was paralyzed. Then she rushed to the window and raised it. What she saw caused her to catch her breath. Gustaf lay motionless on the ground.

Olina quickly leaned out and looked toward the eaves. August leaned over, gazing at his brother with anguish covering his face.

"What happened?" Olina's question sounded shrill even to her own ears.

August shook his head. "I don't know for sure. He was going for more shingles. . .and then he was—" August couldn't continue.

"Come down right now." Olina turned and hurried toward the front door.

She ran around to the side of the house and crumpled beside the still unmoving body. She doubled over and sobs tore from deep within her.

When August came around the house, he knelt on the other side of his brother. Tears were making their way down his cheeks. "He's not dead, Olina."

Olina looked up.

"See. He's breathing." August pointed to Gustaf's chest, which was moving with each breath.

"Should we move him into the house?" Olina looked toward the structure.

"That might not be a good idea." August stood. "What if something is broken? We could injure him more. . . . I'm going for the doctor."

Olina scrambled to her feet. "What can I do?"

"Stay with him." August strode across the yard toward his horse, but he swerved to head to the wagon, then stopped and turned to look back at Olina and Gustaf. "Maybe you should cover him with something warm."

Olina ran into the house and up the stairs to her bedroom. She jerked the quilt from her bed and grabbed her pillow. After hurrying down the stairs and around the house, she gently cradled Gustaf's head in her arms while she pushed the pillow under it. Then she covered him with the quilt and pushed it in close to his body all around. It became soiled, but she didn't care. Nothing was important except Gustaf.

As Olina gazed at his face, her heart felt as if it had burst open, and all the love that had been building for Gustaf poured forth. She loved him with her whole heart. Olina didn't know when this had happened, but she really loved him. More than she had ever loved Lars. More than she had realized was even possible. That love hurt because Gustaf was injured.

"Father God," Olina wailed, "please help Gustaf." She pulled the bottom of her skirt up and wiped the tears from her face, but they continued to pour from her eyes. "I love him, Father God. Please don't take him away from me just when I've discovered that I love him."

Olina reached and pushed his hair from his forehead. Then her hand continued around his cheek and came to rest on his strong neck. Olina could feel the blood pulsing through the vein there. Surely he wouldn't die while his pulse was so strong.

"Please, God, I beg You. Let him not be badly hurt. I don't care if he'll never be mine. I love him enough to want the best for him. Let him be okay. I want to see him every day." The last sentence ended on a sob.

The first thing Gustaf became aware of was the cold hard ground beneath him. He fought to open his eyes but was unable to keep from drifting back into the blackness.

The next time he fought his way up out of the dark, he noticed that he felt warmer. Something soft was under his head, something warm had settled over him, and someone was tucking it in around his body. It felt good. He tried to open his eyes, but he still couldn't. Then he heard the voice.

Olina, sweet Olina, was praying. For him. She said that she loved him. He wanted to try to open his eyes again but decided against it. He would wait to hear what else she had to say. When her hand touched his head, he almost flinched because it surprised him so much. As it continued down his face, he reveled in the feel of her soft flesh against his. He would remember the way it felt as long as he lived. When her hand rested on his neck, Gustaf knew she could feel his pulse. His heartbeat had quickened so much at her touch. He couldn't wait any longer. He had to look at her.

Olina was studying Gustaf's face when his eyes fluttered open. She tried to pull back, but one of his arms snaked out from under the quilt, and his hand grabbed hers. When she relaxed, his touch became gentle. She was unable to tear her gaze from his eyes. They seemed to hold her captive, and she read an answering love in them. Could it be that he loved her as she loved him?

Before long, August, Gerda, and the doctor hurried around the side of the house.

"I see that he has recovered consciousness." The doctor's voice boomed.

Startled, Olina turned and tried to get up, but Gustaf didn't let her hand go, so she sank back onto the ground beside him.

The doctor set his black bag on the ground beside Gustaf and took out his stethoscope. He listened to Gustaf's breathing through his chest and took his pulse.

"Do you have any pain, son?" the fatherly man asked.

Gustaf looked toward the man. "Yes. I kind of hurt all over."

"Is there any place that it is localized?" The doctor started probing his body, searching for broken bones.

"I don't think so, sir." Gustaf moved first one arm and then the other. "Maybe I'm just sore. I know I had the breath knocked out of me."

"He was knocked unconscious for several minutes," Olina informed the doctor.

"Well, can you move everything?" The doctor watched as Gustaf moved his arms, his legs, and his head. "Does anything hurt worse when you move it?"

"Not that I can tell." Gustaf tried to sit up, and the doctor gave him a hand.

"Are you dizzy?" The doctor looked at Gustaf's pupils.

"No, sir. Is it all right if I stand up?"

The doctor helped him to his feet. Then he looked at the ground where

Gustaf had been lying. "If you were going to fall off a house, it's a good thing you picked this place to land."

Gustaf looked down, too.

"See? There's enough grass to cushion your fall, and there are no rocks to harm you." The doctor touched his shoulder. "Come inside, son. I would like to do a thorough examination to be on the safe side."

Olina followed the men into the house. She was glad that nothing seemed to be seriously injured.

Chapter 19

After the doctor finished the examination, he and Gustaf came back downstairs. Olina looked up expectantly, waiting for the doctor's verdict.

"Well, young man, you are lucky." The doctor nodded his head as he spoke.

"I believe that God protected me," Gustaf told him. "Maybe my guardian angel caught me and lowered me to the ground."

The doctor glanced at the others before he answered. "If that's what you want to think." He put his bag down on a chair and dug through it. After pulling out a package, he placed it in Gustaf's hand. "This is Epsom salt. Go home. Take a hot bath and put some of this salt in your bathwater. It should take out the soreness. Didn't I hear that your folks have one of those newfangled water heaters at your house?"

"Yes." Gustaf took the proffered remedy. "I'm glad we do. It'll come in handy today."

After the doctor drove off in his buggy, August looked at Gustaf. "You take my horse and ride home. I'll bring your wagon later."

"Why?" Gustaf looked as if he was going to refuse. "What are you going to do?"

August gestured toward the roof. "Go up there and finish what we started."

Gustaf shook his head. "I'll do it another day."

"No need for that. It won't take me long." August glanced from Gustaf to Gerda and Olina. "When I'm finished, I'll bring the girls home for dinner. By that time, you might be feeling better."

August accompanied Gustaf to the horse. It looked to Olina, who was watching from the window, as though Gustaf was arguing about it, but August must have won, because Gustaf mounted the horse. August loaded more shingles onto his shoulder before he started back up the ladder. While he finished the roof that afternoon, Olina wished for Gustaf's part in the hammering rhythm.

When August, Gerda, and Olina arrived at the Nilsson farm for dinner, Olina was glad to see Gustaf sitting in the parlor. She stopped in the doorway and watched him. He was engrossed in reading his Bible. It allowed her a few undisturbed moments to study him. As if someone had told him that she was there, Gustaf glanced up. He smiled then rose slowly.

The Other Brother

"Come in, Olina," he said, his voice husky with emotion.

Olina caught her breath. "P—perhaps I should see if your mother needs any help with dinner." She turned to go.

"Come in, Olina. We are alone, and we need to talk."

Olina's right hand fluttered to her throat. "Right now?" Her question sounded breathless, even to her own ears.

Gustaf looked around. "Now would be a good time."

Olina took one step into the room. It seemed to be filled with the presence of Gustaf, leaving little space for her. She took a hesitant breath. There wasn't even enough air for both of them to breathe comfortably.

Gustaf walked toward her. "Are you suddenly afraid of me, Olina?"

She shook her head in denial. Gustaf stopped right in front of her, but he didn't reach out to her. Olina didn't know what to say to him. All afternoon she had wondered if he had heard any of the words of her prayer. He was standing so close that the heat of his body reached out and enveloped her.

"You weren't afraid of me this morning, dear Olina." The soft words were for her ears alone, and the endearment touched her heart.

Olina dropped her gaze to his muscular chest, but that didn't help her breathe any easier. "Why do you say that, Gustaf?"

A gentle chuckle rumbled from him, causing his chest to rise and fall. "Do you love me, Olina?"

Her wary gaze flew to his. Once again, she saw the loving expression from that morning. "Why do you ask?"

Gustaf reached out and pulled her into his arms. With her nestled against his chest, he rested his chin on top of her head. Olina was glad she had worn her hair in a simple chignon at the nape of her neck. Nothing was in the way of his chin. Its touch felt like a caress. She closed her eyes and sighed.

"I heard a voice calling me out of the darkness this morning."

Olina's eyes flew open. That startling statement answered the questions she had wrestled with all day. He had heard her. But how much had he heard?

As if she had spoken the question aloud, Gustaf answered. "I heard you praying for God to heal me. You told Him that you love me." He leaned back a little and placed one finger under her chin, raising it until her gaze met his. "You wouldn't lie to God, would you? Do you love me?"

A large lump in her throat kept Olina from voicing her answer, so she nodded.

"Enough to marry me, Olina?"

Olina's heart almost burst with happiness.

Before she could answer, Gerda came from the kitchen. "Olina, Gustaf—" She stopped short. "I'm not interrupting anything, am I?"

"Yes."

"No."

Gustaf and Olina answered at the same time. Then they burst out laughing, but Gustaf didn't release Olina from the shelter of his arms.

"Is there something you would like to tell me?" Gerda looked from one to the other.

"Yes."

"No."

Once again, they answered in unison.

Now Gerda was laughing with them. "Well, Gustaf keeps telling me 'yes,' and Olina keeps telling me 'no.' Which is it?"

Olina could feel a blush creep up over her neck and face while Gustaf answered. "Yes, we'll have something to tell you but not right now. You'll know what's going on soon enough."

Gerda rolled her eyes and went back into the kitchen. "Mother, is it time to ring the dinner bell?" Gustaf and Olina could hear her elevated tone. "Father and August are in the barn, but Gustaf and Olina are in the parlor."

The next thing Olina heard was the dinner bell. Although it was the most wonderful place she had ever been, Olina pulled herself from Gustaf's embrace and put her hands on her cheeks to try to cool them.

"That won't take away your becoming blush." Gustaf touched his forefinger to the tip of her nose, then turned toward the kitchen, but he whispered into her ear as he went by. "I will get an answer to my question before the evening is over."

The meal Mrs. Nilsson had prepared was a veritable feast. A succulent ham was accompanied by roasted potatoes, green beans, and the last tomatoes from the garden. Fresh churned butter melted into the hot rolls. Some of the butter dripped down Olina's chin when she took her first bite. She patted her chin with her napkin and glanced toward Gustaf once again. His face held a secret smile that touched her heart.

Although everything tasted wonderful, Olina couldn't eat more than a few bites. Her stomach did flip-flops every time she glanced up at Gustaf to find his intent gaze trained on her face. Soon she was moving the food around her plate instead of putting it in her mouth. Gustaf wanted to marry her.

Father God, is this Your plan for me? When Olina asked the question in her heart, she felt a peace there, but the turmoil in the rest of her body continued. What was the matter with her? Was this jumpy feeling in the pit of her stomach a prelude to some illness?

Olina was drawing circles in the gravy on her plate with her fork when she felt Gerda's foot nudge hers. She looked up to find every eye in the room trained on her. The blush that had died down once more stained her cheeks.

"I asked you, dear, if you were feeling all right." Mrs. Nilsson looked concerned. "You've hardly eaten any of your dinner. I hope you're not getting sick."

"No." Olina smiled at her hostess. "I guess I have had too much excitement for one day." Olina didn't look directly at Gustaf, but out of the corner of her eye, she could see his smile widen.

"Yes, well." Mr. Nilsson harrumphed to clear his throat. "I wanted to tell you girls how proud I am of you."

Everyone's attention turned toward the head of the table.

"Why is that, Father?" Gerda asked.

"I can't help but worry about you." He looked toward Gustaf. "Of course your brother keeps me informed about how you're doing, but I wondered if you needed any monetary help." Olina started to comment, but before she could, Mr. Nilsson continued. "When I was at the bank this afternoon, I asked Mr. Finley if I needed to put some money into your account. He informed me that you each had a very healthy account indeed."

"It helps that Gustaf isn't charging us any rent." Gerda smiled at her brother.

He laughed in return. "No rent except several hot meals each week."

"Which you don't need, since your mother feeds you quite well." Olina looked him full in the face for the first time during the meal.

His gaze was so intent that she couldn't look away. "It's a good time to make sure you are safe and don't need anything."

Everything around them seemed to fade away, leaving only Gustaf and Olina, with an invisible, mysterious connection—even across the table.

Finally, Mrs. Nilsson arose from her chair and began cleaning off the table. Gerda quickly assisted her. When Olina also started to help, Gustaf asked her if she would take a walk with him.

"I need to keep the stiffness worked out of my body." His eyes compelled her more than his words. "Please accompany me."

They strolled halfway down the long drive in companionable silence before Gustaf brought up the subject that was on both of their minds.

"Are you ready to give me your answer, Olina?"

At his words, Olina stopped and turned toward him. Before she could answer, he laughed. Gustaf took her hands in both of his. "Are you going to make me kneel and ask you again? It might be hard for me to get up afterward."

The picture of her trying to pull the tall, strong man up caused Olina to laugh, too. "Yes. I love you enough to marry you."

After a moment, Gustaf asked, "Do I hear a 'but' at the end of your sentence?"

"I want to marry you, but I need to make things right with *Fader*. When you shared that scripture with me about forgiving as God would forgive, it made me realize that I need to forgive *Fader* as much as I must forgive Lars. I've finally come to the point where I have forgiven him in my heart. I was planning to write a letter to him asking his forgiveness for going against his wishes. Would you wait for the wedding until I can write him? I've come so far since I started listening to the Lord again, but I still feel I can't move on with my life without taking care of this matter."

Gustaf pulled her into his embrace again. Cradling her against his strong chest, he whispered, "You are so special. I'll wait as long as you need me to. I do believe that God intends for us to be together."

Olina nodded against his chest. "I do, too."

"It'll give me time to court you properly."

Gustaf liked the feel of Olina in his arms. As they stood with her soft, warm body pressed against his leanness, he thought of her strawberry-colored mouth. He wondered how it would feel to press his lips to hers and savor the sweetness that was the essence of Olina. She must have sensed some of what he felt, because she raised her face from against his chest and looked up into his face.

Gustaf's gaze dropped to her trembling lips. He lowered his head slightly, then hesitated, to give her time to pull away. Olina's adoring gaze never wavered, so he continued his descent.

Gustaf had never kissed a woman. He had never felt this burning desire to taste a woman's lips before. The first touch was tentative and gentle. Gustaf savored Olina's sweetness, then settled his lips more firmly against hers.

For a moment, or an eon of time, he reveled in the feel of Olina. All too soon, Gustaf broke the earth-shattering kiss. He once again cradled her head against his chest. He felt sure she heard his heartbeat thunder against her ear. How easily he could have lost himself in their togetherness. But Gustaf knew that if they were going to wait awhile before marrying, he needed to protect Olina from his strong human urges. *Father, help me be the man she needs.*

When Gustaf and Olina gazed into each other's eyes, she felt it to her very foundation. She had never realized how strong the connection between two people in love could be. Then Gustaf's gaze dropped to her lips. She could feel the intensity of his attention. It caused her to lick her lips because they felt dry.

As Gustaf's head lowered toward hers, Olina held her breath. She knew that he was going to kiss her. For an instant, he hesitated. She recognized that he was giving her a chance to step back. But Olina didn't want to. She welcomed his kiss with all the love she felt for him.

Gustaf was so strong. His muscles were rock hard, but his lips were soft. His gentleness reached toward her. And then the kiss deepened. Everything faded from Olina's awareness except Gustaf. Wrapped in his love, she felt protected. Her arms crept around his waist.

Too soon, Gustaf broke the kiss, but he pulled her against his chest. . .and his beating heart. She could tell by the rhythm of the heartbeats that he was as affected by their kiss as she was.

Gustaf turned toward the house and started walking with one arm around Olina, holding her securely by his side. "Now we must tell my family, but I don't think they'll be surprised."

Chapter 20

That night, Olina wrote a long letter to her mother, explaining all that had happened. She included another to her father, asking for his forgiveness. After writing a note to *Tant* Olga, she enclosed all the missives in one envelope addressed to her great-aunt. Olina sealed the envelope then placed both hands on the thick bundle and prayed over it, asking God to direct every word to the hearts of those receiving them. When she finished this task, her heart felt lighter.

During the rest of the autumn, Olina and Gerda were busy with their dressmaking. News of their expertise spread, and some women even came from other towns to order dresses from them.

Olina no longer felt the need to protect her financial security as she had, so she and Gerda purchased things to make their cottage more homey. They chose fabric to make all new curtains and even bought a few small pieces of furniture. Tables and lamps added warmth to the living room. Scraps of fabric were fashioned into pillows that made the sofa more inviting.

Gustaf kept his promise to court Olina. He escorted her to every party and social that was held in Litchfield or at any of the surrounding farms. It wasn't long until everyone knew that the two planned to marry. They received many congratulations, even from Anna Jenson, who was being courted by one of the other young farmers in the area.

Olina hoped that she would hear from her father in a month or two after she sent the letter. By mid-November, she went every day to the post office, which was located in the mercantile, to check for a letter. Every day that didn't bring an answer caused a heaviness in her heart. She feared that her father was still angry with her. How would she ever have total peace if he continued to shut her out?

Thanksgiving was fast approaching. Olina had never experienced this holiday, since it was distinctly American. She was excited when the family began preparations. In addition to their grain crops, the Nilssons raised cattle. However, for Thanksgiving, August went hunting for venison. When he brought in a large buck three days before the holiday, the whole family worked on preparing the meat. The two hindquarters were smoked, much like the hams of a pig. The forelegs were roasted, and the rest of the meat was made into sausage, then smoked.

On Thanksgiving Day, their church hosted a community-wide celebration.

The Other Brother

A morning service allowed everyone to express thanks to God for their blessings that year. Olina thanked God for bringing her to America and giving her Gustaf to love, but a small part of her heart ached for the loss of her Swedish family. She prayed silently for God to intervene there, too.

The pews were moved into a storeroom, and tables and benches were brought in for the dinner. Everyone had prepared their best.

The Nilssons shared the roasted forelegs and one hindquarter of their deer. Others brought ham, pork chops, beef roasts, or chickens. Olina imagined that the tables groaned under the weight of all the food. Vegetable dishes, pies, cakes, pastries, hot breads, fresh churned butter. The aromas started her mouth watering long before the meal began.

Soon after Thanksgiving, everyone was preparing for Christmas. Olina and Gerda worked together to make all the members of Gerda's family some new garment. While they were visiting at the farm, Gerda sneaked around and measured her father's and Gustaf's shirts. The young women offered to do August's laundry with theirs, so they were able to measure his shirt, too.

Pooling the amount of money they could afford to spend, they bought the best fabric available in Litchfield. They made each man a new dress shirt. Mrs. Nilsson would receive a wool suit, complete with a silk waist to wear with it.

One week before Christmas, Olina went to town to pick out lace for the dress she was secretly creating for Gerda. When she finished making all her purchases, she went to the corner where the post office was located. Once again, she was disappointed to find no letter from Sweden waiting for her. With her head down against the cold wind, she started the walk toward the cottage. She didn't notice the vehicle driving by until she heard her name called.

Olina almost dropped her package. The voice calling her sounded so much like her mother's voice that tears pooled in her eyes. When she looked up, she saw August driving a buggy from the livery. The tears blurred her vision so that she didn't recognize the woman sitting on the other side of him.

"Olina." August stopped right beside her. "Look who has come to visit you."

He jumped from the buggy and turned back to help the woman to the sidewalk. Olina reached into her reticule and withdrew a handkerchief to wipe her eyes. When she looked up, she saw that her ears had not deceived her.

"*Mor!*" Olina dropped the package and threw her arms around the woman her heart had missed all these months. With tears streaming down her face, Olina hugged her mother as if she would never let go.

"Darling, don't cry," Brigitta Sandstrom said in Swedish, as she pulled back from the embrace to look at her daughter's face. "I only wanted to make you happy."

Olina was used to conversing in English, but she easily went back into her native tongue. "Oh, you have. These are happy tears." Then Olina looked around. "Where is *Fader*?"

Brigitta and August looked at each other. August picked the package up from the wooden sidewalk. "Olina, I'll take you and your mother to your house. We'll be there in a few minutes and then you can talk all you want."

"Could *Fader* not come?"

"Come, dear." Brigitta took Olina by the arm. "This wind is so cold. Let's get in out of it, and I'll tell you all about it."

Olina was so pleased to be with *Mor* that she climbed into the buggy for the ride. Thankfully, it took only a few minutes.

Once they arrived at the cottage, Gerda hurried to the kitchen to make a pot of tea. Olina was glad that she and Gerda had baked Christmas cookies the day before.

Mrs. Sandstrom and Olina sat on the sofa holding hands and devouring each other with their eyes. "Mother, what are you doing here?"

Brigitta laughed at her daughter. "I've come to help plan a wedding." She pulled Olina into another hug. "Have you set a date yet?"

Olina leaned back from her mother's arms. "I wanted to wait until I heard from *Fader*. Where is he?"

After standing up, Mrs. Sandstrom paced once across the parlor. With her back still turned toward her daughter, she started explaining. "Your father couldn't come, Olina." She turned around and looked into Olina's face. "I brought some bad news."

Oh no. Please, God. Her thoughts became jumbled. She wasn't even sure what she was asking Him for. She had realized when *Moder* didn't tell her anything in town that something bad had happened, but she hadn't wanted to believe it was possible. Now she could no longer deny it.

Mrs. Sandstrom crossed the room and sat beside her daughter. "There's no easy way to say this. Your father became sick. I believe it was his hard-heartedness toward you that brought the sickness on. I prayed for him so much, but he kept getting sicker and sicker."

She pulled a hanky from her sleeve and wiped the tears that were making trails down her cheeks. That caused Olina to realize how wrinkled they had become. As she looked more closely at her mother, Olina realized that she had lost weight, and her hair, which had still retained the golden color when Olina last saw her a month before she left Sweden, was streaked with silver. When had her mother become old? It had been only nine months since Olina last saw her. Nine months shouldn't have done that much damage. Unless something terrible had happened.

"Finally, your father told me that we must contact you. He wanted to make peace with you. I told him that I would write you a letter the next morning, but before the sun came up, he left us."

Olina pulled her mother into her arms, and the two women cried together. They weren't aware of Gerda entering the room, but when they stopped crying, they found a tray—with a pot of tea, two cups and saucers, and some cookies—sitting on the table in front of the sofa. Olina poured each of them a cup of tea, but neither of them picked up a cookie.

After taking a few sips from the bracing brew, Mrs. Sandstrom set her cup and saucer back on the table. "That day, we received your letter telling about Gustaf and asking your father to forgive you. I'm so sorry he wasn't able to say this himself, but I know that he would accept your apology and welcome you back into the family."

Olina smiled at her mother through her tears. "I hope so. I wouldn't set a date for the wedding because I was waiting to hear from *Fader*."

Mrs. Sandstrom patted Olina on the knee. "I know, dear. That is why *Tant* Olga urged me to come to America and talk to you in person."

Olina smiled. "*Tant* Olga?"

"*Ja*, for sure." Mrs. Sandstrom returned her smile. "I already turned the farm over to the boys. When Sven got so sick, I couldn't help them at all. All my time was taken with caring for him. Then he died, and Olga asked me to live with her. That way the boys would know that the farm is theirs. Sven and I saved enough money for me to live on for the rest of my life. I won't have many expenses living with Olga, and she needs me."

Olina looked up as Gerda came into the parlor with a carpetbag in her hand. "Are you going somewhere?"

Gerda went over and hugged Mrs. Sandstrom, then Olina. "I wanted to give you and your mother some time alone. August put her luggage in my room. He and I have been having tea in the kitchen. Now he'll take me home. I'll stay with my parents for a few days."

Mrs. Sandstrom stood up. "You don't have to do that, Gerda. I can sleep here on the sofa."

"No need for that." Gerda turned and called August. "I'm ready to go."

August came in and took the carpetbag from her. Then he helped her into her heavy coat. "It's cold. You probably should take a blanket to wrap up in during the drive."

Gerda went upstairs and returned quickly with the cover. "Don't be surprised if Gustaf comes for dinner tonight. I'm sure he'll want to be with the two of you."

After Gerda and August left, Olina and her mother planned a special meal for when Gustaf came. It was good to work together in the kitchen again. Gustaf arrived as they were putting the finishing touches on the food.

Olina answered his knock. He gave her a quick hug before he greeted her mother. Soon they were seated at the table sharing the special meal.

"How long are you staying in Minnesota?" Gustaf asked.

"I planned to stay for a while. It's such a long journey. One of my cousins is staying with *Tant* Olga until I return." Brigitta glanced at her daughter. "I want to be here for the wedding, and I know Olina needs some time to mourn her father's death."

Gustaf put his fork down and looked from mother to daughter. "For sure, that's right. I know Olina was anxious to hear from him." He reached over and placed his hand on Olina's shoulder. "How are you doing?"

Olina's eyes glistened with unshed tears. "I'll be okay. It will just take some time."

"I want to be here for the wedding." Brigitta took a bite of the *gräddbakelse* she had made because it was such a favorite of Olina's.

"Maybe we should set the date tonight." Gustaf studied Olina for a moment. "Do you think we could do that?"

"*Moder*, can you stay until April?" Olina asked.

"*Ja*, for sure."

Gustaf and Olina soon decided that they would exchange their vows on Saturday, April 9. That would give them plenty of time to plan the wedding, and Olina and her mother would have time to enjoy each other.

Since Christmas was only a few days away, Gerda and Olina were busy with a few last-minute orders for Christmas presents. Gustaf brought Gerda to the house every morning so she and Olina could work together. After two days, he took Mrs. Sandstrom back to the farm with him to visit with her old friend, Ingrid.

That day Gerda and Olina went to town to purchase fabric so they could make Mrs. Sandstrom a suit similar to the one they were making Mrs. Nilsson. They finished in time for the family Christmas at the farm.

Olina woke on her wedding day to the sun streaming through her window. She was used to getting up at dawn and making breakfast, but Gerda must have beaten her to it. The fragrant aroma of coffee beckoned Olina to the warm kitchen.

"Well, sleepyhead, I see you finally woke up." Gerda was pouring a cup of coffee as Olina entered the room.

"Yes. I didn't think I would ever go to sleep. I was so excited thinking about today." Olina stretched and yawned before she sat at the place Gerda set for her at the table. "When I did go to sleep, I slept like a baby." Gerda placed a plate filled with pancakes and sausage in front of Olina.

Olina gasped. It was so much food. "I can't eat all of this."

"You need to," Gerda urged. "You might not be able to eat lunch, and you must keep up your strength. I don't want you fainting before you walk down the aisle."

It was here. Her wedding day. Olina could hardly believe it. So much had gone into the preparations for the day. Her mother wanted to make her wedding dress. Olina and Gerda told Mrs. Sandstrom that she should learn to use the sewing machine, but she insisted on making the dress by hand. Her stitches were tiny and even, a labor of love.

The wedding was scheduled for one o'clock, because Gustaf and Olina were catching the four o'clock train. They were taking a honeymoon trip to San Francisco.

❧

Gustaf stood beside the preacher at the front of the church. His father was standing at the back of the church with Olina's dainty hand resting on his arm. Since her father wasn't there to escort her down the aisle, she asked Gustaf's father. It made both Bennel and Gustaf very proud.

Gustaf caught his breath at the vision of loveliness. Olina wore a dress of white silk brocade. A single row of flowers, formed into a coronet, now adorned her golden tresses. She looked like an angel. His angel.

Tears formed in his eyes. *Thank You, Father, for bringing her to me.*

The pastor's wife began playing the organ, and Olina walked toward him.

I'll care for her, Father, as You have cared for me. I'll love her and cherish her.

❧

Olina had never seen the suit Gustaf was wearing. He must have bought a new one for the wedding. She was amused. He wore a suit so seldom, but it meant a lot to her that he would purchase a new suit for their wedding. He was such a thoughtful man.

As Olina and Mr. Nilsson walked down the aisle, tears blurred Olina's vision. It didn't matter that she couldn't really see the people who surrounded them. *Father, thank You for what You planned for me. Thank You for helping me come to the place that I could recognize Your plans. I will love and cherish Gustaf for the rest of my life.*

His
Brother's
Castoff

To my two grandsons,
Timothy Van Zant and Austin Waldron.
You are precious to me, and I love you very much.

Special thanks go to my wonderful husband, James.
Without your support, no book would be written in our home.
Thank you for loving me and allowing me to be all that God intends.

Chapter 1

Minnesota—September 1894

Fingers of early morning sunlight slipped between the panels of heavy draperies and bathed Anna Jenson's face with warmth. She slowly opened her eyes, then squeezed them tight against the brightness. Sitting up against her pillows, she stretched her arms above her head and smiled. She pulled her heavy dark braid across her shoulder and began at the bottom to carefully work the hair loose from its confinement. Then she ran her fingers through the soft length to be sure there were no tangles.

Today was a special day. Gerda Nilsson and Merta Swenson were coming to help Anna work on her wedding dress. Gerda and her sister-in-law Olina had helped design the gorgeous gown. They also ordered the fabric from Paris. For the first time in her life, Anna would wear silk. She felt beautiful just thinking about walking down the aisle with the material swishing around her.

Finally, she would be married. One month from today. She pictured her fiancé, Olaf Johanson, with the unruly black curls that danced across his forehead. Kind, steady Olaf, whose blue eyes twinkled when he smiled at her. They would have a good life together. His farm wasn't as large as her father's, but it would be able to support them and the family they would have.

Anna wondered how many children God would bless them with. Maybe she would have a baby by this time next year. She hoped it wouldn't take too long. She wanted a boy first. A boy with his father's dark curls and twinkling eyes. Maybe a girl would be next. Of course, it didn't matter which came first, but she hoped she would have both sons and daughters. Olaf would have to build on to the tiny farmhouse to make room for their children. She looked forward to their planning together the addition to their home.

Shaking her head, Anna got up and started dressing. She couldn't stay in bed daydreaming about her wonderful life with Olaf. If she did, she wouldn't be ready when her dress arrived. Gerda and Olina had made it using their sewing machine. This would be the first time Anna would try it on since they stitched it together. Today she would get to see what she looked like in the beautiful gown.

Of course there was still a lot of handwork to be done on the dress. That was why Gerda and Merta were coming. The three friends would sew yards and yards of lace on the skirt. Anna looked forward to finishing the special garment, but she also anticipated spending time with her two best friends. The three young women always had a lot of things to talk about. Since both Gerda and Merta lived in Litchfield, they could catch her up on all the new happenings in town.

Anna hurried down the stairs, almost skipping because she was so happy. When she entered the kitchen, she was surprised. No one was there except her mother.

"Where is everyone?"

Margreta Jenson looked up from the pie crust she was rolling out. A smudge of flour decorated one of her cheeks. "They've all eaten and gone out to see about the horses."

"So early?" Anna picked up a slice of apple her mother had prepared to put in the crust and sucked the cinnamon and sugar from it before popping it into her mouth.

"It's not so early, for sure. You slept a little late today, Anna." Margreta smiled at her only daughter. "There is some food for you in the warming oven."

Anna hugged her mother. "*Tack så mycket*, I mean, thank you very much. Sometimes I forget to speak English, even after all these years."

"I do, too." Her mother nodded. "But Soren wants us to use English. It helps us when we are around other people. America is our home now, not Sweden."

"Father is right." Anna folded up a large dish towel and used it to protect her hand from the heat while she lifted the warm plate from the oven. "It smells good, and I'm hungry."

"When do you think Gerda and Merta will arrive?"

Anna poured herself a glass of milk and brought it to the table. "I'm not sure. Probably as soon as they are finished with cleaning up after breakfast, so I need to eat quickly." After bowing her head for a brief prayer, she took a bite of the still-warm biscuit that dripped with melted butter. She couldn't keep from licking a wayward drop from her thumb, even though her mother would say it wasn't polite if she had seen her do it. Thankfully, Mother was fitting the top crust onto the pie.

The sound of a carriage coming down the drive interrupted Anna before she took her last drink of milk. "It sounds as though they are here." She gathered her dishes and took them over to the sink.

Before she started running water in the dishpan, her mother said, "Don't bother with that, Anna." Margreta placed the apple pie into the oven. "I'll wash your dishes while I'm cleaning up from this pie."

Anna glanced at her. "Are you sure?"

"*Ja*, for sure. You go be with your friends." Margreta used both hands to shoo her daughter from the kitchen.

Anna was thankful to have such a wonderful mother. She hoped that when she had children she would do as good a job.

"So, what do you think?" Gerda looked up and down Anna's body, checking how the dress fit.

Anna turned slowly and looked over her shoulder. She could only see part of the dress in the mirror at one time, so she moved around to get the whole picture. She liked what she saw. The full skirt rippled with every move she made. Because she was taller and had a larger frame than most of the girls she knew, she always felt awkward and less feminine. This dress did something to her figure that made it look graceful.

She smiled at Gerda. "It's more beautiful than I imagined it would be." Anna grabbed her friend and gave her a big hug.

Gerda pulled back. "I don't want to crush it. Now take it off, and we'll start sewing on the lace."

Anna went behind the screen her mother had moved into the parlor for her to use while they worked on the dress. As she changed into her regular clothes, she thought about the reflection of herself in the wedding gown. Everyone would be surprised when she walked down the aisle. She could imagine Olaf's stunned expression when he first saw her coming toward him. A special spark—of passion perhaps—would light his beautiful eyes. It would be wonderful—a moment Anna would cherish all her life.

"Anna," Gerda called to her. "I brought several pieces of lace for you to choose from. I thought we might put some around the neckline and even on the sleeves."

Anna stepped around the screen. "Let me see what you have."

Gerda was sitting on the settee with several pieces of the lace in her lap. Some were round medallions, some diamond shaped or irregular. Merta had lifted one and held it up to the light from the window. It was curved at the top and fell into a V-shape.

"This would be beautiful on the bodice, at the neckline."

The three friends chose what lace to use and pinned it to the dress. Then they started sewing it on, using tiny, almost invisible stitches. Gerda worked on the bodice while Merta and Anna added lacy ruffles to the skirt.

Gerda glanced up from her work. "Anna, it's so good to see you happy."

Anna looked up and smiled. "I am happy, and it's wonderful."

Gerda hesitated, as if she were afraid to go on. Anna could tell that something was on her friend's mind.

"What did you want to say to me? We've been friends long enough to be honest with each other, haven't we?"

Gerda nodded and bent over her sewing. "I'm glad you were able to get over the hurt my brother caused."

"That's ancient history, Gerda." Anna knew that deep inside there was a painful place that wouldn't go away, but she didn't want to think about it right now. "Gustaf and Olina are so right for each other. I know that."

Merta tied off her thread. She snipped it close to the fabric, then started threading her needle again. "You know, I was surprised when you and Gustaf started keeping time together."

Anna looked at her with a questioning expression. "Why do you say that?"

"You remember that my family came to America right before the Nilssons did. When they first arrived, I thought August was the one who was interested in you."

"August?" Anna and Gerda said in unison. Both of the young women laughed.

"Yes." Merta sounded positive.

Gerda shook her head. "August has always been so shy. Why would you think he was interested in Anna?"

"He was always looking at her, especially if he thought no one would notice. His eyes had a longing expression in them." Merta started sewing again. "I saw it several times. I kept waiting for him to say something to you."

Gerda laughed. "August wasn't like that. I think you're imagining things."

"Maybe so." Merta sounded doubtful.

And maybe not. Anna remembered many times when she had caught August looking at her. Even on the night when Gustaf had broken off their relationship. There was a party at the community center. Often that night Anna had felt as though someone was staring at her, and when she looked up, it was August. She had passed it off at the time, but could he have been interested in her? If he was, why hadn't he said something after Gustaf stopped coming over? That would have been a good time to start a relationship, but he had done nothing to indicate that he was interested in her. Well, it was too late now. One month from today, she would become Mrs. Olaf Johanson.

The young women worked together most of the day so they could finish the dress. At noon, Mrs. Jenson brought tea and delicate sandwiches into the parlor. She ate with them and caught up with what was going on in town. Anna was glad that her mother had a good relationship with her friends. The four of them enjoyed visiting and sharing. This had been true as long as Anna could remember.

When everyone was through eating the sandwiches, Margreta brought pound cake for dessert. After lunch, she went to town to do some shopping.

Around midafternoon, the last stitch was made in the beautiful gown. Anna tried it on again. With the addition of the various pieces of lace, Anna was awestruck by her reflection in the mirror. The time before her wedding couldn't go by fast enough for her.

After thanking her friends once again for their diligent work, she stood on the porch and watched them drive down toward the road. She carefully took her wedding gown upstairs to her bedroom and hung it in the wardrobe.

Anna returned to the parlor. She had just finished putting her needles, thread, and scissors into the sewing basket when she heard someone ride up on a horse. Someone who was in a big hurry. Anna felt sorry for the horse's having to run so fast, even if summer's heat had given way to the milder weather in September. After going to the window, she peeked out through the lace curtains.

Olaf was stepping onto the porch. Anna went into the foyer and opened the front door.

"Come in." Anna smiled up at him. Although she was tall, he towered above her. His twinkling eyes smiled down at hers.

Olaf carelessly put one arm across her shoulders and dropped a casual kiss on her cheek. Anna wished he would kiss her more romantically. It was only a month until they would be married. Surely a different kiss would be in order. But Olaf was a perfect gentleman when he was with her. Maybe too much of a gentleman. Anna wanted him to exhibit some passion about her and their approaching marriage. It had taken him a year to ask her to marry him, and then he wanted to wait over nine months for the wedding. Somehow his affection for her felt lukewarm, not passionate. She wondered what it would be like to have Olaf sweep her into his arms and kiss her the way she had seen her father kiss her mother when they didn't know anyone was watching.

Anna put her arm around Olaf's waist as they walked to the parlor. "You seem to be in a hurry."

"I wanted to tell you my good news." It was evident that Olaf was excited about something. *Maybe something about the wedd—* Before she finished that thought, he continued. "Angus McPherson has asked me to guide him on a hunting trip into Montana."

"Who is Angus McPherson?" Anna stepped back and folded her arms. Why in the world did that make him so excited? For some reason, she had an uncomfortable feeling in the pit of her stomach, almost as if something were wrong. *Lord, please, not now.* The thought came before she could stop it. Dread started to build until it almost consumed her. She could taste it. She tried to push it down, but it continued to grow.

"He's a man who has come over from Scotland because he heard about the good elk hunting in Montana." Olaf reached to push back a tangle of black curls that had fallen across his brow, almost covering his eyes.

All Anna could think about was that Olaf needed a haircut soon. She hoped he would get one before the wedding. "Just when will this hunting trip take place?" She was thinking of everything that still needed to be done before the wedding. Since she was the only daughter in the family, her mother wanted it to be special. And Anna did, too. She thought Olaf agreed with her, but now she wasn't so sure.

He placed both his hands in the back pockets of his waist overalls and rocked on the balls of his feet before he answered. "We leave on Monday." He looked at the floor instead of at her. It felt as if he didn't want to see her reaction. He must have known she wouldn't be happy about it.

"And how long will you be gone on this trip?" Why was it so hard to get all the details from Olaf? They never communicated the way she and Gustaf had. Why was she thinking about Gustaf at a time like this? She had been over him for a long time. She was glad he and Olina were so happy. Their daughter was a year old, and Olina was expecting their second child. Anna helped with little Olga whenever she could.

"It will take at least three weeks." Olaf rubbed the carpet with the toe of his boot, outlining the floral design. Was he trying to wear a hole in the rug?

"Three weeks!" Anna knew that she sounded like a shrew, but she couldn't help raising her voice. She placed her fisted hands on her hips the same way her mother did when she was upset. "Our wedding is only a month away."

"Aw, Anna." Olaf took hold of her shoulders with both hands. Finally, he looked at her. "I know when the wedding is, and I'm looking forward to it as much as you are." He gathered her into his arms and leaned his chin on the top of her head. He held her a moment before he continued. "But this is a chance for me to make a lot of money. It'll really help us. I can start adding on to the house soon after the wedding."

Anna leaned back in his arms and looked up at his face, once again wishing he would pull her into a passionate kiss. "Olaf, please don't go. I have a bad feeling about it. Please stay here. . .because you love me."

Olaf flung himself away from Anna and went out into the foyer, the force of his boot heels making loud drumbeats on the wooden floor. Then he turned to look back at her. "You know that I love you, Anna." His voice boomed through the nearly empty house, and the words didn't sound loving. He had never spoken so harshly to her before. "But I am going on this trip."

"Do you, Olaf?" Anna shouted, trying not to cry. "Do you really love me?"

Olaf jerked the door open, banging it so hard against the wall that Anna was afraid the glass would break. Before he exited, he told her in a monotone voice, "I'm not going to be controlled by a woman, not even one I love. I'm not going to live my life that way, so we should start our life together the right way. I love you, Anna, and I promise I'll be back in plenty of time for the wedding."

He slammed the door behind him and stomped across the porch. He didn't even kiss her good-bye. Anna felt sorry for the horse as Olaf jumped into the saddle and galloped away. She leaned back against the door and covered her mouth with her hand to stifle a sob. One thing gave her a little hope. Olaf had promised to be back for the wedding, and Olaf never broke his promises.

Chapter 2

October

August Nilsson bent over the anvil in his blacksmith shop in Litchfield, pounding a horseshoe. Although a cool breeze blew through the large open doorway, the fire in the massive forge and his own hard work caused sweat to run down his forehead. He swiped at it with the back of his hand. Then he reached into the hip pocket of his denim overalls and pulled out a bandanna. He wiped the sweat from his forehead and the back of his neck before hanging the bandanna from his back pocket.

August liked working with molten iron. His arms had grown powerful as he beat it into shape time after time. No one knew that his aggressive strokes were fueled by more than just the need to create useful things. No one knew that he fought against jealousy every day of his life. Jealousy that burned as hot as the flames in the forge. Jealousy that threatened to destroy him if he didn't keep it under control.

For years he had carried on this battle within—losing more often than he cared to admit, even to himself. Everyone thought of August as the quiet Nilsson brother. He never gave anyone any trouble. He was a model of decorum, at least outwardly.

His younger brother, Lars, had always gotten into one scrape after another. August often wondered if Lars would ever grow up. It had taken him years to settle down. He finally did, but he had left a path strewn with colossal messes, not the least of which was the one when he had sent Olina Sandstrom the money to come to America to marry him. Before she arrived, he had already moved to Denver and married another woman. August had been surprised when Olina forgave Lars. Everything had finally worked out when Olina and Gustaf married.

Gustaf was the older brother. The perfect older brother. The brother August had been jealous of most of his life.

He wasn't sure when it had started. Maybe something happened when he was very young, something he couldn't even remember. But he knew that the jealousy always had been there, eating away at him. As he grew older, he tried to control it, but he was never able to completely destroy it. The jealousy was like a disease with no cure.

The Nilsson family had immigrated to America. August was still in his teens when they came to Minnesota from Sweden. He was the only one in the family who hadn't wanted to leave their native country, but he didn't express his opinion in the family discussions before they came. After all, he was the quiet one. No one expected him to have any objections. Everyone else was so set on coming. Especially Gustaf. And Gustaf usually got what he wanted. *Ja*, that was for sure.

The first time the Nilsson family attended church in America, August lost his heart to Anna Jenson. He tried not to let anyone know that he was watching her, but he was aware of every move she made. She was tall, with dark hair cascading down her back that first time he saw her. Before long, she had started wearing it up, as the other young women did, but August had never forgotten how it looked, swinging as she walked, barely brushing her hips.

August was not as tall as Gustaf, but even at nineteen, he was a big man. That's why he made such a good blacksmith. He was strong and muscular. But he was also shy. So he quietly studied Anna every time he was near her, trying to work up the courage to talk to her. He liked the fact that she was tall and strong.

August had never been interested in small girls. He felt clumsy around them. He was afraid he would hurt them without meaning to. Even though she wasn't dainty, Anna had a grace about her—not like some tall women who slumped to appear shorter. He liked everything about her.

Before he worked up the courage to speak to Anna for the first time, Gustaf sat beside her and introduced himself. She had smiled up at him. August liked watching her eyes flash, and a smile spread across her face as she talked. Why couldn't he be like Gustaf? He should have spoken to her first. Then she would have been smiling up at him instead of his brother.

After that first day when Gustaf spoke to her, Anna had not paid attention to any other man. She had followed him around every time they went to church. Soon she and Gerda had become best friends. They spent a lot of time together, either at the Nilsson farm or at the Jensons'. August tried to harden his heart against her, but when no one was looking, he feasted his eyes on her beauty, wishing he were his older brother so she would notice him.

After a couple of years, Gustaf and Anna started keeping time together. Since then August had a major, ongoing battle with the jealousy. He would pray, begging God to take it away. But the next time he saw Anna and Gustaf together, there it would be, making its way back into his heart. He was glad when his father let him move to town and apprentice as a blacksmith. He didn't see Gustaf as often, so he was able to control the jealousy a little more.

"Are you trying to beat that horseshoe to death?" Gustaf's voice penetrated August's dark thoughts.

August stopped what he was doing, took the bandanna from his back pocket, and wiped the sweat from his face again before he turned toward the doorway.

"That iron doesn't shape itself, you know." Gustaf laughed with August. "What brings you to the smithy? Do you have something I need to fix?"

Gustaf dusted off the front of the worktable that was next to the wall, then leaned against it. "Can't I just come to visit my brother?"

"*Ja*, for sure." August stuffed the bandanna back into his pocket. As he joined Gustaf against the table, he crossed his arms over his chest, placing his hands under the opposite arms. "So how's Olina doing?" Whenever he was with Gustaf, he was better able to control his emotions. It was after Gustaf left that the tormenting thoughts would do battle in his mind.

Gustaf shook his head. "This time she has a lot more morning sickness. It's hard on her, since she has to take care of Olga, too."

"But she's okay, isn't she?" August really cared about his sister-in-law.

"*Ja, Mor* assures me this is normal." August was sure that Gustaf was glad their mother lived so close so she could help sometimes. "I wish I could take some of it away from her. I want to protect her."

August wondered what it would feel like to have a woman to love and cherish. Would he ever know that feeling? He couldn't imagine ever loving a woman the way Gustaf loved Olina.

The two men shared a moment of companionable silence before August asked another question. "So, how's my favorite niece?"

"You mean your only niece, don't you?" Gustaf chuckled. "Now that Olga is walking all over the place, Olina has her hands full. That's why I don't come to town as much as I used to. When I'm not at the farm helping *Fader*, I stay home to give Olina some relief. And Olga loves me. When I come home, she runs across the room with her arms outstretched and wants me to pick her up, even before I have time to clean up."

A stab of jealousy penetrated August's carefully constructed defenses. Here he was twenty-six years old, and still he had no family. If Gustaf hadn't spent so much time with Anna, maybe he would have spoken to her. Maybe he would be the one with a wife and child—and another on the way.

When Gustaf broke off his relationship with Anna, August could have tried to establish one with her. But jealousy raised its ugly head. He didn't want his brother's castoff. If he hadn't fought jealousy so long, maybe he would have started something with Anna that could have led to a permanent relationship. Before he was able to overcome his aversion to having Gustaf's leftovers, Olaf Johanson had already captured Anna's affections.

"Well, I only stopped by to tell you that Gerda is staying at the house to fix supper tonight so that Olina won't have to. She told me to ask you to come." Gustaf stood away from the table and brushed off the back of his trousers.

"I won't turn down a home-cooked meal, that's for sure." August got tired of eating at the boardinghouse, and he wasn't able to cook in his room. Occasionally, he would go to the hotel dining room to eat, but by far his favorite place to eat was at the house of one of his relatives. And Gerda was a wonderful cook. This would be a good evening, getting to see Olga and having a home-cooked meal.

As Gustaf ambled out the door, August picked up the horseshoe with the tongs and held it in the flames of the forge. While he watched the iron change color, he fought the demons that threatened to consume him, bringing them under control once again. Sometimes it was very hard to do, and today was one of those days. He didn't want them to accompany him to his brother's house later and ruin the evening for him.

When August started to knock on the door of Gustaf and Olina's house, he heard Olga shriek with glee. Probably Gustaf was teasing her or chasing her. She liked to be chased. Her little legs would pump as she rushed across the room, often falling into a heap of laughter. Someday maybe he would have a daughter.

Before his knuckles connected with the door, it flew open. Gerda looked into his face, laughing. "Come in, August. You're just in time for all the fun."

August stepped inside. Olga looked up at him and laughed out loud. She put her hands on the floor and pushed her little bottom into the air before she stood up. Then she rushed toward him with her arms outstretched.

"Unka, Unka, up!"

August bent down and grasped her under her arms. He lifted her into a high arc that ended with him showering her neck with kisses as he gathered her close to his chest. By the time he was through, they were both breathless with laughter.

"Is anyone hungry?" Gerda looked from one brother to the other. "Or are you going to spend all evening playing?"

"August, it's good to see you." Olina descended the stairs looking regal but a little pale. She stood on tiptoe and kissed his cheek then took her daughter from his arms. "Come, Olga. Let's eat supper."

After they finished eating, August told Gustaf and Olina that he would help Gerda clean up. He enjoyed spending time with his sister. She kept him up on what was going on better than anyone else did.

After she had told him all about what was happening on the farm, he asked, "So how is the dressmaking business?"

"We're very busy." Gerda hung the tea towel on the edge of the cabinet and took off her apron. "It's hard to keep up with all the orders." She leaned close to him and whispered, "I'm trying to protect Olina from having to do much. She gets tired so easily."

August nodded. "I can see that. Have you thought about getting someone else to help out?"

August pulled out a chair from the table and sat in it. Gerda did the same.

"I thought about asking Anna, but she is working so hard on the wedding. And then she will have a home of her own to take care of."

Olaf Johanson kept his promise to Anna. He returned before the wedding. Two days before the wedding. But he wasn't riding his horse. He came home in the bed of a wagon, completely wrapped in canvas. Even his face.

Now Anna knew why she'd had such a bad feeling about the hunting trip. Maybe God was trying to tell her something. She had never been able to get that thought to dissipate the whole time Olaf was gone. Why couldn't he have listened to her when she tried to tell him? Had he ever cared about her feelings? Perhaps their whole marriage would have been that way, with him trying to control her and not letting her express who she was and what she felt.

Here she was on what was supposed to be her wedding day, getting ready to go to her fiancé's funeral. Her white silk dress was carefully packed away in a trunk, and she wore black wool gabardine. She wasn't even eligible to wear widow's weeds, because she wasn't a widow. But she felt like one. Once again, her heart had been ripped to shreds.

The service was held in the community center out on the prairie. Olaf's parents didn't want the funeral to be in the white clapboard church in town. They had only gone there on rare occasions, instead preferring the family feel of the services held in the structure that was so near their farm. Anna hadn't even had any say in the plans for the service. She would have preferred that the funeral be held in the building in town. It seemed more like a church than this one did. She couldn't keep from remembering all the parties she had attended here.

The edifice was used as a schoolhouse and for community functions as well as for church. The last time Anna had been here was for a party. The room had been draped with gaily colored paper streamers. Today it was so stark. Stark and cold. Cold and dreary.

At the front of the room, Olaf's handcrafted pine box was covered with autumn leaves since it was too late for any flowers. Actually, there weren't many leaves left either. It had taken Anna and Gerda a long time to find enough to cover the top of the casket. At least his family had let her take care of that detail.

During the service, Anna sat on the front bench beside Mrs. Johanson. Gerda sat beside her. Anna didn't think she would have been able to get through this without Gerda's friendship. Tears trailed down Anna's cheeks, and Gerda pressed a handkerchief into Anna's hand. She wiped her tears away and returned the handkerchief before they filed out of the building, following the pallbearers to the open wound in the ground.

When they stood beside the grave and listened to the preacher recite the

Lord's Prayer, Anna couldn't remember what had gone on during the service inside the building. It was a blur in her mind. Everything since Olaf's body arrived home was a blur. Everything except the pain in her heart. That pain was focused and sharp and penetrating.

Why were her last words to Olaf spoken in anger? Why hadn't he loved her enough to listen to her warning? She didn't even want to think about what this day should have been.

When the graveside service was over, Gerda guided Anna back inside the building. Several women had turned the community center into a place to serve dinner to the family and friends of Olaf. Although the room was still stark and bare, the smell of food permeated every corner. Anna looked at the table spread with a bounty of dishes, and her stomach churned. She fought back the feeling of nausea. Hadn't enough happened without her throwing up in front of everyone?

"May I fill a plate for you?" Gerda sat in the chair beside Anna.

Anna shook her head. "Not now. I couldn't eat a thing."

Gerda patted her hand. "If there is anything I can do, just tell me."

Anna nodded without speaking, tears streaming down her cheeks again. Gerda took another pristine white handkerchief from her pocket and handed it to Anna. She must have known that Anna would need more than one.

When the men finished shoveling the dirt on the coffin in the grave, they came into the building for something to eat. They had worked up a good appetite both digging the grave that morning and then covering it up after the service.

August looked around the room and saw his sister with Anna. He was glad Gerda was there for her. Anna needed someone right now. His gaze traveled from her hands twisting a soggy handkerchief to her face that was still wet from tears. In his opinion, even the red blotches could not take away from her beauty. His heart constricted at her pain. He wished he could shoulder it for her and shelter her from this storm that had raged against her.

Lustrous, abundant dark brown hair framed her face. The black hat could not hide the highlights that gleamed in the sunlight streaming through the window. August was sure her hair must feel silky and smooth. It had been so long since he had seen Anna with her hair down, but sometimes a stray curl would make its way from her carefully constructed hairstyle. He would love to see her hair hanging in waves again. He wished it was his right. For a moment August was lost in a fantasy world, and the jealousy receded, but it didn't depart.

When he came to his senses, he realized that his thoughts were probably inappropriate. How could he fantasize about Anna when it was the day of her fiancé's funeral? What kind of man did that? August didn't really want to know, and he didn't want to be that man. He gave himself a mental shake.

"Are you going to eat anything?" Gustaf sat beside August and interrupted his thoughts.

"I was waiting until everyone else had filled their plates." August didn't take his eyes off of Anna.

"So you can eat all that's left?" The often shared joke didn't lighten August's mood, but he agreed out of habit.

Before taking a bite, Gustaf followed August's gaze across the room. "What's so interesting about our sister?"

"What?" August looked at Gustaf. *What was he talking about?*

"Or maybe it isn't our sister who has captured your interest." Gustaf turned back toward his plate and lifted a fork full of mashed sweet potatoes.

August got up and went to the table. Anna's two brothers, Lowell and Ollie, were filling their plates.

"Do you think Anna is going to be all right?" August tried to sound casual.

Lowell, the brother who was a year older than Anna, stopped putting food on his plate and stared at August. "What do you mean?"

That surprised August. He took a minute to think about his answer. "I just wondered. Today was supposed to be her wedding day, wasn't it?"

Ollie, a year younger than Anna, nodded. "So what?"

"Well. . ." August was having a hard time putting his thoughts into words. "It might be extra hard on her, losing Olaf that way. . ." He stood there with an empty plate, trying to think of something else to say.

Lowell and Ollie both turned back to piling food on their plates. They didn't seem to be bothered by what was going on with Anna, and they must have dismissed August's question. Suddenly, August's appetite left him. He stared down at his empty plate, then at the long table of food. He could have his choice of almost any food he liked, but after putting only a few spoonfuls on the plate, he returned to his seat by Gustaf.

"What's the matter, brother? Have you lost your appetite?" Gustaf glanced at August's nearly empty dish.

"I guess I worked too hard today. Nothing looked that good." But that wasn't quite true. Something looked good to August, but it didn't have anything to do with food.

Chapter 3

November

Two weeks. It had been two weeks since the funeral. Where had the time gone? Anna pulled back the curtains and opened the window. A cool autumn breeze brought fresh air into the oppressive bedroom. She had spent most of the time mourning in this space. This place that had often been a refuge for her now felt more like a prison cell. She had cried a lake full of tears, and now she felt empty. Empty and used up. Would the pain ever come to an end?

Anna wanted a change, but what? Could anything alter what happened to her? She opened the door of her wardrobe and looked at all the finery there. It bulged with more clothing than most women she knew owned. But Anna loved to sew. She often designed new frocks for herself or her mother. It had been a long time since she had felt like dressing up. She had worn the same old dark, dreary black or brown dresses too long.

Somehow today she couldn't put either of them back on. They lay in a heap on the floor in the corner of her bedroom, a quiet testimony to her tragedy. It didn't seem right to wear anything bright or fashionable, but she had to wear something. Maybe an older house dress.

As her hand hovered over the garments in the polished oak wardrobe, her gaze was drawn to her riding clothes. Although the family made their living raising horses, she hadn't been on her mare in a long time. Anna knew that the open air would do her good. Maybe it would freshen her outlook a little. . .if anything could.

Ollie was mucking out the stalls when Anna walked through the open door of the barn. He leaned the crook of his arm on the handle of the pitchfork and pulled a bandanna from the back pocket of his denim trousers to wipe the sweat from his forehead. "Hi, sis, what're you doing here?"

"What does it look like I'm doing?" As soon as the words slipped between her lips, Anna was sorry that her voice sounded so sharp. She was able to soften it when she continued. "I'm going for a ride."

Ollie smiled as he pushed the hanky back into his pocket and leaned the pitchfork against the stall door. "Do you want me to saddle your horse for you?"

"I have been saddling my own horse since I was nine years old. I haven't forgotten how." This time she was able to force a more teasing tone into her words.

Ollie picked up the pitchfork and thrust the tines under a mound of soiled straw. "Okay. I was just trying to help."

Anna led her mare out of the stall and placed the saddle blanket on her back. When she lifted the saddle to the back of the horse, the creak of the leather was comforting. Comforting and familiar.

"I know you were. Thanks for caring." She gave Ollie the best smile she could muster. She hoped it was enough to keep him from worrying about her.

After leading Buttermilk out into the sunshine, she mounted and turned the horse away from the house. At first, Anna rode at a slow pace, but soon she and the mare flew across the prairie. This had been one of her favorite pastimes since she was old enough to ride alone. She always thought it was the closest to flying a person could ever get. The wind tugged tendrils of hair from the scarf where she had tied it at the nape of her neck. She turned her face in the wind, trying to keep the hair from blowing in her eyes.

Almost before she realized it, Buttermilk turned toward a copse of trees by a gentle stream. They had ridden this way many times before. Had she subconsciously given the horse signals that brought them to this place, or had Buttermilk come here out of habit?

Now, nearly empty branches swayed in the gentle breeze, and leaves covered the ground. Anna and Olaf had often met here. They had seen all the seasons of the year pass by. Anna loved spring with the new green leaves brushing the sky with promise. In summer, the trees had given welcome shade from the hot sun. Even when snow covered the ground and ice outlined the branches, Anna loved this place. But autumn was her least favorite season. In her mind, it symbolized death—the ending of the wonderful life of summer. How appropriate that it was autumn, for death had come into her life, in more ways than one.

In spring and summer, Anna and Olaf usually sat on a large rock beside the stream. In the winter, it had been too dangerous and cold. It was while sitting on that rock watching a beautiful sunset that Olaf asked her to marry him. Why had she come here today? It opened the wounds she was trying to ignore.

Buttermilk slowed her pace as she neared the grove, leaves crunching under her hooves. When they were close to the rock, the horse stopped and bent her head to munch the blades of brown grass that peeked through the carpet of autumn leaves. Anna slid from the horse's back and walked to the rock, but she didn't sit on it. As she stared at the monolith, anger simmered within her. She picked up a dead twig and fiddled with it, breaking small pieces off and dropping them as she stomped up the trail worn around the side of the huge stone. When she reached the flat surface at the top, she stood and looked all around. In every direction, things looked as if they were dying or were already dead.

"Olaf, why did you leave me?" Anna spit the words out as if she couldn't get rid of them quickly enough.

She picked up a small stone that had broken off from the larger block and threw it into the clear water that gurgled below. The splash sent up a spray that fell back into the stream like raindrops. Cleansing raindrops. If only something could cleanse the pain from her heart.

"Why were you so stubborn?" This time, the words were louder, and tears began to make tracks down her cheeks. But they were tears of anger, not tears of grief.

Slowly she picked her way down the side of the rock. With each step, the word *Why?* beat a cadence in her brain. She wanted to hit something. . .or someone. Actually, she wanted to hit Olaf for leaving her. She wanted him to hold her in his arms as she beat furiously against his muscular chest. But he wasn't here. He would never be here again. She leaned over and picked up a rock that peeked out from under the leaves.

"Why couldn't you love me more?" she shouted, as she threw the rock against the large stone.

Again and again, shouted questions accompanied the missiles she hurled against the monument to her unfulfilled love. Each one shattered, just as her heart had shattered. Finally, when her anger was spent, Anna stopped the barrage of words and weapons. She slumped against a tree, exhausted.

Twice she had given her heart freely, and twice it had been broken. No more. She would never give her heart to a man again. She would never risk being this hurt again. She didn't need a man. She could take care of herself.

Anna walked downstream until she came to a spot where there was a narrow sandbar and she could walk to the water's edge. She pulled the scarf from her hair and dipped a corner of the cotton square into the cold water. With the dampened fabric, she washed the dried tears from her face. After wringing the cloth out, she tied her hair back again. Straightening her shoulders, she went to Buttermilk and caressed the beloved animal's neck before mounting and riding toward home. She sat tall in the saddle and held her head high. Today, Anna was determined that her world would change. But deep inside, somehow she knew that this would be hard to accomplish.

Gerda was sitting at the kitchen table talking to Mrs. Jenson when Anna came in from the barn. "Anna, there you are. I was about to give up on you and go home."

Anna looked at her mother. "I'm sorry I didn't tell you what I was doing. I decided to go for a ride this morning." She looked at her best friend. "And I would have waited if I had known you were coming today."

"That's wonderful." Gerda jumped up and hugged her. "It's the first time you've been out of the house, isn't it?"

Anna nodded. "I know. I was becoming a recluse. I'm through with that. Today is a new day." She hoped that Gerda wouldn't recognize the emptiness in her eyes or the forced bravado in her voice.

Taking Gerda's arm, Anna escorted her into the parlor. The last time they sat in this room was when they worked on her wedding dress, but she wouldn't let herself think about that today. Hopefully she would be able to forget that whole time in her life. She needed to move on. . .if she could.

"I should have asked while we were still in the kitchen," Anna said before she sat on the sofa. "Would you like a cup of tea? I think there are some muffins left from breakfast. That's unusual, since Lowell and Ollie eat so much to keep up their strength."

"They're big men." Gerda smiled. "Big men eat a lot to keep them going. Right?" She looked back toward the kitchen. "I love your *moder*'s muffins. Maybe I'll eat one."

Anna smiled, and the two young women headed back to get the food. When they returned to the parlor, Anna set the tray on the table in front of the sofa. After sitting beside Gerda, she poured two cups of the fragrant brew and handed one to her friend. Then she put fresh butter on the still warm muffin and set the small plate beside Gerda's saucer.

"So what brings you by this morning?" Anna stopped suddenly. "That's a silly question. You've been faithful about checking on me every couple of days."

Gerda sipped her tea, then set the cup on the saucer. "Was I that obvious?"

"Actually, I appreciate the love you've shown me. And the understanding. I needed both of them." Anna patted Gerda's hand. "But I turned a corner this morning, I think. I'm going to be all right."

Gerda stood and walked to the window and fiddled with the lace curtains. After turning around, she straightened the crocheted doily under the lamp on the table that was framed by the curtains. Was she nervous? Anna wondered what she had to be nervous about.

"Actually, Anna, I wanted to talk to you about something. I wasn't sure I should, but since you seem better this morning—"

"I would do anything for you, just as you would for me."

Gerda came back around the end of the sofa and dropped down to sit on the edge, turning to face Anna. "The only thing that's wrong with me is that I need you to help with the dressmaking business."

"What about Olina?" Anna knew that Gerda's sister-in-law was also her partner. Besides that, the business was located in the front room of the home Olina and Gustaf Nilsson lived in on the outskirts of Litchfield.

"You know she's going to have a baby. She gets tired quicker with this one, and she has her daughter to take care of. Little Olga can be a big handful sometimes. That's for sure." Gerda laughed. "So if you could help me, it would relieve Olina a lot."

Anna sat a moment lost in thought. Did she want to work? Why not? She was good at making clothing, and it would help her move on with her life. A change of scenery might take her mind off her problems.

"When do you want me to start. . .if I decide to help?"

Gerda smiled and relaxed against the back of the sofa. Had she been afraid to ask Anna? Maybe that was why she seemed nervous earlier.

"Any time you're ready," Gerda said. "Tomorrow wouldn't be too soon."

"All right. I'll be there in the morning if you're sure Olina won't mind."

Gerda hugged Anna. "I talked it over with her before I came. She'll be glad to have the help, too."

"And we work so well together. Remember all the parties we've planned, and we've helped each other make clothing before." *A wedding dress among them.* But Anna shut that thought out of her mind. It was 1894, and in this modern time, more women were working outside the home. Tomorrow she would enter the world of business.

August hurried to finish shoeing the horse Gustaf had left with him. Then he was going to clean up and ride the horse to Gustaf's house. Gerda had asked him to come by the Nilsson home for lunch today. She was fixing the meal so Olina wouldn't have to, and she wanted August to eat with them.

He walked the horse to the livery and tied it in a stall before he went to his room. For some reason, he felt like sprucing up a bit. After a good washup in his room, he got some hot water for a shave. It was unlike him to shave in the middle of the day, but he hadn't shaved that morning, and he didn't want to look like a mountain man or trapper when he went to eat. Gerda was always teasing him about his bad habit of not being careful about his grooming.

While August swished his brush around the bar of soap in his shaving mug, he whistled a happy tune. He smeared the foamy suds over his face. Then he opened his straight razor and started by sliding it up his neck. He was glad that he had stropped his razor at the end of his last shave. Its sharp edge sliced through the softened hairs as if they were butter. After he rinsed the residue from his face, he applied a little bay rum shaving lotion. Then he preened in front of the mirror.

"This blacksmith cleans up pretty good, if I do say so myself."

The happy melody was still playing in his head when August dismounted in front of the house. Since it was already noon, he decided to tie the horse to the hitching post and take it to the barn after he ate. When the door opened following his rap on it, August stood and stared.

He saw a vision of loveliness framed in the doorway. Anna. She was wearing a green dress that brought out the highlights in her hazel eyes. This was the first time he had seen her in anything but black since the funeral. Actually, this was the first time he had seen her at all. She hadn't come to church or to town that he knew of, at least not in the last two weeks. He had heard from Gerda that Anna hardly left her room. What was she doing here?

Anna didn't know that they were expecting August to eat with them. When the knock sounded on the door, she thought it might be one of the many customers of the thriving dressmaking business. She opened the door to see if she could help instead of bothering Gerda or Olina.

Although she was tall, she had to look up into the face of the man standing there. August. He was wearing a blue plaid shirt that made his eyes seem more blue than gray. He looked fresh and clean, his face newly shaven. For an instant, she wanted to test the smoothness with her fingertips.

What was wrong with her? This was August. Gerda's brother. The strong, shy, quiet Nilsson brother. Then a snippet of a thought flitted through her mind. A phrase that Merta had uttered when they had been working on her wedding dress. Something about August being interested in Anna. For some reason, he had captured her gaze, and she caught a glimpse of something she couldn't define.

"Are you two going to stand there gaping at each other, or are you going to invite my brother in?" Gerda came up behind Anna. "Dinner is on the table. You're just in time."

Gerda took August by the arm and led him to the table. Anna gave her head a slight shake to clear her thoughts and followed her friends.

Mrs. Braxton ordered three new dresses for the upcoming holiday season. And Marja wasn't a patient person. She was anxious to get the garments, even though it was still over a week before Thanksgiving.

Normally Anna used the sewing machine, stitching up the major seams of the designs. When she finished each dress, Gerda did the handwork and added the decorations. But today Gerda wasn't in the sunny workroom. She had gone to town. August wanted her to help him bring something to the house. Probably for Gustaf or Olina.

Ever since Anna started working with Gerda, August was always underfoot. If he wasn't helping Gustaf with some repair on the house, he was running errands or doing other things for Gerda. Didn't that man have a job of his own that he needed to see about?

The thought wasn't fair, and Anna knew it. August was a hard worker. Mr. Simpkins had employed him for several years. Recently, Mr. Simpkins decided to retire and move to California where his daughter and her family lived. August had saved enough money to buy him out, so he did. Now he was the only blacksmith in town. That kept him plenty busy.

Maybe he didn't have much of a social life since he spent so much time over here. Anna laughed. Who was she to comment on the social life of others? Hers consisted of eating dinner with her family and working with Gerda. Sometimes she took a break and played with Olga so Olina could get some rest. But that was the extent of her activities. Of course, that wasn't a bad thing. Since she started working here, she could relegate to the dark recesses of her mind all the events that had plagued her while she was holed up in her room for those two weeks. Thoughts she didn't want to entertain but that never actually left her for long.

Anna finished stitching the skirt to the bodice of the dress. When she lifted the garment and repositioned it, the material filled her lap. She hoped she wouldn't crush it too badly.

"Oh good, you're finished." Gerda breezed into the room from the door that opened onto the front porch. "I wanted to try this out."

Anna looked past Gerda to see August enter carrying something that was wrapped in brown paper. Legs stuck out from the paper, two at one end and one near the other end of the contraption.

"What's that?" Anna stood and folded the dress over the back of the chair where she had been sitting.

"It's an ironing table." Gerda smiled up at her brother. "August built it for us. Now we don't have to clear off the cutting table to iron something."

August pulled off the paper that had protected the top. The table was long and thin with padding tied around it. He had even tapered one end to make it easier to slip items on it.

Anna glanced over at the potbellied stove where their irons rested when not in use. "Maybe we should set it near the stove. That way we won't have to carry the flatirons so far."

"Good idea." August moved the contraption and situated it a comfortable distance from the irons. "How's this?"

Anna thought he was asking Gerda, but he turned questioning eyes toward her. "It looks fine to me." She picked up the dress she had been working on. "I'll try it out."

After laying the garment on the new addition to the workroom, she picked up one of the flatirons, using the thick pad of fabric they kept nearby to protect their hands from the heat of the iron handle. While she applied heated pressure to the dress, she peeked at August, who was carrying on a conversation with Gerda.

His Brother's Castoff

Why hadn't she ever noticed how handsome he was? He was so quiet he didn't draw attention to himself. The work he did helped him develop extremely muscular arms and chest. His shirt stretched tight over them whenever he moved. Anna almost wished he had been the one who had sought her out first. With his gentle nature, he probably wouldn't have broken her heart the way Gustaf and Olaf had. What was she thinking? Here she was still mourning the loss of Olaf. How could she compare him to another man?

All the time August talked to Gerda, he was aware of every move Anna made. As she bent over the ironing table and pressed the heavy, hot iron into the fabric, he hoped she wouldn't burn herself. He knew it was impossible not to get burned occasionally when you used one of those. He remembered many times Gerda, and even his mother, had to deal with a blister on their hands or arms from ironing.

A war raged within him every time he came to this house and found Anna here. When he looked at her, all the longing he felt for her from the first time he saw her surged to the surface. Along with it came the fierce jealousy. Jealousy of Gustaf for capturing her heart before he tried. Even jealousy of a dead man for the time he had held her heart in his hands. Why couldn't he get past this jealousy? Maybe some day he would be able to think of Anna as something more than his brother's castoff. But not yet. Not today.

Anna thought she had gotten used to August's appearance at the Nilsson house, but it always startled her. She had moved the sewing machine in front of the window so the sunlight would help her see what she was doing. While she concentrated on keeping the gathers even as she sewed a ruffle onto the skirt of one of the dresses for Mrs. Braxton, she became aware of a wagon stopping in front of the house. She hoped it wasn't Marja coming for the dresses. They weren't quite ready.

When she finished the seam, she looked up, and there he was mounting the front steps. Today August didn't look like a blacksmith. Anna had never seen him in buckskins before. If she hadn't known better, she would have thought he was a trapper. If he quit shaving, he would have made a good mountain man with blond whiskers and strong muscles under the leather clothing. She had never been drawn to those untamed men when they came into town. They were often unwashed and smelly. Anna knew that August usually smelled faintly of bay rum shaving lotion. For a moment, she could imagine those strong leather-clad arms holding her—

"Who is that?" Gerda asked from her place by the ironing table. "I can't see from here."

Anna was glad that Gerda interrupted her crazy thoughts. "It's August." She stood up, placed her fists against her waist, and stretched her back. She had been sitting at the sewing machine too long without moving. "What's he doing here? He didn't come for lunch, did he? I thought we were going to eat sandwiches made from yesterday's leftovers for our noon meal."

Gerda placed the iron back on the stove and went toward the door. "We are. But it's too early for lunch. I think he's going hunting. He said that his contribution to the community Thanksgiving dinner would be a deer, since he doesn't cook."

Hunting? August is going hunting? Fear clutched Anna in a tight grip. Her heart ached. Something of what she felt must have shown on her face when Gerda turned toward her.

"Anna, what's the matter? You're white as a sheet."

"Nothing." Anna reached for the back of the straight chair where she had been sitting. Now she felt dread, but not the uncanny dread she had felt when Olaf left to go on his last hunting trip. Would she always feel this way when someone she knew went hunting? Surely not.

Gerda came and put her arm around Anna. "Have you been working too long? Maybe we should take a break."

August knocked on the door of the workroom instead of the door to the rest of the house. Gerda quickly went to let him in.

～

When Gerda opened the door, August looked past her to where Anna leaned on the back of a chair. Sunlight streamed through the window and bathed her in a golden glow that should have gilded her beauty. Instead, she looked frail, almost as if something was wrong with her. He wondered what it was. He had always thought of Anna as strong. That was one of the things he loved about her, her strength. But she didn't look strong today.

"Come in." Gerda stepped back to make room for him. "We were just going to take a break. Do you have time for a cup of coffee with us before you go?"

August looked from Anna's pale face to Gerda's cheerful one. "Sounds good, for sure. The wind has a bite in it today. This trip could be a cold one. Wouldn't hurt to warm up first."

Gerda put her arm around his waist as they started toward the kitchen. "So what really brought you over here?"

August glanced back at Anna. He was going to stop Gerda, but Anna had turned to follow them. "Gustaf said I could use his new rifle. It's more accurate than mine, and I don't want to stay out in the cold any longer than I have to."

～

Anna was glad to hear August's last statement. It made her feel better, but not much. She followed them into the kitchen.

"Where is Olina?" August looked around the warm room.

"She took Olga to see her grandmother."

Anna picked up the coffeepot that sat on the back of the cookstove, poured August a mugful, and set it on the table in front of him. Then she poured hot water into a teapot and set tea to steep. Gerda uncovered a pan of cinnamon rolls that were left from breakfast.

"I would have come over sooner if I had known you had cinnamon rolls." August forked two onto the plate Gerda set in front of him.

"How long will you be gone?" Anna kept her back to the table. She didn't want anyone to know how important his answer was to her.

When he didn't answer, she turned around. No wonder. He was chewing the big bite that was missing from one of the rolls in front of him. Always the gentleman, he wouldn't talk with his mouth full.

"As soon as I see a large deer and kill it, I'll field dress it and return to town." He took a swig of the hot coffee.

Anna wondered how he could drink it so fast. She always let her tea cool off a bit before she sipped it.

"There's a storm brewing, and I don't want to be out in it too long. Maybe it'll only snow this time."

Anna could imagine him huddled in the cold. She didn't welcome this feeling of sympathy for him. She didn't want to feel anything for any man. Her life would be much more uncomplicated without men.

August had been gone barely half an hour when feathery flakes started floating past the window. Could it have been only an hour before that sunlight poured through the same window? Where was August now? Where would he camp? Did he have plenty of warm clothes? Could he find enough dry wood for his campfire? Why did he have to go hunting alone? Anna wished the questions wouldn't dance through her mind, taunting her. She could hardly wait until August came back, hopefully driving his own wagon.

Chapter 4

Not a day had gone by since August left that Anna didn't hope to hear his wagon come to the house. At least the storm had only held snow. Although several inches covered the ground, the air hadn't warmed up enough to thaw any of it, so there wasn't much ice. Anna knew that August was a careful hunter. He was skilled at making camp and building a fire—all the things that were needed to be successful. But the longer he was gone, the more her mind filled with pictures of the day Olaf had returned in the bed of the wagon. And August didn't have anyone with him to bring him home.

Why did she care? It seemed as if Anna asked herself that question a million times. August was just a friend, but he was a good friend. Her best friend's brother. Anyone would care under those circumstances. Why did her concern feel like much more than that?

Gustaf went out to the farm one morning, leaving Olina and Olga with Anna and Gerda. Olina was having a hard day, and Olga was full of energy. She had been inside for the last week. Gerda bundled Olga up in several layers of clothing and took her outside to play in the snow. Anna decided to stay indoors and work on one of the many dresses clients had ordered. That way she could keep a discreet watch on Olina.

Anna liked the fabric for the new outfit. It was a rich mulberry wool with a soft touch. As Anna smoothed the fabric out across the top of the cutting table, she imagined herself in a suit from the dark purple fabric. A fitted jacket with a short peplum spreading over a full skirt. She would line the jacket with lavender silk. A blouse of the same silk with a froth of ruffles to fill the V neckline. Even with the blouse, the suit would be dark enough for someone who had lost her fiancé to death. Maybe she should leave work early enough today to go by the mercantile and purchase the fabric on her way home. She didn't want the store to sell out before she got some.

The sound of hoofbeats mingled with the shouts of laughter coming from the yard. Anna glanced out the window. It was just Gustaf returning home. She looked back at the piece of paper containing the customer's measurements. Then she realized what else she had seen. Gustaf was carrying his rifle. The rifle August had taken hunting with him.

Anna couldn't have stopped herself from going to the window if she had tried.

She wanted to be sure. Gustaf tied the horse to the hitching post and started up the sidewalk to the house, and he carried the rifle. Anna didn't realize that she was holding her breath until she released it. Why did she feel as if a heavy load had been lifted from her shoulders? She didn't want to look at the answer to that question.

Anna had made the first slice through the fabric with her scissors when Gerda and Olga tumbled through the door. Gerda set Olga in a corner near the window and gave her a bucket of wooden spools to play with.

"So why did Gustaf come home early?" Anna tried to sound disinterested, but she knew she failed.

Gerda came over to watch. "He wanted to talk to Olina." She fingered an edge of the fabric. "I like the feel of this wool, don't you?"

Anna nodded while she continued cutting. "I thought I saw him carrying the rifle August borrowed." Anna didn't look up from her work. She didn't want Gerda to see how relieved she was.

"Yes, August arrived at our house a few minutes before Gustaf left the farm to come home." Gerda turned and leaned against the end of the table. "He brought two deer. I think Gustaf wants Olina and Olga to go out to the farm with him. They're probably going to spend the night."

Anna pulled the blades of the scissors away from the fabric to protect it and looked at Gerda. "Why would they do that?"

"Have you forgotten what tomorrow is?"

Tomorrow? Thursday. "Thanksgiving." Anna had tried to put it out of her mind. She wasn't looking forward to all the celebrating.

"It'll take all afternoon to process the meat." Gerda started picking up and putting away all the things that were out of place in the room. "One deer will be kept for our family's meals, and the other will be roasted for the community Thanksgiving dinner. It'll take all night. *Far* and August are building the fire in the pit Gustaf dug. The fire'll have to burn down to coals before they put the deer in it."

Anna laid the scissors on the table, being careful to close the blades so there wouldn't be a mishap. "Are you going with them?"

Gerda nodded. "Yes. The whole family will be preparing for the big feast."

"I can finish this Monday." Anna started to put on her coat and scarf. "I want to stop at the mercantile on the way home anyway."

When August arrived at the community center for the Thanksgiving shindig, he immediately started looking for Anna. If she came, it would be the first event she had attended since the funeral. Because she hadn't started coming to church again, he was afraid she wouldn't be here either. He decided that if she didn't come, he would take food to her house for her.

He came early with his mother and sister to help set everything up. Gustaf and his father would bring Olina and Olga when they brought the roasted deer meat right before noon.

While Gerda swept the floor, August helped set up tables across one wall of the large room. Then he placed chairs all around the other three sides. Each time he passed a window, he glanced toward the road that led to the Jenson horse farm. And each time, the road was empty, making his heart grow heavier and heavier.

After they had worked for a couple of hours, the room looked festive. Gerda and Mother had a knack for decorating. All that was missing was the food that would soon cover the tables. The sound of a buggy coming down the road drew August to the window, but it wasn't the Jenson buggy.

Other vehicles joined the first in rapid succession. People filled the tables with food and the room with merriment as they greeted neighbors and caught up on recent activities. August leaned one shoulder against the back wall and watched everyone. He didn't feel much like socializing. Besides, no one would probably notice if he wasn't there. He wasn't exactly the life of the party. He wasn't sure anyone would even be aware if he walked out the door and didn't return.

He decided to try out his theory, but before he reached the door, it burst open. Lowell and Ollie Jenson carried in baskets laden with food. Behind them, Mrs. Jenson was talking to Anna as they entered the warm building. The temperature had risen above freezing and started melting the snow, but there was still a chill in the air.

August sat in one of the chairs by the wall and crossed his ankle over his other knee. He leaned the chair back against the wall and tried to act nonchalant. Of course, if his mother saw him, she would probably come tell him to sit with all four legs of the chair on the floor. She wouldn't care that he was an adult who'd been living on his own for several years. He decided not to tempt her, so he uncrossed his legs, dropped the chair back down, and leaned his elbows on his knees. With his hands dangling between his long legs, he watched Anna as she sidled up to the table and made sure her brothers had put each dish in the proper place.

Anna had a look like a lost little girl. She glanced around the room and moved toward a back corner. August knew that she hadn't wanted to come. He got up and followed her.

"I'm glad you're here, Anna."

The sound of her name startled Anna. She turned around and looked at the top button of August's shirt. Where had he come from? She hadn't noticed him in any of the clusters of men she passed. What was he doing standing so close to her? For some reason, she liked the way he said her name. She'd heard him say it many times before, but somehow it sounded different today.

"I almost didn't." Anna lifted her gaze to his face.

Today August wasn't wearing buckskins, but he looked every bit as virile without them. His denim trousers were new, and his shirt was a blue that brought out the color of his eyes. Anna was close enough to step into his arms. She shifted back to give herself some space and took a deep breath. Mingled with the tantalizing scents of food that permeated the air was the distinctive aroma of bay rum shaving lotion. This was only August, Gerda's brother. Why was his presence crowding her, even though he stood a couple of feet away?

Anna decided that her emotions were too raw. She had told Mother that she wasn't ready to be in a crowd, and she must have been right.

When Anna arrived home that evening, she was tired, but it was a good tired. The day had gone better than she hoped. No one asked her about Olaf. People seemed to understand that she didn't want to talk about what had happened. The women drew her into several conversations. The most prominent subject was the clothing that she and Gerda had been producing in their workroom. Several of the women wore garments with their distinctive touches. Those conversations helped Anna relax. Before the day was over, other women mentioned that they were going to stop by the shop and talk about holiday dresses. It looked as if she and Gerda would have their hands full, at least for the next month. And that was a good thing.

The only uncomfortable times Anna experienced were when she was too close to August. Her longtime friend had grown into a strong, handsome man. Were all the other young single women blind? He should've had plenty of feminine attention. That would've kept him from seeking her out every chance he got. Or so it seemed to her.

Anna was sure that August only felt sorry for her. He couldn't have been feeling anything else. But his presence made her uncomfortable. She didn't need this. Didn't he realize that there was something wrong with her? That some strange phenomenon kept a man from loving her enough? That fact had been amply demonstrated in the past. Gustaf had seemed ready to ask her to marry him before Olina arrived. But that changed fast enough. And Olaf had loved her in his own way, she supposed. But it was a lukewarm love at best. Her feelings and desires hadn't meant much to him, had they? If they had, she would be married right now.

Well, she wasn't going to put herself through that agony again. Her life was full with friends and her work. That's all she needed. Wasn't it? She would never marry. That was for sure.

⁕

The day after Thanksgiving, August was back at work. The heat from the forge staved off the chill from outside. He was even able to leave the door open without the room getting too cold. He added more fuel to the fire, then turned to look at all the items that needed repairing. They were lined up on one table in the order in which he had received them. A testimony to his hard work. Anna's brothers would be here any minute with several horses that needed shoeing. He'd get back to the other things after they left.

Every time August turned around, he was reminded of Anna. Beautiful Anna. He couldn't take his eyes off her yesterday. She wasn't wearing one of the brighter colors she favored before she lost Olaf, but the warm brown of her suit brought out the rich darkness of her eyes. August liked the way her eyes changed color according to what she wore. Although she had her hair pulled into a figure-eight bun fastened at her neck, she looked soft and feminine. August was disgusted that he hadn't taken his chance when he had it. She should be loved, not mourning a loss.

These thoughts brought him full circle to the jealousy he had to fight all the time. If he had been less shy, he would have spoken to her before Gustaf did. Now look at him. He didn't know if he would ever marry. She was the one woman he could love. But not now.

August picked up an iron bar and held it in the flame of the forge. After it was red hot, he placed it on the anvil and bent it into a horseshoe shape. The pounding didn't work out his tension as it usually did. He held the bar back in the fire to reheat so he could pound it flat. When that was accomplished, he plunged it into the tub of cold water that sputtered and spit as it cooled the finished product.

It took almost an hour to form as many horseshoes as he thought he would need. When he laid the last one on the bench, Ollie and Lowell rode up to the door. Each one led two horses behind their own mounts.

Gerda was already hard at work when Anna arrived at the workroom on Monday morning. She watched as Anna took off her coat and hung it up.

"So, what are you working on?" Anna moved toward the table. "I think I'll finish cutting this out."

"Okay." Gerda held up the waistband of the skirt she was hemming. "I just now finished this. It's a good thing. Mrs. Larkin is coming to pick it up this morning."

Anna picked up her scissors and bent over the fabric for the suit, which was still spread across the table. She slid the scissors back into the place where she had stopped cutting the day before Thanksgiving. Carefully, she followed the outlines she had drawn on the fabric.

Gerda stood and started folding the skirt. "I was glad you came to church yesterday. We have missed you there."

Anna continued cutting. "I know, and I missed being there." She reached the end of the long side of the skirt, so she had to turn the scissors a different direction. She moved around the edge of the table so her hand wasn't at an uncomfortable angle to cut the rest of the garment. "It wasn't as bad as I thought it would be."

"Bad?" Gerda stopped folding and walked over to Anna. "Why would going to church be bad?"

Anna carefully laid the scissors down and stood up, looking her friend in the eye. "I thought that everyone would be sympathetic. . .or ask questions or something."

Gerda smiled. "Oh, Anna. Everyone cares about you, but no one wants to make you uncomfortable."

"I know that. And it helps."

Olina knocked on the door that connected to the parlor, then opened it. "I want to talk to you two."

Anna pulled up a chair and offered it to Olina. Then she sat on a stool that was beside the cutting table.

"What's on your mind?" Gerda picked up the folded skirt and placed it on the shelf where the finished articles were kept.

"Now that Thanksgiving is over, we need to think about Christmas."

"Isn't it a little early?" Anna asked.

"Not at all." Olina leaned forward as if she were eager. "I love Christmas." Anna nodded. "I always have, too."

Olina looked up at her. "I know that you have your own family, but I really need help here. That buggy ride out to the farm gets harder and harder. I would like to have Christmas for the family here at our house, but I can't do it by myself. Would you two help me?"

Anna thought a minute. "I might have to spend Christmas Day at home with my family, but I could help you prepare. That is, if you give us time to work on all the orders we have."

Olina clapped her hands. It reminded Anna of the way Marja Braxton at the mercantile always clapped her hands when she was excited. Maybe Olina was picking up some of her habits.

"August said he would help us, too."

When Anna started home, riding on Buttermilk, she revisited the conversation with Olina. Did Anna really want to spend that much time with August? It might not be too bad. . .if she could remember that he was only a friend. She wondered why she was thinking so much about him. She was supposed to have been in love with Olaf, and it had been only a couple of months since he died. She should still feel devastated, shouldn't she?

She had been so upset when Gustaf turned away from her love for him.

Wasn't she turning away from her love of Olaf in the same way?

A thought struck Anna in the heart. Maybe she hadn't loved Olaf any more than he loved her. Was she truly in love with him, or was she only in love with the idea of being a wife and mother? Anna didn't like what she saw deep inside her heart.

She had liked Olaf. A lot. They had fun together, but something was missing from their relationship. Up until now, she had felt that the lack was one sided. Only Olaf didn't express the love she needed. Maybe the reason he didn't love her enough was because she didn't really love him either. Perhaps on some level, he understood that. It could be that the love they felt for each other wasn't strong enough to carry them through all the stresses of married life. Maybe God hadn't wanted her to marry Olaf. Maybe He didn't want her to be married at all.

Why is life so complicated?

Anna pushed aside these thoughts and put her mind to the plans for Christmas. That was what she needed. Something to keep her busy.

Anna felt that she reached a turning point during that ride home. She was strong. An independent businesswoman. Her life was full. She didn't need anything else. Especially not a man.

Chapter 5

January 1895

As Anna drove the buggy toward the dress shop, her thoughts returned to Christmas. Not only did she spend holiday time with her own family, but she had been included in the festivities at the Nilssons'. Since most of their celebrations took place at Gustaf and Olina's house, and since Olina needed Gerda and Anna to help her, Anna's time had been completely filled. She knew that if she had had much time to think, she would have had a hard time with the holiday. As it was, she was able to close off her heart from the pain and fill her life with the busyness Christmas brought to her.

Another benefit of her activities was the fact that she felt competent. While she was helping with all the cooking, decorating, and gift preparation, her confidence grew. More and more, the idea of her independence blossomed within her. Any doubts or lingering desires for a marriage and children were quickly pushed into some far recess of her mind. She made a concerted effort to forget that they were there.

During the holidays, Olina had talked to Gerda and Anna. She wanted Anna to take her place in the dressmaking business. Olina would have her hands full with her home and family. Anna had wondered how she and Gerda would continue to work, since they were using the room at Gustaf and Olina's house for a workroom. Olina told them that it was not an imposition, since Gerda was family anyway. Now Anna was half owner of a successful business.

Although the remnants of the latest snowfall had turned mushy, Anna didn't have any problems getting to work that morning. She felt proud of herself as she drove the buggy through the open door of Gustaf's barn. She was so lost in her thoughts that she didn't wonder why the barn door was open on such a cold day.

"Anna, let me help you."

Almost before she could turn her head, two large hands rested on her waist and strong arms lifted her down from the conveyance. When she glanced up, she was standing much too close to August.

"What are you doing here?" She couldn't keep her question from sounding breathless.

"Aren't you glad to see me?"

The twinkle in his eyes reached a place dangerously near her heart. Anna took a couple of steps back, almost tumbling over the barn cat.

"I just didn't expect you to be here at this time of day."

She started removing her soft leather gloves. The sooner she got the horse into a stall, the better. Who knew how long August would be there?

The jingle of the harness caused Anna to look up from her hands. August was already leading the horse toward the stall she usually used. He grabbed a brush on the way.

"You don't have to do that."

August smiled back at her. "I know I don't, but I want to." He continued toward the stall.

Anna stood watching him as if she were dumbfounded. Why was he doing this? After a moment, she mumbled, "Thank you." Then she turned and hurried out of the barn as if something were chasing her.

When she was halfway to the house, she heard August give a hearty laugh followed by, "You're welcome."

What was so funny? She shook her head and rounded the side of the house. She wondered if Gerda had arrived. When she entered the workroom, she found a note telling her that Gerda had gone to the mercantile. It was a little early in the day for that, wasn't it? Without another thought, Anna turned her attention to the many garments that needed work. She thought that when the holidays were over, the orders would slow down. But it had been a good year, and that didn't happen. The more often women in the area wore their new dresses, the more orders she and Gerda received. Actually, they could use a larger workroom. If only that were possible.

"Anna!"

Gerda's exuberant greeting as she entered the front door startled Anna. She looked up from the gabardine skirt she was cutting out.

"Guess what!" Gerda threw off her navy wool cape, letting it slip to the floor, then started pulling off her knitted gloves.

Anna put the scissors on the table and turned to lean against it, crossing her arms. "I'm sure I don't know."

Gerda grabbed Anna and hugged her. "It's the most wonderful news."

Anna could hardly catch her breath because Gerda was hugging her so hard. "Well, tell me before you squeeze me in two."

Gerda pulled away and laughed. She walked over to the heavy laden shelves along the back wall of the workroom.

"See how crowded we are."

Anna nodded, hoping that Gerda would hurry and tell what was making her so excited.

"How would you like to have a larger workroom?"

Had she read Anna's mind? Anna turned, picked up the scissors, and started cutting again. "That would be nice, but I'm sure that if Gustaf were to add a room to the house, it wouldn't be for us."

Gerda dropped onto the stool beside the cutting table. "That's not what I'm talking about." She leaned her elbows on the end of the table that wasn't covered with material. "When I was in town, the Braxtons asked if we would like to have a dress shop in the mercantile. They think it would help the store if we did. Johan even offered to give us space for a larger workroom as well as a display area. Both Johan and Marja think it will bring more customers into the store and increase their sales."

Anna had stopped cutting halfway through Gerda's explanation. She laid the scissors down and leaned back against the edge of the table, crossing her arms. "What did you tell them?"

"That I needed to talk to you. What do you think?"

Anna stood deep in thought. A dress shop in town. She could just picture a dress form in the front window featuring a beautiful outfit. Lace panels pulled back with cord ties gave a pleasing frame for the display. A real salesroom and a workroom, maybe room for storage.

She turned toward Gerda and smiled. "I like it. How would it work?"

Gerda stood and went to pick up her cape and gloves from where she dropped them. She hung the garment on a hook on the wall. "Remember when the Braxtons bought the building next door to the mercantile and expanded into it? They have been trying to update the merchandise they carry. It's the 1890s, and our city is growing. They want to be more modern. They think the dress shop would be a welcome addition to the mercantile. They would let us have a portion of the right side of the store. We would probably need to get our brothers to help with the remodeling we need to do, but we could have a salesroom with a workroom behind it. And the workroom would be twice as large as this one. Johan said that they would only charge us a small percentage of sales for rent."

"I like it. Let's do it." This only added to Anna's feeling of being an independent modern woman. Oh yes, she would have a fulfilling life as a successful businesswoman. And if Gerda ever decided to marry and have a family, then Anna would run the store by herself. Maybe this was what God had planned for her life all along. If it hadn't matched her plans for herself, that didn't matter. She took the new idea to heart, pushing everything else to the back of her mind.

It was a good thing it was the middle of winter. Otherwise, Gerda and Anna wouldn't have had the help they needed to open the dress shop. Ollie and Lowell were glad to be working inside. So were Gustaf and August.

All four of the men showed up at the mercantile on Monday morning to start the renovation. Anna and Gerda arrived at about the same time as their brothers. Mr. Braxton quickly took them to the section he had set aside for the new venture.

Anna looked at the area that had been roped off. It was such a small part of the store, but even empty as it was now, it was so much larger than their workroom at Gustaf and Olina's house.

"I thought that we could put up a wall going from the front between the windows all the way to the back of the building." Mr. Braxton made a sweeping gesture with his arm. "It would mean taking down one wall, so you would have access that far back."

Anna was amazed. She had assumed that the dress shop would only extend to the wall that separated the store from the storeroom behind it. If he was going to let them have that area, too, they would have plenty of room to work and ample space for storage.

"Are you sure you want us to have all that space?" Anna asked Johan. She didn't want any misunderstandings. If she was going to be a successful business-woman, she needed to start right now by taking care of every detail.

"Oh, yes." Johan nodded. "It will almost be as though you have your own separate store."

Gerda and Anna walked along the rope, looking at the empty space. Then they went into the storeroom to see how much more space was available to them. When they came back into the main part of the store, their brothers were making plans with Johan.

August looked toward the two young women. "I think we should ask Anna and Gerda exactly what they want."

"Of course," Johan agreed. "Gerda and Anna, how much of this space do you want for your salesroom and how much for the workroom?"

Gerda and Anna looked at each other. Anna wondered if they knew what they were getting themselves into. There were so many decisions to make.

"Why don't we get started on taking the wall to the storeroom down? That would give them some time to discuss what they want." August picked up a ham-mer and saw, then started toward the back wall. The other men followed him.

Anna was glad she had thought to bring a pencil and some paper. She and Gerda stood beside one of the empty counters and started discussing what they wanted, drawing it on the paper. It took about an hour, but they agreed about what was needed.

Anna walked toward the hardworking men with confidence, while Gerda went to the front of the store to look at the windows. The excitement of the day had reinforced Anna's determination to become a very successful shopkeeper.

She started to show her drawings to her brothers. August, Gustaf, and Johan noticed and joined them.

"We would like a wall that goes all the way from the front to the back of the building, with a door from the mercantile into the display area and a door from the storeroom of the mercantile into our storage area. The only entrances into the workroom will be from the salesroom and the storeroom."

After showing the men the drawings she and Gerda had made, Anna walked over to the place where the wall between the display area and working space should be. With a defining gesture, she marked the exact line where it would be placed. Gustaf took a piece of chalk from his pocket and drew a line on the floor. Turning, Anna marched through the hole the men had made in the wall.

"We don't need as much area for storage as you do, Mr. Braxton, so we want our other wall right here." Anna used her right hand to slice through the air in the exact spot.

Once again, Gustaf used the chalk to mark the place.

August watched Anna as she gave directions to the men. A different Anna had emerged today. An Anna who was strong, in command of the situation. Who even showed a slightly hard edge. He wasn't sure he liked that. No longer could he see the sparkle that usually lit her eyes. During the holidays, it had finally started coming back, but now it looked as if it had been entirely extinguished. She had been more and more like the old Anna he had fallen in love with so many years ago. Suddenly, that Anna had once again disappeared to be replaced by this stranger. This. . .businesswoman.

Even though a new century was fast approaching, August wasn't sure he agreed with the modern women he saw emerging all around him. He wanted women to be like his mother. A homemaker, wife, and mother whose main focus was her family. Not a shopkeeper who ran a successful business. If a woman needed to work, that was one thing, but couldn't she keep some of the more desirable qualities?

"Hey, brother, are you going to help us, or are you going to stand there and stare?" Gustaf interrupted his thought process.

August turned around and walked toward the remnants of the wall they were removing. Only a little more work, and they could start building the new walls.

On Tuesday, Gerda and Anna designed the workroom, while the men built the long wall that would divide their shop from the mercantile. They drew the plan for shelves and tables that would make their work easier. Of course, they would be able to bring most of the things they had been using at Gustaf and Olina's house. All except the built-in shelves. They had enough work to keep all four brothers busy for a couple of weeks, maybe longer.

"Anna." Mr. Braxton spoke only to her, as if he, too, recognized that she was in charge. "I have ordered a new sign for over the mercantile. Have you ever met Silas Johnson?" When Anna shook her head, he continued. "He's a painter who moved to town about six months ago. His fancy lettering made him an instant hit with the merchants. He's doing our sign. Do you want a separate sign from the mercantile?"

Gerda had been listening to the conversation. She turned to Anna. "That would be good, but we need to decide what to name our part of the store. Do you have any ideas?"

Anna thought for a minute. "What about the Dress Emporium?"

"Oh, I like that. Wouldn't it be wonderful if we could have the letters painted on the glass?" Gerda started doodling on the tablet they were using for their plans. "Maybe in an arc like this." She printed block letters on the paper to illustrate what she meant. "But with the same kind of fancy letters that the Braxtons are using for the mercantile."

Marja had been stocking shelves a little ways from where her husband was talking to their new tenants, so she had heard the conversation. "That would really give both stores an elegant look, wouldn't it?" She clapped her hands as she usually did when she was excited. "We'll have the painter do both at the same time."

It had taken three weeks for the Dress Emporium to be finished. While the men worked at the store, Gerda and Anna stayed in the workroom at Gustaf and Olina's house. There were too many orders from customers for them to take three weeks off. But every day they both went to check on the progress of their new space.

One day when Anna stepped into the mercantile, August met her. "I think you need some windows in the work area."

For a moment, Anna was lost in his intent gaze.

"They will give you much more light to work by."

"Yes. . .that's a good idea." She stepped back to give herself breathing space.

The next time Anna went to the store, she was amazed at the amount of light they had in the workroom. The men had put three windows on the outside wall. She was touched by August's thoughtfulness in making the suggestion.

As she returned to the Nilsson home, she started planning in her head where they should put the stove, the Singer sewing machine, the ironing table, and the cutting table. There was so much room. It was a real blessing.

The men finished their work on Thursday, so everyone planned to help Anna and Gerda move in on Friday. That way the first day of business would be Saturday, when many of the people from outlying farms came into town to shop.

"What are we going to display in the window?" Gerda came through the door carrying a basket with sewing notions in it. "We need something to catch people's attention."

Anna glanced at the dress form she was taking to the workroom. Then she looked at the big window in the front of the store. An idea began to form in her mind. Why not?

"I'll take care of the window." Anna turned toward Gerda. "You set up the rest of the salesroom. I have to go home for something." With that, Anna strode from the building and mounted her mare that was tied to the hitching post in front of the mercantile.

With determination, she rode toward home, her head buzzing with plans. Before long she returned to the store driving a wagon with a trunk in the back.

August came out of the store when she stopped the wagon. "Do you need help with that trunk?" He liked the way Anna looked. The cold breeze had put a lot of color in her cheeks. "I'll get it for you." After August hefted the trunk onto his broad shoulders, he started toward the door of the dress shop. "Where do you want it?"

Anna hurried to keep up with him. "In the workroom. Over in the empty corner. I'll take care of it from there."

August could tell that she was excited about something. He wondered what it was. He wished he had time just to look at her, but there was still a lot that needed his attention. How could he ever have let his jealousy keep him from trying to establish a romantic relationship with Anna? Now her whole attention was being poured into this store. Would there ever be room in her life for him? Had he waited too long?

Chapter 6

W hat are you doing?"

Gerda's loud entrance startled Anna. She looked up from the dress she was pressing to where Gerda stood in the doorway with her arms full of packages.

"Is that your. . . ?" Gerda looked troubled.

"Yes, it's my wedding dress." Anna returned the flatiron to the stove and picked up another one.

Gerda came into the room and dropped the packages on the table that sat in the middle of the room. "Why are you pressing your wedding dress?"

Anna remained intent on her task, pushing the heated iron carefully across the cloth that covered the delicate silk. Although most brides wore other colors, she had followed the example of the English Queen Victoria and chosen white.

"I won't ever wear this dress."

Gerda didn't pick up on Anna's meaning. "Because you didn't marry Olaf doesn't mean you won't ever get married. But what are you going to do with it?"

Anna placed the cooling flatiron back on the stove and exchanged it for one that was ready to be used, ignoring Gerda's first comment. "It will make a wonderful display. I'm going to put it on the dress form in the window. With the lace curtains you and Marja picked out, it should draw attention to the store."

After once again placing the flatiron on the stove, Anna carefully picked up the dress and carried it into the salesroom without wrinkling it. She gently laid it on the counter, then went to the window and pulled the form back a little.

Gerda followed. "What if someone wants to buy it?"

Anna stopped what she was doing and thought a moment. "Then I guess we'll sell it. . . That's what we're in business for, to make money." She gathered up the dress and started fitting it on the form. "What do you have in those packages you brought in?" Anna hoped to take Gerda's attention off the wedding dress, and it worked.

"I'll show you." Gerda went into the other room and returned with two of the packages.

She dropped them on the counter and started untying the string around one. When she pulled back the brown paper, handmade crocheted items spilled out.

"Olina thought we could sell these in the shop. She crochets when Olga takes a nap." Gerda picked up a pair of lacy gloves. "We can put these things on the counter or a shelf right now. Maybe we could bring in a highboy or some small tables to place around the room. Then we could display these and other accessories to go with the dresses women order from us."

Anna finished placing the form with the wedding dress in the center of the window. Then she came over to look at what Gerda had. "That's a good idea, and it'll help Olina, since she doesn't feel like working in the shop."

While Anna started arranging the items from the first two packages, Gerda retrieved the others from the workroom. When they had everything displayed to their satisfaction, both women turned around and surveyed the shop.

"This looks good." Anna stood with her arms crossed.

"Yes," Gerda agreed, "I think we're ready for business tomorrow."

"Not quite," Marja said from the doorway to the mercantile. "We have something for you."

When Gerda and Anna turned, they saw Johan carrying in a lovely screen decorated with a hand-painted still life made up of many soft colors of roses.

"What lovely flowers!" Gerda walked over to Johan and leaned over to examine them more closely.

Anna joined her. "I don't think I've ever seen a lovelier screen."

"When the women come for fittings, they can change clothes behind it." Marja smiled at them.

Anna straightened up and turned to Marja. "You don't mean this screen is for us?"

"Yes." Marja folded her hands in front of her waist.

Anna thought about the cost of such a screen. "We could pay you for it. We were planning on buying one later."

Marja shook her head. "No, it's our little gift for your new store."

"Where do you want it?" Johan asked.

Gerda and Anna looked at each other. "The workroom," they said in unison.

They followed Johan, and Anna showed him the corner where the screen should be placed. He unfolded the four panels and arranged it across the corner Anna indicated. It was over five feet tall, so it made a wonderful, private place, and the pretty flowers were a welcome addition to the room.

"Now"—Marja clapped her hands—"you're ready for business."

Several people brought tools to the blacksmith shop to be repaired. And most of them wanted theirs fixed before they returned to their farms late in the afternoon. So August was busy. He was glad. With all the time he had spent helping Anna and Gerda with the dress shop, he welcomed the income from the repairs. But while he was working on these things, his mind was half on his work and half on the new store on Main Street. He couldn't help wondering how potential shoppers were accepting the Dress Emporium.

August knew it looked good, even though he hadn't been back after helping Gerda and Anna move in the larger items. He wondered what changes they had made to turn it into the store they wanted it to be.

When August was finally finished with all the work, he went to clean up, even taking a bath and shaving. Usually, he waited to shave on Sunday morning before going to church. Maybe it wouldn't hurt his face too much to be shaved late in the afternoon and then the next morning, too.

As he walked down the sidewalk with his boots sounding a drumbeat on the wood, August was surprised to see what was in the window of the Dress Emporium. Usually he didn't pay that much attention to women's fashions, but he knew instinctively that it was a wedding dress. He stopped and admired the intricate lacy designs scattered over filmy material. He knew that the only thing that would have made the dress more beautiful would have been if Anna was wearing it. Wearing it and walking down the aisle of the church. Walking down the aisle of the church to meet him. His heart started beating the speed of the clacking wheels on the steam engine of a train that was pulling into town. He hoped he wasn't just torturing himself with these thoughts.

August pushed open the door to the Dress Emporium. "So who's getting married? I didn't hear about any weddings coming up."

Anna looked up from folding several pieces of fabric on the counter. "August, come in and shut the door. It's hard to keep the shop warm on a cold day like today."

Gerda didn't ignore his question. "No one we know is getting married soon."

August looked from his sister to Anna. "Then whose wedding dress is in the window?"

When Anna gasped, August wondered why. His strong gaze held her captive for a moment that stretched into an eon.

Finally, Gerda blurted, "It's Anna's."

When she did, something flickered in Anna's eyes. Something August didn't understand. Why was she selling her wedding dress? Anna tore her gaze from his and dropped hers to the items on the counter.

Gerda must have felt the uncomfortable silence, because she tried to fill it. "It's the dress we made for Anna to wear when she was going to marry Olaf." The statement ended almost in a whisper.

August turned to stare at the dress for a moment.

"I didn't know," he murmured, then glanced toward Anna. "I'm sorry I brought it up."

Anna turned to replace the folded fabric on the shelves behind the counter.

"It's okay. I knew that everyone would see it when I put it in the window."

August walked over to the counter and leaned across it toward Anna. "Why are you selling the dress?"

Anna didn't turn around. She stood with one hand on the bolt of fabric so long that August thought she wasn't going to answer his question.

"I'll never wear it."

August wasn't sure what Anna meant, but he didn't like the way it sounded. So final. Emotions roiled within him. Emotions he couldn't even name. Why hadn't Anna turned toward him to answer? Was he making her uncomfortable? That wasn't what he wanted to do.

He moved back from the counter and looked around him. "I really like what you've done with the store."

Anna turned around, and Gerda hurried over to hug him. "Thanks, August."

"Have you had many customers?" He was talking to Gerda, but he couldn't keep from glancing at Anna out of the corner of his eyes. For a moment their gazes met, then Anna turned and went into the workroom.

Gerda looked toward the doorway where Anna had disappeared. "Yes, a lot of people stopped in to see the store. We have several orders for dresses, and we even sold some of the gloves and scarves that Olina crocheted."

August laughed. "It sounds as if you had a good day. I came to take you and Anna to the hotel for dinner."

"I'll ask her."

While Gerda was in the workroom, August moved to the wedding dress and looked at it more closely. If his hands hadn't been so rough, he would have touched its softness. He should have realized that it was Anna's. Not many women in town were that tall. He still wanted to see Anna wearing the dress. It would set off her dark beauty.

When Gerda and Anna returned from the workroom, August couldn't catch a glimpse of the Anna of a few minutes before. She had once again turned into the modern businesswoman who had emerged the last three weeks.

On Monday, Gerda and Anna arrived at the shop at the same time. Immediately, they set to work on the orders they needed to finish right away. Before long, Marja breezed into the workroom.

"I have an idea." Her clap indicated that she was excited about it. "We need to plan a special opening celebration for the Dress Emporium."

Gerda looked up from the handwork she was doing. "But we're already open."

"Oh, the special opening doesn't have to be the first day of business." Marja nodded for emphasis. "We were open two weeks before we had our special opening. You can make sure that everything is all right with your store, and you have enough time to let people know to come."

Anna turned from the machine where she was sewing the seams of a blouse. "What do you do for this opening?"

Marja sat on a trunk that was near the cutting table. "When we had ours, we had posters printed and hung them around town. We also handed them out to every customer who came into the mercantile. We could do that for yours, too."

Gerda put the skirt she had finished hemming on a shelf and turned around. "But what do we have to do that day?"

Marja smiled. "You're open for business, but it would be nice to have some tea or coffee for your customers. We could even bake cookies to serve people. Something like that would keep people talking about the Dress Emporium."

Anna wanted to do whatever it took to make the store successful. It would be proof that she could take care of herself—that she didn't need a man to make her life complete.

The day of the special opening dawned bright and clear. Anna and Gerda arrived at the shop early to get everything ready.

"I wonder if anyone will even come?" Anna couldn't keep from doubting.

"Well, I'm here." A masculine voice boomed from the doorway of the mercantile. "I heard there were coffee and cookies for hungry men." August's laugh filled the room.

Anna laughed with him. "I'm not sure they're for men. . .unless you want to order a dress or buy some lacy gloves."

Gerda giggled and hugged her brother. Then she poured him a cup of coffee and gave him two large oatmeal raisin cookies.

"Is that all I get?" he teased, as he took a big bite of the spicy treat.

Anna tried to look stern. "We want to have enough for real customers."

August stopped chewing for a moment and took a swig of the beverage.

"I might be a customer. Have you thought of making clothing for men?"

The question shocked Anna, and she could tell from the look on Gerda's face that she was also surprised.

"Why don't you buy your clothing from the mercantile?" Anna blurted.

August's mouth was full of a bite of cookie, so he chewed it up before he answered. "I could, but they don't often have anything that really fits me."

Anna knew why. A big man with a barrel chest and muscled arms, he couldn't wear regular-sized clothing. Then a picture of herself trying to take his measurements dropped into her mind. Heat climbed her neck and cheeks. She was sure that everyone in the room could see them glow.

"That's why I ask *Moder* to make my shirts. I can usually find trousers and overalls that fit. It's the shirts that are a problem." August set his empty cup down.

His Brother's Castoff

"*Mor* won't let me pay her, so I thought maybe the two of you could help me. I'm a grown man. I shouldn't be taking advantage of my mother's generosity."

"Could you bring us one of the shirts *Mor* made you so we can use it for a pattern?" Gerda probably didn't know that she was rescuing Anna from her thoughts.

"I'll bring one the next time I come."

Anna looked toward the stacks of material they had on the shelves behind the counter. "Would you like to pick out the fabric you want us to use? We have several pieces that would work for a man's shirt."

The rest of the opening went well. A steady stream of people came into the shop all day. Some only wanted to look at the new store, but many of them became customers. At the end of the day, Anna and Gerda agreed that the opening had been successful.

Several months went by, and winter melted into spring. The Dress Emporium was thriving so much that Gerda and Anna could barely keep up with the orders. One day Marja entered their workroom full of excitement. "I have another idea," she said when she was barely into the store.

Gerda and Anna put down the items they were working on and went out into the shop to give her their full attention.

"So tell us." Anna leaned on the empty counter.

Marja wandered around the shop fingering various items as she talked. "I'm tired of living above the store. Even though we expanded the apartment when we bought the building next door, it's still above a store." She picked up a pair of gloves and started trying them on. "The mercantile has been successful for several years. I've convinced Johan that we should build a house to live in." She pulled the gloves off and laid them back on the small round table. Then she turned toward Anna and Gerda. "We won't want the apartment to sit empty. Johan suggested that we offer it to the two of you. Would you like to live here over your shop?"

Anna looked at Gerda. For a moment, they were both speechless. Living over the store would have advantages. They would be close. If they wanted to go home for a few minutes, they could. It wouldn't take them long to get home after work either. Ideas buzzed through Anna's head. It would add to her independence. After all, she was in her midtwenties, not a child anymore.

Gerda looked hopeful. . .then doubtful. "I'm not sure *Mor* and *Far* would let me live in town."

Suddenly, Anna doubted whether her parents would agree either. But it was something she had to try. "We won't know until we ask them, will we?"

Marja looked from Gerda to Anna. "The question is, if your parents agree, would you want to live there?"

"Yes," Gerda and Anna said at the same time, and they grabbed each other and hugged.

"It would be wonderful," Anna gushed, sounding more like a child than a businesswoman.

August was tired when he finished shoeing two teams of horses. He would have liked to go back to the boardinghouse and maybe read a book after eating, but Gerda had been insistent that he go to their parents' home for dinner. When he had bathed and put on clean clothes, he did feel better. After mounting his big stallion, he set out in the cold evening air.

Mother had outdone herself with the meal, and August ate more than he usually did. That was saying a lot, because he never pushed back from the table very soon. All through the jovial meal, he wondered why Gerda had insisted that they all come home, but she didn't mention anything special. After everyone was through eating, she asked Gustaf and August to help her clean up the dishes while Olina and Olga entertained their parents. When they finished putting everything away, Gerda urged them into the parlor.

"Okay, Gerda." Bennel Nilsson looked at his daughter. "What is the big secret? We're all anxious to hear it."

Gerda glanced around the room while Gustaf scooped up his tiny daughter and sat on the velvet sofa beside his wife. "I wanted all of you here so we could make a good decision."

"About what?" August wanted her to hurry and get it over with so he could return to town.

"Well. . ." Gerda rubbed her hands down the sides of her skirt as if her palms were sweating. "Marja made an offer to Anna and me today. She and Johan are going to build a house to live in." She glanced around the quiet room, as if trying to see if there was a reaction to what she said. "They don't want the apartment above the store to be empty when they move, so she asked if Anna and I would like to live there."

The silence was deafening before pandemonium broke out with everyone speaking.

Bennel held up his hand. "Let's not all talk at once." They all quieted down. "Let's look at this rationally."

"There are some good reasons to do it." Gerda sounded breathless but eager.

"And there are equally as many reasons not to do it," her father added. "I'm not sure I would be comfortable with you living in town. It could be dangerous."

August had been watching Gerda's hopeful face. When Father said that, her hopes seemed to melt away.

"It might be a good idea." August winked at his sister. "And since I live in town, I could keep an eye on Gerda and Anna." Especially Anna. It would be good to have her so close. He could go by the store or the apartment to check on his sister, and Anna would be there, too. The thought made his heart beat a little faster. Maybe with Anna close by, he could break through the facade she had built around herself and reach the woman he knew was deep inside. Maybe Anna would wear that wedding dress for him. He was tempted to buy it the next time he went to the store.

Chapter 7

Anna had a headache. This discussion was making her tired and cranky. All she wanted was for it to be over so she could go to bed. Why had she thought it would be a good idea to wait until after dinner to ask her parents about moving to town when the Braxtons finished building their new house? If she had asked earlier, maybe the decision would be made by now. She rubbed her temples in a circular motion, trying to relieve the stress and pain.

"Anna, dear, are you all right?" Margreta Jenson leaned toward her daughter.

Anna looked up and nodded. She didn't want them to stop talking before a decision was made. The right decision, that she and Gerda could move into the apartment.

Ollie had always been closer to Anna than Lowell, even though Lowell was only one year older and Ollie one year younger than she was. His sympathetic perusal soothed her.

"I've listened to all the concerns you've brought up, *Fader*." This was the first addition Ollie made to the conversation. "I agree that we need to be careful of our Anna."

Soren Jenson gave a tight smile and nodded. He seemed to be glad that his son agreed with him.

"But," Ollie continued, "Anna is a grown woman. I feel that she and Gerda would be as safe in town as they are riding alone from the farms to the store each day. Maybe even safer. Besides, one or the other of us usually goes into town at least every other day. Sometimes more often. We could always check on them."

Soren tented his fingers and leaned his chin against them. Sitting with his eyes closed, he often used this position when he was thinking.

"You know that August Nilsson lives in town." Finally, Lowell sounded as if he were on Anna's side in this. "He'll go by to see Gerda when he can, and the Braxtons have treated the girls almost as if they were family. This might be a good thing for Anna. I, for one, am glad to see her so interested in something after all she's been through."

Lowell looked at Anna as if he were sorry to bring it up and cause her further pain. But she knew what he was doing, and she appreciated it.

Soren leaned forward with his forearms on his legs, hands dangling between his knees. "Okay, boys. You've convinced me."

Anna smiled.

"But," he continued as he sat up and looked at her with a stern expression, "at the first sign of trouble, Anna's coming home. That's my final word on it."

The next morning, Anna strode into the Dress Emporium late. After her bout with the headache, she had overslept. At least this morning, she felt good. As she walked into the workroom, she took off her coat, riding hat, and gloves.

Gerda sat in a straight chair by a window as she sewed buttons on a shirt for August. Anna was glad he had picked out that particular plaid. A thin line of bright yellow set off the interwoven blues and grays—hues that complimented his coloring.

Gerda let the shirt drop into her lap as she looked at Anna. "Well, how did it go at your house last night?" When Anna grimaced, Gerda continued, "Was it that bad?"

After placing her gloves in the pocket, Anna hung her coat and hat on a large hook on the back wall. "It went on a long time. I don't think *Far* would have agreed if it hadn't been for Lowell and Ollie."

Gerda smiled. "I know what you mean. Our discussion wasn't that long, but I'm thankful that August said he would check on me often. I think that made the difference."

Anna turned and laughed. "Your parents said it was okay, too?"

Gerda put the shirt on a table and came to give Anna a hug. "Yes. Can you believe it? It's really going to happen."

"Have you told Johan and Marja yet?"

"No, I was waiting to see if everything went okay at your house. My parents wouldn't let me live here alone."

When Gerda and Anna went to talk to Marja, they found her at the back counter poring over several books. She looked up as they approached. "You both look happy. Do you have good news for me?"

After the young women finished explaining that they were going to move into the apartment, Marja told them to come behind the counter with her. She wanted them to see the books of house plans that she was studying. Johan had ordered three from different architectural firms so Marja could pick out the house she wanted.

"How long will it take for the plans to get here?" Anna wanted to know.

"Oh, we already have them." Marja smiled. "We've even ordered the lumber and supplies required by the plans. They are coming on a railcar today. I'm looking at the books again because they're interesting."

Gerda opened the one from Palliser & Palliser Company in Connecticut. Anna picked up the *Specimen Book* from Bicknells & Company in New York.

"Which house plan did you choose?" Anna glanced from the book she held to Marja.

Marja picked up *American Domestic Architecture* from John Calvin Stevens and Albert Winslow Cobb in New York. "I liked the houses in this one best." After she flipped through the pages, she placed the open book on the counter so all three of them could look at it. "I chose this one."

Spread out before them was a house like no other in Litchfield. It had two stories and an attic with a triple window in the gable that faced the front. Windows at ground level indicated a basement, too.

"They have plans for a house with a basement or without. I think we'll do the one without. It won't take as long to build. I'm anxious to have the house finished."

"It's a big house for only two people." The minute the words left her mouth, Anna was sorry for what she said. She put the fingers of her right hand over her mouth as if to catch the words, but it was too late. She knew that although they had wanted children, Johan and Marja had never had any.

"That's all right, Anna." Marja gave her a quick hug. "We have a large family. When they come to visit, we don't have room for many of them. Most of them have to stay at the hotel. With this house, we can invite all of them for Christmas, and they can stay with us. That's what we are planning to do this year."

Anna was grateful for the way Marja thought about everyone else's feelings. It helped her, but she decided to be more careful with her words in the future.

"Actually, I'm through with these books right now." Marja closed them one at a time and stacked them on top of each other. "If you girls would like to take them to look at, you can."

The idea brought a pang to Anna's heart. She hadn't been able to completely get rid of the desire to have a home and a family to go with it. Looking at house plans would be too much, but Gerda didn't share her aversion.

"Thank you, Marja," she said, as she gathered them into her arms. "We'll return them when we've looked at them all."

"I have an idea." Marja seemed always to be full of new ideas. "Why don't I take you up to the apartment? I don't think you've been there since we enlarged it."

When they arrived at the top of the stairs that went up the outside of the building, Marja pulled a skeleton key from her pocket. After swinging the door open, she gestured for Gerda and Anna to go in before her.

Anna had always loved the look of the parlor. Marja had a good eye for decorating. The furniture contained decorative pillows and doilies, as well as many knickknacks. Pleasing prints of floral paintings adorned the walls, along with family portraits.

Anna and Gerda had been in the dining room and kitchen of the apartment but never in the bedroom. They were amazed to find that there were two separate bedrooms. When they moved in, they would have plenty of privacy. Anna was even more glad that they would be living there soon.

⌒⌇

The large Scandinavian community at Litchfield was a close one. They helped each other whenever needed. Everyone at the church knew Johan and Marja. When Johan announced that they were going to build a house, the men started planning how they could help. Many of the families had built their own homes when they came to Minnesota. And there had been several times when there had been a community-wide barn raising when a neighbor needed a place for his animals.

Johan hired a carpenter to oversee the work, and most of the men in the church planned to give one week to help with the building. This was a major social event, too. The women would cook plenty of food for everyone.

On Monday, August didn't open the blacksmith shop. He had worked especially hard to finish all the projects on Saturday. He planned to help Johan all week if there were no emergencies that needed his attention. Everyone was going to be there the first day they started the house, but the rest of the men would divide into two work teams that would alternate days. That way they could keep up with what needed to be done at home, too.

When August arrived at the lot where the house was going to be built, only a few others were there. They had much farther to come than those who lived in town.

"August, my friend," Johan hailed from the vacant lot next door, where he stood beside stacks and stacks of lumber and other building supplies. "Welcome." Johan strode over to where August stood. "I'm thankful for your help with our project." He clapped August on the back.

August laughed. "You never know when you can return the favor for me."

"I would like that."

I would, too. August looked forward to building a house for himself and his family, when God saw fit to give him a wife. Although he had helped with other houses and barns, he had never worked on anything as elaborate as what Johan had planned. There was even a stack of red bricks with boards holding them up out of the snow. August had never used house plans drawn by an architect before.

It didn't take long for the area to fill with men carrying tools. The carpenter divided them into teams and assigned them specific tasks. August was glad that he and Gustaf were on the same team. They always worked well together. At least since they were adults, they had. Soon the sound of saws and hammers filled the air, interspersed with conversations that often had to be shouted over the other sounds. The crisp air had a festive feeling, even though they were working hard.

August's stomach had given a rumble loud enough for his teammates to hear when the first wagon containing women pulled into the vacant lot on the opposite side from the materials. The aromas of various foods wafted on the slight breeze, enticing the men's attention.

When August walked over to the first wagon, another conveyance joined it. He was glad to see Gerda and Anna in the second vehicle.

"Do you ladies need help setting up?" He couldn't take his eyes off Anna.

Her cheeks were kissed into a becoming pink by the cool air, and strands of hair had worked their way out of her severe bun. He liked to see the thin cloud of dark hair that surrounded her face, giving it a soft frame.

Gerda stretched her leg over the wagon wheel and dropped to the ground. August immediately moved to the other side where Anna was gathering together a couple of bags that were at her feet. He reached up and placed his large hands on her waist. When he lifted her down, it felt as if she weighed no more than a feather.

Anna had been aware of August from the first moment she had seen him while they were driving up. She tried to ignore the feelings that stirred inside her. When his hands touched her waist, the connection was powerful. She was thankful that he let go of her as soon as her feet reached the ground. She looked up to thank him and found him standing much too close for comfort. She took a step backward and moved around him so she could start unloading the food.

"Let me set up some tables first." August marched across to the supplies and found a couple of sawhorses that weren't being used. He brought them back, set them a few feet apart, and started laying lumber on them.

Gustaf came up carrying two more sawhorses. "That table won't be large enough, if I know our women. Let's use these, too."

Anna watched the brothers as they worked together. She was glad that they were her friends. They were two godly men who lived their faith. It was too bad that she and Gustaf weren't meant to be together. Actually, she wasn't meant to be married to any man. Or so it seemed. She couldn't understand why God had created her with this flaw, whatever it was, that kept a man from loving her enough. Maybe He wanted her to love Him more. . .and be an independent businesswoman. Anna shook her head and went to join the other women as they spread sheets on the wood and started placing heaping bowls and platters of hot food on the makeshift tables.

Marja came to where Gerda and Anna worked. "I wanted to talk to the two of you."

Anna turned toward her, but Gerda continued arranging food while she listened.

"I have ordered some furniture for the parlor in the new house. If you would like, I can leave the parlor furniture in the apartment for you to use. Then all you would need to find would be bedroom furniture for each of you."

Margreta Jenson walked up while Marja was speaking. "Anna, you may take the furniture from your bedroom at the house. Your father and I talked about it last night. We wanted to help you that way. And we probably have some tables and lamps in the attic that you can use."

Gerda stopped what she was doing and turned toward them. "*Mor* and *Far* told me last night that I can have the furniture from my bedroom, too. They still have quite a few things that Mrs. Johnson left when she sold the farm to them. It's all stored in our attic. *Mor* said that we can take our pick of anything we need. Oh, Anna, God is working everything out so well."

By the end of the first week, all of the internal and external walls of the house were completed. August planned to give some time each day to help with the finishing. It was a good thing that Johan had hired a woodworker to do the banisters and kitchen cabinets. He had even brought a bricklayer from Minneapolis. August was going to learn as much as he could from each of these men. While he worked on the house, he began to envision a house he would someday build. Maybe he would borrow one of those books from Johan. Those detailed plans made a big difference in how fast they could build. With all the help, the Braxtons could probably move in two or three weeks. A month at the most.

When he finished working on Saturday, he stopped by the Dress Emporium to talk to Gerda. Anna was busy with a customer, but Gerda was in the workroom ironing a dress. He stood in the doorway watching Anna as she talked to a young woman and her brother. The brother had helped with building the house this week. They were fairly new to town, but he had been a hard worker.

"August, did you come to see me?" Gerda was finished with the dress.

"Yes." August watched her place the flatiron back on the stove. "I was wondering how soon after the Braxtons move to their house that you and Anna will want to move into the apartment."

Gerda glanced toward the showroom. "We've been talking about that. Both of us want to move as soon as we can. Tomorrow afternoon Anna is going to come to our house so we can look at the furniture that is stored in the attic. We'll pick out what we want to use."

"That sounds like a good idea. I suppose you want all your brothers to help you get your furniture to the apartment."

Gerda placed her hands against her waist and tried to frown at him. "Of course we do. What are brothers for?"

After they shared a laugh, August started back through the store. He glanced toward Anna and the people she was waiting on. He couldn't help noticing how the man was trying to flirt with Anna. A sword pierced his heart. A remnant of the jealousy he thought he had conquered spilled inside him, spreading its venom. He clenched his fists and strode out the front door to keep from saying or doing anything that would upset Anna. When he reached the sidewalk, he turned and glanced through the window. Anna was laughing with the man about something. The sword thrust deeper inside him.

Chapter 8

August spent every free hour he had working on the house with Johan and the others. As he pounded nails or wielded a paintbrush, he was fighting to get the jealousy under control again. He only went back to the Dress Emporium one time after seeing the farmer flirt with Anna. Anytime August saw Anna, the picture of her laughing up at the man flew into his mind. When he was back at the boardinghouse in the evening, that thought led to others. Memories of all the times Gustaf had been with Anna, when August wished he had been the one with her.

The more August tried to fight the feelings of jealousy, the harder the thoughts assaulted his mind. He knew what the apostle Paul was talking about when he taught about the fiery darts of Satan. August felt sure that these memories were part of Satan's attack on him. He longed for the time when he had been able to control his thoughts.

So as he worked, he tried to stay away from as many of the other men as he could. He was afraid to participate in the conversations. Afraid some of this poison would spill out and be revealed to others. And he didn't want anyone else to know his shame.

"August," Gustaf called to him when it was about quitting time. "How would you like to come over for dinner tonight? I think Gerda and Anna will be there to cook so Olina will have a rest."

August finally turned toward his brother, but he kept his gaze on the ground. "Actually, I am so tired that all I want is a hot bath and to go to bed." When he looked up at Gustaf's face, he could tell that Gustaf didn't think he meant what he said, but he turned back to do the last few strokes of painting he was working on.

The workers would be finished with the Braxtons' house that week. Marja and Johan would move in next week, then Gerda and Anna would be ready to take possession of the apartment.

Anna woke early and dressed in old clothes. Moving day had finally arrived. After eating the breakfast her mother prepared while Anna was dressing, she hurried back upstairs to pack the rest of her things. While she latched her last carpetbag, she heard the wagon pull around to the front of the house. Ollie and Lowell were such good brothers. They insisted that they could get all of her bedroom furniture on the wagon. If they couldn't fit the other things on there with it, Ollie told her he would hitch up the buggy, and she could take the extra items in that.

Anna was halfway down the stairs carrying two bags when Ollie came through the door. Lowell was right behind him.

"Good morning, sleepyhead." Ollie reached to take the bags from her hands.

"You are such a tease." Anna held tight to the handles. "I can get these. You two can start with the big pieces."

In less than an hour, everything was loaded and they were headed to town. Anna would probably be there before Lowell and Ollie. Their wagon was piled high with heavy items. All she had in the buggy were her carpetbags and a trunk.

When they got out on the road, Anna pulled around the wagon. "I'll see you in town, slowpokes." Anna waved at her brothers as she passed.

She was not surprised to see that Gerda, August, and Gustaf were already at the apartment. They had two loads of furniture to bring from the Nilsson farm. Anna felt that God was smiling on her the way He provided all their needs for furnishings. Neither she nor Gerda would have to buy anything right away. Of course, they might want to add some decorating touches of their own to all the donated items.

August was coming out the door of the apartment when Anna started up the stairs. She smiled up at him, but he brushed past her as if he was in a real hurry. What was wrong with him? Maybe he was grouchy because he had to get up so early this morning.

"Anna." Gerda stood in the doorway and called to her. "Come see how wonderful everything looks." She swept her arm toward the opening to usher Anna inside.

Anna took a deep breath. Home. This was her home. Hers and Gerda's.

About the time everything had been unloaded and placed where the young women wanted them, Margreta Jenson and Ingrid Nilsson arrived with baskets of food. They bustled around the kitchen setting the table for their six hungry children and themselves.

"*Moder*"—Anna grabbed her and hugged her—"and Mrs. Nilsson, how thoughtful you are. This food smells heavenly."

"I couldn't agree with you more." Gustaf followed his nose to the kitchen.

Soon they were all seated at the large dining room table.

"Gerda," Anna looked around the room, "I thought the table was too large for the two of us when you showed it to me in the attic. But there's plenty of room for it and all the chairs. You've even brought the china cabinet. It's elegant, and we have room for company."

His Brother's Castoff

While they shared conversation as well as food, Anna noticed once again that August seemed quieter than usual. Perhaps something was wrong with him. She hoped that he wasn't sick or something. He had been working hard to help the Braxtons finish building their house. Maybe he was exhausted. She wondered if any of his family had noticed the change in him.

August hoped no one noticed that he was trying to keep out of Anna's way. He tried to act natural. Maybe it was working.

When they finished eating, he returned to the smithy and stirred up the coals in the forge. It didn't take long to get the answer to his unasked question.

About an hour and a half after August left, Gustaf walked through the open door. The sun reflecting off the remnants of the last snowfall cast his shadow across the room. August turned from what he was doing.

"Are you going to tell me what's bothering you?" Gustaf came right to the point.

August looked at the determination on Gustaf's face and decided not to try to lie to him.

"What makes you think something is bothering me?"

"I know you well enough to know when something is bothering you. You were pretty sullen the last week or two that we were building the house. Gerda tells me that you haven't been to the store to check on her for quite a while, and didn't you promise *Far* that you would?"

August looked down and scuffed the dirt floor with the toe of his boot. "She hadn't moved to town yet."

"But you used to go see her several times a week." Gustaf sounded stern now. "And I saw how you've been avoiding Anna. Has something happened to cause you to be rude to her?"

August snorted. He wasn't going to get out of this discussion. He wished that he could disappear into the ground. He didn't want to bare his soul to Gustaf, especially since he had been jealous of him for so long. He looked toward the ceiling. Gud, *now would be a good time to intervene.* When nothing happened, he looked at his brother, noticing for the first time that his eyes were filled with compassion. Gustaf really cared.

August turned back to the forge and closed the damper. This could take a long time, and he didn't need a roaring fire getting out of control.

"I'm not sure I know how to tell you what's wrong."

"August, I'm your brother. I love you, and anything you tell me will remain between the two of us." Gustaf leaned against the table that ran along the wall of the smithy. It was his favorite place when he came in to talk to August.

August joined him there. At least it would be easier to explain if they weren't face-to-face. "I'm fighting some fierce spiritual battles."

After a long pause, Gustaf said, "I know that you don't drink, or gamble, or chase women. So tell me what the battle is about."

"Jealousy." The word hung in the air between them for a long time.

When August didn't say anything else, Gustaf finally asked, "What kind of jealousy?"

August stood up and stalked across the smithy. He stood with his back to his brother, watching the flames grow smaller and smaller as he recited the ugly truth in a monotone.

"I've been jealous of you as long as I can remember. You were the perfect son. And I wasn't." August didn't want to see the expression on Gustaf's face at this pronouncement. "When we came to America, I fell for Anna the first time I saw her. But I was the quiet son. The shy one. Before I could work up my courage to speak to her, there you were charming her. The jealousy increased every time I saw you together."

Finally August couldn't stand it any longer. He turned around to look at Gustaf. His head was bowed, and he looked as if he had been hit in the stomach with a poleax. August hated to rock the boat or upset anyone. This had been harder than he thought it would be. He knew as he looked at the way Gustaf's shoulders drooped that he loved his brother even though he was jealous of him.

Gustaf raised his head. "When I told Anna that I couldn't see her anymore, why didn't you approach her after that?"

August didn't want to speak this out loud, but he had come this far. He might as well reveal all the ugliness. "I didn't want your castoff."

Gustaf's stricken eyes met his. "How could we have gone so wrong?"

Once more August was disgusted. Disgusted at himself for his weakness. "*We* haven't gone wrong. *I* have."

Gustaf came toward August and put his arm over his shoulders. "I think we need to go down to the church. If we sit and talk there, maybe God will give us some special insight."

August nodded. He followed Gustaf out into the cold, sunny day. After closing the big double doors, he dropped a board across them. Gustaf waited for him, and they walked the mile to the church in silence.

Once inside the cool building, the brothers sat on the front pew looking at the cross hung on the wall behind the pulpit. Silence stretched between them, but it wasn't uncomfortable. Each man listened for the voice of God to speak into his heart.

Gustaf got up and stepped onto the platform. On a shelf behind the pulpit, he found the extra Bible the pastor kept there. Picking it up, he returned to sit beside his brother. After turning through several books, he stopped and started reading.

"Here's a verse for you." Gustaf looked up at August before he continued reading. " 'Set me as a seal upon thine heart, as a seal upon thine arm: for love is strong as death; jealousy is cruel as the grave: the coals thereof are coals of fire, which hath a most vehement flame.' I found this in the Song of Solomon the other night."

August looked at him. "I can honestly say that's not a book that I've ever read."

"It says that love is strong as death and jealousy as cruel as the grave. You work with hot coals. You know what they can do when they are allowed to burn hotter and brighter."

August nodded. In the past, he had often studied God's Word. Many times he had been refreshed with a new revelation when he read a familiar passage. But lately he hadn't spent much time in Bible study.

"God said that jealousy can burn like a blazing fire. Jealousy can consume you and destroy you the way fire destroys. Jealousy can burn up all that is good inside you."

August thought about that for a minute. "I know that's true. It has been like a fire in my belly, devouring the goodness in me."

"Not all the goodness." Gustaf turned several more pages in the Bible. "Proverbs 27:4 says, 'Wrath is cruel, and anger is outrageous; but who is able to stand before envy?' 'Envy' here is just another word for jealousy."

"I haven't been standing very strong before it." August put his elbows on his knees and dropped his head into his hands. "I've tried, and things get better. Sometimes the good times last a long time. Then once again I will be overcome with the jealousy."

Gustaf started murmuring words that were too soft for August to hear, but he knew that his brother was praying. When Gustaf finished, he sat as if he were listening again. After a few moments, he once again turned some of the pages.

" 'All the paths of the Lord are mercy and truth unto such as keep his covenant and his testimonies.' That's what Psalm 25:10 says. August, you need to get rid of that jealousy."

August raised his head. "Don't you think I would if I knew how?"

Gustaf patted him on the shoulder. "Maybe part of the problem is that you have been trying to fight it alone. God wants us to share our burdens with those who love us. Besides, there's nothing for you to be jealous of from me. I love you, and I always have. You know that Anna wasn't the person God intended for me to marry. I'm sorry I monopolized her and stood in your way. Can you forgive me?"

August was amazed. Gustaf hadn't done anything wrong. He was an honorable man, both with Anna and with his brothers, and he was apologizing. August looked deep into his own heart. How could he not forgive his brother? "I want to, and I'll try."

"That's all I ask. And I don't want jealousy to destroy the man God intends you to be."

When August got back to the boardinghouse that evening, he did something that he hadn't done for quite awhile. He read his Bible. He reread the verses that Gustaf shared with him, but he read other passages, too. When he finished, he bowed his head and prayed. For the first time in a long time, he wasn't burdened down with jealousy.

The next morning, he went by the apartment to see if Gerda and Anna would accompany him to church. When he first saw Anna, his heart nearly flipped over. She was so beautiful.

"Of course we'll go to church with you." Gerda took his arm. "We were dreading walking all that way by ourselves."

August hit his forehead with his palm. "Why didn't I think to bring a buggy?"

"It's okay," Anna said as she picked up her reticule. "I don't mind the walk. We sit too much when we work."

During the service, August had a hard time keeping his mind on the sermon. Anna was sitting on the other side of Gerda. He was aware of every tiny move she made. She rearranged her skirt several times. Once she hid a cough behind a handkerchief she pulled from her handbag. He had been so intent on Anna that the service was over before he realized it.

August took Gerda's arm when she started to get up. "Would you two beautiful ladies let me take you to lunch at the hotel? We could celebrate your move."

During the meal, August tried not to be too obvious about watching Anna. She was the epitome of a gracious, independent woman. But he wished for so much more. At least she hadn't mentioned the new farmer he had seen at the Dress Emporium. There had been no need for August to be jealous of him. It was another lie of Satan that tormented him far too long.

August planned to take a nap after the large meal, but when he returned to his room, he sat in the chair and stared out the window. The feelings he had for Anna were the kind a man should have for the woman he planned to marry. What could he do about that?

He prayed and asked the Lord if Anna was the woman he should marry. The peace that filled his heart seemed to be God's blessing on the match. But August knew that Anna wasn't ready for marriage yet. She was too intent on her new life.

"How can I help her love me?" August knew there was no one there to answer him, so he got up and paced across the room and back. "I'll just have to pray for her and find ways to show her my love." So he started making plans.

Chapter 9

Anna turned the skirt she was working on so she could sew the other side seam. When she did, she twisted her hips a little to make them more comfortable. She had been sitting at the sewing machine in one position for too long.

"Have you noticed how often August has been coming by the shop?" Anna didn't take her gaze from her work when Gerda spoke to her. The young women often talked while working and were not distracted from their respective tasks.

"He did promise your father that he would check on us often. That's the main reason you were allowed to move into the apartment with me."

Anna came to the end of the seam and stopped pedaling. She cut the thread and tied the two pieces in a knot close to the fabric to keep the seam from pulling apart. She pivoted on her seat, enjoying the cushioning.

Gerda glanced up from the lace insertion she was sewing into a sleeve. "But did he promise to make us a padded sewing chair, too?"

"No. August was being kind." Anna turned back to the sewing machine and started on another seam.

"Yes, he was." Gerda shook the sleeve out before starting to baste it to the rest of the blouse. "Your brothers Lowell and Ollie promised to check on us, too, but they don't come every day. . .and they don't bring us gifts all the time, either."

"August doesn't bring gifts all the time."

"The new display tables he made. . .a book of poetry for the apartment. . . flowers for the showroom. . .a box of Irish linen handkerchiefs with embroidered flowers and dainty lace edging. Actually, he only brought the handkerchiefs to you. Remember, I wasn't here, and he knew I would be spending the day with Olina. Those were only for you."

Anna stood up and held the skirt by the waist so she could shake out any wrinkles. She could feel the heat warming her face. Probably another one of her blushes. Why did she do that? People with fair skin were supposed to be the ones to blush, not her.

"I tried to tell him that he shouldn't give them to me, but he was insistent. . . and they were so pretty. . ."

Gerda laughed.

Anna started folding the skirt. "Well, the padded chair he brought to use with the sewing machine was for both of us."

"August knew that you use the machine much more than I do. I think he made it with you in mind."

Anna laid the folded skirt on the shelf to wait for Gerda to sew the hem by hand. It was time for her to take a break, and she needed to get away from this conversation. She walked into the showroom.

No one had come into the shop all day. She wondered if the Braxtons' store had been busy. Sometimes Wednesdays were slow days for both the mercantile and the Dress Emporium. She decided to go ask Marja about their customers, so she hurried toward the door to the mercantile. She glanced down for a moment and barreled into a rock-hard wall. A warm wall covered with plaid. Plaid with arms that gathered her against it.

At the sound of a deep chuckle, Anna looked up into the eyes of the person she had been talking about for the last half hour. Did their words cause him to arrive? She felt breathless and comfortable all at the same time.

August couldn't believe his good fortune when Anna practically ran into his arms. He knew she was in a hurry to get somewhere and hadn't noticed him. But the feeling of her against his chest was wonderful. He wanted her to stay there forever. *Please, Lord.*

Anna looked up at him. After stepping back, she murmured, "Sorry," and the color in her cheeks intensified.

"That's all right." August chuckled. "I enjoyed it."

Anna hurried around him and headed toward Marja Braxton. What was she running from—him or her own emotions? He hoped it was her emotions. Maybe his prayers and showering her with love were making a difference.

He entered the Dress Emporium. When Gerda wasn't in the showroom, he continued on to the workroom.

"How's my favorite sister?"

Gerda was ironing something soft and white. "I'm your only sister." She placed the flatiron in its holder on the stove and turned around. "What brings you to the shop today? Not more presents?"

August shook his head slightly and looked out the window. He hoped his sister didn't notice how embarrassed he was. He hadn't wanted her to realize what he was doing. Anna was supposed to be the one to notice. "Gustaf came by the smithy this morning. *Mor* is having one of the hired hands bring dinner to their house tonight so Olina won't have to cook. She said that she'd fix enough for me, too." He moved closer to the window so he could look the other way down the street.

"Anna isn't here right now."

"What?"

"Anna isn't here right now."

When August turned to look at her, she was grinning at him. "Why did you say that?"

"That's why you come so often, isn't it? To see Anna."

His sister was much too perceptive, but he wasn't going to tell her that.

Gustaf had told August to come right in when he arrived, so August opened the door and walked in. Taking a deep whiff of the tantalizing aroma of his mother's cooking, he followed his nose to the kitchen. Gustaf had Olga in the high chair that August had built for her. She was banging a spoon on the table while her father set the plates around the edge.

"Do you need some help?" August lifted Olga from her perch.

"Unka!" she screamed before throwing her arms around his neck and squeezing. "High."

August swung her up and down while Gustaf finished getting the food on the table. "You're pretty good at that."

Gustaf looked up from what he was doing. "Kitchen work is awkward for me, but it's one way I can help Olina." He folded his arms across his chest. "She's miserable today."

"Is she coming down for supper?"

"I don't know. I'll go ask."

While Gustaf was upstairs, August started feeding his hungry niece.

After the meal was over, Gustaf started back up the stairs. Olina hadn't wanted to eat when everyone else did. She told him to see if she was hungry when they finished.

August took Olga to the parlor.

"Horsey, Unka."

He had been heading for the rocking chair, but he chose the settee instead. He sat down and crossed his legs. After lowering Olga to sit on his top foot, he kept a tight hold on her hands and started moving his foot up and down.

"Ride a little horsey, up and down."

The trouble with starting this game was that Olga never wanted to quit. It was one of her favorite things to do. After what seemed like a thousand times of kicking his leg up and down giving Olga a ride on his foot, August was glad that his brother finally returned. Gustaf rubbed his hand over his eyes as he came into the room.

"Does Olina want her supper now?" August pulled Olga up into his lap. His leg was tired, so he was glad for this reprieve.

"No." Gustaf reached down and took his daughter. He hugged her tight.

"She has gone into labor. I feel so helpless, watching her hurt."

August stood. "I'll take Olga to town. I'm sure Anna would be glad to spend time with her. I can bring Gerda back. Then I'll go to the farm to get *Moder*."

Anna had taken her hair down to prepare for bed. She brushed it out before making a long braid. She liked to have it out of her way when she changed from her everyday clothes to her nightdress. When she finished brushing, a loud knock sounded on the door to the apartment. Who could that be? Maybe Gerda would see.

"Anna," Gerda called through the wall. "Can you answer the door? I'm not dressed."

The knock sounded again, more insistent this time. It must be important. Anna pushed her hair behind her back and hurried across the parlor.

"Who is it?" she called through the door.

"August."

What could he want at this time of night? Then Anna heard a tiny voice. She pulled the door wide to allow August to enter with his burden. The night was cool, so Olga was bundled into a quilt. Anna took her and started unwrapping the large cover.

"Why are you and Olga on our doorstep?" Anna glanced to where August had stood, but he had disappeared out the door.

Olga began whimpering again. Anna pulled her close and hummed as she patted her back. This little girl should be asleep by now.

Gerda came into the parlor. "What are you doing with Olga?"

"I don't know." Anna dropped a kiss on the little girl's droopy head.

Gerda went to the door. When she opened it, August arrived at the top of the stairs with his arms full.

"Olina is going to have the baby soon. I brought Olga to you, Anna." He placed a large cloth bag on the settee. "Here are all the things she'll need tonight. Do you mind taking care of her?"

Anna looked at August's concerned expression. "Of course not. I love Olga."

"Are you going to take me to Olina?" Gerda was already heading toward her bedroom. "That's wonderful." She turned back and hugged her brother before she left the room. "I'll throw together a few things in case I have to stay with her awhile."

When August and Gerda left, Anna sat in the rocking chair until Olga slept soundly. She laid Olga on the carpet in her bedroom while she pushed her bed against the wall. Then she put the little angel on the bed close to the wall. After changing her own clothes, she climbed in beside her and started praying for Olina.

Anna decided not to open the shop the next morning. She wanted to wait until she heard from Gerda. After she and Olga had breakfast together, she spent the morning playing with the little girl. Every time she picked Olga up, her heart longed for a child of her own.

Anna knew that her whole being reacted whenever August was around, and it had seemed that he might be interested in her, but she couldn't trust those feelings. Her relationship with Gustaf had seemed strong, but it wasn't enough for him to love her. Then, when she was going to marry Olaf, she loved him, but he didn't love her enough to heed her warnings. No, feelings weren't enough to overcome whatever it was that was wrong with her that kept a man from loving her enough.

After lunch, Anna rocked Olga so she would take a nap. When she was asleep, instead of putting her down on the pallet, Anna held her and imagined that she was holding her own child. Tears streamed down her cheeks as she grieved for what she would never have.

Anna heard the key turn in the door before Gerda quietly stepped into the room. Anna was thankful that Gerda probably knew Olga would be napping. She turned her face away, trying to hide the tears. With one hand, she wiped her cheeks before she greeted Gerda.

"Has Olina had the baby?"

Gerda sank onto the settee. "No. She's having a long, hard labor. *Mor* told me to come help you with Olga."

She reached to take her niece from Anna's arms. After hugging her softly, she laid her on the pallet in Anna's bedroom. When she returned to the parlor, Anna had finished drying her cheeks. She hoped there weren't too many other traces of crying on her face.

"Do you want me to stay with Olga, or should I go open the shop?" Gerda hid a yawn behind her hand.

"Did you get any sleep last night?"

Gerda shook her head.

"Why don't you take a nap while Olga does? She should be tired enough to sleep a long time. We played all morning." Anna started for the door. "I'll go to the shop."

The sun was starting to go down when August rode into town. All day he had a hard time thinking about anything but Anna with her beautiful hair hanging down her back. When he had seen her, for a moment it chased all other thoughts from his head. He wanted to touch the waves that tumbled like a waterfall down her back. He was sure the strands would feel soft as silk. He had had to leave abruptly to retrieve Olga's things. It allowed him time to take control of his longings.

Anna was locking the door to the shop when he stopped in front of the store. She quickly turned. "Have you heard anything yet?"

He dismounted and came to stand by her. She stepped farther into the waning sunlight.

"Olina and Gustaf have a son." A smile split his face.

"How is Olina?"

"Mother and son are doing fine. Do you want me to take Olga now?"

Anna shook her head. "Why don't we keep her here another night? That will give everyone time to get a little rest." She quickly turned and headed toward the stairs at the side of the building.

August wished he had some reason to accompany Anna to the apartment. But he felt as if she had dismissed him from her presence. Would he ever understand that woman?

When August went to the post office to pick up his mail, the postmaster asked if he wanted to take Gustaf's to him. Olina had received a fat packet from Sweden. August thanked the man and headed to the boardinghouse. The mail could wait until morning.

After August had eaten, he fell into bed. Even though he was exhausted, sleep eluded him. *Lord, what am I going to do about Anna?*

August didn't expect an answer, but a quiet voice spoke into his mind.
Love her.

How was he supposed to do that? He thought that was what he had been doing.

Pray for her.

Somehow, lying on his back didn't seem the right way to pray. So August got up and opened his Bible on the edge of the bed. Then he dropped to his knees on the floor beside the open book. He prayed for Anna's heart to heal and for her relationship with the heavenly Father to increase. And he prayed that somehow Anna would come to love him as much as he loved her.

It was early afternoon before August could pick up Olga to take her home. This time, he rode his stallion. Olga always enjoyed being cradled in August's lap while he was on the big horse. They had often ridden this way, with her snuggled close against his chest.

When they arrived, Gustaf was already waiting at the hitching post. August knew that he had missed his young daughter, and Olga lunged into her father's arms with a squeal. August hoped that someday he would have a daughter who loved him as much.

He followed Gustaf into the house, carrying Olga's bag and the mail, which had been in his saddlebags. "The postmaster gave me your mail. Olina received something from Sweden."

His Brother's Castoff

Gustaf put Olga down, and she ran into her grandmother's arms. "Olina will want to see this. Why don't I take it up first? We'll bring Olga to see her *moder* and baby brother later."

He bounded up the stairs. August stayed in the kitchen with their mother. Soon Gustaf returned.

"The letter is from Olina's mother. Her great-aunt Olga passed away, and she left Olina quite a bit of money." Gustaf went to the stove and poured a cup of coffee. After taking a sip, he continued. "I've been saving to build onto the house. We'll need room now that we have two children and are planning to have more. Olina wants me to start as soon as possible." He turned a chair backward and straddled it with his crossed arms leaning on the back. "I don't suppose you'd be able to help me any time soon, would you?"

Since Gustaf had already drawn plans for the rooms he wanted, August agreed to help him. Even working only part of each day, they should be able to complete it in less than a month.

It took two weeks for all the building materials Gustaf ordered to arrive. When August finished work that afternoon, he rented a wagon from the livery and drove a load to Gustaf. It took them two more trips with both that wagon and Gustaf's to retrieve all of it. August promised to take the next day off to help get the framing up.

Gustaf clapped August on the shoulder. "Why don't you come for breakfast? *Mor* is still here, and I know she'll be glad to make enough for both her sons."

"I've never been known to turn down my mother's cooking."

They had finished enjoying thick slabs of ham, red-eye gravy, mounds of scrambled eggs, and piping hot biscuits dripping with butter when several men on horses rode up to the house. Gustaf excused himself from the table and went to see who it was. August started to help his mother clear the table.

"You go on now. I'll take care of this." Ingrid Nilsson had to stand on tiptoe to kiss her son's cheek.

August went out to join Gustaf. About a dozen men from their church were milling around the front yard. August wondered how they found out that Gustaf needed help. He was sure Gustaf hadn't told anyone else. But secrets were hard to keep in this close-knit community. Everyone cared about his neighbors. Probably Johan told them that the supplies had arrived. With all this help, they would finish the addition quickly.

Gustaf divided up the work among the men according to their areas of expertise. When everyone started work, Gustaf and August worked side by side.

August tried to keep his mind on the rooms they were building, but he had a hard time not thinking about Anna. Sometimes he even whispered a prayer for her when she made her way into his thoughts.

At noon, several women arrived, bringing food for the whole crew. August had enjoyed all the talk the men engaged in when they worked, but after he filled his plate, he sat down under a tree away from the crowd. Soon Gustaf joined him.

"You've been distracted today, haven't you?" Gustaf picked up a piece of fried chicken and bit into it.

August finished chewing before he replied. "Yes. At least it didn't interfere with my work."

"Is it Anna?"

August nodded. "I've been praying for her every day. And I try to go by there as often as I can. I'm not sure how to get through to her."

Gustaf laughed. "I hear you've been taking presents to the girls—especially Anna."

"Did she say something about that?"

"No." Gustaf picked up half a roll dripping with butter, popped it into his mouth, and chewed it up. "Gerda has noticed that everything you do directly affects Anna."

August looked up from his plate. "Do you think Anna knows?"

"I'm not sure. I think you would be good for Anna, and I want to see her happy. I'm going to start praying more earnestly for the two of you. That God would show you His will for your lives."

Chapter 10

In early May, Anna changed the navy wool suit that was in the window of the shop. Many women had asked about the new fashions for spring and summer. Anna and Gerda kept up with the new clothing, hats, and accessories offered in the catalogues and fashion magazines they received. Anna had made herself a new spring outfit, but she was going to leave it in the window for a while before she wore it. Made of soft cream-colored lawn, it was sprigged with tiny blue flowers. The clean lines looked good on Anna's tall frame, but the style could be adapted to many figure types. When she returned the dress form to the window, she glanced at the traffic outside. As the weather warmed, the streets were often filled with people moving about—on foot, on horseback, or in a variety of conveyances.

Her gaze drifted to a buggy she had never seen before. The brass fittings were shined until they sparkled. Even though it came from the direction of the road out of town, the vehicle was so clean, it looked as if it had recently been washed.

The man driving it was dressed in a suit that would have looked good on a banker back East. With his cravat arranged in that manner, Anna thought she could see the sparkle of a diamond nestled in the folds. Surely he wasn't wearing a diamond stickpin in Litchfield, Minnesota. Anna had never seen one before, but she had read about them in the fashion magazines she and Gerda subscribed to.

Sitting beside the man was an exquisitely beautiful young woman. She looked much too young to be his wife. Maybe she was his daughter. Anna couldn't help wondering what had brought them to this Midwestern town.

"Did you see that couple?" Anna hadn't realized that Gerda stood behind her until she spoke.

"Yes. I wonder who they are."

Anna didn't have to wonder long, because later that afternoon, the newcomers entered the mercantile. After browsing through the merchandise for half an hour, they came into the Dress Emporium. Anna was rearranging several of the displays on the small tables that were scattered around the room and on the sideboard by the wall.

"Oh. . .Father. Look at this wonderful shop." The young woman released her hold on the man's arm and picked up a triangular lacy shawl. She pulled it around her and tried to look over her shoulders to see the back.

"We have a large mirror." Anna pointed toward the cheval glass.

When the young woman walked over, Anna tipped the top of the frame forward a little so the girl could get a better look. She preened before the mirror. The soft blue shawl set off the color of her eyes. When she shook her head, black ringlets tumbled down her back. Anna had seen pictures of china dolls that looked like this girl.

"I like it." The young woman smiled at the man who had been standing to the side watching her every move. "May I have it. . .Father?"

He came to stand behind her and looked over her shoulder at her reflection in the mirror. "How could I deny my precious daughter anything her heart desires?"

The question sounded innocent enough, but Anna wondered at the undercurrent she sensed pulsing between the two. Then she was distracted when the man walked toward her.

"May I introduce myself?" His smiling eyes sought out Anna's. He extended his hand toward her. "My name is Pierre Le Blanc, and this is my daughter, Rissa."

When Anna reached to shake his hand, he instead grasped the tips of her fingers and lifted them to his mouth. When his lips touched her, shivers went up her spine. She had never had a man kiss her hand before, but she had read about it in books. His moist lips moved ever so slightly against her fingers, causing his moustache to tickle her.

Anna didn't know what to think about this. It wasn't unpleasant, but the awkwardness she felt made her stand aloof. She hoped that he would recognize that she didn't welcome his advances. Unfortunately, that aloofness seemed to draw the man more than if she had fawned over him. When Anna moved toward the counter, Mr. Le Blanc followed her. She stepped behind the wooden structure, hoping to put space between them, but the man leaned casually on the counter as if he were trying to get closer to her.

❧

August had taken a horse back to the livery stable when the fancy buggy pulled in the door. The dandy who was driving it looked down his nose at the big blacksmith. August didn't like to feel like some sort of insect being flicked away by the man. *Who does he think he is?*

"Here's the horse I shod." August addressed Hank, the owner of the livery, and ignored the newcomer. "Do any of the other horses need shoeing?"

When Hank shook his head, August returned to the blacksmith shop. He hurried to finish his work because he wanted to go to the Dress Emporium and see if Gerda or Anna knew who that man was. For some inexplicable reason, August had the feeling that the man was up to no good.

When August finally arrived at the shop, Anna was nowhere around, but he found Gerda in the workroom. "Did you see the new man who came into town this morning?" August didn't mean for his question to sound harsh, but it did.

Gerda looked up from her work. "Hello, brother, I'm glad to see you, too." She put the garment she was hemming on the table and went to hug him. He was sure she was glad that he took time to clean up before he came to see her. "Now what is this about the new visitors in town?"

"Did they come here?"

Gerda nodded but looked away from her brother's scrutiny.

"So what are you not telling me?" August leaned his shoulder against the doorframe and crossed his ankles. He hoped he looked relaxed, but he didn't feel it.

"Mr. Le Blanc and his daughter came into the shop earlier." Gerda turned toward August.

"He has a daughter?"

"Yes, her name is Rissa. Kind of a strange name, isn't it? And she's very beautiful—in a china doll kind of way."

August digested that piece of information. "How old is his daughter?"

"I don't know. She was very dainty. At first, I thought she was only a girl, but after she was here awhile, I realized that she was probably a young woman. Why are you so interested in them?"

August stood up away from the door facing and walked over to look out the window, with his arms crossed over his chest. "I didn't see the girl. Only the man. . .and he wasn't very friendly."

Gerda laughed. "He wasn't very friendly to me either, but he was to Anna."

August felt a slow burn start in his stomach and move upward inside him. A return of the old jealousy? "Just how friendly was he?"

Gerda liked to tease her brothers, and she took the chance to do it now. "Well. . .he did kiss her hand."

August whirled around to face her. "Kiss her hand?" burst from his lips. "Why did he kiss her hand?"

Anna walked in the room in time to hear the outburst. "It was only a friendly gesture."

August glared at her. "Friendly gesture? Well, here's a friendly gesture for you." He stomped toward Anna, took her by her shoulders, and pressed his lips to hers.

It was a brief kiss, but suddenly everything changed for August. He hurried out the door as if he were being chased. Why in the world did he do that? Anna looked shocked, and he felt as if his heart had been ripped out. He wanted the first time he kissed Anna to be special. Tender, soft, and a prelude to a long life together, not a jealous gesture in anger. Now he had ruined everything. His inability to control jealousy had caused Anna pain.

While August ran away, Anna stood touching her lips with the fingertips of her right hand. Why had August done that? She had begun to feel drawn to him, and here he had kissed her in anger. What had she done to make him angry? When she looked at Gerda, she had returned to hemming the dress, and a smile covered her face. What was there to smile about?

Before Anna could ask her, the bell over the door of the shop jingled. Anna went to see who had entered and found Mr. Le Blanc and Rissa.

"My daughter would like to order some dresses." When the man smiled at her, Anna felt it in the pit of her stomach.

This man, who had started all the problems with August, intrigued Anna. She decided to try to get to know him better. Nothing would come of it, but he did seem to be interesting. She had never been one to flirt, but there could be a first time for everything. *We'll see what August thinks of that!*

"What did you have in mind?" Anna should have been asking the girl, but she turned toward the man.

Although he smiled at her, it didn't reach his eyes. They were piercing, intense, with some secret hidden in their depths. "Whatever Rissa wants is all right with me. She knows what she likes."

Anna took Rissa to the counter where several fashion magazines were stacked. While the girl leafed through the pages, Anna often glanced toward the man. Every time she saw him, his gaze was on her. Soon she began to feel uncomfortable. No man had ever concentrated on her for such a long time.

"I want to have four summer outfits made." Rissa drew Anna's attention from her father. Anna glanced down at the magazine she had open. "I like this dress." She turned the pages to show Anna two more styles. Then she waved a hand toward the summer frock on the dress form in the window. "Can you make that style in my size?"

"Of course." Anna had taken a tablet from under the counter. She wrote down the page number in the magazine. Then she added the style from the window. "You need to pick out what fabrics you want us to use."

"Do you need me to help you?" Gerda stepped through the door.

Anna turned toward her. "I'll let you help Rissa choose her fabrics, and I'll talk to her father about the costs involved."

The man raised one eyebrow at Anna's words. "Oh, it doesn't matter how much they cost. I want Rissa to have what she desires. We can afford it." A mocking smile crossed his face.

"I didn't doubt that for a minute." Anna smiled at him then.

While Gerda and Rissa continued to look through the stacks of fabric, Mr. Le Blanc started asking Anna about the town of Litchfield. The conversation was a pleasant one, but after the Le Blancs left the store, Anna realized that she hadn't found out anything about them. And once again, Mr. Le Blanc kissed her hand before he left the store. His gallantry was a pleasant change from what Anna was used to, but she liked the kiss from August better, even if it hadn't meant anything to him. Strong emotion had been the reason for it, even if it had been the wrong emotion.

August was across the street and one block down before he turned to look back at the store. That's when he noticed that the Le Blancs were in the Dress Emporium. He wanted to go back but knew he had no reason to go into the women's store. Maybe he should go to the mercantile. Surely there was something he needed to pick up.

When August entered the establishment, he was glad to see that both Johan and Marja were busy with other customers. He casually made his way to the side of the store nearest the dress shop. He browsed through the merchandise while keeping a close eye on what was transpiring in the next room.

He didn't like the way that man looked at Anna. When she was busy with his daughter, his eyes raked Anna from the top of her head to her feet. And he spent too long on specific parts of her body. August's blood began to simmer. The nerve of that man.

August wished that he hadn't made such a fool of himself earlier with Anna. He knew that she wouldn't listen to a thing he said about that snake oil salesman. A man like him had to be planning some kind of scam. August decided to keep a close watch on him.

Over the next three weeks, Mr. Le Blanc and his daughter insinuated themselves into Litchfield society. They attended church every Sunday. August noticed that they were always slightly late, and when they arrived, they didn't slip in quietly. Everyone in the room knew when they arrived. They invited key people to small *soirees*, as Rissa called them, in their hotel suite. Everyone who was invited was someone important—such as the mayor, the banker, the sheriff, the stationmaster, and the owner of the hotel.

Unfortunately, since Anna and Gerda were business owners, they were often included in the festivities, especially Anna. However, although he was the owner of a business, August was never invited. Neither were Hank or any of the farmers. Only people Le Blanc thought had quite a bit of money. . .and Anna.

When the parties were held downstairs in the hotel, August was able to keep an eye on the proceedings. But when they were in the sitting room of the Le Blancs' hotel suite, he could only guess what went on. What August observed didn't make him change his mind about the man. Something wasn't quite right about him.

The Dress Emporium had received a new shipment of fabrics, and Anna was arranging them on the shelves when August arrived. He came into the shop and leaned on the counter.

"I've come to apologize to you."

Although Anna kept her back to him, she was aware of his every move. She had tried to stay out of his way ever since that unfortunate kiss. Now here he was only a few feet from her. So close she could feel the heat emanating from him, helping her remember the feel and taste of his lips.

"And what do you have to apologize for?" Anna didn't think her heart could take him saying he was sorry for kissing her. There had been only short periods of time since that fateful day when she didn't remember every nuance of that connection, even though it was brief.

"Anna, please look at me." When she turned around and their gazes connected, he continued. "I'm sorry I was angry when I kissed you."

He hadn't said he was sorry that he kissed her, only that he was angry when he did. That was interesting.

"Why were you angry? I hadn't done anything to upset you." Anna crossed her arms and stood her ground.

He nodded. "You're right. I wasn't angry at you. It was that man."

Anna took a deep breath. "Mr. Le Blanc?"

"Yes." August stepped back from the counter and stuffed his hands into the back pockets of his denim trousers.

"You never have liked him, have you?" Anna's question caught August off guard.

"No, I don't trust the man."

Anna looked as if he had said something bad about her. "What did he do to make you not trust him?"

How could August make her understand? He knew that he was right. The man never looked August in the eyes. He had a smooth way of talking, but when August looked at his eyes, there was no light in them. Only a confidence man talked that smoothly. August had seen them at work on more than one occasion. The man had to be a confidence man, but August had no way to prove it.

"That man is up to no good."

The sound Anna made wasn't very ladylike. "I think you're jealous because you weren't invited to any of the parties."

"Jealous? Of that man? Hardly. . .but he's not honest."

August could tell that Anna was getting exasperated. "He was totally honest with Gerda and me. He spent a lot of money in this store. How can you say he's not honest?" Anna was raising her voice a little more with each word she said.

August did the same. "That man is up to no good. Mark my words. You'll see that soon enough."

Anna came around the counter and stood toe to toe with August, and her finger on his chest punctuated each word. "I can't believe you're so pigheaded. He was kind to me, and I won't let you say bad things about him."

"I've seen the way he looked at you when you didn't notice. He was devouring you with his eyes in a very unsavory manner. No decent woman would want a man looking at her like that." August knew that he was shouting, but he couldn't stop himself.

Anna turned and marched to the door of the workroom. There she whirled around. "I can't believe you would stoop so low as to say something like that. I guess you'll be glad to know that he and his daughter left town this morning after picking up the dresses we made for her. We'll probably never see them again." When Anna went through the door, she slammed it shut behind her. The sound reverberated off all four walls of the store.

August stood there stunned. He had done it again. Lost his temper with Anna. What in the world was wrong with him?

Thankfully, it was time to close the shop. When August walked out, Anna came from the workroom and locked the door to the mercantile. She grabbed her coat, gloves, and handbag and hurried out the front door. She didn't want to cry until she got in the apartment, but it took every ounce of strength she had to hold the tears inside. After fumbling with the lock and key, she finally secured the front door.

When Anna closed the apartment door behind her, her reserves were gone. She dropped into the rocking chair and covered her face with her hands. The tears she had been holding back came in a flood, as if a dam inside her had broken. With a keening wail, she rocked and sobbed. Why had God done this to her?

That's where Gerda found her when she returned home, rocking and crying. Anna wished that she had thought about going to her own bedroom. Maybe then Gerda wouldn't have been so concerned about her.

"Anna!" Gerda dropped the bags she was carrying and hurried to the rocking chair. She knelt on the oval braided rug and took Anna's hands in hers. "What happened?"

Anna had carried this load too long by herself. She was tired. Without thinking, the words tumbled out.

"August is angry with me. . .and he doesn't like Mr. Le Blanc. . .and he yelled at me, and—"

"Who yelled at you? Mr. Le Blanc?"

"No, August yelled at me, and he was angry when he kissed me, and—"

Gerda stood up and put her hands on her hips. "August kissed you again?"

"No!" Anna knew that her thoughts were jumbled, and what she was saying didn't make much sense.

Gerda pulled Anna up from the chair and wrapped her arms around her friend. After hugging her for a moment, she led Anna to the settee where they both sat down. Then Gerda began to pray.

"*Fader Gud*, Anna is upset. Please bring a peace and calmness to her so we can discuss what is bothering her. Give us wisdom as we try to discern Your will in the matter. In Jesus' name, amen."

Inexplicably, Anna felt a calmness descend upon her. After sitting still for a short time, her thoughts began to make sense.

"Now, Anna," Gerda said. "Start at the beginning, and tell me what's wrong."

Anna stood up and removed her coat while she explained what had happened in the store earlier with August. Gerda sat quietly and listened.

"I think maybe August is jealous of the attention that Mr. Le Blanc is giving you."

That was a new thought to Anna. August jealous? Why would he be jealous?

"Haven't you noticed how attentive he is to you?" Gerda asked.

Anna hadn't thought of August as being attentive to her. He was only a good friend, wasn't he? "Why do you think he's paying any attention to me?" Anna sat down again and clasped her hands in her lap.

"Oh, Anna." Gerda put her hand over Anna's. "I've suspected for some time that August is interested in you. Before Mr. Le Blanc came, I even thought you might be interested in him. Now I'm not sure."

Anna sat for a moment, deep in thought. Then she stood, walked across the room, and looked out the window, staring at nothing in particular. "I can't let myself think about a man that way."

"Why not?" Gerda came to stand beside her. "Every woman looks forward to marriage someday."

Anna looked at Gerda with a stricken expression on her face. "That's not God's plan for me."

Gerda put her hands on her hips. "Why do you say that?"

Anna took a deep breath. Gerda had been her best friend long before they were partners in the business. If she couldn't tell her, who could she tell? Maybe Gerda's prayers would help her accept what was happening to her.

"I don't know when it started, but I do know that there is something wrong with me. Something that keeps a man from loving me enough." For a moment, the words hung in the air between them.

"Anna, how can you say that?" Gerda pulled Anna into her arms and patted her back. "Nothing's wrong with you."

"Gustaf couldn't love me enough. . .even though we were together for years." Anna tried to speak the words evenly, but her voice had a catch in it.

"You know that Olina was the right woman for him, don't you?"

Anna nodded. "Olaf didn't love me enough either. I knew that he shouldn't go on the hunting trip. I begged him not to go. . .if he loved me. He went anyway, not even considering my feelings."

Gerda dropped onto the settee. "I'm so sorry, Anna. I didn't know. But that doesn't mean that something is wrong with you. He wasn't the right man to love you the way God wants you loved."

"If you say so." Anna wasn't convinced. She walked over to the table by the rocking chair and started straightening the doily on top.

Gerda went to her bedroom and returned with her Bible. She opened it and searched for a particular passage. "I want to read something to you. I read it last night, and God brought it back to my mind. Here it is, Matthew 10:29–31: 'Are not two sparrows sold for a farthing? and one of them shall not fall on the ground without your Father. But the very hairs of your head are all numbered. Fear ye not therefore, ye are of more value than many sparrows.' God made you special, Anna, and He has a plan for you. Maybe you haven't found it yet."

"Read those words to me again." Anna dropped into the rocking chair, leaned her head against the back, and closed her eyes.

After Gerda finished reading the verses, Anna sat and let them soak into her heart.

Gerda began to turn the pages in her Bible again. "Here's another Scripture. Psalm 139:13–16: 'For thou hast possessed my reins: thou hast covered me in my mother's womb. I will praise thee; for I am fearfully and wonderfully made: marvellous are thy works; and that my soul knoweth right well. My substance was not hid from thee, when I was made in secret, and curiously wrought in the lowest parts of the earth. Thine eyes did see my substance, yet being unperfect; and in thy book all my members were written, which in continuance were fashioned, when as yet there was none of them.' Anna, these words apply to you, too. You were fearfully and wonderfully made according to God's plan. You are altogether lovely, as He created you to be. Nothing is wrong with you. And He cares about everything that happens in your life. He understands your desires to have a husband and children, and in His timing, He will bring it about."

These added words were a balm to the wounds in Anna's heart. When Gerda began to pray for her, she sat and listened. She felt the presence of the Lord stronger than she had in a long time, and the pain in her heart started to recede.

Chapter 11

August was glad that he needed to make horseshoes today. While he pounded the red-hot iron bar flat, he berated himself. "Why were you so stupid?" *Bang. . .bang.* "How could you have yelled at Anna?" *Bang. . . bang.* "She'll never know that you love her."

"You're right about that." August hadn't noticed that Gustaf had walked into the blacksmith shop until he spoke above the pounding.

August dropped his chin against his chest and took a deep breath before turning to face his brother. "I guess you heard every word I said." It was a statement, not a question.

"You weren't exactly speaking softly." Gustaf had a twinkle in his eye that August didn't want to see. "I'm surprised that everyone couldn't hear you. It's a good thing the smithy is on the edge of town."

August knew the fiery forge caused his face to redden, but now there was an additional reason. He hoped that no one passing in the street heard what he said.

"There wasn't anyone walking by." Gustaf must have read August's thoughts. He often did that. Sometimes August didn't mind, but more often than not, it drove him crazy.

"Good." August nodded. "So what brings you here today?" He glanced toward the table where he kept things waiting to be repaired. He didn't see anything added to the carefully arranged items already there. "You didn't bring me any work, did you?"

Gustaf slid his hands into his back pockets and rocked up on the balls of his feet. August knew he did that when he wanted to discuss something serious.

"No, I only thought that you might need someone to talk to."

"Because of what I was saying when you came in?" August studied his brother's expression, trying to discern what he was concerned about.

"No, Gerda talked to me about what happened in the Dress Emporium yesterday."

August stared at the floor. He scuffed the dirt with the toe of his boot, drawing overlapping ovals. "I'm not very proud of that."

"You shouldn't be," Gustaf quickly agreed. "Can you take a break, or do you have too much work?" He glanced around the shop.

August looked at the nearly empty table. "Nothing that I need to rush to finish. Where do you want to talk?" Since there were no chairs in the smithy, it wasn't conducive to long conversations.

"The church worked really well last time. Do you want to go there?"

The brothers were each lost in their own thoughts as they trudged to the church. When they were inside the building, Gustaf led the way to the front pew. After sitting, he bowed his head. August knew his brother was praying. He wanted to pray, too, but instead he sat silently, hoping the feeling of peace he always received at church would soak into him today. However, it seemed to be far away.

Gustaf spoke first. "You're still having trouble with jealousy, aren't you?"

"I don't feel the strong jealousy of you that poisoned my life before." August leaned his forearms on his thighs and let his huge hands dangle between his knees. He studied the wooden floor between his work boots. "It's been coming out about other things now."

"That isn't healthy."

August nodded. "I know. That's why I was berating myself when you came into the smithy."

"Maybe we didn't do enough when we talked last time. I've been reading about roots of bitterness." Light pouring through the one stained-glass window cast a warm, multicolored glow over Gustaf's face. "You have to get to the very bottom of them before you can dig them out of your life. Maybe we need to find the root of the jealousy in your heart."

That made sense to August. He sat up and put his arms along the back of the handmade wooden pew, drumming his fingers on the polished surface. "Do you have any idea how I can do that?" He would welcome any help he could get. He had wrestled with this problem far too long.

Gustaf sat silent so long that August thought he wasn't going to answer. "I've been praying about that ever since Gerda told me what happened yesterday. I feel the Lord is telling me that we need to go as far back in your memory as we can. You told me you were jealous of me before we came to America. Do you know how long you felt that jealousy in Sweden?"

For several minutes, August studied the wooden cross that hung behind the pulpit. His thoughts returned to their native land and the life they lived there. "I don't remember ever not being jealous. . .of you."

Gustaf stood and paced toward the platform, but he didn't step up on it. He turned around to face August. "Were you jealous when you were. . .say, ten years old?"

August thought a few minutes while he reconstructed in his mind what he felt when he was ten. "Yes."

"What about when Gerda was born?"

August remembered that Gustaf got to hold their baby sister more often than he did. That had never seemed fair to him. He nodded. "Yes."

"Okay, before that. . . What about when Lars was born?"

It took August awhile, but he remembered when Lars was a baby. Gustaf had been very proud of the new little brother. Suddenly, August could see with clarity into his long-ago memories.

Before Lars was born, Gustaf had doted on August. As the little brother, August had followed him around like a puppy, and his older brother was proud of him. He helped him do a lot of things. They were real buddies, always together. August could hear his father's voice saying how his two boys were inseparable and how proud he was of them. August didn't feel anything but admiration for his big brother. He was stunned. It took him awhile before he could articulate what God had revealed to him.

He finally looked up at Gustaf, his beloved older brother. "I was not jealous of you before Lars was born." He hated to admit that. What would Gustaf think of him now, knowing that jealousy of a baby brother had caused all the heartache?

Gustaf smiled. "I'm so glad. I was afraid we wouldn't be able to find the root of your jealousy. I've prayed since yesterday that God would reveal it to one of us. He answered my prayers. I praise Him for that."

August looked up at the ceiling. "I remember that you were so proud of me. We went everywhere together. *Fader* even told people how proud he was of his two sons." He dropped his head and studied the floorboards. "Then when Lars was born, you didn't spend as much time with me." The words sounded so petty coming from his mouth.

Gustaf moved to sit beside August on the pew. "Brother, I'm so sorry that I caused this."

August looked up at him. "You were only a boy. You didn't do anything any other brother wouldn't."

Gustaf put his arm across August's shoulders. "I think it'll help if I ask for your forgiveness and you choose to freely give it to me."

August had tears in his own eyes when he looked into his brother's teary eyes. "Of course I forgive you. I"—he cleared his throat before he could continue—"love you."

The brothers clutched each other in a strong embrace while they wept for the special times they had lost. When they finally stood, each pulled a bandanna from his pocket and wiped his face. August couldn't believe how much lighter he felt. It was as if the weight of an anvil had been lifted from his heart.

"This was a turning point in my life." August smiled at Gustaf. "Thank you for helping me."

"Jealousy has been a habit in your life a long time, but I believe God will help you break it if you let Him."

When the two men returned to the blacksmith shop, they both walked with a spring in their steps. August expected Gustaf to leave when they reached his horse that was tied to the hitching post outside the building, but instead he came into the smithy.

After leaning against the table, Gustaf crossed his arms over his chest. "So, what are you going to do about Anna?"

August didn't have a ready answer. He had been wondering the same thing. What could he do about Anna? After yesterday, she probably thought he was a lunatic, or worse.

"I don't know." He started straightening things on the table even though they weren't in disarray.

"Do you love her?"

August stopped what he was doing and faced his brother. "You get right to the heart of the matter, don't you?"

Gustaf didn't say a word but gave August time to consider his answer.

August leaned against the table beside his brother and crossed his own arms. "Yes, I love her, for all the good it'll do me."

"Does she know?"

After thinking a minute, August said, "She ought to."

Gustaf blew out an exasperated breath. "Why should she? Have you told her?"

"Of course not, but I've been showing her in a lot of ways."

"What kind of ways?"

August started listing them. "I've made them a cushioned sewing chair. I bought a book of poetry for the apartment. I try to fix everything that needs fixing. I go to see her almost every day."

Gustaf straightened away from the table and brushed off the back of his jeans. "You have a lot to learn about women, brother. None of that was for only Anna. Gerda shared them."

"Well, I did buy her some pretty handkerchiefs. They had dainty needlework flowers on them. They reminded me of her when I saw them in the mercantile. On impulse, I bought them and took them to her."

Gustaf smiled. "That's a step in the right direction. Now stop doing things that can be for both Gerda and Anna. Make sure that everything you do to show her you love her is for Anna alone. And eventually, you'll need to tell her how you feel."

"I kissed her."

Gustaf laughed. "Oh, I heard about that kiss. Remember, Gerda was there. I don't think that one counts. You probably need to do something to make her forget that one. A while back, didn't you tell me that you were going to pray about whether Anna was the woman God wanted you to marry?"

August moved away from the table. "Yes, and I feel that God told me she was. That's why I've been trying to do things for her. So she would start having feelings for me."

"If God has told you she's the one, pour all your efforts into wooing her." Gustaf headed out the door, but he turned back. "You're not getting any younger, you know."

After her conversation with Gerda, Anna couldn't get August out of her mind. Was he as interested in her as Gerda thought? If so, why did he yell at her? Wouldn't a man who loved her want to protect her, not yell at her?

Protect her? That was an idea. Maybe August thought he was protecting her from Pierre. . .Mr. Le Blanc. The words that August said about the way Mr. Le Blanc looked at her left an uncomfortable feeling in Anna's heart. She had allowed the man to become a friend. Had he been unsuitable? If so, why hadn't she noticed? Besides, she wouldn't even have paid any attention to him if it hadn't been for August's irrational accusations when the Le Blancs first came to town.

Anna didn't need all this turmoil in her life. If August was interested in her, he needed to learn how to treat a woman. And it wasn't by yelling at her in her own store. Anna hoped there weren't many customers in the mercantile. She was sure that whoever was there heard every word she and August exchanged. Anna hadn't even been able to face Marja or Johan since the confrontation.

August hadn't been showing interest in her. He had been trying to control her, telling her what to do. She didn't need that. It reminded her too much of the last words Olaf spoke to her before he left on that hunting trip. Anna didn't want a man who controlled her without taking into consideration what she felt about anything. She wanted one who would love her the way her father loved her mother. He was the head of the household, but he wasn't heavy-handed about it. If Anna were to marry, she would be glad to be a helpmeet, as the Bible said, to a man who wasn't overbearing.

Too much had happened in the last few days. Anna was tired of all the turmoil. The best thing for her to do would be to stay out of the way when August was around. Then he couldn't yell at her again.

After his conversation with Gustaf, August plotted his next move. He would win Anna's love or die trying. She was worth it. He could face anything with her by his side. And the family they would have would be such a blessing.

The next time he went to the dress shop, Anna wasn't there. Gerda said that she had left for a few minutes. So he decided to come back later. Once again,

Anna had left before he got there. August went into the mercantile to look at the newer merchandise. The Braxtons were always adding things to the store. Recently, it was a larger shelf of books. He was browsing through the titles when he heard Anna and Gerda talking in the dress shop.

He picked up a book of poetry by Emily Dickinson. The slim volume was bound in soft, maroon leather. Anna would like it. Gerda had said that Anna enjoyed the book of poetry he bought for the apartment. After paying for the volume, he asked Marja to wrap it up for him. Then he went into the dress shop. Gerda was rearranging some of the merchandise in the showroom.

"August, you've come back." Gerda spoke louder than usual.

He wondered why she spoke so loud, then he heard a door closing. It sounded as if it came from the workroom. When he asked about Anna, Gerda told him that she wasn't in the shop.

As he walked toward the boardinghouse carrying the package wrapped in brown paper and tied with string, he wondered what was going on. Was Anna hiding from him? Of course, he couldn't blame her. He would have to figure out a way to get her to see him. Maybe he could go to the apartment after dinner and deliver this book.

August finished the delicious meal Mrs. Olson prepared, then he went upstairs and shaved again. He wanted to look as nice as possible when he saw Anna. He even changed into his best pants and shirt. When August started toward the mercantile building, he couldn't see any light in the windows of the apartment. The bedrooms were on the front of the building. Maybe the girls were in the parlor or the kitchen. But when he arrived at the top of the stairs, there wasn't a hint of light coming from the windows. They weren't home. All that trouble for nothing. But that was all right. He would try again tomorrow. August was patient. He would do whatever it took to win Anna's love.

Chapter 12

June

Anna enjoyed poetry. The words sang in her heart. After eating lunch in the apartment, she picked up the book of poetry August brought by two evenings ago. She decided to sit and read a few pages before she returned to the shop so Gerda could have lunch.

When she sat in her favorite rocking chair, instead of opening the volume, her fingers stroked the texture of the smooth surface. She lifted the book close to her face. The scent of the new leather reminded her of August. The other book of poetry he bought had been for both her and Gerda, but this one was inscribed inside from August to her. She would never understand that man. He had aggravated her when he yelled at her. She placed the fingertips of her right hand over her lips, once again feeling the memory of his lips on hers. When he kissed her, it touched more than her mouth. Even in his anger, his lips had felt soft and velvety.

If truth were known, Anna hadn't wanted the kiss to end so quickly. She had often wondered what it would feel like to be kissed on the mouth. Gustaf had never kissed her, and when Olaf did, it was on the cheek or forehead. But August had touched her lips, and she couldn't forget the feeling. He was such a confusing man. Either yelling at her, kissing her, or doing nice things. Maybe all the good things could outweigh the other.

When Anna realized how long she had sat daydreaming, she put the book down and went to the bedroom to check her hair in the mirror over her wash-stand. Gerda had waited long enough for her lunch.

August had the doors of the smithy wide open. It was June, and the heat from the forge called for a cool breeze. But this spring had been pretty dry. He would welcome a storm if it brought the wind to cool things off.

For some reason, today the forge smelled hotter, smokier. August went to the door to get a whiff of fresh air. When he stepped outside, he realized that the smell of fire and smoke didn't only come from the forge. The livery stable that was a little ways down the street had smoke pouring out through the door and every window. It billowed from the opening to the hay loft and formed a wreath around the entire roof of the building.

Fire!

August wondered about the proprietor, but Hank stepped from the inferno, leading two horses. So August ran as fast as he could toward the fire bell. By the time he reached the bell, Hank had tied those two horses to hitching posts and headed back toward the stable. August pulled the rope hard several times until people carrying buckets started running down the street toward him. They would form a bucket brigade, dipping water from Lake Ripley. It was a good thing the livery was at the edge of town, near the body of water.

In other circumstances, they would have used the fire wagon. The trouble was that both the wagon and the horses that pulled it were kept in the livery. It was too late to get to the wagon, but Hank was leading the fire horses from the burning barn when August returned.

Gerda and Anna were working on a wedding dress that a customer needed by the end of the week. After they had sold Anna's wedding dress soon after the Dress Emporium opened, many brides ordered their gowns from them. Anna had finished sewing the last seam on the machine when the fire bell startled them. They both ran out on the sidewalk to see what was happening. They were appalled by what they saw.

"What do you think we should do?" Gerda shaded her eyes with one hand. "They need help with the bucket brigade."

"Most of the town is heading that way, but if we both go, we'll never finish this dress in time. I wouldn't want to disappoint the bride, would you?"

Gerda nodded. "You're right. At least I can pray while I work on it. Be sure to come back as soon as you can and let me know what is happening."

Anna left Gerda in the workroom, grabbed a bucket, and hurried to join the brigade from the lake. While she ran, she searched the sky for even a hint of a cloud. Rain would be especially welcome right now. It could do more than any bucket brigade to put the fire out.

When she reached the line of people, she looked toward the lake. There were fifty or more people passing full buckets one way and empty buckets back. Her brother Ollie let her get in line in front of him. He was near the end of the brigade closest to the livery. She would be able to see all that was happening.

Anna handed her empty bucket to Ollie and took the full one he was passing forward. Then she exchanged buckets with the person in front of her. By the time she turned back to Ollie, he held another full bucket. Even though the work was repetitious, it allowed her the opportunity to watch August without him being aware of it.

When she ran to get in line, she noticed that August was the one who rang the fire bell. She watched him go to some of the horses tied along the street and try to calm them.

It was so like August to care for the animals. Probably that was one reason he wanted to be a blacksmith. He knew how important it was for animals to be treated right. Anna had heard several men say that his horseshoes were some of the best, and they complimented August on treating the animals with care while he shod them. It was another thing to like about him. Too bad he was so bossy with her.

While she was watching him, August looked her way. She turned around, intent on passing the buckets quickly. When she glanced at him again, he was headed toward the owner of the livery stable.

"Are all the horses out?" August called to Hank.

"No. There's one more. I've tied all the others to hitching posts." He pointed down the street where August had been trying to calm down the skittish horses that were dancing around, pulling on their leads.

August knew that horses didn't like fire or smoke. It might take a lot to calm them. He wished he could help them, but right now, the fire was more important. The livery building was wooden and filled with so many things that burned easily. Hay fueled the flames, sending them higher and higher. They had broken through the roof by the time August neared the building. Sparkling embers danced in the air above the fire. At least there wasn't any wind to blow them toward the other wooden buildings.

Although the buckets were being passed from hand to hand at a fast clip, the small amount of water poured on the raging fire didn't seem to affect it at all. August started toward the open doorway of the stable.

"Hey, you can't go in there!"

Anna heard the shout about someone going into the building, and she looked toward the livery. Who was that man walking so close to the inferno?

"There's still one horse inside!"

Right after August's shouted statement, the shrill whinny of a scared animal pierced the air. To Anna's horror, August continued toward the raging fire. In an instant, he was swallowed up in the roiling smoke.

"No!" She couldn't leave the line, but she wanted to.

The thump of her heartbeat in her throat almost choked her. August, dear August. For the first time, she realized that she truly loved him. And it might be too late. She might never get the chance to tell him. What he was doing was heroic, but it was also stupid. Who in his right mind would rush into a burning building? But Anna knew his tender heart made him want to rescue the frightened animal. She began to pray frantically that his efforts wouldn't be in vain. She begged God to bring both August and the horse out of the inferno.

※

August pulled the blue bandanna from his hip pocket and tied it around his face, leaving only his eyes uncovered. If he wanted to find the horse, he needed to see. Before he entered the stable, he should have asked Hank which stall the horse was in, but he couldn't go back now. The overpowering heat almost brought August to his knees, but he heard the animal's horrible scream again. The sound gave him a direction to go.

Thick smoke obscured most of the things around him. He stumbled over burning pieces of wood that had fallen from the beams. He didn't know how much time was left before the roof would cave in. Flames licked upward on the walls and scrabbled across the floor. August stamped the flickers near his feet, keeping them at bay for a short time. At least he had on heavy boots.

One more agonized cry from the animal brought August to his stall. The horse was so overcome with fear that August had a hard time catching hold of its bridle, which, thankfully, someone had left on the animal. He grabbed the lead line that lay across the stall divider. He attached it to the bridle and tried to lead the horse toward the door.

When the animal refused to move from its stall, August pulled the bandanna from his own face and quickly covered the horse's eyes. Then he jerked on the lead line and moved as swiftly as possible toward the stable doors. August knew that if he didn't get there very soon, neither he nor the animal would survive. The air was full of burning bits of debris that were constantly falling through the thick haze.

Smoke and heat seared August's lungs, so he tried to hold his breath. Choking and coughing, he stumbled forward pulling the horse as hard as he could. *Oh, Gud, please help us. Let us reach the door in time.*

※

Anna stood horrified, as did many others in the brigade. She held her breath for what seemed an eternity, crying out to God to save August. Finally, the majestic animal and man came through the smoke-filled opening. August stumbled and fell to his knees. With a shrill cry, the horse reared up on his hind legs and pulled his lead away from August. The bandanna fell from its head, and the horse shot away from the heat and smoke. Hank ran toward one of the other horses and jumped on its back. He took off after the runaway. Anna knew that he wanted to bring it back safely.

When Anna looked back toward August, he was lying on the ground, much too close to the burning building. She passed off the bucket she held, gathered her skirt with both hands, and started running toward him.

One of the men tried to stop her, but she pushed past him. It took three men to hold her and keep her from rushing into danger.

"Stop! We have two men going to get him!" It took awhile for the words to soak into Anna's fear-crazed brain. Finally, she stopped writhing and twisting, trying to get away from the hands that held her.

"He has to be all right! He just has to!" Then she burst into tears.

Gustaf and Ollie ran toward August's still form. Anna was thankful for brothers. They would take care of August. She wondered where Lowell was. When she glanced around looking for him, he was coming from the direction of the doctor's office. Carrying his black bag, Dr. Bradley hurried after Lowell.

August couldn't remember when breathing had hurt so much. Not even the time the plow horse kicked him when he was only ten years old. It was agony to take a breath. He tasted smoke and flames. He smelled smoke and flames. The only way to get a breath was to cough some of the smoke out of his lungs. When he did, he sputtered, trying not to scream from the pain.

Finally aware that two men were carrying him, he tried to open his eyes, but even that was hard. When he glimpsed Ollie and Gustaf, he relaxed as much as he could without becoming dead weight to them.

Lowell and Dr. Bradley met them in the middle of the street. The doctor told the two men to lower August to the dusty ground. People gathered close around, and August felt as if he couldn't breathe at all.

"All right now!" Doc's voice thundered. "Everybody back! Give the man some air!"

When people moved back, it brought some relief, but not much. Doc's hands roved over his form, seeking, searching. Doc put a stethoscope against August's chest and listened.

"He doesn't seem to have any burns on his body. He's just breathed in too much smoke."

"What can we do to help him?" August was glad his brother asked the question that was screaming in his mind. "Should I take him out to the farm?"

August glanced at Doc in time to see him shake his head. "I would like to have him here in town so I can keep an eye on him."

"I don't feel good about taking him to the boardinghouse. There wouldn't be anyone to look after him," Gustaf said.

"You can take him to the apartment."

Anna had come to stand by Lowell. The sound of her voice was a soothing balm to August's heart. He tried to smile at her but didn't think she noticed. She was intent on her conversation with the doctor.

"That's a good idea," Gustaf agreed. "I'll go get *Moder*. She'll want to take care of him."

Chapter 13

A nna rushed to the Dress Emporium and burst through the front door. "Gerda, August has been hurt!"

Gerda placed the wedding dress she was hemming on the cutting table and hurried into the shop toward her best friend. "How bad is he?"

So she could catch her breath, Anna stopped beside the counter and leaned one hand on it, placing the other over her heart. "I don't think he's burned, but he went into the livery stable to rescue a trapped horse. When they came out, August fainted." Anna had never swooned in her life, but she felt as if she could crumple into a heap right now.

Gerda put the fingers of her right hand over her mouth, and tears started making their way down her cheeks. After she sobbed a moment, she took a deep breath and asked, "Is he going to be all right?"

Tears were also streaming down Anna's cheeks, and she didn't even try to wipe them off. "Lowell went to get the doctor. Doc wants August to stay in town. I told them they could bring him to the apartment. I hope that's all right with you."

Gerda grabbed Anna and held her tight. "Of course, I want him here. I want to take care of him."

Anna clutched her also. "Gustaf has already gone to get your mother. Lowell and Ollie will bring August to our place."

The two young women decided to close the dress shop. If anyone needed anything, they could come back later. Everyone in town would understand.

Lowell and Ollie met them at the bottom of the outside stairs. Their shoulders supported August's arms, and he was trying to walk, even though the other two men carried most of his weight. That was probably why it had taken this long for them to arrive.

The two women preceded them up the steps, and Gerda immediately went into her own room to prepare the bed for her brother. Anna stood by the door and watched, feeling helpless, while her brothers helped August across the parlor and down the short hall to the bedroom. Before she shut the outside door, Dr. Bradley reached the top of the stairs.

After showing the doctor to Gerda's bedroom, Anna dropped into her rocker. Unmoving, she stared unseeing at her hands, which were clasped in her lap. It was hard waiting for the doctor to finish tending to August.

Lowell and Ollie soon joined her in the parlor. They didn't sit. Instead, they prowled around as if they couldn't settle down. Anna knew they were probably as worried as she was.

She glanced up at them. "Has Doc almost finished with August?"

Lowell continued to pace the room, but Ollie dropped onto the settee across from her. "He was still working with him when we came out."

"Did he say anything about how badly August is hurt?"

Before he could answer, Gerda came down the hall and joined them. "Dr. Bradley said that he would talk to us when he's finished, but he was sure that August would recover."

Anna let out the breath she hadn't even realized she was holding. August would be all right.

Lowell and Ollie decided to go back and join the battle against the fire. Although the livery stable was a total loss, the townspeople were still trying to make sure the fire didn't spread to any other structures. All buildings in the vicinity were also wooden and could easily burn.

Gerda went to the kitchen while Anna continued to sit in her rocker. She remembered how she felt when she saw August run into the burning building. Love had welled up and overtaken her completely. She wanted, more than anything, to be able to express that love. But Anna knew that she had had strong feelings twice before. She began to wonder if she could trust her emotions. Nothing she experienced had led to a lasting relationship. Maybe this new love wasn't strong enough either. Anna felt confused, but she didn't want to completely let go of these feelings. They seemed to be different from before, but she couldn't be sure. Life—or was that love—was much too confusing.

By the time Dr. Bradley had finished with his thorough examination, August was exhausted. He had been having such a hard time breathing, and Doc said that was making him even more tired. Unfortunately, there wasn't much Doc could do for August. He said it would take time for all the smoke to get out of his lungs. Until then, he wanted August to take it easy.

"I'll make sure he does." Ingrid Nilsson stepped through the door just as the doctor made that statement.

August was glad to see his mother, even though he hadn't wanted to bother her. He tried to smile, hoping it didn't look like a grimace. Although he didn't have any blisters on his skin—and that was a surprise—it felt as if he had worked two days in the sun without any shade. His skin was tight and dry. He was sure that if he could see in Gerda's mirror, he would be red, too. If he smiled too much, his face might crack.

"Now, Doctor, what do I need to do to help my son?"

Dr. Bradley smiled. "I'm glad you're here, Mrs. Nilsson. I know you'll take good care of him."

August knew his mother. She always wrote everything down. She took a small tablet and pencil out of her handbag and wrote down everything the doctor told her. *Moder* was careful like that.

"Keep the windows open so he has fresh air to breathe. If anyone has time, have them fan him. That will help move the air from the windows to where he is in the bed. You might even send over to the ice house and get him some ice. Chip small pieces off the block for him to eat. That should help him start to cool down." Doc turned and looked at August. "And make sure he drinks a lot of liquid. He's probably pretty dry after being in that fire. It was like a giant oven."

When August's mother turned her attention from the doctor to her son, she asked another question. "And what should I do for his skin? It's awfully red and dry."

"Any kind of lotion you have would be good. Or if you don't have any, use butter or lard. But be careful when you are smearing it on him so you don't damage his skin any more than it already is."

Well, great! August couldn't help thinking about Anna being in the same apartment. *I'm going to look like a greased pig. That should really make her love me.*

Soon after the doctor left, Johan and Marja Braxton arrived at the top of the stairs. When Anna opened the door, she was surprised. Both of them carried folding cots.

"We thought you might need these for tonight." Marja put her cot down and leaned it against the wall beside the door. She took Johan's from him, and he left. "I knew that with two extra people up here, you need a place for them to sleep."

Anna thanked her. "We'll put one in my bedroom and the other in Gerda's. That's where August is. He probably needs someone in there with him all night."

Mrs. Nilsson came out of Gerda's bedroom. "Marja, how nice to see you."

Marja handed Ingrid a small tin. "Here's some salve. We've had good results using it on burns. Maybe it will help August."

"Thank you." Mrs. Nilsson hugged her friend.

"Another thing we've done when someone has a burn is put mint compresses on it. The herb has a cooling effect. Johan is going over to the garden to pull some of mine. He'll bring it up here for you."

Ingrid smiled. "How thoughtful you are, Marja."

"The women at the church want to help, too, so they've made a list of people who will bring meals to you the next few days."

Anna was surprised. "There are three women here. We could take care of the cooking."

Marja turned toward her. "We know you can." She put her hand on Anna's arm. "But August is always so helpful to everyone else. This is a way to show how much we love him."

All Anna could do was nod, because her throat was tight and her eyes were full of tears.

How long was he going to have to stay in this room? August was tired of the confinement, even though it had only been three days. He sat up on the side of the bed. He had to sit there for a few moments. All this inactivity would make any man feel a little woozy. Of course, the fire had sapped his strength, too. While he waited for his head to clear, he flexed his stiff hands. The blaze had left them dry, cracked, and sore.

He was glad that no one had taken away his clothes. He reached across to the chair and got his trousers. After carefully pulling them on, he stood up, walked to the window, and leaned both hands against the facing. His gaze swept up and down the street. There was a lot of activity outside. That was good. Everything was back to normal. At the end of the street, he could barely make out the pile of burned-out rubble that used to be the livery stable. At least nothing else burned.

When Gustaf came to see him the day after the incident, he told August that he had banked the fire in the forge and closed up the smithy. August was thankful to have such a thoughtful brother. How could he have let petty, childish jealousy rob him of the close relationship they should have enjoyed all those years? He was thankful that God had helped them overcome that obstacle.

Over the last few days, August often questioned his own sanity. *What kind of idiot runs into a burning building?* But then the memory of the agonized cry of the crazed animal rang through his head, and he answered his own question. The kind of idiot that he was, and he would do it again without a moment's hesitation. The best thing about all that happened was that not a single animal was destroyed in the fire, or even injured.

His mother, sister, and Anna had been taking care of him. The ice soothed his throat those first two days, and the salve that the Braxtons contributed helped his skin, even though it didn't smell very good. The mint compresses had been the most pleasant part of the treatment. At least they hadn't used butter or lard on him. He had been spared that indignity.

The three women had taken turns fanning him. When one would tire, another would take her place. There hadn't been much talking during that time. His throat hurt too much. Besides, Doc had suggested that he give his voice a rest.

Lying there covered up to his chin with a sheet, August had loved Anna with his eyes. The only problem was that she didn't look straight at him when she was in the room. She would sit and fan the fresh air toward him. Sometimes, she even read to him from the Bible or that book of poetry he bought her. The sound of her voice was music to his ears—and his heart. Then she would relinquish her place to his mother or sister. They never left Anna in the room alone with him more than a few minutes.

Why was Anna so aloof?

"What are you doing up?" Gerda tried to help August back to bed, but he shook her hands off.

"I'm not an invalid. I need to move around to keep up my strength. I'll be going back to work soon."

Gerda put her hands on her hips the same way their mother often did. "Not before Doc says you can."

August dropped onto the side of the bed. "When is he coming again?"

"Later today, I think." Gerda sat in the chair beside him.

"Good. Is Anna working at the Dress Emporium right now?"

He didn't like the look in Gerda's eyes when she answered. "Why do you want to know where Anna is?"

August got up again and walked back to the window. He leaned his left arm against the facing and studied the street again. He didn't want Gerda to read anything in his expression. "I need to talk to you about her."

When he turned back around, Gerda had crossed her arms. "I'm listening."

After August told Gerda how aloof Anna had been, he asked her if she knew of anything he had done to make Anna mad or to hurt her. At first, he thought Gerda wasn't going to answer. She just sat there. Then she bowed her head, and he knew she was praying. He decided to pray, too.

After a period of silent contemplation, Gerda started telling August how worried she was about Anna. She finished by telling him that Anna thought something was wrong with her that kept a man from loving her enough.

"That's the most ridiculous thing I've ever heard. There's nothing wrong with Anna."

"I told her that, but I don't think she believed me, even though I shared Scriptures with her about how special God had created her. At first, I thought she understood, but now I'm not so sure."

That gave August something to think about. When Gerda left to start dinner, he kept mulling over what she had said. He picked up his Bible and asked God to show him how he could help Anna. He was more determined than ever to marry her.

Chapter 14

When Dr. Bradley came to check on August later that day, he found him sitting in the rocking chair in the parlor of the apartment.

"Doc, I want to go home." August got up and walked toward the door. "And I want to go back to work."

The doctor didn't even examine August this time. He turned toward Ingrid, who had opened the door, and smiled. "I think he's ready."

She nodded and took hold of August's arm with both hands. "I believe you're right." She smiled up at him. "You can't keep a Nilsson man down very long."

August knew that it was probably too late in the day to get much work done. It would take too long to get the forge hot enough. He would start early the next morning. After gathering up all his belongings that had made their way into the apartment, he headed toward the boardinghouse. In one way, he was glad to be out of that apartment. It had almost seemed like a prison to him. But in another way, he would miss seeing Anna so often. He would have to work on ways to accomplish that.

On the way home, he noticed a poster on the front window of the mercantile. The first barn dance of the summer would be Saturday night. Anna liked to dance, so he would ask her to let him escort her to the festivity. He whistled a happy tune the rest of the way to his room.

The next day was Friday, and August only worked until noon. He didn't have many things on his table to finish. As soon as people realized that he was open again, that would change. But he was glad to be able to quit after only five hours. It would take him a little while to build back to his original strength.

After closing the smithy, he went over to the Dress Emporium. Gerda and Anna were in the shop when he arrived.

"How are my two favorite girls today?"

Both of them looked up from their individual tasks when they heard his voice. By their expressions, he could tell that Gerda was glad to see her brother. Anna was a little wary of him. That was all right.

"I came to ask if I could take the two of you to lunch at the hotel. I want to thank you for the use of your apartment."

Anna was quick to answer. "Oh, you don't have to thank us for that."

"I know." August smiled straight into her eyes. "I want to. Please let me do this for you."

218

His Brother's Castoff

Anna couldn't look away from the pull of August's intense gaze. What was it about this man? Everything about him interested her. Those eyes that sometimes looked cloudy and gray were as blue as Lake Ripley. If she wasn't careful, she could drown in their depths. She was glad when he finally looked at his sister, wasn't she?

"What do you say?" he asked.

Anna glanced at Gerda, who was smiling. Anna was trying to think of a kind way to turn him down when she heard Gerda accept for both of them. How could she? Being with August was dangerous to Anna's peace of mind.

When they arrived at the hotel, they were shown to a table by the window. Tantalizing aromas caused Anna's stomach to growl. She was mortified. Now she wished she had eaten a good breakfast. She glanced up and caught a twinkle in August's eyes.

"It's a good thing I came along when I did." He laughed. "I rescued you from dying of hunger."

Anna joined his laughter. The rest of the meal was spent in pleasant banter as they consumed the delicious food. While he escorted them back to the store, Anna realized that she had more fun at lunch than she had experienced in a long time.

After they unlocked the door to the Dress Emporium, Gerda hurried through the shop and opened the door that connected to the mercantile. Then she went into the workroom, leaving Anna and August alone in the display room. Anna started straightening the accessories on the sideboard by the outside wall. She kept her back to August, but she was totally aware of him.

"Thank you for lunch."

When he spoke, his voice came from close behind her. "You're welcome, Anna."

She liked the way he said her name. It sounded different from the way anyone else had ever said it. As if her name was special. She wanted to turn toward him so she could see the expression on his face. But she was afraid to. He was standing much too close.

"I want to ask you something."

The words sounded husky, almost intimate. She wanted to shake that thought out of her head, but if she did, he might think she didn't want him to ask his question.

"What is it, August?" She almost couldn't get the words out.

He stepped back a little, so she turned toward him. He slid his hands into the front pockets of his trousers. She wondered if he was trying to hide his hands. What a silly thought!

"There's a barn dance tomorrow night. Are you going?"

Anna looked up into August's face, studying his expression. "I hadn't planned on it."

He shuffled his feet, as if he was nervous. "I want to go, but not alone. Maybe you could go with me. I know how much you like barn dances." Finally, he smiled.

She had always liked parties. All kinds of parties. She loved being around people, and it had been a long time since she felt like going to a party. Maybe it was time to go again.

"It's okay, Anna. You don't have to go if you don't want to." His voice sounded tender.

"But I do want to go. Thank you for asking me. You're a good friend."

A good friend. Anna had called him a good friend. That was nice, but August wanted so much more than friendship from her. August paced across his room at the boardinghouse and leaned one hand on the window frame. He stared out the window and watched birds flit around in the tops of the trees across the street. Had he only heard what he wanted to when he asked God if Anna was the woman he should share his life with? He was glad that he had time before the party to ask Him once again. After praying a few minutes, he listened very carefully for God's answer. Just as it happened before, he felt that God was telling him yes. So he asked God how to reach her with his love.

It was too bad that the livery stable had burned down. He wanted to rent a nice buggy to take her to the dance. Instead, he had to borrow a vehicle from his brother. Since Gustaf and Olina were also going to the party, they would be using the buggy. So August borrowed the farm wagon.

Before he picked up Anna, he cleaned the wagon as much as he could. He put one of the quilts his mother had given him on the seat to pad it for Anna. He wanted her to be comfortable on the hard wooden bench. He planned to be especially attentive to her at the party. He would look for ways to show his affection for her.

The ride out to the Madsens' farm, where the dance was being held, was pleasant. August kept up a lively conversation with Anna. That in itself was surprising. He was the quiet Nilsson brother, but since he had been coming to the dress shop often, he had been talking more around Anna. She was surprised that she enjoyed the ride so much. Of course the padded seat helped. August had explained about wanting a buggy, and she was impressed by his thoughtfulness. He was a nice man. No wonder her heart was filled with strong emotions toward him. It would be so easy to love him completely, but there was still that question in her mind.

They arrived at the large barn, which was overflowing with the light of the many lanterns hung around the walls, and anticipation filled Anna's heart. It had been too long since she had been to a dance. The musicians were already playing. There were two fiddlers and a banjo player, and one man played a harmonica. A square dance was starting. August pulled Anna into a square that was forming at one end of the barn.

It didn't take long for them to catch up with the other dancers. They moved through the intricate patterns shouted out by the caller. Every time August held her in his arms for a twirl, it seemed to Anna as if he held her a little tighter than anyone else did. When that set was over, Anna felt breathless. . .and warm.

"Let me get you some cider," August whispered in her ear.

He left her sitting on a bale of hay and quickly returned with two cups of the cool liquid. When he sat beside her, their shoulders rested against each other. She liked the feeling of him next to her. A wall of strength. The faint scent of bay rum filled the air and mingled with the aromas of hay, food, and cider.

Before long another farmer asked Anna to be his partner. When she looked at August, he nodded. While that set of square dances continued, Anna often glanced at August. Every time she saw him, he was watching her every move. She thought he would dance with someone else, but he didn't.

The next song was a waltz, and August claimed Anna as his partner. Although they only touched in three places—his hand on the back of her waist, her hand resting on his shoulder, and their other hands clasped—she felt a strong connection between them. For a large man, he moved with a grace that not many men had. He led her smoothly around the floor. She felt as if she were floating on air. Too soon the song ended, and another farmer asked her to share a square dance with him.

As before, August didn't dance with anyone. He sat on a bale of hay and sipped a cup of cider, never taking his eyes from her. Why didn't he dance with someone else, or at least go talk to some other men?

This pattern continued for most of the evening. August danced with Anna about half the time. He asked for all the waltzes and the lively polkas. When they were getting refreshments, he never left her side. While they were together off the dance floor, he carried on conversations with her. But when they waltzed, he whirled her across the floor and seemed to be communicating something to her with his eyes. She wasn't sure what it was.

The only part of the evening that was uncomfortable was when she was with another man. August always agreed to share her company, but while she danced with someone else, he stared at her. The longer this went on, the more Anna's memories of another party surfaced. The evening Gustaf told her he only wanted to be her friend. August had stared at her that night, too. Finally, Anna had all she could take.

August knew something was bothering Anna when she stalked across the floor toward him. She was not smiling. He didn't want everyone to hear whatever she had to say to him.

He stood when she got close. "How about taking a walk in the cool night air with me?"

Anna seemed surprised, but she agreed. He held out his arm. When she rested her hand in the crook, he led her out the door and across the barnyard to a bench that sat under a spreading maple tree. Moonlight illuminated the area, but they were hidden in the shadows. Across the fence that surrounded the pasture, a cow lay in the tall grass. Her calf snuggled close to her, and they were both asleep.

"What's bothering you, my Anna?"

For a moment, the silence was broken only by sounds of the night. In the distance, bullfrogs croaked, and a cow lowed in the pasture. August could tell by the expression on Anna's face that she was surprised by what he said.

She ignored the name he called her and answered the question with one of her own. "Why were you staring at me all evening?"

August was glad that she had been watching him, too. "Ah, Anna, I couldn't help it. Your loveliness is breathtaking."

The comment seemed to make Anna speechless. Then she said, "But you didn't answer my question."

August tried to ignore the excitement that was building inside him. Anna looked down at her hands, which were clasped in her lap. He placed his hand over hers. Above them, the leaves fluttered in the soft breeze, making a whispering sound as they touched.

She turned to look at him. "I was remembering another party when you watched me all evening, too."

He smiled. "And when was that? I've watched you at many parties."

Anna gasped and started to pull her hands out from under his. "It was the night that Gustaf took me home the last time. He told me that he only wanted to be friends."

He slid his arm across her shoulders and searched her face, trying to read her emotions. "And that made you unhappy, didn't it?"

"I loved him. . .and thought he loved me." The words were so quiet that August almost missed them.

Footsteps crunched along the gravel walkway. He glanced to see who was coming, but the person continued on to the house without noticing them under the tree.

"Are you still upset about that night?" August pulled her closer and settled her head against his shoulder. "Later you did plan to marry Olaf."

Anna relaxed in his embrace. "I still love Gustaf, but more like a brother. I know Olina is the woman for him."

August rested his chin on her head, inhaling the sweet fragrance of her hair. He wished he could stay here with her forever.

"Olaf didn't love me enough."

"He wasn't the man for you either." August paused, then continued. "Anna, I would like to court you."

Anna was surprised when August said that. Wasn't he only a friend? Oh, her feelings for him were strong and deep, but were they enough? And would his feelings continue if they courted?

"I'm afraid."

He pulled away and looked at her. "You, Anna? You're strong and fearless."

"But not in the ways of love."

He laughed. "You are a delight to me. *Ja*, that's for sure."

She was confused. "Why do you say that?"

"I've been praying about a relationship with you. I want to tell you what the Lord showed me about you." He turned to face her. He took both her hands in his and looked straight in her eyes. " 'Thou art all fair, my love; there is no spot in thee.' That's the verse God showed me for you. You know that in the Bible it talks about spots and blemishes. This verse tells me there is not a single blemish in you. You are perfect the way God made you."

Anna could hardly believe her ears, but her spirit heard and drank in every word. They were an added balm on her wounded heart, to help finish the healing the Lord had already started.

"Yes."

Once again Anna's voice spoke in a whisper. August wondered what she meant.

"What?"

"Yes." This time when Anna answered, it was stronger. Then she laughed, her voice playing a melody in his heart. "I would like to be courted by you."

August could hardly believe it. She had agreed. This was wonderful! He had thought it would take longer.

"I mean right away." He saw the stars twinkling in Anna's eyes, even though they were under the shade of the tree.

"Right away would be nice." Her shy smile touched his heart.

August didn't want to return to the party, but he knew they had been outside as long as they should. This time he danced every dance with her. He never took his eyes off her, but she didn't seem to mind. Tomorrow the courtship would start in earnest.

Chapter 15

When August arrived home that night, he fell to his knees and dropped his head into his hands. "Help me be what Anna needs, Lord. Show me the best ways to express my love to her. I've waited so long."

On Monday morning, he didn't go to the smithy first. After breakfast, he drove the wagon back to Gustaf's. On the way, he noticed that the open fields between town and the house were full of wildflowers. He was glad he had walked over to pick up the wagon the day before. On his way back into town, he gathered colorful blossoms. Instead of going to his place of business, he went to the Dress Emporium. It wasn't open, so he climbed the stairs to the apartment. Each step built his anticipation for glimpsing Anna's lovely face again. Had it only been a few hours since he had seen her? It felt like an eternity.

Gerda answered his knock. August peeked around the large bouquet and winked at her. She stepped back.

"Anna, it's for you," she called, turning toward the dining room.

⌘

Anna set her cup of tea on the table and went into the parlor. A rather large bouquet filled the doorway and hid whoever was carrying it. Black-eyed Susans, butterfly flowers, wild geraniums, trillium, and columbine—some of her favorites. She put her hand to her chest to still the fluttering of her heart. Without seeing him, she knew it had to be August. He was aware of how much she liked wildflowers. It was one of the things they discussed on one of his many trips to visit her at the shop. The only way he could have gotten those was to pick them this morning. She could picture him walking through a field of wildflowers, filling his arms with the multicolored blossoms. No one had ever before done anything like that for her.

"Come in, August. Would you like a cup of tea, or should I make you some coffee?" Anna's voice sounded breathless, but she couldn't help it. He could think whatever he wanted to about that.

When he stepped over the threshold, Anna thought that she would like to have him in her home every day. . .for the rest of her life. She only hoped their love was strong enough to last that long.

Gerda offered to take the flowers and put them in a vase. "If we have one large enough," she said with a chuckle.

August slid his hands into the front pockets of his jeans. Anna wondered why he was nervous today. She wanted to make him feel comfortable. "You didn't say whether you wanted tea or coffee."

He glanced toward the dining room. "Whatever you and Gerda are having is fine."

Anna nodded. "We're finishing our breakfast with a cup of tea." She led the way to the table. "Have a seat. I think there's another cup in the teapot, if that's what you want."

"Tea'll be fine."

After the wonderful time they had over tea, August came to the Dress Emporium at noon with a picnic basket. While they were visiting that morning, Anna and Gerda had told him how busy they were. He decided that they might like to spread a picnic on the table in the workroom. That way the young women wouldn't have to take time from their work to prepare the noon meal.

When Anna helped August put the tablecloth that he had packed in the basket on the cutting table, their hands brushed. His touch was light as a feather, but it caused excitement to zing up her arm. She quickly glanced at his face. He looked as surprised as she felt. Maybe he had felt a spark, too. She hoped so.

In addition to eating the wonderful food, the three friends laughed and joked a lot.

"I didn't know you could cook, August." Anna grinned up at him. "You might make someone a good wife."

August almost choked on the piece of fried chicken he was chewing. "A good wife?"

She laughed. "Yes, you could do the cooking and clean up the kitchen." She reached for another hot roll.

He had a thoughtful look on his face when he took her hand in his. "I wish I could cook if it would make you happy, Anna, but Mrs. Olson prepared this lunch for me."

Oh, August, you make me happy. Anna wished she were brave enough to say the words, but she wasn't. . .at least, not yet.

Not only did August come at noon, he came to the store after he finished work. He asked if there was any way he could help them. He looked at Anna when he asked the question, but Gerda put him to work carrying crates of new fabrics from the storeroom to the showroom. A new shipment had arrived on the morning train. The stationmaster delivered them right after noon, but Gerda and Anna hadn't had time to unpack the merchandise.

Gerda came back into the workroom. "Anna, why don't you show August where you want the bolts of fabric placed." She sat down and started sewing lace on a blouse.

Anna wondered if Gerda was giving her and August time to be alone. When she stepped into the front room, he had set the final wooden crate on top of the stack.

"Do you have a crowbar to open these?" He leaned one arm on the top box. "I'll do it for you."

She had been opening crates ever since they opened the Dress Emporium, but she was glad he wanted to do it for her. She told him where he would find the tool in the storage room. While he was gone, she walked to the front window and looked out at the busy street. Litchfield was growing, and every day activity increased. An ice cream shop had opened down the block. Of course, all the new people coming into town gave her and Gerda a lot of business, and she was glad.

Soon her mind filled with the man who was helping her. *Lord, I love him so much.* If only her heart was at peace. Her thoughts were interrupted by August returning. Immediately, he started opening the top crate. It was full of bolts of silk.

"Anna, maybe you should unpack this. I'm afraid all the calluses on my hands would snag it. It's too pretty to damage."

She turned around and glanced at him standing beside the counter. Tall and strong with blond hair and those penetrating eyes that changed color to match what he wore. Looking at him caused her heart to beat faster. He was thoughtful in so many ways. His tender side balanced his virility. Why hadn't she seen it sooner? What would her life have been like if he had been the first man to seek her out?

After helping her unpack the crates, he asked her if he could pick her up for church the next Sunday. "Monday, I'm going to Minneapolis to buy a buggy. I don't want to take you anywhere else in a farm wagon. You deserve to ride in style."

❧

When August went to the station to catch the eastbound train, he was surprised to see Anna and Gerda waiting for him on the platform. It was more pleasant waiting for the train to arrive since they were there, especially Anna. But the wait wasn't long enough. The loud train was right on schedule. It was the first time in his life he wished for his ride to be late.

Before he boarded the car, he took Anna's hands in his. "Thank you for coming. I should be home in a couple of days."

Anna reached up and placed a light kiss on his cheek. Then she blushed and turned around. Gerda stood back and smiled.

On the long ride, August had time to think about that kiss. During the whole time, the spot on his face still felt the imprint of her soft lips. It didn't matter that the touch had been as fleeting as the flutter of a butterfly's wings. Anna had kissed his cheek. He knew it was a silly thought, but he didn't even want to wash his face. He was afraid the feeling would go away. If only they were already married.

He wished he was going to return to their home instead of a lonely room in the boardinghouse.

Minneapolis had grown since the last time he was there, and across the river, the state capital of St. Paul was equally bustling. August couldn't keep from thinking of the many new directions his life had taken. As a boy in Sweden, he never would have imagined that as an adult, he would be a black-smith in the state of Minnesota in the middle of the great country, the United States of America. He would raise his family here, but someday he wanted to take them back to the land where he had been born. They needed to know their heritage.

While he shopped for the right buggy, August learned a lot about what was going on in the rest of the world. There were major changes in transportation, and he wasn't sure he was ready for all of them.

Anna began to worry when August hadn't returned by Thursday evening. What if there had been a train wreck and he was hurt? But she knew if that was true, the news would have reached Litchfield by now. However, something could have happened to him in Minneapolis. Or driving the buggy home. She whispered a prayer for his safety several times during the day, and she couldn't go to sleep that night. She had tried, she really had, but sleep eluded her.

Finally, Anna got out of bed and pulled on her housecoat. After tying the sash, she stood by her window watching the quiet street below, soaking up the peaceful-ness of midnight. The whistle of the westbound train whined in the distance. She almost wished August hadn't left town. She didn't mind riding in a farm wagon with him if that meant he was all right. Her attention was drawn to movement at the end of the street. The shiny paint of a large black surrey glinted in the moon-light. The light was so bright that she could see the red fringe that decorated the roof. A beautiful black stallion pulled the buggy, and August sat on the seat.

Anna smiled to herself. *Thank You, Lord.* Suddenly, Anna yawned, and her eyes felt heavy. She settled into bed with a satisfied sigh. August was home, and all was well.

Because August had so much work waiting for him, it was Friday evening before Anna saw him. He came into the Dress Emporium right before closing time. Anna looked up when the door opened.

"Are you through for the day?" August's voice floated across the room to caress her ears.

"Just about. Why?" Anna couldn't take her eyes off his imposing figure in nice trousers and a white shirt. She wondered why he was dressed like that. She was more used to seeing him in denim trousers or overalls and a plaid work shirt.

"I want to take you for a ride in my new surrey." When August smiled at her, Anna could hardly catch her breath. She had never felt this way before. What was wrong with her?

While they stood there staring at each other, Gerda walked in. "August, when did you get back?" She rushed across the room and hugged him.

Anna wished that she could have done that. She remembered the night of the dance. He had held her in his arms under the tree while they talked. It felt good. . .and so right.

"What are you doing here all dressed up?" Gerda voiced the question in Anna's mind.

August looked above Gerda's head to where Anna was standing. "I came to take Anna for a ride."

"So go, both of you." Gerda made a shooing motion with her hands. "I can close the store by myself."

Anna started patting her hair the way women did when they thought something was out of place. August thought she looked wonderful, but he would give her time to freshen up if she wanted to.

"I need to go get the horse and buggy. I'm keeping them in Gustaf's barn until the livery stable is rebuilt." He smiled into Anna's eyes, which looked green today to match her dress. "I'll be back to pick you up in a few minutes. Is that all right?"

Anna nodded. "Come to the apartment to get me." She followed him out the door.

When August returned, Anna was waiting in the parlor. They went down to the new vehicle standing by the boardwalk.

"It's beautiful, August." Anna clasped her hands. "So shiny. And the horse matches it so well."

Soon they were heading out of town. The slight breeze increased as the horse picked up speed. Anna gave a tiny shiver, and August pulled her toward him.

"I missed you while I was gone," he whispered against her hair. It was a good thing the horse was well trained, because August didn't want to have to pay that much attention to him.

"I missed you, too." Anna pulled away from him a little. "Actually, I was worried about you. I was afraid something bad had happened, since you took so long to come home."

He laughed. He knew this showed how much she cared. "I didn't want to worry you. It took me longer than I thought it would to find the right surrey and horse."

She smiled and moved back closer to him. "Tell me about Minneapolis."

August told her about all the new things he had seen in the large city. "I even had to go into St. Paul to find the right horse. And do you know what I saw there?"

"No, what?"

"A horseless carriage."

Anna looked puzzled. "What is a horseless carriage?"

"Someone took a buggy and put an engine on it. It ran without having a horse pull it."

Since it was almost dark, August didn't want to go too far from town. At a crossroads, he turned the buggy around and headed back. "I don't think anything will come of it, even though people told me that a lot of those contraptions are being used in France. It was very noisy. It scared the horses. I can't ever imagine it sharing the roadways here with the dependable horses we have."

August often came to take Anna for a ride. The more time they spent together, the more she fell in love with him. His kindness and devotion touched a place in her heart that hadn't ever been touched before. Not by Gustaf, not even by Olaf. Hardly a day went by when August didn't come by for lunch or dinner. Even Gerda had started setting a place for him when she was the one preparing the meal.

Anna began thinking about what marriage to a man like August would mean. The dream of a husband and family that she had decided was not God's plan for her became more possible every day. She could imagine strong sons like their father and a few girls who would be tall like her. The more she thought about these things, the less her heart hurt, until one morning she awoke with the knowledge that all the old pain was totally gone.

About two weeks after August asked Anna if he could court her, he went to the mercantile for supplies.

"I know you like books." Marja glanced over toward the bookshelf display. "We have some new ones."

August decided to browse through them before he returned home. There were several novels he hadn't read, but the book that caught his eye was *Sonnets from the Portuguese* by Elizabeth Barrett Browning. When he opened it, he found that it was not a recent publication, but he hadn't ever seen it before. It was bound in the same leather as the Emily Dickinson book he had bought Anna, but it had an added ribbon bookmark bound into it. When he opened it to the marked page, these words caught his eye: "How do I love thee? Let me count the ways."

By the time he finished the poem, he knew that he had to buy this book for Anna. A plan began to form in his mind.

After Marja Braxton wrapped the parcel for him, he took it into the dress shop. Anna was waiting on a customer in the front room. He walked around studying the displays until she was finished.

Then he went to the counter and leaned on it to get closer to Anna. "I have something for you."

She smiled. "I wondered what you were looking for as you walked all over the shop. I thought you were familiar with everything in here. And I was sure you didn't need any of that lace you were studying so intently."

He put the package on the counter between them. "When you open this, please read what's on the page where the bookmark is. I'll be back to pick you up after work. We're going for a ride."

Anna shook her head. The man swaggered as he went out of the store. And he didn't ask if she would go riding with him today. He told her. She waited for the old feelings of being controlled to come over her. But they didn't. She had come to know August's heart. He wasn't overbearing. If he said they were going for a ride, there must be a good reason. She knew he would never intentionally do anything to hurt her. She couldn't help wondering what he was planning.

No one was in the shop, so she went to the workroom. Gerda had gone to the post office, so she was alone. She tore the paper off the book and opened it to the page August told her to read. After the first line, she read slowly to let the words soak into her heart. It expressed how she felt about him, too. The words *freely. . .purely. . .passion. . .smiles. . .tears* touched something deep in her heart. Once again, she read every word. They were so beautiful, and August wanted her to read them for a reason. Thoughts of what that reason could be brought excitement bubbling up from the depths of her heart. She could hardly wait for the ride later that afternoon.

When Gerda returned, Anna told her that she was taking the rest of the day off. She didn't tell her why, even though Gerda looked surprised. When Anna reached the apartment, she went to her wardrobe and looked at all her dresses. Since she was part owner of a dressmaking business, she had more to choose from than most women. She took several out and laid them on the bed. One by one, she picked them up and held them in front of her as she gazed in the looking glass. Finally, she picked a soft green lawn with tiny white flowers and trimmed with lace.

After taking a long soaking bath, she spritzed on some rose water before she dressed. Working deftly with her fingers, she pushed her hair into a pleasing arrangement decorated with a ribbon the same shade as her dress. She thought she would be ready long before August came, but she had just dropped into her rocking chair in the parlor when a soft knock sounded.

She opened the door and caught her breath. August must have spent most of the afternoon getting ready, too. He was smooth shaven, every hair in place. His clothes looked new, and his shoes so shiny that, if she were close enough, she could probably see her reflection in them.

For a moment they stood and looked at each other, then August said in a voice that was husky with emotion, "My Anna. . .you're so beautiful."

They drove out of town toward Lake Ripley. Anna was aware of how their shoulders touched every time the surrey hit a bump. Too bad the buggy had such good springs. She almost wished it was the farm wagon. She liked the feel of August's warm strength when it touched her.

As they rode along, they talked about many things.

"Anna, when you opened the Dress Emporium, you were so. . .strong and forceful." August kept his gaze on the road ahead. "You said that all you wanted was to be a successful businesswoman. Do you still feel that way?"

Anna sighed. "No, August. I really wanted a home and family all along. I just didn't think it would ever happen. I love the store, and I would want to keep the business. . .at least until I have children."

August started around the lake, but he didn't go all the way. Instead, he pulled into a copse of trees that shaded them from the evening sun. Anna was glad. The cool breeze off the water would keep them comfortable on the hot summer day. Birds flitted from tree to tree, calling to each other, and dragonflies flew among the reeds that grew in the shallow water nearby.

After stopping the vehicle, August sat there looking at Anna. She could see the love in his eyes, love such as she read about in the poem he had marked.

"I have a question to ask you." He stopped and cleared his throat.

Anna waited for him to continue, listening to the wind as it softly blew through the trees.

When he started again, the words came out in a torrent. "Anna, I have loved you so long. I can't imagine my life without you. I know this is soon after I asked if I could court you, but I can't wait any longer. . . . Will you marry me?"

The words Anna had been waiting for all her life fell into her heart. She had never heard a man declare his love for her so deeply and sincerely. Warmth flooded her, chasing any remnants of the old feelings that were hiding in the hidden corners of her heart. She tried to answer, but her voice wouldn't work, so she nodded, never taking her eyes from his intense gaze.

August reached to pull her into his arms. The strength of his touch comforted and excited her. He lowered his head until their breath mingled. For a moment he hesitated, as if asking her if he could continue, but she closed the distance between their lips. Tentatively, she touched his. Once, twice. The softness and sweetness were more wonderful than she had ever imagined. A kiss given in love was so much more than the one she had received in anger. She could lose herself in the feelings that overcame her.

When Anna touched her lips to his, August thought he was in heaven. He settled his more firmly on hers and poured all his love into the effort. All the longing. All the passion. Everything around them faded. The only reality was Anna in his arms, returning his kiss with a fervency he had never imagined. He wanted it to last forever, but he knew that would not be a good idea. Reluctantly, he pulled back and rested his forehead against hers. It took several minutes for his breathing to return to normal, and he wasn't the only one.

"Did you read the poem?"

"Yes," she whispered and caressed his cheek with the fingers of one hand. "And it spoke to my soul."

"I'm not good with words, but those could have come straight from my heart to yours."

He pulled her closer against his chest and nestled her head against his neck. "Anna, I have yearned for you so many years. And as my older brother told me, I'm not getting any younger. . . . If it isn't all right with you, I'll understand."

Anna waited for him to continue, then she asked. "August, what are you trying to say to me?"

"I want to get married as soon as possible." The words once again tumbled from him. "Please don't make me wait too long."

Anna sat up and laughed. "You have no idea how happy those words make me. I have wanted a man who felt passion for me."

August's laughter burst forth. "That's what you've got, my Anna. *Ja*, that's for sure!"

Epilogue

September 21 was a cold autumn day with crisp air and bright sunshine. Anna felt as if God was smiling on her wedding day. So much had happened in the last two months. Their brothers and many of the neighbors had helped August build their new home. They would live between Gustaf and Olina's house and the edge of town. Both of their families had helped them gather enough furniture so they could move into the house right away. God wasn't just smiling on her wedding day, He was smiling on her whole life.

Olina and Gerda had designed a wedding dress that was more beautiful than the one Anna had planned to wear before. As Gerda helped her dress in her finery, she thanked God for giving her such a wonderful man. Finally, she understood that August was the one God had created for her to love. Life had a funny way of leading a person down the wrong path. That was what had happened in Anna's life. Or maybe she had made choices that had helped her go the wrong way, but she was thankful that God had brought her back to the right man. She knew that their life together, with God as the center, would be rich and full. Only a few hours, and they would be man and wife—and her life would never be the same.

When Anna walked down the aisle toward the man who was the other half of her heart, love was a beacon shining from his eyes. She was glad that she had chosen to wear a veil. She didn't want August to see the tears in her eyes. He might not understand that they were tears of happiness and joy.

When the organ started playing, August looked at the door at the back of the sanctuary. Anna was covered with a cloud of creamy fabric that was decorated with lace.

Gud, thank You for giving this woman to me. How could he have ever thought of her as his brother's castoff? She was the best gift God had given him, besides Jesus. She fulfilled all the longings in his heart for a wife and family. He was thankful God had helped him win the battle over jealousy. Now he was free to love Anna the way God wanted her to be loved.

Double Deception

To my oldest granddaughter, Marissa Waldron, who is a joy to my heart.
I will enjoy watching you grow into the beautiful woman God intends you to be.
And every book is dedicated to the man who has shared his life with me since 1964,
James Allan Dooley, the love of my life, the man God created to be my husband.

Chapter 1

July 1895

T his is the town." Pierre Le Blanc leaned toward Clarissa Voss, who shared the front seat of the surrey with him. A gentle breeze ruffled the fringe that decorated the roof of the carriage, bringing welcome relief from the summer heat.

"What's so special about this place?" The young woman glanced around. The town seemed nice enough, but nothing made it stand out from the others they'd visited. And they'd visited many over the years. "Oh, look. An ice cream parlor." She started to point, then remembered it wasn't polite. So many things her mother had taught her were drifting out of her life, no matter how hard she tried to hold on to them.

Pierre frowned at her. "You must remember, *Rissa*"—he emphasized the name—"that you have been here before. This is where you had that lovely ensemble made."

Clarissa looked down at the claret-colored silk. It had more ruffles and flounces than she liked, but it was one of the most fashionable dresses she had worn in a long time. It reminded her of the clothing she and her sister wore before their mother died. Barely realizing what she was doing, she picked at the ruffles on the skirt as she looked up again.

They were turning from the street that ran beside the railroad tracks onto a thoroughfare leading through the middle of downtown Litchfield. If anyone had told her four years ago that she would go to Minnesota, she would have laughed and asked where Minnesota was. She never was good in geography, and New Orleans was so far from here—in more ways than one.

Clarissa wished for the quiet streets around their family home. It was situated far from the busy part of town, far from the French Quarter. She longed to hear the soft Southern drawl that had filled the air with a familiar melody. The farther north they moved, the more clipped the speech became. She sighed, longing to see her mother again. If only that were possible.

Pierre stopped the surrey in front of a store with a large sign emblazoned across the top story of the building: BRAXTON'S MERCANTILE. Clarissa looked at the brightly colored words with fanciful letters and curlicues. Her gaze dropped to the windows filled with merchandise. All kinds of merchandise. Then her attention was drawn to the window at the far end.

The words *Dress Emporium* were painted on the glass, but they didn't obstruct the view of the window with its lacy sheer curtains held open by ruffled tiebacks. In the center of the window stood a form displaying an ensemble that included a hat. The chapeau rested on the shoulders of a beautiful, but simple, elegant gown in a lovely shade of blue, and an ostrich feather in the same hue was draped around the brim of the hat. Clarissa knew she would look good in that ensemble. She liked the simpler lines of the garment, and the color would bring out the sky blue of her eyes. She could imagine herself with her abundant black curls pulled up in an elaborate style with a long curl hanging down one side against the soft fabric of the dress. The hat would rest atop the hairstyle, and the wide brim would protect her creamy complexion from the sun. She would feel like a Southern belle again in that dress and hat—instead of what she had become.

"Is that where you had this dress made?" She glanced at the man who shared the seat with her.

Pierre looked at the store before he answered. "Yes." He climbed down from the surrey and came around to help her alight. "We told you all about the people and what transpired when we were here."

Clarissa pulled her light cape closer around her. The breeze felt cooler, and the dress bared her shoulders. The ensemble would be more appropriate for a party than day wear. "Is there any way we could buy the dress and hat displayed in the window of the Dress Emporium?" She was surprised she had the courage to voice the question running through her mind.

Pierre frowned. He jingled the coins in his pocket as if counting how many he had. He always did that when they talked about money. "I suppose it would be good business. But we won't purchase it if it's too expensive. Just try not to seem too interested. Remember—that always drives the price up."

Pierre drew Clarissa's hand through the crook of his arm, and they sauntered into the cool recesses of the mercantile. Clarissa blinked her eyes at the bright light inside. It had looked dark from the outside, but gaslights were scattered along the four walls. She was amazed by the abundance of the merchandise displayed there. They hadn't frequented a store with such a wide variety in a long time. Perhaps this wasn't such a backwater town after all. They wandered around the store and browsed through the items. Soon they reached the open doorway that led to the dress shop.

Pierre looked around the room until he spotted a tall young woman with dark brown hair piled on top of her head in an almost haphazard manner. "Good afternoon, Miss Jenson."

The woman turned toward them. "Hello, Mr. Le Blanc, Rissa. When did you get back in town?"

Pierre removed Clarissa's hand from the crook of his arm and moved closer to Miss Jenson.

Anna, Clarissa thought. *They said her name is Anna.*

"We've just arrived." He turned toward Clarissa. "Come, Rissa—say hello to Miss Jenson."

The woman held out her hand to Clarissa. "Remember, I told you to call me Anna. How lovely you look in that dress."

Clarissa took the proffered hand and gave it a dainty shake. "Yes. Thank you—Anna."

Pierre hovered near the woman. She moved away then and walked behind the counter that spread across the back of the room.

"How may I help you?"

Pierre followed her and leaned on the counter. Clarissa hated the way he flirted with almost every attractive woman they met.

"We'll be in Litchfield longer this time, and I'd rather not stay at the hotel. I want Rissa to be in a better, more homey environment. Do you have any suggestions?" He paused, and when Anna didn't say anything he continued. "Are there any good boardinghouses in town? Maybe in a quiet neighborhood?"

Anna lifted a bolt of fabric from the counter and placed it on a shelf behind her. Clarissa got the feeling she was trying to move away from Pierre. And Clarissa didn't blame her. If only she could put a lot of distance between herself and Pierre. Oh, if only Mother hadn't died.

Anna turned back around. For a moment, she looked as if she were thinking. "The only boardinghouse I know of is the one Mrs. Olson runs." She picked up another bolt of fabric and fussed with it. "When Mr. Olson died, she was left alone in a large two-story house. So she opened the boardinghouse. That might meet your needs. It's on the residential side of town."

"It sounds perfect." Pierre inched down the counter closer to where Anna stood. "You've been so helpful, just as you were when we were here before."

Anna turned to place the bolt on the shelf beside the others. Clarissa walked around the room. The shop carried a lot of accessory items. She noticed a display of lacy white gloves arranged attractively on a small table.

"These are lovely." Clarissa picked up one and pulled it on her left hand. It fit perfectly.

"Olina Nilsson crocheted them." Anna glided around the end of the counter and across the room toward Clarissa. "She's staying home with her two children, and this gives her an outlet for her creative abilities." She picked up the other glove. "Here, try them both on."

Pierre had worked his way around the room to the window display. "Rissa, this dress is lovely. How do you like it?"

Before Clarissa could respond, Anna said, "I tried to get you to use that color when you were here before, but you said you weren't fond of it. I knew it would look good on you with your coloring."

Clarissa inspected the garment. White crocheted lace outlined the neckline. "These gloves would go so well with that dress, wouldn't they—Father?" How she hated calling him that, but he insisted she use that form of address when they were in public.

Pierre looked at her from under hooded eyelids. Clarissa could tell he didn't like her hesitation, and she knew she would hear about it when they were alone, but she didn't care. She was so tired of this charade. If only it could end—but there seemed little hope of that.

He turned toward Anna and gave her a warm smile. "Do you think this would fit Rissa?"

"Yes, I made it soon after you left, and the measurements are very close to hers." Anna smoothed an imaginary wrinkle on the back of the dress.

"Then we'll take it and the hat—and the gloves."

Anna was smiling when she turned around. She led the way to the counter and started to write the sales slip while Pierre pulled his wallet from his pocket.

"Anna, where do you want me to put this?" Ollie Jenson, Anna's brother, called to her as he came through the opening to the workroom, carrying a rocking chair.

"Over there by the window." She gestured toward a spot.

Ollie looked around the back of the chair and saw two people silhouetted against the light from the window. As he drew closer to them, he realized it was Mr. Le Blanc and his daughter. He remembered her being standoffish when they were there before. His brother, Lowell, had said she wasn't that way at all, but that's how she was around him.

"Look who's here." Anna nodded toward the couple.

"Mr. Le Blanc." Ollie spoke to the man while he set the chair near the window; then he glanced toward the woman. "Miss Le Blanc."

For an instant it seemed to Ollie as if she winced. But why would she wince when he spoke to her? Then her eyes lighted up with such a dazzling smile that it almost took his breath away. The warmth in that look touched something deep inside him. He should have tried to get to know her better during their previous visit.

Mr. Le Blanc had flirted shamelessly with Anna on his last trip. The first time he met her, he'd kissed her hand in a regal manner. Ollie decided he could be just as regal as Mr. Le Blanc. He looked into Rissa's eyes and gently took her hand in his. He lifted it to his lips and placed a light kiss on her fingertips.

He was pleased to see a blush stain her cheeks—and relieved she didn't rebuff him. He must have misunderstood when he met her before. How could he have ever thought this exquisite creature was standoffish? Lowell was right; she was friendly and intriguing. Mr. Le Blanc's voice penetrated his thoughts.

"Anna, please join Rissa and me for dinner. We could take you to the restaurant in the hotel."

Anna looked startled. The man was asking her out. It was sure to set August Nilsson off again. August had been terribly jealous of the man on the last visit. Later, he and Anna had worked everything out, and now they were planning their wedding.

"Thank you for the kind invitation, Mr. Le Blanc." Anna stepped around a table and started rearranging the stack of gloves. "My fiancé and I will be dining with his family tonight."

Now the man looked startled. "I'm sorry. I didn't realize you were engaged."

"That's all right, Mr. Le Blanc." Anna smiled at him. "August and I have just recently decided to get married. You couldn't have known. Now let's get these items wrapped up for you."

She went to the window display and removed the hat and dress. Ollie had liked that dress ever since Anna and Gerda finished it. It would look good on Miss Le Blanc. He hoped he would have a chance to see her in it. He wished it could be when he escorted her to one of the frequent socials, but they probably wouldn't be staying long enough for that to happen. A man could hope, though.

Ollie watched Le Blanc while Anna finished the sale. Something about that man made Ollie uncomfortable. He wasn't sure what it was. He decided to make an effort to get to know the Le Blancs better, especially Rissa. He definitely didn't sense anything wrong with her.

Ollie left the shop and headed out of town to the farm. Once there he sought out Lowell, who was working in the barn. "You'll never guess who I just saw in town."

Lowell looked up from the horse he was currying. "So why don't you tell me instead of keeping me guessing?"

He was always so serious. Ollie often told him he should take time to have more fun. Ollie picked up a currying comb and went into the stall adjoining the one where his brother was busy. He set to work on the palomino while he talked. "You remember earlier in the summer when that Le Blanc family came to town?"

"Sure." Lowell stopped and leaned his arms on the half wall that divided the enclosures. "What about them?"

"They were in the dress shop when I took the rocker to Anna." Ollie stood and looked his brother in the eyes. "I believe you're right about Miss Le Blanc. She was much friendlier today."

Lowell frowned. "What do you mean, friendlier?"

"I don't know. I had the impression she was glad to see me."

"So?"

"So you were right." Ollie returned to currying the horse. "But I don't think I like her father."

Lowell looked thoughtful. "I never did warm up to him myself. What did he do today?"

The horse stamped its hoof, and Ollie had to move to keep his own foot from being stepped on. "He asked Anna if he could take her to dinner at the hotel."

Lowell raised his brows. "That's not a good idea."

"Oh, Anna set him straight. She told him she and August are going to be married. Le Blanc didn't seem to like that a bit."

Lowell put his hands in the back pockets of his jeans. He rocked up on the balls of his feet then down again. "I never felt at ease around that man. It's too bad Rissa is kin to him. I wouldn't mind knowing her better."

Ollie didn't like what his brother said. He wanted that privilege himself. When he and Lowell were younger, they used to wrestle, trying to see who was stronger. Since becoming adults, they'd been best friends as well as brothers. But right now, Ollie wanted to punch him. Where had that thought come from? What was happening to him? Surely that little filly with the black hair and blue eyes couldn't come between them. A picture crept into his thoughts. A warm smile with twinkling eyes. Cheeks stained with a becoming blush.

This could be a real problem.

Chapter 2

S oon after Ollie left the dress shop, August Nilsson arrived. Anna studied her hands for a moment before she began rearranging the items on the counter. Clarissa wondered why she appeared so nervous, then she remembered Pierre telling her August was jealous of him on their other trip. The big man looked muscular—and nice. She couldn't blame him for being jealous. Pierre was up to no good. He left one or more broken hearts in every town they exited. Even after such a short time, Clarissa liked Anna Jenson. She was glad a man like August was going to marry her. They looked good together with his blond handsomeness and her dark coloring.

"August." Anna hurried from behind the counter and took his arm when he entered. "Look who's come back to town."

The two men eyed each other for a moment, and the air crackled with tension; then August stepped forward and extended his hand. "It's good to see you, Le Blanc."

Pierre hesitated a moment, then reached out. After all, it wasn't good for his business to antagonize anyone this early in the game. He clasped August's hand and smiled. Clarissa wondered why no one besides her could tell how insincere that smile was. The only time he gave a real smile was when he was counting his ill-gotten gains. She didn't want him hurting these people. If only she could do something about it—but she hadn't even figured out a way to escape from his clutches herself. Oh, she had dreamed about it often enough. Either she escaped, or someone rescued her, but those dreams were like the fairy tales her mother used to read to her. They weren't real.

August turned toward her, and Clarissa smiled. She never wanted to use people the way Pierre did. She hoped he could see her smile was sincere.

August smiled at her warmly. "And I'm glad you're back, Rissa. Are you staying in town long?"

Pierre stepped behind her. He placed his hands on her shoulders and gripped—hard. When she tried in an unobtrusive way to pull away, he wouldn't let go. She might as well stand still. It would hurt less. But she didn't like his touching her, whether he was hurting her or not.

"Actually, we want to spend the rest of the summer here." Pierre was so close, his breath moved tendrils of her hair. It was all she could do to keep from

243

shivering in disgust. "Maybe longer."

Anna clasped August's hand and looked up into his face. "Pierre and Rissa don't want to live in the hotel. Do you think Mrs. Olson has any vacant rooms?"

August smiled at Anna. Clarissa hoped someone would look at her like that someday, but with the way they lived their lives, it was unlikely. Her mother would roll over in her grave if she knew what Pierre had done since she died. This was not the life Mother had wanted for her daughters.

"Yes. Just yesterday a family moved out. Their house had burned, and they lived in the boardinghouse while it was rebuilt. Mrs. Olson said something at breakfast about cleaning up those rooms today. She was wondering where she would find more boarders." August turned toward Pierre. "Maybe you're the answer to her prayers."

Pierre moved around Clarissa. She was sure that last statement had made him squirm. She knew he didn't believe in prayers, but she wished she knew more about them. Before her father had died, the family attended church and had family devotions together, but she had been so young she couldn't understand much of it. Since she had been traveling with Pierre, they hadn't gone to church. They were often on the run by the time they'd stayed in a town no longer than a week.

"That's good. Nilsson, would you be so kind as to tell me how to find this boardinghouse?" Clarissa hated the sound of Pierre's voice, especially when he was trying to ingratiate himself into the society of a town.

August dropped a quick kiss on Anna's cheek, and a blush stole over her face. Clarissa remembered that before he died, her father and mother had had a relationship like the one August and Anna seemed to have. And it was the kind of relationship she wanted with a man. Not one such as her mother and Pierre had. She'd heard them arguing about the money he spent. He'd been attentive to her before they married but stopped as soon as he had the ring on her finger.

"I'll do more than that." August moved toward the door. "I can take the two of you there myself."

Pierre rented the two adjoining rooms on the second floor of the boardinghouse, then left Clarissa in her room with her carpetbag and the new ensemble they'd purchased. He said he was going to pick up her trunk. Clarissa was glad to have time away from him for a while.

After hanging up the new dress, she opened her bag and started putting her unmentionables in the drawers of a polished oak highboy that sat beside one window. Then she turned around and surveyed her surroundings. It was so long since she'd had a room of her own in a real house. This one was large and airy. Since it was a corner room, she had windows on two sides, so light poured in between the priscilla curtains, bathing the room in golden brightness. She opened one window and drew in a breath of fresh air. Then she opened a window on the other wall, and a breeze blew through, cooling the room a bit.

When they had lived in New Orleans, Clarissa's room had been about this size, so it made her feel as though she had come home. Even the wallpaper with a soft cabbage-rose pattern resembled the paper she had chosen when she was just nine years old. The tall brass bed gleamed in the sunlight, and the plush quilt that covered it repeated the colors of the wall covering. She went to the bed and sat on the edge. The soft mattress was inviting. She had slept on the hard ground too long.

Clarissa took off her dress and petticoats and slipped into her dressing gown. Then she went back to the bed. Stretched out on top of the covers, she felt cradled in the softness. Turning on her side, she nestled her head into the down pillow. She was going to rest only a few minutes, but before long, she drifted off to sleep, dreaming about her beautiful, loving mother and the wonderful life that had disappeared like a vapor.

Ever since Ollie told Lowell about seeing the Le Blancs in town, he sensed Lowell's withdrawal from him. What was the matter with the man? He'd only agreed with him. That Le Blanc gal was a prize, and he'd told Lowell so.

Lowell had always been quieter than he, but now his quietness bordered on sullenness. Ollie was tired of it. He saddled one of the horses and rode off down the road to exercise it. A buyer from the cavalry was coming in a few days, and he wanted all the horses in top form. People sought their family's ranch out because of the quality of the horses they raised. It was a good business that provided a comfortable living for the whole family.

He headed to his favorite place. The prairie grass grew tall and blew in the wind. Here and there a copse of trees provided welcome shade from the hot summer sun. And the frequent pools of shimmering water gave the horses plenty to drink. As he galloped across the prairie, his mind returned to the time when he had been in town. He could feast his eyes all day on that pretty little woman. She had been dressed in a pretty gown with ruffles and lace, but he could imagine her with her ebony hair pulled back and tied with a scarf. That's the way Anna wore hers when she was riding Buttermilk.

He wished Rissa was wearing riding clothes now and galloping beside him across the prairie. He was sure her sky blue eyes would light up, and the wind would bring out the roses in her creamy cheeks. He wondered if she knew how to ride a horse. Maybe he should ask. He could teach her anytime she wanted to learn.

He slowed the horse to a trot and turned back toward the farm. Wasn't there any reason for him to return to town?

Pierre carried Clarissa's trunk upstairs and stayed in her room while she unpacked it. She wished he wouldn't. It made her uncomfortable when he was in her room. She didn't like the way his eyes slid over her body, half hidden behind his lowered eyelids. She felt somehow as if she needed a bath.

"Did you notice the variety of merchandise in Braxton's Mercantile?" He sat in the straight chair and propped his foot on the knee of his other leg.

Any minute, Clarissa expected him to lean the chair back against the wall. She hoped he would—and that the chair would slip. She knew her thoughts weren't kind, but when had he ever been kind to her? She was only a means to an end for him. A tool. A pawn.

"Yes," she answered distractedly. "It's a nice store."

"Do you realize what that means?"

She turned and looked at him. His voice betrayed an excitement she hadn't seen in him for a long time. "What?"

Pierre stood and took out a cheroot.

Clarissa frowned. "Please don't smoke in my room. It's so smelly."

He struck the match and held it to the tip of the rolled tobacco. After the smoke wreathed his head, he threw back his head and laughed. She wondered why he was so happy—besides the fact he was tormenting her with his smoke. She walked to the window and breathed in a lungful of fresh air.

He followed her and stood so close she could feel his breath on her neck. "If you weren't so valuable to me as a daughter. . ."

He left the sentence dangling, but she knew what he meant. He often hinted he found her desirable. The thought sickened her. She wasn't entirely ignorant of the ways of men and women. She cringed and moved back to finish unpacking the trunk.

He took another long draw on the thin cigar and blew the smoke toward her, then continued their conversation about the store as if he hadn't stopped. "Because of the variety of merchandise, I can tell this town has wealth. Now if we can figure out how to transfer much of it to my pockets."

Clarissa shuddered. Her heart broke for the nice people she had met. If only there was a way to stop him.

❧

Ollie pulled up at the blacksmith shop where August was plunging a horseshoe into the bucket of water to cool it. Steam hissed and shot up into the air.

August turned his face away and saw him standing in the doorway. "Ollie, what brings you here?"

"I want you to check the shoes on the horse I rode into town." Ollie stood with his hands shoved into the front pockets of his jeans. He glanced toward the table where August kept the things that needed repair. He was thankful it was nearly empty. He wouldn't be wasting August's time.

Ollie walked farther into the shadows of the shop. "Do you know who was at the Dress Emporium this morning?"

August placed the cool horseshoe on a pile of similar pieces of metal. "I went by to see Anna earlier, and the Le Blancs were there. Is that who you're talking about?"

Ollie nodded. "How do you feel about that?"

August laid his tongs on the worktable. He pulled out a bandanna from his back pocket and mopped sweat off his face. "It's fine with me. I know I was jealous of him when he was here before, but not now." He stuffed his bandanna into his pocket. "I even took the Le Blancs over and introduced them to Mrs. Olson. They want to stay in the boardinghouse instead of the hotel this time."

Ollie was surprised. "Does that mean they'll be here awhile?" He hoped he didn't sound too eager.

August nodded. "It looks that way."

"Did you two get settled in the boardinghouse?" Anna asked when Clarissa and Pierre entered the dress shop. She moved behind the counter and leaned both arms on it.

Pierre strode to the front of the counter and leaned on it, too, close to Anna. "Yes, it's just what we wanted. Rissa even has a corner room. Very nice."

Anna shifted closer to the shelves lining the wall behind the counter. Clarissa didn't blame her. Pierre was much too forward. One day he would go too far.

"Is there some other way I can help you?" Anna's smile wasn't as broad as it had been earlier.

Pierre straightened and glanced around the store. "Yes, Rissa is so taken with the wonderful outfit we bought her this morning that she'd like to order four more."

Clarissa stifled a gasp. Pierre had told her he wanted to go to the store, but she assumed he meant the mercantile. He'd talked about it so much in her room. But they went into the dress shop instead, and now he was ordering her more dresses. He hadn't said a word about that before they came. She hoped he wasn't planning on using this as a way to get close to Anna again and cause trouble in her relationship with August.

"That's wonderful!" Anna exclaimed. "If you could leave Rissa with us for a while, Gerda and I will help her choose the styles and fabrics that would best suit her."

Clarissa knew Pierre didn't want to leave her there alone, but she was glad. She'd like to spend part of the afternoon with the two women without him hovering over her. It had been a long time since she'd visited with other young women. After Pierre left, Anna took her into the workroom.

"Gerda, look who's come back." Anna moved around Clarissa. "You remember Rissa Le Blanc, don't you?"

"Rissa, how nice to see you again." Gerda, the seamstress, had a beautiful face and pale blond hair. "Will you be in town long?"

Clarissa felt shy around the woman. What was she supposed to know about her? Maybe Pierre hadn't told her everything. "I think we'll be here awhile."

"They're staying at the boardinghouse." Anna sat on the chair by the sewing machine. "Her father wants us to make four new dresses for her."

"That's very nice," Gerda said, smiling.

Clarissa could understand her delight. When Pierre was there before, he'd ordered four ensembles. That would make eight from this one shop. Even though he spent money in each town, he seldom established a strong relationship with any one business.

No one was in the front room of the Dress Emporium when Ollie entered, but the bell above the door announced his arrival. Gerda quickly came through the curtain that covered the opening to the workroom. There was a door, but Gerda and Anna didn't like to shut it during business hours. They also didn't want everyone seeing into the workroom, so just last week he had helped them hang the curtain.

"What can I do for you, Ollie?"

"Is Anna here?" He always felt a little out of place in a woman's shop.

"Sure. Come on back."

He followed Gerda into the workroom, and there, by one of the windows, Rissa Le Blanc stood bathed in a golden glow. The light gave tiny blue highlights to her coal black hair. And her smiling eyes sparked fire in his heart. Something in this woman called to something deep within him, and it took his breath away.

Clarissa returned to her room after she and Pierre ate dinner in the boardinghouse. She was glad to be alone. She wanted to revisit the events of her day, in particular the time she'd spent in the dress shop with Anna, Gerda, and Ollie. Especially Ollie.

He stayed a long time, and the four of them talked and laughed like old friends. She didn't have any friends, but she was sure that was what it felt like. Litchfield seemed to be the home she had hoped for, a place where she could belong. Where she could be accepted for who she was. But these people had no idea who she was, and she wasn't about to tell them. If they ever found out, it would be over. The friendship—and everything else.

She paced back and forth in the room, wringing her hands. She had to stop Pierre, but how? She couldn't allow him to hurt these people as he had so many others. Just how long had this been going on? She usually tried to forget, but tonight she remembered.

She and her sister had been happy when they lived on the plantation with her mother and father. It was a wonder the family had held on to the plantation through the War between the States, but they had. After the war, her grandfather struggled to make ends meet. When her mother and father married, her father helped her grandfather try to turn the plantation around.

Her father died when she was only six years old, and her mother couldn't take care of the property. Then, with her father gone, her grandfather had sold the property and used the money to buy the house in New Orleans. There her mother met and married Pierre. Her wedding day was the beginning of the prison in which Clarissa now found herself.

She wished she were a man. If she were a man, she could stop Pierre, but what could a young woman do? Since he was her guardian, he had the law on his side. Of course he wouldn't have it if anyone ever found out about his illegal activities. She wished she had enough courage to tell someone, but Pierre had threatened her and her sister. Mari wasn't as strong as she was, so Clarissa knew she had to protect her.

Clarissa wanted to be friends with Anna, August, Gerda, and Ollie. Maybe she should just enjoy what she had as long as it lasted. It would end soon enough.

Chapter 3

Lowell let out his breath and frowned. Every time he needed help, Ollie was missing. Then later he would return from town. When Lowell asked him what he was doing in Litchfield, Ollie said he went to get something repaired then visited the Dress Emporium. Their father had asked them to check on Anna, but since she'd become engaged, August was at the store often enough to keep her safe. She didn't need Ollie almost every day.

"Where have you been?" Lowell asked Ollie this time as he rode into the barnyard. "You didn't go to town again, did you?"

Ollie didn't say anything, but Lowell wasn't going to let him off the hook. They had a horse farm to run, and he couldn't do it by himself.

Finally, Ollie spoke. "Yeah, I was in town."

Lowell stepped between his brother and the doorway to the barn. "Just why did you have to go today? You were there yesterday—and the day before—and every day this week. You do have things to do around here, you know."

Ollie looked at Lowell. "I do my share of the chores." He raised his voice. "You haven't had to do anything I usually do. I make sure everything is taken care of before I go."

Lowell raised his own voice. "Sometimes things come up, and I need help, and you aren't here."

Ollie stared at him until Lowell moved from the doorway. Then Ollie led his horse inside. Lowell followed his brother into the cool interior shadows and stood watching as he unsaddled the animal and rubbed him down. For a long time, neither of them said anything.

Finally, Lowell walked over to the stall and leaned one elbow on the half wall. "I suppose you saw Rissa again." It was a statement, not a question.

Ollie stopped grooming the horse and stood silent for a minute. Then he turned toward him. "Yes, I saw her. She was visiting with Anna and Gerda. They've become friends. I think it's good for Rissa. I don't think she's ever had any women friends."

Lowell snorted as he stood up. "Maybe that's because she's just a girl." He crossed his arms over his chest.

"You haven't seen her lately, have you? I wouldn't call her a girl." Ollie resumed working on the horse. "She's a little thing, but she's all woman."

Lowell knew she was a woman. He remembered when the Le Blancs had been in Litchfield earlier in the spring. He carried a picture of her in his head, which he often allowed to take over his thoughts. Lowell wanted to touch her ebony curls. He was sure they would be soft as silk. Her lilting laugh played like a harp in his heart. Her sky blue eyes were appealing, but they looked a little shy. That part of his memory didn't agree with all Ollie had told him about Rissa now. She didn't sound as reserved as he remembered. Maybe it was time for him to see for himself.

"I'm going into town for feed," he told his brother.

He could feel Ollie's gaze boring into his back as he hitched the horses to the wagon. He didn't care. Perhaps if he saw the girl again, he wouldn't be so haunted by these thoughts.

He hadn't driven into town for a while. Usually, he left that to Ollie, who enjoyed talking to people. Lowell liked people, but he wasn't as outgoing as his brother. When he pulled up in front of the mercantile, he glanced at the Dress Emporium. He would order the feed, then check on his sister. He loved Anna, even though she was more like Ollie. She was his baby sister and always would be. He was only one year older than she was, and she would soon be a married woman.

He tied the reins to the hitching post and turned around to come face-to-face with the woman who had filled his thoughts for so long. Standing bathed in the glow from the bright summer sunshine, she was more beautiful than he remembered.

"Hello, Miss Le Blanc."

She stared at him as if she didn't know who he was. What was wrong with her? Maybe she had forgotten meeting him. Ollie had taken up so much of her time since she'd come back to town that she might have forgotten there were two Jenson brothers.

"I know you haven't seen me for a while. I'm Lowell Jenson." He tipped his cap.

She finally gave him a tight smile. "You're Ollie's brother, aren't you?"

Lowell nodded.

"You look a lot like him." She tilted her head and studied him from another direction. "You could almost be twins." Then she continued down the boardwalk away from him.

He entered the mercantile and browsed through the merchandise, not seeing what was in front of him. His thoughts about the young woman distracted him so much he almost forgot to order the feed. After he and Johan had loaded the gunnysacks into the wagon, Lowell went to see Anna in the dress shop.

He always felt ill at ease in the feminine place. All those female fripperies that covered every surface in the room made him nervous. He liked clean, uncluttered space. He hurried through the store to the workroom so as not to disturb anything.

Anna looked up and smiled. "Lowell, how nice to see you." She crossed the room to where he stood and gave him a hug.

He hugged her back stiffly with one arm. He never understood why she and Ollie liked all this touching, but he did love her.

"So how are you doing?" Anna took an interest in everyone around her.

"Fine." He shoved his hands into the back pockets of his jeans. It was the safest place to keep them. "I had to come for feed—for the horses."

Anna raised her brows. "Why didn't you ask Ollie to get it for you? He was here earlier."

Lowell rocked up on his toes and back down. "I know, but I hadn't been to town for a while. I thought I might as well come."

Anna opened her mouth, but Lowell stopped her before she could ask any more questions. "I need to get back to the farm. It's time to feed the horses."

She just nodded and walked out to the wagon with him, then hugged him again.

On the ride home, he mulled over what had happened in town. He remembered Miss Le Blanc—Rissa—being friendlier to him when she was there before. Now it was almost as if she had never met him. It was Ollie's fault. He had turned her against him. It was the first time in Lowell's life he'd felt drawn to a woman, and Ollie had already messed it up. His brother could have any woman he wanted, so why did he choose the one who interested Lowell? He had been so disappointed when the Le Blancs left town the first time. Lowell had started to think he might have a chance to establish a relationship with Rissa this time. Now he wasn't so sure.

Ollie hurried across the barnyard to help Lowell unload the sacks of feed. Neither one spoke or looked at the other as they carried the sacks into the storeroom. They just stared at the ground as they tramped back and forth. When they'd put away the last sack, Ollie started unhitching the horses.

"You don't have to do that. I can take care of it." Lowell didn't want his brother to do him any favors.

Ollie stared at him, then turned back to the horses. "It's okay. I don't want you saying I don't do my share around here."

Lowell put his hands on his hips. "You've done enough as it is." He knew it sounded harsh, but he didn't care. He had worked himself into a frenzy over that woman.

Ollie stopped what he was doing and turned to face him. "Just what do you mean by that?"

Lowell glared at him. "As if you didn't know." He turned to walk off.

His brother grabbed him by the shoulder and jerked him around.

It was too bad he was now as big and strong as Lowell. "Why did you do that?"

"I want to know what you're talking about."

"You've turned that girl against me," Lowell blurted out.

Ollie's mouth dropped open, and he shook his head. "I don't know what you mean. I haven't done anything."

Anger clouded Lowell's thoughts, raising the timbre of his voice as his temper grew. "Then why didn't she seem to know me when I was in town?"

"You went to town to see Rissa?" Ollie almost choked on the shouted question. "I can't believe this! Why would you do that? You knew I was spending time with her!"

They stood toe-to-toe, glaring at each other with fists clenched. Lowell never would hit his brother, but if he hit first—

"Boys, I want to have a word with the two of you."

The sound of their father's voice was like a bucket of cold water splashing against the anger they both felt. They turned and saw him standing in the doorway to the barn. "Let's go inside and sit down."

They followed their father into the shadowy dimness of the building and sat on two bales of hay. The older man towered over his sons.

"I don't like what I've been seeing and hearing lately." He looked at Lowell, then at Ollie. "I don't know what has gotten into the two of you, but we can't run a successful horse farm if you're bickering all the time. It's not the way brothers should treat each other."

Lowell stood and turned away. He wondered how much his father had heard. Probably a lot since they were so loud. He didn't like his father treating him as if he were still a child.

He turned back around. "We'll take care of it, Father." He glared at his brother. "Won't we?"

Ollie glanced from Lowell to his father and back.

Their father looked at each brother in turn. "Just see that you do."

It had been two weeks since they had come to Litchfield. Clarissa had enjoyed every minute of the time. Now she would have to leave, and she didn't want to. Pierre told her after breakfast to be ready to depart by nine o'clock this morning. So here she was in the parlor waiting for him to come with the surrey.

"There you are, Rissa, dear." Mrs. Olson bustled into the room with a picnic basket over her arm. "Your father asked me to fix up this food for you to take on your outing today. He said you might be gone until after dinner tonight. Where are you going?"

Clarissa turned from watching out the front windows. "He wants me to see as much of the beautiful Minnesota landscape as possible while we're here. We'll probably take several trips to explore before we leave."

"You be careful," Mrs. Olson said. "It may be 1895, but some parts of our state are still pretty wild. Don't stray too far off the beaten path."

Clarissa laughed. "I am sure we won't go anywhere dangerous."

The sound of horses and the wagon pulled her attention back to the window. She took the heavy basket from their landlady and again thanked her before stepping out onto the front porch.

"There you are, Rissa." Pierre came up the walk and relieved her of her burden. "The sooner we get on the road, the more we can see." He stowed the basket in the back, then helped Clarissa onto the seat. He clicked his tongue at the horses, and they started toward the main thoroughfare from town. When they had ridden completely out of sight, Pierre turned the wagon onto an overgrown trail.

"Why didn't you bring the surrey?" Clarissa asked. "It's so much more comfortable to ride in."

"As you know, we'll have to cross a lot of rough terrain to reach the campsite. It wouldn't be good for the surrey. This wagon is fine." Pierre's eyes gleamed. "What's the matter, Rissa? Don't you want to leave the comforts of town?"

She glared at him, crossed her arms, and turned away. The wagon hit a deep rut, and she almost fell out. She grabbed the edge of the seat and clung to it while Pierre's laughter pealed across the rolling plains.

No, she didn't want to leave the comforts of town or anything else that was there, especially Ollie Jenson. She wouldn't see him again for two weeks, and a lot could happen in two weeks. How she hated this life! She was glad Pierre had left her in town when he returned to the campsite a week ago. She'd hoped he would do it again, but he hadn't. They rode for over an hour in silence. The sun moved higher in the sky, and Clarissa unfurled her ruffled parasol and held it over her head to protect her face from the damaging rays.

"You're not very talkative today, Rissa." Pierre finally broke the silence. "You're not pouting, are you?" She glared at him again. "It won't do you any good, and it puts the most unbecoming wrinkles on those creamy smooth cheeks."

He raised his hand as if he might touch her face, and she quickly turned away. She hated it when he touched her, and he knew it. She thought he did it just to torment her.

After crossing the grassy prairie, they entered an area of rolling hills dotted with rocks and scrub brush. Traveling deeper into the hills, they came to trees with thick undergrowth. Pierre had to concentrate on his driving there, and Clarissa was glad. It kept his attention away from her. She began to wonder what they would find when they reached the campsite. At least the overhanging branches protected her from the sunlight, so she was able to put her parasol away.

She enjoyed listening to the sounds in the woods. Birds flitted through the top branches, calling to each other in a melodious cacophony. Sometimes she caught sight of colorful plumage. Besides the usual browns, she saw an occasional flash of yellow, red, or blue. Clarissa wished she were as free as those birds. She was sure small animals lived among the underbrush. She could hear scrambling interspersed with the sound of the horses' hooves clopping on the rocky soil.

Finally, they pulled into a large clearing hidden deep inside the tangle of tall trees and thick underbrush. Clarissa wondered how Pierre had found it in the first place, but he had always managed to find a similar campsite, no matter what state they were in.

A young woman, dressed in trousers and a man's shirt, hopped out of the caravan wagon that sat under a small grove of trees near the center of the clearing. She gave a vigorous wave and started running toward the wagon. Her long ebony curls were unfettered, so they flew out behind her like a flag fluttering in the wind.

"Clari!" she shouted.

After all his years in the family, Pierre understood how close the sisters were, so he stopped the wagon and let Clarissa clamber over the wheel. She ran toward her sister with her arms outstretched. "Mari!"

It felt so good to hold Mari in her arms again. Clarissa had never liked being separated from her twin, but about the only time they spent together was traveling from one place to another in the caravan. As soon as they reached a destination, Pierre would set up the confidence game so they were never seen at the same time. Their few hours together before they switched places had to suffice. But it never did. Of course, occasionally Pierre had to scout a new location. Then he would take the girls to an out-of-the-way place, and they stayed together for a few days. Precious days that were too few.

When the sisters finally quit dancing around and hugging each other, Clarissa walked with Marissa back to the campsite. Pierre had passed them and driven the wagon under the trees. He unhitched the horses and hobbled them in a grassy spot close enough to the small lake where they could graze and drink their fill. He pulled the basket Mrs. Olson had fixed for them from the back of the wagon and opened it. Soon they were enjoying fried chicken, homemade bread, fresh vegetables, and apple crumb cake. Mrs. Olson had even put homemade pickles in the basket. It was a wonderful feast.

"This is delicious." Marissa wiped her mouth on a napkin. "Do you eat like this all the time, Clari?"

Clarissa nodded. "Mrs. Olson is a very good cook."

Marissa smiled at her. "Don't eat too much, or our clothes won't fit you." The sisters laughed.

Pierre didn't join them. "I watch to see she doesn't. It's too important."

His comments put a damper on the festive feeling the young women had been sharing. The real reason they were apart always did that.

"Pierre." Marissa was usually the one who didn't complain. "Please, please let us stop. Don't we have enough money yet?"

His glare could have turned fresh milk to clabber. "Don't start."

"But you know how much we hate what we're doing," Clarissa agreed with her sister. "Why do we have to continue?"

Pierre started packing the things back into the basket. "If this is the thanks I get for bringing you fresh food—"

"I'm sorry, Pierre." Marissa was almost crying. "I really do appreciate it. Don't take it away."

He looked from one girl to the other. "Don't worry. You'll be eating well for a while. You're going back to town with me. It's Clarissa who won't have the food."

He stared at her. She knew he wanted an apology, but it stuck in her throat. Then she remembered she would have only smoked meat, canned beans and peaches, biscuits, and whatever she could scrounge from the woods. "I'm sorry, Pierre. Please don't take the food away."

He laughed such an evil laugh that it sliced into Clarissa's spirit. How could they fight him? He always told them they were as guilty as he was and would go to jail if he did. Would being in prison be any worse than how they lived now? She often wondered.

After lunch, Pierre unloaded other things from the wagon. He had rented it the day before and gone into a neighboring town to buy supplies, which he'd hidden under a tarp.

"Look, Clarissa—I bought some eggs and bacon. They'll last a few days if you store them in that cool spring that feeds the lake."

"Thank you, Pierre." Clarissa almost choked on the words, but she knew if she didn't say them he would retaliate, maybe even against Mari. That hurt more than when he did something to her. Her sister wasn't as strong as she was.

While Pierre lay under a tree and dozed, the sisters explored the area together. Mari showed her some wild gooseberries. In the last few days, she had picked some and used them to make desserts for herself; but more would ripen for the next week or two so Clarissa could enjoy them too. Mari also took her upstream to a waterfall with an indentation in the rock behind it. She said she used it to bathe and wash her hair. Clarissa knew she would enjoy that too. This was much better than most of their campsites had been.

Just as they returned to camp, Pierre sat up and stretched. "It's about time to start back, so get ready."

The girls went into the caravan and switched clothing. While they were changing, Clarissa told her sister about the four dresses Pierre had ordered from the Dress Emporium. She had already taken one to her room in the boarding-house, but the other three weren't started yet. The Dress Emporium was busy, and Pierre had told Anna and Gerda there was no hurry for the dresses.

Clarissa also told Mari how she had become good friends with Anna and Gerda and Anna's brother. She tried to make the transition as easy on her sister as she could, but it was always harder for Mari than it was for her.

Before Mari got into the wagon to drive off with Pierre, Clarissa hugged her. It was hard to let go, knowing that for the next two or more weeks the only person she would see was Pierre when he came to bring her more provisions. It wasn't as hard on Mari when she was the one to stay at the camp. She was quieter, but Clarissa liked to have people around her. It would be lonely.

Clarissa watched them drive away until the shadows swallowed up the wagon in the forest. Then she went into the caravan, threw herself on the bed, and cried herself to sleep.

Chapter 4

Marissa twisted around on the wagon seat so she could see her sister as long as possible. Every time they were separated, she felt as if her heart were torn apart. They were two different and distinct personalities, but Marissa felt as if Clari were her other half—the brighter, smarter half. Marissa longed for the days before Pierre married their mother. She and Clari had been together constantly. During the early days of the marriage, he started separating them as much as he could. He told Mother their close relationship was unhealthy, and they would never develop into the women they should if they didn't do more things apart.

Unfortunately, Mother agreed with him. Clari adapted well with the new activities, but Marissa had never adjusted. While Clari became more outgoing, Marissa withdrew into herself. That was why this confidence game they were pulling was so painful. Every time it happened, something died inside her. She felt guilty, dirty, and unredeemable. Of course, it didn't help when Pierre told her she was as guilty as he was. It reinforced what she already felt.

"You can turn around now," Pierre sneered. "You won't see her for two weeks." Then he laughed. An evil laugh that echoed through the thick forest and bounced back to haunt her.

Marissa turned toward the front of the wagon and straightened her shoulders. She wouldn't let him know how much he hurt her. If she did, he'd only chide her more harshly.

Marissa didn't like this journey through the forest. It was too shadowy. It reminded her of one of the enchanted forests in the fairy tales Mother had read to them. Any moment, she expected an ogre to step out from behind a tree and attack, or at least growl. She enjoyed life in the pleasant glade, but now she was back in the evil forest. Even the sound of birds singing had quieted with the coming of twilight—twilight that made the forest shadows darken. Would they never get through this horrible place?

Though much of the journey to Litchfield took them over uneven ground, Marissa didn't mind it. They were out in the open, away from the shadows that mirrored the darkness deep inside her.

When they reached town, the streets were silent—all except the one where the saloon was located. At least they didn't drive down that one. Near the train depot, Pierre turned the wagon across the tracks and into a quiet residential area. When he pulled up in front of a lovely two-story Victorian house, Marissa studied it with interest. The pleasant aroma of the evening meal wafted on the air, causing her stomach to give an unladylike growl. Before Pierre could help her down, she climbed over the wheel of the wagon. She didn't like his touching her. Clari had told her she didn't either, but both of the sisters had noticed he took every opportunity to do so.

"Mr. Le Blanc, Rissa, I was afraid you weren't going to make it back before dinner was over." Marissa looked up at the motherly woman who had come out on the front porch. "All the other boarders are eating now. Come on in. I set places for you, just in case."

Marissa followed her through the door into the front hall. She was glad they weren't staying at the hotel. Living in this house, she could pretend she was like most people.

"Rissa, dear, did you enjoy the sightseeing?"

Marissa looked into the woman's kind face and smiled. "Yes, the day was very interesting."

That seemed to satisfy the woman's curiosity. She led Marissa into the dining room. All conversations around the large table ceased as everyone looked at Marissa. She wanted to sink into the floor, but she stiffened her backbone and smiled. She saw at least one person she knew. August. *Let's see—what was his last name? Nilsson, wasn't it?*

The big blacksmith stood and pulled out the chair next to him. Marissa sat in the proffered seat and gave him a shy smile.

When Marissa was finally alone in the room she and Clari shared, she sank onto the chair and wilted. The evening meal had been difficult for her. She had to pretend she knew all those people. Clari had told her about them, but the information was sketchy. This room was heavenly, though. A real room in a real house. For a moment, she felt like a regular person. Then reality set in. She actually enjoyed the time at the campsite. She could relax and be herself there. Here she would have to be alert all the time, playing a role. The role of Rissa Le Blanc, a fictional person who didn't have anything in common with Marissa Voss. She sighed and hung her head.

She allowed a few moments to feel sorry for herself; then she resolved to make the most of this wonderful room while she had it. She walked over to the bed and pressed both hands on it to test the mattress. Clari had said it was soft. Marissa hadn't imagined how soft. She crossed to the highboy and opened the drawers, one at a time, to familiarize herself with where each thing was stored. After reopening the third drawer, she extracted a nightgown and dressed for bed. By the time she nestled into the welcoming cocoon, she had pushed her negative thoughts into a hidden recess of her mind. She could play this part as well as Clari did. Their very lives depended on it.

When Marissa walked through the door of the Dress Emporium the next morning, Anna and Gerda weren't in the showroom. They must be working in the back. It gave her time to refamiliarize herself with the shop. Lots of new accessories were cleverly displayed on various pieces of furniture. She walked around the shop and fingered several delicate, handmade lace items. Olina Nilsson must have been busy to create all these lovely things. Even the shawl Pierre had purchased before had been replaced, but the new one was white instead of blue. She might ask him if she could have that one, too. He didn't often turn down anything she asked for when other people were around. He wanted to appear wealthy and generous. But, as the girls played a part, he was playing his.

The curtains that separated the shop from the workroom parted, and Anna came through the opening. "I thought I heard the bell." She smiled at Marissa. "Rissa, I'm so glad you came by. We've finished your second dress. I want you to try it on." She led the way into the back room where Gerda sat hemming a dark skirt.

The dress they had finished for her was beautiful. Marissa went behind the screen and changed into it. When she came out and looked at herself in the cheval glass, she was pleased with what she saw. She would enjoy wearing this gown. After changing into her other clothes, she looked at the fabric Anna was spreading on the cutting table.

"Is that for one of my other dresses?" Marissa asked.

Anna nodded. "We'll try to get both of them finished before we have to start anything else. I know your father told us you weren't in a hurry, but we don't want to take too long, do we?"

Gerda agreed, and Marissa looked around the room. They had so much fabric, lace, buttons, and other notions. The variety fascinated her. She glanced again at the fabric on the table. It was a vibrant emerald green. Marissa knew she would never feel comfortable wearing that color. Why did Clari always pick such intense colors? Marissa was happier in softer shades.

"Anna"—Marissa gave her a pleading look—"would it be all right if I changed the color, since you haven't cut it out yet?"

Anna glanced at Gerda, then back at Marissa. "Are you sure? I thought you loved this shade of green."

"I do." Marissa almost choked on that lie. "But since it's summer, maybe I should wear lighter colors. Do you have a softer green?"

Anna folded up the fabric, then looked thoughtfully at Marissa, who had to turn away from the intense scrutiny. "Let's go see what's on the shelves in the shop."

Marissa was glad when she spied a bolt of light green, a softer color with a tiny white flower woven into it. She pointed toward the bolt. "I like that piece. Would it work as well?"

Anna pulled it from the shelf and spread it across the counter. "It might look better in the other style we haven't made yet."

Marissa ran her hand gently across the smooth fabric. "I would like that."

Gerda joined them in the front room. "That piece won't work as well with this pattern—"

"We're going to use it for the other style," Anna interrupted her.

Gerda looked confused. Marissa hoped she wasn't making too much trouble for the two women. She knew Clari liked them, and she hoped she would get to know them better.

"What about this pattern?" Gerda held up the picture of the style they had planned to use for the emerald-colored lawn material. "What fabric should we use for it?"

Marissa was drawn to a light lavender silk. "Could we use this?"

She couldn't understand why the other two women looked so stunned. What had she done now? How could she fix the problem if she didn't know what it was?

"Or, if not, maybe you could suggest some other material."

Anna spoke first. "No. That's all right. We'll use whatever you want. After all, the dress is for you." She picked up the two bolts of fabric and carried them into the workroom, leaving Gerda and Marissa alone.

Marissa walked over to the shawl that was arranged over a rocking chair. She didn't remember that piece of furniture being in the dress shop when she was here before. She picked up the garment and draped it around her shoulders. Then she walked to the mirror and studied how it looked on her.

She turned back around and found Gerda watching her. "I like this. I think I'll ask Pierre to buy it for me the next time he comes with me."

When Marissa returned to the boardinghouse, she pondered what had happened at the dress shop. Almost every time she looked at Anna or Gerda, they had a funny expression on their faces. It made her feel odd. Did they know who she was and what she was doing? Was that why they kept looking at her that way?

When she was alone at the campsite, Marissa enjoyed reading novels. Pierre was glad to supply plenty of them. One of her favorites was *The Scarlet Letter* by Nathaniel Hawthorne. Now she felt as if she wore a sign as Hester did in the book. How fitting her dress was in red, which was not a color Marissa liked to wear. Only hers wasn't a letter *A* for adultery. Would it be a *C* for criminal or an *L* for liar?

She threw herself across the bed. "Mother, why did you have to die and leave us in the hands of that man?" Her crying tired her out. She slept the rest of the day and through the night on top of the covers of her bed.

One of the horses had thrown a shoe. Ollie almost wanted to send Lowell to town instead, since he so often complained about Ollie not doing his share of the work. But this was work. And Ollie wasn't going to let him change what he did. He was an adult, and he wasn't doing anything wrong.

The closer he got to town, the more his thoughts turned to Rissa. It would take a little while for August to shoe the horse. He might have to wait in line, so he should have time to go to the dress shop. If Rissa wasn't there, he'd check the mercantile and the ice cream shop. He knew she liked ice cream.

At the blacksmith shop, August was waiting on a stranger. Ollie tied the horse he'd led into town to the hitching post in front of the shop. He told August he'd return in about an hour to check on the work. That should give August time to finish what he was doing.

He rode his own horse to the dress shop, then hitched him in front of the mercantile. He glanced up and down the street. Rissa was just coming out of the ice cream shop. He leaned his arms on the saddle and watched her cross the street, heading for the Dress Emporium. He couldn't ask her to get an ice cream with him, but he could go in and visit with her. She didn't look up before she pushed the door open. That was strange. He never before had seen her walk with her eyes studying the boards in the sidewalk. He hoped nothing was wrong with her.

He opened the door, and the shop bell tinkled. Rissa glanced back toward the entrance. Her gaze encountered his. She blushed and looked at the floor, then turned and hurried into the workroom.

Ollie followed her through the curtains. Both Anna and Gerda looked up when his boots sounded on the wooden floor.

"Ollie!" Anna jumped up and came over to hug him. "It's good to see you. You haven't been coming to town as often as you did." She turned a puzzled look at Rissa, who was studying a folded dress lying on one of the shelves.

He thought it odd that Rissa hadn't greeted him warmly. He'd come to town in hopes of basking in her sunny smile, but something must be wrong.

Before he had a chance to ask her if she wasn't feeling well, she scooted through the curtains. "I'll come back when you're not busy," she said softly to Anna.

The bell on the front door tinkled.

Ollie furrowed his brows. "Is something wrong with Rissa?"

Anna and Gerda glanced at each other.

"Is anyone going to tell me what's going on?" He didn't care if he did sound frustrated. He was.

⌒≈

Lowell saw Ollie as soon as he returned to the farm. "Did you just get back from town again?"

"Now don't start in on me." Ollie frowned. "I had to take the palomino. She threw a shoe."

Lowell stepped back. "Okay." He hesitated a moment. "Did something bad happen while you were in town? You weren't in this kind of mood before you left, were you?"

Ollie stopped and took a deep breath, then looked at Lowell. "Something funny is going on, and I don't understand it."

"So what seems to be the problem?"

Ollie kept staring at Lowell. Finally, he took off his cap and tapped it against his leg. "I don't understand that woman."

Lowell didn't have to ask what woman. He knew it was Rissa. What had she done now?

It had been a dry summer. The wind blew a little whirlwind of dust around their booted feet. Ollie kicked at the small dust funnel as if it were a living thing.

"It was almost as if she didn't know me. She hurried out of the dress shop right after I got there." He rubbed the back of his neck with his other hand. "When I asked Anna and Gerda if Rissa was okay, they told me she had been acting strange for a couple of days. She even changed the color of fabric for two of the dresses they're making for her."

Lowell slipped his hands into the back pockets of his jeans. He could think better in that position. "Isn't that just something women do? Change their minds? Remember all the times Anna has changed hers without any reason."

Ollie turned to walk away when Lowell heard him mutter, "But she didn't even smile at me."

Lowell pitched clean hay into the stalls he'd mucked out while he mulled over what Ollie had told him. He decided he would see for himself what was going on. Without telling anyone, he saddled his horse and set out across the fields. He could get to town faster that way instead of on the road. He turned his horse down the street toward the mercantile and saw Rissa enter the front door of the Dress Emporium. Good. He would go there first.

When the bell over the door tinkled, Rissa turned from where she was talking to Anna at the counter. Their gazes met, and hers went straight to his heart. She looked so vulnerable. Some pain was hidden in the depths. He wanted to take her in his arms and tell her everything would be fine, but he didn't have the right. He wished he did.

"Lowell!" Anna crossed the room and gave him one of her exuberant hugs. "I'm glad to see you again." She linked her arm with his and pulled him toward the back of the store.

Rissa continued to gaze at him, but she had shuttered the pain, only allowing him to see her sweet smile. Nothing seemed to be wrong with her, except that now she recognized him. Not like the last time he was in town. The smile she gave him was reminiscent of the ones she had bestowed on him when the Le Blancs came to Litchfield earlier in the spring.

Marissa was glad to see Lowell Jenson enter the shop. Ollie's presence seemed to overwhelm her. Somehow Lowell made her feel at ease. He was restful. She wished she could stay in Litchfield forever. Maybe get to know Lowell better. Perhaps then she could lead a normal life—with a home and family. She would have to stop thinking about it, though. He wouldn't even look at her if he could see her scarlet letter. If he knew the truth about who she was and what she'd done. She'd tried to push all that into a quiet place in the back of her mind. Lowell's presence brought it to the forefront. She felt imprisoned by circumstances. Circumstances and an evil man. An evil man named Pierre Le Blanc.

Chapter 5

On the way to the farm, Lowell took off his cap and stuffed it in his back pocket. He liked to feel the wind blow through his hair. It made him feel much cooler on a hot summer day. His thoughts were filled with Rissa Le Blanc. When he saw her in town, her glistening black curls were tied away from her face with a ribbon the same color as her blue eyes. It made her look more approachable than when she wore an elaborate hairstyle. She was more beautiful than he remembered, but the pain he glimpsed deep in her eyes disturbed him. What could have put it there? Had someone treated her badly, or was it something else? It made Lowell wonder about her father. No matter how many times they met, Lowell had never felt any warmth from the man. Surely he wouldn't abuse his own daughter. But something or someone had hurt her.

After he considered the things Anna and Gerda had told him when he was in town, he had to agree that Rissa was acting strangely. It wasn't any one thing she did that would cause concern; but when they were added together, it was almost as if she were a different person than the young woman he had seen a couple of weeks ago. He had heard about people who put on one face for some and another for others. People like that couldn't be trusted. But he couldn't believe Rissa was like that.

Something in his heart wanted to know her better—to help her. But how could he?

When Lowell arrived at the farm, he searched for Ollie. He and his brother needed to talk. They had to heal the breach between them. It was important to their parents—and to both of them, too. Lowell had noticed their father had not seemed as strong as he used to be. Maybe he and Ollie could take more of the responsibility for the harder work from him. Father wasn't a young man anymore.

Finally, Lowell found his brother training one of the colts with a bridle. As Ollie led the young horse around the pasture, he talked to him and rubbed his neck in a soothing manner. Lowell leaned his arms on the top rail of the wooden fence and hiked one of his booted feet onto the lower rail. He took his cap from his pocket and put it on to shade his eyes from the bright sun. Ollie was good with the young animals, that was for sure.

His brother looked up; then he led the horse over to the fence and tied the lead line to the top rail. "Did you want to see me?"

Lowell gazed at his brother. He loved him, in his own way, even if Ollie did make him angry sometimes. Maybe they could work this out. "I've been thinking about what *Fader* said earlier."

Ollie crossed his arms over his chest and stared at him. "And—?"

Lowell moved away from the fence and stuffed his hands in his back pockets. "And I think he's right."

Ollie stared hard at him but didn't say anything. Why was it so hard for Lowell to get his brother to talk to him? He talked to everyone else. After untying the lead line, Ollie started toward the stable with the young horse. Lowell followed him into the cool darkness of the barn. He sat on a bale of hay and watched Ollie carefully remove the bridle from the animal before he opened the door that led to the pasture. The colt walked through the doorway, then ran toward his mother.

Lowell leaned both forearms on his thighs and let his hands dangle between his knees. "Are you going to talk to me about this or not?"

"What do you think we can do?" At least Ollie must have been thinking about it, too.

"Well, do you like the way things are going?" Lowell looked up at him.

"No, but we don't seem to agree on much right now."

Lowell stood up from the bale of hay and thrust his fingers through his windblown hair before stuffing his hands into his back pockets. "You mean, we don't agree about Rissa Le Blanc."

Ollie nodded. "That's all we don't see eye-to-eye on, isn't it?"

A headache was starting at the back of Lowell's neck. He rubbed the spot, but it didn't help. "I guess I shouldn't tell you that when I was in town earlier Rissa was friendlier than the last time I was there—but that's what happened."

Lowell kept looking down at the ground, then finally glanced up at his brother. Ollie's green eyes were like ice and bored into Lowell's.

"I don't understand that woman at all." Ollie stomped across the barn and picked up a pitchfork. He started toward the bale where his brother had been sitting only a few moments before.

Lowell didn't want to be in the way when Ollie started wielding that tool. He stepped closer to the door. "I hate for this to come between us." Silence fell over the room. Even the sound of the pitchfork slicing through the hay had ceased. "And I hate to upset *Fader*. Maybe we could just not talk about her—and maybe we could act friendly when we're working together." At the door, he turned and studied his brother.

Ollie was still holding the pitchfork. "We could try that."

Lowell nodded and walked out into the hot sunshine. Why couldn't the two of them agree? Were they so different? Maybe it was because they were adults now and their ideas weren't the same. Somehow they had to protect their father's health. He hadn't even mentioned that fact to his brother.

His ride and the talk with Ollie had made Lowell thirsty. A cold glass of water pumped straight from the well would taste good right now, so he headed up to the house. When he rounded the end of the porch, he saw his father sitting on the top step with his head drooping against his chest. He looked as if he would have fallen if he hadn't been leaning against the post. Lowell hurried toward him.

"*Fader!*" Lowell couldn't recall his father ever stopping work before lunch and taking a rest. "Are you all right?"

His father didn't look up when Lowell sat on the step beside him. Lowell was trying to decide what to do when his mother rushed out the front door.

"What's the shouting about?" Then she saw her husband. She dried her hands on her apron, then dropped to her knees on the floor beside him and put her hand on his shoulder. "He's burning up. I can feel it through his shirt."

Father didn't look at her, either. She threw her arms around him and pulled him back against her with his head cradled against her chest. "Lowell, he's terribly sick. Go to town and bring Dr. Bradley as fast as you can."

Lowell stood and looked down at them. "Let me help you get him up to bed first."

Mother clutched Father more tightly. "No! When you get your horse, send Ollie to help me." She started rocking back and forth and praying softly in Swedish. If he didn't already know how upset she was, that would have told him. Mother hardly ever spoke Swedish anymore.

Lowell raced to the barn. Ollie was hanging the pitchfork on its hook. He let go of the handle and turned. "Lowell, what's the matter?"

"*Fader* is very sick." Lowell saddled his horse as quickly as he could. "He's on the front porch with *Moder*. She needs your help getting him to the bedroom."

Ollie ran out the stable door just before Lowell galloped through. All the way to town, Lowell wondered what the problem could be. "*Gud*, please help me find Dr. Bradley. Let him be in town and not out on one of the farms!"

He was thankful God answered his prayer. The doctor was in his office finishing sewing up a deep puncture wound in Kurt Madson's leg. Some farm families took care of things like that at home, but Kurt's wife, Ellie, had always been squeamish, and she was going to have a baby, so she had driven him to the doctor's office. Lowell helped her get Kurt into the wagon while Dr. Bradley grabbed his bag.

Most days Doc kept his horse tied to the hitching post out front in case of an emergency. Lowell was glad they wouldn't have to wait for him to saddle the horse or hitch up a buggy. He wanted to get back to the farm before something terrible happened to his father.

On the ride, Doc shouted questions, and Lowell answered them over the sound of the horses galloping. By the time they arrived at the farmhouse, Doc knew as much as Lowell did about his father's condition.

Ollie was pacing on the front porch, watching the road from town. He met them at the hitching post. "I'll take care of your horse, Dr. Bradley. You go on up to see about *Fader*." He led the animal toward the barn. Lowell knew his brother would cool the horse down, give him a good brushing, and make sure he was fed.

Dr. Bradley had been to their home a number of times, but Lowell escorted him up the stairs to the bedroom his parents shared. Doc went through the door and shut it behind him. Lowell knew they didn't need him getting in the way, but he didn't want to go very far. So he hunkered down beside the door. He could hear parts of what was happening in the bedroom, but he didn't learn much. Fear for his father filled Lowell with dread. Bowing his head, he started to pray but soon ran out of words. He didn't know what else to say.

Often enough he had read the Scripture passage in Romans, chapter eight, about the Spirit making intercession. So while his heart grew heavier the longer the doctor took, he allowed the Spirit to pray for him, expressing to the heavenly Father his anguish about his earthly father.

It seemed like hours before Dr. Bradley opened the door. Lowell stood and studied his face. What he saw didn't give him much hope. The doctor looked as worried as Lowell felt.

"I'm not going to lie to you, Lowell." Dr. Bradley, a short, rotund man, looked up at Lowell's face. "I'm not sure what's wrong with your father, and I'm not sure I can help him."

Lowell could hear his mother's soft sobs and his father's heavy breathing coming from the bedroom. "What are we supposed to do?"

"These fevers can be severe. We often don't know what brings them on." The doctor started toward the staircase. "I gave your mother a list of things that might help."

Lowell followed him to the barn. Ollie was attacking bales of hay with the pitchfork. His brother was as worried as he was, but he didn't ask any questions. When anything bad was happening, Ollie always tried to hide from it as long as he could. He often lost himself in the mundane tasks around the farm, waiting and watching. Before the doctor mounted his horse, Lowell pulled his wallet out and removed the usual fee.

"You don't have to pay me right now." Doc put his foot in the stirrup and threw his other leg over the back of the mare. "I may not be able to help your father."

Lowell held the greenbacks up to him. "You were available to come when we needed you, and we like to stay current with our accounts."

The doctor stared hard into Lowell's face before he accepted the money and stuffed it in the pocket of his vest. When he was gone, Lowell and Ollie both sat on a bale of hay. Almost in unison, they dropped their heads into their hands.

After a short time, Ollie raised his head. "The doctor's expression was grim. How bad is it?"

Lowell stood and pushed his hands into his back pockets. "He doesn't know."

Ollie jumped up and started prowling around like a nervous barn cat. "What are we going to do?"

Lowell rocked up on the balls of his feet, then dropped his heels with a thud onto the dirt floor. "I've been praying a lot."

"So have I."

"We're going to run this horse farm to the best of our abilities and help *Mor* do all Doc said to do to help *Far*."

Chapter 6

"You will go because I said you will." Pierre leaned closer. His whispered words hissed across the table, which was draped in a white linen tablecloth and set with fine china.

Marissa closed her eyes and sighed. She was glad no one was sitting close to them in the large dining room of the hotel. They ate most meals at the boardinghouse, but Pierre occasionally took her to the restaurant for the evening meal. Usually the room was full, and he felt the exposure would help them with the confidence game he had planned. Except today he probably was wasting his money. In a way, Marissa was glad. Everything went his way much too often.

Tonight only two other tables were being used, and the people didn't look familiar. She thought they must be travelers spending the night at the hotel on their journey to somewhere else. None of them seemed to be aware that she and Pierre were sitting across the room from them.

"Why this sudden interest in church, Pierre?" She brought her attention back to the subject they were discussing.

He glared at Marissa. She was sure he was unhappy with her calling him by his first name, but she hated calling him Father. Marissa didn't remember much about her own father. She and Clari had been so young when he died. She knew he was tall, with black curly hair much like theirs. He often pushed his curls back from his forehead. The gesture was familiar. When she was a young child, he seemed extremely tall to her. He gave her rides on his shoulders, and she felt as if she could almost touch the puffy clouds that floated in the sky above them. He ran through the open fields on the plantation, holding on to her feet to keep her from falling from her perch. If she got off balance, she would clutch his ears, and he would tell her to be careful not to pull them off. When he sat on a grassy knoll, she would carefully climb down and sit beside him as they studied the clouds, trying to find animals hiding in them. They would laugh together. Life had been full of happiness—and freedom.

"Haven't you noticed how important church is to the people who live here?" Pierre said sharply.

Marissa was sorry he'd interrupted her pleasant memories. "Yes, all the ones we know go to church."

"At least the important ones do. They're the people we want to impress.

270

Double Deception

You're doing a good job with Gerda, Anna, and the Braxtons. I'm afraid Clarissa was getting a little too friendly with them. I was glad it was time to switch the two of you when I did. I didn't want her ruining anything." Pierre whispered the last sentence because the waitress was approaching the table with their plates of steaming food.

Little did he know Marissa also felt a growing friendship—especially with Gerda and Anna. The only friend she had ever had was her sister, but these women were drawing her out of her shyness. They really cared about her. If only she and Clari could stay here in Litchfield. If only they could live normal lives. If only they weren't pulling a confidence game. If only Pierre would let her and Clari go free. But she couldn't live on *if onlys*.

Pierre had ordered steaks for them, and they smelled delicious. They practically covered the plate, leaving little room for the green beans and mashed potatoes that crowded around the edges. Marissa didn't want to eat. All the pressures in her life were at war in her stomach, but she knew Pierre would be concerned if she didn't eat at least part of the meal, so she cut a piece of the tender meat. She followed that bite with a morsel she pinched off the hot buttered roll. It melted in her mouth. The more she ate, the hungrier she got, so soon she was enjoying the food as much as Pierre appeared to be.

Maybe it was because his attention had been drawn away from her to a striking woman who had come into the restaurant to dine alone. She was probably single. Married women didn't dine out alone. Everyone was looking at her, but Pierre's focus was different. His eyes devoured the woman while he mindlessly forked the food on his plate into his mouth. The looks he gave her made Marissa feel uneasy. She glanced around to see if anyone else noticed. She was thankful no one did.

If circumstances were different, Marissa was sure he would have tried to make contact with the woman. Marissa knew that often when Pierre left the sisters alone at a campsite he went into a different town to spend time with women. Mother would be distressed if she knew the kind of women he pursued. Many young women Marissa's age didn't know about that kind of female, but she had found out about them in some of the books she'd read. She wished Pierre would make a mistake here in Litchfield, such as trying to get friendly with the wrong kind of woman. She had heard of several down at the saloon, but she hadn't seen any. If he did that, maybe the people would recognize what kind of man he was. Maybe it would bring freedom to her and Clari. At least she could dream about such a wonderful thing happening.

It had been a rough week. Lowell and Ollie did all their father's work in addition to their own chores, but that wasn't the hard part. Knowing their father was lying in bed, getting weaker every day, brought an emotional turmoil that sapped their strength. Their mother hardly left his side. It was all they could do to get her to go to sleep at night. Sometimes the only way was for one of them to sit with their father. This added activity drained them further. Lowell didn't remember being this exhausted.

When Anna found out about Father, she had come home and cooked a meal. Then every day after that, some woman from the church brought the noon meal. There was often enough to feed them dinner, too. The brothers were working so hard that they weren't as hungry as usual. At least they didn't notice their hunger.

When the Saturday evening chores were finished, Lowell went to his parents' bedroom and insisted his mother get some rest.

"Are you boys going to church tomorrow?" She turned her weary eyes toward him.

Lowell shook his head, thinking that would be the end of the discussion, but he should have known better.

"And why not?" Mother sounded more like her usual self. "Church is important. Besides, our friends will want to know how Soren is doing and pray for him."

Lowell didn't want to add to his mother's distress, so he agreed to go.

"You'll take Ollie, too, won't you?" she insisted.

Lowell glanced at his brother, who was leaning against the door facing. Ollie gave a slight nod, and Lowell smiled at his mother. "Of course. We'll both go."

Not only had the week been hard, but Saturday night, Father didn't sleep well. His restlessness kept everyone in the house awake, trying to ease his pain and help him. He didn't want to take the medicine Doc had left for him, so it was an almost impossible task. When Lowell and Ollie finally went to bed, they overslept. They knew that if they didn't want to be late for church, they would have to hurry to finish the chores and eat breakfast. Lowell was tempted to tell their mother they wouldn't go.

In addition to the horses that provided most of their livelihood, they also had the usual assortment of farm animals to provide food for the family. It took Lowell awhile to milk their two cows while his brother took care of the chickens and pigs. When he arrived back in the kitchen with the buckets of milk, his mother was cooking breakfast. He knew she hadn't gotten as much sleep as he had, but she was up early so he and Ollie could get to church. He didn't have the heart to tell her he wasn't going. He just hoped he could stay awake for the pastor's sermon.

They had a new pastor who was only a little older than Lowell. Joseph Harrelson had been in Litchfield for a few months, and in that time, Lowell had gotten to know him well. His sermons were biblical and thought provoking.

Lowell had grown in his walk with the Lord from listening to them. That was one reason he was so concerned about this thing that was happening between him and his brother. He knew he should talk to Pastor Harrelson about the problem, but he'd been too busy. When Father was better, he would make the time. Lowell felt as if it were stunting his spiritual growth, and he didn't want that to happen.

The singing had started before Lowell and Ollie rode their horses into the churchyard. But they weren't the only people who were late. A buggy pulled up while they were tying their horses to a hitching post. Pierre Le Blanc was driving, and Rissa sat on the seat shading herself from the hot sun with a dainty ruffled parasol that matched her dress. Her black curls were pulled up in an elaborate style, topped by a small hat that perched like a mother bird on a carefully built nest. A thin veil draped her face, making her look more intriguing. . . mysterious. . .inviting.

Lowell swallowed hard and glanced at his brother out of the corner of his eye. Ollie was smiling at the woman. Once again, the knowledge that something had come between him and his brother pierced Lowell's heart. When he looked back at Rissa, she sent a shy smile his way. He walked over to the buggy.

"May I help you down?" He didn't care what her father or his brother thought.

Rissa held out her graceful hand, and he clasped it gently. With his other hand, he supported her arm as she stepped from the conveyance. She was such a tiny woman, as light as a feather. After both slippered feet were firmly on the ground, he reluctantly released her. She reached down to straighten her skirt.

"You look lovely this morning, Miss Le Blanc." He couldn't keep his voice from sounding husky.

She glanced up at him and blushed. "Please, call me Rissa." She lowered her eyes and brushed an invisible speck from her sky blue silk dress.

Lowell tipped his hat, and Mr. Le Blanc came around the buggy and took Rissa's arm. They headed toward the door of the church, leaving Lowell with his brother.

"What do you suppose they're doing here?" Ollie watched them until they were inside. "I've never seen them in church before, and we haven't missed a Sunday since they've been in town."

"I'm sure she has come to worship, as we all have." Lowell wished his brother wasn't so interested in her.

Ollie didn't look convinced. "Something's not quite right about her or her father. I can't imagine either of them worshiping. They're here for some other reason."

Lowell stood where he was while his brother entered the building. Ollie had to be wrong about Rissa. Lowell would slip in later, but right now he needed some time alone.

◑∕∽

When Marissa and Pierre entered the church, the congregation was singing a song she had never heard before. Even though it was about the blood of Jesus, it sounded soothing instead of gruesome. Marissa had never liked to see blood—hers or anyone else's. She had even fainted a time or two when she or Clari was injured as a child. But the music and the words washed over her, warming something deep inside.

Pierre led the way down the aisle to two seats on the second pew. Marissa didn't like to be the center of attention, but she couldn't help it when Pierre was around.

" 'What can wash away my sin? Nothing but the blood of Jesus; What can make me whole again? Nothing but the blood of Jesus.' " Everyone else in the room sang with great gusto, as if they meant every word.

Mother had died when Marissa and Clari were ten, but before that, she had told them stories of children from the Bible. Marissa remembered baby Moses in a basket, little David who killed a giant with his slingshot, and baby Jesus in a manger. Could that be the same Jesus everyone was singing about? How could that baby take away your sins and make you whole? She faintly recalled a story about a Jesus who died; maybe that was the One they were singing about.

When the preacher began his sermon, Marissa listened to every word, although she didn't understand many of the things he said. Once, she glanced at Pierre, and he looked bored. She was sure he wasn't listening to the preacher.

It was hot in the room even though the windows were all open. Marissa took out a folding fan from her reticule and unfurled it. The rhythmic movement of the fan didn't take her concentration from the sermon.

She didn't understand it all. He said you couldn't commit a sin for which Jesus wouldn't forgive you if you asked Him. Marissa wondered what kind of sins these people could have committed. She was sure none of them had done anything as bad as the things Pierre made her and Clari do. She wished she could talk to someone about what had been going on in her life, but she couldn't. None of these people could know what she had done—or what she was going to have to do later. They wouldn't understand, and if Pierre found out, he would punish her for talking about it. Of course, he always made sure her clothes would cover any bruises.

After the service, Pierre spent a lot of time talking to various people he considered important. As a result, the two of them were among the last ones to head home. On the way back to the boardinghouse, Marissa told him she wanted to talk to him about something important. He looked at her from under hooded eyes, studying her as a snake studies its prey. And that's what she felt like—Pierre's prey.

When they finished eating with the other boarders, he led her to the surrey. They drove toward Lake Ripley. Near the lake, he pulled into a grove of trees and let the horses graze on the green grass that was growing close to the water. Because of the dry summer, most of the other grass had turned brown.

"Now, Marissa, what did you want to talk about?" Pierre scowled.

Marissa sat with her hands clasped tightly in her lap. She took a deep breath and looked down at her hands while she talked. She didn't want to see his expression. If she did, she might not be able to continue.

"I don't want to do this anymore." For a moment, the only sound she heard was the birds fluttering from branch to branch above them. Nothing else moved in the heat.

"I know that. You and Clarissa have made your wishes known often enough." Pierre spoke in a monotone.

He removed a cheroot from the pocket of his vest and lit it. She had told him often enough that she didn't like for him to smoke around her, so he blew the smoke in her direction. He liked to torment her. She ignored it. She didn't want to be sidetracked from her purpose.

"I mean it this time." Marissa turned away and took another deep breath, then blurted out, "I want a fresh start, a new life."

Pierre gave a mirthless laugh. "And you think you can do that? Make a fresh start?"

Marissa dropped her gaze back to her hands and nodded.

"It was that church service, wasn't it?" Pierre sneered. "You believe all those fairy tales, don't you?"

He flicked his ashes over the side of the buggy, but some landed on her dress. Since they weren't on fire anymore, they did no damage. She brushed them from her skirt and ventured a glance in his direction. His eyes were gleaming.

"Do you think any of those fine people in the service today would give you a chance if they knew what you've done? Don't think such silly thoughts. You're a criminal. You have been for many years. You're as guilty as I am. That's what everyone will think if we are ever caught." He took another long draw on the awful-smelling little cigar.

Tears made their way down her cheeks. Pierre didn't care about them, but she couldn't stop.

"There is no way out of the life we lead. Even if you left me, how could you afford to live? The only thing you could do is sell your body." He knew that thought would disgust her. He always used that argument when she or Clari begged him to stop their life of crime.

A slight breeze shook the trees above them, but it wasn't what caused the chills to run up and down Marissa's spine. Pierre's words did.

"You wouldn't want to do that, would you?" His voice was quiet but harsh.

The very thought was abhorrent to her. She shook her head, and the hope that had started to take root in her heart withered.

❧

Lowell and Ollie rode back to the farm in silence, each lost in his own thoughts. Lowell had slipped into the service right before the sermon. Joseph's words went straight to his heart. He knew the Lord wouldn't like this breach between Ollie and him.

After the service, while everyone was visiting in the churchyard, many people had asked about their father. Their friends committed to pray for him and for the family. Some even offered to help with the chores, but Lowell told them everything was under control right now. During that time, he watched Rissa and her father. Le Blanc seemed to be working the crowd, much as a politician would. What did he want from these people? It had to be something.

Several times Lowell caught Rissa looking at him. She gave him a shy smile, and he returned it. Just when he decided to go over and talk to her, Ollie approached her. Lowell didn't know what he said, but she didn't smile at him. Soon Ollie moved away. Now, on the trip home, the chasm between the brothers was as wide as it had ever been. How could they overcome it?

❧

Marissa didn't feel like talking to anyone after the discussion yesterday with Pierre. So she stayed in her room. She didn't go to the Dress Emporium or the mercantile as she usually did. The words she had heard at church still tugged at her heart. She longed for what seemed to be just out of reach.

"Rissa." A knock on her door accompanied Pierre's voice. "I need to talk to you."

She opened it reluctantly. He stepped into the room and pulled the door shut behind him. He walked to the window, then looked out while he talked to her.

"Our chance is coming up soon." He turned and smiled at her.

Those words struck fear in her heart. She didn't want the chance to come anytime, especially not soon. When it did, her life here was over.

Pierre pulled a handbill from his pocket. He thrust it toward her. An artist's rendition of a circus parade, complete with a woman riding an elephant, marched across the top of the handbill. The circus was coming to town.

"I talked to the front man for the circus. They're making Litchfield their last stop before the circus train heads for their winter quarters in Florida. After I talked to him, I checked around town." He turned and smiled. "No one here has ever seen the circus. That's good for us. Most everyone will attend out of curiosity. This town will be ripe for the picking. We should have no trouble with our plans." He rubbed his hands together and gave his evil smile. Then he stuck one hand in his pocket and jingled the coins there.

For a moment, Marissa felt brave. "I've never seen a circus, either. I want to go."

Pierre frowned. "You won't be going. Clarissa will. You are much better at the other part of the plan than she is."

With his words, the last vestiges of hope she had hidden in her heart died.

Chapter 7

Lowell hoped the doctor would be able to help his father. Every day Father suffered more and grew weaker. Dr. Bradley couldn't find what caused the terrible fever. It had to be some kind of infection, but what? Doc told Lowell he had sent telegrams to several colleagues in other states, trying to find out if anyone had seen symptoms like this. He also ordered medical books to add to his library. When he wasn't treating patients, he studied them, trying to find something that would explain this malady so he could treat it.

As Lowell worked on the farm, he prayed for his father, and he prayed for Doc to find an answer that would bring relief. Of course, a miracle would be welcome, too. But most days he felt as if his prayers didn't get past the roof of the barn. If he was in the pasture, he was sure they got caught in the treetops nearby. God seemed far away. Lowell figured the problem he and Ollie were having hindered his prayers.

Of course, he and Ollie no longer exchanged cross words. They just didn't talk to each other when no one else was around. They didn't seem to have anything left to say. A tiny woman with black curly hair and sky blue eyes stood between them. Even though she was short, her presence provided a wall that neither of them could—or would—scale.

Lowell didn't like what was happening, but every time he decided to agree with Ollie about Rissa, he remembered the hurt he had glimpsed deep in her eyes. He couldn't believe she was the kind of person his brother thought she was. He didn't think she was devious or two-faced. Lowell had seen a purity within her, but something held her captive. He was beginning to believe it was her father. What kind of hold did he have on her? Lowell hoped he could help her find a way to get away from whatever was causing her such pain. He had never seen any bruises on her body, but most of it was always covered, so he couldn't be sure. If Le Blanc was beating her, Lowell would gladly show him how it felt.

Ollie enjoyed spending time with the horses. They were undemanding and loved him unconditionally, not like some people in his family. While his brother did the other chores on the farm, Ollie took care of the horses. With soothing words and gentle hands, he fed them, groomed them, and slowly trained each one.

All the time he spent in the stable or pasture, his thoughts were constantly drawn toward the woman who kept him tied in knots. Only a couple of weeks ago, he'd spent every minute he could squeeze out of his busy day in town with Rissa. Her smiling eyes and quick wit drew him like a magnet. She had been interested in him. He had seen it in her eyes and heard it in the lilt of her voice. He didn't know a lot about women, but he knew that for a certainty. Now she was an iceberg—cold and unmoving. She had time to smile at Lowell, but it wasn't the same as the smiles they had shared before.

Something wasn't right. No one could change his mind about that. He couldn't help believing Pierre Le Blanc was behind the change in Rissa. Ollie was sure Le Blanc didn't approve of all the time he spent with her, so he did something that caused her to change her opinion of Ollie. But what? What lies had he told her? He wanted to rush into town and confront the man, but he knew that wasn't wise. Sometimes he wished he could throw caution to the wind and follow his heart.

It would have helped if he could talk to Lowell about this, but any mention of Rissa raised an insurmountable barrier between the two of them. It was better not to talk about her at all. They could never agree anyway.

When they were younger, Ollie looked up to Lowell. He was the best brother a boy could have, always looking after him and teaching him things. As they grew older, they became best friends as well as brothers. That was one reason they worked so well together. In such a short period of time, all that had changed. They were like strangers, and their estrangement affected every facet of their lives, even the other members of the family.

Since it was almost lunchtime, Ollie led the colt he was working with into the stable. After seeing to the horse's needs, he headed up to the house to see if he could help get the meal on the table. Sometimes the women who brought the food served it; other times they didn't. He wanted to be sure Mother wasn't disturbed. She needed to stay with Father.

Ollie was washing his hands in the kitchen sink when he heard his mother call. "Ollie, is that you?" Somehow she always knew which son it was. They must sound different, even when they weren't talking.

He hurried up the stairs, taking two steps at a time. His mother met him in the hall outside the door to his parents' bedroom. She reached to hug him, and he gathered her into his arms, hoping to comfort her somehow.

"I'm glad you've come into the house." Her voice was muffled against his broad chest, but he didn't have any trouble understanding her. "Your father insists he must speak to his lawyer." She pulled back and looked up at Ollie's face. "I told him I would send whichever one of you came into the house first. Would you please go into town and bring Mr. Jones out here as quickly as you can?"

Ollie glanced through the partially open door and saw his father was asleep. He looked so frail, almost as though he were wasting away. "Yes. I'll go right now. I can eat when I get back."

His mother patted him on the shoulder. "You are such a good son, Ollie." Then she returned to the rocking chair next to the bed.

Ollie watched her pick up her knitting. Even though her hands flew, performing the intricate needlework, she never took her eyes from his father's still form. Her lips formed soundless words, and he knew she was praying.

Lowell was eating his lunch when Ollie and another man rode up. He left his half-empty plate and went to open the front door. The two men had reached the porch. "Ollie. . .Mr. Jones?" He opened the door wider, and the lawyer immediately started up the stairs. Lowell looked at his brother with a questioning expression.

Ollie shrugged. "I'm famished." He headed toward the kitchen.

Lowell followed him. "Are you going to tell me what's going on?"

Ollie dished up some beef stew with corn bread, then answered his brother's question. "*Fader* insisted on seeing his lawyer. *Moder* asked me to get him." He turned toward the table where Lowell sat. "That's all I know."

Just after Ollie sat down, their mother came into the kitchen. She said she had taken some broth up to Father earlier, but she hadn't eaten lunch. After filling a bowl from the food in the warming oven, she joined them.

For a few minutes, the only thing they did was eat. Then Lowell put his fork down and asked, "Do you know why *Fader* wants to talk to Mr. Jones?"

She shook her head. "He didn't tell me, and he didn't want me to stay in the room." She pushed her food around the bowl with a spoon.

Lowell had noticed she didn't eat much these days. He almost wished he hadn't asked his question. He hoped it wouldn't keep her from finishing lunch.

The three of them tried to make casual conversation, but it was sporadic. They took turns glancing at the ceiling as if they could see into the bedroom above and hear what was transpiring.

When he finished lunch, Lowell went outside to split some logs for the stove. But he couldn't keep his mind on what he was doing. He was afraid the ax might slip and cut him. Besides, it was hot. When he went into the kitchen to pump a glass of cold water from the well, he saw Mother in a rocking chair in the parlor. She usually worked on needlework when she was there, but now she just sat still and stared out the window. Her hands lay idle in her lap.

Lowell stepped out on the porch and prayed for his mother and father. Just as he finished and looked up, he noticed someone galloping on a horse toward the house. Dr. Bradley leaped from his mare and quickly tied her to the hitching post. Lowell met him halfway.

"I think I've discovered what's causing the infection!" Doc rushed toward the house, and Lowell had to hurry to keep up with him. "We can't lose any time treating it, if it's not too late already!"

A thought invaded Lowell's consciousness—one he had pushed from his mind before, not letting it near. What if it was too late? He couldn't lose his father. He just couldn't. He still needed him. So did Mother—and Ollie.

Mother must have heard the commotion, because she opened the screen door before they reached it. "Come in, Dr. Bradley. What can I do to help?"

"Bring some boiling water up to the bedroom, along with clean pieces of material for compresses."

Before he could rush up the stairs, Mr. Jones came down. He tipped his hat to Lowell's mother and left quickly.

"What was he doing here?" the doctor asked.

Lowell followed him up the stairs. "*Far* wanted to see him. He's been up there for a couple of hours."

Doc frowned, then entered the bedroom and closed the door. Lowell hurried back downstairs to carry the hot water for his mother. She opened the door for him, and he set the large pan on the bedside table.

"I hate to do this, Lowell." Doc had already rolled up his sleeves to his elbows. "But I'm going to have to ask you to let your mother and me take care of your father."

Lowell glanced around the room. He wanted to help. But when he looked at his mother, he knew it would be better for her if he didn't make a fuss.

When Lowell came back downstairs, he wanted to throw something—or hit someone. If he were younger, he might have done one of those things. Instead, he went out to the front porch and sat on the top step. Ollie saw him and walked over from the barn to join him. They sat and waited. Neither of them wanted to voice the fear that had invaded their hearts. It wasn't long before the doctor came out to join them, but it seemed like an eternity.

"I'm sorry." Doc was rolling his sleeves back down and buttoning the cuffs. "I did all I could. The infection had been in his system too long."

Ollie jumped up. "Tell me he's not de—"

When his younger brother dropped his head into his hands and sobbed, Lowell went to him. He knew why his brother couldn't finish that word. How could their father be dead? As boys, Lowell had always taken care of Ollie and tried to keep him from getting hurt. Now he couldn't stop Ollie's pain; he felt the same thing.

Lowell looked at the doctor. "What caused the fever?" Tears clogged his throat.

"I finally heard from a colleague. He works near a horse farm in Kentucky. This kind of thing has happened there. If you're not careful, you can get an especially virulent infection from horse manure. Your mother and I looked your father over, and we found a cut on his shin. I think that's where the infection entered his body. But we were unable to treat it. If only I had found this out sooner, I might have been able to help him."

Lowell could tell from the expression on Doc's face that this had hurt him almost as much as it did them.

"Boys," Doc continued, "I want you to be especially careful." He looked stern. "Don't ever go into the barn or anywhere there is horse manure if you have an untreated open cut or sore. It could be deadly." He clapped his hat on his head and walked toward his horse with his head and shoulders slumped. He mounted and headed toward town, but he didn't seem to be in a hurry. His horse walked slowly down the road.

The next day passed in a blur. Lowell knew his mother, Anna, Ollie, and he had made several decisions together, but he wasn't sure what they were. Mother spent most of the time in tears. Lowell fought to keep from crying. When he looked at Ollie, he could tell he was having the same battle. Once Doc reached town, word spread quickly. August brought Anna to the house so she could be with the family. A couple of neighbor women came and helped Mother get Father ready for the viewing. The town had an undertaker, but he was a stranger. They didn't want to take Father to him. Neighbors and church members sat with them around the clock until the funeral. Bennel, Gustaf, and August Nilsson worked together to build the casket.

After the service in church, Gustaf and August drove the wagon carrying the casket to the knoll above the Jenson house where Father wanted to be buried. He and Mother had already decided to have the family cemetery in the small grove of trees on that hill. Father's was the first.

After a brief graveside service, Lowell and Ollie decided they would build a white picket fence to enclose enough ground for the next few generations of Jensons. They would also order a headstone from a stonemason in St. Paul.

Now most of the neighbors had gone home, and Mother was finally resting. Lowell and Ollie sat on the front porch drinking glasses of lemonade someone had brought to them. Soon August and Anna joined them and sat on the swing, and August put his arm around Anna.

"How are we going to get along without *Fader*?" Ollie's plaintive question reached out to Lowell.

It repeated the one that had haunted Lowell. What would they do? He didn't want to think about it today, but he couldn't ignore it for long.

"I always thought he would be here for my children." Lowell glanced at his brother. "I wanted him to teach my sons the things he taught us. He could do a much better job of it than I'll be able to."

Ollie nodded. "Life doesn't always happen the way we think it will, does it?"

Lowell leaned his head against one of the pillars holding up the roof of the porch. He closed his eyes, trying to keep the tears at bay. Men weren't supposed to cry, but he was having a hard time not doing so. According to the wet trails making their way down Ollie's cheeks, his brother shared the same problem.

After a few moments, Lowell became aware of the sound of a horse making its way toward the house. Probably another neighbor bringing food or something else for Mother. He opened his eyes and turned to look at the lone rider. Mr. Jones dismounted at the hitching post in front of the house. Lowell wasn't sure he was glad to see him. Lawyers often didn't bring good news. Surely if he had bad news, he would have waited to come another day.

Mr. Jones walked up to the porch. He took off his hat and held it in both hands as he looked at the brothers. "I'm sorry to come on such a sad day, but it was your father's instructions I should come the day he was buried."

Lowell glanced at his brother. Ollie just stared at the lawyer.

Lowell turned and did the same thing. "Our mother is resting, and this isn't a good time. Can't you come back later?"

"No." Mother's voice came through the screen door. "I'm up now, Lowell. Ask Mr. Jones in for a cool drink. I'm sure he's thirsty on such a hot, dry day."

Lowell and Ollie led the way into the parlor. August and Anna followed the lawyer. It was even hot in the house. If there had been any kind of wind, it would have blown through the open windows and cooled the room some, but there wasn't even a hint of a breeze. One of the women who was cleaning the kitchen brought a pitcher of lemonade and a glass for Mr. Jones; then she left the family alone with the lawyer. When Lowell looked at his mother, her red-rimmed eyes seemed to fill her face.

After taking a long swallow of the drink, Mr. Jones reached into the pocket of his suit jacket and removed a folded document. He cleared his throat. "This isn't my favorite thing to do, but it goes along with being a lawyer." He unfolded the pages and started reading, "I, Soren Jenson, being of sound mind. . ."

All the legal terms droned on and on. When he finished reading, Mr. Jones asked if there were any questions. Lowell was too stunned to think of any. Ollie just sat there with his hands clasped between his knees.

Mother looked at Lowell with a wan smile on her face. "Do you understand?"

"I think so." He turned toward the lawyer. "It means Ollie and I own the horse farm as equal partners. Right?"

Mr. Jones nodded.

"And we're not allowed to sell our shares for at least a year."

"Your father was specific about that provision. He mentioned there had been some. . .tension between you for a while. By the way, that information will remain confidential between us. He hoped that by adding this provision he could help you get over this situation. By working together for a year, I mean." He cleared his throat again. Then he picked up his glass of lemonade and took another swallow.

Mother nodded. "That sounds like a good idea to me."

After Mr. Jones left, Lowell went to the barn and sat on a bale of hay. He loved this place. Surely Father knew that. He never wanted to sell it. He and Ollie were having a bit of a problem right now, but they were family. And this horse farm was their heritage. They would have worked together even without that will. Lowell hadn't realized the situation between Ollie and him had affected the rest of the family so much. It was their own fault Father felt he had to put this in a legal document. Lowell dropped his head into his hands and sobbed.

Chapter 8

If she lived to be one hundred years old, Marissa would never understand Pierre. Of course, he was hardly ever nice to her or Clari. Since the Sunday when they attended church, he had been more brusque with her than before. She was sure it was because of their conversation later that afternoon. And he didn't take her to church again. Most days Pierre disappeared soon after breakfast. He often told her not to leave the boardinghouse, because he would soon return. That was never true. Day after day she stayed in her room reading the books he brought her. She spent a lot of time alone, and he never returned until dinnertime.

Well, today would be different. He could go away if he wanted to, but she wouldn't stay meekly in her room as he ordered. She was going to the Dress Emporium. She wanted to see Gerda and Anna. She missed talking to them.

After breakfast, he left with the usual admonishment. Marissa went upstairs and looked through her clothes, trying to decide which dress would be coolest to wear. Even though Minnesota was much farther north than any place they had been before, the month of August was hot here. If the wind wasn't blowing, she sweltered even with her windows open, and it hadn't been windy for days.

She hadn't finished dressing before Pierre knocked on her door. Why hadn't he stayed away today as he had before?

She went to the door but didn't open it. "Just a moment. I'm changing into something cooler."

"Well, hurry up." Pierre usually tried to sound nicer when they were in the boardinghouse, but not today.

She fastened the buttons on the front of her bodice, then opened the door. He pushed past her and closed the door behind him.

"I'm going to take you out to the camp. You may pack one carpetbag. I told Mrs. Olson we would be gone for a few days. I want to get on the road before it gets too hot."

When he left, Marissa sat on the side of the bed trying not to cry. She had always liked being in the campsite instead of in whatever town they were visiting. Not this time. She had made friends, and she didn't want to leave them. She wished she could stop Pierre, but he couldn't keep her from thinking what she liked. With a sigh, she stuffed several items into the carpetbag, along with some new books.

On the way to the woods, Pierre was quiet. He looked as if he had a lot on his mind. Marissa didn't want to make him mad at her, so she didn't talk, either. But she could think about anything she wanted to. She hadn't seen Lowell Jenson since the day they went to church. She wondered what it would be like if she could just be herself around him. He always paid attention to her, and his smiles reached something deep inside.

His brother, on the other hand, was sort of strange. Marissa didn't know exactly what it was about him, but she had the feeling somehow he didn't trust her. There was a very good reason not to trust her, but he couldn't know about that. So being around him made her uncomfortable.

Marissa wondered why Pierre had told Mrs. Olson they would be away a few days. She hoped that was true. Maybe he would leave her with Clari at the camp for a while. She and Clari could relax and enjoy each other's company. She could hardly wait to talk to her sister about the Jenson brothers.

Pierre had always told Clari and her it was important to keep the camp a secret. Each time he went, he found a different way to go, to keep from making a trail someone could follow. This trip was longer than before. Pierre drove the horses faster than usual, so Marissa bounced around on the seat. She gripped the seat to keep from falling out of the wagon. At least she would see her sister soon. It had been a long time since they were able to spend more than a single day together. Marissa hoped they could be together for at least a week. And she hoped Pierre would be nowhere around so she and Clari could relax.

When they reached the forest, Marissa closed her eyes so she wouldn't see the dark shadows; but she couldn't shut out the unidentifiable sounds that brought out her hidden fears. She was glad when the wagon entered the sunshine again. She opened her eyes and scanned the clearing, looking for some sign of Clari.

Clarissa was at the creek washing her clothes when she heard a wagon. She grabbed up her wet clothing and darted behind a tree. Carefully working her way toward the sound, she peeked from behind each tree before she ran to another one. Finally, she caught sight of Pierre and Mari in the wagon, which was fast approaching the campsite. She ran to the caravan and put her wet clothes on the top step. Later she could spread them on bushes to dry.

She turned and saw Pierre pull on the reins to stop the horses. "Mari!" Clarissa ran and helped her sister alight from the wagon.

"Clari!" Mari hugged her so hard she could hardly breathe. Clarissa hugged her back; then they danced around, laughing and holding each other's hands.

Pierre stood and glared at them. He knew how much they loved each other—and how much they didn't love him.

"Stop that and come help me unload the wagon."

He sounded harsher than she remembered. Either he was upset, or Clarissa had been in the camp so long she wasn't used to him anymore.

After they unloaded the supplies, Mari reached under the seat and pulled out a carpetbag. Clarissa turned a questioning face toward Pierre.

He stood in the shade of a tall tree, so his face was in shadows. "Yes, Marissa will stay with you awhile." Clarissa couldn't keep from smiling. She didn't care if it made him angry.

Mari stared at Pierre for a moment. "Pierre, please let us stop this criminal activity."

He frowned. "We've already discussed this enough, and I'm tired of your whining." He took a menacing step toward Mari.

Clarissa moved between them. "I agree with Mari. How long will you make us continue to do this?"

When Pierre laughed, it pierced Clarissa's heart. He sounded so evil. "I'm all the family you have left. I have to take care of you. Why do you question everything I do? You have nice clothes and plenty of food to eat. Most women would be happy with that."

Mari stepped up beside Clarissa. "But it's wrong, and you know it's wrong."

Pierre glared at her before he turned to Clarissa. "I made the mistake of taking Marissa to church. She has had all kinds of ideas since then."

Mari placed her fists on her hips. "I only want to live a normal life—as Gerda and Anna do." Clarissa was proud of her for taking a stand.

Pierre took Mari by the shoulders and shook her. "I told you I didn't want you to mess anything up. You weren't supposed to make friends. That's why I brought Clarissa to the campsite earlier. She was too friendly."

Clarissa watched Mari's eyes fill with tears when Pierre grabbed her. Soon they became twin waterfalls down her cheeks. Clarissa wanted to intervene, but this had happened enough times in the past that she'd learned not to try to stop him. He wouldn't listen, and both she and her sister would be hurt far worse than Mari was today. So Clarissa clamped her teeth together and stifled her impulse to yell at him and pound him with her fists.

Mari jerked herself from his hold. "I haven't been the kind of friend to them they were to me. I want to live an honest life." She crossed her arms over her chest and thrust her chin out. Clarissa had never seen her timid sister like this.

Once again Pierre laughed. "Don't worry. We won't be here long enough for you to do that. As soon as I come back, we'll set everything in motion." He turned and sauntered toward the wagon. "I have some business to take care of getting ready for the game we'll pull in Litchfield. I don't know how long it will take, but I think it'll be about two weeks." He turned and gestured toward the large pile of items they had unloaded from the wagon. "That's why I brought so many supplies."

Marissa's eyes widened.

"You're going to leave us for two weeks?" Clarissa's voice squeaked out the last word.

Pierre nodded. "If you're careful, you'll be all right."

"What if something happens?" Marissa's voice quavered. Her bravado had been short lived.

"Nothing's going to happen." Pierre sounded disgusted. "You have a gun, and I'm going to leave one of the horses with you. If you have an emergency, you can go into town but not Litchfield." He pulled a paper from his pocket. "Here's a map that will lead you to Wayzata. You can go there in an emergency. But if I come back, and you've gone there for any other reason, you'll wish you hadn't." That last sentence was no idle threat.

Clarissa knew Mari was probably shaking in her shoes. "What about money— if we have an emergency?"

Pierre pulled a pouch from the pocket of his vest and threw it toward Clarissa. She surprised herself by catching it in midair. She was also surprised by how much the pouch weighed. He really meant he wouldn't be back for at least two weeks. Maybe he wasn't ever coming back. Maybe this was his way of getting rid of them, and this money was a payoff. Wouldn't that be wonderful?

Pierre unhitched the horses from the wagon and took them to the stream for a drink. When he returned, he hitched only one horse to the wagon. Clarissa and Mari stood and watched him in silence. They would talk after he was gone. As he drove away from them, he turned around and gave a cavalier wave just before he entered the surrounding forest.

When they could no longer see him, Mari crumpled into a heap, weeping as if her heart were broken. Clarissa sat on the ground and gathered her into her arms. She held her sister until she was cried out. Then Clarissa stood and pulled Mari up with her.

She dried Mari's eyes with her handkerchief, then stuffed it back in the pocket of her trousers. "Think about it, Mari. Pierre will be gone for two whole weeks."

Marissa felt unfettered, and she knew her sister did, too. Free. It was wonderful. Marissa wished it could be forever. They opened the crates and worked together to store the provisions in the caravan. Then they ran and played in the glade as if they were still children. In the evening after eating, they sat around the campfire and talked.

"Tell me what has been happening in town," Clari inquired.

After Marissa told her about becoming friends with Anna and Gerda, Clari asked, "How is Ollie Jenson?"

"Okay, I guess." Marissa looked at Clari. "I was more interested in Lowell."

Clari laughed. "He was too quiet for me. Ollie is more fun."

Marissa understood what was going on. "You're interested in Ollie, and I'm interested in Lowell. Wouldn't it be wonderful if we could be ourselves around them?"

Clari looked thoughtful. "Oh, yes. I know it can never happen, but what if it could?" She gazed up at the clouds. "What if we were living normal lives—being ourselves—and they knew there were two of us? I wonder if they would court us the way Mother told us Father courted her."

"We wouldn't dress alike," Marissa added. "Our clothing would reflect our individual personalities. You could be Clarissa Voss, and I could be Marissa Voss, and Rissa Le Blanc would be no more."

The next morning, the sisters went to the waterfall. They stripped down to their unmentionables and romped in the pool at the base before they showered and washed their hair under the waterfall. While they let their hair dry, Marissa told Clari about the Sunday she and Pierre had attended church.

The song that had touched her heart still played through her mind. She sang as much of it as she could remember.

"I can't believe you're singing about blood." Clari sat up straighter. "You never liked it."

"I know, but something about the song soothes me. I don't know why."

"What does it mean?" Clari asked.

"I wish I knew." Marissa tried to remember what the preacher said. "In the sermon, the pastor talked about Jesus saving us from all our sins. He said we can't commit a sin Jesus won't forgive."

Clari looked confused. "I remember Mother telling us about baby Jesus in a manger, and we see things about Him at Christmas. Is this the same Jesus?"

"I think so."

"But how could that baby save us from all our sins?"

Marissa shook her head. "I don't know. I think I remember Mother telling us a little about an older Jesus, too. One who died. I'd hoped Pierre would take me to church again so I could hear more of what the preacher had to say and maybe find out. I didn't even get a chance to ask Gerda and Anna about it. Pierre didn't let me go back to the Dress Emporium before he brought me out here."

When Clarissa got up the next morning, Mari was still sleeping. After leaving her sister in bed, Clarissa took a walk through the grove around the campsite. She liked early mornings. They were the only cool times of the day. She went back to the berry patch and picked some berries for breakfast.

The rest of the day was spent much like the first one. When evening came, the sisters cooked dinner, then sat watching the fire die down.

Mari got a dreamy expression on her face. "I've been thinking about Lowell and Ollie again. What if they did court us?"

Clarissa put her hands in the grass behind her and leaned her weight on them. "That would be wonderful!"

"It would mean we were living normal lives. Maybe we would be in Mrs. Olson's boardinghouse, and Pierre would be gone. I wish he could be sent to prison. He deserves it." Mari drew her knees up and put her arms around her legs. "If only he could be caught, and we wouldn't. But that is impossible."

Clarissa leaned forward. "Don't start thinking bad thoughts. We need to enjoy this time together. If we lived in the boardinghouse and Lowell and Ollie were courting us, I wonder how long it would take them to ask us to marry them."

Mari leaned her chin on her knees. "Maybe they would do it at almost the same time. We could have a double wedding."

Clarissa sighed. "We've never really been to a wedding. It's silly for us to make up these stories."

"Oh, Clari, I would just die if I didn't have a little hope!"

Chapter 9

Because Ollie and Lowell were used to doing all the work around the horse farm, they had no trouble continuing after their father died. Their problems were mostly confined to their personal relationship.

They worked well together, but when they arrived back at the house in the evenings, they maintained a shaky peace at best. Every conversation led to things they disagreed about. Their differing opinions about Rissa Le Blanc affected many other things they discussed. Neither one could understand his brother's position, so discussions were short and tense. Ollie realized he was as much to blame as his brother.

The situation affected Mother, too. Ollie knew it broke her heart. In addition to the grief she felt at the loss of Father, this was too much. She tried to hide how it hurt her, but Ollie recognized the signs of her pain. And he was sure his brother did, too. That's why they had almost stopped talking to each other once they returned to the house after work.

One evening, Ollie asked Lowell to accompany him out to the barn when they finished dinner. He used the pretense of wanting to show him how one of the colts was progressing, but he figured Lowell had guessed he wanted to talk to him about something else. As long as he could remember, his brother had been able to read him like a book.

"Why did you ask me to come out here?" Lowell didn't lose any time getting right to the point.

His belligerent stance alerted Ollie to the fact that the discussion might not go as he had hoped. He walked over to the closest stall and leaned his arms on the top rail, his back to his brother. It was often easier to talk to Lowell if he wasn't looking at him.

"*Moder.*"

Lowell was quiet so long Ollie finally turned to look at him.

"What about *Moder?*" Lowell asked.

"I'm sure you know how much our estrangement affects her."

Lowell nodded and rubbed the back of his neck. Then he dropped his hands to his sides. "Do you have any idea how we can overcome this? If we start talking about Rissa Le Blanc, we only argue. You think she is not what she seems, and I want to help her."

"I know." Ollie looked at the floor. He scuffed an oval in the dirt with the toe of his boot. Then he erased it. "We work together well, though."

"In the evenings, when we should be enjoying conversation, we are so careful about what we say to each other. I think about Rissa a lot. Maybe you do, too. So I want to talk about her, but we're back to the problem." Lowell crossed his arms over his chest, tucking his hands under his arms. "How are we going to get past that?" He rocked up on the balls of his feet, then down again.

Ollie pushed his hands into his hip pockets, something Lowell usually did. Maybe he was more like his brother than he had thought. "How about if I let you have the house?"

"What?" Lowell looked confused. "Have the house? What are you talking about? Where would you live?"

"I've figured that out. I could build a house on another part of the property." Lowell opened his mouth, but Ollie held up his hand to stop him. "Let me finish. We'll both want to marry someday. When we do, we'll have separate homes. I don't think either one of us plans to sell his part of the horse farm. There is no reason we can't run it together."

Lowell seemed to be mulling over this information. "That's right. Do you have a spot in mind?"

"I think so. When I was out riding yesterday, I noticed it again. I was reminded that when I was younger I used to ride out there. It was my favorite spot on the farm. Tomorrow maybe we could go over there and look it over. If you agree I can use the land, I'll start building as soon as I can."

Lowell scratched his head. "I'm not sure how that would help, but it's okay with me."

Ollie looked his brother in the eyes. "Mother can live with you in the main house. It's been her home for so long. Maybe we could even eat meals together as we do now. That would make the transition of my living in another house easier on her."

Lowell didn't take his gaze from his brother's. "That should work, and she could see both of us in the evenings as she does now. Maybe it could help ease the tension, too."

The only thing that will ease the tension will be for us to work out the problem about Rissa Le Blanc. Ollie knew that wouldn't happen any time soon. His brother was interested in her—very interested. If she were the woman Ollie knew a few weeks ago, he would be interested in her, too, but evidently she had changed. That's why he didn't trust her. But his brother wouldn't hear any talk against her.

When Lowell awoke the next morning, it was later than usual. He could hear the sounds of his mother in the kitchen. The aroma of bacon and biscuits that usually met him when he returned from milking the cows wafted up the stairs. It was no wonder he slept so late, because it had taken him a long time to get to sleep. His mind wouldn't let go of what he and Ollie discussed in the barn. Intermingled with those thoughts were musings about Rissa Le Blanc and pain over losing his father. He wished Father were here so he could talk to him. Maybe he could make some sense of what was happening. Lowell's thoughts had been so jumbled that he couldn't settle down. He took off his boots so he wouldn't make any noise and paced the floor of his room for hours after they all retired.

If Rissa hadn't come into their lives, he and Ollie might never have disagreed the way they did now. Thoughts of the woman warmed Lowell's heart. The memory of her soft voice and the enticing fragrance that enveloped her haunted him night and day. He wanted to get to know her better. Thoughts of having her in his life forever never left him, but Ollie's opinion of her intruded on those ideas.

Lowell hurried to don his clothes; then he took the stairs two at a time. When he arrived in the kitchen, Ollie was bringing in two buckets of warm milk. Lowell stopped short in the doorway and looked at his brother.

"You didn't have to do the milking for me."

A slow smile covered Ollie's face. "I wanted us to get an early start on our ride."

Lowell could see their friendly conversation pleased their mother. She beamed, and the twinkle had returned to her eyes.

After a hearty breakfast, the brothers set off. Since they both enjoyed a good gallop, Lowell followed Ollie's lead as they let the horses stretch their abilities to the limit. Soon Ollie slowed down. Lowell did, too.

When Ollie turned his horse toward a hill, Lowell followed him. On the top of the hill, a grove of trees stood sentinel over a bluff. The small stream that flowed through the farm ran along the base of the cliff. Ollie dismounted his horse, then tied him to one of the trees. When Lowell had finished tying his horse, he went to stand beside Ollie, who was looking out over the valley surrounding the stream. The vista was beautiful and familiar. A small lake on the near horizon glistened in the bright sunshine. Since it was morning, birds flitted from branch to branch above them, and a gentle breeze whispered through the trees, cooling both the men and the horses. This site was the perfect place to build a house. The trees would serve as a windbreak in the storms of winter. Because the hill was the highest spot around, no one could sneak up on it. It was thirty years since the war, and the country was tamer now, but outlaws occasionally still roamed outlying areas.

"I think you've chosen wisely." Lowell turned toward Ollie. "I hope a house here will make you happy."

Ollie looked surprised. "You really mean that, don't you?"

Lowell nodded and threw his arm across Ollie's shoulder as they walked back to where the horses were waiting.

That evening, Ollie completed drawing plans for the house he had already been working on. He tried not to think about Rissa, but he could picture her in each of the rooms. He knew he needed to forget the woman. She was bad news for him and his brother. No woman who changed that much in only a couple of weeks would be a good wife, but he couldn't help wondering what life with her would be like—if she were the woman he remembered.

Ollie planned to build a two-story house. It would be almost as large as the main house because he wanted several children. He needed plenty of room for the family God would give him and his wife. He could imagine Rissa descending the stairs toward him with an eager smile lighting her blue eyes. He would hold out his arms, and she would slip into his embrace, her dark curls tumbling over his arms. Ollie stopped staring into space and shook his head. He had to stop this nonsense.

The next day, Ollie made a trip into town to order materials for the house. When he was finished, he sauntered into the Dress Emporium to see Anna.

After they had visited for a few minutes, Anna asked, "Have you heard about the Le Blancs?"

Ollie shook his head. "What about them?"

"August said Mrs. Olson told them Pierre and his daughter were out of town for a few days, but they said they were coming back in a week or two."

Ollie wished he didn't care, but he was glad he might see Rissa again soon. He hoped she would once more be his lively companion, for a while anyway.

Because he had telegraphed the order, the supplies arrived by train a couple of days later. About fifty men from the church—including Johan Braxton as well as August, Gustaf, and Bennel Nilsson—came to help build the outside walls and put on the roof. They put in most of the studs on both the lower floor and the upper story in a few days. Ollie wanted to finish the inside of the house by himself. He could come over most evenings after dinner. While it was still summer, he would have enough light to work several hours. It was a good way to relieve his frustrations.

Lowell worked hard to finish the chores. He even repaired some of the tack they had let go for a while.

Ollie returned from town, and Lowell stepped out of the barn to meet him. "I want to ask you something."

Ollie dismounted and led his horse into the stable. Lowell followed him.

"Ask away, brother." Ollie started to remove his horse's saddle.

Lowell leaned against the tack room door frame. "I want to go on a hunting trip—if that's all right with you."

Ollie turned around, still holding the saddle. "Why wouldn't it be all right with me?"

"Well, you would have to do all the chores, and you want to work on your house."

Ollie glanced around. "It looks as if you have things under control, so it won't be too much more work." He took the saddle into the tack room and put it up. "How long will you be gone?"

Lowell moved away from the door frame. "I don't know. I have a lot to think about. You know I like to be alone to work things out in my mind."

The next morning long before dawn, Lowell loaded a pack animal with the provisions he would need on a hunt. Besides food, he packed ammunition for his rifle and a tarp in case it rained. It had been a dry summer, but one never knew when a summer storm would blow across the plains. At least he wouldn't need a tent. It was warm enough to sleep under the stars. Lowell always enjoyed lying on his back looking up at the indigo canopy filled with tiny lights that winked and glowed above him. When he did, he felt closer to God than at any other time. A God who could create that vast expanse had to be powerful enough to help him with any difficulty. He hoped that by the time he came home, God would help him overcome his problems.

After the provisions were loaded, he saddled his horse. He walked the two horses slowly by the house because he didn't want to wake either his mother or Ollie. When he was far enough away that the sound wouldn't disturb them, he mounted his horse and headed toward the northwest. It had been a long time since he had ventured in that direction. Because the land had a wilder, untamed feel to it, he usually hunted in other places. But today he wanted to get as far from civilization as he could. He just hoped he wouldn't encounter a gang of outlaws.

Lowell rode across the plains until he came to an area that was pocked with canyons and gullies. The sun was coming up, and he stopped to eat some cold biscuits and bacon his mother had cooked for him last night when he told her he was going hunting. He stopped beside a small, clear stream that tumbled over rocks. He dipped up some of the cold water with a tin cup. If he had wanted to take the time, coffee would have tasted good with the biscuits, but he was in a hurry to move farther into the wilderness.

After watering his horse, Lowell mounted and started down a gully. He was surprised to see signs of recent wagon tracks. They were faint because of the rocky soil, but here and there a distinct impression caused by the rim of a wagon wheel led deeper into the gully. Slowly, he followed the trail. Sometimes it disappeared altogether when solid rock lined the gully. Eventually, he would pick up the trail again farther on. He had never heard of anyone taking a wagon into this country. Usually travelers kept to the south where the undulating plains were easier to traverse. He wondered if a new band of outlaws he hadn't heard about yet was operating there. He would be careful—just in case.

Lowell followed the trail deeper and deeper into the wilderness where scrub brush grew from tiny patches of soil that clung to the rocks. He entered a valley surrounded by cliffs. The floor of the valley contained a dense forest. One time, when he was about twelve years old, his father had brought Ollie and him here. Lowell remembered a clearing in the forest where scattered clumps of trees created shelter good for camping. They had spent several days exploring the area. A stream entered the valley from the north ridge of the canyon and tumbled over rock formations until a waterfall, about fifteen feet tall, emptied into a pool of clear water. He and his brother had played in that pool when they got hot.

After that summer, Father didn't take them on any camping trips so far from home. He had decided to start raising horses, and all three of them worked too hard to be gone so long.

Lowell made his way through the thick trees that surrounded the valley. The dense undergrowth would be a good hiding place for bandits. He hoped he wasn't making a mistake coming here. If he could find the waterfall, he wanted to camp near it if it was safe. The tranquility of the glade might help him sort out his thoughts. Maybe God would even give him a solution to the dilemma.

Before Lowell reached the clearing, he heard faint voices. Someone was in the valley. He almost turned back, but what if it wasn't outlaws? What if someone else had found this place of refuge? The valley was large. It would be easy to camp out of sight from the others. They didn't have to have any contact, but he did want to check them out first.

He found a place where the undergrowth was thinner. After taking some rope from his pack, he tied both horses to trees, leaving enough slack so they could graze on a patch of grass. He slowly made his way around the valley, staying in the protective cover of the trees and underbrush. Occasionally, he stopped and studied the glade, trying to see where the voices were coming from. Soon he spotted a caravan wagon sitting under a spreading maple tree. All around it were other indications of human habitation—clothing hung on bushes to dry, a campfire that had burned down to a few coals, and a horse staked near the wagon. Lowell was glad he was good at tracking and keeping quiet or the horse would have already announced his presence.

If he remembered right, and he was sure he did, the waterfall was on the other side of the tree where the wagon sat, just through some underbrush. He glanced in that direction and saw two figures coming through the trees. They were talking and laughing, but he couldn't see them very well. He couldn't understand anything they were saying, either, but they had to be young, because their voices weren't deep yet. They were dressed in shirts and trousers, and their dark hair made their faces stand out. If only he were close enough to see their features, but they were a light blur in the shadows.

When the two emerged into the sunlight, Lowell could tell they were women. Evidently, they had been in the pool or under the waterfall, because their long black hair glistened with water as it hung down their backs. They walked over to the bushes where the clothes had been spread. One of the women removed what was there while the other woman began to spread more to dry.

Lowell felt like an invader. He wondered if any men were with the women, but he doubted it. They were dressed in shirts and trousers themselves. If they were traveling alone, they probably tried to pass themselves off as young men to protect themselves from unwanted attention. Lowell wondered what their story was. He tried to decide whether to approach them or find another place to camp. Just then, one of the women danced across the clearing with her hands raised to the sky. His attention was drawn to the other one, who stood quietly watching her.

When he looked back at the exuberant one, he was shocked. If he didn't know better, Lowell would have thought she was Rissa Le Blanc. Drying tendrils of curly hair danced in the air around her head. She was close enough for him to see her face clearly. He shrank back deeper into the shadows and slipped completely behind a large tree trunk. He took a deep breath and peeked again.

"Marissa, the sun feels so good after the cool water." She whirled to look back at the other woman. "Come join me. We can walk instead of dance if you want to."

Lowell felt as if he had been kicked in the chest by his horse. Marissa. Rissa could be short for that. But she had called the other woman Marissa. Was this her sister? How could they look so much alike? Unless they were twins.

He leaned against the tree with his hands on his knees. What was going on here? Should he approach these women? And where was Le Blanc?

Lowell slid down the trunk until he was sitting on the ground. He took a deep breath and bowed his head while dangling his arms across his raised knees. *Now would be a good time for You to talk to me*, Gud. *What am I supposed to do?*

❧

Marissa knew how tired Clari was of this isolation. She did everything she could to make their time together exciting, but Clari had gone too far this time. Dancing in the sunshine. Marissa supposed she had to join her. Their skin needed to be the same shade for the game to work. Maybe she should just stay in the shade. If Clari were too tan, perhaps Pierre would call off the plan. Marissa knew that wasn't a possibility, but it felt good to think so.

This time when they were together, the sisters had talked more than they had ever done before. It was the first time Marissa told Clari what was deep in her heart. She wished they could just drive the wagon into Litchfield and tell their friends who they were. Gerda and Anna would understand, wouldn't they? But what about Lowell and Ollie? Ollie was as important to Clari as Lowell was to her. Would telling them the truth destroy their fragile friendships? Marissa would never know. Pierre would see to that. As soon as the plan was executed, they would leave town, never to return again. If only there was a God who could take away her sins. Then maybe she would have a chance. But Pierre dashed that hope every time she tried to voice it.

Raising her hands above her head, she stepped into the sunlight and slowly turned around. Clari was right. It felt good to move around in the light and warmth, but Marissa could never move with the reckless abandon of her sister, even if they were alone in this obscure wilderness.

Lowell sat still for a few minutes until a thought dropped into his mind. If he were to show himself, he probably would scare the young women. They might not even wait to see who he was. He had noticed a rifle leaning against the tree beside the wagon. They might shoot him in their haste.

He made his way back to the horses, took a long swig from his canteen, and untied them. He led the pack animal over to his horse, mounted him, then headed toward the slight trail that led in the direction of the clearing. He rode along as if he didn't know anyone was there—as if he were a hunter who happened on the valley.

He didn't look up until he was completely out of the trees and in the sunlight. Then he glanced around as if he were hunting for a place to camp. The young women still cavorted around the clearing. His horse saw the one staked near the caravan and whinnied.

The other horse raised its head and perked its ears, and the two young women stood as still as statues. After a moment, they turned and looked in his direction; then they ran into the shelter of trees beside their wagon.

"Hallo!" he shouted.

The women continued their headlong plunge into the shadows. One grabbed the rifle as she ran past. They took a position behind the wagon, and with the barrel of the rifle protruding, one leaned her head out so she could watch his approach.

"I'm not going to bother you," he called out when he was closer. "I've been hunting and need to get some fresh water from the waterfall. I won't disturb you." He continued to ride past the campsite.

One of the young women stepped out from behind the wagon. She still carried the rifle, but it wasn't raised so high. "Lowell Jenson, is that you?" The other young woman stepped up beside her.

Lowell stopped near them. He took off his hat and looked down at one of the women. "Rissa Le Blanc?" He glanced at the other one. "Or are you Rissa Le Blanc?"

In the face of the second young woman, he recognized the one he had been dreaming about. That hint of hurt was still in her eyes. Sky blue eyes surrounded by a smudge of long black lashes. She quickly averted her face but not before he noticed her slight smile.

The first woman still pointed the rifle at him, but he dismounted and stood beside his horse, patting his neck, watching them from the corner of his eyes. He didn't want to spook the young woman into pulling the trigger.

"Where is Pierre?"

The women turned to each other, a look of fear in their eyes. The one with the rifle stiffened.

"Why do you want to know?" she asked, her voice trembling.

Lowell faced them. "I was just wondering. I don't want to disturb you, though." He continued to hold his horse's reins and the lead line to the pack animal. "I just wanted to camp here, but if that isn't all right with you, I won't. I do need some fresh water for myself and my horses." He continued walking toward the stream that led from the pool at the base of the waterfall. He forced himself not to look back at the two young women.

Marissa heard the horse's whinny, and her heart started to pound wildly. Then she saw a man riding toward them. Clari grabbed her hand and pulled her toward the wagon. When he spoke, Mari was surprised. The voice she had grown to love, the voice that echoed in her memory, was there in the campsite with them. Could it really be Lowell Jenson?

Even though she couldn't look at him after she and Clari stepped away from the wagon's protection, Marissa was happy to see him. She watched him longingly as he led his horses toward the pool; then she looked at her sister.

"What will we do, Clari?"

Clari turned toward her sister. "I don't know. If we aren't hospitable to him, he will wonder why, but Pierre would be angry if he found out."

Marissa looked at the place where the man and two horses had disappeared into the shadows. "Clari, it's Lowell."

"Yes, I know, but now he knows there are two of us. What if he tells someone?"

"He won't hurt us."

Clari looked worried. "We have to tell him something when he returns from the waterfall. But what?"

"I wish we could tell him the truth." Marissa couldn't keep from glancing in the direction he had gone. "Maybe we could."

"No!" Clari's whisper was almost a shout.

Chapter 10

Lowell had more on his mind as he headed home than he did when he left. The short time he'd spent with the twins filled his head—and heart—with a myriad of questions. At least he knew there were two girls. Come to think of it, he still didn't know their names, except that one of them was Marissa. They were evasive and ill at ease while he was there, so he didn't prolong his visit. The story they told him was nothing short of incredible. Incredible and unbelievable. Unbelievable and probably a lie.

The girl whose name was Marissa didn't look him in the eye as they were telling their wild tale. He wished she had. He could hardly wait to get to the farm and talk to Ollie. But first he was going by town to ask August for a favor.

Lowell made good time getting to Litchfield. He stopped outside the blacksmith shop and tied his horse close to the watering trough. Lowell was glad no other horses were tied there. Maybe his future brother-in-law was alone.

When Lowell stepped through the door into the shadowy interior of the shop, he took off his hat and used it to fan himself. The summer heat was bad enough without getting close to the blazing forge. He didn't know how August could stand it.

August looked up from the plow he was shaping. "What brings you here this time of day?"

"I need to ask a favor."

August set the plow on the dirt floor, laid his tools on the workbench, then rubbed his hands on his jeans. "What do you need?"

Lowell combed his fingers through his hair. He didn't want to tell August too much, but he also didn't want him to be suspicious. "I want Ollie to go somewhere with me, and we need someone who is familiar with the farm to look after the animals. I know it's asking a lot, but could you do that for us?"

"Sure." August crossed his arms over his massive chest. "How long are we talking about?"

"Maybe just today, maybe longer."

"I don't have a lot of work right now. Let me bank the fire in the forge, and I'll ride out with you." August started toward the blaze. "You can show me what I need to do."

Lowell turned his hat around and around in his hands. "We'll be really grateful."

Ollie looked out at the sound of horses' hooves and saw Lowell and August riding up to the barn door. He laid aside the saddle he'd been cleaning and stepped out into the sunlight.

"Lowell, what are you doing back so—?"

"I need you to go somewhere with me," his brother said quickly, interrupting him. "August will take care of the animals while we're gone. I'll tell you about it on the ride. Just saddle your horse, and we'll head out. I have enough provisions for both of us."

Lowell showed August what needed to be done while Ollie prepared his horse for travel. Within minutes, the brothers were heading northwest away from the farm.

When they were out of sight, Ollie pulled up under the shade of a tree in a small grove. "Are you going to tell me what's happening? I'm not riding any farther without an explanation."

Both brothers dismounted and tied their horses to a tree. Lowell walked over and sat on a fallen log near the horses. Ollie followed him but remained standing.

"You're not going to believe what I have to tell you." Lowell got a faraway look in his eyes. "I went up that canyon where *Far* took us camping that time, just before we started raising horses. You remember, near the waterfall."

Ollie nodded.

"When I reached the clearing in the forest, someone was camping there. I was afraid it was outlaws, but it wasn't. It was two beautiful young women."

"What are you talking about? What young women?"

Lowell stood and paced near his brother. "Rissa Le Blanc has a twin sister. Both of them were there."

Ollie dropped to the log. "Okay, come sit down and tell me about it."

Lowell lowered himself to the log. "They have a caravan wagon, a horse, and a rifle. And they were dressed in shirts and trousers. Le Blanc was nowhere around."

Ollie's eyes widened. "What were they doing there?"

"Well, that's where the story gets weird. They told me a tale about their being twins. One doesn't live here. She's been in New Orleans. But she came to visit her sister. They wanted time together, and Le Blanc took them out there in the wilderness to get to know each other better. He's coming back in a week or so to get them. Supposedly, the one from New Orleans will return there when he gets back, and he and Rissa will come to Litchfield."

Ollie quickly stood to his feet. "That doesn't make any sense."

"I know." Lowell stood again and brushed off the back of his trousers. "The sister called Marissa is like the Rissa I know. The other one is more like the Rissa you know."

Ollie stared at his brother.

"Do you think one of them has been out there all the time—and they changed places sometimes?"

Lowell nodded. "It looks that way to me. I've never felt good about Le Blanc, and after I left the young women, I had more suspicions about him. The whole time I was in the clearing, I felt as if they were very disturbed about my being there. That they were hiding something. And Marissa wouldn't look at me."

Ollie let out a deep breath. "We have to find out what's going on."

Lowell started toward his horse. "That's what I thought. That's why I came to get you now. I want us to get there before they have time to run away. Somehow I have the feeling they're in trouble and need help."

"Well, what are we waiting for, brother?"

Marissa watched Lowell disappear into the trees. She wished she could have talked to him alone. Clari had done all the talking, and Marissa couldn't even look at his face. She hated lying to him. Now she had no hope he would ever be interested in her. She knew it was only a fairy-tale wish, but she had a hard time letting it go.

She turned to her sister. "What are we going to do?"

Clari usually had good ideas but not now. "I don't know." She dropped onto the top step of the caravan.

Marissa crossed her arms over her waist. "Do you think he believed us?"

"I don't know. I wish you had watched his face. You know Lowell better than I do. Maybe you could have seen if he believed."

Marissa started wringing her hands. "Oh, Clari, I couldn't look at him and lie to his face."

"What do you mean? We've been lying to them all the time we've been here."

"But I didn't want to." Marissa rubbed her sweaty palms down the sides of her trousers.

Clari stood and looked at the place in the forest where they had last glimpsed Lowell and his horses. "Do you think I like to lie?"

"What if he comes back?"

"Pierre gave us a lot of money. Maybe we should leave. We could go to Wayzata and take a train somewhere."

For a moment, Marissa wished they could do what Clari suggested, but she knew it was no use. "And what would we do when we got there? Pierre said no one would give us a job. And I'm not going to. . .sell my. . .body as he said we would have to."

Clari rubbed her hand over her eyes. "Maybe we could teach school. Some small towns have a hard time getting a teacher. At least Mother made sure we could read, write, and work arithmetic. A lot of people don't know even that much."

Marissa clutched her sister's arm. "Pierre would find us. I know he would, and when he did, we would pay for running away."

"How long has he been gone? It's been over a week, hasn't it?"

Marissa nodded.

"Maybe everything is okay. Lowell probably went somewhere else to camp, and he won't bother us again."

"I hope you're right." Marissa shook her head. "I really hope you are."

Ollie followed Lowell down the gully into the canyon that led to the valley around the waterfall. His mind was filled with memories. Even though it had been years since Father had brought them there, he remembered every detail with clarity. He and Lowell had laughed and pretended to be outlaws while they followed their father. Although Father was often a stern man, he seemed amused by the boys' antics. These vivid scenes playing through his mind brought tears to Ollie's eyes. He wished Father were with them today. He would help them know what to do when they reached the valley.

Soon they arrived where Lowell had left the packhorse. He pulled up the stake and put it back in the pack; then he took the horse's lead and set off through the thick forest, with Ollie following.

By the time they rode out of the trees, it was nearing dusk. Ollie saw the caravan sitting under a tree with a horse hobbled nearby but no sign of the young women. The two men rode slowly across the clearing, scanning the area.

Ollie wondered why he had never come back to this peaceful place. A gentle breeze sighed through the trees, and he could hear birds settling down for the night and small animals moving around. Even the horse near the wagon seemed calm and not alarmed at their arrival, perhaps because of Lowell's visit earlier that day.

Lowell stopped with Ollie beside him.

"What do we do now?"

Lowell dismounted, then looked at him. "We wait. They have to be here somewhere."

Within minutes, the two young women came from the direction of the waterfall. Even though they wore shirts and trousers, they didn't resemble men. Ollie had never seen a woman in trousers. The girls didn't look as feminine as he thought they should, but they were still beautiful.

They were talking animatedly and didn't notice the two men. Then suddenly they stopped, their eyes wide. One sister stepped behind the other, and the one in front moved forward.

"Lowell—Ollie, how nice to see you."

Ollie tipped his hat. "Rissa—or whatever your name is."

The girl blushed. "My name is Clarissa." She gestured toward the other woman. "This is my sister, Marissa."

Marissa didn't look at him.

Clarissa turned toward Lowell. "Why did you come back?"

Lowell kept staring at Marissa, but she refused to look up.

"We'd like to camp in this meadow. Perhaps we could set up our campsite a little ways from yours. We could share one fire—maybe even our supper." He glanced at Clarissa.

Clarissa's cheeks flushed scarlet. She looked at Ollie, then back at Lowell.

"How long will you be staying?" Her voice trembled.

Couldn't Lowell see how uncomfortable she was? Ollie wanted to intervene, but he didn't.

"Probably just for one night," Lowell told Clarissa, then looked back at Marissa.

"Pierre may come back soon. He won't like it." She was beginning to sound like the Rissa Ollie remembered.

"Do you expect him tonight?" Lowell stood with his arms crossed over his chest.

Ollie was sure his brother intimidated the young women. Why couldn't he let up a little?

"No." The soft reply came from the woman named Marissa. She was looking at Lowell. "He won't be back tonight. Maybe not for a few days."

Lowell unfolded his arms and stuck his hands in his back pockets. "Then we'll be gone before he returns."

Lowell was glad when Marissa and Clarissa agreed to let them bed down close by. It didn't take long to set up their camp. Then he and Ollie gathered wood to make a fire.

The brothers cooked their canned beans while the sisters prepared their meal. Lowell opened a tin of peaches and offered another tin to the young women.

"Thank you," Clarissa said, taking the can. "We've made enough biscuits if you'd like some."

They sat around the campfire and began to eat.

Lowell smiled and leaned forward. "I don't want to hurt you, but Ollie and I don't believe the story you told me this morning."

The sisters stopped eating and glanced at each other; then Marissa turned toward him. He saw again the pain in her eyes and wanted to take her in his arms and comfort her.

Marissa lowered her head. "You're right. It was a lie." She looked up into his eyes. "I never wanted to lie to you, Lowell."

The soft timbre of her voice went straight to his heart, melting it. Lowell moved closer to her.

"Marissa, I know something is wrong here." He took her hand. "And I think it has to do with your father."

She pulled her hand away and stood quickly. "He's not my father!" Then she clapped her hand over her mouth and looked at her sister with tears in her eyes.

Clarissa pulled her into her arms and patted her back. "It's all right, Mari." Clarissa looked over her sister's shoulder at Lowell. "Now see what you've done!"

Marissa stepped away. "Don't blame Lowell. It's all Pierre's doing." The two women stared at each other. "We've wondered if our new friends in Litchfield would understand. Now would be a good time to find out."

Clarissa shook her head. "No. Pierre would be very angry."

Ollie stood up and turned toward Clarissa. "Who is Le Blanc, and what kind of hold does he have on you?"

Marissa covered her face with her hands and burst into tears.

"Hush, sister," Clarissa said gently, holding her and patting her back again. "It will be all right. It must be."

Marissa finally stopped crying, and the two women walked over to the woods, then disappeared among the trees.

"I think it's time for us to pray for them," Lowell said, bowing his head.

Tonight Ollie was glad Lowell wasn't talkative. His own thoughts occupied him. He finished praying and watched the woods, hoping the girls were safe. It was dark now. They'd probably been here long enough to know how to get around at night. He looked up. The moon and stars shone brightly overhead, illuminating the dark sky, but even with the brilliance the shadows of the grove might obscure a tree root or something else they could trip on. He was about to search for them when they stepped into the circle of light.

Clarissa led the way to the side of the campfire opposite where the two men waited. "We've decided we can trust you. We'll tell you what you want to know." Marissa stood behind her and nodded. "We are Clarissa and Marissa Voss. Pierre is our stepfather."

Clarissa Voss. Ollie liked the sound of that name much better than the one she used when he first met her. "So why did you call yourselves Rissa Le Blanc?"

Clarissa looked at him. "Pierre thought we should go by Rissa when we were in town, because it's part of both our names. We never told anyone our last name was Le Blanc. People assumed it was, and Pierre forbade us to say otherwise."

Lowell frowned. "What kind of hold does Le Blanc have on you?" His voice sounded harsh as he repeated Ollie's earlier question.

Marissa stepped up beside her sister. When she spoke, her voice was gentler. "Why don't we all sit down? Clari and I will tell you the whole story."

The brothers had pulled two logs near the fire before supper, and now they sat opposite the girls on the logs.

"We came from a Southern family," Marissa explained.

Lowell chuckled. "We could tell that."

Marissa smiled. "Our family owned a large plantation before the War between the States."

Ollie had learned about the war through studying history in school and from the stories his father told them.

"Somehow our family retained the plantation throughout the war," Clarissa added. "Our grandfather was able to run it, hiring workers to help him. When our mother and father married, Father took over the plantation."

"I remember wonderful times with our father before he died." Marissa was staring into the fire. "He was tall, and he loved us very much."

"But he died when we were young." Clarissa went on with her story, ignoring the interruption. "When we were about seven years old, Grandfather sold the plantation, and we moved to a large house in New Orleans with him and our mother."

"So New Orleans wasn't exactly a lie." Lowell stared at Marissa until she looked at him and shook her head. Lowell smiled. "I'm glad."

Ollie saw something pass between them. He glanced at Clarissa, and she was staring at him. He smiled. Oh yes, this was the woman he remembered.

Clarissa cleared her throat. "Grandfather died after we moved into town. It wasn't long before Mother met Pierre. He swept her off her feet, and they were married soon after that. I think she was just lonely. Then, about two years later, Mother contracted malaria. She never recovered."

"Actually, that was a blessing," Marissa said. "She didn't know Pierre was a confidence man. If she had lived longer, I don't think he would have been able to hide it from her." Marissa gave a deep sigh. "But he inherited what was left of the family fortune—and us."

Ollie stood and stuffed his hands in his front pockets. "Didn't you have any other family to take care of you?"

Clarissa shook her head, and her abundant black curls swirled around her shoulders. Ollie liked her hair hanging free instead of up in an elaborate style.

He could just imagine how soft it must feel.

"It didn't take Pierre long to go through the fortune. I think he gambled it away." Clarissa looked at Marissa, who had her head down. "He sold the house, and we started moving around the country. We were only twelve years old then. He said he'd worked out the 'greatest confidence game of all.' He forced us to do what he wanted. If we tried to rebel, he beat us."

Lowell slammed his fist against the log and jumped up. "Why didn't anyone stop him?" He looked from one sister to the other.

"Oh, he never left bruises where anyone could see them," Marissa said. "After we were older, he quit striking us."

"Because I stood up to him," Clarissa said.

Her sister nodded. "But he threatened to sell us into. . .a house of. . .ill repute if we didn't do what he wanted."

Lowell paced away from the fire and stood gazing up at the starry sky.

He turned back to the girls. "So what is this 'greatest confidence game of all'?"

Clarissa put her head in her hands, rubbed her face, then answered. "He takes one of us into a town and leaves the other in a remote campsite. Sometimes he switches us so we both have a chance to be in town."

"But I usually prefer being in the camp because I like to read," Marissa said.

Lowell turned to her, a look of compassion on his face.

"While Pierre is getting to know 'all the right people,' he is scouting possible places for us to rob. Then when a big event happens, which most of the people attend, he takes me with him to the event." Clarissa glanced at Marissa.

"And I rob the places he has told me to." Marissa dropped her head into her hands and sobbed again.

Lowell walked over to her and gently put his hands on her shoulders.

"If anyone happens to see Marissa and comes to the hotel to arrest me, Pierre has many witnesses to the fact that he and I were at the event. We leave town at once and never return."

Ollie looked at Lowell, his brother's face reflecting his own shocked feelings. The poor women. "How long has this been going on?"

Clarissa stood. "Almost eight years."

"Eight years!" Ollie exclaimed. "How many towns have you been to?"

Clarissa turned away from him and sighed. "I don't know. At least two or three a year—maybe more some years."

Anger welled up inside Ollie. How could that man have done this? It was a wonder the women weren't ruined. "What about the friends you've made? Didn't anyone try to help you?"

Marissa finally looked up. Trails of tears still stained her cheeks. "We've never made friends before. Pierre kept us away from people. He'd always tell them he's very protective of his daughter, and they believed him." She stood beside her sister. "You two and Gerda and Anna are the only friends we've had since Mother died."

Ollie shuddered to think what could have happened to them. He thanked God for bringing them to Litchfield. Somehow he and Lowell had to rescue them from Le Blanc. The women had been held captive by his evil mind.

Chapter 11

Lowell and Ollie camped far enough away from the young women so as not to bother them, but they kept the other camp in sight. They wanted to protect Clarissa and Marissa if the need arose during the night. They spread their bedrolls close together on the ground, then lay down on them without taking off their boots.

Lying on his back, Lowell gazed up at the stars. He was tired, but he couldn't sleep. His mind went over and over the story he had heard that evening. It was more fantastic than the lie the young women had told him earlier, but he believed every word. Marissa looked at him while she talked, and he could read the sincerity in her gaze. His heart nearly broke when the twins relayed all that had transpired in their lives since their mother died. He knew it wasn't right to want to hurt anyone, but if Le Blanc had been there, Lowell probably would have done so. What kind of man used young women for his own ill-gotten gain? No kind of man. He had no conscience. He and his brother had to devise a scheme for helping the Voss sisters escape from him.

"Ollie." Lowell kept his voice low.

"Yes?"

"Ah. You can't sleep, either?"

"No. We have to help them." Ollie raised his head and leaned on one elbow. "I've been trying to figure out a way."

Lowell sat up and crossed his legs. "Whatever we do, we need to do it soon."

Ollie moved to a sitting position also. "I believe the sheriff would take into consideration the fact that they were forced to do what they did."

Lowell nodded. "I'm sure he would, too."

A gentle breeze started blowing across the prairie grass that filled the large clearing, bringing welcome relief from the heat of the day. It had not cooled down much after sundown. Lowell turned his face into the wind. Just then, a rustling in the grass caught his attention. In the bright moonlight, he glanced at a place where the grass was moving more than anywhere else. He glimpsed the light glinting off shiny fur. Probably some nocturnal animal out foraging for food. Lowell watched it disappear into the underbrush.

"I'd like to talk to the sheriff. What do you think?" Ollie asked.

Lowell turned to his brother. "That's a good idea. But when?"

"Well, I can't sleep. I think I'll go now."

"Sheriff Bartlett will be asleep." Lowell chuckled. "He might not like you waking him in the middle of the night."

Ollie stood and straightened his clothes. "I think this is important enough to wake him. Besides"—he glanced toward the other camp—"I think we should do something before Le Blanc returns. Every minute we waste might be dangerous for them."

Lowell stood, then placed his hand on his brother's shoulder. "Just be careful. It's dangerous to ride across unfamiliar territory in the dark." He hesitated. "I'm glad the problem between us was just a misunderstanding. I'll be praying for you while you're gone. I don't expect to get any sleep, either."

Ollie walked his horse the short distance to the tree line; then he mounted the horse and let him pick his way through the underbrush. Dark shadows made it harder, but while he rode, he prayed for protection. Once out of the forest, he stepped up the pace, though he still had to be careful on the uneven, rocky ground through the canyon and gully.

When he arrived at Litchfield, it looked like a sleeping town. The only lights were down the street at the saloon. He made his way up Main Street to the sheriff's office and jail. Bartlett, a widower, lived in a room behind the office. Ollie went around the building and tapped on the darkened glass of the window. He waited a few minutes, then tapped again. Immediately after the second tap, he saw a kerosene lamp flare, then Bartlett holding the lamp by the window. He motioned to Ollie to go around to the front.

"What brings you here at this time of night, Ollie?" The sheriff closed the door behind him. "Is there a problem at the farm?"

Ollie shook his head. "It's something else. I'm sorry to bother you at this hour, but I thought it was important."

The sheriff eased into the chair behind his desk. Ollie sat across from him; then he began to relate to him what the Voss sisters had told him and his brother. Bartlett leaned back in his chair and listened carefully.

At the end, the sheriff sat forward and looked him in the eyes. "Do you believe the story?"

Ollie nodded. "When Lowell first saw them this morning, they told him a lie; but later, when he took me back, we were able to convince them to trust us."

The sheriff chuckled. "I'm sure you were. So where is Le Blanc now?"

"I don't think the twins know for sure. He left them in the camp and said he had some business to attend to. He told them he'd be back in a couple of weeks."

"Twins." The sheriff scratched the stubble on his jaw. "That's really something, isn't it?"

Ollie stood and walked over to the desk. "The robbery will take place when the circus comes."

Sheriff Bartlett looked up at him. "That would be a good time. Most of the people in town will attend the performance. It's the first time the circus has ever been in Litchfield. It's not long off, is it?"

"I know. That's why I didn't wait until morning to see you."

The sheriff stood and opened the bottom desk drawer. He withdrew his gun belt and strapped it around his hips.

"Um, there's one other thing." Ollie stuck his hands in his front pockets. "Clarissa and Marissa don't know I've come to see you. Lowell and I wondered if you could somehow arrange to keep from prosecuting them if they help you capture Le Blanc."

The sheriff grabbed his hat off the hook by the door, shoved it on his head, then turned back to Ollie. "Let me think about that on the ride. How far did you say they were from town?"

Dawn was peeking over the treetops when Clarissa heard horses coming through the woods. She had dozed off and on all night. In one way, she felt as if a burden had been lifted from her shoulders. But she was also afraid of what would happen now. She thought she could trust Lowell and Ollie, especially Ollie. What if she was wrong? What if their decision to be truthful backfired and they ended up in prison? Would that be any worse than the life they were living? For the first time since she had become an adult, she knew what it meant to have friends. If that was taken away from her and Mari, it might as well be prison.

Two men burst through the trees across the clearing and headed straight toward their camp. In the dim light of early morning, she recognized Ollie. Where had he gone this early? And who was the other rider? She could see Lowell moving around the campsite across the way. For a moment, she was afraid it was Pierre. But why would he be riding with Ollie, and where was the wagon? She shaded her eyes from the rays of the rising sun to get a better view.

"Who's that?" Mari spoke from just behind her.

Clarissa whirled around. "I don't know who the other one is, but Ollie is one of them."

"Then everything is all right, isn't it?"

As they drew closer, Clarissa noticed the other man was wearing a star on his shirt. Her heart dropped like a rock in the pool at the base of the waterfall, and she felt as if she were drowning. What had Ollie done? Had he turned them in to the sheriff? She hoped Marissa didn't notice, but when her sister grabbed her shoulders, she could feel her trembling.

"Oh, Clari, it's the sheriff." Mari's voice caught on a sob. "What are we going to do?"

Ollie dismounted and started toward her. She glared at him, and he quickened his pace.

"Don't worry, Clarissa. Everything's going to be all right."

His whispered words did nothing to calm the storm raging inside her.

The sheriff was an older man with kind, clear blue eyes, but Clarissa knew he wouldn't go easy on criminals. She had heard about him while she was in town.

Lowell walked over to him. "Sheriff Bartlett. Good to see you." The older man extended his hand, and Lowell shook it.

Clarissa wanted to scream at them. Everyone was being polite, and she was worried about her future—hers and Mari's. She wished they would dispense with the pleasantries and get to the point. Were they going to jail—or not?

"Sheriff, I want you to meet Clarissa and Marissa Voss." Ollie gestured to each woman.

The sheriff reached up and tipped his hat. "Ladies."

Clarissa looked at him. "So, Sheriff, why are you here?"

"I want you to tell me your story. Then we'll see where we go from there."

Clarissa let out a little breath; then, with her sister's help, they both related the story. Mari's voice trembled at first, as did Clarissa's, but soon they relaxed. Clarissa watched the sheriff. He kept his gaze focused on the one who was talking—never showing any emotion, positive or negative.

When they were finished, he cleared his throat. "Well now, we have a situation here, don't we?"

Clarissa wondered what he meant by that.

"I think I can be of help to you if you will help me."

"What do you mean?" Clarissa asked, almost feeling hopeful.

"If you will help us catch Le Blanc in the act, we won't prosecute you. Even though you've committed many crimes, I believe you when you say he forced you. I'd like to put him behind bars."

And I'd like to help you. Clarissa let out a deep sigh. The sheriff believed them and was offering a way out of their bondage to Pierre. She smiled and looked at her sister. Mari nodded. Clarissa turned back to the sheriff. "Just tell us what we have to do."

The women sat down with the sheriff and the two brothers and planned how they would catch Pierre. They decided it would need to be during the robbery or when he had the stolen goods. After a while, the three men mounted their horses and rode toward the forest. Near the trees, Lowell turned and made his way to his camp. He loaded the supplies onto the packhorse, then rode off with the sheriff and Ollie. Clarissa wondered what Ollie and the sheriff had talked about while they waited for Lowell.

Just before he disappeared into the trees, Ollie looked back at the camp where she and her sister waited. She returned his wave and felt a sense of loss when he was gone. It had only been two days, but she had relaxed around him more than she had in town. She hoped that when this was over they could get to know each other better.

It was nearing dusk later that day when Pierre rode up in the wagon. Marissa was glad he hadn't come any sooner.

"Pierre, you're back. It hasn't been two weeks yet."

"Aren't you glad to see me, Marissa? I just couldn't stay away from my two lovely daughters any longer." His laugh echoed in the open stillness around them.

All evening, Pierre would start sentences, then stop midway and laugh, a gleam in his eyes, as if he had a secret. Marissa didn't care. She didn't want to know anything about him or where he'd been. She was sure he'd spent part of the time with unsavory companions, some of them women. How she hated him and what he had done to her. She imagined her life would have been much like that of Gerda or Anna if she'd never known him. Maybe it wasn't too late. She certainly hoped not. But Pierre wasn't the only one with a secret, and the one she and Clari shared would put him in prison. It was hard for her to act natural around him. She was glad when he said Clarissa would be going into town with him this time. It would be easier to wait at the camp for the fateful day. The only thing Marissa regretted was that she would have to commit one more crime, but it would be the last. And Pierre would be out of their lives forever, she hoped.

Chapter 12

It was the last day of August, and the circus train was coming that morning. The railroad agent had posted a sign to let everyone know when it was due. By the time they could hear the huge mechanical monster in the distance, chugging toward the station, gawkers crowded the platform. Others were scattered along both sides of the tracks. Young mothers sat on the benches beside the depot holding toddlers and babies. Children darted in and out among the crowd as though they were playing hide-and-seek with each other, and the more daring boys stood at the edge of the platform and hung out over the tracks to wait for the engine's approach.

Ollie leaned against the depot wall watching the activity. Lowell was taking his turn at keeping watch on Marissa in the camp. Of course, she didn't know he was there, but the brothers had decided they wouldn't leave her alone in the wilderness.

Ollie scanned the crowd, looking for Clarissa. He didn't see her, but Le Blanc was there, watching everything with a huge smile on his face. The excitement would help his scheme succeed. Ollie glanced down Main Street. Since most of the people who were in town were at the station, the thoroughfare looked deserted, except for the shop owners who stood near their doors in case a stray customer needed an item. Even the saloon keeper and a few of the women sauntered toward the tracks and clustered in small groups a short distance from the crowd. At least the women were dressed modestly. It was a wonder they were awake this early since they'd worked so late at night.

"The train's here!" someone shouted. "I can see it coming!"

Smoke belched from the smokestack on the powerful engine, and cars spread down the track as far as the eye could see. More than fifty long railroad cars, Ollie guessed.

When the whistle blew, the stationmaster made his way out onto the platform and tried to get the crowd to move back. Finally, the sheriff and his deputy came to help him. Within moments, the people had moved to a safer distance, and the stationmaster stepped up beside the huffing engine as its shrieking brakes brought it to a halt. He spoke to the engineer, then directed him to move to a side track that ran beside the main line. After all the cars were on the other track, he turned the wheel that threw the switch, leaving the tracks ready for the next train to pass through town.

People emerged from the railroad cars and moved quickly to perform their duties.

The ringmaster, in a uniform covered with gold braid and fringe, lifted a megaphone to his mouth. "Come one, come all—to the greatest spectacle you've ever seen! At precisely two o'clock, the circus parade will begin!" He turned toward another part of the crowd. "Come see the performers and fee-ro-cious wild animals from the jungles of Africa! The parade will start at that end of Main Street." He swept his white-gloved hand down the street. "And it'll come this way and go out to the field beside Lake Ripley. See the greatest little show under the big top right after the parade!"

The clock on the depot chimed ten o'clock. Ollie guessed it would take about four hours for the workers to set up the mammoth tent pictured on the flyers around town. He noticed Le Blanc leaning against the depot wall writing in a notebook. Ollie wished he could see what he was writing, but he didn't want to alert the man to his interest.

After most of the people had dispersed from the area, Ollie decided to go home and get his mother. She might enjoy the excitement. He'd take her to eat at the hotel. Since he and his brother wouldn't be home at lunchtime, she probably wouldn't fix herself anything, either. Ollie was worried about her not eating right since Father died. Her clothes were beginning to hang on her thin frame. Perhaps someone else's cooking would perk up her appetite.

He figured she could spend a little time with Anna, then watch the parade with her from the front of the Dress Emporium. After that he'd try to get the two women to go with him to the performance. He wanted everything to seem normal to Le Blanc.

The hotel restaurant was crowded when Ollie arrived with his mother; but one group left, and they were given that table. His mother ate more than she had in some time. After dropping her off at his sister's store, Ollie sauntered up the street, stopping and talking to people as he went. Finally, he stepped into the sheriff's office, as if paying a friendly visit.

"Is everything all set?" Ollie asked Sheriff Bartlett.

Bartlett glanced out the window. "Yes, a friend sent several of his deputies to help us. They're already hidden in the forest around the campsite where the girls are. Mr. Finley told me he was closing the bank during the circus performance, so I asked if he and his family would sit with Le Blanc and his daughter."

"Did you tell him why?" Ollie hesitated. "I mean, do you think it's good for many people to know what's going on?"

"No, I didn't tell him, and I agree with you. But he has a daughter who might enjoy Clarissa."

After reviewing the plans, Ollie left the office and headed toward the bank.

Double Deception

Le Blanc was just coming out of the door.

"Are you and Rissa going to the performance this afternoon?"

"We wouldn't miss it," Le Blanc said with a smile and continued down the street.

Ollie smiled to himself. *I'm sure you wouldn't.*

❧

Clarissa couldn't believe her good fortune. Pierre had suggested she might like to watch the parade with her friends at the Dress Emporium, so he took her there right after an early lunch. He would get Mari and bring her to town, keeping her hidden in the wagon until after the circus performance started. Then she would rob the homes he had listed and return to the wagon to hide again.

I hope Ollie will come by the store while I'm there. She sighed as she remembered his green eyes and wavy brown hair. Soon after she arrived at the Dress Emporium, Ollie came, as well as his mother. She was a lovely older woman. Now Clarissa knew where Ollie got his good looks. He shared many of his features with his mother, even though her brown hair was laced with silver strands that only added to her beauty.

Clarissa watched Mrs. Jenson talking with her daughter and Gerda. How she wished she'd known her mother after she had reached adulthood. The special bond between these two women was evident. A mother would have made a big difference in the way her life and Mari's had turned out. Clarissa had to swallow the tears that clogged her throat. She didn't want anyone to guess anything was wrong. She tried to join in the pleasant conversation but had little to say. She was glad the other women were too busy talking to notice.

Soon it was time to move outside for the parade. The boardwalks were already filling with people. She was thankful no one was in front of the Dress Emporium yet. Gerda and Anna moved chairs from the store and set them under the awnings the Braxtons had recently added to the front of the building. The women would have a comfortable, shaded spot to watch the festivities.

A horse-drawn calliope led the parade. The music it played was lively and different from anything Clarissa had ever heard—tinny and breathy at the same time. Clowns and jugglers followed, then two men leading three huge gray animals. The handlers carried long sticks and walked on either side of the animals, keeping them in line down the middle of the street. A woman in a fancy costume perched on the neck of the first animal. The beasts' long trunks and huge ears swished through the air, stirring up a small breeze, and their feet raised giant puffs of dust that filled the air around them.

"What are those?" Clarissa whispered, staring at them. For the first time, she wished she'd been as interested in books as her sister. Mari would know what they were.

"They're elephants." Anna watched as the animals drew closer. "I saw a picture of one in a book once, but these are the first real ones I've seen."

Clarissa leaned as far back in her chair as she could. What if an elephant stepped on her? It could kill her. But some boys dashed out into the street and tried to get as close as possible to them. One boy even reached out to touch one of the elephant's legs.

"You there, boy!" one of the handlers barked. "Get back before he tramples on you!"

The boy jumped back on the boardwalk, his friends right after him.

Behind the elephants came horse-drawn wagons with colorful cages containing other strange animals. Some of them prowled around the cages and roared at the crowd. This seemed to excite some of the boys, but Clarissa didn't like it. The sound was terrifying coming from such close proximity. In the heat of waning summer, the strong wild animal smells were almost overwhelming. She held a white handkerchief to her nose and didn't breathe very deeply.

After the caged animals passed, other performers wearing fancy costumes and heavy makeup rode horses or walked down the street waving to the people who lined the thoroughfare. Clarissa wondered what they looked like under the garish greasepaint. Then she saw a man carrying a stick that was on fire. He had just reached the street in front of the Dress Emporium when he stuck the burning end into his mouth, then pulled it back out.

Clarissa gasped and shuddered. "Why did he do that?"

"He's a fire-eater," Anna said, her eyes wide. "I've read about them, too, but I've never seen one." She looked from one end of the street to the other. "In fact, most of these things are new to me. I can hardly wait for the performance to start."

When the last of the parade had passed, Ollie returned for his sister and his mother, with Pierre close behind. He offered Clarissa his arm, then escorted her down the street toward the tent. She wished he'd waited until the dust from the parade had settled. She covered her nose again with the now-dingy handkerchief. A brown film blanketed everything.

Smaller tents and booths dotted the landscape around the big tent, and hawkers called out to the people to come inside and behold the "wonders" they boasted about. One was supposed to be a bearded lady, while another purported to house an Egyptian mummy.

The hawker outside one small tent shouted, "Step right up! Buy a ticket now! Inside this tent is General Tom Thumb and a gen-u-wine Feejee mermaid." He looked right at Pierre. "Come on, sir—buy a ticket so you and your lady friend can see these amazing wonders!"

Pierre leaned close to her. "Would you like to see something before the show starts?"

Clarissa shook her head. With the closed tents and the heat, she didn't want to venture inside one, even to see a mummy or a mermaid. And she was appalled the man thought she was Pierre's lady friend.

"Perhaps you'd like a glass of lemonade?" Pierre stopped in front of a small wooden hut.

"Yes, anything to help my dry throat. Thank you."

Clarissa looked around her while Pierre paid for the drinks. She wondered how they'd set up everything in the time since the train had arrived that morning. Many people must have worked together. She sipped the cool liquid as they headed toward the main tent.

Inside she saw seats on raised platforms that looked like stairs around the perimeter of the tent. Sawdust covered the floor, and short barriers defined the different sections. Strange-looking equipment was attached to the tall poles that held up the great canvas, and most of the sides were rolled up to let in what little wind was blowing.

After buying two tickets, Pierre led her to a spot about halfway down one side of the long tent. "Would you like to sit on the front row?"

Clarissa shook her head. "No, not that close. Maybe farther back—up there in the second group of seats. We can still see over the heads of the people in front of us." They climbed up to the second tier, then sat down. Other seats along the rows were filling up, and a short time later, the banker, Mr. Finley, and his family joined them. Clarissa had never met Becky Finley, but soon they were chattering away as if they'd known each other for years.

Both old men and young strode up and down the aisles, calling out, "Roasted peanuts! Popcorn! Get 'em right here!" The atmosphere was festive—and different from anything Clarissa had ever experienced.

Circuses had traveled mainly in the East until recent years, so she and her sister had never been in the same town where one was performing. They would usually pull a con during a community barn dance, an Independence Day celebration, or a similar big event.

Ollie escorted his mother into the tent and found seats where he could look straight across the center ring at Clarissa. Soon August brought Gerda and Anna to sit with them. Ollie knew they were talking, but his attention was trained on the woman sitting across the tent. Today her hairstyle was not as elaborate as usual. It reminded him of the way she looked out at the campsite. A ribbon the color of her dress tied back her hair, and her curls bounced against her shoulders as she moved her head. He gazed at her. *If only someday I could touch those curls. . .*

"Did you hear what I said, Ollie?"

His mother's voice brought him back to the present. "I'm sorry, Mother. I didn't."

"Do you think something will be happening in all three rings at once?"

"I don't know." He smiled at her. "But why else do you think they'd have three rings?"

Just then the ringmaster announced the equestrian events in ring number one. Riders circled the ring while executing tricks on the backs of the horses, sometimes standing, sometimes sitting. One even stood on his hands on the horse's back. Then suddenly, the ringmaster turned their attention to ring number three at the other end of the tent. A man stepped inside a large cage that held two lions and three tigers. He cracked a whip about their heads until they stood on small round pedestals.

"I want to watch both of them, but I can't." Mother looked first at one ring, then at the other.

Ollie smiled at her. He hadn't seen her this animated since Father had died. Maybe it would take her mind off losing him—for a short while anyway. Then Ollie glanced across the ring at Clarissa. She was watching the big cats. One of them roared, and she shuddered. Quickly, she turned to watch the performers on horses. He had never been to a circus, but he didn't want to waste any of the time he could spend appreciating her beauty.

"And now, ladies and gentlemen, turn your attention to the center ring! Those masters of laughter are coming your way!" The ringmaster pointed to the clowns, tumbling and chasing each other into the ring.

Ollie glanced at Clarissa again. She was laughing and clapping her hands. He could feel his own heart tumbling, too. Clarissa—so happy, so beautiful— took his breath away. He wanted to help her be happy for the rest of her life.

Ollie shook his head. He didn't know if she was a Christian, and he knew the Bible spoke plainly against a believer marrying an unbeliever. But he couldn't get rid of the thoughts that filled his head and heart. He hoped he would find out soon if she knew the Lord. For now he would pray.

After the clowns had cavorted around the center ring, the ringmaster announced the high-wire acts. "Oohs" and "aahs" and gasps of breath rippled through the audience as various performers crossed the high wire—walking, riding a bicycle, juggling, and carrying a variety of bulky items. Ollie watched a myriad of emotions cross Clarissa's face at the same time.

The final act took place on the flying trapezes. It was the most spectacular of all. Ollie couldn't keep from watching it, even though he stole glances at the beautiful face across the tent.

<hr/>

Clarissa was glad when the performance was over. Just before the end of the display on the trapezes, she noticed Ollie across the tent from where she sat. How long had he been there? After that, she had a hard time staying focused on the performers. One time, when she glanced at him, he was looking straight at her. She felt as if they were the only two people in the tent. Everything around her faded, and she could hardly breathe. The death-defying heroics of the troop held no more attraction for her. Ollie Jenson filled her mind and heart. If only her life had been different. More like Anna's or Gerda's. Perhaps then they would have had a future together.

As soon as most of the people were out of the tent, Clarissa noticed the circus workers dismantling the equipment. "Do you know where they're going next?" she asked Pierre.

"According to the front man, they'll have to head south for the winter." He helped her climb down from the tier where they'd been sitting. "Most of the wild animals came from Africa, and it's hot there. They can't tolerate the winters this far north."

They followed the rest of the crowd that was headed toward the middle of town. Pierre made a point of greeting many people. Clarissa knew he wanted them to remember talking to him and seeing her. Then, if anyone saw Mari before she slipped away, he could assure them Rissa Le Blanc was indeed at the circus. There would be plenty of witnesses to that fact. She only hoped this would be the last time she and her sister had to go through this.

By the time Clarissa and Pierre reached the place where most of the businesses were, they saw the banker coming out of the sheriff's office. Mr. Finley was talking and gesturing while Sheriff Bartlett listened to him. Pierre hurried toward the boardinghouse and let Clarissa into her room then went back downstairs.

A few minutes later, Pierre knocked on the door to Clarissa's room, then stepped inside. "The sheriff wants to talk to you."

"Did he say why?"

"No, and I didn't ask." Pierre was pacing about the room, clenching and unclenching his fists. "Hurry. I don't want to keep him waiting."

Clarissa crossed the room to peer into her looking glass. She had already rinsed off the thin layer of dust that had covered her face and hands. She tucked a stray curl behind her ear, then left with Pierre.

Sheriff Bartlett stood in the parlor downstairs and waited for them to sit down. "Mr. Le Blanc, I'm afraid someone saw your daughter leaving Mr. Finley's home while he was at the circus. When he arrived home, many of their valuables were missing—including his wife's jewelry. He's very upset."

Clarissa glanced at Pierre out of the corner of her eye. He was looking directly at the sheriff, a calm expression on his face.

"Did Mr. Finley say it was Rissa who robbed him?"

"No. Someone else saw her. He had already come by the office and told me. You see, she was wearing a black shirt and dark trousers. The person who saw her thought it was unusual for her to be dressed that way and for her to be at that house when most people in town were at the circus."

Pierre rose quickly. "Who told you these things?"

"I'm afraid I can't give you that information, but he was someone I trust." The sheriff also stood. He turned his hat round and round. "I'm afraid I'll have to take Miss Le Blanc down to the jail."

Clarissa rose to her feet then. "What?"

"I'm sorry, Miss. It has to be done."

If Clarissa hadn't known he was playing a part, she would have been frightened. "But I was at the circus, too."

"Can anyone substantiate that?"

Pierre interrupted. "Yes, we sat beside the Finleys. Let's go to their house. You'll see that you're wrong."

When they arrived at the residence, everything went the way Pierre had planned it. The Finleys assured the sheriff that Clarissa had indeed sat beside them.

Pierre flew into the rage he had planned for the occasion. "I can't believe you would treat anyone this way! My daughter and I have been fine upstanding citizens while we've lived in your town. And this is the way you treat us? We won't stay in such a place!" He glared at the sheriff, then took Clarissa's arm. "Come, Rissa—we won't spend another night here."

Chapter 13

At the boardinghouse, Pierre sought out Mrs. Olson and told her what had happened.

"Oh, you poor dear." The older woman patted Clarissa's cheek. "How could they think such a thing about you?"

How, indeed? Clarissa knew how, and all this subterfuge made her sick. Of course, they thought she was the one. Mari looked just like her. Clarissa wished she could shout the truth so everyone would hear, but that wasn't part of the plan.

"You have been a gracious hostess, Mrs. Olson," Pierre said in a smooth voice. "If this hadn't happened, we would have been glad to stay here a long time. Wouldn't we, Rissa?"

Clarissa nodded. When this was over, she would never have to hear that hated name again. Rissa. Her name wasn't Rissa. Neither was Mari's. Soon they could tell people their real names.

After Pierre paid Mrs. Olson, they went to their rooms to pack their bags. Clarissa looked around the room. She had loved being here. So had Mari. This was the first time they'd lived in a real house since they left their family home in New Orleans. Even though it had been only a few weeks, it felt like home. Clarissa wondered what would happen after the sheriff arrested Pierre. Had he meant it when he said he wouldn't have to arrest her or her sister? What would they do until Pierre came to trial? What would they do after he was convicted and sent to prison? So many questions raced through her mind. She walked to the window and looked out at the peaceful, tree-lined street. She wished she could come back here and share this room with her sister.

They loaded their bags into the surrey and headed south out of town. When they could no longer see the outskirts of Litchfield, Pierre turned toward the northeast, pulled into a tight grove of trees, and stopped beside a wagon hidden in the underbrush.

"Marissa," he called out softly. "You may come out now."

Clarissa expected to see her sister climb out from under the tarp on the wagon. Instead, Mari stepped from behind the underbrush. While Pierre was unhitching one of the horses from the surrey and hooking it to the wagon, Mari led Clarissa to a small pool of water in the middle of the copse.

"It was too hot under the tarp in the wagon." Mari trailed her fingers in the cool water. "I stayed here while I was waiting for you. I could hear anyone who might be coming and hide in any number of places."

The sisters rested there a few minutes, then returned to find Pierre in a good mood.

"Marissa, I'll let you ride in the surrey with your sister." His eyes gleamed as he climbed onto the wagon seat.

Clarissa was sure he was proud of what he had pulled off today. They'd had to leave a town like this only a few times. Usually, no one saw Mari, and Clarissa and Pierre left at leisure. Pierre liked the excitement of playing out the whole confidence game. More than once, he had boasted of his superiority when they were this successful.

He scoured the area to make sure no one was around; then he drove the wagon out of the copse. Clarissa drove the surrey out behind him with her sister seated beside her.

"How did it go?" Mari whispered.

"We'll talk about it later," Clarissa whispered back.

"Oh, Clari, tell me about the circus," she said then eagerly.

During the journey to the forest and the bit of prairie concealed in its depths, Clarissa told her about the parade, the sideshows and refreshments, and the performances. Mari listened closely. Clarissa wished her sister could have been there. Mari had no doubt seen pictures of some of those things in the books she read and would have loved being there.

Ollie watched Pierre leave town with Clarissa. From a safe distance, he followed the wagon and the surrey when they drove out of the grove of trees. He knew where they were going and could stay far enough away so Pierre wasn't aware of his presence. Soon after they entered the forest, Ollie made his way through the trees to the place where Lowell had camped while he watched over Marissa.

Although Ollie was stealthy, Lowell met him as soon as he drew near. "How did it go in town?"

"Just the way we planned." Ollie dismounted and tied his horse to a tree. "I talked to Sheriff Bartlett. He asked another sheriff to send some of his deputies to help him. They're hiding in the woods somewhere around here."

Lowell smiled. "I know where they are."

The two brothers made their way closer to the tree line so they could observe what was happening.

Pierre stopped the wagon near the caravan and started unloading the stolen goods. The two sisters pulled up beside the wagon. He was smiling and talking excitedly to the girls, holding up various items, turning them around, watching the sun glint off their surfaces.

Soon Pierre disappeared into the caravan and dragged out a couple of wooden trunks. He started packing some of the items into them. He had the two girls help him. It looked as if they were separating the goods according to kind. Ollie watched Pierre place sparkling pieces of jewelry in one trunk and silver items in the other.

Then Pierre climbed back into the caravan to replace one of the trunks, and Ollie scanned the edges of the forest. Deputies were coming through the underbrush. He glanced back toward the campsite, and Pierre was climbing down from the caravan. He picked up another trunk and turned to reenter the vehicle. Sheriff Bartlett stepped forward from the tree line, gun in hand.

"Pierre Le Blanc! Stop where you are!"

Pierre turned slowly around to see men with guns emerge from the forest and move toward the camp. His eyes widened, and his face drained of its color. His moustache even seemed to bristle. Ollie almost chuckled at the expression. He and Lowell were following the deputies.

"Put down the trunk and raise your hands." The sheriff advanced across the wide clearing with rapid strides.

Pierre set the wooden container on the ground and straightened. He glanced toward each of the girls. His eyes narrowed, and he scowled. He lifted his hand toward Clarissa. Ollie's stomach tightened. He wanted to drive his fist into the man's face. He had never felt that way about anyone before.

The sheriff shouted, "Hold it right there, Le Blanc!" Pierre stopped. "Clarissa and Marissa, move over near the trees."

Le Blanc's face darkened. The veins in his neck bulged, and his face turned red with rage.

Ollie and Lowell stopped near the twins, out of the way of the deputies but close enough to see what was happening.

Two deputies stepped to the other side of Le Blanc. One pulled his hands down, and the other handcuffed them behind him. When the cuffs clicked shut, something seemed to snap inside Pierre. He turned to look at the young women.

"How could you do this to me, you ungrateful wretches?" he yelled. Then he spewed out words so vile no one should have to hear them. They ricocheted and echoed through the trees, disgusting Ollie and no doubt devastating Clarissa and Marissa.

"Let's get them out of here." Lowell put words to Ollie's thoughts.

Ollie glanced at the sheriff, who nodded. The brothers quickly moved the young women toward Lowell's campsite. Pierre's screeches followed them, and the twins covered their ears with their hands.

Minnesota Brothers

At the campsite, Ollie and Lowell didn't take time to pack. One of them could return in a day or two to retrieve their belongings. They needed to get the women elsewhere as fast as possible. Ollie mounted his horse and pulled Clarissa up onto his lap, and Lowell did the same with Marissa. They hurried through the forest away from the evil man who was still filling the air with his poison.

Chapter 14

Lowell was relieved when he no longer could hear the foul words spilling forth from Le Blanc. As long as he heard even a faint sound of the man's voice, though, he felt heat rising within him. They emerged from the forest, with Marissa still cradled against his chest. He urged his mount forward; the sooner they arrived at home, the better. He glanced at Ollie. The grim look on his brother's face probably mirrored his own. They needed to get the young women to a safe place. They could talk to the sheriff later.

By the time they reached the farm, their horses had slowed, but Lowell could still feel Marissa shaking in his arms. During the wild ride, she hadn't raised her face from where it pressed against his shirt. But he didn't mind. Having her so close was wonderful. He wanted to protect her from harm and hoped he'd be allowed to do that very thing. Gud, *help me know what to do. Show me what Your will is in this matter.*

Mother stepped out onto the front porch, wiping her hands with the bottom of her large apron. Lowell had seen her do this many times but not since Father died. She didn't look as pale and wan as she had when Lowell left to guard Marissa in the forest. He wondered why.

She came down the steps and waited by the hitching post until both her sons halted their horses. "Who is this with you, Lowell? I recognize the girl with Ollie. This one looks just like her, but why is she dressed like a man?" She placed her hands on her hips. "What's going on, boys?"

Lowell patted Marissa's back. "It's okay. You're safe now," he murmured against her fragrant hair.

Marissa gazed up at him and slowly loosened her hold on his shirt. Then she glanced around her. "Where are we?"

"You're at my home. This is my mother." Lowell gestured toward the older woman, who smiled up at them.

His mother lifted her arms toward Marissa. The young woman slipped down into them, and Mother gathered her into a close hug. They walked over to Ollie's horse where Clarissa already stood on the ground.

Mother hugged her, too. "I'm glad to see you again, Rissa." She turned and put an arm around each girl. "Come—let's go into the house, and you can tell me what this is all about."

Lowell smiled grimly at Ollie, then called to the women, "We'll take care of the horses and join you in a few minutes."

On the way to the stable, Lowell asked his brother, "So what's happened to *Mor*? She seems different."

Ollie chuckled. "I took her to the circus."

~~~

Mrs. Jenson escorted the young women into the parlor. Clarissa wondered how much she knew about what had transpired.

The older woman looked from one sister to the other and smiled. "You're twins. If you were dressed alike, I couldn't tell you apart. Now which one is Rissa Le Blanc?"

Her friendly manner helped Clarissa relax. "Actually, I'm Clarissa Voss, and this is my sister, Marissa."

The change of the last name didn't seem to bother Mrs. Jenson. "Well, Clarissa and Marissa Voss, you are welcome in our home. How about some lemonade and pound cake?"

Marissa nodded to Clarissa.

"Yes, that would be nice." Clarissa rearranged her skirt. It was quite wrinkled from the day's activities.

Just as Mrs. Jenson returned with a tray containing a pitcher of lemonade, glasses, and cake, Ollie and Lowell walked through the door. Clarissa smiled at Ollie, and his eyes lit up, making him even more handsome. Riding away from that awful scene, she had felt so protected in his arms. She didn't want to leave them when they arrived at the farm. Clarissa knew he was just being nice, but she could pretend it meant more to him, too.

"Sit down, boys, and join us." Mrs. Jenson smiled at her sons. "I'm sure it won't spoil your supper." She chuckled.

Lowell and Ollie told their mother what had happened since Lowell found Mari and Clarissa at the campsite. Was it only a few days ago? It seemed like an eternity. An eternity that had changed her life—for the better, she hoped.

Mrs. Jenson was shocked at the news her sons related and clucked over the girls like a mother hen protecting her chicks. Clarissa had feared people would believe she and Mari were as guilty as Pierre, but when Mrs. Jenson smiled, Clarissa remembered how much her own mother had loved her.

"I am so sorry about all this, Mrs. Jenson," Clarissa said softly. "We would understand if you didn't want us in your home, considering what Pierre forced us to do."

The older woman's eyes were moist as she turned to Clarissa. "Did you want to do the things that man made you do?"

"No! Of course not!" both sisters exclaimed at once.

"Oh, you poor dears." The compassion in Mrs. Jenson's voice went straight to Clarissa's heart, softening it. "I can't believe that awful man did such terrible things to you girls."

Marissa was usually the quiet sister. "He was good at putting on an act. He was so believable he could have gone on stage. That's why he could get away with almost any confidence game he planned." She shuddered.

Mrs. Jenson turned toward her older son. "What's Sheriff Bartlett going to do about these precious girls?"

"We're not sure. We'll talk to him later."

"They'll stay right here until he tells us anything different." She nodded firmly.

Ollie crossed the room to his mother and hugged her. "I knew you would say that. Thank you, *Mor*."

The next morning, the sheriff drove up in a wagon with a trunk in the back. Ollie walked out from the barn to meet him.

"I thought the girls might need this." Sheriff Bartlett lifted the trunk down from the wagon. "Should I take it into the house?"

Ollie relieved the older man of his burden and hefted the trunk onto his shoulders. "Come on—let's go in for a cup of coffee. *Mor* made cinnamon rolls for breakfast. She might have one or two left."

"Well, now, I won't turn down your mother's good cooking." He patted his stomach. "I don't get home cooking very often."

Lowell joined them on the porch and opened the door for his brother. Ollie set the trunk in the hallway, and the three men went to the kitchen, where his mother was teaching Clarissa and Marissa how to bake bread.

His mother turned around and smiled. "Welcome, Sheriff Bartlett—how nice to see you."

"Ollie said you might have some coffee and cinnamon rolls left from breakfast." He grabbed his hat from his head and held it in his hands. "I know what a good cook you are, Mrs. Jenson."

Ollie pulled up a chair for the sheriff, and they all sat around the large kitchen table.

"I thought you might need some more clothes," Sheriff Bartlett told the sisters, "so I brought out one of your trunks."

Both girls clapped their hands. "That is so thoughtful!" Clarissa said. "Mrs. Jenson loaned us some of her clothes, but she's a little taller than we are. It'll be nice to have our own things."

Ollie looked at the sheriff. "What's happened to Le Blanc?" He hated to mention the vile man around the twins, but they needed to know, too.

"We arrested him, and he's in jail under heavy guard." Bartlett sipped the hot coffee. "I've wired the district judge. I'm waiting to hear when he'll come to town to conduct the trial." He looked at the twins. "You girls haven't changed your minds about testifying against Le Blanc, have you?"

Marissa's breath came in short gasps, and her hands began to tremble. Clarissa reached over and patted her sister. "I can hardly wait. You did say he'd go to prison, didn't you? Then he couldn't come after us and punish us for testifying."

The sheriff put down the cinnamon roll. "We don't know exactly what'll happen, but with all the evidence against him, I'm sure he'll go to prison for a long time. We'll protect you from him."

Marissa sighed. Ollie glanced at his brother and found Lowell studying her. Ollie sensed his brother was as interested in Marissa as he was in Clarissa. Wouldn't it be amazing if God allowed them to marry the sisters? At least they would remain near each other. The sisters were so close that it would be a shame to separate them with much distance.

Ollie's mother gave him a sharp look, interrupting his thoughts. "Won't we, Ollie?"

Whatever it was, he knew it would be a good idea to agree with her. He nodded, wondering if he would regret it later.

His mother smiled at each young woman. "I told you that you were welcome to stay here until everything is worked out."

Yes, he could agree to that. Clarissa would be close by. He planned to get to know her well while he had the chance.

⟨⟨⟩⟩

They soon received word it would be the first of October before the district judge could hold court in Litchfield. Marissa was glad they'd have almost a month in this wonderful home before they had to face Pierre again. The few days they'd been there had made a big difference in how she felt about herself. Mrs. Jenson took her and Clari under her wing. She seemed to derive great pleasure from mothering them and teaching them new skills. Marissa was learning to cook. Ever since her mother died, she'd wanted to know how to bake. Although she made a big mess in the kitchen, Mrs. Jenson didn't seem to mind. She said messes were easy to clean up. She loved them the way Marissa was sure their own mother would have if she had lived.

Clari enjoyed cleaning and polishing. Mrs. Jenson said Clari's help made her work so much easier. Marissa was glad they were blending into the family so well. Several times each day, either Lowell or Ollie showed up at the house to check on them. It made Marissa feel even more special. It had been so long since she'd felt that way. She enjoyed it. She also relished every minute she spent in Lowell's company. He was quieter than his brother, but he always talked to her.

Double Deception

One night before falling asleep, Marissa was alone with her thoughts. *How is it this family talks about Jesus as if He is a real person, a friend? They mention Him so often around the table.* She recalled the service she'd attended with Pierre. She wanted to know more about this Jesus, but she hadn't the slightest idea what questions to ask.

The first Saturday evening after the twins arrived at the farm, Mrs. Jenson asked if she and her sister would like to attend church with them the next day. Marissa looked at Clari, who shrugged her shoulders.

Marissa turned back to their hostess. "We'd love to."

The next morning, she and Clari dressed with care. They wore different outfits since they didn't own two of one kind. Clari chose a silk suit in a deep, vibrant shade of blue, while Marissa wore a soft green ensemble—the one with tiny white flowers woven in. They fixed their hair in the same style, though. That way they looked alike, but their clothing matched their personalities.

Marissa thought for a moment, then turned to her sister. "I guess most of the people in Litchfield have heard about what happened the day the circus came to town. Especially since Pierre is in jail there." She hesitated. "I'm not sure what to expect from the people at church. They were friendly the other time I visited. But now I wouldn't be surprised if no one speaks to us."

"Oh, Mari, I wouldn't worry about it. If they don't speak to us now, maybe they will later. At least the Jensons do." She tucked in a stray curl, took one more look in the glass, then walked out of the room and downstairs.

Lowell and Ollie rode in the front of the two-seater surrey with the three women in back. Mrs. Jenson kept up a steady stream of conversation on the way to the church. When no one else talked, she asked questions, including all four of the young people in her comments. Marissa was glad, because it helped her relax. She could sense the change in Clari, too.

"Be sure to listen to what the preacher says during the service," Marissa whispered to her sister. "I want to discuss it with you later—if he preaches the way he did the other time."

When they pulled into the churchyard, people gathered around the surrey and greeted them warmly. Many asked to be introduced. Their friendliness let Marissa know they accepted her.

She hoped the preacher would talk about Jesus, and she wasn't disappointed. He preached about Jesus bringing hope and forgiveness. He mentioned some terrible sins, worse than anything she or Clari had ever done. The man said that even if a person had committed murder, Jesus would forgive him if he repented. *Repented?* That was a new word for Marissa. She planned to ask what it meant when they got home.

Clari reached over and took hold of Marissa's hand. Marissa turned to look at her sister and saw her eyes brimming with tears. During the rest of the service, they grasped each other's hands. Marissa knew they both needed what the preacher was talking about. But how did they gain that forgiveness?

At the end of the service, the pastor asked if anyone wanted to accept Jesus into his or her heart. The congregation sang a song with the phrase "O Lamb of God, I come, I come." Marissa wanted to, but she was afraid she didn't know enough. With tears streaming down her face, she listened as everyone sang. While the pastor said the final prayer, Marissa slipped a handkerchief from her reticule and dried her cheeks. She hoped her eyes weren't too red or swollen from crying.

Lowell watched Marissa throughout the service. He sensed that she was being drawn to the Savior. He prayed for her comfort and salvation. The young women needed both of these. Lowell understood what the Bible taught about a believer not marrying an unbeliever. Yet he felt such a strong pull to Marissa. His growing attraction warred with the apparent fact that she didn't know the Lord. Surely God didn't want them to turn these young women out of their home; but the longer they resided there, the more Lowell cared for Marissa. On the ride back to the house, his mother again made sure the conversation didn't lag. But he was lost in his thoughts.

At home the family sat down to the meal Mother had prepared with the help of the twins. Lowell asked a blessing on the food, and they passed the bowls filled with roast beef and vegetables around the table.

After a few moments of quiet, Lowell spoke. "Since *Far* died, we haven't had our family time in the evenings."

Ollie frowned. "We've been together."

"I guess I didn't say what I meant." Lowell cleared his throat. "We need to read the Bible together again."

His mother reached over and patted his hand. "What a wonderful idea, Lowell! I know Soren would want us to continue what he started when we first married."

That evening, after the supper dishes were cleaned up, the women joined the men in the parlor. While Lowell took out his Bible, Mrs. Jenson made room for Marissa and her sister on the settee beside her.

Lowell lowered his frame into the big chair across from the sofa, then turned to Marissa. "Where would you like me to start reading?"

Marissa's eyes widened. Why was he asking her? She didn't know enough about the Book to tell him anything. She shrugged. "We haven't read from the Bible since our mother died, and we were very young then."

Mrs. Jenson squeezed her hand. "That's all right, dear."

"But I do have a question—if it's all right to ask one." Marissa felt comfortable enough with the family to assert herself.

"What would you like to know?" Lowell looked into her eyes.

"Well…this morning the preacher said something about repenting." Marissa glanced at her sister. "Clari and I don't know what that means."

Lowell gazed at her. "Do you know what sin is?"

Marissa looked down at the toe of her slipper that peeked out from under her skirt. "Yes. Most of the things Clari and I have done are sins, aren't they?" She didn't want to cry, but she couldn't keep the catch out of her voice.

"Yes, I'm afraid they are. But sin is more than that. It's anything that keeps us from doing what God wants us to do."

"How can you know what God wants you to do?" Clari's question rang through the room.

Lowell held up the Book that had been resting on his knees. "He tells us in His Word—the Bible."

Marissa glanced up. "What does that have to do with repenting?"

Lowell captured her gaze with his, then smiled, and she sensed he didn't condemn her for the things she had done. "If you choose to turn away from the sins in your life, you are repenting."

For a moment, the room was quiet while Marissa thought about what he had said. She looked at her sister. Once again, tears glistened in Clari's eyes.

"Lowell," Mrs. Jenson said, "read the Gospel of Luke, chapter four, verse eighteen. I memorized it when I was young, and it has encouraged me many times in my life. The Lord has brought it to my mind several times since the young women have been with us. I believe it applies to them."

Lowell opened the Bible to the passage his mother had asked him to read. "'The Spirit of the Lord is upon me, because he hath anointed me to preach the gospel to the poor; he hath sent me to heal the brokenhearted, to preach deliverance to the captives, and recovering of sight to the blind, to set at liberty them that are bruised.' Is that the verse you mean, *Mor*?"

Mrs. Jenson nodded and turned toward Marissa and Clari. "I believe Jesus wants you to know the gospel, the good news that He came to save you from your sins. And the parts about deliverance for the captives and liberty for those who are bruised or hurt refer to what has happened in your lives."

Could it be true? Would Jesus forgive their sins and free them from hurts in their past? It was almost too much to believe. But Marissa wanted to. Tears were streaming down her cheeks too fast to wipe them off. Lowell reached into his back pocket and brought out a clean red bandanna. He handed it to her, and she started blotting her whole face.

When she looked at her sister, she was wiping her face with a matching handkerchief. Probably from Ollie. "Clari, I want what they're talking about."

"I do, too." Clari turned to Mrs. Jenson. "What do we have to do?"

The older woman put her arm around her. "You just pray and tell Jesus you want Him in your life. You're ready to repent and start trusting Him, aren't you? Would you like me to help you with the prayer?" She looked from Clari to Marissa.

Both twins nodded, and Mrs. Jenson led them in a short prayer that was to the point. As Marissa said the words, she sensed a peace like nothing she'd ever felt before sweep through her. Now the tears streaming from her eyes were tears of joy. She and Clari fell into each other's arms.

"Oh, sister!" Clari said. "Isn't it wonderful?"

Finally, Marissa pulled away and looked over at Lowell. His face was beaming, and a light shone in his eyes.

"I want to know all about Jesus!" Marissa exclaimed, and Clari nodded.

The smile on Lowell's face widened. "We'll read the Bible together every night. Then you can ask any questions you have, and we'll try to answer them."

His mother and Ollie agreed. Lowell read more from the Book then, and the words played a heavenly melody in Marissa's heart. She and Clari would have a lot to talk about when they went to their room that night.

Chapter 15

The Jensons had said all she had to do was repent and ask Jesus into her life.

But that's too simple, Clarissa thought later that night when she was alone. *Pierre made us steal from so many people. We'll surely have to do more than that to make up for the sins we've committed.*

But she and Mari had repeated the prayer after Mrs. Jenson anyway. She couldn't describe what washed over her then, but it took away all the dirt clinging to her soul. *I feel clean for the first time,* she marveled. *If Jesus is this powerful, I want to learn everything I can about Him.*

Each evening when the family gathered together after the meal, she drank in every word that came from that big Book and was left thirsting for more.

Lowell said he started with the Gospel of John because it told more about the life of Jesus than any other book in the Bible. On the first day, he read John, chapter one, and she and Mari found out Jesus was the Son of God, who came to live on earth as a man. Ollie read chapter two the next day. He and Lowell planned to alternate reading the Scriptures to the family. One or more of the Jensons would eagerly answer every question Clarissa or her sister asked.

On the fourth day, Ollie read the story of the woman at the well. Clarissa felt confused by what she heard, perhaps as the Samaritan woman had been. But when Jesus told the woman about the living water, Clarissa knew that was what she and Mari were receiving each day—a drink from the fountain of living water.

On Thursday, Ollie had to pick up some supplies in Litchfield. He asked Clarissa if she and Marissa wanted to visit with Anna and Gerda while he took care of his business. They were eager to accompany him. They knew Gerda and Anna were strong Christians and wanted to share what had happened to them with their friends.

The bell over the door to the Dress Emporium brought Anna out into the shop to see who was there.

"Clarissa and Marissa!" She rushed across the store and hugged both girls at once. "Come on back to the workroom. Gerda will want to see you, too."

After living out at the farm, Clarissa could see how much Anna resembled her mother. She had Mrs. Jenson's smile, and her hugs felt just as warm. Clarissa and Mari followed Anna into the back room.

"Look who I found in the front room."

Gerda glanced up from the dress she was hemming; then she quickly stood and crossed the room to hug the girls. "I'm so glad you've come to see us." She clasped her hands in front of her and looked from one to the other. "I wasn't at church the other day when you came, so now you must tell me, which one is which?"

They all laughed, then began catching up on what had been happening. Anna and Gerda had heard the general reports of how Pierre had treated his stepdaughters but not some of the particulars.

"We're so glad Ollie and Lowell rescued you." Gerda's smile was as sincere as Anna's.

Clarissa had worried about how the two women would regard them, but their openness and concern dispelled her fears. Anna and Gerda truly were their friends.

"We have something wonderful to tell you," Mari said, her eyes shining.

Anna and Gerda glanced from one twin to the other.

Clarissa smiled. "Mari had told me about going to church with Pierre some time back. That sermon made her want the forgiveness the preacher talked about, but she didn't know anything about Jesus."

"Except that He was a baby in a manger," Mari interjected.

"Then last Sunday when we both went to church, I heard about Him and wanted that same forgiveness, too. After supper that night, Lowell started reading the Bible to us. We asked questions, and they all answered them for us. Then Mrs. Jenson helped us pray and ask Jesus into our lives."

"And now we're forgiven." Mari's eyes sparkled. "It's as if we're new people."

"Oh, how wonderful! That is the best news of all!" Anna wiped tears of joy from her eyes, and she and Gerda hugged the girls.

"Now every day either Ollie or Lowell reads to us from the Bible." Clarissa moved around the room as she talked. "Just last night Ollie read about the woman at the well."

"Yes, I wish I could read the story again slowly," Marissa said wistfully.

Ollie finished putting the supplies in the wagon and headed toward the dress shop. He had just entered the shop when he overheard what Marissa said. The twins didn't have a Bible. He hadn't thought about that. He left the shop and hurried into the mercantile. He stowed his purchase in the wagon, then went back to the shop to get Clarissa and her sister.

"Are you ready to go?" Ollie asked the girls.

"Oh, no, please don't take them away from us yet!" Anna turned a pleading look at him.

"I need to get back and help Lowell. We have a lot to do today."

Clarissa smiled and placed her hand on Anna's arm. "And we want to help your mother. She's been so kind to us. We're learning so much from her."

Ollie chuckled. "Besides, it's not as if you won't see them again."

On the way to the farm, Ollie could hardly hide his excitement. When would he give his present to them? As soon as they arrived or after dinner? He wasn't sure. Meanwhile, they were chattering happily about their visit. He was glad they'd enjoyed it. He hoped he could give them more happy times—especially Clarissa. The twins looked a lot alike, but he could see the subtle differences. And Clarissa was the one who tugged on his heartstrings. Now they knew the Savior. He prayed every day for the Lord to show him whether Clarissa was the woman He had chosen for him, and every day his heart drew closer to her.

Ollie managed to unload the wagon before his mother called the men into the house for dinner. He put the parcel wrapped in brown paper under his arm and dropped it behind the settee in the parlor. Maybe he would wait until the family was reading the Bible tonight.

The rest of the afternoon, while he worked, he thought about that parcel. He wondered how the young women would receive it and what their reactions would be. Family time couldn't come fast enough for him.

Finally, supper was over, and the dishes were cleaned up. Ollie sat across from the twins so he could watch their expressions while Lowell started reading the fifth chapter of John. They leaned forward on the settee, their gazes fixed on the Bible as he read, apparently listening to every word. After Lowell finished reading, first Marissa asked a question, then Clarissa. During the discussion Ollie said nothing; instead, he listened and observed the girls' reactions. Finally, when the talk quieted, he stood and stretched. Then he casually walked to where he had hidden the parcel. He picked it up and laid it on the table in front of the settee.

"What's that, son?" Mother eyed the bundle.

"It's a gift for Clarissa and Marissa."

The twins turned toward him, their eyes wide. "For us?" they exclaimed in unison.

Clarissa took the package and untied the string. The brown paper fell away, and she and her sister saw two small Bibles inside.

Clarissa looked up at him, her eyes moist. "Oh, Ollie, thank you! This is the best gift we've ever received."

Marissa smiled, her eyes moist, too, and reached for one of the Books. "Yes, thank you so much, Ollie. I shall treasure this always." She ran her hand softly across the smooth leather.

Ollie continued to gaze into Clarissa's eyes. He couldn't look away if he'd wanted to, which, of course, he didn't.

On the way to church on Sunday, Mrs. Jenson talked about the decision the young women had made earlier in the week. "When the pastor asks if anyone wants to accept Jesus, you can go forward and let the whole church know you've asked Him into your lives, if that's what you want to do."

Marissa smiled and nodded. "I felt a strong desire to go to the front of the church at the end of both services I've attended, but I didn't know why."

"That was the Lord calling you." Mrs. Jenson took Marissa's hand in hers. "You don't have to go forward, but the Bible does tell us that if we confess openly that Jesus is Lord and believe in our hearts that God raised Him from the dead, we'll be saved."

Lowell glanced over his shoulder at Marissa. "Pastor Harrelson may ask if you want to join the church. You might like to think about what you'll tell him."

Marissa looked at Clari. What should they tell him? Where would they be after the first of October?

Mrs. Jenson broke into Marissa's thoughts. "You don't have to join the church if you don't want to."

"Oh, we want to, don't we, Clari?"

Clarissa nodded, and Mrs. Jenson smiled. "Then it's settled. You can join the church today."

"But we don't know where we'll be after the trial." Marissa couldn't shake this worry from her mind.

"Are you planning on going somewhere else?" Mrs. Jenson asked.

"No, but we probably need to find a job—or something."

"You'll stay with us as long as you want to. When the Lord provides something else for you, then you may go." Mrs. Jenson's declaration sounded final.

At the beginning of the service, the congregation sang "What a Friend We Have in Jesus." Marissa hadn't heard the hymn before, but it expressed her feelings exactly. No matter what happened later, she and Clari would have one special Friend who would never leave them.

On Saturday, September 21, Anna Jenson and August Nilsson were married. Lowell and Ollie escorted Marissa and Clarissa to the wedding. While Anna and August repeated their vows, Lowell listened with his ears and his heart. He wanted a home and a family. Had God brought Marissa into his life for that purpose? She and her sister had traveled all over the western United States. No one had helped them find a better way of living until they visited Litchfield. Had God planned for him and his family to rescue them from their stepfather? Did He have other plans for these young women, too? Was that why Lowell felt as if his heartstrings were tied to Marissa's?

He had thought she was sweet and quiet. But during the last few weeks, he had watched her spirit emerge like a butterfly from a cocoon. Her love of the Lord gave her an added peace and radiance—a radiance that was like sunshine to his heart. He didn't want to think about her ever leaving his home and family.

At the wedding reception, Lowell observed the love Anna and August showed each other. He knew in his heart he felt the same way about Marissa. Could there be a wedding in their future? When he returned home, he spent a long time on his knees seeking God's will about the relationship that had developed between them.

The next day, as they were preparing for church, Lowell didn't even hear Ollie when he asked him a question, so lost was he in his thoughts.

After dinner, Lowell and his brother set out for Ollie's half-finished house. They had agreed they needed to talk and work off some of the tension they were feeling.

"You haven't been working as diligently on the house lately, but I know you want to complete it." Lowell glanced at his brother as they rode toward the knoll.

"I've wanted to spend as much time as I could around the sisters."

Lowell smiled. "One in particular?"

Ollie laughed. "As if you didn't know!"

They dismounted and walked up the steps to the front porch. The outside walls were finished, and the roof protected the interior from the weather. Inside, though the stairs leading to the second floor were in place, many of the walls were still just studs.

"I need your help to finish this house." Ollie walked through a doorway framed in one wall. "I'm thinking about asking Clarissa to marry me." He turned to look at Lowell, who was smiling. "You're not surprised, are you?"

Lowell shoved his hands into his back pockets and rocked up on the balls of his feet. "No. I knew you were thinking about her the same way I've been thinking about Marissa. Have you prayed about it?"

Ollie rubbed the back of his neck. "It feels as if that's all I've done for a week now."

Lowell nodded but said nothing.

"I believe that's why God brought them to our town. So He could use us to rescue them—and so I could marry her."

Lowell crossed to a window and gazed out. The view from the parlor would be breathtaking, whatever the season. This would make a wonderful home for Ollie's family. "At least they would live close together." He turned to his brother. "They need to be near each other."

They shared a hearty laugh. It felt good.

"Maybe Gustaf will help us some, and even August, after he and Anna have had some time alone together. We've helped both of them when they were building. We could probably finish the inside of the house before Thanksgiving if we try."

Chapter 16

Tuesday, October 1, dawned clear and cool. The bright sunshine couldn't lift the gloom that had settled over Marissa, though. She dreaded this day. How could she face Pierre while she testified against him? But she knew the only way she and her sister could be free from his hold on their lives was to send him to prison for his crimes.

Marissa pictured the room full of people. The knot in her stomach tightened. She had never liked being the center of attention, and everyone at the trial would be looking at her and listening to what she said. She dropped to her knees beside the bed and poured out her heart to Jesus. A short time later she stood, walked to the washstand, and rinsed her face in the bowl of water; she felt stronger than she had in a long time.

Conversation during breakfast was light. The others must have felt the gravity of the day also. Afterward, Marissa and her sister went to their rooms to dress for court; they chose dark clothing to match their moods. Neither one fixed her hair in an elaborate style, instead pulling it back and securing it in a bun on the nape of her neck. And neither girl spoke.

Lowell and Ollie waited for them at the bottom of the stairs. Mrs. Jenson came from the kitchen to join them when they headed for the surrey. Even the trip into town was silent. The others were lost in their own thoughts, just as Marissa was in hers.

When Mother married Pierre, he had been kind to her and Clari. She thought he would be a good stepfather. She was young enough not to know the dark side of life then. Everything around her had been bright and good. After Mother became sick, Pierre began to show his true nature, but only when Mother wasn't around. Marissa wanted to remember the good times before her mother was sick, but the recent past kept intruding on those memories.

The teacher had dismissed the students for the day so the trial could take place in the schoolhouse. The townspeople gathered in small clusters in front of the building talking. Marissa looked away, then closed her eyes and prayed before Lowell helped her alight from the surrey.

Inside the schoolhouse, Pierre sat at a table near the front, but he was turned toward the door. Marissa tried to look away, but his gaze locked with hers, sending cold chills down her spine. He studied her as a rattlesnake studies its prey before striking. She could see his hands clenched into tight fists at his side as they had been in the past before he struck her. Her breath came in short gasps. She felt something almost tangible reaching out from him to pull her back into his grasp. He mouthed some words at her. They looked like, *I'll get you for this.*

Marissa looked at Clari. Her face had paled to the color of chalk. Her eyes wide with fear, she grasped her hands so tightly her knuckles had become white. Marissa wanted to flee from that room and never look back. But she couldn't. She had to testify. She had to tell the truth despite the conflict raging inside her.

Lowell slipped his arm around her waist and pulled her close to his side. He leaned down and whispered into her ear, " 'I can do all things through Christ which strengtheneth me.' "

Marissa had never read that passage, but she knew it had to be from the Bible. Jesus would give her strength. She held her head high and walked with Lowell to the seats the sheriff had saved for them.

The judge entered the room, and everyone rose until he was settled behind the table in the front. Marissa studied his face. He appeared solemn, but laugh lines around his eyes and mouth indicated he wasn't always that way. He looked at her just then and smiled. She took a deep breath and fixed her gaze on the judge.

Marissa had always feared anyone connected with the law, because she was guilty of doing what Pierre had forced her to do. The judge knew what she had done. In fact, Lowell had told her that the judge knew everything about the case before it started. The man smiled at her again as a loving father might smile upon his daughter. She could do what she needed to do.

The judge pounded his gavel on the table, and sudden quiet filled the room. It didn't take long for Sheriff Bartlett to present his case. Three deputies told about capturing Pierre with the stolen goods. Then came Marissa's turn to answer questions. Clari would testify last. Before Marissa arose to take the stand, Lowell gave her hand a squeeze. "I'll be praying for you," he whispered.

Marissa decided not to look at Pierre. Instead, she focused on the man asking the questions and answered every question with the truth.

Lowell's heart pounded in his ears as he watched Marissa approach the witness chair. He hated for her to go up there alone; he knew how difficult it was for her. He could only pray for her strength during the questioning. When she finished, he whispered a prayer of thanks. He wanted to protect her, with his own life if need be. Gud, *I love her with my whole heart. Help me know what You want me to do.* A sense of peace enveloped him.

Marissa finished her testimony and returned to her chair. Lowell stood, took her arm, and escorted her from the courtroom.

"Don't I need to stay?" she asked when they were outside the schoolhouse.

"No. You've done your part. Let's go for a walk."

"What if Clari needs me?"

"She'll do fine. Besides, Ollie will be there for her."

At first they walked in silence, and Lowell held her hand. He wanted to comfort her and never let her go. He guided her away from the crowd to a small park nestled among tall trees. They found a bench and sat quietly for a time. Lowell sensed a great peace surrounding them. Only the birds chirping overhead broke the stillness.

Marissa turned her face toward him and smiled. It was such a sweet smile that he wanted to take her in his arms.

"Marissa, do you have any idea how I feel about you?"

She lowered her gaze to their hands clasped on the bench between them. "I. . .I'm not sure, Lowell, but I'd like to know."

"You're very important to me." He drew her into his arms and rested his chin on the top of her head. "I want to protect you from anything that might hurt you."

She nestled close against his chest. "I'm sure you could," she whispered, then looked up into his eyes.

Lowell's face drifted closer to hers until their lips touched. He felt such a sweet, tender connection between them. Warmth flooded his body. He pulled away and took a deep breath.

"We need to get back and see what the verdict is."

Ollie felt great relief when the trial ended. The judge and jury had been appalled when they heard what Clarissa and her sister had gone through. Because of the evidence and the girls' testimonies, the jury was quick to give Pierre a life sentence. Ollie was glad Lowell had taken Marissa out of the courtroom. When Pierre heard the verdict, his outburst was loud and ugly. Ollie wished Clarissa hadn't heard it, either. The man's vindictive words must have wounded her deeply. The judge immediately restored order to the court, and the U.S. marshal and his deputies led Pierre away in handcuffs. The twins would never have to see him again.

Ollie glanced at Sheriff Bartlett, who nodded. Ollie slipped his arm under Clarissa's and quietly escorted her out the back door before the judge dismissed everyone. He wanted to spare her from the crowds. They walked up the street, hunting for Lowell and Marissa. Finally, they gave up when they reached the church.

Clarissa looked at the open door. "Do you think it would be all right to go inside? I mean, it isn't Sunday, after all."

Ollie smiled at her. "Sure. We can go in anytime. It's the Lord's house, you know."

They walked up to the front pew and sat down. Clarissa bowed her head.

"Dear Jesus, thank You for helping Mari and me get through the trial. Thank You for giving us strength to help put Pierre in prison where he belongs. And thank You for sending Ollie and Lowell to rescue us from him. Amen."

Ollie kept his head bowed after she finished. Her prayer echoed his own thoughts. But he also sent one more silent plea toward heaven.

As they made their way to the back of the church, Ollie reached out and drew Clarissa into his arms. She gazed up at him, and the desire to kiss her lips overcame him. He lowered his head, then hesitated. He wanted to give her a chance to turn away. Instead, she closed the distance between them. Her mouth tasted like honey to him, and he wanted to hold her in his arms forever.

He pulled back, then settled her closer into his arms. "Oh, Clarissa, what am I going to do about you?"

Back at the farm, the sisters went to their rooms to change clothes. Lowell and Ollie followed their mother into the kitchen.

Lowell crossed his arms and leaned against the counter. "*Moder*, we want to ask you something."

She turned around and smiled, waiting for him to continue.

Lowell stood up straight and stuck his hands in his back pockets. Why was he nervous? He should be able to say what was on his mind.

"I want to ask Marissa to marry me." He felt better after the words were out.

Ollie stepped up beside him. "And I want to marry Clarissa."

Mother smiled. "I'm not surprised."

Lowell rubbed his hands on his trousers. Why were his palms sweating? "Is that all right with you?"

Mother laughed. "I would love to have them in the family. They seem like daughters to me already. And they need a family to love them."

Lowell grinned. He felt like shouting. Ollie turned and strode from the room. Lowell could hear the barn door slamming shut, then the faint sound of a joyous whoop.

"What's wrong with Ollie?" Clarissa had just come into the kitchen.

Lowell laughed. "I don't know. Why don't you go see about him?"

"Is anyone going to tell me what's going on?" Marissa asked.

Lowell and his mother laughed, and Marissa raised her brows. A puzzled look was on her face. Maybe he was crazy. Crazy in love.

Clarissa stepped through the barn door. "Oh, there you are, Ollie. Are you all right?"

"Sure. How about if we take a ride after lunch? I'd like to show you something."

"What is it?"

Ollie smiled, his eyes twinkling. "Oh, you'll see." He smiled again.

After lunch, Mrs. Jenson told her and Mari they didn't need to help with the dishes, but they insisted. When they finished, the surrey and two other horses stood in front of the house. Ollie had suggested Clarissa put on a riding skirt, so she dashed upstairs, changed, then hurried back down. Lowell was escorting Mari to the surrey. Ollie had saddled a gentle mare for Clarissa to ride. He boosted her up, then mounted his own horse.

They started across the pasture. Soon they came to a house sitting on a hill. Ollie stopped in front of it and dismounted. He helped her down from her horse, then pulled her into his arms and kissed the top of her head. A shiver coursed through her. She had never felt like this before.

"Are you cold?" he whispered against her hair.

"No." She looked up into his eyes. The clear green deepened as his gaze intensified.

She was quiet for a moment, then asked, "Whose house is this?"

Ollie cleared his throat and led her by the hand up the steps to the front porch. "It's mine, but it isn't finished."

He opened the door, and Clarissa stepped through into what looked like a dream world to her. She knew the house wasn't finished, but she could picture beautiful wallpaper with tiny flowers, pictures of lovely scenes on the walls, a fire in the fireplace, and lace curtains at the windows. How she wished she could live in such a house.

Ollie placed his hands lightly on her shoulders and turned her toward him. "And it can be your home if you'll marry me."

Clarissa caught her breath. Had he asked her to marry him? Were her dreams coming true? Tears filled her eyes.

He gently cupped her cheeks in his strong palms. "Please don't cry. I love you."

"But they're tears of joy, Ollie. I've never been so happy." It was hard to get the words past the lump in her throat.

"Then are you saying yes?" He held his breath.

Clarissa nodded and stood on tiptoe to touch his lips briefly with hers, but he captured her in an embrace that made her feel protected and cherished. The kiss deepened, and her insides felt molten. She could hardly believe this man loved her and she was going to spend the rest of her life with him. God had been so good to her.

Marissa had looked back at Ollie as she and Lowell drove away in the surrey. He was taking Clari riding. Maybe the brothers wanted to help Marissa and her sister celebrate the end of Pierre's hold on their lives. It felt odd to ride in the middle of the day. No one had done any chores before the trial, so she thought the men would need to work when they returned home.

Marissa looked at Lowell. "Where are we going?"

"I thought you might want to go for a ride." He pulled her close to him and kept his arm around her. "I know a place by a stream where we can sit and talk."

Marissa liked sitting nestled close to him. If only it didn't have to end. She would be happy to spend the rest of her life with Lowell, but she knew that was unreasonable. She knew he liked her a lot, but she wished it were more than that. Marissa wasn't sure when she had started loving him, but she had been drawn to him as long as she'd known him. It was only a few months, but it seemed much longer than that. She felt as if her life began when she met him.

Lowell pulled the surrey off the road and parked it under a grove of trees. He helped her alight and led her deeper into the grove. Soon she heard the sound of water gurgling over rocks. The sun shone through the branches above the brook, and sparkles danced on the surface of the water. What a beautiful place!

Lowell stuffed his hands in his back pockets, then pulled them out. She had seen him do this many times, but it was usually when he was nervous. What did he have to be nervous about? She studied his expression. Whatever was on his mind was important.

She touched his arm. "What's the matter, Lowell? Can I help?"

He took her hands in his. "Yes, you can. You can marry me."

Marissa looked at him thoughtfully. "Why do you want me to marry you?" She hoped it wasn't because he felt sorry for her and Clari because they had no home.

He gathered her gently in his arms. "I'm not doing this very well, am I?" He rested his chin on the top of her head. "Marissa, I love you so much it hurts. I can't imagine my life without you in it."

She smiled and looked up at him. "I love you, too, Lowell. And I want to marry you."

She placed her hand on his cheek. He had no doubt shaved that morning, but she could feel a tiny bit of stubble against her palm. His masculinity made her feel safe.

He lowered his head until his lips touched hers. This time he didn't pull away quickly. His kiss awakened every part of her being. The thought that she could experience kisses like this for the rest of her life washed over her, and she poured her love into returning his kiss.

Epilogue

They had chosen the Saturday after Thanksgiving for the wedding day. The dreams Marissa and Clarissa had shared in the forest were coming true. They would have a double wedding, and Lowell and Ollie were the grooms. Mrs. Jenson had offered to move to town and live with Gerda over the Dress Emporium, but neither of the twins would hear of it. Marissa wanted her mother-in-law to continue living in the home she had shared with her husband. She knew she would need the older woman's help. She hadn't learned all she needed to know about running a household and being a wife. Clarissa assured Mrs. Jenson she would need her help, too.

Ollie and Clarissa's house was finished, but all the furniture they'd ordered hadn't arrived yet. They would move in right after the wedding, but it would take awhile before the household was settled.

The day of the wedding was a winter spectacle. It had snowed earlier in the week, and the sun on the white expanse lent a special glow to the bare tree branches encased in ice. Everything sparkled as if celebrating the special day.

Anna and Gerda came to the farm to help the sisters don the dresses they had made for them. They had created the same style but in different fabrics. Marissa wore a pure white brocade and Clarissa a rich cream-colored satin.

August brought a sleigh to take the brides to the wedding. The girls had never ridden in a sleigh and laughed all the way to the church. The horses wore bells on their harnesses, and the merry jingling was the perfect accompaniment to the excitement Clarissa and Marissa felt. The church was filled when they arrived, and some people had even clustered around the doors.

Mrs. Olson played the pump organ while Gustaf escorted Marissa down the aisle to Lowell. Then August walked with Clarissa to Ollie. In their dreams, this had been a fairy-tale ending for the girls' lives, but they both realized this was truly the beginning—of a more wonderful life than either had ever imagined—a life free from deception.

Gerda's Lawman

This book is dedicated to my youngest granddaughter, Amanda.
You are a joy and treasure.
I look forward to seeing what God is going to do in your life.
And every book is dedicated to my husband, James,
who has showered me with his love for most of my life.

Chapter 1

April 1896

Frank Daggett sure hoped that was a town up ahead and not a mirage. He had been in the saddle so long he felt as if it were fused to the seat of his pants. Finally, he could have a bath, a shave, a hot meal, and a real bed. In that order. But the long ride had been worth it. Although he was bone weary, he could sense that indefinable excitement he always felt when he was about to catch his prey. Pierre Le Blanc and his daughter had to be just ahead. His two daughters, if Frank had it figured right. Litchfield, Minnesota, was the end of the line. For him and for the Le Blancs—in more ways than one.

Litchfield looked like a nice enough town, and Frank hoped it wouldn't take very long to bring the Le Blancs to justice. He was ready to get on with his life, and he couldn't until he had finished this one chore. Although he was only thirty years old, he felt ancient. He had seen enough to age him beyond his years. Bad people and their evil deeds had hardened him so much he hardly knew who he was anymore—certainly not the idealistic young man who became a U.S. Marshal all those years ago. He didn't even know where he belonged. Maybe when he finished this quest he could find out. For the first time in over ten years, he could have a life of his own, complete with a home and family, like most men his age.

Because of his obsession with catching Pierre Le Blanc and his daughters, he was no longer a marshal. The Old Man had given him a choice: Give up this pursuit or turn in his badge. The head of the U.S. Marshals taught Frank everything he knew about being a lawman. And like all of the marshals, he had tremendous respect for his superior. Frank had only disagreed with the Old Man about one thing—his decision that the U.S. Marshals would stop pursuing the Le Blancs.

With great reluctance, Frank had removed the star. Since then, he had been on his own as he followed the trail of this confidence man and his family. It was a good thing that Frank had saved so much of his pay over the years and his needs were negligible. A lot of his money remained in a bank back East, waiting for him to get to the point where he could start living a real life. He wouldn't have to worry about finances while he was establishing himself.

Sometimes he had been so close to catching these criminals that he could almost taste victory. But he always arrived after they had left the vicinity. Then it would take him awhile to find their trail again. They committed crimes in such a way that no one could prove they did it. That was why Frank had finally figured out there had to be two girls. And they must be twins to look that much alike. It was the only way they could have pulled off so many seemingly perfect crimes. But Frank knew that there were no perfect crimes. It was about time this family was brought to justice, and he was the man to do that very thing.

Frank stopped his horse in front of the first hotel he came to. He looked up at the second-story windows. They even sported curtains. It was a high-class establishment—nicer than many of the places he had stayed during this long quest. After tying the reins of his mount to the hitching post, he removed his saddlebags from the horse and slung them across his shoulder. He stepped up on the high boardwalk without bothering to go down to where steps had been built. His legs were long enough, and he was too tired to go even that much farther. The steady beat of his boots on the boards and the jingle of his spurs accompanied him through the door. His whole body itched, and he was eager to remove his traveling gear and put on clean clothes.

A young man sat behind the hotel's front desk writing something in a book. His head was bent forward, and Frank was sure the man didn't even know anyone was around until Frank dropped his saddlebags on the counter.

"I'd like a room."

The man looked startled as he slammed the book shut and glanced up. He stood and pulled the hotel register from a shelf under the counter. "Do you want a room that looks out on the street or one in the back where it's quieter?"

Frank wished he could say, "In the back," but he needed to be able to keep an eye on the town's comings and goings. That was the only way he could keep a lookout for the Le Blancs. He just hoped this wasn't another town where rowdy cowboys came to drink late into the night.

"In the front would be fine." Frank reached for his wallet. "Do I need to pay now?"

"How long are you staying?" The man smiled up at Frank.

"I'm not really sure. How about if I pay you for a week, and we'll see if I need to be here longer?"

The man pushed the register book toward Frank, handed him a pen, and moved the ink well closer to him. "That would be fine, Mister. . ." He watched as Frank wrote his name. "Daggett. That'll be five dollars for the week. You're in room three." He turned around and retrieved the key from the numbered cubbyhole behind him.

"Where's the best place to get a bath, a shave, and a meal?"

Gerda Nilsson was just putting the finishing touches on her hairdo when August knocked at the door of the apartment. She shoved one last hairpin into the style to anchor it before she answered the door.

"I'm coming." Thick carpet muffled her footsteps as she crossed the parlor. She opened the door and hugged her brother. "Why didn't you just use your key?"

August returned her hug, then stood back. "I only kept the key because you insisted. It's a good idea for me to check on things for you when you're out at the farm since you're living here alone. But I won't use it for any other reason. You deserve your privacy, too." He looked around the apartment that had also been his wife's home before they married. "I like what you've done with the place. It really expresses your personality."

"Thank you, kind sir." Gerda gave a low curtsy. She and her brother had always enjoyed a playful relationship.

He bowed slightly and nodded. "Are you ready, milady?" August picked up her jacket from the claret-colored velvet settee. He helped her into the wrap, opened the door, and escorted her down the stairs and into the warm spring twilight.

Gerda placed her hand in the crook of his elbow as they walked across the street to the hotel. "It was really nice of Anna to offer to keep Gustaf and Olina's children so we could take them out to dinner for their anniversary."

"She loves those two little ones. *Ja*, for sure. And I do, too. They come over to our house a lot since we live so close."

When they entered the hotel lobby, Gerda looked around the room. She didn't come here often, but she had always liked the friendly, yet elegant, atmosphere. The gaslights around the walls gave a warm glow to the plush carpeting and matching wallpaper. Several potted plants enhanced the décor's sense of opulence. Whenever she came to the hotel, its air of sophistication made her feel that Litchfield was as cosmopolitan as Chicago or New York City.

Gerda's attention was drawn to a man beginning to descend the stairs. He was taller than any man she had ever seen. Although his body was lean, it was muscular. His face was dark and clean-shaven except for a neat mustache. *He must spend a lot of time in the sun*. The top of his forehead was lighter than the rest of his tanned face, evidence that he wore a cowboy hat most of the time. He wasn't dressed like a cowboy, but as he walked down the stairs, he had that bowlegged gait of a man who spent most of his life on horseback. His luxurious, thick dark hair looked wet and was slicked back, but separate locks were pulling into strong waves as they dried.

For some inexplicable reason, she felt drawn to him. Her fingers tingled with the desire to brush back an errant curl that had drooped over his strong forehead. She had never felt that way about any man. For a moment, she held her breath in wonder. His most arresting feature—his eyes—were a clear, icy blue. When his gaze met hers, something passed between them that was both exciting and disturbing. Uncomfortable, Gerda quickly looked away.

What is wrong with me? Maybe it was because all her friends had soul mates, and she wanted one, too. Why did some stranger affect her this way? Gerda was glad that Gustaf and Olina arrived at that moment, and the four of them went into the dining room. She tried to dismiss the man from her thoughts.

Frank stopped halfway down the stairs. What had just happened? He was going to the hotel restaurant to get something to eat, minding his own business, when a vision of loveliness entered the lobby. Her beauty almost took his breath away. He had seen those new calendars painted by the artist named Gibson. She looked as if she had just stepped out of one. She was the right size with curves in all the right places. Her delicate features proclaimed class and character. Her light blond hair was formed into a poufy style and had a cluster of curls nested in the crown. Curly tendrils brushed her cheeks and neck where he wished he could place his lips. He could just imagine what the silky strands would feel like. He would have to stop thinking like that!

When she looked into his eyes, he had felt something he had never felt before. Something that crackled through the room, almost sucking out all the air, leaving nothing to breathe. He wondered if anyone else had sensed it. He glanced around, but no one was paying either of them any attention.

Frank wasn't looking for a relationship yet. If he found one, or one found him, it would have to be a relationship with no strings attached, at least until his mission was over. He wasn't ready to settle down, and that girl had strings dangling off her so long they would really hog-tie a man. Frank almost turned around and went back to his room, but just then his stomach rumbled so loudly he was sure everyone within a mile radius could hear it. He had to get something to eat. If only she and her companions hadn't gone into the dining room.

Frank continued toward the open doorway of the restaurant. His attention was drawn to the table where the woman and her friends were sitting. It was a good thing they were on one side of the room. He would just choose a table on the other side, and that would be the end of it. With the decision made, he looked around the room for an empty table.

He hadn't thought that this town would have many people staying at a hotel, but there were plenty in the restaurant. Perhaps this is why Le Blanc was here. Evidently, Litchfield had some affluent citizens. Most of these people were dressed in more expensive clothing than he'd seen in many places. Finally, he spied an empty table on the exact opposite side of the room from where the woman and her party sat. With the large dining area separating them, he could almost forget she was there.

However, when Frank walked across the room and selected a place to sit, he chose a chair that gave him a clear view of the beauty. He couldn't take his eyes off of her until the waitress came to take his order.

"My name is Molly." The grandmotherly woman smiled at him. She raised her voice to be heard over the din of voices and silverware clanking against dishes in the background. "You're new to town, aren't you? You look like you could use a good meal."

Frank nodded, ignoring her question. No one needed to know his business. "What do you have?"

While the woman recited a list of items, Frank couldn't keep from glancing at the beauty seated across the room. When Molly stopped talking, all he could remember her saying was "pot roast."

"I'll have the roast beef." Frank looked up into her kind eyes. "It's been a long time since I've had any."

"We get lots of travelers through here." Molly's eyes twinkled as she talked. "They always appreciate a good hot meal." She started to walk off then turned back toward him. "Our cook makes hot rolls that will melt in your mouth. And we have plenty of butter to go with them."

"That'll be better than the hardtack I've been eating." Frank had enough of that in the past few weeks to last a lifetime.

When the waitress went to get him a cup of coffee, he glanced toward the table where the vision of loveliness sat. Her every move was grace itself. Her dainty hand fluttered like a butterfly on its way to pick up her glass of water. When she turned to speak to the man on her left, she cocked her head toward him, revealing a profile that looked just liked his mother's cameo. It was the only thing he still owned that had belonged to her, and it was precious to him. He kept that cameo locked in a safe-deposit box in the bank where his savings were.

"Here's your coffee, sir." Molly set the steaming china cup and its saucer in front of him. He glanced up at her, almost sorry for the interruption of his thoughts.

"Thank you." At least he was able to remember his manners. He picked up the cup and took a sip. He liked his coffee hot and strong but not too strong. This coffee was just right. He set the cup down and looked back across the room.

Why did he torture himself this way? That woman had an escort. She might be married. But somehow he didn't think she was. He had spent too many years watching people not to know the signs. And there was no indication that the couple was married or even romantically involved. The other couple at the table was another matter. Marriage screamed from every look and touch they shared.

When Frank glanced around the room again, his gaze stopped on a man who just had to be a banker. No one else in the room wore a waistcoat with a gold watch chain draped across it. Litchfield must have a healthy economy from the looks of this man. Just the kind of town Le Blanc preyed on. Frank wondered if these people had any idea what they were in for. He had to stop the Le Blanc gang before they destroyed any more lives.

His attention quickly returned to the woman sitting across the room. He couldn't seem to keep his eyes off of her.

"Here you are." The waitress set his meal in front of him. "Some folks say we serve the finest food west of the Mississippi."

"That sounds good to me." Frank smiled up at her before picking up his fork.

Steam rose from the plate, bringing with it the pleasant aroma of roast beef. Carrots and potatoes, covered with a generous helping of a rich, brown gravy, surrounded the meat. There was nothing he liked better than good gravy. His stomach growled again. This time louder. He hoped the group across the room couldn't hear it.

The first bite was heavenly. He chewed it slowly, savoring the almost forgotten flavors that reminded him of just how much he had given up to bring Le Blanc to justice. He hoped that, at last, this would be the town where he would arrest the man and his daughters.

The waitress returned with a dish of butter and a basket of hot yeast rolls. "Don't forget to save room for dessert. Tonight we have apple pie."

Could life get any better than this? Frank took his time eating. He wanted to enjoy every minute of this good food. But more than that, he decided to just relax and enjoy watching the beautiful woman. Who knew? Someday he would be ready to settle down. Someday maybe he would find a woman much like her to marry.

When they were seated at a table in the dining room, Gerda decided to forget what had happened in the hotel lobby and concentrate on her brothers and sister-in-law. "Well, Olina, I guess it's nice for you to get to go out without the children."

Olina smiled at her. "Oh yes, it is a real treat, for sure. It was good of you and August to plan this little celebration."

"Actually, it was Anna's idea." August picked up his linen napkin and spread it across his lap.

"Why didn't she come with us?" Olina asked.

Gerda laughed. "You mean besides the fact that she's keeping your children for you?" Olina nodded. "I offered to keep them at the apartment, but Anna thought it would be special for Gustaf's brother and sister to take the two of you out."

August picked up his fork and turned it over and over in his hands as if he were checking its weight. "She really likes having Olga and Sven at the house." He put the fork down and cleared his throat. "She's hoping we'll have a little one ourselves pretty soon. I told her that it has only been a few months since we married, and I enjoy our time together, but I want children pretty soon, too. *Ja,* that's for sure."

Gustaf patted his wife's hand. "Well, we have an announcement to make, and you two will be the first to hear."

Olina blushed and looked down at her plate. "We are going to have another baby this fall."

Gerda got up and went around the table to hug Olina. "I am so happy for you." When she passed Gustaf on the way back to her chair, she hugged him, too. "And I'm happy for you, big brother."

The waitress came to their table. "What are we all having tonight?"

"I think this calls for steaks." August looked at each of them in turn. "Unless you want something else. We have a lot to celebrate."

When the waitress left, conversation flowed around the table, but Gerda's attention was divided. That cowboy was sitting across the room. She could see him when she turned to talk to August. The man seemed to be enjoying his food, but every once in a while, she could feel his gaze on her. Why was he doing that? It made her very uncomfortable. Though she was glad to have this time with her relatives, she couldn't forget the man or the impression he had made on her when they were in the lobby.

It didn't make any sense. She felt drawn to him, even here in the dining room. She was aware when his coffee arrived. While he ate his roast beef and hot rolls, she looked at him from time to time. He had perfect table manners, not like some of the cowboys she had seen. She didn't want him to catch her watching him, so she peeked at him out of the corners of her eyes to make sure it wasn't when he was looking at her.

I am acting like an old maid. Just because everyone else is married doesn't mean anything is wrong with my life, does it? She was a successful proprietor with a comfortable home, good friends, and a family who loved her. But they weren't a husband and children. Then she felt that deep longing she had harbored since she'd become an adult. She wanted to be loved by a man the way *Far* loved *Mor.* The way Gustaf loved Olina. The way August loved Anna. The way Anna's brothers Ollie and Lowell loved their wives. She wanted a home of her own, not just an apartment above a store. And she wanted children. To feel their arms around her neck, to have them call her "Mother." Oh yes, Gerda wanted all those things more than she could tell anyone. *But that cowboy across the dining room is not the man to give them to me.*

Chapter 2

If Frank had been eating in a tavern or even a small café, he would have lit up a cheroot and enjoyed a smoke with his after-dinner coffee, but it didn't seem like the thing to do in this classy restaurant. He didn't want to leave where he was sitting while that beauty was across the room, so he sipped the hot beverage and relaxed in his chair, taking frequent peeks at her. The waitress had filled his cup three more times before the party he was watching got up and left the room.

When Frank emerged from the restaurant, he felt too restless to sleep. Instead of going to his room, he decided to go outside for a smoke. The sun had set and gaslights flickered along the main street, casting indefinite circles of light at regular intervals along the boardwalk. Frank glanced down the street toward the saloon. Light, noise, and tobacco smoke poured out through the swinging doors. When he was younger, he would have felt drawn to the place, but it held no enticement tonight. He fished in the pocket of his shirt for a cheroot and placed the end between his lips. He then pulled a small box of matches from his vest pocket, withdrew one, and returned the box to his pocket. Leaning down, he struck the matchstick against the sole of his boot and applied the flame to the end of the thin cigar. The smoke curled around his head as he moved down the sidewalk away from the doorway and leaned back against the wall.

He wondered where the sheriff's office was. Tomorrow he would need to find it. Frank decided that he would wait and alert the lawman after he'd found the Le Blancs. At that point, he would need assistance, since he was no longer an officer of the law himself. Frank could see a train station past the end of this block. He wondered how often the train came through town. All the lights were off in the depot, so there must not be any more due tonight.

Frank took another draw on his small cigar. Just then a lamp was lighted in the upstairs room across the street. A large sign spanning the building proclaimed it BRAXTON'S MERCANTILE. One of the downstairs windows at the end of the building had DRESS EMPORIUM painted in letters that matched those on the mercantile sign. An elegant dress in some shimmery fabric the color of rich cream was draped over a dress form in that window. Frank liked women's clothing without too many frills. The clean lines of the garment would look good on the woman he had watched during dinner. Of course, with her classic features and perfect figure, almost anything would look good on her. He wondered if she had seen this dress. He also wondered where she lived and if he would ever see her again. *Probably not, so I should just quit thinking about her.* But he wasn't ready to release her from his thoughts.

Earlier in the day, when Frank took his horse to be stabled at the livery, he'd noticed that the building looked as though it hadn't been there long. The wood was new, not weathered like the smithy that stood nearby. It made him wonder why a town this size hadn't had a livery stable before this. A few questions about the new business might help him open a conversation that would lead to the whereabouts of the Le Blancs.

Frank moved away from the wall and leaned against a post that supported the porch. The night felt chilly. He was tired but not sleepy. He figured he just might as well go to his room, so he threw the stub of the cigar in the dirt and stepped off the boardwalk to snuff it out with the heel of his boot. He glanced up and down the silent street before he entered the front door to the hotel.

Frank hadn't lost the feeling that he was close to Le Blanc and his daughters, but it wasn't any stronger now than when he'd come into town. He was pretty sure they weren't at this hotel. He hoped he hadn't missed them once again, but he decided not to dwell on that. It would just keep him from being able to sleep tonight.

As he crossed the hotel lobby, the young man behind the desk looked up over the top of his spectacles. "Do you need anything else, sir?"

"No, thank you. I'm going to turn in for the night." When Frank reached the step on the carpeted stairs where he had first become aware of the woman, he turned and looked at the place where she had stood. He half hoped she would be there now, but that was a crazy thought. As he knew it would be, the spot was empty. So was the rest of the lobby, except for the man behind the desk, who had returned to reading his book.

Gerda was glad to leave the restaurant and get that cowboy out of sight and off her mind. August accompanied her to the door of her apartment. He unlocked the door with his key.

She turned toward her brother and gave him a hug. "Thank you. I'll be fine now."

August looked a little disappointed. He may have wanted to stay and talk awhile, but she was afraid she might blurt out something about that cowboy. Gerda was confident that neither of her brothers had noticed him. She certainly didn't want to call attention to him now.

She was glad she'd left one lamp burning. It gave her enough light to get to the others. For some reason, she didn't want the apartment to be dark tonight.

Gerda walked over to the window and pulled back the curtain. She stayed mostly behind the fabric and looked at the hotel across the street wondering which room was the cowboy's. *Probably one in the back where it's quieter.* Since they spent so much time out on the range, didn't cowboys like to be away from the noise of town? Unless he had gone down to the saloon. Although he was dressed like a gentleman at dinner, he might have headed that way afterward. For all she knew, he was just a snake in the grass like Pierre Le Blanc. But she hoped not. How could she have felt that strong connection in the hotel lobby if the man was like Pierre?

What if he were something besides a drifter? Could Gerda have a relationship with him? What was she thinking? She didn't know if the man was a Christian or even if he was a decent man. It must have been because of the wedding anniversary and all the talk of children. That was why her thinking had gone awry. She was fine just as she was right now.

Then an image came to mind of her old maid aunt who had died when Gerda was a little girl. The woman was dried up. Her skin was wrinkled, and her outlook on life was sour. Unlike Aunt Ada, Gerda loved children. Just because Gerda wasn't married didn't mean she would end up like her aunt. Besides, maybe God just hadn't yet brought the man into her life that He wanted her to marry.

Gerda released the edge of the curtain with a disgusted sigh, then walked into the parlor and picked up the book of poetry August had brought as a housewarming gift after she and Anna moved into the apartment. She sat in the rocking chair and read a few pages but soon closed the volume. Poetry was not what she needed tonight. Too many of the poems were about love. Maybe she should read the Bible. When she picked up the leather-bound book, it fell open to Esther. Gerda read all ten chapters. God had Esther marry a king to save His people from destruction. Surely God had a purpose for keeping Gerda unmarried so long. She wished He would tell her what it was—and soon.

"Father God, forgive me for feeling dissatisfied tonight. Please help me wait for Your plan for my life. Help me be happy and patient until You bring something else—and help me recognize what You are doing when You do. Amen." Praying aloud helped God seem more real to Gerda, as if He were sitting on the settee across the room. Although she felt a calmness settle on her spirit, she wished to hear an audible reply from Him.

She hadn't been dissatisfied with her life until that tall, tan, handsome stranger connected with her across the hotel lobby. Gerda thought her prayer had been sincere, but she didn't sleep very soundly that night. She dreamed disturbing things about growing old alone, and the cowboy from the hotel flitted in and out of her nonsensical dreams at odd times and for no apparent reason.

Frank didn't get ready for bed when he went to his room. He didn't even light the lamp. One of the gas streetlights was right outside his window. He didn't pull the shade down, so he could see all he needed from the glow it provided. Frank stood beside the window and studied the area one more time. The lighted windows above the store had curtains on them. It was probably where someone lived. He wondered who. Maybe the owner of the mercantile.

He looked down to the empty street below. When he glanced back across the street, a woman was pulling the shade down on one of the windows. All he could see was her hand and part of her skirt.

Leaning his weight on the hand that rested on the window frame, Frank wondered how long it would be before he could find the Le Blancs. He would make discreet inquiries tomorrow because he didn't want to alert them that someone was after them. Stepping away from the window, he rubbed his hand through his unruly curls. Sometimes he thought it would be easier to just shave his head when he shaved his face. Then his hair wouldn't be such a problem to control. Maybe it was time to visit the barbershop. He'd noticed a red-and-white-striped pole on one of the buildings near the saloon. A barbershop was a good place to obtain information.

Frank opened his saddlebags and retrieved the papers he had been collecting. Papers that chronicled all the crimes he was sure the Le Blanc gang had committed. Frank wanted to be sure they were in order when he took them to the sheriff.

As he shuffled through the pages he had collected, each one brought uncomfortable memories. If only the Old Man had been with Frank, he never would have insisted that Frank give up. Seeing all the devastation left behind by the Le Blancs, there was no way Frank could do that. As a lawman, he'd tried to protect people from evil people like Pierre Le Blanc. He couldn't allow other people to be destroyed by him, too.

Frank's hand stopped on the information from Cheyenne, Wyoming. He withdrew the slip of paper and moved to the window, reading the words in the glow from the gaslight and the moon. He didn't really need to see the words. He couldn't forget the stricken look on the face of a rancher who had been wiped out when his life savings were taken. Unfortunately, the man—like many others—didn't trust banking institutions. He'd hidden his savings under his mattress. That year had been hard, and the rancher was counting on that money to build up his depleted herd. He was even going to pay his hired hands with some of the cash.

Frank threw the paper down on the bed and stalked across the floor, rubbing the back of his neck. The man had lost heart along with his cash. When Frank left Cheyenne, the rancher was contemplating going back East to work in his brother's store—something he had declared he would never do.

Frank sat on the side of the bed and replaced the paper in the stack. He straightened the stack and started to slip it back into his saddlebag.

There was another face that Frank couldn't banish from his thoughts. A woman from Topeka, Kansas. The Le Blancs had taken jewelry from her—jewelry that had been in her family for over five generations. It had come from Europe with the ancestors who'd settled in Kansas while it was a wild land. When Frank met the woman, her eyes were red from weeping. She had shut herself off from most people, but the sheriff convinced her to talk to the marshal. She mourned the loss of the legacy she wanted to pass on to her daughters. While Frank questioned her, she showed him a portrait a traveling painter had done of her wearing some of the jewelry. They were beautiful pieces. Ever since then, he had been on the lookout for them in every town he passed through as he followed the trail of the Le Blanc gang.

Frank wondered what Le Blanc did with the jewelry and silver he stole. There wasn't much of a market for things like that in smaller towns. Perhaps he took it back East to sell. If so, Frank knew the owners would never see them again. It was a shame for a family to lose heirlooms like that.

While he undressed and got ready for bed, his thoughts returned to the graceful beauty. She was the kind of woman a man brought home to Mother, if his mother were still alive. He didn't know that for a fact, but he thought he could tell that much about her. She walked with a regal bearing. The beauty would make a good mother for some man's children. Were the men in this town blind, or just stupid, to let a woman like her remain unmarried? Then another thought hit him. Was she a widow? Maybe she had been married. Perhaps there were children.

He could be mistaken about her. Maybe she was married but didn't wear a ring for some reason. But he couldn't dismiss the feeling that she was unattached. Frank had been good at reading people. He had to be in the business he was in.

Frank shook his head to clear it of the thoughts that haunted him. He crawled between clean sheets, which smelled like sunshine, and pulled up the colorful quilt that had been draped across the end of the bed. He was glad to be in a hotel that believed in cleanliness. He had slept plenty of times in beds with used sheets.

❧

Frank rode his horse, following Pierre Le Blanc and his two daughters, who were in a fancy buggy. They stayed just far enough ahead that he could barely make out their features, but he was sure it had to be them. They turned off the road and drove up to a farmhouse. A woman came out to meet them. She stood straight with glorious, light blond hair that was pulled up into a poufy hairstyle. He couldn't take his eyes off her. Her graceful hand waved toward him. He started to raise his but remembered what he had been doing when he saw her, so he didn't return her salute.

He glanced toward the Le Blancs, but they had disappeared. So had the buggy they were riding in. Nothing lay between him and the woman on the porch. He was no longer riding a horse, though he didn't remember dismounting. He strode across a grassy field toward the beauty who was now clothed in a creamy, shimmery dress that somehow looked familiar. The cool breeze blew the skirt out behind her, and the wisps of hair that fell around her shoulders also billowed in the wind. She smiled at him as if she were waiting for him.

"Welcome home."

Her melodious voice drifted on the spring breeze and caressed his ears. Her arms spread wide as if to emphasize the words, and he walked into her embrace. When her arms closed around him, she lifted her face to receive his kiss. He wanted to put his arms around her when he kissed her, but he couldn't move them. He struggled against the bonds that held him, but the more he struggled, the tighter they became.

Frank shook himself, and his eyes opened. He glanced around the unfamiliar place. In the light streaming through his window from the gaslight and a bright moon, he saw the flowered paper covering the walls above the wainscoting. Wind blew through the open window, and the curtains danced in the breeze. He glanced down. His body was trapped inside a cocoon of covers that wouldn't let him move. Frank snorted a derisive laugh. He must have been sleeping restlessly to become this entangled in his bedding.

Frank extricated himself from his bonds, got up, and walked to the window. Nothing moved outside, and the windows across the street were dark. He was probably the only person in town who was still awake.

The dream had seemed so real. He could almost smell the sweet woman who had thrown her arms around him and offered her lips for his kiss. He wished they had connected in the dream before he had awakened. Inner desires tormented him with things that could never happen.

Chapter 3

Frank knew this night would be a long, sleepless one. It was quite awhile before dawn, but he dressed anyway. He stood at the window, leaning with both hands on the window frame, and studied the quiet street below. In the dream, the house had looked like his parents' old homestead when he was a boy, only with new paint. Often, his mother had waited on the porch and watched for his father the same way the woman in his dream had. In fact, when he first saw her standing there, she was wearing a dress much like the ones his mother wore. Perhaps the dream was trying to tell him something. Was he was ready to settle down and have a family similar to the happy family he grew up in?

The moon had moved across the sky while he slept, and its beams highlighted the dress in the window across the street. It shone like a pearl on black velvet, nestled against the darkness of the store's interior. Now he realized it was the dress the woman in his dream wore.

With a disgusted shake of his head, Frank turned toward the door. Maybe a walk in the cold night air would clear his head of the thoughts that plagued him. He needed to focus on the reason he came to this town. When he stepped out of the front door of the hotel, a nippy breeze caused gooseflesh to rise on his arms. He didn't care. Taking a cheroot from his pocket, Frank struck a match to light it. After taking several draws on it, he realized it didn't give him the satisfaction he usually felt when he smoked. He looked at the glowing tip before he flicked it into the dirt of the alley he was passing. He smashed it with the heel of his boot before continuing. His steps caused too much noise when he walked on the boardwalk, so he stepped out into the street. Frank couldn't remember when he had ever felt so restless. It was something more than just being near the object of his search. He couldn't put a name on the feeling, but he didn't like it at all. He was used to being completely in control of his emotions as well as his body.

The moon was three-quarters full, and it was sinking near the horizon. Frank glanced toward the east and could see the first, faint predawn light. He wondered how long it would be before the restaurant at the hotel would start serving breakfast. He went back into the lobby and up to his room to stretch out on his bed and wait until he smelled food cooking.

When Gerda opened the Dress Emporium the next morning, Clarissa Jenson was her first customer. Gerda was glad that someone had come to the shop so early. It would help take her thoughts off the man who had invaded her dreams. Although they hadn't made any sense, his presence was overwhelming, clouding her mind.

"Clari!" Gerda and Anna had picked up the habit of calling the twin sisters by the shortened names they used for each other. "What brings you out so early in the morning?"

Clarissa gave Gerda a quick hug. "Ollie and I have the house fixed up the way we want it. It's a good thing, too." A dreamy expression covered Clarissa's face like a veil. "Soon there will be something else to take all my attention."

"You don't mean. . . ?" Gerda wondered if this couple was going to have a child before her brother August and his wife, Anna, would. The Nilssons had been married longer, and they wanted a child so much.

Clarissa nodded. "We're going to have a baby. So I need you to make me some clothes to wear while I'm expanding."

"I'm so happy for you." Gerda hugged Clarissa again. "You've had too many bad things happen in your life. I'm glad that has changed."

Clarissa stepped back and rubbed her hands down her skirt. "The good things started several months ago when Pierre was sent to prison—and when God brought Ollie into my life."

She went over to the counter where several fashion books were arranged and started leafing through one. "Do you have any ideas about what I'll need?"

"I always enjoy creating lovely clothing to help women hide their growing figures while they wait for the birth of their child." Gerda must have sounded wistful, because Clarissa looked concerned. Gerda didn't want her to think she was unhappy. "Why don't we go to the ice cream parlor to celebrate when we've finished choosing styles and materials?"

Clarissa walked to the display of fabrics on the shelves behind the counter and started running her fingers over different pieces, feeling their textures. "Actually, Mari and I are meeting there at ten o'clock, but you could join us. I'm afraid I've been craving one of those chocolate sundaes." She patted her flat stomach for emphasis. "Having a baby makes a woman want strange things sometimes. A couple of days ago, I mentioned to Ollie that I would really like one of the pickles from the barrel in the mercantile, and he came to town and bought some."

It took until almost ten o'clock for Clarissa to make up her mind about what fabrics to use for her new outfits. Gerda couldn't help remembering how concerned she and Anna had been when Rissa Le Blanc kept changing her mind about the colors and styles of the dresses they were making for her. How surprised they had been to find out that there was no Rissa Le Blanc! Instead, the twins were playing a part their stepfather had created. Finally, the two dress-makers understood. Although the twins looked a lot alike, their tastes were very different. Their styles fit their personalities. Clarissa was more outgoing, and Marissa was the quieter sister. Gerda loved both of them.

Frank fell into a deep, dreamless sleep just before dawn. When he finally awoke, he cleaned up before he went to the dining room to see if he could get a late breakfast. Some places served all day and others only at mealtime. He hoped this restaurant was one that didn't have specific hours.

Molly, who had waited on him the night before, met him at the door. "How can we help you, Mr. Daggett?"

"Molly, I'm afraid I overslept." He smiled at the older woman. "Do you think I could still get some breakfast?"

"Let me go ask Cook. I know she has started on lunch, but maybe she can do something for you. If not, I can make you some toast."

She headed toward the kitchen, and Frank sat down at a table near the window. He didn't think he could make it until lunch on only a couple pieces of toast, even if he loaded them with butter and jelly. A newspaper was lying on the table, so he picked it up and perused it until she returned.

"It just so happens that there is still some flapjack batter left. How does that sound?" A smile accompanied the waitress's question.

When Frank agreed, she returned to the kitchen. Before long, she came back, but she didn't have just buckwheat flapjacks with a tin of maple syrup. The cook was kind enough to make him bacon and eggs, too. He left the hotel forti-fied for a full day's activities.

The sun was high in the sky when he stepped onto the boardwalk. He pulled the brim of his Stetson low to shade his eyes from the glare off the windows across the street.

Frank glanced down toward the saloon. All seemed to be quiet on that end of town. When he looked across the street, he was astonished to see Rissa Le Blanc exiting that dress shop he had noticed the night before. It had to be her. She looked exactly like the drawing one of their victims had made of her. He was right. Pierre and the other girl, if there was another girl, must be nearby. Here in Litchfield, Minnesota. When Frank had first headed this direction, he had been afraid it was too far north for this Southern family. His gut instincts kept urging him on. And he had learned long ago to trust his instincts.

Frank had even started to wonder if he had lost his touch, but since they were here, now he knew he hadn't. All he had to do was keep an eye on this girl and let her lead him to Pierre. He wanted to catch that villain and make him and his accomplices pay for all the crimes they had committed.

Trying to act nonchalant, Frank sidled down the boardwalk in the direction the girl took. He kept his head down, so she wouldn't notice that he was watching her from under the brim of his hat. Soon the Le Blanc woman went into the ice cream parlor. He continued walking toward the store. When he reached it, he leaned against the wall and pulled his knife and a small block of wood from his pocket. While he whittled on the wood, he could keep up with what was going on inside.

After he took a few small shavings from the wood, he studied the ice cream parlor from the corners of his eyes. Rissa Le Blanc sat at a table near some planters that looked remarkably like brass spittoons. She looked at the door as if she were waiting for someone. Maybe Le Blanc. Frank's senses sharpened and his blood pumped through his veins at an accelerated rate. He took a deep breath and exhaled. He could almost smell victory.

From the doorway of the Dress Emporium, Gerda watched Clarissa walk across the street toward the ice cream parlor. When she started to turn back into the store, she saw the cowboy head up the street. He seemed to be watching Clari. Of course, she couldn't blame him. Clarissa was a very beautiful woman. When Clari went into the ice cream parlor, he sauntered toward it as if he were following her. He didn't look eager, as he might if he wanted to flirt with her. It was more like he was stalking her. Gerda got a funny feeling deep inside. Something wasn't quite right. She felt that Clarissa was in danger or. . .something. Maybe he was someone from Clarissa's past, someone who had been swindled. Gerda didn't think he was a lawman. Didn't they usually wear badges? He wasn't wearing one, although he did look more like a cowboy than he had at dinner last night. She could hear his spurs jingling as he walked down the boardwalk.

When he stopped and leaned against the building outside the ice cream parlor, she studied him intently. She wasn't sure, but she thought he was watching Clarissa, even though he looked like he was whittling. He looked as if he were a spring that was wound really tight.

Gerda stepped back inside and rushed into the back room for her wool cape and her reticule then went out the front door, trying to appear nonchalant. She locked the door to the Dress Emporium and hurried across the railroad tracks toward August's blacksmith shop. He would know what to do to protect Clarissa and Marissa.

When he noticed the beauty exiting the dress shop, Frank was distracted from both watching the Le Blanc girl and whittling. The woman turned and locked the front door of the store. *She must be the proprietor. No wonder the dress in the window would look good on her. She probably created it.*

The image of a woman pulling down the window shade above the dress shop returned to Frank's mind. It was probably her. Now that he thought about it, the bit of skirt he had seen did resemble what she'd worn at dinner last night. He had watched her long enough that he should have recognized it when he saw it later. He just wasn't thinking of her being there, so it hadn't occurred to him. Again, Frank wondered if anyone else lived there with her—like a husband or children.

When the woman swept down the street and past the depot, he wondered where she was going in such a hurry. He glanced back into the confectionary shop. Rissa Le Blanc still sat at a table by herself. He started whittling again. Someday, he needed to learn how to really make something when he whittled. For now, it was merely a ploy he used to appear busy when he was tailing someone. No one knew he just chipped small pieces off the block of wood until it was as small as a toothpick. Then he'd throw it away and start on another block.

He'd gotten the idea from watching his grandfather whittle when he was a small boy. The things that emerged from the blocks of wood Gramps worked on were wondrous. The toy soldiers, small animals, even sailing ships his grandfather had whittled had given Frank hours of enjoyment as a child. It was too bad he had never learned the craft from Gramps.

It was still a cool spring, but before Gerda arrived at the blacksmith shop, she wished she had left off the wool cape that matched her dress. She hurried because she didn't want to be too late meeting with Marissa and Clarissa. By the time she arrived at the open door of the smithy, she was almost out of breath. Her shadow must have alerted her brother to her presence, because he turned from what he was doing.

"Gerda, come in." A smile spread across August's face. "What can I do for you? Do you have something for me to fix?"

She put her hand to her throat and took a deep breath. "No, I don't need anything repaired. But I do need your help. I don't know what to do!"

August rushed over to her and looked deep into her eyes. "What has upset you?"

"Well, I don't know if it's anything or not." Her words tumbled out in rapid succession. "But that cowboy is following Clari, and I don't want anything to happen to her. Especially now that she's going to have a baby."

August looked confused. "Slow down, sister. You're talking too fast. Now what cowboy?"

Gerda pulled off the cape and draped it over her arm. "Well, there's this cowboy. He's new in town. He was at the hotel last night when we had dinner."

August nodded. "I saw him, but I didn't pay that much attention to him.

Why do you think he's following Clarissa?"

Suddenly, Gerda wondered if she had made too much out of what she'd seen. He could just be a drifter. Maybe he just happened to walk down the street after Clarissa did. It could all be merely a coincidence. What if she was mistaken? Deep inside, the worry wouldn't go away.

"He watched Clarissa go to the ice cream parlor. Then he followed her but stopped and leaned against the outside wall and started whittling. Then I got this uncomfortable feeling about it. I just don't want anything bad to happen to Clarissa or Marissa. They're meeting there for a treat."

August put his arm around her shoulders. "I've learned to trust women's intuition. Even if there isn't anything wrong, I'll go check it out." He went to the table and took off his apron. Then he banked the fire in the forge. He turned toward the door. "You go back to the store, and I'll take care of it."

Gerda shook her head. "I can't. I'm supposed to meet Clari and Mari at the ice cream parlor. We're going to celebrate together."

August laughed. "Oh, yes, you did mention something about a baby, didn't you?"

"Yes, she and Ollie are expecting. You don't think it'll make Anna feel bad, do you?"

"Don't worry about that." He closed the door and dropped the board into the holders. "She'll be happy for them. Our time will come. You go ahead, and I'll follow at a slower pace. I don't want the man to know we're together. Just be careful."

Chapter 4

While Frank watched the beauty walking rapidly down the road, he mechanically continued to work on the block of wood with his knife. He liked the way her hips swayed with each quick step. If only his life wasn't so complicated. He shook his head. The woman surely was a temptation to him. Suddenly, he felt the tip of the sharp blade nick his finger. The words that came to mind weren't suitable for mixed company, and there was more than one woman in his vicinity, so he kept them to himself. He looked down in time to see a large drop of blood leave his finger and make its way to the toe of his boot. He quickly closed his pocketknife with his other hand and shoved both it and the block of wood into his pocket.

Frank didn't want to leave his post, but he needed to take care of the wound he had carelessly inflicted on himself. How could he have been so stupid? He knew better than to let his mind wander. His finger was bleeding pretty fast now. He pulled out his bandanna and wrapped it around his fingertip. After glancing in the window of the ice cream parlor to make sure Rissa was still there, Frank started toward the hotel. She was sitting at the table and looked as if she were waiting for someone. Maybe Le Blanc would be here soon. But they couldn't know that he was looking for them. He should be able to make it to his hotel room and back before they were ready to leave the store.

While he was in his hotel room, he called himself all kinds of unflattering names for the harebrained stunt he had pulled. The tip of his finger was awkward to bandage, and now the digit throbbed enough to make him extremely uncomfortable. He might have a hard time pulling his gun with it, but at least it was his left hand. If he needed to use his guns quickly, he might only have one good trigger finger, but it should be enough. His aim was always on target. In his business, you often had only one chance before someone else shot you.

Frank glanced toward the ice cream parlor when he exited the hotel. Another girl, who looked remarkably like the one sitting at the table, was just going through the door. Only this young woman had on a different dress. Her hair was in a simpler style, too. He was right. How he wished the Old Man could see them. He'd change his tune now. There *were* two girls, and they were in that building together! Frank paused. Something didn't feel right. He had never heard of both of the young women showing themselves at the same time. He'd have to be careful. Maybe Litchfield was their base of operations and everyone here knew both of the young women. Maybe their neighbors didn't know what they did for a living.

He took up his post against the ice cream parlor, but this time Frank had left the block of wood in his hotel room. He started to pull out a cheroot. However, he didn't want to be smoking when they exited the shop. Frank reached up and pulled the brim of his Stetson lower.

Before his hand reached his headgear, the beauty from the Dress Emporium walked past him. She looked him straight in the eye. The disdain in her expression cut him just as much as the knife blade had cut his finger—maybe even more. Why did he care what she thought of him? She was just a pretty woman he had enjoyed watching. Nothing more. Right?

When Gerda first glanced toward the ice cream parlor, the cowboy was gone. She had probably bothered August for nothing. She wondered if she should go back and tell him. But she wasn't exactly sure where he was right now. She slowed down after she crossed the railroad tracks. It wouldn't look ladylike for her to rush down the street.

When the stranger emerged from the hotel and started down the street, she hoped he was going somewhere else. By the time she arrived at the ice cream parlor, he had taken up his post again, leaning against the wall. She gave him her most withering expression as she passed. Maybe he would take the hint and leave. Unfortunately, he just stared back at her, but his expression was unfathomable. If only his eyes weren't so blue. Each time she looked into them, they touched a place deep inside, piercing through all her defenses. Even though she suspected the cowboy of stalking Clarissa, Gerda felt drawn to him as she had never felt with any man before.

Gerda really wanted to enjoy her time with her friends, but it would be hard to forget that the cowboy was just outside the building. All the worries she harbored about him returned—and brought a few friends with them.

"Gerda." Clarissa smiled up at her when she stopped by the table where they sat. "I was about to think you weren't coming."

"I'm sorry I kept you waiting." Gerda pulled out a chair and sat with them. "What shall we order?" She always felt as if she were sitting in a park when she came to the ice cream parlor. The flowers on the mural painted around the wall were so realistic she could almost smell them.

The friends discussed all the offerings, then Gerda went to the counter to order a phosphate for herself and ice cream sundaes for both Marissa and Clarissa. Gerda had to wait behind a woman and young child who were having a hard time deciding what they wanted. After ordering, Gerda returned to the table where Clarissa and Marissa sat talking.

While they waited for the treats to be concocted, Marissa blurted, "I have a surprise to tell you." Both young women leaned forward, eager to hear. "I've just been to see Dr. Bradley."

"Oh, Mari, are you sick?" Clarissa exclaimed. She reached across the table and took her sister's hand.

"I hope not." Gerda cared about the twins as though they were her sisters.

"It's nothing like that." Marissa smiled and glanced down before raising her head again.

Clarissa looked worried. "Then why did you go to the doctor? Is something wrong with Lowell or Mother Jenson?"

Marissa laughed. "I can't keep the secret any longer. Lowell and I are going to have a baby."

For a moment they all talked at once, so no one could understand what anyone was saying. The proprietor brought their treats on a tray and set them on the table.

Marissa tasted the sundae, then looked from Gerda to Clarissa. "I am so happy. Both Lowell and I want lots of children. When I told him that I thought I might be expecting a baby, he wanted me to come right to town and have the doctor check. So I can't stay too long. He'll want to know what I found out."

"Mari, this is so wonderful!" Clarissa clapped her hands. She glanced at Gerda, then at her sister. "I'm going to have a baby, too! I found out for sure yesterday. Ollie is so proud, his chest puffed out like a peacock's."

Marissa's smile broadened more. "Oh, Clari, I'm so glad!"

Gerda watched the twins share a special look. They often did that, but today the look was different. Gerda knew it was because they were both expecting a child. Would she never get to share that feeling? Why was God denying her a husband and children when they were her heart's desire?

"Do you girls always do the same thing at the same time? Your husbands proposed to you on the same day. You had double weddings, and now you're both going to have a baby."

"It'll be wonderful for our babies to each have a cousin almost the same age." Clarissa reached across the table and took her sister's hand again.

"And one that lives so close, too," Marissa added, returning the strong grip.

The sisters started giggling. Soon Gerda joined them. Even with her disappointment, she was happy for her friends. Out of the corner of her eye, she could see that the young worker behind the counter was smiling at them. Soon the word would be all over town that everyone was having babies. Of course, in a town like Litchfield, it was hard to keep secrets.

The man standing outside the building came into Gerda's thoughts. She knew he was hiding something. She hoped that soon his secret would be revealed, too. Then the man could move on and her thoughts would return to normal. Wouldn't they?

Frank couldn't believe it. Not only did the beauty go into the ice cream parlor, but she sat at the table with the Le Blanc sisters. They were obviously close friends. Could she be in cahoots with them? Was she part of the gang? He didn't want to entertain that thought, but it wouldn't let him go. Time would tell.

Was Le Blanc coming to join them? While Frank kept watch on the women in the shop, he also scanned the street looking for the confidence man who had hoodwinked so many people across the country. The man was a menace to society. Le Blanc insinuated himself into a community, making the citizens think that he was someone important. He flashed money around and hosted parties until everyone he considered special in that town knew him. Then Le Blanc pulled a fast one on his victims. Now Frank knew how he had accomplished it. Exactly the way Frank had figured it out a few months earlier. Today was the first time he had evidence that his theory was correct.

Le Blanc only let the people in town meet one of his daughters. Then during some kind of community event, the other daughter robbed many of the people who were in attendance. If anyone saw her, Le Blanc had proof that his daughter was with him at the event. He soon left town, and no one was sure who had committed the robberies. In some of the towns, the sheriff was still looking for another perpetrator of the crimes.

Frank wondered which of the young women at the table was actually Rissa. What was the other woman's name? Did both of them participate in the crimes, or only one? He hoped he would find out when he took them into custody later today.

The only fly in the ointment was the presence of the other woman—the beauty. Last night he had been so sure that she was a decent, upright citizen. How could he have been so wrong? Was she Le Blanc's mistress or accomplice. . .or just his friend? If she was a proprietor here in Litchfield, how did she fit in the picture of the other places where Le Blanc had been? Or was she just a new acquaintance of the gang? He sure hoped so. It was going to hurt him to have to take her into custody. But a lawman always did his duty, even when it hurt. And no matter if the Old Man had made him turn in his badge, he was still a lawman at heart.

Frank glanced up and down the street again. He had watched several people go in, then come out of the mercantile carrying packages wrapped in brown paper. Several people came and went at the bank. Wagons and men on horseback traveled up and down the street at frequent intervals. When Frank had first seen Litchfield on the horizon, it had looked like a sleepy town, but he had been wrong about that. It was a thriving, vital town. It seemed like a nice place to live and bring up a family. That woman in the ice cream parlor was affecting him. He hadn't had so many thoughts about a family in a long time.

If Le Blanc was going to join the women, Frank wished the scoundrel would do it soon. Frank was getting tired of standing in this spot. He peeked into the window. The young women were busy talking. It didn't look as if they would be ready to leave any time soon. Frank decided to stroll up and down the street. He could look into the windows of other businesses to see if he could spot Le Blanc. Maybe by the time he got back here, the women would be finished visiting. He would keep a sharp eye on the place and not get too far away in case they came out.

Gerda saw the cowboy when he walked past the front of the store. It was all she could do to keep from shouting, she was so glad to see him go. Perhaps it was just a coincidence that he came along when he did. He just happened to choose to lean against this building. That's all.

"What do you think, Gerda?" Clarissa's words brought Gerda's attention back to the conversation at the table.

"About what? I'm afraid I was distracted."

Clarissa looked toward the window. "What distracted you, Gerda? Was it that cowboy walking down the street?"

Gerda hoped she wasn't that obvious. "Of course not." After a good laugh, she asked what they had been talking about.

"Marissa wants you to make her some clothes, too. Will you have time to do both?"

"It would be my pleasure. Besides, Anna still comes in to work a couple of days a week. She has her hands full keeping up that big house, and she helps Olina with the children sometimes."

"Let's go back to the Dress Emporium so Marissa can pick out her fabrics and styles," said Clarissa. Gerda stood and glanced across the shop toward the now-empty counter.

"I'm going to pay for our treats. Just wait for me."

When she got back to the table, both of the sisters were standing. As the trio stepped out into the sunlight, their eyes had to adjust to the brightness.

"Just hold it right there!" The rich baritone voice came from behind Gerda, and expressions of horror covered Marissa's and Clarissa's faces as they stared over her shoulder.

Gerda turned to see what was going on and came face-to-face with the cowboy. The man had both of his six-shooters trained on the women!

Chapter 5

Frank watched the three women finish their treats. When they seemed ready to leave the building, he pulled his hat lower on his forehead and turned to wait for them. His body was wound tight as an eight-day clock as he watched them glide toward the door as though they were walking on clouds. His hands hovered near his pistols while he tried to figure out how to handle the next few minutes. He hadn't seen the sheriff or Le Blanc, and now that he was so close, he worried that the women were about to slip away from him. How was he ever going to keep up with three women? If they split up, which one should he follow? Which one would lead him to Le Blanc? Before he could decide, the women were at the entrance. Making a lightning-quick decision, he pulled his guns. It would be better to have the three women in custody than to let any of them get away to warn Pierre. Maybe Le Blanc would come out of hiding to rescue them. Frank hoped so. The women stepped outside and froze with shocked expressions on their faces.

"Just hold it right there!" Frank bit out. "You're all under arrest."

The beauty was the first to react. "Arrest!" she screamed as she whirled toward him. Frank was surprised at the volume of her shriek. "You can't arrest us! We're not criminals! Besides, you aren't a lawman!"

Frank didn't know what kind of reaction he had expected, but it wasn't this. Why couldn't they just come quietly? He didn't want to create a disturbance. He simply planned to apprehend them, take them to the sheriff, then slip out of town. There was no need for anyone besides the sheriff and the Le Blanc gang to even know why he was here—or that he wasn't a real lawman anymore. Because he didn't want any of them to get away, Frank didn't dare look to see if anyone else in the street had noticed the hullabaloo.

"I'm a retired U.S. Marshal, and I'm taking you to the sheriff." Frank tried to keep his voice low but authoritative.

"We'll go to the sheriff with you," the beauty said just as quietly, then took a deep breath as if fortifying herself. "He'll straighten this all out."

Suddenly, a strong arm snaked around Frank's neck, almost choking him. Who could it be, and how did the man get there without making any noise on the boardwalk?

The man holding him was much larger than and too strong to be Le Blanc.

Muscles bulged as the man's arm tightened around Frank's neck. Quickly, Frank holstered one gun and fought to pull the arm from around his neck so he could breathe easier. It tightened even more. Breathing was becoming more difficult for Frank. Black spots danced before his eyes, and he dropped the other gun. He heard it bounce off the boardwalk and hit the dirt street.

A deep voice sounded from over his shoulder. "Gerda, take the gun from his holster, and I'll let him go."

Frank hoped she would hurry. He didn't want to pass out right here in the middle of town. Just as he was about to lose consciousness, he felt the gun being lifted away. The arm around his neck loosened slightly, and his vision cleared in time to see the beauty raising the pistol, which she then pointed straight at him.

Frank was glad no one he knew lived in this town. He would never be able to live down the fact that he'd let a criminal, a female one at that, get the drop on him.

When August told her to get the gun, Gerda straightened her spine and stood taller. She didn't have to be afraid of the man while August held him. She reached over and took the weapon gingerly. When she felt its weight in her hand, something happened. It gave her a sense of power. She lifted the barrel and turned it toward the cowboy. *Let's see how you like having a gun pointed at you.* She glanced at August and nodded.

"All right, cowboy, I'm going to let you go, but don't make any sudden movements or Gerda will shoot you."

Gerda couldn't believe what August said. She would never shoot anyone. And even though she knew she shouldn't, Gerda felt something for this cowboy. She wasn't sure what it was, but she couldn't shoot him even if he did make a sudden move. Whatever she felt for him, it made her uncomfortable. A vision of the barrel of a gun pointed at her temple returned, and something inside her snapped.

"How could you?" She waved the barrel of the gun toward him. "What were you trying to do with these guns? Kill innocent women?" The look on the man's face would have been comical to Gerda if she hadn't been so angry. "I can't believe I felt so drawn to you when I first saw you. You're nothing but a common criminal yourself."

Gerda glanced from the gun in her hand toward the man's face. The expression in his eyes reached out to her, and she burst into tears. Clarissa grabbed the gun from Gerda and turned it back toward the cowboy. August pulled the man's hands behind his back and held them with one giant hand. He turned the cowboy toward the sheriff's office, and they started walking.

Marissa pulled a handkerchief from her reticule and gave it to Gerda. Then she patted her friend on the back. Gerda was mortified. People were staring. Some were whispering among themselves. She didn't think she would ever live this down. Marissa took her arm, and they followed the others toward the sheriff's office.

Sheriff Bartlett must have heard the disturbance, because he was running toward them.

❧

Frank didn't know when he had ever been so glad to see a sheriff. Now the man would rescue him from this gang. But something wasn't quite right. If they were criminals, why did the strong man want to take him to the sheriff—unless he was part of the gang, too? *Maybe the whole town is in on this with the Le Blancs. Stay calm, Frank. Don't lose your edge.*

When they were all inside the small office, the sheriff offered his only two chairs to the Le Blanc sisters. "I'm sorry I don't have another chair, Gerda." He smiled at the beauty, and Frank didn't like the way it made him feel.

Gerda. Frank liked the sound of her name. It fit her Scandinavian good looks.

"It's all right." She paced across the small space. "I'm too upset to sit down."

The burly man who had grabbed Frank in front of the ice cream parlor put his arm around Gerda. Frank didn't like that either. Was this woman some kind of doxy? How could she seem so pure and untouched if she was that kind of woman?

"Calm down, sis." The big man's words were a balm to Frank's troubled heart. She was the man's sister. But that didn't clear up anything. They could still both be part of the Le Blanc gang.

The sheriff took Frank's gun from Clarissa. He laid it on his desk. At least it was no longer pointed at Frank.

"Now who's going to tell me what's going on?" The sheriff held up one hand. "And I want to hear one person at a time. Clarissa Jenson, since you were holding the gun on this man, why don't you start?"

Jenson. Her name was Jenson, not Le Blanc. Frank's jumbled thoughts kept him from hearing all the woman said.

"And he was pointing his guns at us," she finished.

"Where is his other gun?" The sheriff looked at each person in turn.

The other twin, who seemed more reserved, spoke up. "I have it. When August grabbed him, it fell into the street, so I picked it up. . .in case we needed it, too. I didn't like touching it, so I put it in my reticule to carry it over here."

"Mari, you hate guns!" The Jenson woman looked at her sister with a worried expression on her face.

"I know, but I couldn't let him hurt Gerda or August."

The woman was trembling like a maple leaf in the breeze. She pulled the gun from her handbag and, holding it between her thumb and forefinger, gave it to the sheriff. He placed it beside the one on his desk.

377

"Thank you, Marissa." The lawman looked at Frank. "All right. Who are you, and why are you bothering these fine folks?"

Frank stared the man straight in his eyes. They weren't shifty. The corrupt lawmen he had known before wouldn't look him in the eyes. This man did. Maybe he was honest. Frank had to take that chance.

"Frank Daggett, former U.S. Marshal. I've been on the trail of a gang of robbers who have carried out confidence games in many states. I have documents detailing their crimes which I intended to deliver to you once I had placed the gang in your custody." He stopped at the irony—it had turned out a little different than he'd anticipated.

Frank looked at the sisters as he gestured toward them. He was sure they would be cowering in their chairs. Instead, they were smiling. Maybe he had made a mistake. His glance shot back to the sheriff, and he was smiling, too. A sense of doom settled over Frank. Why hadn't he stopped when the Old Man told him to?

He heard a burst of laughter. The brother and sister were almost doubled over with mirth. The sheriff's guffaw joined theirs.

When Frank turned to look at him, the lawman was holding Frank's guns out to him. "You might as well take these, since you're not a criminal."

Frank returned his weapons to their holsters, then asked, "Is anyone going to let me in on what's so amusing here?"

The sheriff sat on the corner of his desk. "You drew your guns on these three women because you thought they were criminals. Right?"

Frank nodded.

When he did, Gerda glared at him. "You thought *I* was a criminal?" She placed her fisted hands on her waist with her arms akimbo.

He nodded again, unable to voice the answer to the question.

"I've never been so insulted in my life." She whirled around and started toward the door.

Her brother followed her, and the sheriff turned toward the twin sisters. "I wouldn't want Lowell and Ollie to think you were in trouble. You can go, too. I'll explain everything to Mr. Daggett."

The door closed behind them, and the sheriff looked at Frank. "This is really something! You're about," he said as he counted on his fingers, "six months too late."

Frank felt as if he had stepped into the middle of a discussion and had been asked a question about what had gone on before. "I don't understand. Six months too late for what?"

"Maybe you should sit down while I tell you all about it." The sheriff motioned toward the chair that had recently been vacated by one of the twins. "Actually,

I admire your tenacity—to follow Le Blanc's trail so faithfully."

Frank ducked his head and rubbed the back of his neck. Tenacity. That's what he had all right. The Old Man had often told him that he was like an old dog with a bone.

"Pierre Le Blanc is a very evil man." The sheriff propped his booted feet on the corner of his desk and leaned back in his chair. "He planned to rob the good folks of Litchfield, just as you figured."

"What stopped him?"

"Well, it was a lot of things. People in this town had become fond of Rissa Le Blanc—especially the Nilsson family." The sheriff dropped his feet back on the floor and leaned forward as if eager to get on with the story. "None of us knew that there were two girls, and neither one of them was really Rissa Le Blanc. Pierre, their stepfather, called whichever one was in town with him 'Rissa.' It was part of each of their names. Clarissa and Marissa. Is this getting too confusing for you?"

Frank leaned his forearms on his thighs. "I had pretty much decided there had to be two girls. That was the only way he could get away with all he did."

The sheriff chuckled. "The man was clever. I'll give him that. He kept one girl in a camp quite a ways from town in an area where not many people ventured. He planned to rob the town while most everyone was at the circus. It was the first time the circus had ever come here, so it was a good plan."

Frank's interest was piqued. "Then what went wrong with his plan?"

"This is where it gets complicated." The sheriff laughed. "Both of the Jenson brothers had a hankering for Rissa Le Blanc. It caused a lot of friction between them."

"I can understand that. They're good-looking women." Frank sat back in the chair and propped one foot on the other knee.

"Lowell is the quieter brother. He decided to go camping to think about things, and he stumbled across their camp. Le Blanc had left both girls there, which they later said was unusual. Lowell went back to the farm to get his brother. When they returned, they learned about Le Blanc's scheme and convinced the girls to help us catch Pierre in the act."

"That could have been dangerous, couldn't it?"

"Yes, but the girls felt as if they were their stepfather's prisoners. It was a way for them to finally be free of him." The sheriff stood up. "So that's why you are six months too late. That's when we had the trial that put Le Blanc in prison for life."

Frank stood up, too. "What can you tell me about the Nilssons?"

"That's another interesting family. Good folks. They came from Sweden, originally." The sheriff sat on the front corner of his desk. "There are three brothers and one sister. Gustaf works the farm with his dad, August is the blacksmith in town, and Lars moved to Denver. Gerda is part owner of the Dress

Emporium. She lives in an apartment above the store."

The door burst open, and Hank, the owner of the livery stable, came in. "Sheriff, I need to talk to you." He stopped short when he noticed Frank. "Sorry, I didn't mean to interrupt."

"That's all right." Frank picked up his hat from the floor beside where he had been sitting. "I was just going." He turned toward the sheriff. "I'll buy you coffee sometime, Sheriff."

When Frank arrived at the hotel, everyone in the lobby looked at him as he headed toward the stairs at the back of the room. Just what he needed. Everyone in town would talk about him until something happened to take their minds off what he'd done. He hoped that event would come soon. Of course, Frank could leave town now. The Old Man might give him his badge back. Probably, the Old Man already knew about Le Blanc being in prison and was expecting Frank to come back. But he didn't want to leave town without trying to get to know Gerda Nilsson. Frank wondered why no man had claimed her for his own. She seemed to be beautiful through and through. How could he ever have thought Gerda was a fallen woman? He was going to have to make that thought up to her somehow.

Frank paused with his boot resting on the bottom step. He glanced at the desk clerk. Just as Frank suspected, the man was watching him. When Frank looked at him, he quickly averted his gaze to something behind the counter.

After raking his fingers down his bristly cheek, Frank decided that what he needed most was a bath and shave. "Would you have hot water sent up to my room?"

The desk clerk glanced up at him. "Yes, sir."

Frank continued up the carpeted staircase. It was a good thing the Jenson brothers found the campsite and rescued the sisters from Le Blanc's clutches. It was a shame that their stepfather had been able to hold them in servitude. The sheriff had assured Frank that even though it had gone on so many years, the young women hadn't become corrupted. If Frank believed in a God, he would have been sure that God had protected them all that time. But Frank had never been able to believe that a loving God would allow all the bad things he'd seen in his lifetime. He could remember his mother and grandmother praying for him when he was a little boy, but when he left home, he put all that behind him.

After he had scraped the whiskers from his cheeks, he gathered up his clothes and went down the hall to the bathroom. At least this hotel had all the modern amenities. Some of the places Frank had stayed didn't. In those places, the proprietor hauled up a large galvanized tub and lots of hot water for a person to take a bath in the bedroom.

Frank immersed himself in the warm water and began to lather his arms.

with the lye soap. It would have been nice to have something a little kinder to his skin. Maybe he would go to the mercantile and see what they had for sale. He could buy something better to use. That was a good excuse to go to the store. What reason could he use to go into the Dress Emporium? He had never been to a circus. Maybe he could ask Gerda about it.

Gerda swept through the door of the sheriff's office, glad that August accompanied her. Out on the street, everyone stared at the two of them while they walked to the Dress Emporium. She was tempted to keep the store closed. She didn't want anyone coming in asking questions. Wasn't it enough that they were the spectacle of the day?

However, Clarissa and Marissa were coming to choose patterns and fabrics for Marissa's new clothing. Gerda couldn't turn them away.

If she could only keep from thinking about that cowboy—that former U.S. Marshal. The gall of the man, thinking she was a criminal! How could she ever have been drawn to him? God surely had a man in mind for her, and he wouldn't be someone who could think something like that about her. Gerda hoped she would never see the man again. Maybe he would leave town as soon as he knew the whole story. It couldn't be soon enough for her.

Chapter 6

When Frank finished bathing and dressing, he went to Braxton's Mercantile. He was pleasantly surprised to see all the merchandise the store had to offer. He had been in a lot of businesses scattered all across the country. This establishment would compare favorably with many in large cities like Chicago. He hadn't thought he would find such an assortment of high-quality goods tucked away here in the heart of Minnesota. Frank browsed through the sundries and picked up some scented coal tar soap. He held the paper wrapping to his nose to check the fragrance. It had a nice, masculine aroma, and coal tar soap was easy on the skin. Sitting on the shelf alongside the bath soap was an assortment of shaving bars and brushes. The brush he had been using was wearing out, so he chose one with bristles that didn't seem too soft or too stiff. Since no one else was nearby, he tested it by swirling it against his cheek. It felt good, so he added it and two bars of shaving soap to the things he was carrying and headed toward the counter at the back of the store.

At that point, Frank realized that several other people were shopping in the large establishment. He could feel their eyes trained on him. He didn't want to turn around and see if they were talking about him. The walk toward the man at the counter was uncomfortable. Frank didn't like to be the center of attention, and he wondered why he hadn't just stayed in his hotel room until everyone forgot what happened.

Frank had been talked about before, but he didn't like it. He held his head a little higher and continued down an aisle between shelves containing an assortment of men's clothing. Perhaps it was time to replenish his wardrobe. He'd kept his possessions to a minimum while he was on the trail of the gang. How long had it been now? Frank didn't want to think about the number of years that he had wasted chasing a phantom.

He would have to make some decision soon about what to do now. He could go and ask the Old Man for his job back, but Frank wasn't sure that was what he wanted to do. When the talk died down, Litchfield, Minnesota, might be the place for him to settle into a normal life. If it wasn't too late for that. And gnawing at the back of his mind were the words Gerda had blurted when she was holding the gun on him. She'd felt the same strong sense of connection he had that first time he laid eyes on her in the hotel lobby.

When he reached the counter, the man behind it smiled at him. *That's a good sign.* Frank decided to act as if nothing out of the ordinary had happened.

"I'm Frank Daggett." He set the soaps and brush on the wooden structure. The man with sandy red hair and lots of freckles had blue eyes that sparkled with friendliness.

"Glad to meet you, Mr. Daggett. I'm Claude Dawson." He reached for the merchandise Frank had laid on the counter.

"This is a real nice store you have here, Mr. Dawson." Frank turned and perused the rest of the refreshingly clean establishment while he leaned on the counter with one arm.

"Oh, I'm not the proprietor." The clerk shook his head. "I work for the Braxtons. Please call me Claude."

Frank straightened away from the counter and smiled back. "All right, Claude. If someone wanted to settle in Litchfield, what is there to do here?"

Claude looked him up and down as if assessing his attributes. "Well, I'm just working to make enough money to move to California. I almost have enough saved, so you could take my place here. Or there are a couple of businesses for sale. What have you done before?"

Frank decided that maybe the sheriff was a closemouthed man if word of what happened hadn't even reached the clerk in the store. "I've been in law enforcement, but I want to settle down. I like the looks of the town."

"Claude, did you receive my shipment from Boston?" The feminine voice sounded from across the room, but it was coming closer. "I need it as soon as. . ."

As the melodious words stopped abruptly, Frank turned and smiled. "Hello, Gerda."

⁓

When had that lawman come into the store? Gerda felt flustered. She probably hadn't recognized him because he had cleaned up since their infamous encounter earlier that morning. She couldn't keep from staring into his blue eyes. The clear, icy color had turned warm in a way she hadn't anticipated. She wanted to look away, but she couldn't tear her gaze from his eyes. *Animal magnetism.* That's what that man had. Where had she heard that term? Probably in one of those dime novels she had been reading since Anna had moved out of the apartment. The man's body was sleek, like a cougar, all sinews and strength.

Gerda could feel heat make its way up her neck and into her cheeks. She couldn't just stand here and gawk at the man. Why was he still here? Didn't the sheriff tell him what had happened?

"No." Claude's voice penetrated the fog in Gerda's brain. "The freight wagon hasn't come from the station yet. I'm not even sure if the train has arrived. Maybe it's behind schedule."

I have to get out of here. "Thank you, Claude." She wheeled and hurried back to her own store. All the way, she could feel the cowboy's gaze on her back. When she arrived in the workroom, she leaned against the wall and tried to catch her breath. Why didn't the man just leave town? There wasn't anything here for him. She fanned her face with her hand then pressed it to her chest to try to slow her racing heartbeat. If he left right now, it wouldn't be too soon for her.

Gerda. Frank rolled her name around in his head as he headed to his hotel room with his purchases from the mercantile. *Gerda Nilsson.* A name that fit her Nordic beauty. If he were to settle here, maybe he could build a relationship with her. Of course, it might not be a good idea. He had experienced so much of the hard side of life, and seen even more, that he wasn't sure he was fit to establish a relationship with a woman like her. She was the kind of woman he had dreamed about all his life, but now that he had met her, he didn't feel worthy.

Frank couldn't stay cooped up in this hotel room, even if it was a nice, large one. He put on his Stetson and stepped out on the boardwalk. He had only seen this end of town and the street down to the livery. If he explored more, maybe he could work off some of his nervous energy.

When he walked by the sheriff's office, the man stepped out the door. After giving Frank an appraising glance, he commented, "You clean up real nice. I would hardly recognize you as the man who came into my office earlier today."

Frank liked the man's wry humor. During their previous discussion, Frank had come to appreciate the older man's thoroughness in dealing with hard topics. "I couldn't go around town looking like I'd been on a cattle drive."

Sheriff Bartlett stepped back a little and gestured toward the interior of the building. "Would you like to come in for a cup of coffee? I keep a pot on the stove. Of course, it won't be as good as you get in the hotel, but it's hot and black."

Frank followed him into the dimly lit room. The sheriff took a clean mug from the shelf on the wall near the stove. After pouring the steaming brew, he handed the white cup to Frank. He took a quick taste. It wasn't bad at all.

"So what are you going to do now?" the sheriff asked after he set his own cup on the desk. "Go back into the marshal service?" Bartlett sat in the chair behind his desk and crossed his booted ankles on top of the desk. He placed his hands behind his head and leaned back, looking Frank straight in the eyes.

Frank dropped into a chair that sat near an open jail cell. "I've considered it."

"You shouldn't have any problem getting back on. Good men are hard to find, and you are persistent," the sheriff added with a chuckle.

Frank glanced out the open door at a wagon that was coming down the street. A man and woman sat on the seat, and several children dangled their legs off the back. "I've been thinking about settling down. I was planning on walking around town. From what I've seen of it, Litchfield might be a good town to settle in."

"Yep," the sheriff agreed. "Most of the time, it is. We don't often have events like the Le Blanc incident." The man dropped his feet back onto the floor with a thud. "How about if I walk along with you? I could give you a personal guided tour."

Frank took a big swig of the cooling beverage and looked down into the nearly empty mug. "You got some place where I can rinse this out?"

"Don't worry about it." Bartlett rose and reached for his hat. "The deputy will take the cups home, and his wife will wash them with her dishes." He led the way out the door.

The sheriff took Frank down the street in the direction he had already been. The lawman introduced him to all of the proprietors along the way.

Soon they arrived at the barbershop. "I really could use a trim." Frank reached up, removed his hat, and pushed some curls off his forehead.

"Let's go in and chat awhile with Silas." Frank followed the sheriff as he stepped through the doorway. "I've brought you a customer," he said to the man behind the chair.

"Just have a seat over there." The barber pointed with his scissors, then he went back to snipping and talking to the man sitting in front of him.

By the time Silas was finished cutting Frank's hair, Frank knew more than he really wanted to know about most of the people in town. What was it about barbers that they liked to talk so much?

"Do you want to go into the saloon?" Sheriff Bartlett asked when they were back out on the sidewalk. "They serve lunch there, and there aren't too many people drinking at this time of day."

Frank followed him through the swinging doors. It had been quite awhile since he had stepped into a saloon. He had forgotten how they smelled. No matter how much they cleaned up a bar, they couldn't get the smell of liquor and tobacco smoke out of the wood. Frank used to like to drink, but he hadn't had time while he was following Le Blanc. He had needed all his wits about him in case he ever found the scoundrel.

A barmaid dressed in red satin brought bowls of stew and some corn bread to the two men after they were seated at a round table. She smiled at Frank and leaned over farther than was necessary when she set his food down. Maybe he had been feasting his eyes on pure women long enough that she seemed tawdry and pitiful to him. He turned his attention to his companion, and the woman walked away in a huff. If Frank decided to settle down here, he knew he wouldn't be frequenting this establishment. He started eating quickly because he wanted the meal over as soon as possible. The sheriff was eating pretty fast, too.

Once Gerda got her heartbeat to settle down, she decided to close the shop.

Anna wasn't coming today, and Gerda had to eat lu___. She went upstairs and pulled out the bread she had made two days bef___. It didn't look that inviting, but she had to eat something. While she s___ambled some eggs, she grilled two pieces of bread in a buttered skillet. Some days she went to the hotel to keep from having to cook for one. August had taken her to the boardinghouse to eat with him several times, too. But today she didn't want to be around other people. Too many things had happened to upset her. For a day that had started with so much promise, it really had deteriorated quickly. The bright part of the day had been spending time with Marissa and Clarissa.

It was wonderful that the sisters were going to have babies. However, that thought brought a sharp pain to Gerda's heart. The pain was followed by the image of the cowboy talking to Claude in the store downstairs. Every detail of how he looked was vivid in her mind's eye. He was no longer dressed like a trail bum. He was even more devastatingly handsome dressed in nice clothes, although curls still fell across his broad forehead, almost reaching his eyes. What was there about him that was different from the other men she had known? They all paled in comparison to his good looks. But looks weren't everything.

After choking down the last of her eggs and toasted bread, Gerda went into the parlor and picked up her Bible. She clutched it to her chest and dropped her chin against it. "Father God, please help me. Please tell me that You have a man picked out for me. I have been patient, but now my desire for a husband and family has brought temptation into my life. I feel undeniably drawn to an unacceptable man. God, please take away the temptation. Father, it would be a blessing if the man would just leave town today. Help me be strong. In Jesus' name, amen."

Gerda knew that God heard her, but the prayer seemed to hang in the air around her. She sighed. When she opened her Bible, it fell open to the sixth chapter of Second Corinthians. Soon, verses 14 through 18 jumped out at her.

> *Be ye not unequally yoked together with unbelievers: for what fellowship hath righteousness with unrighteousness? and what communion hath light with darkness? And what concord hath Christ with Belial? or what part hath he that believeth with an infidel? And what agreement hath the temple of God with idols? for ye are the temple of the living God; as God hath said, I will dwell in them, and walk in them; and I will be their God, and they shall be my people. Wherefore come out from among them, and be ye separate, saith the Lord, and touch not the unclean thing; and I will receive you, and will be a Father unto you, and ye shall be my sons and daughters, saith the Lord Almighty.*

Gerda knew she should not feel drawn to that man. For some reason, she was sure he was not a Christian. She knew that when God brought a man into her life for her to marry, he wouldn't be an unbeliever. She had to fight this strong attraction she felt for the former lawman.

After sitting there for a few more minutes, Gerda put her Bible on the table beside her rocking chair. She stepped out on the platform at the top of the stairs and turned around to lock her door. As she turned and glanced down the street, she saw the man she had been thinking about come out of the saloon. *It must be a sign from God. He must be showing me that the man is not a godly man.* With a firm nod of her head, she walked down the stairs to open the shop.

When Frank stepped through the swinging doors of the saloon after he and the sheriff had finished their meals, his gaze was drawn to the staircase that led up the side of the mercantile building. Gerda Nilsson stood on the platform at the top, and she was looking his direction. Why had he agreed to go into the saloon with the sheriff? Instinctively he knew she would not like the fact that he was there. It would probably be a setback that would be hard to overcome in his pursuit of the woman of his dreams.

"If you were to settle here, what would you do?" The sheriff's question drew Frank's attention from his thoughts.

"I don't have to go to work immediately. I've saved most of the money I've made over the years. It will give me time to look around and find just the right business to invest in." Frank glanced once again toward the mercantile building, but Gerda was nowhere in sight.

The sheriff walked a few steps without saying anything. "There are a few possibilities. I could introduce you to the owners."

Frank nodded. "That would be nice. And I'm going to need a place to live. Although the hotel is nice, it's not a home."

The sheriff seemed to be lost in thought. After a few minutes of the two men walking back through town, he finally made a suggestion. "I've run down the list of the houses I know to be empty. If you want a wife and family, your best bet might be Mrs. Nichols's home."

"Why do you say that?" Frank's interest was piqued.

"Well, it's pretty new, and it hasn't been lived in very long. Would you like to see it?"

At Frank's agreement, the sheriff led the way to the lawyer's office where they obtained a key to the house, then he accompanied Frank across the railroad tracks and into an area that was mostly homes.

"This area is really pretty." Frank looked at the trees whose branches stretched across the street, almost meeting. "I like all the shade."

Sheriff Bartlett nodded. "That's why I've stayed around here. I think you'll like this house. Oliver Nichols had been a widower for several years. He didn't have any children, so he was lonely. Everyone thought he was crazy when he advertised in several newspapers for a bride."

"Sometimes that works, but sometimes it doesn't," Frank agreed. "Did he get many answers?"

The lawman turned to his right down another tree-lined street. "I don't guess anyone knows how many he got. He didn't share them with anyone. At least we know that a young woman from Ohio answered. They kept up quite a correspondence while Oliver had the house built for her. After it was finished, everyone in town was invited to the large wedding. It was a really happy affair."

"So what happened?"

"They had only lived in the house a few months when Oliver died of a heart attack. His grieving widow soon returned to Ohio to live with her parents."

"How long ago was that?" Frank wondered if the house would be in disrepair since it had sat empty for a long time.

"It was only a little over a year ago."

The neighborhood was dotted with mature trees that were just beginning to bud. When the sheriff stopped in front of a white wooden fence, Frank turned to look the same direction. Situated at the end of that area of town, the house, which was set back quite a ways from the street, was surrounded by a small grove of trees. Through the nearly bare branches, Frank glimpsed the second story and attic complete with gables and lots of gingerbread decorations. It was just the kind of house that needed a family.

"It doesn't look as though it is vacant." Frank turned toward his companion. "It's been well taken care of."

"The lawyer sees that it is. No one wants to buy a derelict home."

Frank nodded. "I understand that. But why hasn't it sold before now?"

The sheriff led the way up the stepping-stones toward the structure. "It's more house than most new people in town want right away. And the price is a little too high for most folks. I hope that's not a problem for you."

"If I like it, I'm sure the price wouldn't be a deterrent."

After touring the home, Frank knew he was going to buy it. Whether he made any headway with Gerda Nilsson or not, he wanted to live in this house. Someday he'd fill it with a family. The two men started back down the street toward the business part of town so Frank could talk to the lawyer about the house.

"You know," the sheriff said, "maybe the good Lord kept this house available for you. He's been known to do things like that."

Frank didn't know about the "good Lord" part of the sheriff's statement, but he was glad the house was still vacant. After conducting his business with the lawyer, Frank went to the bank to make arrangements to have his money transferred to Litchfield. Then he proceeded to the depot to send a telegram to his bank manager, who was a close family friend, back East. He told him to send the contents of his safe-deposit box in a strongbox on the train. If Frank was going to settle in Litchfield, he needed to have all his assets here.

August came into the Dress Emporium just as Gerda finished giving a customer her new clothes. She went to give her brother a hug when the other woman left the shop.

"I'm glad to see you." She stood back and looked up into his kind eyes. "Is Anna well?"

"Yes. She's fine, just not feeling too good this morning. So she won't be in today."

Gerda moved behind the counter and placed the roll of brown wrapping paper back under it. "You didn't have to come all the way over here just to tell me that. I don't expect her until I see her coming."

August leaned his crossed arms on the polished wood. She knew he did that so they would be closer to the same height. He must have something important to tell her.

She stopped what she was doing and looked at him. "What do you want to talk about?"

"You can read me like a book, can't you?" August gave a nervous laugh.

"So what is it?"

August stood away from the counter and stuffed his hands in the pockets of his trousers, another sure sign of his nervousness. "You know how you told me that you're saving your money to buy Mrs. Nichols's house?"

Gerda nodded. For some reason, she knew she wasn't going to like what he had to say. "I almost have enough for a good down payment. Their lawyer said that I could pay part of it off monthly."

August shuffled his feet. "You can't now."

"And why not?" Gerda wished he'd get to the point instead of talking around a subject.

August looked at the brightly colored fabrics that lined the shelves behind Gerda. He couldn't even look her in the eyes. She sighed. Now she knew she wouldn't want to hear whatever he had to say.

"Frank Daggett bought the house."

"Frank Daggett?" Gerda realized that her question was loud and shrill, but she didn't care. "You mean that cowboy lawman?" Maybe August was wrong. Maybe it wasn't too late for her to buy it. Gerda crossed her arms to keep them from trembling. "How do you know that?"

August patted her on the shoulder. "I know it hurts, but it's true. The sheriff's horse threw a shoe, so he came into the blacksmith shop. He told me about spending the day with Frank showing him around town the other day. Frank wants to settle here, so he bought the house. All the papers are signed, and the money should be here soon."

When August finally left, Gerda wanted to crawl into her bed, pull the quilt up over her head, and cry like a baby. Why did that man have to turn her life upside down again? She had hoped that he would leave town soon, but that wasn't going to happen. What was she going to do now?

As if her thoughts had taken on human form, Frank Daggett walked through the front door of the Dress Emporium. Gerda stood behind the counter and glared at him while he moved around the room fingering various items on display.

"May I help you, Mr. Daggett?"

The man looked up with eager anticipation, but his face fell when he saw the expression on hers. Gerda didn't care if her sour look drove the man out of the store. What was he here for, anyway? The answer to that question was too much to contemplate. He must have a girlfriend. . .or a wife. Why else would he buy the house?

"Miss Nilsson." The deep baritone voice was much too smooth. "Please call me Frank. I hope we can be friends?"

Gerda ignored the question implied by his voice. "I occasionally make clothing for my brother, who's hard to fit, but you should be able to find things you can wear at the mercantile next door." After this dismissal, Gerda went through the curtains that divided the store from the workroom. She leaned on the wall beside the doorway and waited until she heard the sound of his footsteps as they led to the outside door. When it closed behind the man, she let out the breath she had been holding. What was she going to do now? She had been saving so long to buy that house. She was tired of living in the apartment above the store. If God didn't bring her someone to marry, at least she would have had a real home. But that man had interfered in her life again. Why wouldn't he just go away and leave her alone?

Chapter 7

That didn't go very well. Frank berated himself all the way to the hotel. For several days, the words Gerda had blurted in front of the ice cream parlor had never left his mind. They interfered with much of his thinking. Of course she had gotten angry both then and in the sheriff's office, but he thought he had given her enough time to get over it. Surely it was all right to follow up on the feelings she inadvertently had claimed. But the encounter in the Dress Emporium had been far from successful.

Frank knew he didn't understand women very well, but Gerda Nilsson was a complicated puzzle that had him completely baffled. In his thoughts, she was pliant and loving, but when they were face-to-face, she was feisty and often disagreeable. Why was he so drawn to her? He had seen her smile at other people, and that smile could light up a room. Unfortunately, the smile was usually for someone else, not him. She was a combination of grace and beauty. No wonder he couldn't get her out of his mind.

The next morning, Frank ate breakfast at a table near the front window of the restaurant. He realized that when he moved into his house, he would have to cook his own meals. Maybe he would still come here to the hotel. He'd had enough of the few things he knew how to prepare to last a lifetime. Perhaps he could hire a housekeeper who could also cook for him.

When Molly came to pour him more hot coffee, he looked up from the newspaper he was reading. Out of the corner of his eyes, he noticed a surrey stop in front of the mercantile. Frank was pretty sure the store was closed today. He wondered who it was and why they were there. He guessed he would never lose the habit of watching what was going on, checking for anything out of the ordinary. It was ingrained in him from all the years in law enforcement.

A man and woman were in the surrey. When the man alighted from the carriage, Frank recognized August Nilsson. He climbed the stairs, leaving the woman in the buggy. In just a moment, August and Gerda came down the stairs. All three were dressed up as if they were going somewhere special.

"Is something going on in town today?" Frank looked up at Molly when he asked the question.

The waitress turned and glanced at the trio across the street. "Oh, they're just going to church."

To church? Frank hadn't thought of that. Since he'd become an adult, Frank hadn't had the time or the inclination to attend those meetings.

"Most people in Litchfield go to church on Sundays." Molly looked back at Frank. "I'll be on my way as soon as I finish waiting on you. Cook and I get there a little late and sit on a pew at the back. Can I get you anything else?"

When Frank shook his head, the woman returned to the kitchen, presumably to get ready for church. Frank continued to study the street outside the hotel. There wasn't much activity. What did church have to offer to cause so many people to attend? If he was ever going to understand Gerda, it might be a good thing for him to find out for himself. He really didn't want to make a late entrance, so he wouldn't go today. But next Sunday, he would get up bright and early and see what it was all about.

Gerda could hardly believe her eyes. When she walked into the church, Frank Daggett was already sitting on the pew where her family usually sat. Gerda hoped that August would notice him and choose another place to sit, but he ushered her and Anna into the other end of that pew. Soon Gustaf and Olina and their children joined them. At least they moved into the seat from the other direction. Now they separated her from the man who filled her thoughts so often.

It had been over a week since she had seen him. She was glad about that. Gradually, she had returned to her old self, often forgetting about him for an hour at a time. But she couldn't control her dreams. At night, he cavorted through her mind in a myriad of situations, always her hero. In the morning, she would have to pray especially hard to overcome the temptation he was to her. Now, here he was, sitting a few feet away, and she wondered why. He didn't strike her as a churchgoer. If he were, why hadn't he been here before? He'd been in town more than one Sunday.

The pastor's opening prayer invaded her thoughts. She bowed her head but didn't close her eyes. She peeked at Frank Daggett to see what he was doing. Didn't the man know anything? His head was up, and he watched the pastor with a thoughtful expression on his face. Well, whatever the reason he was here, maybe it would be good for him.

Gerda had a hard time keeping her attention on the service. She was as aware of Frank Daggett as if he were sitting right beside her. When everyone stood, it seemed to take him by surprise, so he was later than anyone else getting to his feet. Although Olina shared a hymnal with the man, he didn't sing a single word. He probably didn't know the songs. Olina had to share her Bible with him when the pastor read from the scriptures, because he didn't have one with him. Gerda was sure the man didn't own one. She wondered if he had ever seen one before. He kept his eyes trained on the words all through the Bible reading. During the sermon, his attention was on the preacher. For someone who may not have been to church before, he didn't seem nervous.

Frank had been a little uncomfortable when the family sat between him and Gerda. He recognized them as the loving couple who had eaten dinner at the hotel with Gerda and August his first night in Litchfield. It didn't take long for the couple to introduce themselves. Gustaf and Olina Nilsson were kin to Gerda and August. They sat with their children between them, and the woman ended up beside him. She was friendly and shared her songbook and Bible with him. Maybe he would need to buy a Bible if he was going to come to church very often. He couldn't rely on the good nature of whoever sat beside him. He wondered if Gerda would have shared hers with him if they were side by side. He doubted it. That's why he had stayed out of her way all week. He wanted to know more about this religion thing since it was so much a part of her life.

"Mr. Daggett." After the final prayer, the petite blond turned toward him.

"Yes, Mrs. Nilsson."

"We would like you to join us for lunch, wouldn't we, Gustaf?" She turned toward her tall husband.

The man looked Frank straight in the eyes. "Of course."

Frank shook his head. "Thank you. I wouldn't want to be any trouble."

"Oh, it's no trouble. We almost always have people come to the house for Sunday lunch. Most of Gustaf's family will be there, as will our friends, the Jensons. I believe you've met some of them, and I gather your first meeting wasn't especially pleasant," she said with a smile. "I want you to have the chance to get to know them better. Besides, I always cook enough for several extra people, just in case."

What could Frank do but agree? He wasn't sure that Gerda would be glad to see him there, but it might be a chance to make progress with her. "Thank you. I'll follow your carriage."

Gerda had seen Olina talking to Frank. Of course, that was just like Olina. She tried to make everyone feel welcome. That was all it was. But when the others started toward Gustaf and Olina's home for Sunday lunch, Gerda was surprised to see Frank Daggett's horse in the procession of buggies. Surely Olina hadn't invited him to have lunch with them. Gerda knew her assumption was probably wrong. Olina often asked visitors to the services to share their noon meal. Why did it have to be Frank Daggett? Gerda sent a prayer for help winging heavenward.

While everyone was exiting their vehicles, Gerda glanced at the house. It no longer looked like the place where Gerda and Olina started their dress shop back in 1892. At that time, it had been a small, two-story cottage, but after Olina received an inheritance from her great-aunt Olga, Gustaf had turned the modest house into a large family home, complete with an ample dining room equipped for many guests. All of the existing rooms had been enlarged and other rooms added. Recently, red brick had been applied to the outside walls, and all the windows were framed with white shutters that matched the picket fence surrounding the front yard. Usually, Gerda like to visit her brother and his family. But she dreaded entering the house today.

She wished she hadn't accepted the invitation. She almost hadn't, because all the other adults were couples. However, since they were all so close, she'd never felt like just a single person. Now she wasn't so sure. Perhaps she could plead a headache. All this stress could certainly bring one on quickly. Of course, no one knew how stressed she was about the added guest.

Soon everyone was in the house removing their wraps, and the women went to the kitchen to help Olina. The men entered the parlor. Gustaf took the children with them. Gerda knew that Gustaf and Olina wanted them to be tired enough to nap after the meal. If the men played with them before lunch, then the adults could visit afterward without interruption.

Gerda borrowed one of Olina's large, white ruffled aprons. While she was tying it on, she asked, "Are you sure you feel up to having this many people for lunch?"

Olina removed a large roasting pan from the oven. "Thank you for asking, Gerda, but this time I have more energy than I did before Sven was born. Besides, I really enjoy entertaining."

While the other women put the finishing touches on the meal, Gerda helped Anna set the table. First, they spread out an embroidered linen tablecloth that Olina had brought with her from Sweden. Then they set the good china plates around the sides.

"How many people do we have?" Gerda asked.

Anna started counting them. She stopped before she was finished and took hold of the back of a chair.

Gerda rushed to her side. "Are you all right?"

Anna smiled. "Yes, I was just a little dizzy. It's been awhile since I ate breakfast, and I only had some toast."

"You knew it would be a long time before we had lunch," Gerda scolded as she began placing the silverware beside each plate. "Why didn't you eat more?" She glanced up in time to see a blush steal across Anna's cheeks. Gerda put the silverware she was holding on the table in a pile and went to her sister-in-law and best friend. "What aren't you telling me?"

"I'm not telling anyone until I'm sure," Anna whispered. "But I can't keep it from you. Just remember, this is our secret. I haven't even told August what I suspect."

Gerda pulled Anna into a hug. "I'm so happy for you. I know how much you've wanted a baby. I will pray that it's true."

Anna reached up and wiped a tear from the corner of her eye. "I know. It's too wonderful."

Gerda went back to placing the silverware beside the other plates. She knew that she should be glad for August and Anna, and she was. But her happiness for them mingled with sadness for herself. What was wrong with her? When she looked in the mirror, the woman who gazed back at her wasn't unattractive. She had always been a pleasant companion, hadn't she? Why was she still unmarried? A tear slipped from her eye, and it wasn't a tear of happiness as Anna's had been.

Frank stayed in the background in the parlor while August and Gustaf played with the two blond children. Gustaf had a wonderful family with another child on the way. What did Frank have to show for all his years as a lawman? Now that he owned a house, maybe the wife and family wouldn't be far behind. He enjoyed watching the interaction between the children and their father. Olga, the little girl, loved her uncle August, too. He picked her up and swung her high into the air. Her peals of laughter were a balm to Frank's weary soul. He had just begun to feel comfortable in this home when the women called them to the table.

When Frank saw the bounty spread before them, he was amazed. He hadn't had a feast like this in years, even on holidays, and this was just Sunday lunch. The mingling aromas teased his senses, making him suddenly ravenous. Having a home and family could provide these kinds of blessings to him, too. That thought caused his gaze to seek out Gerda. He didn't like what he saw. For some reason, tears glistened in her eyes. He wished he had the right to go across the room, take her in his arms, and comfort her.

Olina told each person where to sit, and they took their places. Frank was amazed that the room didn't feel crowded, even with all the people clustered around the table. He had been introduced to Ollie and Lowell Jenson in the living room. The brothers looked almost as much alike as their twin wives, Clarissa and Marissa, did. All these other people were related in various ways, yet Frank didn't feel like an outsider. This family was so warm and friendly.

Gustaf pronounced a blessing on the meal. Frank remembered blessings spoken at mealtime while his mother was still alive, but not one had sounded as if the person speaking it was talking to a friend the way Gustaf's did. As the hostess started passing dishes around the table, group conversation started.

"I wish I had been there to see their faces when you drew your guns on these three women." With a twinkle in his eyes, Ollie Jenson looked right at Frank.

Frank was surprised. He thought these men would be upset with him, but they didn't seem to be. "If I had known the truth at that time, I never would have done it. I apologize."

He glanced at Gerda, who was seated across the table from him. She watched him with amazement in her expression. A large mirror with a heavy gold frame hung on the wall behind her. Frank saw not only her beautiful face, but also the reflection of the back of her dainty head. Everything about her caused a tightening in his gut. What was he going to have to do to get her to forgive him and return to the feelings that had connected them across the hotel lobby?

"What did you think when August threw his arm around your neck?" the other Jenson brother asked with a smile.

"At first, I thought there must be more to the Le Blanc gang than I had suspected. I knew Pierre didn't have that much strength. It was all I could do to keep from passing out."

August looked sheepish. "I wasn't trying to hurt you. I was only protecting our women."

"And I don't blame you. I would have done the same thing in your place."

The other men agreed.

"At that point I decided it might be time to hang up my guns. I had already turned in my badge, and I had never let a woman get the drop on me before."

Laughter echoed around the room, but Gerda didn't join in. Frank could tell that she was trying to digest all he said. Would he ever be able to reach her and see her return to being the warm, animated woman he had observed that first day? Something was really bothering her. Was it his presence? Maybe he should finish eating and go back to the hotel to allow her to enjoy the rest of the day with her family and friends.

"So, Frank." Olina looked down the table toward where he sat halfway between herself and her husband at the other end. "What are you going to do if you hang up your guns?"

Every eye in the room was trained on him. Frank cleared his throat. "I've been talking to the sheriff about investing in a business, but we haven't come up with the right one yet."

"But he did help you buy Mrs. Nichols's house." August's statement was not a question. He must know all about it.

Frank nodded. "He was kind enough to take me on a tour of the house after he introduced me to Harold Jones. Then Mr. Jones and I worked out the details. Are you familiar with the house?"

"Yes," August answered. "Actually, Gerda was trying to save enough money to make a down payment on it."

"You were?" Olina asked her sister-in-law. "We didn't know that. We would have helped you."

Frank looked at Gerda. The tears were back, glistening in her eyes.

"I wanted to do it on my own."

The words hung in the air between them, and suddenly Frank understood just how important that house was to Gerda. Without knowing it, he had done something else to hurt her. He wished there were some way he could make it up to her. If he thought she would accept it, he would sign over the deed to her today. But he knew she wouldn't. Maybe he could sell it to her himself, but he didn't want to profit from her, and he somehow knew she wouldn't buy it any other way.

"I understand that house is unfurnished, Mr. Daggett." Anna Nilsson reached out and took Gerda's hand as if giving her a lifeline. "What are you going to do for furniture?"

Frank looked around the table. Everyone seemed to be genuinely interested in his answer. "When my parents died, I inherited all their household goods. It's stored in a warehouse my uncle owns in Philadelphia. I've already sent a letter to my uncle telling him to ship everything to me. I realize it might not be enough to fill that house, but it will be a good start. It should arrive soon."

Gerda felt as if a boulder had lodged itself near her heart. Not only had he bought her house, but the man had furniture to fill it. All of her dreams evaporated like a mist in the morning sunlight. She wanted to excuse herself and leave the room, but she knew that Olina would be hurt if she didn't eat more of the wonderful food than she already had. However, she didn't know how she could get it past the gigantic lump in her chest.

"Mr. Daggett." Olina gestured at each woman around the table. "We are so glad that you've decided to settle in our town. We'd like to help you clean up the house before your furniture arrives, wouldn't we?"

The other women started talking at once, agreeing with her. All except Gerda. Somehow she couldn't push words past the heaviness, either. She knew it would look bad if she didn't help them, but she couldn't agree. Not today, anyway.

"I appreciate your offer, but why don't we wait until my furniture arrives. Then the house would be fresh to move it into."

The man's words made sense, but they didn't change the way Gerda felt. Her world was slowly crumbling around her, and she didn't know what to do about it.

Chapter 8

Frank was pleased that the women had offered to help him prepare his house for the arrival of his possessions. It gave him a feeling of acceptance and finally belonging somewhere. He'd expected Gerda to object, but she didn't. She didn't exactly say that she would help, but she didn't say she wouldn't either. Because she hadn't refused, a tiny flame of hope ignited in Frank's heart—hope that there could be a future for him and Gerda. If he were a praying man, he might ask God to help him, but he wasn't even on speaking terms with God, if there was one. By starting to go to church, he was doing his best to find out if God was real.

It only took a week for the strongbox to arrive with what Frank had stored in his safe-deposit box back East. The banker had also put the money Frank had in his savings account in the box. The key to the strongbox had arrived on the previous train, enclosed in a package addressed to Frank. After he got to the hotel and opened the box, he carried it to the bank wrapped in brown paper. He didn't want to announce the fact that he had a strongbox with him.

"I'd like to talk to the bank manager, please," Frank told the teller when he arrived.

The man went into a back room, then returned accompanied by a spry man wearing a black suit and glasses. "I'm Mr. Finley. What can I do for you, sir?" the manager asked.

"I'm Frank Daggett. Could I speak to you privately, Mr. Finley?"

The manager led Frank into an office lined with dark paneled walls. The furniture in the room could have graced the bank office back East. It gave Frank confidence that this was a prosperous bank.

"I would like to open an account." Frank sat in the wine-colored leather chair across from Mr. Finley. "I would also like to put this strongbox in your safe. It contains some of my family valuables."

The banker smiled at him. "We'd be glad to accommodate you. How much money would you like to deposit in your account?"

When Frank told him, the man's smile broadened. He rose from his chair and extended his hand. "We'll be glad to have you as a customer, Mr. Daggett."

When they had finished the paperwork, Mr. Finley took Frank into the vault. He proudly displayed its strength, reassuring Frank that it was completely safe.

Gerda's Lawman

After that first Sunday when Frank went to church, he had friends in town besides the sheriff. He often saw one or more of the men, and they always included him in conversations and expressed a genuine interest in what was happening with him. Frank couldn't remember a time since he'd become an adult when he'd had true friends. It felt good.

Frank continued to attend church, but he wasn't sure he understood what the preacher was talking about. He had never been one to make any kind of decision without a lot of thought. He listened intently, trying to get a handle on what this religion business was all about.

One Monday, Frank decided to exercise his horse by taking a ride away from town. He took a different direction from any he had taken before. After he had ridden awhile, he came to a place with a wrought iron arch over the entrance. Worked into the arch were the words JENSON HORSE FARM. *This must be owned by Lowell and Ollie.* He turned under the archway and rode up the drive toward a large, white farmhouse surrounded by magnificent stables. He had heard that theirs was the most successful horse farm in five states. Now he understood why. The animals that ran across the surrounding pastures were sleek. Their shiny coats glistened in the morning sunlight. Several colts cavorted after their mothers. For a moment, he stopped his horse and watched. Their manes and tails waved in the wind as they raced across the greening fields.

When he rode up to the house, a pleasant-looking older woman stepped out onto the porch. "May I help you?" she asked as she brushed a wisp of hair up away from the back of her neck with one hand.

Frank tipped his hat. "Good morning, ma'am. I'm Frank Daggett. I was just out riding and noticed the sign. I thought I would stop and visit with Lowell and Ollie."

The woman moved to the top step and used her other hand to shade her eyes from the bright morning sun. A gentle breeze blew her skirt around her ankles. "Oh, Mr. Daggett. I've heard about you. I'm Margreta Jenson, the boys' mother."

Frank dismounted and stood at the bottom of the steps. He removed his hat and ran his fingers through his hair to push the curls back from his forehead. "I'm sure you have. I'm very sorry about the misunderstanding with your daughters-in-law."

Mrs. Jenson smiled. "We've all gotten a good laugh out of that. But we understand why you did what you did. We're just glad that it had already been taken care of."

The sound of hoofbeats coming down the drive captured their attention. They both turned to look. A man with a star pinned to his chest was making his way toward them.

"Oh, Sheriff Bartlett." The woman standing on the porch suddenly sounded a little breathless.

Frank looked at her. One of her hands fluttered to her throat, and she looked somehow younger and more animated than she had while he was talking to her. He glanced toward the sheriff and caught him smiling at her. *Well, well, perhaps I'm not the only one trying to pursue a woman.*

"Good morning, Sheriff," Frank greeted his friend. "What brings you out here today?"

For a moment the man didn't answer. He seemed to be having a hard time taking his gaze off the woman on the porch. Then he turned to Frank.

"I've come to have lunch. Mrs. Jenson invited me."

"We'd be glad to have you join us, Mr. Daggett." Her voice sounded softer and gentler than before.

Frank glanced from one of them to the other. "Thank you, but I think I'll pass. Are Lowell and Ollie around?"

"They're working with the horses in the barn." She gave a vague wave toward the buildings behind the house.

Frank returned his hat to his head. "Thank you, Mrs. Jenson, for the information." He tied his horse to the hitching post in front of the house and started toward the barn. He could hear soft conversation going on behind him, and he smiled. He wondered if Lowell and Ollie realized the sheriff was interested in their mother and she welcomed it.

Frank placed one foot on the bottom rail of the fence then leaned his forearms on the top. Ollie was putting a horse through its paces.

Lowell joined Frank. "What brings you out here today?"

"I was just out for a ride when I noticed the name over your gate." Frank smiled at him. "I thought I'd drop in and see the horse farm I had heard so much about. You have a nice spread here."

"We think so."

Ollie led the animal close to where the other two men leaned on the fence. "Say, Frank, have you decided what you're going to do yet?"

Frank stood back from the fence and shoved his hands in the front pockets of his denim trousers. "Not yet. I'm still looking around."

Ollie tied the lead rope loosely to the top rail. "We have a neighbor who wants to sell his farm."

"Yeah, he wants to move to California," Lowell added. "We thought you might be interested in buying it."

Frank studied the grass that grew around the fence post nearby. "I'm not sure that's quite what I'm looking for. I don't want to be this far from town."

Although his grandfather had been a farmer, Frank hadn't spent much time learning about farming from him, and he had died when Frank was pretty young.

After Ollie turned the young horse he was working with out into the pasture, he stood in the doorway to the barn. "Lowell and I are going over to my house for lunch. Marissa is there with Clarissa, and they're fixing something special. They wouldn't tell us what. You're welcome to join us."

Frank glanced up toward the house where the sheriff and Mrs. Jenson had entered. "You don't all live here?"

Ollie watched his boot as he scuffed the dirt by the door. "We had a real misunderstanding before we found out the truth about Marissa and Clarissa. During that time, I started building my own home on the other side of our property. Now Clarissa and I live there."

Lowell glanced up at the main house. "Besides, we wanted to give Mother and the sheriff a little privacy."

Frank looked from one brother to the other. "I wondered if you knew that they were interested in each other. I also wondered how you felt about it."

"Our father passed away awhile ago." Lowell stopped to clear his throat. "The sheriff was helpful with the girls while all the trouble with their stepfather was going on, and he spent time out here at the farm. I guess you could say that this relationship is another blessing that came from all that happened."

Ollie smiled. "Lowell and I are so happy in our marriages that we want *Mor* to be happy, too."

Just before he reached town, Frank's horse threw a shoe. It was a good thing they were close to town, because Frank wouldn't have wanted to walk too far. Although it was May, the days had started heating up a lot by midday. He didn't want to ride the horse while the hoof wasn't protected. He just hoped August wouldn't be too busy to make a new shoe today.

When Frank walked through the door of the smithy, August turned to greet him. "It's good to see you again." The burly man wiped his right hand on his apron then stuck it toward Frank.

He shook the proffered hand. "I'm afraid this isn't a social call. My horse threw a shoe just outside town. Do you think you could get to it today?"

August turned and went out through the open doorway. "He's a magnificent animal." The big man crooned something into the horse's ear and scratched his head. "Have you had him long?"

Frank patted his animal's neck. "We've been together quite awhile. He's been more than just transportation for me. Sometimes he was my only companion."

August ran his hand down each leg until he came to the one the horse was favoring. He lifted the hoof and looked at it. "I can fix this right now if you want to wait."

After following the blacksmith into the warm building, Frank leaned against a table by the wall. It was close enough to the door that he could feel a slight breeze. August was using some kind of aromatic wood in the forge today. It took away from the unpleasant smoky odor that Frank usually associated with smithies. He watched the other man look through a pile of horseshoes until he found the one he wanted. When he went back out and picked up the unshod hoof and measured it against the horseshoe he had chosen, it was almost a perfect fit. After taking the piece of formed iron to the forge, he held it in the flames with long tongs.

"So have you found a business to invest in?" August looked at Frank instead of the metal that was slowly heating.

"Not yet."

"I don't know if you'd be interested, but Hank over at the livery mentioned that he was thinking about selling. He hasn't been the same since he was burned out last summer. Even though he built the stable back, his heart isn't in it anymore. Would you like to talk to him about purchasing it?"

Frank let his chin rest against his chest while he thought about it. After a moment, he raised his gaze toward the fire, where the horseshoe was beginning to glow. "I don't think I'd be any good at running a livery stable."

August pulled the horseshoe from the fire and took it to the anvil. He only had to pound it a few times to get it to the shape he wanted, but the loud noise prevented further conversation for a time. After the metal was the shape he wanted, he plunged it into a bucket of cold water. A loud hiss accompanied the steam that rose from the bucket.

"I'll keep an ear open when people are talking." August turned to smile at him. "I sure wouldn't want you to leave here now. We're getting used to having you around." With a chuckle, he lifted the horseshoe out of the water and tested the temperature of the metal. Then he went outside to where the horse was tied.

Frank accompanied him outside. "Thanks. I like it here, too." It was fascinating to watch the man. He was like an artist, knowing just where to put the nails to protect the horse and pounding them in with a minimum of strokes.

When he was finished, Frank paid August, then rode his horse over to the livery. When he got back to the other side of the railroad tracks, Frank decided to make another visit to the Dress Emporium. It had been too long since he had seen Gerda. Even though she didn't seem to be interested in him, he wasn't going to give up. He still remembered the words that had burst from her lips the day she'd held the gun on him. They warmed his heart whenever he felt lonely.

Gerda couldn't believe that Frank Daggett was back in the Dress Emporium again. It seemed as though he was always underfoot. This time, he talked to Anna. Gerda tried to look disinterested, but his gaze kept straying toward her even though he was talking to her friend. Picking up a bolt of fabric, Gerda made her way through the curtains into the workroom. There was no hurry to cut out the new outfit that Marja Braxton ordered today, but taking the fabric into the back room gave Gerda a good excuse to leave the area where Frank was. Unfortunately, even from the back room, Frank's melodious voice penetrated Gerda's heart.

She sat on the padded chair in front of the sewing machine and leaned her elbows on the table. Gerda buried her face in her hands and prayed as hard as she could for the Lord to deliver her from the temptation that was Frank Daggett. When she finished and raised her head, she could still hear him discussing yesterday's church service with Anna. The man had been attending services for several weeks. How could he listen to the powerful sermons without becoming a believer? Was he just making a show of being interested in church for some nefarious reason? Of course, he wasn't anything like Pierre Le Blanc had been. When Pierre was in church, he didn't even try to look interested. Frank listened intently to the sermons. He had even started trying to sing some of the songs, but as far as Gerda could tell, he still didn't have his own Bible. He usually sat with Gustaf and Olina, and whoever was nearest to Frank shared a Bible with him.

She got up and put the bolt of fabric on the cutting table. While she measured the amount needed to complete Marja's new suit, her thoughts were filled with Frank. Since that day when he'd tried to arrest her and the twins, Gerda had never seen him dressed like a cowboy. He always wore nice clothes when he came by. His trousers and shirts looked as though they were tailored just for him. She wondered if he already owned them or if he had bought them at the mercantile. She would ask Marja, but Gerda knew that it would only cause Marja to ask questions she didn't want to answer to herself, much less to anyone else.

It was a wonder Gerda was able to cut the fabric straight. Those icy blue eyes, surrounded by long black lashes, twinkled as they looked at her in her mind's eye. Her hands still itched to reach out and brush back the curls that often fell over his forehead. He'd had more than one haircut since he came to town, but nothing tamed those curls. Some men didn't keep their hair especially clean, or else they put too much hair cream on it, so it looked greasy. Frank's never did. Gerda wondered what it would feel like to run her fingers through those curly strands, especially where the hair in the back reached his collar and curled up slightly. She imagined that if she put her arms around his shoulders, she would be able to feel their texture.

Disgusted with herself, Gerda slammed the scissors down on the cutting table. Then she realized that the voices in the next room had silenced. She turned and stared into the face of her best friend, who stood framed between the curtains that divided the room, a shocked expression on her face.

"Gerda!" Anna came all the way into the workroom. "Are you going to tell me what's the matter?"

Gerda didn't want to upset Anna, considering her condition, but what could she tell her?

"I've noticed that you aren't very nice to Mr. Daggett when he comes to the store."

"Just why would he be coming into a women's clothing store, anyway?" Gerda knew her voice was harsh, but she couldn't keep it from sounding that way. "It's not as if he ever buys anything."

Anna patted Gerda on the arm. "I think he just needs friends. Why don't you want to be his friend?"

Unfortunately, "friends" was not what Gerda wanted to be with Frank Daggett. Much to her shame, she wanted more. She had carried this burden in her heart too long. Anna was one of her best friends as well as her sister-in-law, and Anna had taken Gerda into her confidence about the baby long before she told anyone else. If Gerda could tell anyone about what was bothering her, it was Anna.

She turned and looked at Anna. "Can I tell you something in confidence?"

"Of course you can." Anna sat in the chair by the windows. "I'm ready to listen. You have my full attention."

Gerda dropped into the chair by the sewing machine. "I'm not sure how to say this."

Anna leaned forward. "Just start at the beginning."

"I haven't told anyone, but the first time I saw Frank Daggett was the day August and I had dinner with Gustaf and Olina."

"I didn't know that." Anna leaned back and smiled.

"He was coming down the stairs in the hotel lobby while we were waiting for Gustaf and Olina to arrive. I glanced up," Gerda said as a blush moved up her cheeks, "and when our eyes met, it was as if everything within me connected with everything in him. I don't know how to explain it. For a moment, I felt as if we were the only two people in the room."

Anna looked as if she were holding back a chuckle. "That's interesting."

Gerda got up and walked to the window nearest the sewing machine. She held back the curtain and gazed at nothing in particular. "Don't you see? All these years I've waited for God to bring me someone to love, and the only person I've felt anything special for is a man who isn't a Christian. I've been praying for God to take the temptation from me. I just can't get too close to him, because. . ."

After a moment, Anna asked, "Because what?"

Gerda turned away and crossed her arms. "I'm afraid I could fall in love with him very easily. I can't risk that."

When Anna arrived the next morning, she was carrying her Bible. Gerda watched her sit in the chair by the windows and open the book.

"I prayed about you last night. When I started reading the Bible, I found this verse, and it spoke to me about Frank Daggett. Do you want to hear it?"

When Gerda nodded, Anna opened the book to where she had a bookmark. " 'And the Lord said unto Satan, Hast thou considered my servant Job, that there is none like him in the earth, a perfect and an upright man, one that feareth God, and escheweth evil?' That verse describes Frank."

"Read it to me again." Gerda wanted to be sure she heard it right.

Anna read it another time. "That's how Mr. Daggett is. He is an upright man, and he has fought evil all of his life."

"I don't know about that part about him fearing God. I haven't seen any indication of that."

Anna closed her Bible and laid it on the small table that sat near the chair she was using. "He listens to every word the preacher says. If he doesn't know God yet, I'm sure he will soon. You know, Gerda, maybe Frank *is* the man God brought to you."

This statement startled Gerda. She paced across the room. That was something she hadn't even considered. Why would God bring that man to her when there were so many other godly men around? But none of them had ever caused her pulse to race the way it did around Frank Daggett.

Gerda turned back toward her friend. "I saw him coming out of the saloon one day."

"When was that?"

"Soon after he came to town."

"But have you seen him go into the saloon since he started coming to church?"

Gerda thought about it a moment. She had only seen him at the saloon that one time. Could she be wrong about him?

Chapter 9

Frank was sure he would never make any headway with Gerda. Every time he went to the Dress Emporium, she wasn't very friendly. Anna Nilsson always made him feel welcome, but Gerda was either almost rude to him or she hid in the back room. Not only had he scared and insulted her when he tried to arrest her, but he'd unknowingly bought her dream house. What did a man have to do to make up for the mistakes he inadvertently made? He never meant to hurt her.

Frank was walking toward the bank when the sheriff joined him. "I'd really like to talk to you. Would you join me in my office for a cup of coffee? Or should we go to the restaurant in the hotel?"

"Your coffee is fine with me." Frank followed his friend into the building.

After pouring each of them a mugful of the brew, Sheriff Bartlett dropped into his chair behind the desk. He gathered the papers scattered across the top, formed them into a neat stack, and placed them to the side. Then he leaned his forearms on the smooth surface of the desk.

"I'm thinking about retiring."

Frank knew that wasn't the whole story, so he waited to let the man tell it in his own good time. Frank dropped into the other chair and propped one booted foot on his other knee.

"I'm thinking about buying a small farm that's for sale outside town. It wouldn't be too much for me to take care of, and it has a nice little house on it."

Frank crossed his arms over his chest and looked at the older man. "Sounds good, if that's what you want to do."

"There's more to it than that." The sheriff leaned back and gazed off into the distance. "I'm thinking about getting married."

"Mrs. Jenson?"

The lawman nodded. "I knew you probably had that one figured out. I don't want to ask Margreta to marry me while I'm still a lawman. I'm getting too old for this, and I want to enjoy a life with less danger."

"Just how much danger is there here in Litchfield?" Frank hadn't seen much since he'd arrived. Even the men who frequented the saloon didn't cause much of a disturbance.

"Not a lot." Sheriff Bartlett wiped his hand across his clean-shaven jaw.

"The worst that has happened since I've been here was the Le Blanc incident. It could have turned ugly and anything could have gone wrong, but it didn't."

Frank mulled over what the man had said. "Why are you telling me all this?"

"Well, I've watched you as you've considered businesses to invest in. Nothing has appealed to you. I think it's because you're still a lawman at heart. Besides, you're a lot younger than I am."

Frank placed his foot back on the floor and laughed. "Some days I feel younger, but some days I feel older."

"I know what you mean. You sure do see the hard side of life when you're a lawman, but I don't think that's a problem here. Litchfield is a nice, quiet town, and since you want to settle here, it might be a good opportunity for both of us to get what we want. I can't retire until there's someone to take my place, and I won't ask her to share that life with me. She's already lost one husband."

"What about your deputy?"

"Clarence isn't interested in being sheriff. He says being deputy is enough for him."

Frank got up and rubbed one finger across his mustache. "Can you give me a little time to think about it?"

"Sure." The sheriff smiled. "Just don't take too long. I'm not getting any younger."

Business in the Dress Emporium grew almost every week. Gerda liked to keep busy. That way she didn't have too much time to think about Frank Daggett. But she still couldn't get the man out of her mind. No wonder. Every time she turned around, there he was—at church, in the shop, or with her close friends. It wasn't enough that he had taken away the house she had dreamed of buying; now he seemed to be taking all her friends, too.

Anna was a little late coming in on Wednesday. She had started trying to work every day to help Gerda with the added business. "I'm sorry I'm late." Anna breezed through the door. "I had another bout of sickness this morning. I finally was able to keep some toast down."

Gerda looked up from straightening the things that were in disarray under the counter. "If you don't feel like working, I'll understand."

Anna stopped at the end of the counter and peered down at what Gerda was doing. "I'm fine now, and we have so much to do. I want to finish the suit for Mother. I wish she would just let me make things for her at home instead of coming in and insisting on paying for them like any other customer."

Gerda lifted the cash box and placed it on the counter. Using the key attached to the inside of her belt, she opened it. "I need to go to the bank. I didn't have time last week. Now the box is almost overflowing. I don't like keeping this much cash in the store."

"Why don't you go while I work on the suit?"

Gerda had a special, larger reticule in which she carried money to the bank. She didn't want it to look like a moneybag and tempt someone to try to steal it from her on the way. She went into the back room and took the special handbag off the shelf. Then she stuffed the bills into the bottom of the bag and added a handkerchief on top of the money.

"I'll be back soon," she called to Anna, who was now in the workroom.

It was a pretty day. May was still spring, but it felt more like summer. The trees were covered with leaves, and flowers were blooming in several flower beds around town. Gerda loved spring. All the fresh, new growth reminded her that life could be renewed, too. So what if she couldn't buy her dream house. God probably had something else just as wonderful in mind for her. Because she had a lot of money saved, she decided to start looking at other houses that were for sale. Maybe one of them would be just right for her. Anyway, the one Frank bought would have been too large for a single woman living alone.

When she went into the bank, there was a short line at the teller's window. Gerda didn't want anyone to figure out that she was carrying the cash from the store, so she patiently waited until no one else was in line. She glanced around the room and noticed a stranger standing near the door. His hat was pulled low over his brow, so she couldn't tell too much about him. She wondered if he was someone new moving to town. Litchfield did seem to be growing a lot lately.

Soon it was her turn to make a deposit. The teller had just greeted her when she felt something hard touch the middle of her back. Even through the material of her dress, it was cold.

"Don't move," a grating, masculine voice sounded close to her ear.

She started to turn and look at the man, but the hard thing pushed deeper into her back, and she knew it had to be a gun barrel. She couldn't believe a man was holding a gun on her again. For some reason, she felt more apprehensive now than she had the last time. She had known that Frank wouldn't pull the trigger, but she wasn't sure about this stranger. If she just could have seen the expression in his eyes, maybe she would have been able to tell. Cold fingers of fright danced up and down her spine. It took all her willpower to keep from shivering. It was a good thing that her reticule was hanging safely on her arm, or she might have dropped it.

"Don't move." The man turned his attention toward the teller, who stood as if paralyzed behind the metal bars of the teller's cage. "And you there, come around and lock the front door. You do have a key to the front door, don't you?"

The poor teller was shaking so badly he could hardly get the key into the lock. Gerda could hear it scrape around on the metal, and the vibrations from the man were almost tangible in the room. Mr. Jackson was an elderly man who had been at the bank as long as Gerda had lived in the area. As far as she knew, he had worked there long before, as well. When he turned around after securing the door, he returned to his post with his trembling hands raised. His face had blanched almost white. Gerda was afraid the poor man was going to pass out right there.

"Where is the bank manager?" The gruff voice was louder this time.

Mr. Jackson's voice wavered, then became a whisper. "He's in his office."

"Go get him, but if either of you does anything foolish, this woman will not see another day."

Gerda didn't like the sound of that. She could tell from the steely tone of his voice that the man meant every word he said. She had never fainted in her life, but she felt the color drain from her own face. Without moving her body, she took hold of the counter in front of her with her hands to keep from slipping away. She took a deep breath and slowly let it out, trying to gain control of her emotions and her reluctant body.

"How can I hel—" Mr. Finley's question died when he saw the man holding his gun on Gerda.

"If you do what I say, this woman won't be hurt."

Following the robber's instructions, Mr. Finley went into the safe and brought out bags of money. Then he unlocked the door to the alley. Two other bandits entered wearing bandannas pulled over their mouths and noses. They started picking up the bags of money and carrying them outside, presumably to load on their horses. A wagon would be too slow for a quick getaway.

When they had loaded all the bags, the leader told one of them to go into the vault with Mr. Finley and make sure they had all the money. After they returned and told him they had it, the two other bandits went out the back door.

"Let's see what you have in that bag." The robber ripped Gerda's reticule from where she carried it on her arm. "You were here to make a deposit, weren't you?" Gerda looked from her handbag to the robber's face, which was now covered with a handkerchief as the other men's had been. "Well, this is quite a haul right here." He stuffed the bag inside his shirt and gestured with his gun. "The three of you come inside here and lie facedown on the floor."

They went into the teller's cage area and complied.

"What time does your watch say, Banker?"

Mr. Finley fumbled to pull the watch out of its pocket. After telling the robber what he wanted to know, he stuffed it back into its place. The fob fell against the floor making a loud thud in the stillness.

"Take that watch back out. I want you to keep an eye on it, Banker. Don't anyone move for at least fifteen minutes. I'm going to leave one man watching you from outside the back door. If anyone moves, the woman will be shot first."

When she heard the horses ride away, Gerda almost started crying, but she was afraid it would cause the gunman to shoot. The only thing she knew to do was pray.

~

All Frank could think about since the sheriff had talked to him was whether he should become sheriff or not. In one way, it was tempting. He had always been a good lawman. But would it prevent him from having a normal life with the woman he was coming to love? Even if she wouldn't give him the time of day.

Every time he laid his eyes on her, her beauty assailed him. But there was more to Gerda than outward appearances. Her beauty was internal as well. He'd heard all the sayings. Beauty is only skin deep. Beauty is as beauty does. She exemplified all of them—with everyone except him. He only hoped that she would soon forgive him for the pain he had caused her. Frank had waited a long time to settle down. He could wait even longer for a woman like Gerda Nilsson.

Frank had looked into several business ventures, but none appealed to him. Of course, he had enough money saved to live a long time without having to work, but he wanted to be busy doing something worthwhile. And what was more worthwhile than serving as sheriff for this quiet town? In Litchfield, he should be able both to serve as a lawman and to be a family man. Other men did it.

When Frank and the sheriff had finished their discussion, Frank went back to his room at the hotel to think. He didn't want to be distracted by all the activities in town. Finally, he knew that he couldn't make the decision today, so he started back toward the bank to make a withdrawal since he had spent almost all the money he had been carrying. Just before he reached the bank, the front door burst open and three people rushed out. Mr. Finley, the bank manager; Mr. Jackson; and Gerda—and something was definitely wrong.

"There's been a bank robbery!" Gerda ran to him and grabbed the front of his shirt, holding on as if it were a lifeline. "They took all my money!" Then she burst into tears.

Of their own volition, Frank's arms went around her and cradled her head against his chest. He was glad when she didn't pull away. Instead, she nestled close enough that her tears soaked through his shirt, but he didn't care. She was finally in his arms. Then he realized what she was saying.

"He pulled a gun on me, and he threatened to shoot me, and he took all the money in the bank, and he took my bag with the Dress Emporium money in it, and he made us lie down on the floor!" Gerda's rambling was punctuated with sobs.

Frank heard the banker and the bank teller both shout, "I'm going to get the sheriff!" Then the two men ran down the boardwalk, their boots making thudding sounds that resonated up and down the street. Other people turned to stare, both at the men running and at Frank as he held Gerda. He didn't want to destroy her reputation, so he released his arms from around her and started patting her back.

"It's going to be all right. They've gone for the sheriff."

By the time Frank got the words out, the sheriff, accompanied by Mr. Finley and Mr. Jackson, ran toward the bank. The three men went in the open front door of the bank. Frank turned Gerda around, and the two of them joined the men inside.

The sheriff questioned all three of the people who were there during the robbery. "We'll need to send a posse after them right away." He turned to Frank. "Have you ever headed up a posse?"

Frank nodded.

"This robbery could be a diversion," Sheriff Bartlett whispered as he scratched his head. "That's all I can say except that I don't think Deputy Wright and I should leave town, just in case someone's planning another robbery, if you get my drift. Would you be willing to lead the posse?"

"I'll help any way I can." Frank wondered if perhaps the sheriff was expecting a courier or a shipment containing something valuable today.

A large crowd had formed in the street in front of them. August Nilsson and Hank from the livery stood near the front of the group. Frank motioned for the two men to come up on the boardwalk where he and the sheriff stood.

"We need a posse, but I don't want too many people." He placed his hand on August's massive shoulder. "You know these people better than I do. I want you and Hank and four other men who are strong, intelligent, and have cool heads."

August surveyed the crowd. He pointed out each person. "Harold Jones is real levelheaded. Silas is a good rider and shoots straighter than most anyone in the county. Harvey and Charles Stevenson own the farm next to ours. They will do whatever you need them to."

Frank motioned to each man August recommended, and they quickly stepped up beside him. "I'd like you to be part of the posse."

They all nodded in agreement.

Frank hadn't noticed that the sheriff had gone until he returned carrying a deputy's badge.

"Frank, you can't go without me deputizing you." He pinned the star to Frank's chest.

Frank looked down at it. A small lump formed in his throat. It felt so good to be wearing a badge again, even if it was just temporary.

For whatever reason, the robbers weren't careful to cover their tracks very well. It didn't take the posse long to pick up the trail.

August rode beside Frank, their horses never breaking stride as the men shouted to one another. "I think I know where they're headed."

"Where?"

"They're going in the direction that leads to the place where Pierre Le Blanc kept his hidden camp."

Frank halted the posse so they could strategize. "How hard is it to find this place?"

August stopped his mount beside Frank's. "You have to know what you're looking for. That's why it's a perfect hideout."

"Does anyone here know how to get there?"

August's horse took one side step. The high-strung animals sensed the excitement and urgency of their riders. "I've been there. Lowell and Ollie showed it to me after Le Blanc was captured."

After August described to Frank the surrounding territory, Frank divided the other men into three groups of two. They rode to the valley as quietly as possible. Then they left their horses tied at the outer edge of the woods. Soon the seven men worked their way toward the clearing in the center of the valley. They spread out along the perimeter of forest, being careful to stay hidden in the undergrowth.

Sure enough, the three robbers lounged around a campfire. Two counted the money, and one stood guard. Frank signaled the other posse members to move around the perimeter of the woods until they were all near the campsite, which was off to one side of the clearing.

Frank didn't want to jump the gun. He wanted to make an arrest without anyone coming to harm. He hunkered down to watch through the bushes. When the two robbers finished sorting the cash, they started dividing it.

"I want a larger cut." The tall, lean man spoke with a gravelly voice. "This job was my idea, and I planned it."

The man who was standing guard turned around. "Yeah, but we did a lot of the work, carrying those bags and putting them on the horses."

"You wouldn't have enough brains to pull off a job like this," the tall man said with a sneer.

"Yeah, you were real smart, Joe." The younger man looked at their leader with admiration in his expression. "Telling those people that someone would be watching to make sure they didn't move for fifteen minutes. They were so stupid they believed you!" He laughed.

The guard relaxed. "That was pretty smart, too, when you said you'd shoot the woman if the banker didn't cooperate. I guess you knew they'd do anything to protect her. How much was the haul?"

The younger robber looked down at the stacks of bills. "We're not finished counting it all, but there's more than one fortune here."

The guard whistled. "It's all right with me if Joe gets a larger cut. I could buy a ranch and run it for several years on my share, even if it is a smaller cut than he gets."

Frank's temper flared when the men talked about threatening Gerda. He had to take several deep breaths and force himself to remain coolheaded. He was a razor-sharp lawman. He wasn't going to make any mistakes this time.

With the guard not paying attention to what was going on around the camp, Frank knew it was time to attack. He signaled the other men. He watched them raise their guns and point them out between the trees. Then he stepped into the clearing.

"Drop your guns!" He used his most authoritative voice. "The members of a posse have their guns trained on you."

The guard dropped the rifle he was holding and raised his hands, and the young robber who was kneeling beside the money held up his hands, too.

"Take your pistols out of your holsters and throw them over here." Frank kept his steely tone.

The guard and the young robber complied, but the leader stood his ground.

"I don't believe you. There's only one of you and three of us." He pulled his gun and pointed it at Frank. "I can kill you before you get a shot off at any of us."

"Now!" Frank shouted.

The other six men stepped from the cover of the trees and underbrush. Each man was holding a rifle, all pointed at the bank robbers.

"I said drop your guns." Frank looked straight at the leader.

Venom accompanied the man's gaze. Frank suspected he wasn't used to having anyone get the drop on him. Slowly, the man lowered his arm, and his gun thudded to the ground.

Frank spoke to the posse. "Don't take your eyes off of the man you're covering, and if he pulls anything, shoot."

He walked to the leader and frisked him, finding another pistol hidden at his back under his belt and a knife in his boot. A woman's handbag was stuffed inside the man's shirt. Frank figured it was Gerda's. He glanced inside and hoped that all her money was still there.

"Weren't you going to share this with your gang?" Frank asked him.

A glare was the man's only answer to the question. After handcuffing the leader of the gang, Frank motioned Harold Jones over and stationed him beside the robber. Frank then searched the other two men. Neither of them had any hidden weapons, but the younger man had some bills stuffed inside his shirt.

"As the saying goes, there's no honor among thieves." Frank shook his head and ordered Harvey and Charlie Stevenson to guard these two robbers.

August took some rope and tied the captives' hands while Frank gathered up the money and stuffed it into the bank bags.

On the way back to town, the members of the posse were in high spirits. Even though they had to keep an eye on the prisoners, jubilant conversations bounced around the group.

When the ten men rode into town, a crowd quickly gathered. The sheriff met them outside his office.

"I see you caught them pretty quickly." He smiled up at Frank.

"We wouldn't have done it so soon if it hadn't been for August. He told us where to look." Frank didn't mind giving credit where it was due.

The sheriff turned toward August. "How did you know where to look?"

"When I realized which direction they went, I figured they might be where Pierre kept the girls."

The sheriff smiled as he and Frank helped the robbers dismount, then they herded the criminals into the jail cells and removed their bonds. The clang of the cell doors closing was music to Frank's ears.

The crowd outside the sheriff's office was growing. By the time the culprits were behind bars, almost everyone who was in town that day had gathered. The sheriff stepped out the door, followed by Frank.

Sheriff Bartlett raised his hands for silence. "Mr. Daggett led the posse that captured the robbers."

A shout went up. Frank's name and the word "hero" were among the shouts. Frank wanted to step back inside. He was just doing a job. He wasn't a hero.

August Nilsson moved to the front of the crowd and turned to face his friends. "Frank Daggett knew just how to take the men without anyone getting hurt. And we recovered all the money." He pointed to the moneybags hanging on the horses ridden by August, Hank, and Silas.

Gerda was standing at the edge of the crowd. Frank had seen her as soon as he'd stepped through the door. He watched the expressions on her face while the sheriff and August spoke. When she finally looked at him, admiration filled her solemn gaze. The connection he had felt that first day at the hotel once again sizzled through the air. The crowd faded away, and for a moment, he and Gerda were the only two people in the world. He slowly reached inside his shirt and extracted the woman's handbag he had stuffed there. He raised it, and her attention turned from him to what he held in his hand. She smiled and mouthed the words *thank you*. For the first time in a long time, all was right with Frank's world.

Chapter 10

Gerda couldn't tear her gaze from Frank's compelling eyes, which were no longer icy but contained the blue warmth of a summer sky. She had a hard time catching her breath and suddenly felt warm all over. She hoped no one noticed that a blush now covered her cheeks. Or was it a flush? Blushes didn't usually make her feel this hot, and the temperature wasn't high enough today to bring on so much heat.

Her attention was drawn toward the sheriff, who was holding up his hands for silence. "Now seems like a good time to tell you all that I'm ready to retire. I've asked Frank Daggett to take my place." Murmurs through the crowd rose to a crescendo, almost drowning out his next words. "He hasn't said yes yet, but I'm hoping he will." The lawman turned and smiled at the man standing beside him.

The crowd clamored for Frank. Gerda glanced back toward him, and he still looked at her. Once again, she was held in his hypnotic stare. After an almost imperceptible nod, he turned his gaze from hers, and she watched him study the individuals who filled the street between them. A slow smile spread across his face, lighting his features. Then the chatter settled down as if the crowd was waiting for him to speak. Gerda wanted to hear what he would say, too. She knew he still hadn't invested in any business in town, even though that's what he'd said he wanted to do. He had purchased her dream house, but he hadn't moved in. There really was nothing to keep him in Litchfield, but now she didn't want him to leave.

"I've been thinking about Sheriff Bartlett's proposal." The rich tones of his voice carried over the crowd straight into Gerda's heart. "I really want to settle down here, and I've been a lawman all my life, so I've decided to take him up on his offer if you good folks would have me as your sheriff."

The cheers drowned out anything else he might have been planning on saying. All Gerda could hear were the shouts and the loud drumbeat of her heart. But there was still a problem standing between them. Although Frank had been attending church, there was no indication that he had become a believer. Gerda couldn't see any future with the man unless he did, and it wouldn't be sincere if he only became a Christian because she wanted him to. It had to be for himself.

With turmoil churning inside her, Gerda slipped away from the crowd and headed back across the street toward the Dress Emporium. After what she had felt again today, she knew that the future sheriff of Litchfield tempted her. To protect her heart, she would just have to keep her distance. Gerda was glad that Frank was going to stay in town, and she was grateful to him for recovering her money, but she couldn't risk getting hurt. She had lived long enough to see how devastating a lost love could be for a woman. Olina had experienced it. So had Anna. And Gerda had been their friend through all the heartaches. She knew it wasn't something she wanted to endure. Especially not because of Frank Daggett.

When she arrived at the store, Gerda realized that she hadn't gotten the reticule with the money in it. With everyone still in the street gathered around Frank, she would just have to wait awhile. Once the crowd dispersed, she'd go over to the sheriff's office to retrieve it and then make her deposit. She headed into the back room to start working on the orders that needed to be completed this week.

Frank saw Gerda slip away. What had gone wrong? He had felt such a connection with her—just like that first day in the hotel. Now she didn't seem to be interested in what was happening to him. Maybe she didn't want him to become sheriff. He needed to find out right away. It wasn't too late to change his mind. He might not look good in the eyes of the people around him if he withdrew his declaration, but it wasn't them he was trying to please.

He waved to the crowd and stepped off the boardwalk, heading toward the dress shop. When he went through the door, the bell tinkled. He glanced up at the brass clanger above the doorway before perusing every corner of the store. No one was in the shop. Gerda must have gone to the back room. Today, he was going to follow her. He took off his hat and held it in one hand, gently tapping it against his leg as he walked. When he parted the curtains, he had to duck his head a little to go between them. Gerda must have heard him enter, because she turned her startled gaze toward him.

"Mr. Daggett, what do you want?" Frank liked the breathless sound of her voice and the way her hand fluttered toward her throat. "Or should I say, Sheriff Daggett?"

Frank studied her for a moment before answering. A blush stole its way across her cheeks, giving them the look of fresh rose petals. Frank didn't know why he was thinking about flowers. It wasn't usual for him, but his feelings for Gerda caused everything in his life to turn upside down.

"Would you rather I didn't take the job as sheriff?"

Gerda took a quick breath before answering. "I think you'll make a wonderful sheriff. And I want to thank you for getting my money back."

Frank remembered the woman's handbag he was still carrying. He gave it to her, then pulled his hat in front of him and started turning it around with both hands. "I was just doing my job."

Gerda's gaze dropped to the star on his chest. "You're already wearing the badge."

Frank tapped the metal with one finger. "The sheriff deputized me before I took the posse out. I forgot to give it back."

"I suppose you'll just exchange it for the sheriff's star, won't you?"

"If you think it's all right." It was important for Frank to hear her say that she wanted him to be sheriff.

"I, for one, would be glad to have you as our lawman. When would you start?" Gerda turned her attention to the reticule in her hands. Her fingers nervously plucked at it.

"I'm not sure. When I get back across the street, I'll ask Sheriff Bartlett when he wants me to start." He wanted to say something else, but he couldn't think of anything. "Good day, Gerda." Frank made his way through the curtains before he put his hat on his head. He was almost out the door before he heard Gerda's answer.

"Good day, Frank."

He liked the way his name sounded coming from her. Softly, he whistled a happy tune as he headed toward the sheriff's office.

The second week Frank was sheriff, he rode his horse all around town checking for anything suspicious. This job might be the easiest he ever had. Everyone loved him and treated him as if he were someone special. After making a turn through the business section of town, he rode through the residential area across the railroad tracks, ending near the smithy and livery.

June had arrived the week before. It looked as if this summer wouldn't be as dry as last year when the livery burned down. This year, spring rains had nourished a good crop of wildflowers, which sprang up all over the place—in town and outside. Trees that dotted the landscape held abundant leaves in varying shades of lush green. Frank took a deep breath of the fresh-smelling air. A cool breeze kept him from getting hot on his ride. He could only think of one way that life could get any better, but he didn't want to torment himself with that remote possibility.

He took a quick glance around then dismounted his horse in front of the smithy. Maybe August would have time to visit with him. He entered the open door and was greeted by the smoky heat from the forge.

August was facing the door. "Frank, what brings you here? Did your horse throw another shoe?"

"No, I just thought I'd pay you a short visit—if you have the time."

August put down the tongs and mallet he was holding, then wiped his hands on his large canvas apron. Then he pulled it over his head and laid it on the table beside his tools. "I'm ready for a break. Do you want to visit here or outside in the fresh air?"

"Outside would be fine."

The two men had just walked through the door when the stationmaster rode up. "I was glad to see your horse tied here, Sheriff Daggett. A rather large shipment arrived for you today. From somewhere back East."

Frank smiled. "It's probably my furniture."

"Yep," the stationmaster agreed. "Could be. There sure are lots of big crates. I thought you might need whatever it is right away, so I came to find you."

"I appreciate that. But there's no rush."

"I need to get back to the station. Good day, gents." The man wheeled his horse around and rode that direction.

"It sounds as though you're going to need that help we offered." August turned to look back toward a table along the wall of the smithy. "It's a good thing I don't have much left to do. I can complete it today."

"You don't have to help—"

"I was there when our family and friends offered to help you get your house ready. Everyone meant what they said."

"But they didn't know when my things would arrive. They might be busy right now—with planting and all that."

"That has been finished a long time." August looked at Frank with a shrewd expression on his face. "Don't you want us to help you?"

What could Frank say to that? Of course he wanted them to help, but he didn't want to be a bother. Then he remembered that Gerda was there when everyone agreed to help him, and she hadn't said that she wouldn't come. Any time he could spend with Gerda was good, wasn't it?

"When do you want to move your things?" August asked.

"I guess I need to clean the house up some, first."

"Today is Friday. I'll see if everyone can come early tomorrow morning. If all of us help, we can have the house ready for the furniture by tomorrow afternoon. I'm sure I can get my brother and brothers-in-law to help."

August arrived at the Dress Emporium just before noon carrying a picnic basket. Gerda was waiting on a customer in the shop when he came in, so he went into the workroom. When Gerda finished, she put the OUT TO LUNCH sign in the window and pulled down the shade on the door. Then she joined Anna and August. A wonderful meal was spread across the cutting table.

"We waited for you, Gerda." Anna turned from placing plates and napkins along the edge of the table. "August brought us a lunch from Mrs. Olson."

Gerda was glad that she wouldn't have to go up to her apartment to eat alone. Sometimes it seemed that everyone else had someone to share meals with. Of course she could go to either one of her brothers' houses for lunch, but she sometimes felt like a fifth wheel on a wagon when she did.

Gerda hugged her brother. "That was thoughtful of you."

They sat in the chairs that had been pulled close to the table. Then August said grace before Anna passed the food around.

When their plates were full, August started talking instead of eating. Gerda thought that was strange. August loved to eat. He worked hard, and he was a big man. He needed a lot of food to keep him going.

"I wanted to tell you something."

Wondering what it could be, Gerda put her fork down on her plate and waited with her hands clasped in her lap.

"Frank's furniture arrived on the morning train." August leaned forward as if eager to impart the news. "I thought it would be a good thing for all of us to help him tomorrow. I'll go talk to Gustaf and Lowell and Ollie."

Anna clasped her hands in her lap. "That will be so much fun. I've always wanted to see inside that house. If all the women get there early in the morning, we can have it cleaned up in plenty of time for the men to move in the furniture by afternoon."

August looked concerned. "I'm not sure about *all* the women. Several of you need to be careful." He glanced down at Anna's abdomen and blushed.

Anna patted his arm. "Oh, August, it won't hurt us to help Frank. Women have babies all the time, and it doesn't keep them from doing their work."

Gerda knew that it wouldn't be easy for her to go into that house and help clean it. The presence of Frank Daggett in the house she had dreamed of owning might be too much heartbreak for her.

"It might not be good to close the Dress Emporium tomorrow. People come into town on Saturdays, and often we get new business then." That sounded reasonable to her. "Maybe I should keep the store open."

"Nonsense." Anna was adamant. "I'll ask the Braxtons to keep an eye on things. If anyone needs us, they can come by Frank's house." She picked up a forkful of mashed potatoes and smiled at Gerda.

How could Gerda disagree with her?

When Marja came into the dress shop later that afternoon, Anna asked for her help.

"I'll come and work in the Dress Emporium, and Johan can run the mercantile." She clapped her hands as she usually did when she was excited. "That way we can help Sheriff Daggett and still keep both stores open." She wheeled around and started toward the door. "I'll go tell Johan. He'll be so glad we can be of assistance."

Now there was no reason for Gerda not to help. She even thought for a moment about feigning a headache or stomachache in the morning, but she knew that wouldn't be honest, so she resigned herself to being in her dream house most of the next day, with the man of her dreams—and both of them out of her reach.

◈

The day turned out more festive than Frank had thought it would. Not only did the Nilssons and Jensons come to help get the house ready for him to move in, but also other people from the church arrived at various intervals during the first part of the morning. Soon the sound of hammers and saws filled the air as the men did minor repairs to the house that had sat vacant for almost a year. Some of the men even brought paint so they could help with the touch-up work. The women opened all the windows and swept and washed until everything in the house gleamed.

Right before noon, a wagon pulled up in front. Frank didn't have to wonder what the back of that wagon held. The tempting aromas of food wafted toward him, making his mouth water and his stomach growl. Belonging to a community satisfied something inside Frank and gave him something that he hadn't known he was lacking. It was almost unbelievable how much these people accepted him and loved him. Laughter and bantering conversations had rung throughout the house all morning. The only voice missing from all the happy noise was the one he most wanted to hear.

Gerda had been very quiet. She had worked efficiently, accomplishing a lot, but her quietness spoke more to his heart than all the loud chatter. Frank wondered if she was still upset because he had bought the house she planned to buy. He also wondered if there was anything he could do to take away the melancholy that surrounded her. It was odd to Frank that no one else noticed.

While Frank and August set up tables made of sawhorses and planks, the women bustled around and started bringing all kinds of food to cover them. Soon the workers gathered around the bounty, but no one ventured to pick up a plate to fill. For a moment Frank wondered why, then it hit him.

He turned toward the preacher, who looked more like a lumberjack that day since he was dressed in a plaid shirt and denim trousers. "Pastor Harrelson, would you say grace so we can eat what these wonderful women prepared for us?"

Just before Frank bowed his head, he noticed that Gerda looked at him with a bemused expression on her face. He knew what grace was. His mother had always said a prayer before a meal when he was a young boy. Why should Gerda think he wouldn't know about that? Whenever he joined her family for a meal, he always bowed his head when they said grace. That woman surely was a puzzle to him. A puzzle he wanted to solve really soon.

◈

After lunch, several of the men took their wagons to the station to pick up the crates of household furnishings. Gerda was glad they would be gone for a little while. All through the meal, she had felt Frank's gaze on her. She'd tried not to look directly at him, but occasionally she'd cast a sidelong glance his way. It was almost as if he were watching for her reaction to everything that happened today. How she wished she were back at the store where she felt more comfortable doing what she usually did.

During the morning, Olina and Anna had tried to get her to participate in the discussions that went on all around. Although she answered their inquiries, she didn't feel like talking very much. The whole day had the feeling of a festival, but her heart wasn't in that kind of mood.

Although she'd never been inside it before, Gerda had fallen in love with the outside of the house. That's why she'd made inquiries about buying it. She knew that she could change how the inside was decorated if she needed to.

When she first walked into the parlor, she gasped. The wallpaper pattern was one of her favorites. Trellises, green leaves, and cabbage roses made the room feel like a garden. She knew just the kind of furniture she would use in it to make it feel like home.

Her fingers itched to make curtains to frame the windows with shades of fabric that would complement the wallpaper. If all this went on much longer, she might just have the headache or stomachache she'd thought about feigning yesterday.

When she finished in the parlor, she went to the dining room. Once again, the wallpaper pleased her, and she mentally placed a large cherrywood table in the center of the room. Carved lion's paw legs rested on a hand-loomed rug that echoed the wallpaper pattern.

She turned left at the doorway. Quickly, she toured the other rooms, upstairs and down. Everything she saw illustrated the home she hoped to have someday.

Soon the men returned from the station with their wagons loaded down with crates. Frank called Anna and Gerda into the parlor.

"I need a woman's touch to make this house a real home." He smiled at them. "Would you help me decide where to put the furniture?"

How could Gerda refuse graciously? There didn't seem to be any way.

When the men opened the first crate of furniture in the parlor, Gerda could hardly believe her eyes. The settee was the exact style she had imagined. Even the upholstery fabric was the same color. All she wanted to do was go home and spend time by herself. This day was one of the longest she had ever lived.

When everyone had gone, Frank walked through his new house. It wasn't just a house. It looked like a real home. He was glad that he had asked Gerda and Anna to help him decide where to put each piece of furniture. There was something about a woman's perspective that added to each room's uniqueness.

Several of the other women had unpacked all the kitchen items while the furniture was being dispersed. It looked as if it was waiting for a cook to come and prepare a meal. The rest of the house was almost full. Of course, he would need to purchase a few items, but he wasn't in a hurry. He wanted Gerda to help him, but he knew she wasn't ready for that. She had been wonderful working with Anna and him today, but when it was time to leave, he felt her withdraw from him once again.

That woman was an enigma. Would he ever understand her?

Chapter 11

Frank went to the hotel to check out of his room. He loaded his belongings on his horse and rode across town to his house—home. The word had a nice ring to it. It had been many years since he'd had a place to call home.

Frank took his horse into the small stable behind the house. While he groomed him, he familiarized himself with the rest of the structure.

His horse nudged him on the shoulder, trying to get his attention.

"You miss me talking to you, don't you?" He stroked the animal's glossy neck. "How would you like to share your home? I want to get a carriage. I won't ask you to pull it, my friend. There's plenty of room for another horse or two."

He finished grooming his stallion and gave him a scoop of oats. "Now that you've got your supper, I'm going in to enjoy the feast the women left in the kitchen for me. There's enough on the table and in the icebox to keep me from starving tonight and tomorrow."

When he arrived upstairs at the master bedroom, he dropped his saddlebags on top of the bureau. He'd unload them later. There were several boxes marked PERSONAL ITEMS sitting along one wall. Frank couldn't imagine what was in those boxes, but he would find out when he unpacked them. He decided to wait until after church tomorrow to do that. It had been a long day, and he was exhausted. All he wanted to do was try out the bathtub in the bathroom down the hall. A soak in hot water should help relieve the aches from all the activities his body wasn't used to. If he could talk to Mr. Nichols, he would thank him for installing one of those water heaters. Frank had loaded it with wood and lit it before he went to the hotel for his belongings.

He almost fell asleep in the tub, but when the water cooled, it brought him back to full awareness of his surroundings. After a late supper, he went right to bed. He didn't want to be late for the church service the next day.

Once again, this week's sermon made Frank think. Joseph Harrelson was a man of God, but he spoke to the lives of ordinary men—like a lawman who had drifted too long. He helped Frank understand that he needed an anchor, but Frank still didn't know how to find that anchor. He wished he had a Bible so he could reread the verses the preacher shared with them. He wanted to mull over the words. Maybe on Monday he'd go to Braxton's Mercantile and see if they had any Bibles for sale.

After having lunch with August and Anna, Frank returned to his house, once again reveling in the joy of owning a home. The only thing that bothered him was the fact that he didn't have anyone to share his feelings with. *A man needed a wife in more ways than one.* Hard on the heels of that thought came the picture of Gerda as she helped arrange his house. She'd worn a scarf over her hair and tied it behind her neck. Tendrils crept out from under the covering, and she often blew them away from her face. Frank would like to see her in this house every day. Oh yes, she was just the woman this house needed. Although she had helped all day yesterday, she concentrated on the house and what needed to be done instead of paying him any attention.

Frank took off his Sunday-go-to-meeting clothes and slid into denim trousers and a well-worn plaid shirt. Today, he wasn't going to put on the star. He had a deputy who could take care of things this weekend. Once again, Frank's attention was drawn to the boxes by the wall in his bedroom. He might as well open them now.

When he took the lid off the first box, tears pooled in his eyes. There, carefully packed, were various sheets and pillowcases that his mother had lovingly decorated with colorful, embroidered flowers. When he was a lad, he had watched her work by the light of a kerosene lamp while rocking in her favorite chair. The warmth of those memories fueled the tears, and they poured down his cheeks unchecked. He placed the lid back on the box. He would probably use the linens, but he wasn't ready to unpack them yet. Here he was, a lawman who could face down the hardest criminal, blubbering over a few pieces of cloth. It was a good thing no one was watching.

The second box opened to reveal various items carefully wrapped in newspaper. He unwrapped one. It was a tiny shepherd girl made out of china. He remembered it sitting on a table by his mother's rocker. She often looked at it fondly. She said it was a touch of beauty in her life. Other beloved knickknacks of his mother's were also tucked into this box. He decided to store them in one of the bedrooms until he knew what he wanted to do with them. Later he might put a few of them on display in the parlor. They were fond reminders of his mother, and women seemed to like that sort of thing. Similar items were scattered about the parlors of the friends he had made here in Litchfield. Gerda and Anna had several of this style of knickknack on display in the Dress Emporium.

The last box he opened contained his mother's books. She had always been a woman who loved to read. Some of the books, she had read to him. Adventure stories and tales about King Arthur and the Knights of the Round Table. He carried this box downstairs and started placing the books in the empty bookcase that had been set against a wall in the parlor. At the bottom of the box, Frank found his mother's Bible.

This was an answer to a prayer he hadn't even uttered. He had a Bible of his own. Frank thought for a minute until he called to mind the scripture reference Pastor Harrelson used this morning. Then he tried to find it. As he turned through the worn pages, there were many places where his mother had written notes in the margins, and all the family history was recorded on the parchment pages in the center of the book. Frank went to the rocking chair near the window—the one his mother had often sat in. He cradled the large book in his arms as he turned through each section. He knew he held a real treasure in his hands. His mother had been a godly woman. She knew what this book contained, and he vowed that he would, too—soon. Frank sat in the chair and read the verses from the morning sermon. Then he moved into other areas of the book. Before he realized it, the whole afternoon had passed, and the light was becoming too dim to read by.

After spending Saturday at Frank's, Gerda's attraction to the man had multiplied. She pictured him in the house that was furnished much the way she would have done it. Thoughts of her and Frank sharing the home as man and wife tormented her. No matter how hard she tried to banish them, they crept back into her mind. *Oh, Father God, what am I going to do? Please help me get over my attraction to this man.*

Gerda again wished God would answer her audibly. She didn't care if it was thunder from heaven or just a whisper. She just wanted God to tell her what to do. But her apartment was silent, and in the recesses of her mind where she often heard from God, silence also reigned.

On Monday, Gerda opened the store bright and early. She hoped that working on some of the orders for new clothes that were stacked up in the back room would give her something besides Frank Daggett to think about. She chose three different dresses she wanted to start working on today. She cut the dress lengths from the bolts of fabric the customers had chosen. Then she returned the rest of each bolt to the shelves behind the counter in the front of the store.

Gerda had just placed the last of the bolts on a shelf high above her head when she heard the bell above the door jingle. She turned to greet the customer but stopped in midstride. It wasn't a woman looking for something to wear who walked across the floor toward her. As if the thoughts she had been wrestling with had called him to come, the sheriff was striding toward her, his Stetson in hand, his boots beating a rhythm against the polished wooden floor. With each step, her heartbeat thudded just as loudly. The man looked too good in his black twill trousers and starched gray cotton shirt with the silver star shining on his chest. He had removed his hat, and dark curls tumbled across his brow, framing his clear blue eyes. Even his mustache looked as if it had recently been trimmed.

"Well, do I pass inspection?" When Frank spoke, his voice tilted along with his upraised eyebrow.

Gerda gulped, and she felt a blush make its way to her cheeks. *I shouldn't have been staring at him.* She turned away and started rearranging the bolts that weren't in disarray. "What can I do for you, Sheriff?" She kept her head turned far enough that she could see what he was doing, even though her back was to him.

Frank set his Stetson down and leaned on the counter with both hands. "I thought I might be able to do something for you, Gerda."

She liked the way her name sounded coming from him. He always softened his rich baritone voice when he spoke to her. Slowly, she turned and glanced up at him.

"I don't need any help, Frank."

His mesmerizing eyes held a twinkle. "I'm just making my rounds, checking on things. I'm glad everything's all right with you."

Gerda smiled. "Thank you."

"And I want to thank you for all the help you gave me on Saturday." The intensity of his gaze continued to hold her captive. "Without your suggestions, I probably would have lined the furniture up along the walls in each room. My house looks like a home thanks to you. . .and Anna."

Gerda thought the room had gradually gotten very warm. The intensity of the connection she felt to this man was almost tangible. *God, where are You now?*

Frank straightened. He picked up his hat from the counter and held it in front of his waist. "I'll be moseying on down the street. You be sure to get in touch with me if you need me for anything."

Gerda couldn't answer him. She just stood still and watched him walk out the door. When it latched behind him, she leaned back against the shelf behind her and took a deep breath. There seemed to be more air in the room now, and it felt cooler.

She went back into the workroom and sat in the chair by the window. She thought about every second that had transpired in the other room. Then she tried to shut Frank Daggett out of her thoughts, but it didn't work. Maybe praying would help.

"Father God, I don't like what's happening to me. I want to be a wife and mother just as all my friends are. But I can't do that without a husband. Please, Lord, bring me a man to love. Surely You have one for me, and he won't be a man who doesn't profess to believe in You." She sat quietly for a few moments, then whispered, "Amen."

That evening when Gerda finished working, she returned to her apartment. She roamed the rooms restlessly and finally sat down and picked up her Bible. She reread the verses Pastor Joseph used yesterday. Once again, she agreed with what the pastor said. She was thankful God had provided such a strong man of God to share His Word with the congregation.

Gerda knew her problem was that she was alone. Everyone she knew had someone. Even former Sheriff Bartlett and Mrs. Jenson were getting married. She wanted a husband and family, and she didn't want to wait very long before she had them.

She leafed through the pages of her Bible. When her hands stilled, the book was open at First Corinthians. She began reading the words, trying to find some comfort. One verse almost leaped off the page at her.

She reread the words from chapter 10, verse 13.

There hath no temptation taken you but such as is common to man: but God is faithful, who will not suffer you to be tempted above that ye are able; but will with the temptation also make a way to escape, that ye may be able to bear it.

"That's what I'm trying to do, Lord." Gerda spoke the words aloud. "I want to escape from the temptation of Frank Daggett. Father, he's not a believer, but he is such a temptation to me. Please give me a way to escape that temptation."

Two days later, when Anna and Gerda were working together, Olina came to see them. The women had been chatting a few minutes when she said, "I have an idea. Why don't we give Frank a housewarming?"

"That would be wonderful!" Anna took the skirt she had been hemming and placed it on a worktable, then turned to look at her friends. "There are some things he still needs in his house."

Gerda wasn't sure it was such a good idea. It would mean spending more time with the man, and she was just now getting her emotions under control after his visit to the store on Monday.

Anna gestured toward her. "Don't you agree, Gerda?"

How could she not agree? If she didn't, they would both think she was awful. "It wouldn't hurt."

Anna looked at her as if she were crazy. "What a funny way to put it!"

Olina sat on one of the extra chairs. "I'm sure almost everyone will come to honor Frank. He's done so much for the town, and it'll be a way for people to show their appreciation."

Gerda thought that hiring him as sheriff had been a good way to show their appreciation, but she didn't say so.

"When should we have it?" Anna had picked up the tablet they kept in the workroom. She poised a pencil over it. "Do we want it to be a surprise to him, or should we tell him?"

"You know how men are." Olina laughed. "We'd better warn him so his house won't be in disarray."

"Maybe we should ask him first." Gerda looked from one of her friends to the other. "He might not like it."

"What's not to like?" Anna asked. "But I think you're right. We should ask him what date he wants to do it, but we won't give him the option of not having one."

☙❧

Frank hadn't imagined anyone doing anything so wonderful for him. He thought they had assisted him more than enough when they'd helped him get his house ready and then move his furniture in. He'd almost told the women he didn't think this housewarming was necessary, but he was glad he hadn't. Gerda had been involved with it from the beginning, and now she was in his kitchen, looking as if she belonged there. Gerda, Anna, Olina, and the twins who had married Anna's brothers had cooked enough goodies to feed an army, and it was a good thing, because people had been coming by all afternoon.

Not only did they welcome him and share the refreshments, they all brought gifts. Frank was beginning to wonder what he was going to do with all the things they gave him. Some of the women had made lacy doilies to put on his furniture. Others brought things they had canned. He was glad to get all the jams and jellies. He really liked that stuff on his biscuits in the mornings. Many kinds of staples filled his pantry and overflowed onto the cabinets.

Frank wasn't sure why he needed all this food. He hadn't planned on doing a lot of cooking. He'd never really learned how to cook many things. He knew how to boil a pot of beans and fry a pan of corn bread. He could do a good breakfast—bacon or ham and eggs with biscuits. Or he could cook up a pan of mush, but for most of his other meals, he went out. Maybe he would have to ask some of the women to teach him how to cook other things.

A couple of farmers had even brought hay and feed for his horse. He wouldn't have to buy anything for quite a while. August helped him stack the hay bales and sacks of feed in the stable.

"Thank you for all your help." Frank leaned his elbow on the top rail of one of the stalls. "I can't believe the bounty all you folks brought to me."

"That's how people around here are." August moved toward the open doorway. "I'm going to take the wagon home and come back with the buggy to pick up Anna. The springs are better on the buggy."

When the last of the visitors had left, Frank went to the kitchen. "Well, did they eat all the wonderful things you women fixed?"

Anna turned from the dishpan where her hands were busy with a dishrag in the sudsy water. "There are a few things left for you to eat." She nodded toward two plates piled high with cookies and pieces of cake.

Frank smiled at her. "Why don't you let me finish washing those dishes? You go sit down. You've been on your feet all day." He glanced toward the woman who was drying the dishes Anna had finished washing.

Anna looked as if she might object, but she stopped when she saw the direction he was looking. She quickly rinsed off her hands and dried them on one of the towels that had been in a package earlier that afternoon. "I do feel like resting a little. I think I'll try out that rocking chair until August gets here to pick me up." She stepped through the door toward the parlor.

Frank plunged his hands into the warm water and turned his attention toward Gerda. She had kept her distance ever since the Monday morning he'd visited her in the dress shop. He wanted that to change. At first she kept her gaze glued to the plate she was drying.

"Are you trying to rub the flowers off that dish? I don't think they are supposed to come off." Frank chuckled at his own joke.

Gerda glanced toward him. She looked as if she were trying not to laugh. "That was really corny, Frank."

He rinsed another plate and handed it to her. When he did, their fingers brushed. For a moment, he thought she was going to drop the slick china. He grabbed for it, and his hands covered hers as they cradled the dish. She looked up at him, and the strong connection that sometimes came between them sizzled in the air. Frank could feel it, and the blue of her eyes darkened with intensity that held him captive. She gasped, and he felt her grip on the dish tighten, but she didn't look away.

They were standing so close he could see the golden tips at the end of her dark eyelashes. Wisps of blond curls around her face gave her a soft, vulnerable look. Frank wanted to pull her into his arms and place a kiss on the lips that were slightly open in surprise. Her gentle perfume filled his nostrils, and his heart longed for what he didn't have. Frank knew they were in dangerous territory, and he didn't want to frighten her, so he stepped back and released his hold on her hands. She took a deep breath and rubbed the moisture from the plate.

Frank started washing the other dishes. "It's been a wonderful afternoon, hasn't it?"

He sensed Gerda finally relaxing. He had done the right thing in stepping back, but it was one of the hardest things he had ever done. Never in his life had he wanted a woman more than he wanted this one. He remembered what he thought the first time he saw her. That she had strings hanging off her so long that they would really hog-tie a man. Well, he was a man who wanted to be hog-tied now, and he didn't think she was ready to hear that.

Chapter 12

The rest of that week, Frank was eager to get home after work each day. He kept his mother's Bible on the table in the kitchen and read while he ate dinner. He couldn't get enough of it. He hadn't realized that the book contained so many interesting stories. When he read the words Jesus spoke in the New Testament, they tugged on his heart. If only Frank hadn't lived such a hard life. Maybe the words of Jesus could apply to his life, too.

The next Sunday at church, he sat where he could watch Gerda during the service. He always did that. He just couldn't get enough of looking at her. At first, he feasted on her loveliness. She was dressed in a shade of blue that matched her eyes. Although he couldn't see her eyes from where he sat, he knew that color would bring out the sparkle in them. She had her hair pulled up into a hairdo similar to the ones on those calendars that were becoming popular. The hat that rested on top of the pouf had a large, fluffy feather wound around the wide brim. Frank felt sure that feather would tickle any man who got near her. Maybe that was why she wore it.

Soon Joseph Harrelson's words caught his attention and held it. Frank had learned to respect this man. Many of the preachers he had known in the past were either out of touch with the realities of life or were complete hypocrites. Not Joseph. He lived the life he preached about, and he was keenly aware of what his parishioners were going through. They could see God in Pastor Harrelson's life. That was why the church services were always full. People loved Joseph, and they trusted him.

Frank leaned forward in his seat and hung on to every word the man spoke. Words of comfort for the grieving. Words of hope for those who were in despair. Then Joseph began telling about his own life.

"Before I came to know the Lord, I was a young, hotheaded gunman with a chip on my shoulder."

His words surprised Frank. He never would have guessed this about the man.

"I thought I was going to conquer the West with my lightning-fast guns. All I did was dig a deeper hole for my soul to sink into."

The preacher's words called out to Frank. He understood that kind of hole.

"I killed innocent men and misused women."

It seemed to Frank as if Joseph was talking about a stranger he once knew.

"I was finally arrested, convicted, and sent to prison. I thought it was the end of my life, but it was only the beginning. While I was there, a pastor visited me every day. He led me to the Lord and discipled me."

Frank wondered what that meant.

"Eventually, because of the change that had come about in my heart, God arranged for me to be set free from my life sentence. Only God could have accomplished that feat. After that, I couldn't do anything but preach the gospel of Jesus Christ. For the last five years, I've done that, and I've been in Litchfield for the last couple of years."

Frank was so engrossed in the sermon that he hadn't realized it was time for the service to be over. He was so deep in thought about what he'd heard that everyone had left the room without his knowing it, leaving him sitting on the pew. When Frank finally looked around, he was all alone in the house of God, wondering if maybe what Joseph had talked about could also happen to a man like himself. A man who had done more than his fair share of hard living. A man who had made his living with a gun—but on the right side of the law. A man who was ready for a change in his heart and life.

"God, I need some answers." He spoke the words aloud, not expecting an audible reply.

"Can we help?" The voice sounded familiar.

Frank turned to see Gustaf standing in the doorway with August right behind him.

"We wondered why you didn't come out of the building when everyone else did. We told the pastor that we'd check on you so the Jensons wouldn't have to wait for Joseph to get to their house to start eating lunch." Gustaf dropped on the back pew beside Frank. "August and I sent our wives and family home together. We didn't want to leave you here alone if you needed us."

August stood behind his brother with one hand leaning on the end of pew. "We're here if you want to talk."

Frank was flabbergasted. In all of his adult life, he'd never had any friends like these two men. It was still hard for him to understand this kind of friendship. He rubbed his palms down his thighs while deciding what to say to them.

"I've been listening to the sermons and wondering what it's all about. I found my mother's Bible in the things I received last week, and I've been reading it." Frank wanted to stand up and pace, but he decided not to. "After the message today, I have a lot of questions."

August moved to the pew in front of where Frank and Gustaf sat. He dropped onto the seat but turned sideways in it so he could face Frank. "I'm not sure we'll know the answers, but you could ask us anyway. Maybe we can be of some help."

Now Frank couldn't stay seated. He stood and walked around the other end of the pew and along behind it. He leaned his hands on the back of the bench near where he had been sitting. There was something about this place that made him want to open his thoughts and heart to these friends.

"I've been hearing about Jesus and what He did to save people from their sins. I just have a hard time believing that all my sins can be forgiven." He straightened and rubbed the back of his neck with one hand. "It's only recently that I understood I needed this kind of thing."

Gustaf stood and faced him. "Everyone needs salvation."

August looked up at Frank. "A verse that comes to my mind is John 3:16 and the words that follow." He lifted an open Bible toward Frank. "They have been very important to me all my adult life. I've read them so many times, I can recite them. They're right there on that page if you want to follow along. 'For God so loved the world, that he gave his only begotten Son, that whosoever believeth in him should not perish, but have everlasting life. For God sent not his Son into the world to condemn the world; but that the world through him might be saved. He that believeth on him is not condemned: but he that believeth not is condemned already, because he hath not believed in the name of the only begotten Son of God.' You know, I believe that 'whosoever' means me. And it means you, too."

Gustaf added, "I've put my own name into that verse many times. For God so loved the world, that He gave His only begotten Son, that when Gustaf believes in Him, he shall not perish, but have everlasting life. It gives you a different perspective on it."

Frank could understand that. He read from the page before him. "For God so loved the world, that He gave His only begotten Son, that when Frank Daggett believes in Him, he shall not perish, but have everlasting life. I like the sound of that. But is it hard to live out?"

Gustaf gave a deep hearty laugh. "Life doesn't stop having problems just because you receive salvation from your sins. Life goes on, and you have to meet it head-on."

Frank moved back around the pew and sat beside Gustaf. "So tell me about your big problems."

"It's a long story, but I'll try to make it short." Gustaf leaned forward and dangled his hands between his knees. "When Olina came to the United States from Sweden, she was coming to marry our brother, Lars."

"I haven't met him, have I?" Frank leaned his arm along the back of the pew.

"No, he lives in Denver, and he doesn't come here very often."

Frank chuckled. "What terrible thing did he do to cause Olina to marry you instead?"

"He married another woman before she got here. Olina was devastated, and

I didn't make it any better by not telling her right away when I met her at the docks in New York City. I really hadn't wanted to go meet her, but my parents asked me to. It was my plan to put her right back on a boat heading for Sweden. I didn't know that she'd gone against her father's wishes when she came here and she couldn't go back. It took awhile for it all to work out, but eventually we realized that it was God's plan for her to come here, and it wasn't to marry Lars. It was to marry me. God's thoughts and plans are often different from our own, but His way is always best." Gustaf leaned back in the pew and looked across at Frank. "When you have the Lord in your life, it's always easier to face major problems."

Then August turned toward Frank. "And if there is an area of your life that you haven't yielded to Him, it can cause you extreme difficulties. I resented Gustaf a lot of my younger life. I was jealous of him, and because of that jealousy, I almost missed the woman God intended for me to marry."

Frank squinted his eyes. "If I look confused, it's because I am. What are you talking about?"

Gustaf laughed. "I guess it's a lot to tell you all at once. I was keeping company with Anna before Olina came. After she arrived, I knew that because my thoughts were so often on Olina, I didn't love Anna the way she should be loved by a man who wanted to marry her. When I told her that we weren't right for each other, it broke her heart."

August took up the narrative. "I didn't want my brother's castoff. That's how I thought about Anna. It didn't matter that I had been interested in her long before my brother was but was too shy to say anything to her. After he was with her, I didn't want her, even though I did. Does that make any sense?"

Frank tried not to laugh. "I'm glad I'm not the only person who has had a mixed-up life."

"I waited around too long, and Olaf Johanson starting seeing Anna. They were engaged to be married."

This was getting interesting, almost like one of those dime novels Frank had read in the past. "So how did you get her away from him?"

August hung his head a minute before he raised it and continued. "Olaf was killed on a hunting trip right before the wedding. Anna was devastated. The funeral was on the day that was supposed to be their wedding. A lot happened, but eventually all of us listened to the Lord speaking to us, and Anna and I were married. But not until I had faced the jealousy that had consumed my life. The Lord helped Gustaf and me find the root of that jealousy and dig it out of my heart. Just think. If we hadn't listened to the Lord. . .or if we hadn't had Him in our lives, things might not have turned out the way they did."

Frank looked toward the one stained glass window behind the pulpit. The sun shining through the colored pieces of glass painted the room in a warm, multicolor glow. "I can see the need for having Him in my life. What do I do now?"

Gustaf stood and moved into the aisle between the pews. "We could go down to the altar at the front of the church. We'll kneel with you while you tell the Lord that you want Him to be a part of your life."

That sounded better than anything else he had heard that day. He wanted this salvation. He wanted what his friends had in their lives, but he was afraid he wouldn't do it right. These men could help him say the right thing.

August must have read his thoughts. "When you get down there, just tell Jesus that you know you're a sinner. You're sorry for all you've done, and you want Him to come into your life and change it."

That sounded simple enough. Frank hoped it would work with him. They knelt at the altar, and he started speaking, hesitantly at first. Then the words poured out of him. Later, he wasn't sure exactly what all he'd said, but he did remember asking for forgiveness for his sins and telling Jesus that he wanted Him in his life from that point on. Tears were streaming down his face, and he didn't care that these two men were seeing them.

When the three men finally stood, Frank couldn't explain how he felt. It was as though he were a new man. One who hadn't done all the things that had affected his life. His heart was a clean slate, ready to receive whatever the Lord wanted to give him. And he felt lighter, as if a large burden had lifted from his mind and from his soul.

He looked at Gustaf. There was a hint of moisture around his eyes. He glanced at August, who had wet trails down his cheeks. These two friends had shed tears for him, and he loved them more than he had loved any other men he had ever known. A prayer of thanks for their friendship went up from his heart, and he knew that God heard every word of it.

When Frank arrived at home that afternoon, he started to change out of his good clothes. He opened the top drawer of his bureau. There, carelessly thrown aside, were his cigars and matches. He stared at them for a minute. He couldn't remember the last time he had lit one of the smelly things. None of his new friends smoked, and he hadn't wanted to do it around them. Now all desire for partaking in the use of tobacco had left him. Without hesitating, he picked up the cheroots and went downstairs to throw them away. He knew he would never smoke again.

Chapter 13

Soon after Gerda opened the Dress Emporium on Monday, Anna rushed through the door carrying a basket over her arm.

"What's your hurry?" Gerda asked her. "You don't have to be here at a certain time. Actually, you don't have to come to work if you don't want to."

Anna set the basket down. The warm scent of cinnamon and fruit pastries quickly filled the workroom. "I brought you some apple fritters. I know how much you like them, and I'm sure you don't often take time to cook a good breakfast just for yourself."

Gerda knew her sheepish smile revealed the truth of that statement. "At least before I came down, I made a pot of tea to drink while I read my Bible this morning." She moved over to peer under the checkered napkin that covered the goodies. When she lifted the corner, steam escaped, bringing even more spicy fragrance with it. She took a deep breath of the heavenly scent, and her stomach growled in a most unladylike manner. "I think I'll try one of these right now."

She went to the small cabinet that August had built into one corner of the workroom where she and Anna kept a supply of dishes and silverware on one shelf. She set a small plate on the table and lifted a warm fritter from the basket with a fork. She put it on the plate and cut a bite.

"Mmm, this is good." Gerda took her time enjoying the flavor. "Is my well-being the only reason you're here so early?"

Anna busied herself with one of the dresses they were working on. "August suggested that I might want to get here early today." She ducked her head and concentrated hard on the skirt she was hemming.

Gerda put her fork down. "Now why would he do that?"

"I'm not sure, but he was in a good mood when he finally came home from church yesterday. That's all I know."

"Didn't he go home when you did?" Gerda sat in the chair by the window and took another bite. It tasted even better than the first one. If she ate like this every day, she would soon be unable to wear any of her clothes.

"No." Anna looked up. "I rode home with Olina and the children. August and Gustaf stayed to see about something. August came home after a while with a twinkle in his eyes and a big smile on his face. I think he was even whistling a cheery tune. He doesn't often do that."

Soon the bell over the door in the front room jingled. Since Anna had her lap full with the skirt she was working on, Gerda went through the curtains separating the two rooms. Frank Daggett stood in the middle of the room holding a large bouquet of flowers. It should have seemed incongruous for the masculine sheriff to have something so beautiful in his hands, but to Gerda he looked wonderful. She wondered why he was there. And why he was carrying those fresh blossoms.

"Good morning, Gerda." His voice was soft as he said her name. It sounded like a caress.

"Sheriff." Gerda gave a slight nod, not able to take her eyes off him standing tall and regal. Just looking at him made her insides turn to jelly.

Something looked different about him this morning, but Gerda couldn't figure out what it was. He wasn't wearing his Stetson and his hands were full of flowers, but that shouldn't have made that much difference. As usual when he wasn't wearing a hat, curls fell across his forehead. Not for the first time, Gerda felt a strong desire to run her fingers through those dark locks. She took a deep breath. The expression in his blue eyes was warmer than she had ever seen it, but that wasn't enough to give her the feeling that something was drastically different. She just couldn't put her finger on what it was.

"Call me Frank, Gerda. I'm not wearing the star today." Then, as if he had just now realized what he was holding, he stepped closer to her and thrust the bouquet in her direction. "These are for you." He concentrated his attention on her face, almost as if he were trying to memorize every inch of it.

As she reached out to gather the flowers into her arms, Gerda felt a blush stain her cheeks. "Thank you. . .Frank." She buried her nose in the petals, savoring the scent of a summer meadow. "Let's go into the workroom. I have a vase we can put these in."

Frank pulled the curtains back for her, then followed her into the next room.

When they entered, Anna looked up and smiled. "Why, Sheriff Daggett, it's good to see you this morning."

Gerda glanced back at Frank. He reached up as if to tip his hat, then dropped his hand back to his side because his hat wasn't there as it usually was. What was he doing here, and why did he bring her flowers? Gerda didn't get an answer to her question. Frank stayed for a few minutes and shared small talk with the two women, but he didn't say anything about his reason for being there.

Before he left, Gerda was once again captured by his gaze. Everything around them faded away. She allowed herself to get lost in the moment, but soon he glanced toward the window

"I need to get over to the office and relieve the deputy." Frank looked back toward Gerda. "I'll be seeing you soon. Gerda. . .Anna." He nodded at each woman before he exited the room.

Gerda stood where she was, lost in thought.

"Wasn't that nice of the sheriff to bring flowers?" Anna's words broke into Gerda's thoughts. "We should have offered him some of the fritters."

She looked toward Anna and gave her a distracted nod.

Frank pinned on his star, then pushed the hair off his forehead and settled his Stetson on his head. He walked up one side of Main Street and down the other, then he crossed the tracks and strode toward the livery. Although it was late June, the temperature felt more like late spring than summer. A soft breeze blew through the trees, rustling the leaves. Birds chirped from among the branches, but he couldn't see any. He wondered just how many nests he would find if he were to climb some of those trees and search among the branches as he had done when he was a boy on the farm. The thought of a sheriff doing that brought a smile to his lips.

As he walked by one house, Frank caught the faint scent of the climbing roses on the trellis by the front porch. In other yards, various cultivated flowers added a multicolored patchwork to the manicured lawns. He couldn't ever remember noticing so many things about the landscape. Somehow, the earth felt new this morning. Maybe he should plant some roses or other flowers around his home. For a fleeting moment, he wondered if Gerda would like that. *I know she likes wildflowers.*

He reached the stable and looked inside. Hank was feeding some of the animals that were in the many stalls.

"Hank, is everything all right?"

The other man looked up. "Just fine, Sheriff."

Frank headed toward the smithy. The doors were wide open, so August must already be working.

When Frank darkened the doorway, August glanced toward him. "Ah, Frank, how are you this morning? Still feeling as good as you did yesterday?"

Frank took off his hat and gently tapped it on one leg while he talked. "Every bit as good. Does this feeling ever go away?"

August laughed. "It's really new to you. You'll get used to it, and some days you might not even notice, but the Lord's presence is always with you, and it changes everything in your life."

Frank stepped into the shaded interior of the building. August hadn't fired up the forge yet, so it was still comfortable.

"I took a big bouquet of those wildflowers you told me about to Gerda this morning."

Frank leaned against the table that ran along one wall of the smithy, then placed his hat on a clear spot behind him.

August joined him. "How did that go?"

"All right, I guess. We just talked a few minutes, and I left."

"Did Anna offer you some of the apple fritters she made this morning?"

Suddenly, Frank realized that there had been a spicy fragrance in the work-room of the dress shop. He had concentrated on Gerda so much that he hadn't let it sink in. He chuckled.

"I didn't even notice them when I was there. I was. . .looking at Gerda."

August laughed hard. "You have it bad, don't you? Wait until I tell Gustaf. He'll appreciate this."

Frank crossed his ankles and looked down at the toes of his boots. "I've never tried to woo a woman before. I'll try to remember all you and Gustaf told me about her. I just don't want to scare her away before I can ask her to marry me."

August laughed again.

Frank shook his head. "You sure are getting a lot of fun out of my predica-ment, August. Maybe it was a mistake to talk to you and Gustaf yesterday."

"No, Frank, we're glad you're interested in Gerda." He tried to smother another laugh and failed. "That's why we're going to help you with your courtship."

Frank tried to frown at him but didn't quite make it. "And I appreciate that. I just hope the flowers are a good enough hint."

When Frank walked away, his thoughts returned to his desire for a wife and children.

And not just any wife would do. It had to be Gerda Nilsson.

When Gerda went to her apartment for lunch, she couldn't get Frank out of her mind. The picture of the tall lawman standing in the middle of a women's dress shop holding a bouquet of flowers had set her heart beating almost double time. She hadn't been able to settle down to anything for more than a few minutes the whole morning. Now, here she was trying to eat a light lunch, but the food didn't hold her interest either.

Gerda had set the bouquet on her dining room table. It took up too much space in the workroom. Besides, with it up here, maybe this afternoon she could concentrate on what needed to be done. She laid her fork on her plate and looked at the vase. She propped her elbows on the table—something her mother had told her never to do—then dropped her head into her hands.

Father God, I prayed for You to bring me a man to love. I asked You to remove the temptation of Frank Daggett, but You haven't. What am I supposed to do?

The food on her plate still didn't look appetizing. She took it over to the cabinet and covered it with a tea towel, then set it in the icebox. Maybe she would eat it for dinner.

Gerda paced through the dining room and into the parlor, then back again.

The second time around, she stopped to look at the flowers. The only way Frank could have gotten a large bouquet like this was to pick them this morning. For some reason, she couldn't picture him out gathering wildflowers, but here they were—on her table. If he was going to go to that much trouble, why didn't he tell her why he'd brought them to her?

Soon Gerda returned to the dress shop. Anna was only working half a day today. She had gone home at lunchtime, so Gerda would be alone. Maybe she could get something accomplished this afternoon. She sat at the treadle sewing machine and looked out the window before she started sewing the seams on a light blue dimity dress for the mayor's daughter. Soon she was lost in getting as much of the sewing done as possible. She almost didn't hear the bell jingle when the shop door opened.

In a repeat of the morning, when Gerda went out front, Frank was standing in the middle of the room. This time, he held a small package. From the looks of it, she surmised he had probably wrapped it himself.

Gerda stood still and looked at him. "Do you need something, Frank?"

"Actually, I brought you something." He thrust the badly wrapped package toward her.

She took it. "Why are you doing all this?"

Frank's gaze bored into hers with an expression that looked almost like yearning. "I'm really interested in you, Gerda." He reached his hand toward her before dropping it to his side.

Gerda glanced at the present in her hands. She moved to the counter and laid it down before she began opening it. The small box held a delicate china shepherdess. She gently picked it up and examined it. Anything to keep her attention off Frank. Because he wasn't a Christian, she didn't know what to say to his declaration.

"This is exquisite." She glanced up at the tall lawman who was studying her intently.

"It belonged to my mother." He blew out a deep breath. "I thought you might like to have it."

"I would, but maybe you should keep it in your family." She extended the figurine toward him.

"I don't have a family."

Such a mournful-sounding phrase.

Once again she was captured by his tender expression. What could she say? But she didn't want him to get the wrong impression.

"Frank, I don't know how to say this, but. . .you don't profess to be a believer. You are a good friend, but that's. . .all we can be." Her voice ended almost in a whisper.

If anything, his expression turned even more tender. "Gerda, I am a believer. I asked Jesus into my heart and life yesterday after church."

She studied his face. He seemed sincere, but could she trust appearances? What if he was just saying what he thought she would want to hear? "That's wonderful, Frank."

They stood and gazed at each other for another long moment. Then Frank dipped his head toward her. "I'll let you get back to work. I should as well."

With that, the lawman walked out the front door. Gerda stood staring after him, cradling the delicate figurine in her fingers.

What am I going to do, Lord? After this hurried prayer, Gerda went to the workroom to finish what she had started. She took the small china ornament and set it on the windowsill where she would see it from the sewing machine. After each seam, her attention was drawn to the gift. She stared at it for a few minutes before starting the next seam. *At this rate, I'll never finish the dress.*

Gerda looked at the watch that hung from the brooch on her blouse. It was getting late enough that she probably should close the store for the day. She was about to step through the curtains into the front room of the shop when the bell over the door jingled again. Her heart leaped, then beat frantically. Her hand fluttered to her throat, trying to still her racing heartbeat. Was Frank back again? If so, what would he bring this time?

She pulled back one side of the curtains that covered the doorway, revealing her brother August. She smiled at him and went to give him a hug.

"You seem a little jumpy today, sister." His usually gruff voice sounded as though he was amused by something.

Gerda went behind the counter and leaned her forearms on the top. "No, I'm fine." She set the shepherdess she was carrying on the counter beside her.

"What's this?" The ornament was almost lost in August's huge hands. He turned it over and over and looked at it. "It's really pretty. Dainty, too."

Gerda couldn't take her gaze from the piece of porcelain. "Fra—Sheriff Daggett brought it to me this afternoon." She took it from her brother. "He said he's interested in me."

"And what do you think about that?" August stuffed his hands into the front pockets of his denim trousers.

"I think maybe he means romantically."

"I'm sure he does." August chuckled.

"I told him that I couldn't be interested in him more than just as friends because he's not a believer in Jesus." Gerda set the porcelain girl on the counter again.

"What did he say to that?"

Gerda wondered why August was so interested. "He told me that he asked

Jesus into his life yesterday. I hope he wasn't just saying that because he knew I would want to hear it."

August cleared his throat. "He wasn't. I was with him."

Gerda arched her brows, but before she could ask the question, August continued.

"Gustaf and I noticed that Frank hadn't come out of the church when everyone else did. We went to see if he needed any help."

Gerda was glad that her brothers were so observant.

"Frank had a lot of questions after Joseph's sermon. We answered them the best we could. After reading John 3:16, Frank wanted to ask Jesus into his life. Gustaf and I knelt at the altar with Frank and helped him pray to receive Jesus. I've never heard anyone more sincere than Frank was."

Tears pooled in Gerda's eyes. *That could change things*. Was it possible that Frank *was* the man God intended for her to have?

Chapter 14

The whole evening, Gerda couldn't get her conversation with her brother out of her mind. August didn't have any reason to lie to her, so she believed him. He was there when Frank knelt at the church altar and asked Jesus into his heart. So was Gustaf. Surely Frank didn't do it just to impress her. If so, why spend so much time asking questions about what Pastor Harrelson said? Besides, in his sermon on Sunday, Joseph had told about his life as a gunman before he gave his heart to Jesus. Frank had lived by the gun, too, but he hadn't broken the law. He upheld it. God could reach out to him just as well as he could reach into that prison to save Joseph Harrelson.

All the time Gerda dressed for bed, she thought about Frank. She brushed her hair one hundred strokes before plaiting it in a loose braid for sleep, remembering every expression on his face during each of his visits to the store that day. Looking at that tall man with a bouquet clutched in his masculine hands touched something deep inside her. Those hands were working hands—strong hands, bronzed by the sun, with fingers that could wield a hammer as well as a gun. She wondered how gentle those fingers would feel if they brushed her cheek.

Frank brought gifts to her and treated her with respect, even as his gaze seemed to devour her every expression. His eyes were like quicksilver, always changing. The blue going from light to a medium hue as he seemed to be memorizing her features. When his gaze connected with hers, his eyes were aflame with something that Gerda wasn't ready to put a name to.

She set her hairbrush down, walked over to her rocking chair, and picked up her Bible. When she sat down, it fell open in her lap at the first chapter of Job. Maybe his story of woe would take her mind off the puzzle that was Frank Daggett, handsome lawman and new Christian.

When she got to the eighth verse, she stopped.

Hast thou considered my servant Job, that there is none like him in the earth, a perfect and an upright man, one that feareth God, and escheweth evil?

These words fell into her heart. She remembered the day Anna brought her Bible to the shop and shared this verse with her. If God was bringing it to her attention more than once, maybe God saw Frank in a different way than Gerda had seen him all along. Maybe He saw the man Frank was going to become, not the one he had been. Maybe Frank was becoming an upright man who feared God and turned from evil. From what she knew, he certainly fought evil every chance he got.

Gerda bowed her head and closed her eyes. *Father God, are You trying to tell me something? I have begged You to take the temptation of Frank Daggett out of my life and heart, but he's still there. Now he knows You. Is he the man You prepared for me? Is he the reason I haven't felt drawn to any other man?*

She opened her eyes and lifted her head, then looked across the room at the empty settee. "God, I wish You were sitting there talking to me. I want to hear Your voice. I am so uncertain. Why does it have to be so hard to know for sure that I'm hearing from You?"

About midmorning on Tuesday, July 1, Frank went into the Dress Emporium. Gerda and a customer were looking at a stack of bolts on the counter. The colors of the fabrics ranged from indigo blue all the way through the colors of a rainbow and beyond. The woman seemed to be having a hard time deciding which to choose, so Frank walked around the store and looked at all the doodads sitting on shelves and furniture. Gerda or Anna had skillfully draped lacy things around them to display the items in an artistic manner. What was it about women that they could do that naturally? Frank knew he had never arranged anything to look that good. He pictured things lined up and in order, but usually they were boring to look at. That's why a man needed a woman to bring beauty into his life. A woman like Gerda.

When the customer finally went out the front door, Frank turned from where he was studying a display of gloves, handbags, and scarves. Gerda stood close behind him.

"Can I help you with anything, Frank?" The wary look that had been on her face yesterday was gone, and in its place was peace. Frank took that as a good sign.

"I came to ask you something, Gerda."

Her eyebrows lifted as if in question, but she didn't ask one.

"The picnic." Frank cleared his throat. She was so close that his nostrils filled with the delicate fragrance of some flower, but he wasn't sure what it was. Roses, maybe. He just knew that it came from Gerda. It drew him toward her like a bee to honey. He wanted to take her in his arms and bury his face in her abundant corn-silk-colored hair, but he held back. "Would you accompany me to the Independence Day picnic?"

Gerda stared into his eyes as if looking for something. "That would be nice. I can make a basket of food to take."

"No need." Frank wanted to cradle her cheek in his hand. He was sure it would feel soft and smooth. Instead, he stuffed both hands into his pockets. "I'll bring everything. All you have to do is get ready."

"Why, Frank." Gerda chuckled low in her throat. The sound caused a trembling in Frank's midsection. He had never had that happen before. "I didn't know that you could cook, too."

He laughed with her. "I wouldn't want the meal to be a disaster. Bacon or ham and eggs aren't right for a picnic. No, I'll have Mrs. Olson at the boarding-house do the basket. I often eat there, and she's a good cook. She sure likes to mother the single men who frequent her place."

Gerda walked over to the counter, talking to him as she went, so he followed. "I didn't know you still ate there—since you moved into your house."

"It's easier than trying to cook for myself. As I said, my cooking abilities are limited."

She walked around the counter and reached behind it to lift something off the shelf. "I never thanked you for your gift." She held the figurine that had belonged to his mother in the palm of her hand. Her fingers caressed it as she talked. "I enjoy looking at her. I often put her near me when I'm working."

Frank leaned one hand on the counter. "Does she make you think of me, Gerda?" For some reason, the answer to this question was very important to him.

She didn't take her eyes off his, and hers twinkled. "Oh, I don't need reminders to think of you." She must have realized how that sounded, because she looked down and blushed.

Frank smiled. That was the best thing anyone had ever said to him. He was glad it was Gerda who'd said it. "Well, I'll come by your apartment at about ten o'clock on Friday."

"I'll be ready." Her whispered words reached him just before he went out the door.

～ॐ～

Gerda awoke early on Friday. Her stomach fluttered too much to eat any breakfast, so she just made a pot of tea. She took a leisurely bath and trimmed and buffed her nails until they had a healthy shine. After splashing on some rose water, she braided her hair and fastened it into a figure-eight bun at the nape of her neck. It took her a long time to decide what to wear. She tried on three different dresses before settling on a navy skirt and a crisp, white middy blouse with a sailor collar. The braid on the collar matched the color of the skirt. She liked the way the outfit emphasized her waist, and it wouldn't be too dressy for a picnic.

Gerda sat on the settee listening to the traffic in the street. Too restless to stay seated, she went into her bedroom and peeked between the ruffled curtains. It looked as if everyone in town was headed in the direction of Lake Ripley. The people in Litchfield really liked to celebrate freedom. She glanced at the watch pinned to her collar. It was only 9:30.

When she sat in the rocking chair with a book of poetry, she didn't mind the wait. She enjoyed the rhythm and beauty of the words and the emotions they spoke about. Before she knew it, footsteps were coming up the wooden stairs. Gerda put down the book, looked at her watch again, and smiled. *Frank must have been eager, too. He's early.*

The knock was gentle but firm, just like Frank. Gerda opened the door. The man who stood there took her breath away. He was not the cowboy or the lawman. Frank was dressed in navy twill trousers and a navy-and-white-striped shirt. Without his hat, guns, and boots, he looked younger, more carefree. She liked what she saw.

"Gerda, you look wonderful." His eyes showed his appreciation.

"So do you." Gerda stood there for a minute just looking at him. "Would you like to come in?"

Frank glanced past her. "I don't think that would be a good idea. You're here alone, aren't you?"

His thoughtfulness touched Gerda's heart. "Do we need one of my quilts to spread on the ground?" She turned to go get one.

"I brought one. Let's go down to the buggy."

Frank closed the door behind her and held her arm as they descended the stairs. The warmth of his touch spread up and down her arm, tingling as it went. When they rounded the corner of the store, Frank gestured toward a surrey with a fringed top. Its horse was tied to the hitching post.

"I haven't seen this buggy at the livery stable. Where did you rent it from?"

Frank helped her down from the boardwalk and up into the buggy. "It's mine, Gerda. I went to Minneapolis on Wednesday. It took me awhile to find just the one I wanted and the right horse to pull it. I drove it back yesterday." He untied the animal and climbed up on the seat beside her. "I couldn't take you places on my saddle horse, and I didn't want us to have to walk everywhere."

Gerda could hardly believe it. Frank had bought a buggy to take her places. The thought brought visions of being with him through all the seasons of the year—with autumn leaves falling, in the snow, when spring flowers were budding. . .

All the way to Lake Ripley, their conversation was light and refreshing, but she was constantly aware of the lithe man sharing the seat with her. His hands on the reins were skilled at controlling the horse, and muscles in his arms rippled as he moved with the action of the surrey. Occasionally, when the buggy hit a bump in the road, their shoulders touched. Each time it happened, Gerda's heart leaped. She hoped she wouldn't be breathless by the time they reached the picnic area.

The day was perfect. Although the sun shone brightly, it was cool under the trees where a gentle breeze blew across the lake. They spread their quilt near other members of her family. Soon everyone was visiting. At about eleven o'clock, the men decided to play a baseball game before lunch.

"I've never played before." Frank looked doubtful.

"That's all right." Gustaf clapped him on the shoulder. "We'll teach you."

Gerda was proud of Frank. It didn't take him long to get the hang of it, and he could hit the ball farther than any of the other men. As she watched him run and play, something inside Gerda melted. This man was amazing in every way.

Olina sat down beside Gerda. "I was surprised to see you come with Frank. Is he calling on you now?"

"This is the first time he has asked me to go anywhere with him." Gerda felt a blush creep over her cheeks.

Anna smiled. "I think it won't be the last."

I hope not. Gerda didn't dare say her thoughts aloud. She didn't want there to be too much talk about them.

Frank's team won the game. She was glad that her brothers were on his side.

The men jumped around as if they were boys. They clapped each other on the back and shouted.

"Playing baseball is hot work." Frank took his handkerchief from his back pocket and mopped his brow.

"Let's go wash up." Gustaf led the way to the stream that fed Lake Ripley.

The men washed their hands and faces in the cool, clear water. Gerda enjoyed watching the way Frank interacted with the others. He wasn't the sheriff today. He was just a man enjoying his friends, and it was a good thing. When the men returned to where the quilts were spread, water droplets decorated Frank's hair, looking like diamonds nestled in the curls.

The men had brought Pastor Joseph to eat with them. Before they said the blessing, Frank asked if he could tell them something. Gerda stood back and listened to every word he said. Each syllable sounded as if it came straight from his heart.

"I want to thank Joseph for the sermons he's been preaching, especially the one last Sunday." He nodded at the pastor. "And I want to thank August and Gustaf for taking the time after the service to answer all my questions. Because of these three men, I have accepted Jesus as the Lord of my life."

Everyone clapped and cheered. Other groups scattered around the lake looked at the ruckus, probably wondering what was going on.

After Joseph said a blessing for those gathered near, he sat on the quilt with Gerda and Frank. She was glad their pastor had joined them. The discussion centered on the Bible, and she enjoyed hearing what they talked about.

"Frank, have you thought about being baptized?" Joseph asked.

Frank put down the piece of fried chicken he was eating. He sat for a moment mulling it over.

"I think I'd like that."

"We could do it before we leave today. In Lake Ripley. The water isn't too cold, and I wouldn't mind riding home in wet clothes. They would probably dry out pretty quickly."

Frank looked at Gerda as if asking her permission. She knew it wasn't her place to tell him what to do, but she wanted to let him know that it was fine with her. She gave him a slight nod.

"All right, Preacher, we're going to have a baptism today."

As neighbors wandered from quilt to quilt, Frank relished the intervals when he and Gerda were by themselves. They shared stories of their childhoods and youths. The more he heard about Gerda, the more he loved her. He only hoped that the same was true for her.

As she talked, he watched the expressions that flitted across her face. She was so animated. He loved everything about her. The wind blew tendrils around her neck and face, and he wished that it would be appropriate for him to push them out of her way. He could imagine the feel of her silky hair in his fingers. One day, maybe it would be his right to touch her in such an intimate way. He could hardly wait.

About four o'clock, Joseph returned, bringing quite a crowd with him. He had found three more people who wanted to be a part of the baptism. Soon everyone who had scattered around the lake joined them on the side that held a small beach. The pastor took the four candidates for baptism to the edge of the water and decided what order they would go in. The sheriff would be last.

Frank watched as the man of God waded out into the water until it was up to his waist. Each person went to him, one at a time. He spoke solemn words over them, then helped them bend over backward until they were completely under the surface of the lake. As they each came up out of the water, their faces beamed. When it was his turn, Frank went to his pastor and good friend. He listened to the words the man spoke over him and relaxed in his arms. When Frank came up out of the water, he knew that his face was shining, too. It was as if the symbolic baptism magnified the cleansing he had received when he accepted Jesus as his Savior. Some of the water streaming down his face wasn't from the lake.

Gerda stood on the bank holding his quilt ready to wrap him in it, but he didn't need it. He wanted to just drip dry.

"Why don't you put it on the buggy seat? That way, I won't get you wet as we drive home."

A heavenly melody was playing in his heart, and he knew it would continue until the day he died.

❧

Frank often called on Gerda after the picnic. They spent time with her family or took walks in the evening or drove through the countryside in the surrey. Every time they were together, they bonded on a deeper level. Gerda knew she didn't want to think about the possibility of Frank ever not being a part of her life.

Finally, one day, Frank put his arm around her when they were driving in the country. He pulled her against his side. Gerda thought she might faint from the wonderful way it felt to be so close to him. Every time he held her arm to help her across the street or her hand as they walked in the twilight, the connection had caused her to melt inside. But to be so close to him was heavenly. She sighed and nestled closer.

Although June and July had been cooler than usual, August was a scorcher. People were uncomfortable in the heat, and disagreements often broke out, keeping Frank busier than usual. He even had to lock a couple of troublemakers in the jail, so he had to keep an eye on them. It had been a couple of days since Gerda had seen him, and she was missing their times together. Frank was becoming a necessity to her.

Gerda went into the mercantile to ask Marja Braxton a question. While she was there, a young man with low-slung guns came through the door. When Gerda first saw him, a shiver of apprehension coursed down her spine. Something wasn't right about this man. The two women watched him as he made his way around the store. He didn't really seem to be looking for anything in particular. Finally, he arrived where they were standing by the cash register. Because he made Gerda uncomfortable, she decided to go back to the dress shop. She could keep an eye on what was going on from there. When she turned to go, he pulled his guns and pointed one at her and one at Marja.

"You're not going anywhere." His harsh words brought Gerda back to stand near her friend.

"How much money do you have in that?" He nodded toward the register, never taking his eyes off of Marja and Gerda.

"Not very much." Gerda could tell from the sound of her voice that Marja was just as scared as she was. "We haven't been very busy today."

Gerda glanced at Marja, and she looked pale. Gerda inched closer to the older woman in case she fainted.

The gunman had to be in his teens, he looked so young. He pulled a dirty pillowcase from inside his shirt. "Put all the money in this." Then he shoved it toward Marja.

Marja was shaking so badly Gerda didn't think she would be able to move. "I'll do it for you," she whispered to her friend. Marja nodded, and Gerda took the bag from his hand.

She opened the drawer and removed the bills from each compartment, stuffing them in the case. Then she scooped up the coins and put them into the bag. She tied a loose knot in the end to keep the money from coming out. She didn't want anything to upset the man. He might shoot one of them. He took the bag and stuffed it back inside his shirt. Now it wasn't as flat as it had been when he came in. Through his shirt, it looked like a tumor on his stomach. Gerda almost giggled at that thought, but she knew it was because she was close to becoming hysterical.

"Lay facedown on the floor." His words sounded harsh.

Gerda was getting tired of this. She hadn't seen a robbery in all her life until this year. Now she had experienced two. She got as close as she could to Marja and slid her hand over to clasp Marja's icy one. They heard the robber clomp to the door.

Frank was sitting in his office thinking about Gerda. One day soon, he was going to ask her to marry him, but he wanted to plan the right time to do it. It had to be perfect. . .for her.

Hank from the livery ran to the door of his office. "Come quick, Sheriff! Someone's robbing the mercantile!" The man was so excited his voice trembled, and he was almost gasping for breath.

Frank jumped up and grabbed his guns. "How many men? I didn't hear a gang ride into town."

"It wasn't no gang." Hank hurried along with Frank as he went toward the store. "I was just going in when I noticed a man in the back holding his guns on Marja and Gerda. I ran over here as fast as I could."

Frank's heart dropped to his toes when he thought about a man holding a gun on Gerda again. For a moment, red-hot anger swelled within him. Then reason returned. Frank was a lawman. He had to think rationally. Besides, he didn't think a Christian should be having such hateful thoughts. This was the hardest thing he'd had to face since becoming a believer.

Why had he taken so long to get around to asking Gerda to marry him? He hadn't wanted to rush her, but what if the man's trigger finger got itchy? He might shoot either one of the women with very little provocation. Frank hoped he'd get there in time to avert a tragedy.

When the man ran through the door, Gerda got up and rushed to look out the windows at the front of the building. She got there just in time to see the gunman run straight into Frank. The two men crashed to the boardwalk in a tangle of arms and legs. In the struggle to get free from the mess, the thief's pistol fired, even though he seemed to be trying to shove it into his holster. Frank went still. The kid jumped up and sprinted across the street. Hank and the stationmaster tackled him before he reached his horse. They held him and looked back toward the boardwalk.

She could hardly believe her eyes. Frank was lying in a pool of blood. She ran to him and dropped to her knees, frantically feeling for his pulse. At least it was strong.

Gerda shouted to Hank. "Please! Go get Dr. Bradley!" The pool of blood didn't seem to be getting any larger, and Gerda was afraid she would hurt him if she tried to move him. Then she began to weep over the man she loved with all her heart.

Frank could hardly believe it. That juvenile robber shot him while he was trying to catch hold of him. His shoulder felt like it was on fire. He gritted his teeth and shut his eyes. Before he opened them again, Gerda had dropped to the boardwalk beside him, and she was yelling for someone to get the doctor. He relaxed and kept his eyes shut. There was nothing else he could do until the doctor got there.

Gerda's hot tears began falling onto his face, and she started praying for him. Her prayer warmed his heart.

"Oh, God. I love Frank and can't live without him. Please make sure he stays alive."

Oh, he was alive all right. He hurt a lot, but he was alive and aware of every word she said.

Frank slowly opened his eyes and gazed into Gerda's troubled face. "Gerda, will you marry me?"

She looked startled, but she nodded just before Doc took her place beside Frank.

Chapter 15

Y ou're lucky, Sheriff," the doctor said as he finished bandaging Frank's shoulder. "It's just a flesh wound. It bled a lot, but it wasn't that bad." He started putting his supplies back into the cabinet.

"Thanks, Doc." Frank grimaced. "It hurts, even if it is a flesh wound."

The doctor walked back toward him and grinned. "I didn't say it wouldn't hurt. I just meant it's not as bad as it could have been if it had torn the muscle or hit a bone."

Frank started to stand up so he could put on his shirt.

"Stay seated, Sheriff," Doc said as he helped Frank ease the shirt over his shoulder. "You might want to be careful for the first week. Give it time to heal." Dr. Bradley picked up a large square of white cloth. "You should wear this sling for at least that long."

He folded the cloth into a triangle and tied the ends around Frank's neck. Then he helped slide Frank's arm into the fold. It did take some of the pressure off the wound.

"I'll give you some laudanum to take for the pain. Wait until you get home, then put a few drops in a glass of water. It'll help you sleep." The doctor handed Frank a small, brown glass bottle with a cork in the top. "While you sleep, your body will begin to heal. The longer you stay up fighting the pain, the longer it'll take."

Doc walked over and glanced into his waiting room. "Are one of these men going to take you home?"

August must have been watching, because he quickly came to the door. "I'll take him."

"He doesn't need to ride a horse right now."

Frank tried to smile at them. He wasn't sure it worked. "I didn't ride my horse to the office today. I walked."

"I'll go get your buggy. It has the best springs of any in town. It should ride smooth enough if we take it slow." August quickly went out the door.

Frank was glad when they got up the stairs in his house. August helped him out of his clothes and into bed. Then he went downstairs to get a glass of water for the laudanum. While he was gone, Frank tried to ignore the excruciating pain burning in his shoulder by thinking about Gerda. He couldn't believe he had blurted those words to her out in the street. She deserved better than that. Besides, he really wanted to tell her how he had fallen in love with her over the time he had been in Litchfield. She needed to hear all of it. When he was better, he would rectify that.

All Gerda thought about that afternoon were Frank's last words to her. She wondered if he knew what he had said. He had been shot, and he had lost quite a bit of blood. Besides, he had to be in a lot of pain. Maybe he was out of his head. She wanted to see him so she could know whether he meant it.

When it was almost evening, Anna came to see Gerda.

"August told me that Doc said Frank needed strong beef broth today. I've made some. Would you like to go with me when I take it to him?"

Tears rolled down Gerda's cheeks, and she hugged Anna. "Thank you. I wanted to see how he is doing, but I knew I couldn't go see him alone."

August met Gerda and Anna at the house. He went up to check on Frank while the women put the pot of broth on the stove to heat it some. It shouldn't be too hot for Frank to drink, but it needed to be warm. Gerda was surprised to see how clean and neat everything was. She knew how messy her brothers had always been. If they lived alone in a house, she was sure it would have looked messy most of the time. Maybe Frank paid someone to clean for him. She hadn't heard anyone say they were doing it, but surely a man wasn't this neat. There weren't even any dirty dishes in the sink. She would have expected him to leave his breakfast dishes until later in the day. Maybe she didn't know Frank as well as she thought she did.

August came downstairs. "You can take the broth up to Frank now."

Anna picked up a tray with a mug of the steaming liquid on it. Gerda followed her carrying a napkin. August accompanied them back upstairs. He went in the bedroom first and helped Frank sit up against his pillows.

When August opened the door again, Gerda and Anna entered. Frank looked pale and his eyes were glassy. Gerda tucked the napkin into the neck of his shirt. When the back of her fingers brushed against the warm flesh of his throat, her hands trembled. To be so close to him—and he was so drowsy he didn't even seem to know who was ministering to his needs. Anna set the tray down and went toward the door.

"Where are you going?" August put his arm around his wife.

"I think we'll need to spoon the broth into his mouth. He won't be able to hold the mug and drink."

"I'll go." He dropped a quick kiss on her forehead and glanced down at her abdomen, which was beginning to protrude. "You just wait up here."

A pain shot through Gerda's heart at this display of affection. She wanted to be married, and Frank had even asked her, but she still didn't know if he was aware of doing so.

The next day, several people came to check on Frank and bring him something to eat. He sort of remembered Gerda being here the first day, but he wasn't sure. The laudanum really clouded his mind. He hoped he hadn't done or said anything to offend her, because he was pretty sure she hadn't returned. Of course, many people in town wanted to help him. Someone probably worked out a schedule to keep them from all coming at once.

By evening, Frank decided not to take any more laudanum. The pain had lessened some, and he would rather be able to think straight, even if he hurt. Mrs. Olson came the next morning. Frank was thankful she'd brought a more substantial meal for breakfast. He would never gain the strength he needed if all he did was eat broth and soup. The bacon with scrambled eggs and hot biscuits were the best he had ever tasted. Of course, it could be just because he hadn't had any real solid food since he was shot.

After Mrs. Olson left, Frank got up and dressed himself. He took his time, and although it hurt, he was able to slip into his clothes and boots. He didn't mind putting the sling back on when he was finished. His shoulder needed relief from the pressure. He made his way down the stairs and out to the stable. He planned to feed the horses, but they were already munching on grain when he went into the building.

"Whom should I thank for that?" he whispered as he rubbed the saddle horse's neck.

He stepped back outside. The morning air was pure and fresh, and he filled his lungs with a large breath. It was a bright, sunny day, but it hadn't gotten too hot yet. In the trees above him, Frank could hear birds chattering as they hopped from branch to branch. The two kinds of chirping suggested there were baby birds in a nest up there. It gave him a good feeling, so he decided to try to take a walk. He could always turn back if he needed to.

After going a couple of blocks, he circled around to the other side and made a complete loop back to his house. Although he felt a little tired, he knew it wouldn't take him long to regain his strength. He was determined that this wound wouldn't keep him down.

The next morning, Frank went all the way to his office. He moved slowly as he stepped up onto the boardwalk before opening the door.

"What are you doing here, Sheriff?" Deputy Clarence Wright got up from his chair so fast it almost fell over. "I didn't expect you for several more days."

Frank smiled. "Just thought I'd check and see if everything is all right." He sat at his desk and sorted through the papers on top.

When he got up, he went back to the cell where the young man who shot him was being held. "Where you from, young man?"

The scruffy man turned away from Frank. He clenched the bars in the window so tight that his knuckles turned white. He was just a kid.

"What's your name?" Frank waited awhile for an answer that never came. Frank walked back into his office. "What's being done for the prisoner?"

"I'm making sure he is fed." Clarence glanced back toward the belligerent youth. "My wife fixes extra, so I know it's good food."

Frank nodded. "I'm sure it is."

"I've wired the U.S. Marshals to see if the kid is a known criminal."

"Did he tell you his name?"

"Naw. I just used a description." Clarence shoved his hands into his back pockets.

Frank reached for the doorknob and nodded. "You're doing a good job, Deputy."

Frank crossed the street and headed toward the Dress Emporium. No one was in the front room, but the curtains parted immediately after he closed the door behind himself.

"Frank! What are you doing here?" Gerda's voice sounded breathless.

He smiled. "I couldn't wait any longer to come see you." For a moment he studied her face, drinking in the appearance of her creamy complexion, corn-silk-colored hair, and full, red lips.

An expectant look dropped into Gerda's blue eyes. She seemed to be waiting for something.

"I wanted to ask if you would let me take you to dinner tonight. . .at the hotel."

Her expression changed to one of concern. "Are you sure you should be out yet?"

Frank walked over and leaned his good hand on the counter. "Gerda, I'm a strong, healthy man. It doesn't take that long for me to heal. I don't want to just lie in bed. It'll make me weaker."

A smile lit Gerda's face. "I'd love to go to dinner with you, Frank."

Gerda closed the shop a little early and went to her apartment to get ready. She wanted to look her best tonight. She just hoped that Frank wasn't overdoing it. When he said he was a strong, healthy man, she'd wholeheartedly agreed with him—in her mind. It was hard to believe that the man was wounded. He was an imposing presence in the midst of all the feminine wares in her shop. He wasn't wearing a hat, so his curls were a riot framing his handsome face. His eyes were bright and clear, and the sling didn't detract from his virility.

Surely there was a special reason he wanted them to go out tonight. Maybe he was going to say something about his proposal. Or maybe he was going to tell her that he had been delirious. That thought caused Gerda to stop and sit down. *Please, God, don't let him be sorry for what he said. I don't think I could take it if he is. Please let him be the man You want for me.* What a change from all those months she'd prayed to be freed from the temptation he presented! Now she was asking God to keep him in her life.

Gerda had just finished putting her hair up in a new, soft style when a knock sounded on the door. She patted her coiffure and took one more look in the cheval glass. She was pleased with her reflection.

"Frank." When she opened the door, she had to hold on to it to keep from trembling. Tonight, he looked devastatingly masculine. His muscles filled out his shirt in a wonderful way.

He continued to stand on the landing outside the door. "If you're ready, we can go."

When they arrived at the restaurant in the hotel, Frank asked to be seated as far away as possible from the other diners. After Molly took their orders, he reached across the table with his good hand and took one of Gerda's. He gently rubbed his thumb across her fingers, and a sparkling sensation shot up her arm straight to her heart. As their clasped hands rested on the white linen tablecloth, they sat and gazed at each other. Gerda felt the same strength of connection she had felt that first day in the hotel lobby. What was it about this man that he had that kind of effect on her?

"Dear, dear Gerda," Frank said in a husky whisper. "I must tell you what I feel for you."

With each word, Gerda's pulse accelerated until she was sure her heart would jump out of her chest. Breathlessly, she waited for him to continue.

"I'm sorry I blurted those words in the street."

Gerda felt as if she had slammed against a wall. She dropped her gaze to their hands and started to pull away, but he held her fingers in a tight grip.

"I'm not sorry for the words, just for the time and place. I was frightened for you when I heard that robber had a gun on you. I felt I had waited too long to express my love to you."

Gerda raised her eyes and saw love radiating from his face.

"I've felt a strong connection with you since the first time I laid eyes on you. I believe you felt it, too."

She nodded. "It scared me." She could barely get the words out past the anticipation that had invaded her entire being.

He chuckled. "Me, too. I didn't understand it. It was more than just a physical attraction. Oh, don't get me wrong. I saw how beautiful and desirable you were."

Gerda felt a blush stain her cheeks. She ducked her head.

"Look at me, Gerda." Frank's expression was earnest. "I didn't really understand the connection until after I accepted Jesus into my heart. I believe that God saved you for me. He knew that the best way He could reach me was for me to stay here and become a part of this town. I learned from you and all our friends the truth as it was lived out every day. If I hadn't felt that connection with you, I would have moved on. It was part of God's great plan for my life."

Gerda could believe that. "All my close friends and family had someone special, and I had been praying for God to bring me a man to love. Although I felt the connection to you, I knew you weren't the man He would want me to marry. I even thought that you said you'd accepted Jesus just because you knew I wanted to hear it. I'm sorry for that."

Frank smiled. "What made you change your mind?"

"August told me about the Sunday you talked to him and Gustaf. I knew you wouldn't have asked all those questions if you were just doing it for me. I recognized that it was real."

The waitress came with their food, so Frank let go of Gerda's fingers. He couldn't eat with one arm in a sling and the other holding her hand.

They savored a portion of their tender roast beef, potatoes, gravy, and hot buttered rolls, but soon they continued their discussion.

"What I feel goes way beyond the physical. I believe that God created us for each other."

Gerda nodded her agreement.

"I felt my love for you grow every time I saw you. You were an honest, godly woman in every situation. I saw how you treated everyone you came in contact with. When I bought that house, even before I knew you had wanted it, I dreamed of you sharing it with me. . .as my wife. I can't imagine any other woman in my life."

Gerda put her fork down on her plate and rested her hands in her lap. "I must confess that I prayed earnestly for God to remove you from my life because you were such a temptation. I would never marry an unbeliever, but you were never far from my thoughts. That's why I tried so hard not to be around you. Did you know that I was hesitant when the rest of my family wanted to help you?"

Frank laughed and laid his good hand on the table. "It's funny, but it was as if I could sense so much about you. I knew, and I wondered about it. Little did I know that you felt I was a temptation."

Gerda reached across and touched his hand. "That first night after I saw you in the hotel, I dreamed about you."

Frank turned his palm up under her hand and gripped it. "I dreamed about you, too. You were waiting for me to come home. When I woke up, the dream disturbed me so much that I couldn't go back to sleep. I didn't think I had anything to offer a woman like you, and I really didn't at the time. But now I do. Gerda, will you marry me and share my home. . .and be the mother of my children?"

His proposal took her breath away. The images it brought to mind flooded her whole body with heat. Gerda wondered if he could feel it through her hand. She couldn't take her eyes from his intense gaze. She welcomed the love pouring from him into her heart, and she hoped he could feel hers radiating to him. The sound of voices and silverware against china faded away, and it was as though they were the only two people on earth. For a moment, Gerda felt as if the windows of heaven had opened and God was pouring His blessing on their relationship.

"I love you so much." Frank's words penetrated her heart. "And I will love you until the day I die. Please don't make me wait too long for the wedding."

Gerda gave a soft laugh. "Why, Frank, how could I?"

When they had finished eating, Frank wanted to get Gerda alone, but he also wanted to protect her reputation. "Do you feel like a stroll this evening?" He eased her chair back as she arose from the table.

She looked up at him. A smile gave a gentle glow to her face. "Of course, the evening is beautiful."

He wondered how she could know that, since she hadn't even glanced out the window the whole time they were in the restaurant. Maybe she felt the same way he did—that all was right with the world now that they had defined their relationship.

As they walked along, talking about nothing and everything, Frank was oblivious to everything but the beautiful woman by his side—the woman who would soon be his wife. He hadn't planned to go anywhere in particular, but he wasn't surprised when they arrived at his house—soon to become their home.

Frank was glad he had hung a porch swing near the trellis he'd built for the climbing roses he'd planted earlier. They weren't very tall, but they were already blooming. Every morning the fragrance of those roses, touched with dew, reminded him of Gerda. Although it would cause tongues to wag if they went inside the house, he knew they could sit on the porch and talk as twilight deepened.

Once they were seated in the swing, Frank reached into his coat pocket. He pulled out a velvet pouch and handed it to Gerda. "The first time I saw you, your delicate features made me think about this cameo. It belonged to my mother.

I hoped the day would come that I could give it to you because you were going to become my wife."

"Thank you, Frank." Gerda opened the pouch and slid the brooch into her hand. The gold filigree that framed the stone gave it a delicate design. "I will wear it on our wedding day."

Frank gently rocked the swing with one foot. "How long do you need to plan a wedding?"

"Well, I'm sure all my family and friends will want to help." Gerda smiled up at him, making his heart beat double time.

He didn't want to wait any longer than necessary for the wedding. "Are you going to make me wait a long time?"

Gerda ducked her head. "No, Frank. I'm as anxious as you are."

Even in the waning light of day, Frank could see the blush that stained her cheeks. "Can you be ready in a month?"

Gerda nodded and looked into his eyes. "How does the last Saturday in September sound to you?"

"Just fine." He slid his arm around her shoulders and pulled her close into his embrace.

By the time they arrived at that decision, twilight had disappeared, and the summer night sky sparkled with a million bright stars. Frank was glad the moon was shining from the other side of the porch, casting the two of them into the shadows. He felt as if he had wanted to kiss Gerda all his life. Now the time had come, and he wanted her to experience all his love for her, wrapped up in that kiss.

When Frank pulled her against his side with his good arm, Gerda knew what was going to happen, and she welcomed it. She turned her face up toward his. In the shadows, his eyes shone brightly. She gazed into them, and her throat went dry. Without thinking, she moistened her lips as his face drifted toward hers. She closed her eyes so she could savor every nuance of her first kiss. When his lips gently touched each of her eyelids, she felt tears pool under each lid at his tenderness. As his lips feathered across her cheeks, his soft mustache tickled in a most delicious way. The anticipation building inside her made her feel as if she might explode with delirious happiness.

Finally, his lips touched hers tentatively as though he wanted her to become familiar with the shape of them. His wonderful mouth finally settled firmly on hers. When the kiss eventually deepened, Gerda felt as if their very essence mingled in an indefinable way. She gave herself up to the kiss, pouring all her love for this man into it.

When their lips parted, Gerda gazed into the face of her beloved. "I'm glad God sent a lawman to capture my heart," she whispered.

Frank pulled her closer and settled his chin against her hair. "I am, too, Gerda. I am, too."

A Letter to Our Readers

Dear Readers:

In order that we might better contribute to your reading enjoyment, we would appreciate your taking a few minutes to respond to the following questions. When completed, please return to the following: Fiction Editor, Barbour Publishing, Inc., P.O. Box 719, Uhrichsville, OH 44683.

1. Did you enjoy reading *Minnesota Brothers* by Lena Nelson Dooley?
   ❑ Very much—I would like to see more books like this.
   ❑ Moderately—I would have enjoyed it more if _____
   _____
   _____

2. What influenced your decision to purchase this book?
   (Check those that apply.)
   ❑ Cover   ❑ Back cover copy   ❑ Title   ❑ Price
   ❑ Friends   ❑ Publicity   ❑ Other

3. Which story was your favorite?
   ❑ *The Other Brother*   ❑ *Double Deception*
   ❑ *His Brother's Castoff*   ❑ *Gerda's Lawman*

4. Please check your age range:
   ❑ Under 18   ❑ 18–24   ❑ 25–34
   ❑ 35–45   ❑ 46–55   ❑ Over 55

5. How many hours per week do you read? _____

Name _____

Occupation _____

Address _____

City _____ State _____ Zip _____

E-mail _____

If you enjoyed

Minnesota Brothers

then read:

California CHANCES

Three Brothers Play the Role of Protector as Romance Develops

One Chance in a Million by Cathy Marie Hake
Second Chance by Tracey Bateman
Taking a Chance by Kelly Eileen Hake